EX LIBRIS

VINTAGE CLASSICS

BORIS PASTERNAK

Boris Pasternak was born in Moscow in 1890 and after briefly training as a composer resolved to be a writer. He published a large number of collections of poetry, written under the burden of Soviet Russia's stringent censorship, before publishing his most famous work, *Doctor Zhivago*, in 1958. This novel won him the Nobel Prize for Literature but the USSR's hostility to the West meant he was forced to turn it down. He died in 1960.

Together, Richard Pevear and Larissa Volokhonsky have translated works by Tolstoy, Chekhov, Gogol, Bulgakov and Pasternak. They were twice awarded the PEN/Book-of-the-Month Club Translation Prize (for their translations of Dostoevsky's *Brothers Karamazov* and Tolstoy's *Anna Karenina*) and their translation of Dostoevsky's *Demons* was one of three nominees for the same prize. They are married and live in France.

BORIS PASTERNAK

Doctor Zhivago

TRANSLATED BY
Richard Pevear and Larissa Volokhonsky

WITH AN INTRODUCTION BY
Richard Pevear

VINTAGE

1 3 5 7 9 10 8 6 4 2

Vintage
20 Vauxhall Bridge Road,
London SW1V 2SA

Vintage Classics is part of the Penguin Random House
group of companies whose addresses can be found at
global.penguinrandomhouse.com

 Penguin
Random House
UK

This Russian-language work was first published
in Italian with the title *Il Dottor Zivago* in 1957
by Giangiacomo Feltrinelli Editore, Milano, Italy

First published in Great Britain in 1958 by Collins and Harvill

This translation was first published in Great Britain in 2010
by Harvill Secker and by Vintage Classics in 2011

www.vintage-books.co.uk

A CIP catalogue record for this book
is available from the British Library

ISBN 9781784871925

Printed and bound by Clays Ltd, St Ives plc

Penguin Random House is committed to a sustainable future
for our business, our readers and our planet. This book is made
from Forest Stewardship Council® certified paper.

CONTENTS

INTRODUCTION

> I would pretend (metaphorically) to have seen nature and universe themselves not as a picture made or fastened on an immovable wall, but as a sort of painted canvas roof or curtain in the air, incessantly pulled and blown and flapped by a something of an immaterial unknown and unknowable wind.
>
> — BORIS PASTERNAK
> Letter (in English) to Stephen Spender, 22 August 1959

I

The first edition of *Doctor Zhivago*, the major work of one of the most important Russian writers of the twentieth century, was an Italian translation published in 1957. The next year translations of the novel into English and a number of other languages appeared and Russian-language editions were published in Italy and the United States. But it would take another thirty years and the reforms of perestroika before the novel could be published in Russia. Those circumstances and all that determined them made the reception of the book highly problematical at the time of its appearance.

Pasternak had spent ten years, from 1946 to 1955, writing *Doctor Zhivago*. He considered it the work that justified his life and his survival, when so many of his fellow Russians had perished during the first decades of the century from war, revolution, famine, forced labour, and political terror. After Stalin's death in 1953 came a period known as the Thaw, when there was a general easing of the mechanisms of repression and ideological control. The ban then in place on Pasternak's work (he had been in and out of favour time and again over the years) was lifted, and in 1954 he was able to publish ten poems from *Doctor Zhivago* in the journal *Znamya* ('The Banner'), where the title of the novel was mentioned for the first time. In January 1956, he sent the completed work to *Novy Mir* ('New World'), the most liberal of Moscow literary magazines, and it was also under consideration by Goslitizdat, the state publishing house.

In March 1956, Nikita Khrushchev, first secretary of the Communist Party and virtual head of the government, made a 'secret speech' to the twentieth party congress denouncing the crimes of Stalin. This speech, which immediately became known all over the world, seemed to herald a further opening up of Soviet society. But in fact the thaw was brief. Stirrings of liberation following Khrushchev's speech, especially in such satellite countries as Hungary and Poland, worried the party leadership and caused them to tighten the controls again. The Poznan protests at the end of June were crushed by military force, as were the Polish and Hungarian uprisings later that same year.

The chill made itself felt in literary circles as well. In September 1956, the editors of *Novy Mir* returned the manuscript of *Doctor Zhivago* to Pasternak with a detailed letter explaining that the spirit of the novel, its emotional content, and the author's point of view were incompatible with the spirit of the revolution and the Marxist ideology that was the theoretical foundation of the Soviet state.

Pasternak was not surprised by the rejection. He had anticipated it, and in anticipation had even taken an extraordinary step, which surprised and outraged the Soviet authorities when they learned of it. In May 1956, an Italian Communist journalist by the name of Sergio d'Angelo visited Pasternak at his country house in Peredelkino, a writers' village near Moscow. He had heard about the existence of *Doctor Zhivago* and offered to place it with the Milanese publisher Giangiacomo Feltrinelli (also a Communist) for publication in Italian translation. According to d'Angelo's account, Pasternak, after hesitating for a moment, went to his study, brought out a copy of the novel, and handed it to him with the words: 'You are hereby invited to watch me face the firing squad.' Since 1929, when Evgeny Zamyatin and Boris Pilnyak were vilified in the press for publishing their works abroad, no Soviet writers had had direct dealings with foreign publishers. Zamyatin had been forced to emigrate, and Pilnyak had eventually been shot. Pasternak knew that very well, of course, but he was intent on seeing *Zhivago* published abroad, if it could not be published at home, and was prepared to face the wrath of the authorities.

When publication of the Italian translation was announced for the autumn of 1957, the news caused great uneasiness in the Soviet literary bureaucracy. Pressure was put on Pasternak to make Feltrinelli return the manuscript for revision, telegrams were sent to Milan, and finally, in October 1957, Alexei Surkov, the head of the Writers' Union, went to Italy to speak with the publisher in person. But Feltrinelli refused to delay the novel's release and had already licensed translation rights to publishers in other countries. As Lazar Fleishman wrote in *Boris Pasternak: The Poet and His Politics:*

Nothing promoted the swift growth of interest in *Doctor Zhivago* more than these clumsy attempts to prevent its publication. The novel became an international sensation even before its release. Its first printing of 6,000 was sold out on the first day, 22 November. Prospective publications in other European languages promised to become similar bestsellers. The release of the Italian translation was accompanied by a deluge of articles and notices in the European and American press . . . No work of Russian literature had received such publicity since the time of the revolution.

In the spring of 1958, rumours began to circulate that Pasternak was a likely candidate for that year's Nobel Prize in Literature. In fact, his name had been mentioned for the prize a number of times before. The Nobel Committee's attention was not drawn to him solely because of *Doctor Zhivago*. But the novel, and the politics of the Cold War, certainly had much to do with his nomination this time. On 23 October 1958, it was announced that the prize had indeed been awarded to Pasternak. The Swedish Academy's telegram cited him 'for his important achievement both in contemporary lyric poetry and in the field of the great Russian epic tradition'.

The next day the head of the Moscow section of the Writers' Union, Konstantin Fedin, who was Pasternak's friend and neighbour in Peredelkino, and who had spoken enthusiastically of *Zhivago* when he first read it in 1956, called on him and tried to persuade him not to accept the prize because of its political implications. But Pasternak refused to be persuaded. He sent a telegram of acceptance to the Swedish Academy that read simply: 'Immensely thankful, touched, proud, astonished, abashed.' On 25 October, the attacks on him began with an article in *Literaturnaya Gazeta* ('The Literary Gazette') suggesting that the publication of the book and the award of the prize were merely a political provocation. On 26 October, the campaign expanded to the national press with a vicious article in *Pravda* ('Truth'). On 27 October, Pasternak was tried in absentia by the governing board of the Writers' Union and expelled from the union, which meant losing his right to living quarters and all possibility of earning money by his work. His house in Peredelkino was surrounded by the secret police, and it was hinted that if he went to Sweden for the award ceremony, he might not be allowed to return. This last possibility, along with the danger in which he had put those closest to him, finally led him to refuse the prize. On 29 October, he sent a second telegram to the Swedish Academy: 'In view of the meaning attributed to this award in the society to which I belong, I must refuse the undeserved prize that has been bestowed on me. Do not take my voluntary rejection with any ill will.'

Though this second telegram might seem to be a capitulation on Pasternak's part, it shows no repentance and clearly places the blame on Soviet society. In official circles this was taken as a still greater offence. The attacks on him continued. And the fact that very few of those who attacked him had read the book was no obstacle. At a meeting in Moscow on 31 October, some eight hundred writers voted in favour of a resolution asking the government to 'deprive the traitor B. Pasternak of Soviet citizenship'. The text of the resolution was published in *Literaturnaya Gazeta* the next day. In response, Pasternak's close friends drew up a letter to Khrushchev in his name, asking that this extreme measure not be carried out. Pasternak contributed only two brief sentences to the letter: 'I am bound to Russia by my birth, my life, and my work. I cannot imagine my fate separated from and outside Russia.' The letter was published in *Pravda* on 1 November and eased the tensions somewhat. A second public statement, also drawn up with very little participation from Pasternak, was published in *Pravda* on 6 November and more or less ended the 'Nobel scandal'. Pasternak died a year and a half later. In December 1989, his son, Evgeny Borisovich Pasternak, was finally able to go to Stockholm to receive his father's Nobel medal and diploma.

Pasternak had maintained friendships with some of the best of the proscribed writers of his time – Boris Pilnyak, Osip Mandelstam, Andrei Platonov, Mikhail Bulgakov, Anna Akhmatova – who are now acknowledged as among the major figures of twentieth-century Russian literature. He also befriended and encouraged younger dissident writers like Varlam Shalamov and Andrei Sinyavsky. But he was the first to oppose the Soviet regime and its ideology so openly and so effectively. And yet Pasternak was not at all a political man; the public realm and the conflict of ideologies did not interest him. *Doctor Zhivago* speaks in the name of something else entirely.

That 'something else' caused a certain confusion among readers and critics in the West when the novel first appeared. It was criticised for not being what it was never meant to be: a good, old-fashioned, nineteenth-century historical novel about the Russian revolution, an epic along the lines of *War and Peace*. It was also praised for being what it was not: a moving love story, or the lyrical biography of a poet, setting the sensitive individual against the grim realities of Soviet life. Western Marxists found that Pasternak failed to portray the major events and figures of the revolution –

something he never set out to do. Others devised elaborate allegorical readings of the novel, though Pasternak stated explicitly, in a letter to Stephen
Spender (9 August 1959), that 'a detailed allegorical interpretation of literature' was alien to him. Critics found that there was no real plot to the novel,
that its chronology was confused, that the main characters were oddly
effaced, that the author relied far too much on contrived coincidences.

These perplexities are understandable, but they come from a failure to
pay attention to the specific composition of the novel, its way of represent-
ing reality, its way of making experience felt. *Doctor Zhivago* is a highly
unusual book, an incomparable book in the most literal sense. Pasternak
suggested its unique quality in his reply to a letter from an English school-
teacher:

> The objective world in my habitual, natural grasping, is a vast infinite
> inspiration, that sketches, erases, chooses, compares and describes and
> composes itself . . . living, moving reality in such a rendering must have
> a touch of spontaneous subjectivity, even of arbitrariness, wavering,
> tarrying, doubting, joining and disjoining elements . . . Over and above
> the times, events and persons there is a nature, a spirit of their very suc-
> cession. The frequent coincidences in the plot are (in this case) not the
> secret, trick expedients of the novelist. They are traits to characterise
> that somewhat wilful, free, fanciful flow of reality. (Letter in English to
> John Harris, 8 February 1959; published in *Scottish Slavonic Review*,
> 1984)

To embody this 'living, moving reality' required formal innovation, and
therefore *Doctor Zhivago* had necessarily to be an experimental novel. But
it is not experimental in a modernist or formalist way. Modernism is essentially defined by absence (Godot never comes). Pasternak's vision is defined
by real presence, by an intensity of physical sensation rendered in the abun-
dance of natural description or translated into the voices of his many characters. Pasternak delights in the pathetic fallacy: in his world so-called
inanimate nature constantly participates in the action. On the other hand,
there is no historical or psychological analysis in his narrative, no commentary on the causes of events or the motives of characters. This gives a feeling
of chaos, random movement, impulsiveness, chance encounters, sudden dis-
ruptions to the action of the novel. The trains and trams keep breaking
down. But owing to the breakdowns, surprising new aspects of life appear.
The Russia of three revolutions, two world wars, civil war, and political terror is portrayed in living detail, but from unexpected angles, and with no
abstract ideological synthesis. Pasternak portrays happening as it happens,

which is what Tolstoy also set out to do. But in *Doctor Zhivago* the seeming chaos of events will suddenly be pierced through by forces of a higher order, coming from a greater depth in time – folkloric, cultural, ultimately religious – which are also really present, which reassert their continuing presence, in the most ordinary everyday life. Now, fifty years after its first publication, when the circumstances of the Cold War are more or less behind us, we may be able to read the novel in a new way, to see more clearly the universality of the image that Pasternak held up against the deadly fiction of his time. As Viktor Frank wrote in his essay 'Vodyanoi Znak' ('Watermark: The Poetic Worldview of Pasternak', 1962): 'Pasternak rolled the stone from the tomb.'

2

Boris Leonidovich Pasternak was born in Moscow on 10 February 1890. His father, Leonid Osipovich Pasternak, was a painter and illustrator; his mother, Rozalia Isidorovna Kaufman, was a concert pianist. They belonged to the cultivated Jewish milieu of Odessa, and moved to Moscow only a few months before Boris, the eldest of their four children, was born. Leonid Pasternak had considerable success as an artist, taught at the Moscow School of Painting, Sculpture and Architecture, and became an outstanding portraitist, which led to a close acquaintance with Leo Tolstoy, whose works he illustrated and of whom he painted several portraits, the last just after the writer's death in November 1910 at the railway station in Astapovo. The twenty-year-old Boris accompanied his father to Astapovo on that occasion.

   The young Pasternak showed considerable talent for drawing and might have become an artist himself, but in the summer of 1903, while the family was staying in the country, he chanced to meet the composer Alexander Scriabin, whom he overheard composing his Third Symphony at the piano in a neighbouring house, and decided that his real calling was music. For the next six years, he devoted himself to a serious study of composition. But at a key moment in 1909, after playing some of his compositions for Scriabin, who encouraged him and gave him his blessing, he abandoned music. Meanwhile, he had discovered the poetry of Rilke and had joined a group of young admirers of the Symbolists that called itself Serdarda – 'a name', as he wrote later, 'whose meaning no one knew'. And he had begun to write verse himself.

   It was a member of Serdarda who persuaded Pasternak to give up music in favour of literature, but it was Scriabin himself who suggested that he

switch his field at Moscow University from law to philosophy. He graduated in 1913, after six years of study, including a semester at the University
of Marburg under Hermann Cohen and Paul Natorp, but by then he had
decided to abandon philosophy. In the summer after his final examinations,
he stayed with his parents in the country, and there, as he recalled, 'I read
Tyutchev and for the first time in my life wrote poetry not as a rare exception, but often and continuously, as one paints or writes music.' His first
book, A Twin in the Clouds, was published in December of that year.

Pasternak described these metamorphoses in his two autobiographical
essays, Safe Conduct, written between 1927 and 1931, and People and Situations (published in English under the titles I Remember and An Essay in
Autobiography), written in 1956. Different as the two books are in style
and vision, they both give a good sense of the extraordinary artistic and
philosophical ferment in Russia in the years before the First World War. The
older generation of Symbolists had begun to publish in the 1890s, the second generation, which included Alexander Blok and Andrei Bely, in the
early years of the twentieth century. Then came the new anti-Symbolist
movements: the Futurists (Vladimir Mayakovsky and Velimir Khlebnikov,
among many other poets and painters), whose manifesto, A Slap in the Face
of Public Taste, was published in 1912; and the Acmeists (Nikolai Gumilev,
Osip Mandelstam, Anna Akhmatova), who favoured Apollonian clarity
over Symbolist vagueness. In his essay 'The Morning of Acmeism', Mandelstam wrote banteringly:

> For the Acmeists the conscious sense of the word, the Logos, is just as
> splendid a form as music is for the Symbolists.
>
> And if, among the Futurists, the word as such is still creeping on all
> fours, in Acmeism it has for the first time assumed a more dignified ver-
> tical position and entered upon the stone age of its existence.

Which gives at least a small idea of the lively polemics that went on in those
years.

Pasternak first associated with the younger Symbolists around the journal
Musaget and its publishing house. To a gathering of this group, in 1913, he
read a paper entitled 'Symbolism and Immortality'. The text was later lost,
but in People and Situations, he summarised its main points:

> My paper was based on the idea that our perceptions are subjective, on
> the fact that the sounds and colours we perceive in nature correspond
> to something else, namely, to the objective vibrations of sound and
> light waves. I argued that this subjectivity was not the attribute of an

individual human being, but was a generic and suprapersonal quality, that it was the subjectivity of the human world and of all mankind. I suggested in my paper that every person leaves behind him a part of that undying, generic subjectivity which he possessed during his lifetime and with which he participated in the history of mankind's existence. The main object of my paper was to advance the theory that this utterly subjective and universally human corner or portion of the world was perhaps the eternal sphere of action and the main content of art. That, besides, though the artist was of course mortal, like everyone else, the happiness of existence he experienced was immortal, and that other people centuries after him might experience, through his works, something approaching the personal and innermost form of his original sensations.

These thoughts, or intuitions, were to reach their full realisation decades later in *Doctor Zhivago*.

In January 1914, Pasternak and some of his young friends shifted their allegiance from the Symbolists to the Futurists, forming a new group that called itself Centrifuge. There were other groups as well – the Ego-futurists and the Cubo-futurists, the latter including Vladimir Mayakovsky, whom Pasternak met at that time. These groups were all somewhat fluid and loosely defined, and their members kept forming new alliances and creating new antagonisms.

On 1 August 1914, the First World War broke out, which somewhat curtailed the skirmishing among literary movements. Pasternak was exempted from military service because of an old injury caused by a fall from a horse in 1903, which had left him with one leg slightly shorter than the other. He supported himself by working as a private tutor and later as a clerk in the office of a chemical factory. In connection with this work he spent the winters of 1915 and 1916 in the region of the Urals, which forms the setting for most of Book Two of *Doctor Zhivago*. During that time he wrote the poems of his second book, *Above the Barriers,* published in 1917. When news of the February revolution of 1917 reached him in the Urals, he immediately set out for Moscow.

In the summer of 1917, between the February and October revolutions, Pasternak found his true voice as a poet, composing poems that would go into his third book, *My Sister, Life,* one of the major works of twentieth-century Russian poetry. He knew that something extraordinary had come over him in the writing of this book. In *Safe Conduct,* he says:

When *My Sister, Life* appeared, and was found to contain expressions

not in the least contemporary as regards poetry, which were revealed to
me during the summer of the revolution, I became entirely indifferent
as to the identity of the power which had brought the book into being,
because it was immeasurably greater than myself and than the poetical
conceptions surrounding me.

Between that summer and the eventual publication of the book in 1922
came the Bolshevik revolution and the harsh years of War Communism,
years of hunger, confusion, and civil war. In 1921, Pasternak's parents and
sisters immigrated to Berlin. (After Hitler's accession to power they immigrated again, this time to England, where they remained.) Pasternak visited
them in Berlin in 1922, after his first marriage, and never saw them again.
He himself, like so many of his fellow poets and artists, was not opposed to
the spirit of the revolution and chose to stay in Russia.

My Sister, Life was followed in 1923 by *Themes and Variations,* which
grew out of the same lyric inspiration. In the later twenties, Pasternak felt
the need for a more epic form and turned to writing longer social-historical
poems dealing specifically with the ambiguities of the revolutions of 1905
and 1917: *Lieutenant Schmidt* (1926), *The Year 1905* (1927), *The Lofty
Malady* (1928), and the novel in verse *Spektorsky,* with an extension in prose
entitled 'A Tale' (1925–1930). *Spektorsky* covers the pre-revolutionary
years, the revolution, and the early Soviet period, almost the same span of
time as *Doctor Zhivago.* Its hero, Sergei Spektorsky, a man of indefinite
politics, apparently idle, more of a spectator than an actor, is in some ways
a precursor of Yuri Zhivago.

At the same time, Pasternak kept contemplating a long work in prose. In
1918 he had begun a novel set in the Urals, written in a rather leisurely, old-
fashioned manner that was far removed from the modernist experiments of
writers like Zamyatin, Bely, and Remizov. Only one part of it, *The Childhood of Luvers,* was ever published. He also wrote short works such as
'Without Love' (1918) and 'Aerial Ways' (1924), which sketch situations or
characters that would reappear in *Doctor Zhivago.* And in 1931 he completed and published his most important prose work before the novel, the
autobiography *Safe Conduct.*

In 1936 Pasternak went back to his idea of a long prose work, this time
to be narrated in the first person, and in a deliberately plain style, as the
notes and reminiscences of a certain Patrick, covering the period between
the revolutions of 1905 and 1917. Here there were still more foreshadow-
ings of the later novel: Patrick is an orphan who, like Zhivago, grows up in
the home of a family named Gromeko and marries their daughter Tonya;

there is a woman reminiscent of the novel's Lara Antipova, whose husband is also a teacher in Yuriatin in the Urals; and Patrick, like Zhivago, is torn between his love for this woman and for his wife. Some sections from the notes were published in magazines between 1937 and 1939, but the manuscript was destroyed in a fire in 1941. The cover, which survived, bears two crossed-out titles: *When the Boys Grew Up* and *Notes of Zhivult*. The odd name Zhivult, like the less odd name Zhivago, comes from the Russian root *zhiv,* meaning 'alive'.

Pasternak found it impossible to continue work on the *Notes* in the face of the intensification of Stalin's terror in the later thirties, particularly the great purges that began in 1937. As Lazar Fleishman has written:

> All previous historical explanations and evaluations acquired new and unstable meaning in light of the repression directed against the old guard of revolutionaries, and in light of the unprecedented, bloody catastrophe that the great revolution turned out to be for the entire population in 1937. These events dramatically changed Pasternak's attitude toward Russia, the revolution, and socialism.

Pasternak always had a double view of the revolution. He saw it, on the one hand, as a justified expression of the need of the people, and, on the other, as a programme imposed by 'professional revolutionaries' that was leading to a deadly uniformity and mediocrity. His doubts began as early as 1918 and increased as time went on.

After Lenin's death in 1924, there was a power struggle within the Communist Party leadership, essentially between Stalin and Trotsky, which ended with Trotsky being removed from the Central Committee in 1927, exiled to Alma Ata in 1928, and finally expelled from Russia in 1929. Stalin became the undisputed head of state and ruled with dictatorial powers. In 1928, he abolished the New Economic Policy (NEP), which Lenin had introduced to allow for private enterprise on a small scale, and instituted the first Five-Year Plan for the development of heavy industry and the collectivisation of agriculture. On 23 April 1932, a decree on 'The Restructuring of Literary Organisations' was published, aimed at ending 'stagnation' in literature by putting a stop to rivalries among literary factions. This led to the creation of the Soviet Writers' Union, a single body governing all literary affairs, of which every practising writer was required to be a member. And in October 1932, Stalin defined 'socialist realism' as the single artistic method acceptable for Soviet literature. The Writers' Union drew up a statute at its first congress in 1934 defining socialist realism as a method that 'demands of the artist the truthful, historically concrete representation of reality in its revolutionary development. Moreover, the truthfulness and historical concreteness of reality must be linked with the task of the ideological transformation and education of workers in the spirit of Communism.' The historical theory behind socialist realism was the dialectical materialism of Marx; its necessary representative was the positive hero.

Pasternak made two trips to the Urals during that period. In 1931 he was sent as a member of a 'writers' brigade' to observe the Five-Year Plan in action and report on its successes – in other words, to be 're-educated'. He was curious to see what changes had occurred since his last trip there fifteen years earlier. What he found disturbed him very much – not the scale of the construction, but the depersonalisation of the people. He quit the brigade early and returned home. In the summer of 1932, the official attitude towards Pasternak improved and a collection of his poems, entitled *Second Birth*, was published. He was rewarded with a new trip to the Urals, this time for a month's vacation with his second wife, Zinaida Neuhaus, and her two sons. Here for the first time he saw the results of the forced collectivisation of agriculture, which had led to the breakdown of farming on a vast scale and a famine that cost millions of peasant lives. These disastrous effects of Stalin's policy went entirely unreported in the Soviet press. He wrote a letter to the directors of the Writers' Union detailing what he had seen, but it was ignored.

In another letter, written to his parents in Berlin in the spring of 1933, on Hitler's accession to power, Pasternak defined the tragedy that was being played out in Europe with remarkable clarity and in terms that reveal the essence of his historical understanding as it would finally be embodied in *Doctor Zhivago:*

> . . . however strange it may seem to you, one and the same thing depresses me in both our own state of affairs and yours. It is that this movement is not Christian, but nationalistic; that is, it runs the same danger of degenerating into the bestiality of facts. It has the same alienation from the age-old, gracious tradition that breathes with transformations and anticipations, rather than the cold statements of blind insanity. These movements are on a par, one is evoked by the other, and it is all the sadder for this reason. They are the left and right wings of a single materialistic night. (Published in *Quarto*, London, 1980)

After the appearance of *Second Birth*, Pasternak entered a more or less silent period, in terms of publication, which lasted until 1941. But he did address congresses of the Writers' Union several times during those years. In an important speech to a plenum session of the union, held in Minsk in February 1936, he said:

> The unforeseen is the most beautiful gift life can give us. That is what we must think of multiplying in our domain. That is what should have been talked about in this assembly, and no one has said a word about it . . . Art is inconceivable without risk, without inner sacrifice; freedom and boldness of imagination can be won only in the process of work, and it is there that the unforeseen I spoke of a moment ago must intervene, and there no directives can help.

He went on to describe the inner change he was undergoing:

> For some time I will be writing badly, from the point of view that has been mine up to now, and I will continue to do so until I have become used to the novelty of the themes and situations I wish to address. I will be writing badly, literally speaking, because I must accomplish this change of position in a space rarefied by abstractions and the language of journalists, and therefore poor in images and concreteness. I will also be writing badly in regard to the aims I am working for, because I will deal with subjects that are common to us in a language different from yours. I will not imitate you, I will dispute with you . . .

To earn his living during this time, Pasternak turned to translation. In 1939, the famous director Vsevolod Meyerhold invited him to make a new version of *Hamlet*. Other commissions for Shakespeare plays followed during the war years, but the work on *Hamlet* had a profound effect on Pasternak (twelve versions of the play were found among his papers). During the war years, there was a spirit of genuine unity among the Russian people in the opposition to a real enemy, after the nightmarish conditions of the terror – a spirit reflected in the epilogue to *Doctor Zhivago*. Pasternak believed then that the changes brought about by necessity would lead to the final liberation that had been the promise of the revolution from the beginning. What came instead, starting in August 1946, was a new series of purges, an ideological constriction signalled by virulent denunciations of the poet Anna Akhmatova and the prose writer Mikhail Zoshchenko, new restrictions on film and theatre directors, and the 'bringing into line' of the composers Shostakovich and Prokofiev. And a campaign also began against Pasternak, who was effectively silenced as a writer until after Stalin's death.

Pasternak lived through a profound spiritual crisis at this time, what might be called his 'Hamlet moment'. The change in him is suggested by the two versions of the poem 'Hamlet' that he wrote in 1946. The first, written

in February, before the denunciations of Akhmatova and Zoshchenko, has
just two stanzas:

> Here I am. I step out on the stage.
> Leaning against a doorpost,
> I try to catch the echoes in the distance
> Of what will happen in my age.
>
> It is the noise of acts played far away.
> I take part in all five.
> I am alone. All drowns in pharisaism.
> Life is no stroll through a field.

The second, written in late 1946, consists of four stanzas:

> The hum dies down. I step out on the stage.
> Leaning against a doorpost,
> I try to catch the echoes from far off
> Of what my age is bringing.
>
> The night's darkness focuses on me
> Thousands of opera glasses.
> Abba Father, if only it can be,
> Let this cup pass me by.
>
> I love the stubbornness of your intent
> And agree to play this role.
> But now a different drama's going on,
> Spare me, then, this once.
>
> But the order of the acts has been thought out,
> And leads to just one end.
> I'm alone, all drowns in pharisaism.
> Life is no stroll through a field.

This second version, adding the figure of Christ to those of Hamlet and the
poet, gives great depth and extension to the notion of reluctant acceptance
of the Father's stubborn intent. Pasternak draws the same parallel in the
commentary on *Hamlet* in his *Notes on Translating Shakespeare*, written
in the summer of 1946: 'From the moment of the ghost's appearance, Hamlet gives up his will in order to "do the will of him that sent him". *Hamlet* is
not a drama of weakness, but of duty and self-denial . . . What is important

is that chance has allotted Hamlet the role of judge of his own time and servant of the future. *Hamlet* is the drama of a high destiny, of a life devoted and preordained to a heroic task.'

Early in his career, Pasternak had likened poetry to a sponge left on a wet garden bench, which he would wring out at night 'to the health of the greedy paper'. Now it has become an act of witness, the acceptance of a duty. The second version of 'Hamlet' became the first of Yuri Zhivago's poems in the final part of *Doctor Zhivago*. With the new resolve that had come to him, Pasternak was able to take up the long prose work he had been contemplating all his life and finally complete it.

RICHARD PEVEAR

TRANSLATORS' NOTES

Russian names are composed of first name, patronymic (from the father's first name), and family name. Formal address requires the use of the first name and patronymic; diminutives are commonly used among family and friends; the family name alone can also be used familiarly, and on occasion only the patronymic is used, usually among the lower classes.

Principal Characters:
Yúri Andréevich Zhivágo (Yúra, Yúrochka)
Laríssa Fyódorovna Guichárd, married name Antípova (Lára, Lárochka)
Antonína Alexándrovna Groméko, married name Zhivágo (Tónya, Tónechka)
Pável Pávlovich Antípov (Pásha, Páshka, Páshenka, Pavlúshka, Patúlya, Patúlechka)
Innokénty Deméntievich Dúdorov (Níka)
Mikhaíl Grigórievich Gordon (Mísha)
Víktor Ippolítovich Komaróvsky (no diminutives)
Evgráf Andréevich Zhivágo (Gránya)

There is an extraordinary play with the names of minor characters in the novel. They are all plausible, but often barely so, and they sometimes have an oddly specific meaning. For instance, there is Maxím Aristárkovich Klintsóv-Pogorévshikh, whose name has a rather aristocratic ring until you come to Pogorévshikh, which means 'burned down'. Others are simply tongue twisters: Anfím Efímovich Samdevyátov, or Rufína Onísimovna Vóit-Voitkóvskaya. There are too many of these names for us to comment on them, but the Russian-less reader should know that for Russian readers, too, they are strange and far-fetched, and that Pasternak clearly meant them to be so. Dmitri Bykov, in his *Boris Pasternak* (Moscow, 2007), thinks they suggest a realm alien to Zhivago – deep Siberia, the city outskirts – and almost a different breed of man.

The place-names for the parts of the novel set in the Moscow region and western Russia are real; the place-names in the Urals – Yuriatin, Varykino,

Rynva – are fictional. And there is a corresponding difference in 'worlds' – the one more historical, the other more folkloric. The novel moves from the one to the other and back again. There is also a double sense of time, marked by two different calendars, civil and church-festal, the first linear, the second cyclical. Sometimes the most mundane moment suddenly acquires another dimension, as when the narrator, describing the end of a farewell party, says: 'The house soon turned into a sleeping kingdom.' We have tried to match as closely as possible the wide range of voices, the specific cadences, and the sudden shifts of register in Pasternak's prose.

The poems of Yuri Zhivago, which make up the final part of the novel, are not merely an addendum; they are inseparable from the whole and its true outcome – what remains, what endures. Some clearly reflect moments in the novel; we even overhear Zhivago working on several of them; but it is a mistake to try to pinpoint each poem to a specific passage or event in the novel. In translating them, we have let the meaning guide us, and have welcomed poetry when it has offered itself. We have sacrificed rhyme, but have tried to keep the rhythm, especially when it is as important as it is in 'A Wedding,' which is modelled on a popular song form called the chastushka. Above all, we have tried to keep the tone and terseness of the originals, which are often intentionally prosaic.

Book One

Part One

THE FIVE O'CLOCK EXPRESS

I

They walked and walked and sang 'Memory Eternal',[1] and whenever they stopped, the singing seemed to be carried on by their feet, the horses, the gusts of wind.

Passers-by made way for the cortège, counted the wreaths, crossed themselves. The curious joined the procession, asked: 'Who's being buried?' 'Zhivago,' came the answer. 'So that's it. Now I see.' 'Not him. Her.' 'It's all the same. God rest her soul. A rich funeral.'

The last minutes flashed by, numbered, irrevocable. 'The earth is the Lord's and the fullness thereof; the world, and those who dwell therein.' The priest, tracing a cross, threw a handful of earth onto Marya Nikolaevna. They sang 'With the souls of the righteous'. A terrible bustle began. The coffin was closed, nailed shut, lowered in. A rain of clods drummed down as four shovels hastily filled the grave. Over it a small mound rose. A ten-year-old boy climbed onto it.

Only in the state of torpor and insensibility that usually comes at the end of a big funeral could it have seemed that the boy wanted to speak over his mother's grave.

He raised his head and looked around from that height at the autumn wastes and the domes of the monastery with an absent gaze. His snub-nosed face became distorted. His neck stretched out. If a wolf cub had raised his head with such a movement, it would have been clear that he was about to howl. Covering his face with his hands, the boy burst into sobs. A cloud flying towards him began to lash his hands and face with the wet whips of a cold downpour. A man in black, with narrow, tight-fitting, gathered sleeves, approached the grave. This was the deceased woman's brother and the weeping boy's uncle, Nikolai Nikolaevich Vedenyapin, a priest defrocked at his own request. He went up to the boy and led him out of the cemetery.

2

They spent the night in one of the monastery guest rooms, allotted to the uncle as an old acquaintance. It was the eve of the Protection.[2] The next day he and his uncle were to go far to the south, to one of the provincial capitals on the Volga, where Father Nikolai worked for a publisher who brought out a local progressive newspaper. The train tickets had been bought, the luggage was tied up and standing in the cell. From the nearby station the wind carried the plaintive whistling of engines manoeuvring in the distance.

Towards evening it turned very cold. The two ground-level windows gave onto the corner of an unsightly kitchen garden surrounded by yellow acacia bushes, onto the frozen puddles of the road going past, and onto the end of the cemetery where Marya Nikolaevna had been buried that afternoon. The kitchen garden was empty, except for a few moiré patches of cabbage, blue from the cold. When the wind gusted, the leafless acacia bushes thrashed about as if possessed and flattened themselves to the road.

During the night Yura was awakened by a tapping at the window. The dark cell was supernaturally lit up by a fluttering white light. In just his nightshirt, Yura ran to the window and pressed his face to the cold glass.

Beyond the window there was no road, no cemetery, no kitchen garden. A blizzard was raging outside; the air was smoky with snow. One might have thought the storm noticed Yura and, knowing how frightening it was, revelled in the impression it made on him. It whistled and howled and tried in every way possible to attract Yura's attention. From the sky endless skeins of white cloth, turn after turn, fell on the earth, covering it in a winding sheet. The blizzard was alone in the world; nothing rivalled it.

Yura's first impulse, when he got down from the windowsill, was to get dressed and run outside to start doing something. He was afraid now that the monastery cabbage would be buried and never dug out, now that mama would be snowed under and would be unable to resist going still deeper and further away from him into the ground.

Again it ended in tears. His uncle woke up, spoke to him of Christ and comforted him, then yawned, went to the window, and fell to thinking. They began to dress. It was getting light.

3

While his mother was alive, Yura did not know that his father had abandoned them long ago, had gone around various towns in Siberia and abroad, carousing and debauching, and that he had long ago squandered and thrown to the winds the millions of their fortune. Yura was always told that he was in Petersburg or at some fair, most often the one in Irbit.

But then his mother, who had always been sickly, turned out to have consumption. She began going for treatment to the south of France or to northern Italy, where Yura twice accompanied her. Thus, in disorder and amidst perpetual riddles, Yura spent his childhood, often in the hands of strangers, who changed all the time. He became used to these changes, and in this situation of eternal incoherence his father's absence did not surprise him.

As a little boy, he had still caught that time when the name he bore was applied to a host of different things. There was the Zhivago factory, the Zhivago bank, the Zhivago buildings, a way of tying and pinning a necktie with a Zhivago tiepin, and even some sweet, round-shaped cake, a sort of baba au rhum, called a Zhivago, and at one time in Moscow you could shout to a cabby: 'To Zhivago!' just like 'To the devil's backyard!' and he would carry you off in his sleigh to a fairy-tale kingdom. A quiet park surrounded you. Crows landed on the hanging fir branches, shaking down hoarfrost. Their cawing carried, loud as the cracking of a tree limb. From the new buildings beyond the clearing, pure-bred dogs came running across the road. Lights were lit there. Evening was falling.

Suddenly it all flew to pieces. They were poor.

4

In the summer of 1903, Yura and his uncle were riding in a tarantass and pair over the fields to Duplyanka, the estate of Kologrivov, the silk manufacturer and great patron of the arts, to see Ivan Ivanovich Voskoboinikov, a pedagogue and populariser of useful knowledge.

It was the feast of the Kazan Mother of God,[3] the thick of the wheat harvest. Either because it was lunchtime or on account of the feast day, there was not a soul in the fields. The sun scorched the partly reaped strips like the half-shaven napes of prisoners. Birds circled over the fields. Its ears drooping, the wheat drew itself up straight in the total stillness or stood in shocks far off the road, where, if you stared long enough, it acquired the look of moving figures, as if land surveyors were walking along the edge of the horizon and taking notes.

'And these,' Nikolai Nikolaevich asked Pavel, a handyman and watchman at the publishing house, who was sitting sideways on the box, stooping and crossing his legs, as a sign that he was not a regular coachman and driving was not his calling, 'are these the landowner's or the peasants'?'

'Them's the master's,' Pavel replied, lighting up, 'and them there,' having lighted up and inhaled, he jabbed with the butt of the whip handle towards the other side and said after a long pause, 'them there's ours. Gone to sleep, eh?' he shouted at the horses every so often, glancing at their tails and rumps out of the corner of his eye, like an engineer watching a pressure gauge.

But the horses pulled like all horses in the world; that is, the shaft horse ran with the innate directness of an artless nature, while the outrunner seemed to the uncomprehending to be an arrant idler, who only knew how to arch its neck like a swan and do a squatting dance to the jingling of the harness bells, which its own leaps set going.

Nikolai Nikolaevich was bringing Voskoboinikov the proofs of his little book on the land question, which, in view of increased pressure from the censorship, the publisher had asked him to revise.

'Folk are acting up in the district,' said Nikolai Nikolaevich. 'In the Pankovo area they cut a merchant's throat and a zemstvo man[4] had his stud burned down. What do you think of that? What are they saying in your village?'

But it turned out that Pavel took an even darker view of things than the censor who was restraining Voskoboinikov's agrarian passions.

'What're they saying? Folk got free and easy. Spoiled, they say. Can you do that with our kind? Give our muzhiks their head, they'll throttle each other, it's God's truth. Gone to sleep, eh?'

This was the uncle's and nephew's second trip to Duplyanka. Yura thought he remembered the way, and each time the fields spread out wide, with woods embracing them in front and behind in a narrow border, it seemed to Yura that he recognised the place where the road should turn right, and at the turn there would appear and after a moment vanish the seven-mile panorama of Kologrivovo, with the river glistening in the distance and the railroad running beyond it. But he kept being mistaken. Fields were succeeded by fields. Again and again they were embraced by woods. The succession of these open spaces tuned you to a vast scale. You wanted to dream and think about the future.

Not one of the books that were later to make Nikolai Nikolaevich famous had yet been written. But his thoughts were already defined. He did not know how near his hour was.

Soon he was to appear among the representatives of the literature of that time, university professors and philosophers of the revolution – this man who had thought over all their themes and who, apart from terminology, had nothing in common with them. The whole crowd of them held to some sort of dogma and contented themselves with words and appearances, but Father Nikolai was a priest who had gone through Tolstoyism and revolution[5] and kept going further all the time. He thirsted for a wingedly material thought, which would trace an impartially distinct path in its movement and would change something in the world for the better, and which would be noticeable even to a child or an ignoramus, like a flash of lightning or a roll of thunder. He thirsted for the new.

Yura felt good with his uncle. He resembled his mother. He was a free spirit, as she had been, with no prejudice against anything inhabitual. Like her, he had an aristocratic feeling of equality with all that lived. He understood everything at first glance, just as she had, and was able to express his thoughts in the form in which they came to him at the first moment, while they were alive and had not lost their meaning.

Yura was glad that his uncle was taking him to Duplyanka. It was very beautiful there, and the picturesqueness of the place also reminded him of his mother, who had loved nature and had often taken him on walks with her. Besides that, Yura was pleased that he would again meet Nika Dudorov, a high school boy who lived at Voskoboinikov's and probably despised him for being two years younger, and who, when greeting him, pulled his hand down hard and bowed his head so low that the hair fell over his forehead, covering half his face.

5

'The vital nerve of the problem of pauperism,' Nikolai Nikolaevich read from the corrected manuscript.

'I think it would be better to say "essence",' Ivan Ivanovich said, and introduced the required correction into the proofs.

They were working in the semi-darkness of the glassed-in terrace. The eye could make out watering cans and gardening tools lying around in disorder. A raincoat was thrown over the back of a broken chair. In a corner stood rubber hip boots with dry mud stuck to them, their tops hanging down to the floor.

'Meanwhile, the statistics of deaths and births show . . .' Nikolai Nikolaevich dictated.

'We need to put in "for the year under review",' Ivan Ivanovich said, and wrote it in.

The terrace was slightly draughty. Pieces of granite lay on the pages of the brochure so that they would not fly away.

When they finished, Nikolai Nikolaevich hurried to go home.

'There's a storm coming. We must be on our way.'

'Don't even think of it. I won't let you. We'll have tea now.'

'I absolutely must be in town by evening.'

'Nothing doing. I won't hear of it.'

The fumes of the lighted samovar came drifting from the garden, drowning the scent of nicotiana and heliotrope. Sour cream, berries, and cheesecakes were brought there from the cottage. Suddenly word came that Pavel had gone to bathe in the river and taken the horses with him for a bath. Nikolai Nikolaevich had to give in.

'Let's go to the bluff and sit on a bench while they set out tea,' Ivan Ivanovich suggested.

Ivan Ivanovich, by right of friendship with the rich Kologrivov, occupied two rooms in the steward's cottage. This little house with its adjoining garden stood in a dark, neglected part of the park with an old semicircular driveway. The driveway was thickly overgrown with grass. There was no movement on it now, and it was used only for hauling dirt and construction trash to the ravine, which served as a dry dump site. A man of progressive ideas and a millionaire who sympathised with revolution, Kologrivov himself was presently abroad with his wife. Only his daughters Nadya and Lipa were living on the estate, with their governess and a small staff of servants.

The steward's little garden was set off from the rest of the park, with its ponds and lawns and manor house, by a thick hedge of black viburnum. Ivan Ivanovich and Nikolai Nikolaevich skirted this growth from outside, and, as they walked, the sparrows that swarmed in the viburnum flew out in identical flocks at identical intervals. This filled the hedge with a monotonous noise, as if water were flowing along it through a pipe ahead of Ivan Ivanovich and Nikolai Nikolaevich.

They walked past the greenhouse, the gardener's quarters, and some stone ruins of unknown purpose. Their conversation got on to the new young forces in science and literature.

'You come across talented people,' said Nikolai Nikolaevich. 'But now various circles and associations are the fashion. Every herd is a refuge for giftlessness, whether it's a faith in Soloviev,[6] or Kant, or Marx. Only the solitary seek the truth, and they break with all those who don't love it sufficiently. Is there anything in the world that merits faithfulness? Such things are very few. I think we must be faithful to immortality, that other, slightly stronger name for life. We must keep faith in immortality, we must be faithful to Christ! Ah, you're wincing, poor fellow. Again you haven't understood a thing.'

'M-m-yes,' grunted Ivan Ivanovich, a thin, tow-headed, mercurial man, with a malicious little beard that made him look like an American of Lincoln's time (he kept gathering it in his hand and catching the tip of it in his lips). 'I, of course, say nothing. You understand – I look at these things quite differently. Ah, by the way. Tell me how they defrocked you. I've long been meaning to ask. I bet you were scared. Did they anathematise you? Eh?'

'Why change the subject? Though, anyhow, why not? Anathematise? No, these days they do without cursing. There was some unpleasantness; it had its consequences. For instance, I can't hold a government job for a long time. They won't allow me in the capitals.[7] But that's all rubbish. Let's go back to what we were talking about. I said we must be faithful to Christ. I'll explain at once. You don't understand that one can be an atheist, one can not know whether God exists or why, and at the same time know that man does not live in nature but in history, and that in present-day understanding it was founded by Christ, that its foundation is the Gospel. And what is history? It is the setting in motion of centuries of work at the gradual unriddling of death and its eventual overcoming. Hence the discovery of mathematical infinity and electromagnetic waves, hence the writing of symphonies. It is impossible to move on in that direction without a certain uplift. These discoveries call for spiritual equipment. The grounds for it are contained in the Gospel. They are these. First, love of one's neighbour, that highest form of living energy, overflowing man's heart and demanding to be let out and spent, and then the main component parts of modern man, without which he is unthinkable – namely, the idea of the free person and the idea of life as sacrifice. Bear in mind that this is still extremely new. The ancients did not have history in this sense. Then there was the sanguinary swinishness of the cruel, pockmarked Caligulas, who did not suspect how giftless all oppressors are. They had the boastful, dead eternity of bronze monuments and marble columns. Ages and generations breathed freely only after Christ. Only after him did life in posterity begin, and man now dies not by some fence in the street, but in his own history, in the heat of work devoted to the overcoming of death, dies devoted to that theme himself. Ouf, I'm all in a sweat, as they say. But you can't even make a dent in him!'

'Metaphysics, old boy. It's forbidden me by my doctors; my stomach can't digest it.'

'Well, God help you. Let's drop it. Lucky man! What a view you have from here – I can't stop admiring it! And he lives and doesn't feel it.'

It was painful to look at the river. It gleamed in the sun, curving in and out like a sheet of iron. Suddenly it wrinkled up. A heavy ferry with horses, carts, peasant women and men set out from this bank to the other.

'Just think, it's only a little past five,' said Ivan Ivanovich. 'See, there's the express from Syzran. It passes here at a little after five.'

Far across the plain, a clean little yellow and blue train, greatly diminished by the distance, rolled from right to left. Suddenly they noticed that it had stopped. White puffs of smoke rose up from the engine. Shortly afterwards came its alarmed whistling.

'Strange,' said Voskoboinikov. 'Something's wrong. It has no reason to stop there in the marsh. Something's happened. Let's go and have tea.'

6

Nika was not in the garden, nor in the house. Yura guessed that he was hiding from them because he was bored with them and Yura was no match for him. His uncle and Ivan Ivanovich went to work on the terrace, leaving Yura to loiter aimlessly about the house.

There was a wonderful enchantment about the place! At every moment you could hear the pure, three-note whistling of orioles, with intervals of waiting, so that the moist, drawn-out, flutelike sound could fully saturate the surroundings. The stagnant scent of flowers wandering in the air was nailed down motionless to the flowerbeds by the heat. How reminiscent it was of Antibes and Bordighera! Yura kept turning right and left. Over the lawns in an auditory hallucination hung the phantom of his mother's voice; it sounded for him in the melodious turns of the birds and the buzzing of the bees. Yura kept being startled; time and again it seemed to him that his mother was hallooing him and calling him somewhere.

He went to the ravine and began to climb down. He climbed down from the sparse and clean woods that covered the top of the ravine to the alder bushes that spread over its bottom.

Here there was damp darkness, windfall and carrion; there were few flowers, and the jointed stalks of horsetail looked like rods and staffs with Egyptian ornaments, as in his illustrated Holy Scriptures.

Yura felt more and more sad. He wanted to cry. He fell to his knees and dissolved in tears.

'Angel of God, my holy protector,' Yura prayed, 'set my mind firmly on the true path and tell dear mama that it's good for me here, so that she doesn't worry. If there is life after death, Lord, place mama in paradise, where the faces of the saints and the righteous shine like stars. Mama was so good, it can't be that she was a sinner, have mercy on her, Lord, make it so that she doesn't suffer. Mama!' – in heart-rending anguish he called out to her in heaven as a newly canonised saint, and suddenly could not bear it, fell to the ground, and lost consciousness.

He did not lie oblivious for long. When he came to, he heard his uncle calling him from above. He answered and started to climb up. Suddenly he remembered that he had not prayed for his missing father, as Marya Niko-laevna had taught him to do.

But he felt so good after fainting that he did not want to part with this feeling of lightness and was afraid to lose it. And he thought there would be nothing terrible if he prayed for his father some other time.

'He'll wait. He'll be patient,' he all but thought. Yura did not remember him at all.

7

On the train, travelling in a second-class compartment with his father, the attorney Gordon from Orenburg, sat the second-year student Misha Gordon, an eleven-year-old boy with a thoughtful face and big dark eyes. The father was moving to work in Moscow, the boy had been transferred to a Moscow school. His mother and sisters had long been there, busy with the cares of readying the apartment.

The boy and his father had been on the train for three days.

Past them in clouds of hot dust, bleached as with lime by the sun, flew Russia, fields and steppes, towns and villages. Wagon trains stretched along the roads, turning off cumbersomely to the crossings, and from the furiously speeding train it seemed that the wagons were standing still and the horses were raising and lowering their legs in place.

At big stations the passengers rushed like mad to the buffet, and the setting sun behind the trees of the station garden shone on their legs and the wheels of the carriages.

Separately, all the movements of the world were calculatedly sober, but as a sum total they were unconsciously drunk with the general current of life that united them. People toiled and bustled, set in motion by the mechanism of their own cares. But the mechanisms would not have worked if their chief regulator had not been a sense of supreme and fundamental carefreeness. This carefreeness came from a sense of the cohesion of human existences, a confidence in their passing from one into another, a sense of happiness owing to the fact that everything that happens takes place not only on earth, in which the dead are buried, but somewhere else, in what some call the Kingdom of God, others history, and still others something else again.

To this rule the boy was a bitter and painful exception. His mainspring remained a sense of care, and no feeling of unconcern lightened or ennobled it. He knew he had this inherited trait and with self-conscious alertness caught signs of it in himself. It upset him. Its presence humiliated him.

For as long as he could remember, he had never ceased to marvel at how, with the same arms and legs and a common language and habits, one could be not like everyone else, and besides that, be someone who was liked by few, someone who was not loved. He could not understand a situation in which, if you were worse than others, you could not make an effort to correct yourself and become better. What did it mean to be a Jew? Why was there such a thing? What could reward or justify this unarmed challenge that brought nothing but grief?

When he turned to his father for an answer, he said that his starting points were absurd and one could not reason that way, but he did not offer anything instead that would attract Misha by its profound meaning and oblige him to bow silently before the irrevocable.

And, making an exception for his father and mother, Misha gradually became filled with scorn for adults, who had cooked a pudding they were unable to eat. He was convinced that when he grew up, he would untangle it all.

Now, too, no one would dare to say that his father had acted wrongly in rushing after that madman when he ran out onto the platform, and that there was no need to stop the train, when, powerfully shoving Grigory Osipovich aside and throwing open the door of the carriage, the man had hurled himself headlong off the speeding express onto the embankment, as a diver throws himself off the deck of a bathing house into the water.

But since the brake handle had been turned not by just anyone, but precisely by Grigory Osipovich, it came out that the train went on standing there so unaccountably long thanks to them.

No one really knew the cause of the delay. Some said that the sudden stop had damaged the air brakes, others that the train was standing on a steep slope and the engine could not get up it without momentum. A third opinion spread that, since the man who had killed himself was an eminent person, his attorney, who was travelling with him on the train, had demanded that witnesses be summoned from the nearest station, Kologrivovka, to draw up a report. That was why the assistant engineer had climbed the telephone pole. The handcar must already be on its way.

In the car there was a bit of a whiff from the toilets, which they tried to ward off with eau de cologne, and it smelled of roast chicken gone slightly bad, wrapped in dirty greased paper. The greying Petersburg ladies, powdering themselves as before, wiping their palms with handkerchiefs, and talking in chesty, rasping voices, all turned into jet-black Gypsy women from the combination of engine soot and greasy cosmetics. As they passed by the Gordons' compartment, wrapping the corners of their shoulders in shawls and turning the narrowness of the corridor into a source of fresh coquetry, it seemed to Misha that they hissed, or, judging by their compressed lips, meant to hiss: 'Ah, just imagine, such sensitivity! We're special! We're intelligentsia! We simply can't!'

The body of the suicide lay on the grass by the embankment. A streak of dried blood made a sharp black mark across the forehead and eyes of the broken man, as if crossing out his face. The blood seemed not to be his blood, flowing from him, but a stuck-on, extraneous addition, a plaster, or a spatter of dried mud, or a wet birch leaf.

The little bunch of curious and sympathising people around the body kept changing all the time. Over him, frowning, expressionless, stood his friend and compartment companion, a stout and arrogant lawyer, a pure-bred animal in a sweat-soaked shirt. He was weary from the heat and fanned himself with a soft hat. To all questions, he replied ungraciously through his teeth, shrugging and without even turning: 'An alcoholic. Can't you understand? The most typical consequence of delirium tremens.'

A thin woman in a woollen dress and lace fichu approached the body two or three times. This was old Tiverzina, a widow and the mother of two engineers, who was travelling free in third class with her two daughters-in-law on a company pass. The quiet women, their kerchiefs drawn low, silently followed behind her, like two nuns behind their mother superior. The group inspired respect. People made way for them.

Tiverzina's husband had been burned alive in a railroad accident. She stopped a few steps from the corpse, so that she could see it through the crowd, and sighed as if making the comparison. 'To each as it's set down at birth,' she seemed to say. 'Some die by God's will, but this one, see what a notion took him – from rich living and a fuddled brain.'

All the passengers on the train came in turn to see the body and went back to their carriages only for fear that something might be stolen from them.

When they jumped down on the tracks, stretched their limbs, picked flowers, and took a little run, they all had the feeling that the place had just emerged only thanks to the stop, and that the swampy meadow with its knolls, the wide river, with a beautiful house and a church on the high bank opposite, would not be there had it not been for the accident that had taken place.

Even the sun, which also seemed like a local accessory, shone upon the scene by the rails with an evening shyness, approaching as if timorously, as a cow from the herd grazing nearby would if it were to come to the railway and start looking at the people.

Misha was shaken by all that had happened and for the first moments wept from pity and fright. In the course of the long journey the suicide had come to their compartment several times and had sat talking for hours with Misha's father. He had said that his soul felt relaxed in the morally pure quiet and comprehension of their world, and he had questioned Grigory Osipovich about various legal subtleties and cavils to do with promissory notes and donations, bankruptcies and frauds. 'Ah, is that so?' he kept being surprised at Gordon's explanations. 'You dispose of a much more merciful set of statutes. My attorney has different information. He takes a much darker view of these things.'

Each time this nervous man calmed down, his lawyer and compartment companion came from first class and dragged him off to drink champagne in the dining car. This was the stout, insolent, clean-shaven fop of an attorney who now stood over the body, not surprised at anything in the world. It was impossible to rid oneself of the feeling that his client's constant agitation had somehow played into his hands.

The father said that this was a well-known rich man, kindly and wayward, already half out of his mind. Unembarrassed by Misha's presence, he had told of his son, the same age as Misha, and of his late wife, and had then gone on to his second family, which he had also abandoned. Then he remembered something new, paled with terror, and began talking nonsense and forgetting himself.

Towards Misha he showed an inexplicable tenderness, probably reflected, and perhaps not destined for him. He kept giving him things, for which he got out at the biggest stations and went to the first-class waiting rooms, where there were bookstalls and they sold games and local curiosities.

He drank incessantly and complained that he had not slept for three months and, when he sobered up even for a short time, suffered torments of which a normal man could have no notion.

A moment before the end he rushed to their compartment, seized Grigory Osipovich by the hand, wanted to say something but could not, and, rushing out to the platform, threw himself from the train.

Misha was examining a small collection of minerals from the Urals in a wooden box – the dead man's last gift. Suddenly everything around began to stir. A handcar had reached the train by a different track. From it jumped a coroner in a visored cap with a cockade, a doctor, and two policemen. Cold, businesslike voices were heard. Questions were asked, something was written down. Conductors and policemen clumsily dragged the body up the embankment, losing their footing in the gravel and sliding down all the time. Some peasant woman began to wail. The public was asked to go back to the carriages and the whistle sounded. The train set off.

8

'Again this holy oil!' Nika thought spitefully and rushed about the room. The voices of the guests were coming closer. Retreat was cut off. There were two beds in the room, Voskoboinikov's and his own. Without thinking twice, Nika crawled under the second one.

He heard them looking and calling for him in the other rooms, surprised at his disappearance. Then they came into the bedroom.

'Well, what can we do,' said Vedenyapin. 'Go for a walk, Yura; maybe your friend will turn up later and you can play.'

They talked for a while about the university unrest in Petersburg and Moscow, keeping Nika for some twenty minutes in his stupid, humiliating concealment. Finally they went to the terrace. Nika quietly opened the window, jumped out of it, and went to the park.

He was not himself today and had not slept the previous night. He was going on fourteen. He was sick of being little. All night he had not slept and at dawn he left the cottage. The sun was rising, and the ground in the park was covered with the long, dewy, openwork shade of trees. The shade was not black, but of a dark grey colour, like wet felt. The stupefying fragrance of morning seemed to come precisely from that damp shade on the ground, with its elongated light spots like a young girl's fingers.

Suddenly a silvery little stream of mercury, just like the dewdrops on the grass, flowed a few steps away from him. The little stream flowed, flowed, not soaking into the ground. Then, with an unexpectedly abrupt movement, it darted to one side and vanished. It was a grass snake. Nika shuddered.

He was a strange boy. In a state of excitement, he talked to himself out loud. He imitated his mother in his predilection for lofty matters and paradoxes.

'How good it is in this world!' he thought. 'But why does it always come out so painful? God exists, of course. But if He exists, then He – is me. I'm going to order it,' he thought, glancing at an aspen all seized with trembling from bottom to top (its wet, shimmering leaves seemed cut from tin), 'I'm going to command it,' and, in an insane exceeding of his strength, he did not whisper but with all his being, with all his flesh and blood, desired and thought: 'Be still!' and the tree at once obediently froze in immobility. Nika laughed for joy and ran off to swim in the river.

His father, the terrorist Dementy Dudorov, was serving at hard labour, which by grace of the sovereign had replaced the hanging to which he had been sentenced. His mother, from the Georgian princely family of the Eristovs, was a whimsical and still young beauty, eternally passionate about something – rebellions, rebels, extreme theories, famous actors, poor failures.

She adored Nika and from his name, Innokenty, made a heap of inconceivably tender and foolish nicknames like Inochka or Nochenka, and took him to show to her relatives in Tiflis. There he was struck most of all by a splay-limbed tree in the courtyard of the house where they were staying. It was some sort of clumsy tropical giant. With its leaves, which resembled elephant's ears, it shielded the courtyard from the scorching southern sky. Nika could not get used to the idea that this tree was a plant and not an animal.

It was dangerous for the boy to bear his father's terrible name. With Nina Galaktionovna's consent, Ivan Ivanovich was preparing to petition the sovereign about Nika adopting his mother's family name.

While he lay under the bed, indignant at the way things went in the world, he thought about that along with everything else. Who is this Voskoboinikov to push his meddling so far? He's going to teach them!

And this Nadya! If she's fifteen, does that mean she has the right to turn up her nose and talk to him like a little boy? He's going to show her! 'I hate her,' he repeated to himself several times. 'I'll kill her! I'll invite her for a boat ride and drown her.'

Mama's a good one, too. Of course, she tricked him and Voskoboinikov when she was leaving. She didn't go to any Caucasus, she quite simply turned north at the first junction and is most calmly shooting at the police along with the students in Petersburg. While he has to rot alive in this stupid hole. But he would outwit them all. He'd drown Nadya, quit school, and run off to his father in Siberia to raise a rebellion.

The edge of the pond was densely overgrown with water lilies. The boat cut into their thickness with a dry rustle. Where the growth was torn, the water of the pond showed like the juice of a watermelon in a triangular cut-out.

The boy and girl started picking water lilies. They both took hold of the same tough, rubbery stem, which refused to snap. It pulled them together. The children bumped heads. The boat was drawn to the bank as if by a hook. The stems became entangled and shortened; the white flowers with centres bright as egg yolk and blood sank underwater, then emerged with water streaming from them.

Nadya and Nika went on gathering flowers, heeling the boat over more and more and almost lying next to each other on the lowered side.

'I'm sick of studying,' said Nika. 'It's time to begin life, to earn money, to go among people.'

'And I was just going to ask you to explain quadratic equations to me. I'm so weak in algebra that it almost ended with me repeating the exam.'

Nika sensed some sort of barb in these words. Well, of course, she was putting him in his place, reminding him of how young he still was. Quadratic equations! And they had not even caught a whiff of algebra yet.

Without betraying how wounded he was, he asked with feigned indifference and realising at the same moment how stupid it was:

'When you grow up, who are you going to marry?'

'Oh, that's still so far off. Probably no one. I haven't thought about it yet.'

'Please don't imagine I'm all that interested.'

'Then why did you ask?'

'You're a fool.'

They began to quarrel. Nika remembered his morning misogyny. He threatened Nadya that if she did not stop saying insolent things, he would drown her.

'Just try,' said Nadya.

He seized her round the waist. A fight started. They lost their balance and fell into the water.

They both knew how to swim, but the water lilies caught at their arms and legs, and they could not yet feel the bottom. Finally, sinking into the ooze, they clambered out on the bank. Water poured in streams from their shoes and pockets. Nika was particularly tired.

If this had happened still quite recently, no further back than that spring, then in the given situation, sitting together thoroughly soaked after such a crossing, they would surely have made a noise, scolding or laughing.

But now they were silent and barely breathed, crushed by the absurdity of what had happened. Nadya was indignant and protested silently, while Nika hurt all over, as if his arms and legs had been broken by a stick and his ribs caved in.

Finally, like a grown-up, Nadya quietly murmured, 'Madman!' – and he, in the same grown-up way, said, 'Forgive me.'

They began to walk up towards the house, leaving wet trails behind them like two water barrels. Their way led up the dusty slope, swarming with snakes, not far from the place where Nika had seen a grass snake in the morning.

Nika remembered the magic elation of the night, the dawn, and his morning omnipotence, when by his own will he had commanded nature. What should he order it to do now, he wondered. What did he want most of all? He fancied that he wanted most of all to fall into the pond again some day with Nadya, and he would have given a lot right then to know if it would ever happen or not.

Part Two

A GIRL FROM A DIFFERENT CIRCLE

I

The war with Japan was not over yet. It was unexpectedly overshadowed by other events. Waves of revolution rolled across Russia, each one higher and more prodigious than the last.[1]

At that time Amalia Karlovna Guichard, the widow of a Belgian engineer and herself a Russified Frenchwoman, came to Moscow from the Urals with two children, her son Rodion and her daughter Larissa. Her son she sent to the Cadet Corps, and her daughter to a girls' high school, by chance the same one and in the same class in which Nadya Kologrivova was studying.

Mme Guichard's husband had left her some savings in securities, which had been rising but now had begun to fall. To slow the melting away of her means and not sit with folded arms, Mme Guichard bought a small business, Levitskaya's dressmaking shop near the Triumphal Arch, from the seamstress's heirs, with the right to keep the old firm intact, with the circle of its former clients and all its modistes and apprentices.

Mme Guichard did this on the advice of the lawyer Komarovsky, her husband's friend and her own mainstay, a cold-blooded businessman, who knew business life in Russia like the back of his hand. She corresponded with him about her move, he met them at the station, he took them across the whole of Moscow to the furnished rooms of the Montenegro in Oruzheiny Lane, where he had taken quarters for them, he insisted on sending Rodion to the corps and Lara to the high school he recommended, and he joked distractedly with the boy and fixed his gaze on the girl so that she blushed.

2

Before moving to the small three-room apartment that came with the shop, they lived for about a month at the Montenegro.

These were the most terrible parts of Moscow, slick cabbies and low haunts, whole streets given over to depravity, slums full of 'lost creatures'.

The children were not surprised at the dirtiness of the rooms, the bed-bugs, the squalor of the furnishings. After their father's death, their mother had lived in eternal fear of destitution. Rodya and Lara were used to hearing that they were on the verge of ruin. They understood that they were not street children, but in them there was a deep-seated timidity before the rich, as in children from an orphanage.

A living example of this fear was given them by their mother. Amalia Karlovna was a plump blonde of about thirty-five, whose fits of heart failure alternated with fits of stupidity. She was a terrible coward and had a mortal fear of men. Precisely for that reason, being frightened and bewildered, she kept falling from one embrace into another.

In the Montenegro they occupied number 23, and in number 24, from the day the place was founded, the cellist Tyshkevich had been living, a kindly fellow, sweaty and bald, in a little wig, who folded his hands prayer-fully and pressed them to his breast when he was persuading someone, and threw back his head and rolled up his eyes inspiredly when he played in society or appeared at concerts. He was rarely at home and went off for whole days to the Bolshoi Theatre or the Conservatory. The neighbours became acquainted. Mutual favours brought them close.

Since the children's presence occasionally hampered Amalia Karlovna during Komarovsky's visits, Tyshkevich began leaving his key with her when he left, so that she could receive her friend. Soon Mme Guichard became so accustomed to his self-sacrifices that she knocked on his door several times in tears, asking him to defend her against her protector.

3

The house was of one storey, not far from the corner of Tverskaya. The proximity of the Brest railway could be felt. Its realm began nearby, the company apartments of the employees, the engine depots and warehouses.

The place was home to Olya Demina, an intelligent girl, the niece of one of the employees of the Moscow Freight Yard.

She was a capable apprentice. The former owner had taken notice of her, and now the new one began to bring her closer. Olya Demina liked Lara very much.

Everything remained as it had been under Levitskaya. The sewing machines turned like mad under the pumping feet or fluttering hands of the weary seamstresses. One would be quietly sewing, sitting on a table and drawing her hand with the needle and long thread far out. The floor was littered with scraps. They had to talk loudly to outshout the rapping of the sewing machines and the modulated trills of Kirill Modestovich, a canary in a cage under the window's arch, the secret of whose name the former owner had taken with her to the grave.

In the waiting room, ladies in a picturesque group surrounded a table with magazines. They stood, sat, or half reclined in the poses they saw in the pictures and, studying the models, discussed styles. At another table, in the director's place, sat Amalia Karlovna's assistant from among the senior cutters, Faïna Silantievna Fetisova, a bony woman with warts in the hollows of her wizened cheeks.

She held a bone cigarette holder with a cigarette in it between her yellowed teeth, squinted her eye with its yellow white, and let out a yellow stream of smoke from her nose and mouth as she wrote down measurements, receipt numbers, addresses, and the preferences of the crowding customers.

Amalia Karlovna was a new and inexperienced person in the shop. She did not feel herself the owner in the full sense. But the personnel were honest; Fetisova could be relied on. Nevertheless, it was a troubled time. Amalia Karlovna was afraid to think of the future. She would be seized by despair. Everything would drop from her hands.

Komarovsky visited them often. When Viktor Ippolitovich crossed the whole shop on his way to their apartment and in passing frightened the fancy ladies changing clothes, who hid behind the screen at his appearance and from there playfully parried his casual jokes, the seamstresses disapprovingly and mockingly whispered after him: 'His Honour', 'Her'n', 'Amalka's Heart-throb', 'Stud', 'Skirt-chaser'.

An object of still greater hatred was his bulldog Jack, whom he sometimes brought on a leash and who pulled him along with such violent tugs that Komarovsky would miss his step, lurch forward, and go after the dog with his arms stretched out, like a blind man following his guide.

Once in the spring Jack snapped at Lara's leg and tore her stocking.

'I'll do him in, the filthy devil,' Olya Demina whispered in Lara's ear in a child's hoarse voice.

'Yes, he's really a disgusting dog. But how will you do it, silly girl?'

'Shh, don't shout, I'll tell you. You know those Easter eggs, the stone ones. Like your mother has on the chest of drawers . . .'

'Yes, of course, made of marble, of crystal.'

'Right! Bend down, I'll whisper in your ear. You take one, dip it in lard, the lard sticks to it, the mangy mutt swallows it, stuffs his gut, the little Satan, and – basta! Paws up! It's glass!'

Lara laughed and thought with envy: The girl lives in poverty, works hard. Young ones from the people develop early. But see how much there still is in her that is unspoiled, childlike. The eggs, Jack – where did she get it all? 'Why is it my lot,' thought Lara, 'to see everything and take it so to heart?'

4

'But for him mama is – what's it called . . . He's mama's . . . whatever . . . They're bad words, I don't want to repeat them. But why in that case does he look at me with such eyes? I'm her daughter.'

She was a little over sixteen, but she was a fully formed young girl. They gave her eighteen or more. She had a clear mind and an easy character. She was very good-looking.

She and Rodya understood that they would have to get everything in life the hard way. In contrast to the idle and secure, they had no time to indulge in premature finagling and sniff out in theory things that in practice had not yet touched them. Only the superfluous is dirty. Lara was the purest being in the world.

The brother and sister knew the price of everything and valued what they had attained. One had to be in good repute to make one's way. Lara studied well, not out of an abstract thirst for knowledge, but because to be exempt from paying for one's studies one had to be a good student, and therefore one had to study well. Just as she studied well, so without effort she washed dishes, helped in the shop, and ran errands for her mother. She moved noiselessly and smoothly, and everything about her – the inconspicuous quickness of her movements, her height, her voice, her grey eyes and fair hair – went perfectly together.

It was Sunday, the middle of July. On holidays you could lounge in bed a little longer in the morning. Lara lay on her back, her arms thrown back, her hands under her head.

In the shop there was an unaccustomed quiet. The window onto the street was open. Lara heard a droshky rumbling in the distance drive off the cobbled pavement into the grooves of the horse-tram rails, and the crude clatter turned to a smooth gliding of wheels as if on butter. 'I must sleep a little more,' thought Lara. The murmur of the city was as soporific as a lullaby.

Lara sensed her length and position in the bed by two points now – the jut of her left shoulder and the big toe of her right foot. There was a shoulder and a foot, and all the rest was more or less herself, her soul or essence, harmoniously enclosed in its outlines and responsively straining towards the future.

I must fall asleep, thought Lara, and she called up in her imagination the sunny side of Karetny Row at that hour, the sheds of the equipage establishments with enormous carriages for sale on clean-swept floors, the bevelled glass of carriage lanterns, the stuffed bears, the rich life. And slightly lower – Lara was picturing it mentally – the dragoons drilling in the courtyard of the Znamensky barracks, horses decorously prancing in circles, running leaps into the saddle, riding at a walk, riding at a trot, riding at a gallop. And the gaping mouths of nannies with children and wet nurses, pressed in a row up against the barrack fence. And still lower – thought Lara – Petrovka Street, the Petrovsky Lines.

'How can you, Lara! Where do you get such ideas? I simply want to show you my apartment. The more so as it's close by.'

It was the name day of Olga, the little daughter of his acquaintances on Karetny Row. The grown-ups were having a party for the occasion – dancing, champagne. He invited mama, but mama could not go, she was indisposed. Mama said: 'Take Lara. You're always cautioning me: "Amalia, see to Lara." So go now and see to her.' And he saw to her all right! Ha, ha, ha!

What a mad thing, the waltz! You whirl and whirl, without a thought in your head. While the music is playing, a whole eternity goes by, like life in novels. But the moment it stops, there is a feeling of scandal, as if they had poured cold water over you or found you undressed. Besides, you allow others these liberties out of vanity, to show what a big girl you are.

She could never have supposed that he danced so well. What knowing hands he has, how confidently he takes her by the waist! But never again would she allow anyone to kiss her like that. She could never have supposed that so much shamelessness could be concentrated in anyone's lips when they were pressed so long to your own.

Drop all this foolishness. Once and for all. Do not play the simpleton, do not be coy, do not lower your eyes bashfully. It will end badly some day. The dreadful line is very close here. One step, and you fall straight into the abyss. Forget thinking about dances. That is where the whole evil lies. Do not be embarrassed to refuse. Pretend that you never learned to dance or have broken your leg.

5

In the autumn there were disturbances at the Moscow railway junction. The Moscow–Kazan railway went on strike. The Moscow–Brest line was to join it. The decision to strike had been taken, but the railway committee could not agree on the day to call it. Everyone on the railway knew about the strike, and it needed only an external pretext for it to start spontaneously.

It was a cold, grey morning at the beginning of October. The wages on the line were to be paid that day. For a long time no information came from the accounting department. Then a boy arrived at the office with a schedule, a record of payments, and an armload of workers' pay books collected in order to impose penalties. The payments began. Down the endless strip of unbuilt space that separated the station, the workshops, the engine depots, the warehouses, and the tracks from the wooden office buildings, stretched a line of conductors, switchmen, metalworkers and their assistants, scrub-women from the car park, waiting to receive their wages.

It smelled of early city winter, trampled maple leaves, melting snow, engine fumes, and warm rye bread, which was baked in the basement of the station buffet and had just been taken out of the oven. Trains arrived and departed. They were made up and dismantled with a waving of furled and unfurled flags. The watchmen's little horns, the pocket whistles of the couplers, and the bass-voiced hooting of locomotives played out all sorts of tunes. Pillars of smoke rose into the sky in endless ladders. The heated-up locomotives stood ready to go, scorching the cold winter clouds with boiling clouds of steam.

Up and down the tracks paced the head of the section, the railway expert Fuflygin, and the foreman of the station area, Pavel Ferapontovich Antipov. Antipov had been pestering the repair service with complaints about the materials supplied to him for replacing the tracks. The steel was not tensile enough. The rails did not hold up under tests for bending and breaking, and, according to Antipov's conjectures, were sure to crack in freezing weather. The management treated Pavel Ferapontovich's complaints with indifference. Somebody involved was lining his pockets.

Fuflygin was wearing an expensive fur coat, unbuttoned, trimmed with railway piping, and under it a new civilian suit made of cheviot. He stepped carefully along the embankment, admiring the general line of his lapels, the straight crease of his trousers, and the noble shape of his shoes.

Antipov's words went in one ear and out the other. Fuflygin was thinking his own thoughts, kept taking his watch out and looking at it, and was hurrying somewhere.

'Right, right, old boy,' he interrupted Antipov impatiently, 'but that's only on the main lines somewhere or on a through passage with a lot of traffic. But, mind you, what have you got here? Sidings and dead ends, burdock and nettles, at most the sorting of empty freight cars and the shunting manoeuvres of "pufferbillies". And he's still displeased! You're out of your mind! Not just these rails; here you could even lay wooden ones.'

Fuflygin looked at his watch, snapped the lid shut, and began gazing into the distance, where the highway came close to the railway. A carriage appeared at the bend of the road. This was Fuflygin's own rig. Madame his wife had come for him. The driver stopped the horses almost on the tracks, holding them back all the time and whoa-ing at them in a high, womanish voice, like a nanny at whimpering children – the horses were afraid of trains. In the corner of the carriage, carelessly reclining on the cushions, sat a beautiful lady.

'Well, brother, some other time,' said the head of the section, and he waved his hand as if to say 'Enough of your rails. There are more important matters.'

The spouses went rolling off.

6

Three or four hours later, closer to dusk, two figures, who had not been on the surface earlier, emerged as if from under the ground in the field to one side of the tracks and, looking back frequently, began to hurry off. They were Antipov and Tiverzin.

'Let's make it quick,' said Tiverzin. 'I'm not afraid of being tailed by spies, but once this diddling around is over, they'll climb out of the dugout and catch up with us, and I can't stand the sight of them. If everything's dragged out like this, there's no point fussing and fuming. There's no need for a committee, and for playing with fire, and burrowing under the ground! You're a good one, too, supporting all this slop from the Nikolaevsky line.'

'My Darya's got typhoid fever. I'd like to get her to the hospital. Until I do, my head's not good for anything.'

'They say they're handing out wages today. I'll go to the office. If it wasn't payday, as God is my witness, I'd spit on you all and personally put an end to all this dithering without a moment's delay.'

'In what way, may I ask?'

'Nothing to it. Go down to the boiler room, give a whistle, and the party's over.'

They said goodbye and went off in different directions.

Tiverzin went along the tracks towards the city. On his way he met people coming from the office with their pay. There were a great many of them. Tiverzin judged by the look of it that almost everyone on station territory had been paid.

It was getting dark. Idle workers crowded on the open square near the office, lit by the office lights. At the entrance to the square stood Fuflygin's carriage. Fuflygina sat in it in the same pose, as if she had not left the carriage since morning. She was waiting for her husband, who was getting his money in the office.

Wet snow and rain unexpectedly began to fall. The driver climbed down from the box and began to raise the leather top. While he rested his foot on the back and stretched the tight braces, Fuflygina admired the mess of watery silver beads flitting past the light of the office lamps. She cast her unblinking, dreamy gaze over the crowding workers with such an air, as though in case of need this gaze could pass unhindered through them, as through fog or drizzle.

Tiverzin happened to catch that expression. He cringed. He walked past without greeting Fuflygina, and decided to draw his salary later, so as to avoid running into her husband in the office. He walked on into the less well lit side of the workshops, where the turntable showed black with its tracks radiating towards the engine depot.

'Tiverzin! Kuprik!' several voices called to him from the darkness. In front of the workshops stood a bunch of people. Inside there was shouting and a child's weeping could be heard. 'Kiprian Savelyevich, step in for the boy,' said some woman in the crowd.

The old master Pyotr Khudoleev was again giving a habitual hiding to his victim, the young apprentice Yusupka.

Khudoleev had not always been a torturer of apprentices, a drunkard and a heavy-fisted brawler. Time was when merchants' and priests' daughters from the industrial suburbs near Moscow cast long glances at the dashing workman. But Tiverzin's mother, to whom he proposed just after she graduated from the diocesan girls' school, refused him and married his comrade, the locomotive engineer Savely Nikitich Tiverzin.

In the sixth year of her widowhood, after the terrible death of Savely Nikitich (he was burned up in 1888 in one of the sensational train collisions of that time), Pyotr Petrovich renewed his suit, and again Marfa Gavrilovna refused him. After that Khudoleev started drinking and became violent, settling accounts with the whole world, which was to blame, as he was convinced, for his present misfortunes.

Yusupka was the son of the yard porter Gimazetdin from the Tiverzins' courtyard. Tiverzin protected the boy in the workshops. This added heat to Khudoleev's dislike of him.

'Look how you're holding your file, you slope-head,' Khudoleev shouted, pulling Yusupka's hair and beating him on the neck. 'Is that any way to file down a casting? I'm asking you, are you going to foul up the work for me, you Kasimov bride,[2] allah-mullah, slant-eyes?'

'Ow, I won't, mister, ow, ow, I won't, I won't, ow, that hurts!'

'A thousand times he's been told, first bring the mandril under, then tighten the stop, but no, he's got his own way. Nearly broke the spendler on me, the son of a bitch.'

'I didn't touch the spindle, mister, by God, I didn't.'

'Why do you tyrannise the boy?' asked Tiverzin, squeezing through the crowd.

'Don't poke your nose in other people's business,' Khudoleev snapped.

'I'm asking you, why do you tyrannise the boy?'

'And I'm telling you to shove the hell off, social commander. Killing's too good for him, the scum, he nearly broke the spendler on me. He can go on his knees to me for getting off alive, the slant-eyed devil – I just boxed his ears and pulled his hair a little.'

'So according to you, Uncle Khudolei, he should have his head torn off for it? You really ought to be ashamed. An old master, grey in your hair, but no brains in your head.'

'Shove off, shove off, I said, while you're still in one piece. I'll knock your soul through your shoes for teaching me, you dog's ass! You got made on the ties, fish-blood, right under your father's nose. I know your mother, the wet-tail, all too well, the mangy cat, the skirt-dragger!'

What came next took no more than a minute. They each grabbed the first thing that came to hand among the heavy tools and pieces of iron that lay about on the machines, and they would have killed each other if at that same moment people had not rushed in a mob to pull them apart. Khudoleev and Tiverzin stood, their heads lowered, their foreheads almost touching, pale, with bloodshot eyes. They were unable to speak from agitation. Their arms were seized and held tightly from behind. At moments, gathering their strength, they would try to tear free, their whole bodies writhing and dragging the comrades who were hanging on to them. Hooks and buttons were torn from their clothes, their jackets and shirts were pulled from their bared shoulders. The disorderly uproar around them would not quiet down.

'The chisel! Take the chisel from him – he'll split his skull.' 'Easy, easy, Uncle Pyotr, we'll sprain your arm.' 'Are we just going to keep dancing around them? Pull them apart, lock them up, and be done with it.'

Suddenly, with a superhuman effort, Tiverzin shook off the tangle of bodies holding him and, breaking free of them, found himself running for the door. They were about to rush after him, but, seeing that he had something else in mind, let him go. He went out, slamming the door, and marched off without looking back. He was surrounded by autumnal dampness, night, darkness. 'You reach them a hand and they bite it off,' he muttered, having no idea where he was going or why.

This world of baseness and falsity, where a well-fed little lady dares to look like that at witless working people, and the drunken victim of this order finds pleasure in jeering at one of his own kind, this world was now more hateful to him than ever. He walked quickly, as if the speed of his pace could bring closer the time when everything in the world would be as reasonable and harmonious as it now was in his feverish head. He knew that their strivings in recent days, the disorders on the line, the speeches at meetings, and their decision to go on strike – not yet brought to fulfilment, but also not renounced – were all separate parts of that great path which still lay before them.

But now his excitement had reached such a degree that he was impatient to run the whole of that distance at once, without stopping for breath. He did not realise where he was going with such long strides, but his feet knew very well where they were taking him.

Tiverzin did not suspect for a long time that, after he and Antipov left the dugout, the committee had decided to start the strike that same evening. The members of the committee at once assigned who among them was to go where and who would relieve whom. When the hoarse, gradually clearing and steadying signal burst from the engine repair shop, as if from the bottom of Tiverzin's soul, a crowd from the depot and the freight yard was already moving towards the city from the semaphore at the entrance, merging with a new crowd which, at Tiverzin's whistle, had dropped their work in the boiler room.

For many years Tiverzin thought that he alone had stopped all work and movement on the railway that night. Only later trials, in which he was judged collectively and the accusations did not include inciting to strike, led him out of that error.

People came running out, asking: 'Why is the whistle blowing?' The response came from the darkness: 'Are you deaf? Can't you hear? It's the alarm. There's a fire.' 'But where is it?' 'Must be somewhere, since the whistle's blowing.'

Doors banged, new people came out. Other voices were heard. 'Go on – a fire! Country hicks! Don't listen to the fool. It's what's called a walkout,

understand? Here's my hat and here's the door, I'm not your servant any-
more. Let's go home, boys.'

More and more people joined in. The railway was on strike.

7

Tiverzin came home two days later, chilled, sleepy, and unshaven. The night
before there had been a sudden cold snap, unprecedented for that time of
year, and Tiverzin was dressed for autumn. At the gate he was met by the
yard porter Gimazetdin.

'Thank you, Mr Tiverzin,' he began. 'You not let Yusup be hurt, you
make us all pray God forever.'

'Are you out of your mind, Gimazetdin? What kind of "mister" am I to
you? Drop all that, please. Speak quickly, you see how freezing it is.'

'Why freezing, you warm, Savelyich. Yesterday we bring your mother,
Marfa Gavrilovna, full shed of firewood from freight yard, birch only, good
firewood, dry firewood.'

'Thank you, Gimazetdin. There's something else you wanted to tell me.
Be quick, please, you can see I'm cold.'

'I wanted to tell you, no sleep home, Savelyich, must hide. Policeman
asked, police chief asked, who come to see you. I say no one come. An assistant come, the engine team comes, railway people. But strangers – no, no!'

The house where the bachelor Tiverzin lived with his mother and his
married younger brother belonged to the neighbouring church of the
Holy Trinity. This house was inhabited partly by certain of the clergy,
by two associations of fruit- and meat-sellers who hawked their wares
from stands in town, but mostly by minor employees of the Moscow–Brest
railway.

The house was of stone with wooden galleries. They surrounded on four
sides a dirty, unpaved courtyard. Dirty and slippery wooden stairways led
up to the galleries. They smelled of cats and pickled cabbage. To the landings clung outhouses and cupboards with padlocks.

Tiverzin's brother had been called up as a private in the war and had been
wounded at Wafangkou.[3] He was recovering in the Krasnoyarsk Hospital,
where his wife and two daughters had gone to visit him and receive him
when he was dismissed. Hereditary railwaymen, the Tiverzins were light-
footed and went all over Russia on free company passes. At the time, the
apartment was quiet and empty. Only the mother and son were living in it.

The apartment was on the second floor. On the gallery outside the
front door stood a barrel, which was filled by a water carrier. When Kiprian

Savelyevich got up to his level, he discovered that the lid of the barrel had been moved aside and a metal mug stood frozen to the crust of ice that had formed on the water.

'Prov and nobody else,' thought Tiverzin with a smirk. 'Can't drink enough, got a hole in him, guts on fire.'

Prov Afanasyevich Sokolov, a psalm-reader, a stately and not yet old man, was a distant relation of Marfa Gavrilovna.

Kiprian Savelyevich tore the mug from the ice crust, put the lid on the barrel, and pulled the handle of the doorbell. A cloud of domestic smell and savoury steam moved to meet him.

'You've really heated it up, mama. It's warm here, very nice.'

His mother fell on his neck, embraced him, and wept. He stroked her head, waited a little, and moved her away gently.

'A stout heart takes cities, mama,' he said softly. 'My path goes from Moscow right to Warsaw.'

'I know. That's why I'm crying. It's going to be bad for you. Take yourself off somewhere, Kuprinka, somewhere far away.'

'Your dear little friend, your kindly shepherd boy,[4] Pyotr Petrovich, almost split my skull.' He meant to make her laugh. She did not understand the joke and earnestly replied:

'It's a sin to laugh at him, Kuprinka. You should pity him. A hopeless wretch, a lost soul.'

'They've taken Pashka Antipov. Pavel Ferapontovich. They came at night, made a search, raked everything over. Led him away in the morning. Worse still, his Darya's in the hospital with typhoid. Little Pavlushka – he's in a progressive high school – is alone at home with his deaf aunt. What's more, they're being chased out of the apartment. I think we'll have to take the boy in. Why did Prov come?'

'How do you know he did?'

'I saw the barrel uncovered and the mug standing on it. It must have been bottomless Prov, I thought, guzzling water.'

'You're so sharp, Kuprinka. That's right, it was Prov, Prov Afanasyevich. He ran by to ask if he could borrow some firewood. I gave it to him. But what a fool I am – firewood! He brought such news and it went clean out of my head. You see, the sovereign has signed a manifesto so that everything will be turned a new way, nobody's offended, the muzhiks get the land, and everybody's equal to the nobility.[5] The ukase has been signed, just think of it, it only has to be made public. A new petition came from the Synod to put it into the litany or some sort of prayer of thanksgiving, I'm afraid to get it wrong. Provushka told me, and I went and forgot.'

8

Patulya Antipov, the son of the arrested Pavel Ferapontovich and the hospitalised Darya Filimonovna, came to live with the Tiverzins. He was a neat boy with regular features and dark blond hair parted in the middle. He kept smoothing it with a brush and kept straightening his jacket and his belt with its school buckle. Patulya could laugh to the point of tears and was very observant. He imitated everything he saw and heard with great likeness and comicality.

Soon after the manifesto of 17 October, there was a big demonstration from the Tver to the Kaluga gate. This was an initiative in the spirit of 'too many cooks spoil the broth'. Several of the revolutionary organisations that took part in the enterprise squabbled with each other and gave it up one by one, but when they learned that on the appointed morning people took to the streets even so, they hastened to send their representatives to the demonstration.

Despite Kiprian Savelyevich's protests and dissuasions, Marfa Gavrilovna went to the demonstration with the cheerful and sociable Patulya.

It was a dry, frosty day in early November, with a still, leaden sky and a few snowflakes, so few that you could almost count them, swirling slowly and hesitantly before they fell to earth and then, in a fluffy grey dust, filled the potholes in the road.

Down the street the people came pouring, a veritable babel, faces, faces, faces, quilted winter coats and lambskin hats, old men, girl students and children, railwaymen in uniform, workers from the tram depot and the telephone station in boots above their knees and leather jackets, high school and university students.

For some time they sang the 'Varshavianka', 'You Fell Victims', and the 'Marseillaise', but suddenly the man who had been walking backwards ahead of the marchers and conducting the singing by waving a papakha[6] clutched in his hand, stopped directing, put his hat on, and, turning his back to the procession, began to listen to what the rest of the leaders marching beside him were saying. The singing faltered and broke off. You could hear the crunching steps of the numberless crowd over the frozen pavement.

Some well-wishers informed the initiators of the march that there were Cossacks lying in wait for the demonstrators further ahead. There had been a phone call to a nearby pharmacy about the prepared ambush.

'So what?' the organisers said. 'The main thing then is to keep cool and not lose our heads. We must immediately occupy the first public building

that comes our way, announce the impending danger to people, and disperse one by one.'

They argued over which would be the best place to go. Some suggested
the Society of Merchant's Clerks, others the Technical Institute, still others
the School of Foreign Correspondents.

During the argument, the corner of a government building appeared
ahead of them. It also housed an educational institution, which as a suitable
shelter was no whit worse than the ones enumerated.

When the walkers drew level with it, the leaders went up onto the semicircular landing in front of it and made signs for the head of the procession
to stop. The many-leafed doors of the entrance opened, and all the
marchers, coat after coat and hat after hat, began pouring into the vestibule
of the school and climbing its main stairway.

'To the auditorium, to the auditorium!' solitary voices shouted behind
them, but the crowd continued to flow further on, dispersing through the
separate corridors and classrooms.

When they managed to bring the public back and they were all seated on
chairs, the leaders tried several times to announce to the assembly that a
trap had been set for them ahead, but no one listened to them. This stopping
and going into the building was taken as an invitation to an improvised
meeting, which began at once.

After all the marching and singing, people wanted to sit silently for a
while and have someone else do the work and strain his throat for them.
Compared to the chief pleasure of resting, the insignificant disagreements
among the speakers, who were at one with each other in almost everything,
seemed a matter of indifference.

Therefore the greatest success fell to the worst orator, who did not weary
his listeners with the necessity of following him. His every word was accompanied by a roar of sympathy. No one regretted that his speech was
drowned out by the noise of approval. They hastened to agree with him out
of impatience, cried 'Shame', composed a telegram of protest, then suddenly, bored by the monotony of his voice, they all rose to a man and, forgetting all about the orator, hat after hat, row after row, thronged down the
stairs and poured outside. The march continued.

While they were meeting, it had begun to snow. The pavement turned
white. The snow fell more and more heavily.

When the dragoons came flying at them, those in the back rows did not
suspect it at first. Suddenly a swelling roar rolled over them from the front,
as when a crowd cries 'Hurrah!' Cries of 'Help!' and 'Murder!' and many
others merged into something indistinguishable. At almost the same

moment, on the wave of those sounds, down a narrow pass formed in the shying crowd, horses' manes and muzzles and sabre-brandishing riders raced swiftly and noiselessly.

Half a platoon galloped by, turned round, re-formed, and cut from behind into the tail of the march. The massacre began.

A few minutes later the street was almost empty. People fled into the side streets. The snow fell more lightly. The evening was dry as a charcoal drawing. Suddenly the sun, setting somewhere behind the houses, began poking its finger from around the corner at everything red in the street: the red-topped hats of the dragoons, the red cloth of the fallen flag, the traces of blood scattered over the snow in red threads and spots.

Along the edge of the pavement, dragging himself with his hands, crawled a moaning man with a split skull. A row of several horsemen rode up at a walk. They were coming back from the end of the street, where they had been drawn by the pursuit. Almost under their feet, Marfa Gavrilovna was rushing about, her kerchief shoved back on her neck, and in a voice not her own was shouting for the whole street to hear: 'Pasha! Patulya!'

He had been walking with her all the while, amusing her with a highly skilful imitation of the last orator, and had suddenly vanished in the turmoil when the dragoons fell upon them.

In the skirmish, Marfa Gavrilovna herself got hit in the back by a whip, and though her thick, cotton-quilted coat kept her from feeling the blow, she cursed and shook her fist at the retreating cavalry, indignant that they had dared to lash her, an old woman, with a whip before the eyes of all honest people.

Marfa Gavrilovna cast worried glances down both sides of the street. Luckily, she suddenly saw the boy on the opposite pavement. There, in the narrow space between a colonial shop and a projecting town house, crowded a bunch of chance gawkers.

A dragoon who had ridden up onto the pavement was pressing them into that nook with the rump and flanks of his horse. He was amused by their terror and, barring their way out, performed capers and pirouettes under their noses, then backed his horse away and slowly, as in the circus, made him rear up. Suddenly he saw ahead his comrades slowly returning, spurred his horse, and in two or three leaps took his place in their line.

The people packed into the nook dispersed. Pasha, who had been afraid to call out, rushed to the old woman.

They walked home. Marfa Gavrilovna grumbled all the while. 'Cursed murderers, fiendish butchers! People are rejoicing, the tsar has given them freedom, and they can't stand it. They've got to muck it all up, turn every word inside out.'

She was angry with the dragoons, with the whole world around her, and at that moment even with her own son. In this moment of passion it seemed to her that everything going on now was all the tricks of Kuprinka's blunderers, whom she nicknamed duds and smart alecks.

'Wicked vipers! What do the loudmouths want? They've got no brains! Nothing but barking and squabbling. And that speechifier, how about him, Pashenka? Show me, dear, show me. Oh, I'll die, I'll die! It's perfect, it's him to a tee! Yackety-yack-yack-yack. Ah, you buzzing little gadfly!'

At home she fell upon her son with reproaches, that it was not for her, at her age, to be taught with a whip on the behind by a shaggy, pockmarked blockhead on a horse.

'For God's sake, mama, what's got into you? As if I really was some Cossack officer or sheik of police!'

9

Nikolai Nikolaevich was standing at the window when the fleeing people appeared. He understood that they were from the demonstration, and for some time he looked into the distance to see if Yura or anyone else was among the scattering people. However, no acquaintances appeared, only once he fancied he saw that one (Nikolai Nikolaevich forgot his name), Dudorov's son, pass by quickly – a desperate boy, who just recently had had a bullet extracted from his left shoulder and who was again hanging about where he had no business to be.

Nikolai Nikolaevich had arrived in the autumn from Petersburg. He had no lodgings of his own in Moscow, and he did not want to go to a hotel. He stayed with the Sventitskys, his distant relations. They put him in the corner study upstairs on the mezzanine.

This two-storeyed wing, too big for the childless Sventitsky couple, had been rented from the Princes Dolgoruky by Sventitsky's late parents from time immemorial. The Dolgoruky domain, with three courtyards, a garden, and a multitude of variously styled buildings scattered over it in disorder, gave onto three lanes and bore the old name of Flour Town.

Despite its four windows, the study was rather dark. It was cluttered with books, papers, rugs, and etchings. On the outside, the study had a balcony that ran in a semicircle around that corner of the building. The double glass door to the balcony had been sealed off for the winter.

Through two of the study windows and the glass of the balcony door, the whole length of the lane was visible – a sleigh road running into the distance, little houses in a crooked line, crooked fences.

Violet shadows reached from the garden into the study. Trees peered into the room, looking as if they wanted to strew the floor with their branches covered with heavy hoarfrost, which resembled lilac streams of congealed stearin.

Nikolai Nikolaevich was looking into the lane and remembering the last Petersburg winter, Gapon, Gorky, the visit of Witte, the fashionable contemporary writers.[7] From that turmoil he had fled here, to the peace and quiet of the former capital, to write the book he had in mind. Forget it! He had gone from the frying pan into the fire. Lectures and talks every day – he had no time to catch his breath. At the Women's Institute, at the Religious-Philosophical Society, for the benefit of the Red Cross, for the Fund of the Strike Committee. Oh, to go to Switzerland, to the depths of some wooded canton. Peace and serenity over a lake, the sky and the mountains, and the vibrant, ever-echoing, alert air.

Nikolai Nikolaevich turned away from the window. He had an urge to go and visit someone or simply to go outside with no purpose. But then he remembered that the Tolstoyan Vyvolochnov was supposed to come to him on business and he could not leave. He started pacing the room. His thoughts turned to his nephew.

When Nikolai Nikolaevich moved to Petersburg from the backwoods of the Volga region, he brought Yura to Moscow, to the family circles of the Vedenyapins, the Ostromyslenskys, the Selyavins, the Mikhaelises, the Sventitskys, and the Gromekos. At the beginning, Yura was settled with the scatterbrained old babbler Ostromyslensky, whom his relations simply called Fedka. Fedka privately cohabited with his ward, Motya, and therefore considered himself a shaker of the foundations, the champion of an idea. He did not justify the trust put in him and even turned out to be light-fingered, spending for his own benefit the money allotted for Yura's upkeep. Yura was transferred to the professorial family of the Gromekos, where he remained to this day.

At the Gromekos' Yura was surrounded by an enviably propitious atmosphere.

'They have a sort of triumvirate there,' thought Nikolai Nikolaevich, 'Yura, his friend and schoolmate Gordon, and the daughter of the family, Tonya Gromeko. This triple alliance has read itself up on *The Meaning of Love* and *The Kreutzer Sonata,* and is mad about the preaching of chastity.'[8]

Adolescence has to pass through all the frenzies of purity. But they are overdoing it, they have gone beyond all reason.

They are terribly extravagant and childish. The realm of the sensual that troubles them so much, they for some reason call 'vulgarity', and they use this expression both aptly and inaptly. A very unfortunate choice of words! The 'vulgar' – for them it is the voice of instinct, and pornographic literature, and the exploitation of women, and all but the entire world of the physical. They blush and blanch when they pronounce the word!

If I had been in Moscow, thought Nikolai Nikolaevich, I would not have let it go so far. Modesty is necessary, and within certain limits . . .

'Ah, Nil Feoktistovich! Come in, please,' he exclaimed and went to meet his visitor.

10

Into the room came a fat man in a grey shirt girded with a wide belt. He was wearing felt boots, and his trousers were baggy at the knees. He made the impression of a kindly fellow who lived in the clouds. On his nose a small pince-nez on a wide black ribbon bobbed angrily.

Divesting himself in the front hall, he had not finished the job. He had not taken off his scarf, the end of which dragged on the floor, and his round felt hat was still in his hands. These things hampered his movements and prevented Vyvolochnov not only from shaking Nikolai Nikolaevich's hand, but even from greeting him verbally.

'Umm,' he grunted perplexedly, looking into all the corners.

'Put it wherever you like,' said Nikolai Nikolaevich, restoring to Vyvolochnov his gift of speech and his composure.

He was one of those followers of Lev Nikolaevich Tolstoy in whose heads the thoughts of the genius who had never known peace settled down to enjoy a long and cloudless repose and turned irremediably petty.

Vyvolochnov had come to ask Nikolai Nikolaevich to appear at a benefit for political exiles at some school.

'I've already lectured there.'

'At a benefit for political exiles?'

'Yes.'

'You'll have to do it again.'

Nikolai Nikolaevich resisted at first but then agreed.

The object of the visit was exhausted. Nikolai Nikolaevich was not keeping Nil Feoktistovich. He could get up and leave. But it seemed improper to Vyvolochnov to leave so soon. It was necessary to say something lively and unforced in farewell. A strained and unpleasant conversation began.

'So you've become a decadent? Gone in for mysticism?'

'Why so?'

'A lost man. Remember the zemstvo?'

'Of course I do. We worked on the elections together.'

'We fought for village schools and teachers' education. Remember?'

'Of course. Those were hot battles.'

'Afterwards I believe you went into public health and social welfare? Right?'

'For a while.'

'Mm – yes. And now it's these fauns, nenuphars, ephebes, and "let's be like the sun".[9] For the life of me, I can't believe it. That an intelligent man with a sense of humour and such knowledge of the people . . . Drop it all, please . . . Or maybe I'm intruding . . . Something cherished?'

'Why throw words around at random without thinking? What are we quarrelling about? You don't know my thoughts.'

'Russia needs schools and hospitals, not fauns and nenuphars.'

'No one disputes that.'

'The muzhiks go naked and swollen with hunger . . .'

The conversation progressed by such leaps. Aware beforehand of the futility of these attempts, Nikolai Nikolaevich began to explain what brought him close to certain writers of the symbolist school, and then went on to Tolstoy.

'I'm with you up to a point. But Lev Nikolaevich says that the more a man gives himself to beauty, the more he distances himself from the good.'

'And you think it's the other way round? Beauty will save the world, mysteries and all that, Rozanov and Dostoevsky?'[10]

'Wait, I'll tell you what I think myself. I think that if the beast dormant in man could be stopped by the threat of, whatever, the lock-up or requital beyond the grave, the highest emblem of mankind would be a lion tamer with his whip, and not the preacher who sacrifices himself. But the point is precisely this, that for centuries man has been raised above the animals and borne aloft not by the rod, but by music: the irresistibility of the unarmed truth, the attraction of its example. It has been considered up to now that the most important thing in the Gospels is the moral pronouncements and rules, but for me the main thing is that Christ speaks in parables from daily life, clarifying the truth with the light of everyday things. At the basis of this lies the thought that communion among mortals is immortal and that life is symbolic because it is meaningful.'

'I understand nothing. You should write a book about it.'

When Vyvolochnov left, Nikolai Nikolaevich was overcome by a terrible irritation. He was angry with himself for blurting out some of his innermost thoughts to that blockhead Vyvolochnov without making the slightest impression on him. As sometimes happens, Nikolai Nikolaevich's vexation suddenly changed direction. He forgot all about Vyvolochnov, as if he had never existed. He recalled something else. He did not keep a diary, but once or twice a year he wrote down in his thick notebook the thoughts that struck him most. He took out the notebook and began jotting in a large, legible hand. Here is what he wrote:

'Beside myself all day because of this foolish Schlesinger woman. She comes in the morning, sits till dinnertime, and for a whole two hours tortures me reading that galimatias. A poetic text by the symbolist A for the cosmogonic symphony of the composer B, with the spirits of the planets, the voices of the four elements, etc., etc. I suffered it for a while, then couldn't take it any more and begged her, please, to spare me.

'I suddenly understood it all. I understood why it is always so killingly unbearable and false, even in *Faust*. It is an affected, sham interest. Modern man has no such quests. When he is overcome by the riddles of the universe, he delves into physics, not into Hesiod's hexameters.[11]

'But the point is not only the outdatedness of these forms, their anachronism. The point is not that these spirits of fire and water again darkly entangle what science had brightly disentangled. The point is that this genre contradicts the whole spirit of today's art, its essence, its motive forces.

'These cosmogonies were natural to the old earth, so sparsely populated by man that he did not yet obscure nature. Mammoths still wandered over it, and the memories of dinosaurs and dragons were fresh. Nature leaped so manifestly into man's eye and so rapaciously and tangibly onto his neck, that everything indeed might still have been filled with gods. Those were the very first pages of the chronicles of mankind, they were only the beginning.

'In Rome that ancient world ended from overpopulation.

'Rome was a marketplace of borrowed gods and conquered peoples, a two-tiered throng, on earth and in heaven, a swinishness that bound itself up in a triple knot, like twisted bowels. Dacians, Herulians, Scythians, Sarmatians, Hyperboreans, heavy, spokeless wheels, eyes wallowing in fat, bestiality, double chins, fish fed on the flesh of learned slaves, illiterate emperors. There were more people in the world than ever again, and they were squeezed into the passageways of the Coliseum and suffered.

'And then into the glut of this gold and marble tastelessness came this one, light and clothed in radiance, emphatically human, deliberately provincial, a Galilean, and from that moment peoples and gods ceased, and man began, man the carpenter, man the tiller, man the shepherd with his flock of sheep at sunset, man without a drop of proud sound, man gratefully dispersed through all mothers' lullabies and through all the picture galleries of the world.'

II

The Petrovsky Lines made the impression of a corner of Petersburg in Moscow. The matching buildings on either side of the street, the entrances with tasteful stucco mouldings, a bookshop, a reading room, a cartography establishment, a very decent tobacco store, a very decent restaurant, in front of the restaurant gaslights in frosted globes on massive brackets.

In winter the place frowned with gloomy haughtiness. Here lived serious, self-respecting, and well-paid people of the liberal professions.

Here Viktor Ippolitovich Komarovsky rented his luxurious bachelor quarters on the second floor, up a wide staircase with wide oak banisters. Solicitously entering into everything, and at the same time not interfering with anything, Emma Ernestovna, his housekeeper – no, the matron of his quiet seclusion – managed his household inaudibly and invisibly, and he repaid her with chivalrous gratitude, natural in such a gentleman, and did not suffer the presence in his apartment of guests and lady visitors incompatible with her untroubled, old-maidenly world. With them reigned the peace of a monastic cloister – drawn blinds, not a speck, not a spot, as in an operating room.

On Sundays before dinner Viktor Ippolitovich was in the habit of strolling with his bulldog on Petrovka and Kuznetsky Most, and at one of the corners, Konstantin Illarionovich Satanidi, an actor and gambler, would come to join them.

Together they would set off to polish the pavements, exchanging brief jokes and observations so curt, insignificant, and filled with such scorn for everything in the world that without any loss they might have replaced those words with simple growls, as long as they filled both sides of Kuznetsky with their loud bass voices, shamelessly breathless, as if choking on their own vibrations.

12

The weather was trying to get better. 'Drip, drip, drip' the drops drummed on the iron gutters and cornices. Roof tapped out to roof, as in springtime. It was a thaw.

She walked all the way home as if beside herself and only when she got there did she realise what had happened.

At home everyone was asleep. She again lapsed into torpor and in that distraction sank down at her mother's dressing table in her pale lilac, almost white dress with lace trimmings and a long veil, taken from the shop for that one evening, as if for a masked ball. She sat before her reflection in the mirror and saw nothing. Then she leaned her crossed arms on the table and dropped her head on them.

If mama finds out, she'll kill her. Kill her and then take her own life.

How did it happen? How could it happen? Now it's too late. She should have thought earlier.

Now she's – what is it called? – now she's – a fallen woman. She's a woman from a French novel, and tomorrow she will go to school and sit at the same desk with those girls, who, compared to her, are still unweaned babies. Lord, Lord, how could it happen!

Some day, many, many years from now, when it was possible, she would tell Olya Demina. Olya would clutch her by the head and start howling.

Outside the window the drops prattled, the thaw was talking away. Someone in the street banged on the neighbours' gate. Lara did not raise her head. Her shoulders shook. She was weeping.

13

'Ah, Emma Ernestovna, dearest, that's of no importance. It's tiresome.'

He was flinging things around on the carpet and sofa, cuffs and shirt fronts, and opening and closing the drawers of the chest, not understanding what he wanted.

He needed her desperately, and to see her that Sunday was impossible. He rushed about the room like a beast, unable to settle anywhere.

She was incomparable in her inspired loveliness. Her arms amazed one, as one can be astonished by a lofty way of thinking. Her shadow on the wallpaper of the hotel room seemed the silhouette of her uncorruption. The nightshirt stretched over her breasts was ingenuous and taut, like a piece of linen on an embroidery frame.

Komarovsky drummed his fingers on the windowpane in rhythm with the horses' hoofs unhurriedly clattering over the asphalt of the street downstairs. 'Lara' – he whispered and closed his eyes, and her head mentally appeared in his hands, her sleeping head with its eyelashes lowered, knowing not that it had been gazed at sleeplessly for hours on end. Her shock of hair, scattered in disorder over the pillow, stung Komarovsky's eyes with the smoke of its beauty and penetrated his soul.

His Sunday stroll did not come off. Komarovsky went several steps down the pavement with Jack and stopped. He imagined Kuznetsky, Satanidi's jokes, the stream of acquaintances he was going to meet. No, it was beyond his strength! How repugnant it had all become! Komarovsky turned back. The surprised dog rested his disapproving gaze on him from below and reluctantly trudged after him.

'What is this bedevilment?' he thought. 'What does it all mean?' Was it awakened conscience, a feeling of pity or repentance? Or was it worry? No, he knew she was safe at home. Why, then, could he not get her out of his head!

Komarovsky went through the front door, went upstairs to the landing, and turned. There was a Venetian window with ornamental coats of arms in the corners of the glass. It cast coloured reflections on the floor and the windowsill. Halfway up the next flight Komarovsky stopped.

Do not give in to this gnawing, martyrising anguish! He is not a boy, he must realise how it would be for him if, from a means of diversion, this girl, his late friend's daughter, this child, should turn into the object of his madness. Come to your senses! Be true to yourself, don't change your habits. Otherwise everything will fly to pieces.

Komarovsky squeezed the wide banister with his hand until it hurt, closed his eyes for a moment, and, resolutely turning back, began to go downstairs. On the landing with the sun reflections he caught the adoring gaze of his bulldog. Jack was looking at him from below, raising his head like a slobbering old dwarf with sagging cheeks.

The dog did not like the girl, tore her stockings, growled and snarled at her. He was jealous of Lara, as if fearing that his master might get infected by her with something human.

'Ah, so that's it! You've decided everything will be as before – Satanidi, the meanness, the jokes? Take that, then, take that, take that, take that!'

He started kicking the bulldog and beating him with his cane. Jack made his escape, howling and squealing, and, his behind twitching, hobbled up the stairs to scratch at the door and complain to Emma Ernestovna.

Days and weeks went by.

14

Oh, what a vicious circle it was! If Komarovsky's irruption into Lara's life had aroused only her revulsion, Lara would have rebelled and broken free. But things were not so simple.

The girl was flattered that a handsome, greying man who could have been her father, who was applauded in assemblies and written about in the newspapers, spent money and time on her, called her goddess, took her to theatres and concerts and, as they say, 'improved her mind'.

And here she was still an immature schoolgirl in a brown dress, a secret participant in innocent school conspiracies and pranks. Komarovsky's love-making somewhere in a carriage under the coachman's nose or in the secluded back of a loge before the eyes of the whole theatre fascinated her by its covert boldness and prompted the little demon awakened in her to imitation.

But this naughty schoolgirl daring was quickly passing. An aching sense of brokenness and horror at herself had long been taking root in her. And she wanted to sleep all the time. From not sleeping enough at night, from tears and eternal headaches, from schoolwork and general physical fatigue.

15

He was her curse, she hated him. Every day she went over these thoughts afresh.

Now she's his slave for life. How has he enslaved her? How does he extort her submission, so that she succumbs, plays up to his desires, and delights him with the shudders of her unvarnished shame? Is it his age, mama's financial dependence on him, his skil in frightening her, Lara? No, no, no. That's all nonsense.

It's not she who is subordinate to him, but he to her. Doesn't she see how he languishes after her? She has nothing to be afraid of, her conscience is clear. It is he who should be ashamed and frightened, if she should expose him. But the thing is that she will never do it. For that she does not have enough baseness, which is Komarovsky's main strength in dealing with the subordinate and weak.

That is where they differ. And that also makes for the horror of life all around. How does it stun you – with thunder and lightning? No, with side-long glances and whispers of calumny. It's all trickery and ambiguity. A single thread is like a spiderweb, pull and it's gone, but try to free yourself and you get even more entangled.

And the base and weak rule over the strong.

16

She said to herself: 'And what if I was married? How would it be different?' She entered on the path of sophistry. But at times a hopeless anguish came over her.

How can he not be ashamed to lie at her feet and implore her: 'It can't go on like this. Think what I've done to you. You're sliding down a steep slope. Let's tell your mother. I'll marry you.'

And he wept and insisted, as if she were arguing and disagreeing. But it was all just phrases, and Lara did not even listen to those tragic, empty-sounding words.

And he went on taking her, under a long veil, to the private rooms of that terrible restaurant, where the waiters and customers followed her with their gazes as if undressing her. And she only asked herself: Does one humiliate the person one loves?

Once she had a dream. She is under the ground, all that remains of her is her left side with its shoulder and her right foot. A clump of grass is growing from her left nipple, and above ground they are singing: 'Dark eyes and white breasts' and 'Tell Masha not to cross the river'.

17

Lara was not religious. She did not believe in rites. But sometimes, in order to endure life, she needed it to be accompanied by some inner music. She could not invent such music each time for herself. This music was the word of God about life, and Lara went to church to weep over it.

Once at the beginning of December, when Lara's inner state was like Katerina's in *The Storm*,[12] she went to pray with such a feeling as if the earth were about to open under her and the church's vaults to collapse. And it would serve her right. And everything would be over. Only it was a pity she had taken that chatterbox, Olya Demina, with her.

'Prov Afanasyevich,' Olya whispered in her ear.

'Shh. Let me be, please. What Prov Afanasyevich?'

'Prov Afanasyevich Sokolov. Mother's second cousin. The one who's reading.'

'Ah, she means the psalm-reader. Tiverzin's relation. Shh. Be quiet. Don't bother me, please.'

They had come at the beginning of the service. The psalm 'Bless the Lord, O my soul, and all that is within me, bless His holy name' was being sung.[13]

The church was rather empty and echoing. Only towards the front were people crowded in a compact group. It was a newly built church. The colourless glass of the window did not brighten in any way the grey, snow-covered lane and the people driving or walking up and down it. The church warden stood by that window and, loud enough for the whole church to hear, paying no attention to the service, admonished some deaf woman, a ragged holy fool, and his voice was of the same conventional, everyday sort as the window and the lane.

While Lara, slowly going around the praying people, copper money clutched in her hand, went to the door to buy candles for herself and Olya, and went back just as carefully, so as not to push anyone, Prov Afanasyevich managed to rattle off the nine beatitudes,[14] like something well-known to everyone without him.

Blessed are the poor in spirit . . . Blessed are those who mourn . . . Blessed are those who hunger and thirst after righteousness . . .

Lara walked, suddenly shuddered, and stopped. That was about her. He says: Enviable is the lot of the downtrodden. They have something to tell about themselves. They have everything before them. So He thought. It was Christ's opinion.

18

Those were the Presnya days.[15] They found themselves in the zone of the uprising. A few steps away from them, on Tverskaya, a barricade was being built. It could be seen from the living-room window. People were fetching buckets of water from their courtyard to pour over the barricade and bind the stones and scraps of metal it was made of in an armour of ice.

The neighbouring courtyard was a gathering place of the people's militia, a sort of first-aid station or canteen.

Two boys used to come there. Lara knew them both. One was Nika Dudorov, a friend of Nadya's, at whose house Lara had made his acquaintance. He was of Lara's ilk – direct, proud, and taciturn. He resembled Lara and did not interest her.

The other was a student at a progressive school, Antipov, who lived with old Tiverzina, Olya Demina's grandmother. When visiting Marfa Gavrilovna, Lara began to notice what effect she had on the boy. Pasha Antipov was still so childishly simple that he did not conceal the bliss her visits afforded him, as if Lara were some sort of birch grove during summer vacation, with clean grass and clouds, and he could express his calfish raptures to her unhindered, with no fear of being laughed at for it.

As soon as she noticed the sort of influence she had on him, Lara unconsciously began to take advantage of it. However, she busied herself with the more serious taming of that soft and yielding nature after several years, at a much later season of her friendship with him, when Patulya already knew that he loved her to distraction and that in his life there was no more turning back.

The boys were playing at the most dreadful and adult of games, at war, and moreover of a sort that you were hanged or exiled for taking part in. Yet the ends of their bashlyks[16] were tied at the back with such knots that it gave them away as children and showed that they still had papas and mamas. Lara looked at them as a big girl looks at little boys. There was a bloom of innocence on their dangerous amusements. They imparted the same stamp to everything else. To the frosty evening, overgrown with such shaggy hoarfrost that its thickness made it look not white but black. To the blue courtyard. To the house opposite, where the boys were hiding. And, above all, to the pistol shots that cracked from it all the time. 'The boys are shooting,' thought Lara. She thought it not of Nika and Patulya, but of the whole shooting city. 'Good, honest boys,' she thought. 'They're good, that's why they're shooting.'

19

They learned that cannon fire might be directed at the barricade and that their house was in danger. It was too late to think of moving in with acquaintances somewhere in another part of Moscow: their area was surrounded. They had to look for a niche closer by, within the circle. They remembered the Montenegro.

It turned out that they were not the first. The entire hotel was occupied. Many had found themselves in their situation. But being remembered of old, they were promised quarters in the linen room.

They gathered everything necessary into three bundles, so as not to attract attention with suitcases, and began putting off the move to the hotel from day to day.

Owing to the patriarchal customs that reigned in the shop, work went on until the last minute, despite the strike. Then, in the cold, dull twilight, the outside doorbell rang. Someone came with claims and reproaches. The owner was asked to come to the door. To soothe these passions, Faïna Silantievna went out to the front hall.

'Come here, girls!' she soon called the seamstresses there and began introducing them in turn to the visitor. He greeted each of them separately with a handshake, feelingly and clumsily, and left, having come to some agreement with Fetisova.

Returning to the big room, the seamstresses began wrapping themselves in shawls and flinging their arms up over their heads, putting them through the sleeves of tight-fitting fur coats.

'What's happened?' asked Amalia Karlovna, just coming in.

'They've tooken us out, madame. We're on strike.'

'Maybe I . . . Have I done you any wrong?' Mme Guichard burst into tears.

'Don't be upset, Amalia Karlovna. We're not angry with you, we're very grateful to you. But the talk's not about you and us. It's the same now with everybody, the whole world. And how can you go against everybody?'

They all went home, even Olya Demina and Faïna Silantievna, who whispered to the mistress as she was leaving that she had staged this strike for the benefit of her and the business. But she would not be appeased.

'What black ingratitude! Just think how mistaken one can be about people! This girl on whom I spent so much of my soul! Well, all right, let's say she's a child. But that old witch!'

'Try to understand, mama, they can't make an exception for you,' Lara comforted her. 'Nobody's angry with you. On the contrary. Everything that's going on around us now is being done in the name of man, in defence of the weak, for the good of women and children. Yes, yes, don't shake your head so mistrustfully. It will be better some day for me and you because of it.'

But her mother did not understand anything.

'It's always this way,' she said, sobbing. 'My thoughts are confused to begin with, and then you blurt things out that just make me roll my eyes. They dump on my head, and it turns out to be in my own interest. No, truly, I must have gone soft in the brain.'

Rodya was at the corps. Lara and her mother wandered about the empty house alone. The unlit street looked into the rooms with vacant eyes. The rooms returned the same gaze.

'Let's go to the hotel, mama, before it gets too dark. Do you hear, mama? Without putting it off, right now.'

'Filat, Filat,' they called the yard porter. 'Filat, dearest, take us to the Montenegro.'

'Yes, ma'am.'

'Take the bundles, and another thing, Filat, please look after the place in the meantime. And don't forget seed and water for Kirill Modestovich. And keep everything locked. Oh, and please come to see us there.'

'Yes, ma'am.'

'Thank you, Filat. Christ save you. Well, let's sit down before we go, and God be with us.'

They went outside and did not recognise the air, as after a long illness. Through the frosty expanse, polished like new, round, smooth sounds, as if turned on a lathe, rolled lightly in all directions. Salvoes and gunshots smacked, splatted, and slapped, flattening the distances into a pancake.

Much as Filat tried to dissuade them, Lara and Amalia Karlovna considered these shots blanks.

'You're a little fool, Filat. Judge for yourself, how could they not be blanks if you can't see who's shooting. Who do you think is shooting, the Holy Spirit or something? Of course they're blanks.'

At one of the intersections a patrol stopped them. They were searched by grinning Cossacks, who brazenly felt them from head to foot. Their visorless caps with chin straps were cocked dashingly over the ear. They all looked one-eyed.

What luck, thought Lara, she will not see Komarovsky for the whole time that they are cut off from the rest of the city! She cannot break with him on account of her mother. She cannot say: Mama, don't receive him. Or else everything will be given away. So what? Why be afraid of that? Ah, God, let it all go to the devil, as long as it's over. Lord, Lord, Lord! She'll fall senseless in the middle of the street right now from revulsion. What did she just remember?! How is it called, that horrible painting with the fat Roman in it, in that first private room where it all began? *The Woman or the Vase*.[17] Why, of course. A famous painting. *The Woman or the Vase*. And she was not yet a woman then, to be likened to such a treasure. That came later. The table was so sumptuously set.

'Where are you running like crazy? I can't go so fast,' Amalia Karlovna wailed behind her, breathing heavily and barely keeping up with her.

Lara was moving quickly. Some force bore her up, as if she were walking on air – a proud, inspiring force.

'Oh, how perkily the gunshots crack,' she thought. 'Blessed are the violated, blessed are the ensnared. God give you good health, gunshots! Gunshots, gunshots, you're of the same opinion!'

20

The Gromeko brothers' house stood at the corner of Sivtsev Vrazhek and another lane. Alexander Alexandrovich and Nikolai Alexandrovich Gromeko were professors of chemistry, the first at the Petrovskaya Academy, the second at the university. Nikolai Alexandrovich was a bachelor; Alexander Alexandrovich was married to Anna Ivanovna, née Krüger, the daughter of a steel magnate and owner of abandoned, unprofitable mines on the enormous forest dacha[18] that belonged to him near Yuryatin in the Urals.

The house was two-storeyed. The upper, with bedrooms, a schoolroom, Alexander Alexandrovich's study and library, Anna Ivanovna's boudoir, and Tonya's and Yura's rooms, was the living quarters, and the lower was for receptions. Thanks to its pistachio-coloured curtains, the mirrorlike reflections on the lid of the grand piano, the aquarium, the olive-green furniture, and the indoor plants that resembled seaweed, this lower floor made the impression of a green, drowsily undulating sea bottom.

The Gromekos were cultivated people, hospitable, and great connoisseurs and lovers of music. They gathered company at their home and organised evenings of chamber music at which piano trios, violin sonatas, and string quartets were performed.

In January of 1906, soon after Nikolai Nikolaevich's departure abroad, the next of these chamber concerts on Sivtsev Vrazhek was to take place. They planned to perform a new violin sonata by a beginner from Taneev's school and a Tchaikovsky trio.

Preparations began the day before. Furniture was moved to free the concert hall. In the corner a tuner produced the same note a hundred times and then spilled out the beads of an arpeggio. In the kitchen fowl were plucked, greens were washed, mustard was beaten with olive oil for sauces and dressings.

In the morning Shura Schlesinger, Anna Ivanovna's bosom friend and confidante, came to bother them.

Shura Schlesinger was a tall, lean woman with regular features and a somewhat masculine face, which gave her a slight resemblance to the sovereign, especially in her grey lambskin hat, which she wore cocked and kept on when visiting, just barely lifting the little veil pinned to it.

In periods of sorrow and care, the conversations between the two friends afforded them mutual relief. The relief consisted in Shura Schlesinger and Anna Ivanovna exchanging biting remarks of an ever more caustic nature. A stormy scene would break out, quickly ending in tears and reconciliation. These regular quarrels had a tranquillising effect on both women, like leeches on the bloodstream.

Shura Schlesinger had been married several times, but she forgot her husbands immediately after the divorce and attached so little significance to them that there was in all her habits the cold mobility of the single woman.

Shura Schlesinger was a Theosophist,[19] but at the same time she had such excellent knowledge of the course of the Orthodox services that even when *toute transportée,** in a state of complete ecstasy, she could not help

*Quite carried away.

prompting the clergy on what they should say or sing. 'Hear me, O Lord', 'again and oftentimes', 'more honourable than the cherubim' – her husky, broken patter could be heard escaping her all the time.

Shura Schlesinger knew mathematics, Hindu mysticism, the addresses of the most important professors of Moscow Conservatory, who was living with whom, and, my God, what did she not know? Therefore she was invited as an arbiter and monitor in all serious situations in life.

At the appointed hour the guests began to arrive. Adelaïda Filippovna came, Gintz, the Fufkovs, Mr and Mrs Basurman, the Verzhitskys, Colonel Kavkaztsev. It was snowing, and when the front door was opened, the tangled air raced past, all as if in knots from the flitting of big and little snowflakes. Men came in from the cold, their deep rubber boots flopping loosely on their feet, affecting one after the other to be absent-minded, clumsy fellows, while their wives, freshened by the frost, the two upper buttons of their fur coats undone, their fluffy kerchiefs pushed back on their frosty hair, were, on the contrary, images of the inveterate rogue, perfidy itself, not to be trifled with. 'Cui's nephew,' the whisper went around, on the arrival of a new pianist, invited to the house for the first time.[20]

From the concert hall, through the opened side doors at both ends, they could see a laid table, long as a winter road, in the dining room. The eye was struck by the bright sparkle of rowanberry vodka in bottles with granular facets. The imagination was captivated by little cruets of oil and vinegar on silver stands, and the picturesqueness of the game and snacks, and even the napkins folded in little pyramids that crowned each place setting, and the almond-scented blue-violet cineraria in baskets seemed to excite the appetite. So as not to delay the desired moment of savouring earthly food, they turned as quickly as possible to the spiritual. They sat down in rows in the hall. 'Cui's nephew' – the whispering was renewed when the pianist took his place at the instrument. The concert began.

The sonata was known to be dull and forced, cerebral. It fulfilled expectations, and moreover proved to be terribly drawn out.

During the intermission there was an argument about it between the critic Kerimbekov and Alexander Alexandrovich. The critic denounced the sonata, and Alexander Alexandrovich defended it. Around them people smoked and noisily moved chairs from place to place.

But again their gazes fell upon the ironed tablecloth that shone in the next room. Everyone suggested that the concert continue without delay.

The pianist glanced sidelong at the public and nodded to his partners to begin. The violinist and Tyshkevich swung their bows. The trio burst into sobs.

Yura, Tonya, and Misha Gordon, who now spent half his life at the Gromekos', were sitting in the third row.

'Egorovna's making signs to you,' Yura whispered to Alexander Alexandrovich, who was sitting directly in front of him.

On the threshold of the hall stood Agrafena Egorovna, the Gromeko family's old, grey-haired maid, and with desperate looks in Yura's and equally resolute nods in Alexander Alexandrovich's direction, gave Yura to understand that she urgently needed the host.

Alexander Alexandrovich turned his head, looked at Egorovna reproachfully, and shrugged his shoulders. But Egorovna would not calm down. Soon an exchange started between them, from one end of the hall to the other, as between two deaf-mutes. Eyes turned towards them. Anna Ivanovna cast annihilating glances at her husband.

Alexander Alexandrovich stood up. Something had to be done. He blushed, quietly went around the room by the corner, and approached Egorovna.

'Shame on you, Egorovna! Really, what's this sudden urgency? Well, be quick, what's happened?'

Egorovna started whispering something to him.

'From what Montenegro?'

'The hotel.'

'Well, what is it?'

'He's wanted without delay. Somebody's dying there.'

'So it's dying now. I can imagine. Impossible, Egorovna. They'll finish playing the piece, and I'll tell him. It's impossible before.'

'They're waiting from the hotel. And the cab, too. I'm telling you, somebody's dying, don't you understand? An upper-class lady.'

'No and no again. Look, five minutes is no big thing.'

With the same quiet step along the wall, Alexander Alexandrovich returned to his place and sat down, frowning and rubbing the bridge of his nose.

After the first part, he went up to the performers and, while the applause thundered, told Tyshkevich that they had come for him, there was some sort of unpleasantness, and the music would have to be stopped. Then, holding up his palms to the hall, Alexander Alexandrovich silenced the applause and said loudly:

'Ladies and gentlemen. The trio must be interrupted. Let us express our sympathy with Fadei Kazimirovich. There is some trouble. He is forced to leave us. In such a moment, I do not wish to leave him alone. My presence may prove necessary. I will go with him. Yurochka, go, my dear boy, tell Semyon to come to the front porch, he's been harnessed up for a long time. Ladies and gentlemen, I am not saying goodbye. I beg you all to stay. My absence will be brief.'

The boys begged Alexander Alexandrovich to let them ride with him through the night frost.

21

Despite the restoring of the normal flow of life, there was still shooting here and there after December, and the new fires, of the sort that always happened, looked like the smouldering remains of the earlier ones.

Never before had they driven so far and long as that night. It was within arm's reach – down Smolensky, Novinsky, and half of Sadovaya. But the brutal frost and the mist isolated the separate parts of dislocated space, as if it were not identical everywhere in the world. The shaggy, shredded smoke of the bonfires, the creak of footsteps and squeal of runners contributed to the impression that they had already been driving God knows how long and had gone somewhere terribly far away.

In front of the hotel stood a blanket-covered horse with bandaged pasterns, hitched to a narrow, jaunty sleigh. The cabby sat in the passenger seat, covering his muffled head with his mittened hands for warmth.

The vestibule was warm, and behind the rail separating the coatroom from the entrance, a doorman dozed, lulled by the sound of the ventilator, the hum of the burning stove, and the whistle of the boiling samovar, snoring loudly and waking himself up by it.

To the left in the vestibule, before a mirror, stood a made-up lady, her plump face floury with powder. She was wearing a fur jacket, too airy for such weather. The lady was waiting for someone from upstairs and, turning her back to the mirror, glanced at herself now over her right, then over her left shoulder, to see how she looked from behind.

A chilled cabby poked himself through the front door. The shape of his kaftan resembled a cruller on a signboard, and the steam that billowed around him increased the likeness.

'Will it be soon now, mamzelle?' he asked the lady at the mirror. 'Mixing with your kind'll only get my horse frozen.'

The incident in number 24 was a minor thing among the ordinary everyday vexations of the staff. Bells jangled every moment and numbers popped up in the long glass box on the wall, showing where and under which number someone had lost his mind and, not knowing what he wanted himself, gave the floor attendants no peace.

Now this foolish old Guichard woman was being pumped full in number 24, was being given an emetic and having her guts and stomach flushed out. The maid Glasha was run off her feet, mopping the floor and carrying out dirty buckets and bringing in clean ones. But the present storm in the servants' quarters began long before that turmoil, when there was nothing to talk about yet and Tereshka had not been sent in a cab for the doctor and this wretched fiddle scraper, before Komarovsky arrived and so many unnecessary people crowded in the corridor outside the door, hindering all movement.

Today's hullabaloo flared up in the servants' quarters because in the afternoon someone turned awkwardly in the narrow passage from the pantry and accidentally pushed the waiter Sysoy at the very moment when he, flexing slightly, was preparing to run through the door into the corridor with a loaded tray on his raised right hand. Sysoy dropped the tray, spilled the soup, and broke the dishes – three bowls and one plate.

Sysoy insisted that it was the dishwasher, she was to blame, and she should pay for the damage. It was night-time now, past ten o'clock, the shift was about to go off work, and they still kept exchanging fire on the subject.

'He's got the shakes in his arms and legs, all he worries about is hugging a bottle day and night like a wife, his nose stuck in drink like a duck's, and then – why'd they push him, smash the dishes, spill the fish soup! Who pushed you, you cross-eyed devil, you spook? Who pushed you, you Astrakhan rupture, you shameless gape?'

'I done told you, Matryona Stepanovna – watch your tongue.'

'Something else again, if it was worthwhile making noise and smashing dishes, but this fine thing, Missy Prissy, a boulevard touch-me-not, done so well she gobbled arsenic, retired innocence. We've lived in the Montenegro, we've seen these screwtails and randy old goats.'

Misha and Yura paced up and down the corridor outside the door of the room. Nothing came out as Alexander Alexandrovich had supposed. He had pictured to himself – a cellist, a tragedy, something clean and dignified. But this was devil knows what. Filth, something scandalous, and absolutely not for children.

The boys loitered about in the corridor.

'Go in to the missis, young sirs,' the floor attendant, coming up to the boys, urged them for the second time in a soft, unhurried voice. 'Go in, don't hang back. She's all right, rest assured. She's her whole self now. You can't stand here. We had a disaster here today, costly dishes got smashed. See – we're serving, running, there's no room. Go on in.'

The boys obeyed.

In the room, the lighted kerosene lamp had been taken from the holder in which it hung over the dining table and moved behind the wooden partition, which stank of bedbugs, to the other part of the room.

There was a sleeping nook there, separated from the front part and strangers' eyes by a dusty curtain. Now, in the turmoil, they had forgotten to lower it. Its bottom end was thrown over the upper edge of the partition. The lamp stood on a bench in the alcove. This corner was lit up harshly from below, as if by theatre footlights.

The poisoning was from iodine, not arsenic, as the dishwasher had mistakenly jibed. The room was filled with the sharp, astringent smell of young walnuts in unhardened green husks, which turn black at the touch.

Behind the partition, a maid was mopping the floor and a half-naked woman, wet with water, tears, and sweat, was lying on the bed, sobbing loudly, her head with strands of hair stuck together hanging over a basin. The boys at once averted their eyes, so embarrassing and indecent it was to look. But Yura had time to notice how, in certain uncomfortable, hunched-up poses, under the influence of strain and effort, a woman ceases to be the way she is portrayed in sculpture and comes to resemble a naked wrestler, with bulging muscles, in shorts for the match.

It finally occurred to someone behind the partition to lower the curtain.

'Fadei Kazimirovich, dear, where is your hand? Give me your hand,' the woman said, choking with tears and nausea. 'Ah, I've been through such horror! I had such suspicions! Fadei Kazimirovich . . . I imagined . . . But fortunately it all turned out to be foolishness, my disturbed imagination, Fadei Kazimirovich, just think, such a relief! And as a result . . . And so . . . And so I'm alive.'

'Calm yourself, Amalia Karlovna, I beg you to calm yourself. How awkward this all is, my word, how awkward.'

'We'll go home now,' Alexander Alexandrovich grunted, turning to the children.

Perishing with embarrassment, they stood in the dark entry, on the threshold of the unpartitioned part of the room, and, having nowhere to turn their eyes, looked into the depths of it, from which the lamp had been removed. The walls were hung with photographs, there was a bookcase with music scores, a desk littered with paper and albums, and on the other side of the dining table covered with a crocheted tablecloth, a girl slept sitting in an armchair, her arms round its back and her cheek pressed to it. She must have been mortally tired, if the noise and movement around her did not keep her from sleeping.

Their arrival had been senseless, their further presence here was indecent. 'We'll go now,' Alexander Alexandrovich repeated. 'Once Fadei Kazimirovich comes out. I'll say goodbye to him.'

But instead of Fadei Kazimirovich, someone else came from behind the partition. This was a stout, clean-shaven, imposing, and self-assured man. Above his head he carried the lamp that had been taken from the holder. He went to the table by which the girl was sleeping and put the lamp into the holder. The light woke the girl up. She smiled at the man who had come in, narrowed her eyes, and stretched.

At the sight of the stranger, Misha became all aroused and simply riveted his eyes on him. He tugged at Yura's sleeve, trying to tell him something.

'Aren't you ashamed to whisper in a stranger's house? What will people think of you?' Yura stopped him and refused to listen.

Meanwhile a mute scene was taking place between the girl and the man. They did not say a word to each other and only exchanged glances. But their mutual understanding was frighteningly magical, as if he were a puppeteer and she a puppet, obedient to the movements of his hand.

The weary smile that appeared on her face made the girl half close her eyes and half open her lips. But to the man's mocking glances she responded with the sly winking of an accomplice. Both were pleased that everything had turned out so well, the secret had not been discovered, and the woman who poisoned herself had remained alive.

Yura devoured them both with his eyes. From the semi-darkness, where no one could see him, he looked into the circle of lamplight, unable to tear himself away. The spectacle of the girl's enslavement was inscrutably mysterious and shamelessly candid. Contradictory feelings crowded in his breast. Yura's heart was wrung by their as yet untried power.

This was the very thing he had so ardently yammered about for a year with Misha and Tonya under the meaningless name of vulgarity, that frightening and alluring thing which they had dealt with so easily at a safe distance in words, and here was that force before Yura's eyes, thoroughly tangible and dim and dreamlike, pitilessly destructive and pitiful and calling for help, and where was their childish philosophy, and what was Yura to do now?

'Do you know who that man is?' Misha asked when they went outside. Yura was immersed in his thoughts and did not answer.

'It's the same one who got your father to drink and destroyed him. Remember, on the train? I told you about it.'

Yura was thinking about the girl and the future, and not about his father and the past. For the first moment he did not even understand what Misha was telling him. It was hard to talk in the cold.

'Frozen, Semyon?' asked Alexander Alexandrovich.

They drove off.

Part Three

THE CHRISTMAS PARTY AT THE SVENTITSKYS'

I

Once in the winter Alexander Alexandrovich gave Anna Ivanovna an antique wardrobe. He had bought it by chance. The ebony wardrobe was of enormous proportions. It would not go through any doorway in one piece. It was delivered dismantled, brought into the house in sections, and they began thinking where to put it. It would not do in the downstairs rooms, where there was space enough, because its purpose was unsuitable, and it could not be put upstairs for lack of room. Part of the upper landing of the inside stairway was cleared for the wardrobe, by the door to the master bedroom.

The yard porter Markel came to put the wardrobe together. He brought along his six-year-old daughter Marinka. Marinka was given a stick of barley sugar. Marinka snuffed her nose and, licking the candy and her slobbery fingers, watched frowningly as her father worked.

For a while everything went smoothly. The wardrobe gradually grew before Anna Ivanovna's eyes. Suddenly, when it only remained to attach the top, she decided to help Markel. She stood on the high bottom of the wardrobe and, tottering, bumped against the side, which was held together only by a mortise and tenon. The slipknot Markel had tied temporarily to hold the side came undone. Together with the boards that went crashing to the floor, Anna Ivanovna also fell on her back and hurt herself badly.

'Eh, dear mistress,' Markel murmured as he rushed to her, 'why on earth did you go and do that, dear heart? Is the bone in one piece? Feel the bone. The bone's the main thing, forget the soft part, the soft part'll mend and, as they say, it's only for ladies' playzeer. Don't you howl, you wicked thing,' he fell upon the weeping Marinka. 'Wipe your snot and go to mama. Eh, dear mistress, couldn't I have managed this whole clothing antimony without you? You probably think, at first glance I'm a regular yard porter, but if you reason right, our natural state is cabinetmaking, what we did was cabinetmaking. You wouldn't believe how much of that furniture, them wardrobes and cupboards, went through my hands, in the varnishing sense, or, on the contrary, some such mahogany wood or walnut. Or, for instance, what matches, in the rich bride sense, went floating, forgive the expression, just went floating right past my nose. And the cause of it all – the drinking article, strong drink.'

With Markel's help, Anna Ivanovna got to the armchair, which he rolled up to her, and sat down, groaning and rubbing the hurt place. Markel set about restoring what had been demolished. When the top was attached, he said: 'Well, now it's just the doors, and it'll be fit for exhibition.'

Anna Ivanovna did not like the wardrobe. In appearance and size it resembled a catafalque or a royal tomb. It inspired a superstitious terror in her. She gave the wardrobe the nickname of 'Askold's grave'. By this name she meant Oleg's steed,[1] a thing that brings death to its owner. Being a well-read woman in a disorderly way, Anna Ivanovna confused the related notions.

With this fall began Anna Ivanovna's predisposition for lung diseases.

2

Anna Ivanovna spent the whole of November 1911 in bed. She had pneumonia.

Yura, Misha Gordon, and Tonya were to finish university and the Higher Women's Courses in the spring. Yura would graduate as a doctor, Tonya as a lawyer, and Misha as a philologist in the philosophy section.

Everything in Yura's soul was shifted and entangled, and everything was sharply original – views, habits, and predilections. He was exceedingly impressionable, the novelty of his perceptions not lending itself to description.

But greatly as he was drawn to art and history, Yura had no difficulty in choosing a career. He considered art unsuitable as a calling, in the same sense that innate gaiety or an inclination to melancholy could not be a profession. He was interested in physics and natural science, and held that in practical life one should be occupied with something generally useful. And so he chose medicine.

Four years back, during his first year, he had spent a whole semester in the university basement studying anatomy on corpses. He reached the cellar by a winding stair. Inside the anatomy theatre dishevelled students crowded in groups or singly. Some ground away, laying out bones and leafing through tattered, rot-eaten textbooks; others silently dissected in a corner; still others bantered, cracked jokes, and chased the rats that scurried in great numbers over the stone floor of the mortuary. In its darkness, the corpses of unknown people glowed like phosphorus, striking the eye with their nakedness: young suicides of unestablished identity; drowned women, well preserved and still intact. Alum injections made them look younger, lending them a deceptive roundness. The dead bodies were opened up, taken apart, and prepared, and the beauty of the human body remained true to itself in any section, however small, so that the amazement before some mermaid rudely thrown onto a zinc table did not go away when diverted from her to her amputated arm or cut-off hand. The basement smelled of formalin and carbolic acid, and the presence of mystery was felt in everything, beginning with the unknown fate of all these stretched-out bodies and ending with the mystery of life and death itself, which had settled here in the basement as if in its own home or at its headquarters.

The voice of this mystery, stifling everything else, pursued Yura, interfering with his dissecting. But many other things in life interfered with him in the same way. He was used to it, and the distracting interference did not disturb him.

Yura thought well and wrote very well. Still in his high school years he dreamed of prose, of a book of biographies, in which he could place, in the form of hidden explosive clusters, the most astounding things of all he had managed to see and ponder. But he was too young for such a book, and so he made up for it by writing verses, as a painter might draw sketches all his life for a great painting he had in mind.

Yura forgave these verses the sin of their coming to be for the sake of their energy and originality. These two qualities, energy and originality, Yura considered representative of reality in the arts, which were pointless, idle, and unnecessary in all other respects.

Yura realised how much he owed to his uncle for the general qualities of his character.

Nikolai Nikolaevich was living in Lausanne. In the books he published there in Russian and in translation, he developed his long-standing notion of history as a second universe, erected by mankind in response to the phenomenon of death with the aid of the phenomena of time and memory. The soul of these books was a new understanding of Christianity, their direct consequence a new understanding of art.

Even more than on Yura, the circle of these notions had an effect on his friend. Under their influence, Misha Gordon chose philosophy as his speciality. In his department, he attended lectures on theology, and he even had thoughts of transferring later to the theological academy.

The uncle's influence furthered Yura and liberated him, but it fettered Misha. Yura understood what role in Misha's extreme enthusiasms was played by his origins. From cautious tactfulness, he did not try to talk Misha out of his strange projects. But he often wished to see an empirical Misha, much closer to life.

3

One evening at the end of November, Yura came home late from the university, very tired, having eaten nothing all day. He was told there had been a terrible alarm in the afternoon; Anna Ivanovna had had convulsions, several doctors had come, they had advised sending for a priest, but then the idea was dropped. Now it was better, she was conscious and asked them to send Yura to her without delay, as soon as he came home.

Yura obeyed and, without changing, went to the bedroom.

The room bore signs of the recent turmoil. With soundless movements, a nurse was rearranging something on the bedside table. Crumpled napkins and damp towels from compresses lay about. The water in the rinsing bowl was slightly pink from spat-up blood. In it lay glass ampoules with broken-off tips and waterlogged wads of cotton.

The sick woman was bathed in sweat and licked her dry lips with the tip of her tongue. Her face was noticeably pinched compared with the morning, when Yura had last seen her.

'Haven't they made a wrong diagnosis?' he thought. 'There are all the signs of galloping pneumonia. This looks like the crisis.' Having greeted Anna Ivanovna and said something encouragingly empty, as people always do in such cases, he sent the nurse away. Taking Anna Ivanovna's wrist to count her pulse, he slipped his other hand under his jacket for the stethoscope. Anna Ivanovna moved her head to indicate that it was unnecessary. Yura realised that she needed something else from him. Gathering her strength, Anna Ivanovna began to speak:

'See, they wanted to confess me . . . Death is hanging over me . . . Any moment it may . . . You're afraid to have a tooth pulled, it hurts, you prepare yourself . . . But here it's not a tooth, it's all, all of you, all your life . . . snap, and it's gone, as if with pincers . . . And what is it? Nobody knows . . . And I'm anxious and frightened.'

Anna Ivanovna fell silent. Tears ran down her cheeks. Yura said nothing. After a moment Anna Ivanovna went on.

'You're talented . . . And talent is . . . not like everybody else . . . You must know something . . . Tell me something . . . Reassure me.'

'Well, what can I say?' Yura said, fidgeted uneasily on the chair, got up, paced the room, and sat down again. 'First, tomorrow you'll get better – there are signs, I'll stake my life on it. And then – death, consciousness, faith in resurrection . . . You want to know my opinion as a natural scientist? Maybe some other time? No? Right now? Well, you know best. Only it's hard to do it like this, straight off.'

And he gave her a whole impromptu lecture, surprised himself at the way it came out of him.

'Resurrection. The crude form in which it is affirmed for the comfort of the weakest is foreign to me. And I've always understood Christ's words about the living and the dead in a different way. Where will you find room for all these hordes gathered over thousands of years? The universe won't suffice for them, and God, the good, and meaning will have to take them-selves out of the world. They'll be crushed in this greedy animal stampede.

'But all the time one and the same boundlessly identical life fills the uni-verse and is renewed every hour in countless combinations and transforma-tions. Here you have fears about whether you will resurrect, yet you already resurrected when you were born, and you didn't notice it.

'Will it be painful for you, does tissue feel its own disintegration? That is, in other words, what will become of your consciousness? But what is con-sciousness? Let's look into it. To wish consciously to sleep means sure insomnia, the conscious attempt to feel the working of one's own digestion means the sure upsetting of its nervous regulation. Consciousness is poison, a means of self-poisoning for the subject who applies it to himself. Con-sciousness is a light directed outwards, consciousness lights the way before us so that we don't stumble. Consciousness is the lit headlights at the front of a moving locomotive. Turn their light inwards and there will be a catas-trophe.

'And so, what will become of your consciousness? Yours. Yours. But what are you? There's the whole hitch. Let's sort it out. What do you remember about yourself, what part of your constitution have you been aware of? Your kidneys, liver, blood vessels? No, as far as you can remem-ber, you've always found yourself in an external, active manifestation, in the work of your hands, in your family, in others. And now more attentively. Man in other people is man's soul. That is what you are, that is what your conscience breathed, relished, was nourished by all your life. Your soul, your immortality, your life in others. And what then? You have been in others and you will remain in others. And what difference does it make to you that later it will be called memory? It will be you, having entered into the composition of the future.

'Finally, one last thing. There's nothing to worry about. There is no death. Death is not in our line. But you just said "talent", and that's another thing, that is ours, that is open to us. And talent, in the highest, broadest sense, is the gift of life.

'There shall be no more death, says John the Theologian,[2] and just listen to the simplicity of his argumentation. There shall be no more death, because the former things have passed. It's almost the same as: there shall be no more death, because we've already seen all that, it's old and we're tired of it, and now we need something new, and this new thing is eternal life.'

He paced up and down the room while he spoke. 'Sleep,' he said, going to the bed and putting his hands on Anna Ivanovna's head. Several minutes went by. Anna Ivanovna began to fall asleep.

Yura quietly left the room and told Egorovna to send the nurse to the bedroom. 'Devil knows,' he thought, 'I'm turning into some sort of quack. Casting spells, healing by the laying on of hands.'

The next day Anna Ivanovna felt better.

4

Anna Ivanovna contrived to improve. In the middle of December she tried getting up, but was still very weak. She was advised to have a good long stay in bed.

She often sent for Yura and Tonya and for hours told them about her childhood, spent on her grandfather's estate, Varykino, on the river Rynva in the Urals. Neither Yura nor Tonya had ever been there, but from Anna Ivanovna's words, Yura could easily imagine those fifteen thousand acres of age-old, impenetrable forest, dark as night, pierced in two or three places, as if stabbing it with the knife of its meanders, by the swift river with its stony bottom and steep banks on the Krügers' side.

In those days Yura and Tonya were having evening dress made for them for the first time in their lives – for Yura a two-piece black suit, and for Tonya an evening gown of light satin with a slightly open neck. They were going to wear these outfits for the first time on the twenty-seventh, at the traditional annual Christmas party at the Sventitskys'.

The orders from the men's shop and the dressmaker were delivered on the same day. Yura and Tonya tried the new things on, remained pleased, and had no time to take them off again before Egorovna came from Anna

Ivanovna and said that she was sending for them. As they were, in their new clothes, Yura and Tonya went to Anna Ivanovna.

When they appeared, she propped herself on her elbow, looked at them from the side, told them to turn round, and said:

'Very nice. Simply ravishing. I didn't know they were ready. Now, Tonya, once more. No, never mind. It seemed to me that the basque was slightly puckered. Do you know why I sent for you? But first a few words about you, Yura.'

'I know, Anna Ivanovna. I myself asked them to show you that letter. You, like Nikolai Nikolaevich, think that I shouldn't have renounced it. A moment's patience. It's bad for you to talk. I'll explain everything to you at once. Though you know it all very well.

'And so, first. The case to do with the Zhivago inheritance exists for the sake of feeding lawyers and collecting court costs, but in reality there is no inheritance, there's nothing but debts and entanglements, and the filth that floats to the surface along with it all. If it were possible to turn anything into money, do you think I would give it to the court and not make use of it myself? But the thing is that the case has been trumped up, and rather than rummage through it all, it was better to renounce my rights to the non-existent property and yield it to several false rivals and envious impostors. Of the claims of a certain Madame Alice, who lives in Paris under the name Zhivago, I heard long ago. But new claimants have been added, and, I don't know about you, but I discovered it all quite recently.

'It turns out that, while mama was still alive, father became enamoured of a certain dreamer and madcap, Princess Stolbunova-Enrizzi. This person has a son by my father, he is now ten years old, his name is Evgraf.

'The princess is a recluse. She and her son live on unknown means without ever quitting her private house on the outskirts of Omsk. I was shown a photograph of the house. A handsome place with a five-window façade, single-pane windows, and stucco medallions along the cornice. And all the while recently I've been feeling as if this house is looking at me unkindly with its five windows across the thousands of miles separating European Russia from Siberia, and sooner or later will give me the evil eye. So what is it all to me: fictitious capital, artificially created rivals, their ill will and envy? Plus the lawyers.'

'All the same, you shouldn't have renounced it,' Anna Ivanovna objected. 'Do you know why I sent for you?' she repeated and at once went on: 'I remembered his name. Remember, yesterday I told you about a forester. His name was Vakkh. Splendid, isn't it? A dark forest horror, overgrown with beard up to his eyebrows, and – Vakkh! His face was disfigured, a bear mauled him, but he fought him off. They're all like that there. With names like that. One syllable. So that it's sonorous and vivid. Vakkh. Or Lupp. Or, say, Faust. Listen, listen. Sometimes they'd come and report something. There'd be some Avkt or Frol there, like a blast from grandfather's double-barrelled shotgun, and in a moment the herd of us would dart from the nursery to the kitchen. And there, if you can picture it, there would be a charcoal burner from the forest with a live bear cub or a prospector from a far-off border with a mineral sample. And grandfather would give each of them a little note. For the office. Money for one, grain for another, ammunition for a third. And the forest just outside the windows. And the snow, the snow! Higher than the house!' Anna Ivanovna began to cough.

'Stop, mama, it's not good for you,' Tonya warned. Yura seconded her.

'It's nothing. Trifles. Yes, by the way, Egorovna let on that you're not sure whether you should go to the Christmas party the day after tomorrow. I don't want to hear any more of that foolishness! Shame on you. What kind of doctor are you after that, Yura? So, it's settled. You're going, with no further discussion. But let's go back to Vakkh. This Vakkh was a blacksmith in his youth. He had his guts busted up in a fight. So he made himself new ones out of iron. What an odd fellow you are, Yura. As if I don't understand. Of course, not literally. But that's what people said.'

Anna Ivanovna coughed again, this time for much longer. The fit would not pass. She could not catch her breath.

Yura and Tonya rushed to her at the same moment. They stood shoulder to shoulder by her bed. Still coughing, Anna Ivanovna seized their touching hands in hers and held them united for a time. Then, regaining control of her voice and breath, she said:

'If I die, don't part. You're made for each other. Get married. There, I've betrothed you,' she added and burst into tears.

5

In the spring of 1906, before the start of her last year of high school, the six months of her liaison with Komarovsky had already gone beyond the limits of Lara's endurance. He very skilfully took advantage of her despondency and, whenever he found it necessary, without letting it show, reminded her subtly and inconspicuously of her dishonour. These reminders threw Lara into that state of disarray which a sensualist requires of a woman. This disarray made Lara ever more captive to the sensual nightmare, which made her hair stand on end when she sobered up. The contradictions of the night's madness were as inexplicable as black magic. Here everything was inside out and contrary to logic, sharp pain manifested itself in peals of silvery laughter, struggle and refusal signified consent, and the torturer's hand was covered with kisses of gratitude.

It seemed there would be no end to it, but in spring, at one of the last classes of the school year, having reflected on how much more frequent this pestering would be in the summer, when there were no school studies, which were her last refuge against frequent meetings with Komarovsky, Lara quickly came to a decision that changed her life for a long time.

It was a hot morning, a thunderstorm was gathering. The classroom windows were open. The city was humming in the distance, always on the same note, like bees in an apiary. The shouts of playing children came from the courtyard. The grassy smell of earth and young greenery made your head ache, like the smell of vodka and pancakes in the week before Lent.[3]

The history teacher was telling about Napoleon's Egyptian expedition.[4] When he came to the landing at Fréjus, the sky turned black, cracked and split by lightning and thunder, and through the windows, along with the smell of freshness, columns of sand and dust burst into the room. Two class toadies rushed officiously to the corridor to call the janitor to shut the windows, and when they opened the door, the draught lifted the blotting paper from the notebooks on all the desks and blew it around the room.

The windows were shut. Dirty city rain mixed with dust poured down. Lara tore a page from her notebook and wrote to the girl sitting next to her at the desk, Nadya Kologrivova:

'Nadya, I must set up my life separately from mama. Help me to find well-paid lessons. You have many rich acquaintances.'

Nadya replied in the same way:

'We're looking for a tutor for Lipa. Why don't you come to us. That would be great! You know how papa and mama love you.'

6

For more than three years Lara lived with the Kologrivovs as if behind a stone wall. No attempts on her were made from anywhere, and even her mother and brother, from whom she felt greatly estranged, did not remind her of themselves.

Lavrenty Mikhailovich Kologrivov was a big entrepreneur, a practical man of the new fashion, talented and intelligent. He hated the moribund order with the double hatred of a fabulously wealthy man able to buy out the state treasury, and of a man from simple folk who had gone amazingly far. He hid fugitives from the law, hired lawyers to defend the accused in political trials, and, as the joke went, overthrew himself as a proprietor by subsidising revolution and organising strikes at his own factory. Lavrenty Mikhailovich was a crack shot and a passionate hunter, and in the winter of 1905 had gone on Sundays to the Silver Woods and Moose Island to teach militiamen how to shoot.

He was a remarkable man. Serafima Filippovna, his wife, was a worthy match for him. Lara felt an admiring respect for them both. Everyone in the house loved her like their own.

In the fourth year of Lara's carefree life her brother Rodya came to see her on business. Swaying foppishly on his long legs and, for greater importance, pronouncing the words through his nose and drawing them out unnaturally, he told her that the graduating cadets of his class had collected some money for a farewell gift to the head of the school, had given it to Rodya, and had entrusted him with choosing and purchasing the gift. And that two days ago he had gambled away all the money to the last kopeck. Having said this, he dropped his whole lanky figure into an armchair and burst into tears.

Lara went cold when she heard it. Sobbing, Rodya continued:

'Yesterday I went to see Viktor Ippolitovich. He refused to talk with me about the subject, but said that if you wished . . . He said that, though you don't love us all any more, your power over him is still so great . . . Larochka . . . One word from you is enough . . . Do you understand what a disgrace it is and how it stains the honour of an officer's uniform? . . . Go to him – what will it cost you? – ask him . . . You won't have me wash away this embezzlement with my blood.'

'Wash away with blood . . . Honour of an officer's uniform,' Lara repeated indignantly, pacing the room in agitation. 'And I'm not a uniform, I have no honour, and you can do anything you like with me. Do you realise what you're asking, did you grasp what he's offering you? Year after year the Sisyphean labour of building, raising up, not getting enough sleep, and then this one comes, it's all the same to him, he'll snap his fingers, and it will all be blown to smithereens! Devil take you. Shoot yourself, if you like. What do I care? How much do you need?'

'Six hundred and ninety-some rubles – let's round it off to seven hundred,' said Rodya, faltering slightly.

'Rodya! No, you're out of your mind! Do you realise what you're saying? You gambled away seven hundred rubles? Rodya! Rodya! Do you know how long it would take an ordinary person like me to knock together a sum like that by honest labour?'

After a slight pause she added in a cold, estranged voice:

'All right. I'll try. Come tomorrow. And bring the revolver you were going to shoot yourself with. You'll turn it over to me. With a good supply of cartridges, don't forget.'

She got the money from Mr Kologrivov.

7

Working at the Kologrivovs' did not prevent Lara from finishing high school, entering the higher courses, studying successfully in them, and approaching graduation, which for her would come in the following year, 1912.

In the spring of 1911 her pupil Lipochka finished high school. She already had a fiancé, the young engineer Friesendank, from a good and well-to-do family. Lipochka's parents approved of her choice, but were against her marrying so early and advised her to wait. As a result, there were scenes. The spoiled and whimsical Lipochka, the family's favourite, shouted at her father and mother, wept and stamped her feet.

In this rich home, where Lara was considered one of their own, they did not remember the debt she had incurred for Rodya and did not remind her of it.

Lara would have repaid this debt long ago, if she had not had permanent expenses, the destination of which she kept hidden.

In secret from Pasha, she sent money to his father, Antipov, who was living in exile, and helped his often ailing, peevish mother. Besides that, in still greater secrecy, she reduced the expenses of Pasha himself, paying some extra to his landlord for his room and board without his knowing it.

Pasha, who was slightly younger than Lara, loved her madly and obeyed her in everything. At her insistence, after finishing his progressive high school, he took additional Latin and Greek, in order to enter the university as a philologist. Lara's dream was that in a year, after they passed the state examinations, she and Pasha would get married and go to teach, he in a boys' high school and she in a girls', in one of the provincial cities of the Urals.

Pasha lived in a room that Lara herself had found and rented for him from its quiet owners, in a newly built house on Kamergersky Lane, near the Art Theatre.

In the summer of 1911, Lara visited Duplyanka for the last time with the Kologrivovs. She loved the place to distraction, more than the owners did themselves. That was well-known, and there existed a consensus concerning Lara on the occasion of these summer trips. When the hot and soot-blackened train that brought them continued on its way and, amid the boundless, stupefying, and fragrant silence that succeeded it, the excited Lara lost the gift of speech, they allowed her to go alone on foot to the estate, while the luggage was carried from the little station and put onto a cart, and the Duplyanka driver, the sleeves of his red shirt thrust through the armholes of his coachman's vest, told the masters the local news of the past season as they got into the carriage.

Lara walked beside the rails along a path beaten down by wanderers and pilgrims and turned off on a track that led across a meadow to the forest. Here she stopped and, closing her eyes, breathed in the intricately fragrant air of the vast space around her. It was dearer to her than a father and mother, better than a lover, and wiser than a book. For an instant the meaning of existence was again revealed to Lara. She was here – so she conceived – in order to see into the mad enchantment of the earth, and to call everything by name, and if that was beyond her strength, then, out of love for life, to give birth to her successors, who would do it in her place.

That summer Lara arrived overtired from the excessive work she had heaped on herself. She was easily upset. A self-consciousness developed in her that had not been there before. This feature lent a certain pettiness to her character, which had always been distinguished by its breadth and lack of touchiness.

The Kologrivovs did not want to let her go. She was surrounded by the same affection as ever with them. But since Lipa was on her feet now, Lara considered herself superfluous in their house. She refused her salary. They made her take it. At the same time she needed money, and to earn an independent income while being a guest was awkward and practically unfeasible.

Lara considered her position false and untenable. It seemed to her that she was a burden to them all and they simply did not show it. She was a burden to herself. She wanted to flee from herself and the Kologrivovs wherever her feet would take her, but, according to her own notions, to do so she would have to repay the money to the Kologrivovs, and at the moment she had nowhere to get it. She felt herself a hostage on account of Rodya's stupid embezzlement, and her impotent indignation gave her no peace.

She seemed to see signs of negligence in everything. If the Kologrivovs' visiting acquaintances made much of her, it meant they were treating her as an uncomplaining 'ward' and easy prey. But when she was left in peace, it proved that she was a nonentity and they did not notice her.

Her fits of hypochondria did not keep Lara from sharing in the amusements of the numerous company that visited Duplyanka. She bathed and swam, went boating, took part in night-time picnics across the river, set off fireworks, and danced. She acted in amateur theatricals and with particular passion competed in target shooting from short Mauser rifles, to which, however, she preferred Rodya's light revolver. She came to fire it with great accuracy and jokingly regretted that she was a woman and the career of a swashbuckling duellist was closed to her. But the merrier Lara's life was, the worse she felt. She did not know what she wanted herself.

This increased especially after her return to the city. Here to Lara's troubles were added some slight disagreements with Pasha (Lara was careful not to quarrel seriously with him, because she considered him her last defence). Lately Pasha had acquired a certain self-confidence. The admonishing tones in his conversation upset her and made her laugh.

Pasha, Lipa, the Kologrivovs, money – it all started spinning in her head. Life became repugnant to Lara. She was beginning to lose her mind. She felt like dropping everything familiar and tested and starting something new. In that state of mind, around Christmastime of the year 1911, she came to a fateful decision. She decided to part from the Kologrivovs immediately and somehow build her life alone and independently, and to ask Komarovsky for the money needed for that. It seemed to Lara that after all that had happened and the subsequent years of her hard-won freedom, he should help her chivalrously, not going into any explanations, disinterestedly and without any filth.

With that aim she went, on 27 December, to the Petrovsky neighbourhood and, on the way out, put Rodya's revolver, loaded and with the safety off, into her muff, intending to shoot Viktor Ippolitovich if he should refuse her, understand her perversely, or humiliate her in any way.

She walked in terrible perturbation along the festive streets, not noticing anything around her. The intended shot had already rung out in her soul, with total indifference to the one it had been aimed at. This shot was the only thing she was conscious of. She heard it all along the way, and it was fired at Komarovsky, at herself, at her own fate, and at the oak in Duplyanka with a target carved on its trunk.

8

'Don't touch the muff,' she said to the oh-ing and ah-ing Emma Ernestovna when she reached out to help Lara take off her coat.

Viktor Ippolitovich was not at home. Emma Ernestovna went on persuading Lara to come in and take off her coat.

'I can't. I'm in a hurry. Where is he?'

Emma Ernestovna said he was at a Christmas party. Address in hand, Lara ran down the gloomy stairs with the stained-glass coats of arms in the windows, which vividly reminded her of everything, and set out for the Sventitskys' in Flour Town.

Only now, going out for the second time, did Lara look around properly. It was winter. It was the city. It was evening.

It was freezing cold. The streets were covered with black ice, thick as the glass bottoms of broken beer bottles. It was painful to breathe. The air was choked with grey hoarfrost, and it seemed to tickle and prickle with its shaggy stubble, just as the icy fur of Lara's collar chafed her and got into her mouth. With a pounding heart Lara walked along the empty streets. Smoke came from the doorways of tea rooms and taverns along the way. The frost-bitten faces of passers-by, red as sausage, and the bearded muzzles of horses and dogs hung with icicles emerged from the mist. Covered with a thick layer of ice and snow, the windows of houses were as if painted over with chalk, and the colourful reflections of lighted Christmas trees and the shadows of merrymakers moved over their opaque surface, as if the people outside were being shown shadow pictures from inside on white sheets hung before a magic lantern.

In Kamergersky Lara stopped. 'I can't do it any more, I can't stand it' burst from her almost aloud. 'I'll go up and tell him everything,' she thought, regaining control of herself, opening the heavy door of the imposing entrance.

9

Red from the effort, his tongue stuck in his cheek, Pasha struggled before the mirror, putting on his collar and trying to stick the recalcitrant stud through the overstarched buttonhole of his shirt front. He was getting ready to go out, and he was still so pure and inexperienced that he became embarrassed when Lara came in without knocking and found him in such a minor state of undress. He noticed her agitation at once. Her legs were giving way under her. She came in, pushing her dress ahead at each step as if crossing a ford.

'What is it? What's happened?' he asked in alarm, rushing to meet her.

'Sit down beside me. Sit down as you are. Don't smarten yourself up. I'm in a hurry. I'll have to leave at once. Don't touch the muff. Wait. Turn away for a moment.'

He obeyed. Lara was wearing a two-piece English suit. She took the jacket off, hung it on a nail, and transferred Rodya's revolver from the muff to the jacket pocket. Then, returning to the sofa, she said:

'Now you can look. Light a candle and turn off the electricity.'

Lara liked to talk in semi-darkness with candles burning. Pasha always kept a spare unopened pack for her. He replaced the burned-down end in the candlestick with a new whole candle, placed it on the windowsill, and lit it. The flame choked on the stearin, shot crackling little stars in all directions, and sharpened into an arrow. The room filled with a soft light. The ice on the windowpane at the level of the candle began to melt, forming a black eyehole.

'Listen, Patulya,' said Lara. 'I'm in difficulties. I need help to get out of them. Don't be frightened and don't question me, but part with the notion that we're like everybody else. Don't remain calm. I'm always in danger. If you love me and want to keep me from perishing, don't put it off, let's get married quickly.'

'But that's my constant wish,' he interrupted her. 'Quickly name the day, I'll be glad to do it whenever you like. But tell me more simply and clearly, don't torture me with riddles.'

But Lara distracted him, imperceptibly avoiding a direct answer. They talked for a long time on themes that had no relation to the subject of Lara's grief.

10

That winter Yura was writing a scientific paper on the nervous elements of the retina in competition for a university gold medal. Though Yura would be graduating as a generalist, he knew the eye with the thoroughness of a future oculist.

This interest in the physiology of vision spoke for other sides of Yura's nature – his creative gifts and his reflections on the essence of the artistic image and the structure of the logical idea.

Tonya and Yura were riding in a hired sleigh to the Christmas party at the Sventitskys'. The two had lived for six years side by side through the beginning of youth and the end of childhood. They knew each other in the smallest detail. They had habits in common, their own way of exchanging brief witticisms, their own way of snorting in response. And so they were riding now, keeping silent, pressing their lips from the cold, and exchanging brief remarks. And both thinking their own thoughts.

Yura recalled that the time for the contest was near and he had to hurry with the paper, and in the festive turmoil of the ending year that could be felt in the streets, he jumped from those thoughts to others.

In Gordon's department a hectograph student magazine was published, and Gordon was the editor. Yura had long been promising them an article on Blok.[5] The young people of both capitals were raving about Blok, he and Misha more than anyone.

But these thoughts did not remain long on Yura's conscience. They rode on, tucking their chins into their collars and rubbing their freezing ears, and thought about differing things. But on one point their thoughts came together. The recent scene at Anna Ivanovna's had transformed them both. It was as if they had recovered their sight and looked at each other with new eyes.

Tonya, this old comrade, this person so clear that she needed no explanations, turned out to be the most unattainable and complex of all that Yura could imagine, turned out to be a woman. With a certain stretching of fantasy, Yura could picture himself as a hero climbing Ararat, a prophet, a conqueror, anything you like, but not a woman.

And now Tonya had taken this most difficult and all-surpassing task on her thin and weak shoulders (she suddenly seemed thin and weak to Yura, though she was a perfectly healthy girl). And he became filled with that burning compassion and timid amazement before her which is the beginning of passion.

The same thing, with corresponding modifications, happened to Tonya in relation to Yura.

Yura thought that in any case they had no business leaving the house. What if something should happen during their absence? And then he remembered. Learning that Anna Ivanovna was worse, they had gone to her, already dressed for the evening, and suggested that they stay. She had protested against it with all her former sharpness and insisted that they go to the party. Yura and Tonya went behind the draperies into the deep window niche to see what the weather was like. When they came out of the niche, the two parts of the tulle curtains clung to the still unworn fabric of their new clothes. The light, clinging stuff dragged for several steps behind Tonya like a wedding veil behind a bride. They all burst out laughing, so simultaneously did this resemblance strike the eye of everyone in the room without a word spoken.

Yura looked around and saw the same things that had caught Lara's eye not long before. Their sleigh raised an unnaturally loud noise, which awakened an unnaturally long echo under the ice-bound trees of the gardens and boulevards. The frosted-over windows of houses, lit from inside, resembled precious caskets of laminated smoky topaz. Behind them glowed Moscow's Christmas life, candles burned on trees, guests crowded, and clowning mummers played at hide-and-seek and pass-the-ring.

It suddenly occurred to Yura that Blok was the manifestation of Christmas in all domains of Russian life, in the daily life of the northern city and in the new literature, under the starry sky of the contemporary street and around the lighted Christmas tree in a drawing room of the present century. It occurred to him that no article about Blok was needed, but one needed simply to portray a Russian adoration of the Magi, like the Dutch masters, with frost, wolves, and a dark fir forest.

They were driving down Kamergersky. Yura turned his attention to a black hole melted in the icy coating of one window. Through this hole shone the light of a candle, penetrating outside almost with the consciousness of a gaze, as if the flame were spying on the passers-by and waiting for someone.

'A candle burned on the table. A candle burned . . .' Yura whispered to himself the beginning of something vague, unformed, in hopes that the continuation would come of itself, without forcing. It did not come.

11

From time immemorial the Christmas parties at the Sventitskys' had been organised in the following fashion. At ten, when the children went home, the tree was lighted a second time for the young people and the adults, and the merrymaking went on till morning. The more elderly cut the cards all night in a three-walled Pompeian drawing room, which was an extension of the ballroom and was separated from it by a heavy, thick curtain on big bronze rings. At dawn the whole company had supper.

'Why are you so late?' the Sventitskys' nephew Georges asked them in passing, as he ran through the front hall to his uncle and aunt's rooms. Yura and Tonya also decided to go there to greet the hosts, and, on their way, while taking off their coats, looked into the ballroom.

Past the hotly breathing Christmas tree, girdled by several rows of streaming radiance, rustling their dresses and stepping on each other's feet, moved a black wall of walkers and talkers, not taken up with dancing.

Inside the circle, the dancers whirled furiously. They were spun around, paired off, stretched out in a chain by Koka Kornakov, a lycée student, the son of a deputy prosecutor. He led the dancing and shouted at the top of his voice from one end of the room to the other: '*Grand rond! Chaîne chinoise!*'* – and it was all done according to his word. '*Une valse s'il vous plaît!*'† he bawled to the pianist and led his lady at the head of the first turn

---

* Great ring! Chinese chain!
† A waltz please!

à trois temps, à deux temps,* ever slowing and shortening his step to a barely noticeable turning in place, which was no longer a waltz but only its dying echo. And everyone applauded, and the stirring, shuffling, and chattering crowd was served ice cream and refreshing drinks. Flushed young men and girls stopped shouting and laughing for a moment and hastily and greedily gulped down some cold cranberry drink or lemonade, and, having barely set the glass on the tray, renewed their shouting and laughing tenfold, as if they had snatched some exhilarating brew.

Without going into the ballroom, Tonya and Yura went on to the hosts' rooms at the rear of the apartment.

12

The Sventitskys' inner rooms were cluttered with superfluous things taken from the drawing room and ballroom to make space. Here was the hosts' magic kitchen, their Christmas storehouse. It smelled of paint and glue, there were rolls of coloured paper and piles of boxes with cotillion stars and spare Christmas tree candles.

The old Sventitskys were writing tags for the gifts, place cards for supper, and tickets for some lottery that was to take place. Georges was helping them, but he often confused the numbering and they grumbled irritably at him. The Sventitskys were terribly glad to see Yura and Tonya. They remembered them from when they were little, did not stand on ceremony with them, and with no further talk sat them down to work.

'Felitsata Semyonovna doesn't understand that this ought to have been thought about earlier and not in the heat of things, when the guests are here. Ah, Georges, you ungodly muddler, again you've jumbled up the numbers! The agreement was that we'd put those for the boxes of dragées on the table and the blank ones on the sofa, and again you've got it all topsy-turvy and done it backwards.'

'I'm very glad Annette feels better. Pierre and I were so worried.'

'Yes, but you see, dearest, she happens to be worse, worse, you understand, you always get everything *devant-derrière.*'†

Yura and Tonya hung around backstage for half the festive night with Georges and the old folks.

* In triple time, in double time.
† Back to front.

13

All the while they were sitting with the Sventitskys, Lara was in the ball-room. Though she was not dressed for a ball and did not know anyone there, she now allowed Koka Kornakov to make a turn with her, passively, as if in sleep, now strolled aimlessly about the room, quite crestfallen.

Once or twice already, Lara had stopped irresolutely and hesitated on the threshold of the drawing room, hoping that Komarovsky, who sat facing the ballroom, would notice her. But he kept his eyes on his cards, which he held fanlike in his left hand, and either really did not see her or pretended not to. The affront took Lara's breath away. Just then a girl Lara did not know went into the drawing room from the ballroom. Komarovsky gave the girl that glance Lara knew so well. The flattered girl smiled at Komarovsky, flushed and beamed happily. Lara almost cried out when she saw it. The colour of shame rose high in her face; her forehead and neck turned red. 'A new victim,' she thought. Lara saw as in a mirror her whole self and her whole story. But she still did not give up the idea of having a talk with Komarovsky and, having decided to put off the attempt to a more suit-able moment, forced herself to calm down and went back to the ballroom.

Three more men were playing at the same table with Komarovsky. One of his partners, sitting next to him, was the father of the foppish lycée stu-dent who had invited Lara to waltz. Lara concluded as much from the two or three words she exchanged with him while they made a turn around the room. And the tall, dark-haired woman in black with the crazed, burning eyes and unpleasantly strained, snakelike neck, who kept going from the drawing room to the ballroom, the field of her son's activity, and back to the drawing room and her card-playing husband, was Koka Kornakov's mother. Finally, it became clear that the girl who had served as pretext for Lara's complex feelings was Koka's sister, and Lara's conclusions had no grounds at all.

'Kornakov,' Koka had introduced himself to Lara at the very start. But then she had not caught it. 'Kornakov,' he repeated at the last gliding turn, taking her to a chair and bowing out. This time Lara heard him. 'Kornakov, Kornakov,' she fell to thinking. 'Something familiar. Something unpleasant.' Then she remembered. Kornakov, the deputy prosecutor of the Moscow court. He had prosecuted the group of railway workers with whom Tiverzin had stood trial. At Lara's request, Lavrenty Mikhailovich had gone to but-ter him up, so that he would not be so fierce at the trial, but could not make him bend. 'So that's how it is! Well, well, well. Curious. Kornakov. Kornakov.'

14

It was past twelve or one in the morning. Yura had a buzzing in his ears. After a break, during which tea and biscuits were served in the dining room, the dancing began again. When the candles on the tree burned down, no one replaced them any more.

Yura stood absent-mindedly in the middle of the ballroom and looked at Tonya, who was dancing with someone he did not know. Gliding past Yura, Tonya tossed aside the small train of her too-long satin dress with a movement of her foot and, splashing it like a fish, disappeared into the crowd of dancers.

She was very excited. During the break, when they sat in the dining room, Tonya refused tea and quenched her thirst with mandarines, which she peeled in great number from their fragrant, easily separated skins. She kept taking from behind her sash or from her little sleeve a cambric handkerchief, tiny as a fruit tree blossom, and wiping the trickles of sweat at the edges of her lips and between her sticky fingers. Laughing and not interrupting the animated conversation, she mechanically tucked it back behind her sash or the frills of her bodice.

Now, dancing with an unknown partner and, as she turned, brushing against Yura, who was standing to the side and frowning, Tonya playfully pressed his hand in passing and smiled meaningfully. After one of these pressings, the handkerchief she was holding remained in Yura's hand. He pressed it to his lips and closed his eyes. The handkerchief had the mingled smell of mandarine and of Tonya's hot palm, equally enchanting. This was something new in Yura's life, never before experienced, and its sharpness pierced him through. The childishly naïve smell was intimately reasonable, like a word whispered in the dark. Yura stood, covering his eyes and lips with the handkerchief in his palm and breathing it in. Suddenly a shot rang out in the house.

Everyone turned to the curtain that separated the drawing room from the ballroom. For a moment there was silence. Then turmoil set in. Everyone began to bustle and shout. Some rushed after Koka Kornakov to the place where the shot had resounded. People were already coming from there, threatening, weeping, and interrupting each other as they argued.

'What has she done, what has she done?' Komarovsky repeated in despair.

'Borya, are you alive? Borya, are you alive?' Mrs Kornakov cried hysterically. 'I've heard Dr Drokov is among the guests here. Yes, but where is he, where is he? Ah, leave me alone, please. For you it's a scratch, but for me it's the justification of my whole life. Oh, my poor martyr, the exposer of all these criminals! Here she is, here she is, trash, I'll scratch your eyes out, vile creature! Now she won't get away! What did you say, Mr Komarovsky? At you? She aimed at you? No, it's too much. I'm in great distress, Mr Komarovsky, come to your senses, I can't take jokes now. Koka, Kokochka, what do you say to that! Your father . . . Yes . . . But the right hand of God . . . Koka! Koka!'

The crowd poured out of the drawing room into the ballroom. In the midst of them, loudly joking and assuring everyone that he was perfectly unharmed, walked Kornakov, pressing a clean napkin to the bleeding scratch on his slightly wounded left hand. In another group a little to the side and behind, Lara was being led by the arms.

Yura was dumbfounded when he saw her. The same girl! And again in such extraordinary circumstances! And again this greying one. But now Yura knows him. He is the distinguished lawyer Komarovsky; he was involved in the trial over father's inheritance. No need to greet him, he and Yura pretend they're not acquainted. But she . . . So it was she who fired the shot? At the prosecutor? It must be something political. Poor girl. She'll get it now. What a proud beauty she is! And these! They're dragging her by the arms, the devils, like a caught thief.

But he realised at once that he was mistaken. Lara's legs had given way under her. They were holding her by the arms so that she would not fall, and they barely managed to drag her to the nearest armchair, where she collapsed.

Yura ran to her, so as to bring her to her senses, but for greater propriety he decided first to show concern for the imaginary victim of the attempt. He went to Kornakov and said:

'There was a request for medical assistance here. I can render it. Show me your hand. Well, you have a lucky star. It's such a trifle I wouldn't even bandage it. However, a little iodine won't do any harm. Here's Felitsata Semyonovna, we'll ask her.'

Mrs Sventitsky and Tonya, who were quickly approaching Yura, did not look themselves. They said he should drop everything and fetch his coat quickly, they had been sent for, something was wrong at home. Yura became frightened, supposing the worst, and, forgetting everything in the world, ran for his coat.

15

They did not find Anna Ivanovna alive when they came running headlong into the house from the Sivtsev entrance. Death had occurred ten minutes before their arrival. It was caused by a long fit of suffocation, resulting from an acute oedema of the lungs that had not been diagnosed in time.

During the first hours Tonya cried her head off, thrashed in convulsions, and recognised no one. The next day she calmed down, listened patiently to what her father and Yura told her, but was able to respond only by nodding, because the moment she opened her mouth, grief overwhelmed her with its former force and howls began to escape her of themselves, as if she were possessed.

She spent hours on her knees beside the dead woman, in the intervals between panikhidas,[6] embracing with her big, beautiful arms a corner of the coffin along with the edge of the platform it stood on and the wreaths that covered it. She did not notice anyone around her. But the moment her gaze met the gaze of her relations, she hurriedly got up from the floor, slipped out of the room with quick steps, swiftly ran upstairs to her room, holding back her sobs, and, collapsing on the bed, buried in her pillow the outbursts of despair that raged within her.

From grief, long standing on his feet, and lack of sleep, from the dense singing and the dazzling light of candles day and night, and from the cold he had caught during those days, there was a sweet confusion in Yura's soul, blissfully delirious, mournfully enraptured.

Ten years before then, when his mother was being buried, Yura had been quite little. He could still remember how inconsolably he had wept, struck by grief and horror. Then the main thing was not in him. Then he was hardly even aware that there was some him, Yura, who had a separate existence and was of interest or value. Then the main thing was in what stood around him, the external. The outside world surrounded Yura on all sides, tangible, impenetrable, and unquestionable, like a forest, and that was why Yura was so shaken by his mother's death, because he had been lost in that forest with her and was suddenly left alone in it, without her. This forest consisted of everything in the world – clouds, city signboards, the balls on fire towers, and the servers riding ahead of the carriage bearing the icon of the Mother of God, with earmuffs instead of hats on their heads, uncovered in the presence of the holy object. This forest consisted of shop windows in the arcades and the unattainably high night sky, with stars, dear God, and the saints.

This inaccessibly high sky bent down low, very low to them in the nursery, burying its head in the nanny's skirt, when she told them something about God, and became close and tame, like the tops of hazel bushes when their branches are bent down in the ravines for picking hazelnuts. It was as if it dipped into the gilded basin in their nursery and, having bathed in fire and gold, turned into an early or late liturgy in the little church in the lane where his nanny took him. There the stars of the sky became icon lamps, dear God became the priest, and everyone was assigned his duties more or less according to ability. But the main thing was the actual world of the grown-ups and the city, which stood dark around him like a forest. Then, with all his half-animal faith, Yura believed in the God of this forest, as in a forest warden.

It was quite a different matter now. All these twelve years of secondary school and university, Yura had studied classics and religion, legends and poets, the sciences of the past and of nature, as if it were all the family chronicle of his own house, his own genealogy. Now he was afraid of nothing, neither life nor death; everything in the world, all things were words of his vocabulary. He felt himself on an equal footing with the universe, and he stood through the panikhidas for Anna Ivanovna quite differently from in time past for his mother. Then he had been oblivious of pain, felt timorous, and prayed. But now he listened to the funeral service as information immediately addressed to him and concerning him directly. He listened attentively to the words and demanded meaning from them, comprehensibly expressed, as is demanded of every matter, and there was nothing in common with piety in his feeling of continuity in relation to the higher powers of earth and heaven, which he venerated as his great predecessors.

16

'Holy God, Holy Mighty, Holy Immortal, have mercy on us.'[7] What is it? Where is he? The carrying out. They are carrying the coffin out. He must wake up. He had collapsed fully clothed on the sofa before six in the morning. He probably has a fever. Now they are looking all over the house for him, and no one has guessed that he is asleep in the library, in the far corner, behind the tall bookshelves that reach the ceiling.

'Yura, Yura!' the yard porter Markel is calling him from somewhere close by. They are carrying out the coffin. Markel has to take the wreaths down to the street, and he cannot find Yura, and besides he has got stuck in the bedroom, because the door is blocked by the open door of the wardrobe, preventing Markel from coming out.

'Markel! Markel! Yura!' they call for them from downstairs. With one shove, Markel makes short work of the obstruction and runs downstairs with several wreaths.

'Holy God, Holy Mighty, Holy Immortal' – gently drifts down the lane and lingers there, like a soft ostrich feather passing through the air, and everything sways: the wreaths and the passers-by, the plumed heads of the horses, the censer swinging on its chain in the priest's hand, the white earth underfoot.

'Yura! My God, at last. Wake up, please,' Shura Schlesinger, who has finally found him, shakes him by the shoulder. 'What's the matter with you? They're carrying out the coffin. Are you coming?'

'Why, of course.'

17

The funeral service was over. The beggars, shifting their feet from the cold, moved closer together in two files. The hearse, the gig with the wreaths, and the Krügers' carriage swayed and moved slightly. The cabs drew nearer to the church. The weeping Shura Schlesinger came out and, raising her tear-dampened veil, passed an inquisitive glance over the line of cabs. Finding the pallbearers from the funeral home among them, she beckoned for them to come and disappeared into the church with them. More and more people were pouring out of the church.

'So it's Ann-Ivanna's turn. Paid her respects, poor little thing, and drew herself a one-way ticket.'

'Yes, she's done flitting about, poor thing. The butterfly's gone to her rest.'

'Have you got a cab, or will you take the number eleven?'

'My legs are stiff. Let's walk a bit and then catch the tram.'

'Did you notice how upset Fufkov is? He stared at the newly departed, tears pouring down, blowing his nose, as if he could devour her. And the husband right there beside him.'

'Ogled her all his life.'

With such conversations, they dragged themselves off to the cemetery at the other end of town. That day there was a let-up after the severe frost. The day was filled with a motionless heaviness, a day of diminished frost and departed life, a day as if created for a burial by nature herself. The dirtied snow seemed to shine through a covering of crape; from behind the fences wet fir trees, dark as tarnished silver, kept watch and looked as if they were dressed in mourning.

This was that same memorable cemetery, the resting place of Marya Nikolaevna. Yura had not found his way to his mother's grave at all in recent years. 'Mama,' he whispered almost with the lips of those years, looking towards it from far off.

They dispersed solemnly and even picturesquely along the cleared paths, whose evasive meandering accorded poorly with the mournful measured-ness of their steps. Alexander Alexandrovich led Tonya by the arm. The Krügers followed them. Mourning was very becoming to Tonya.

Shaggy hoarfrost, bearded like mould, covered the chains of the crosses on the cupolas and the pink monastery walls. In the far corner of the monastery courtyard, ropes were stretched from wall to wall with laundered linen hung out to dry – shirts with heavy, waterlogged sleeves, peach-coloured table-cloths, crooked, poorly wrung-out sheets. Yura looked at it more intently and realised that it was the place on the monastery grounds, now changed by new buildings, where the blizzard had raged that night.

Yura walked on alone, quickly getting ahead of the rest, stopping now and then to wait for them. In response to the devastation produced by death in this company slowly walking behind him, he wanted, as irresistibly as water whirling in a funnel rushes into the deep, to dream and think, to toil over forms, to bring forth beauty. Now, as never before, it was clear to him that art is always, ceaselessly, occupied with two things. It constantly reflects on death and thereby constantly creates life. Great and true art, that which is called the Revelation of St John and that which goes on to finish it.

Yura longingly anticipated his disappearance for a day or two from family and university horizons and would put into his memorial lines for Anna Ivanovna all that turned up at that moment, all the chance things that life put in his way: two or three of the dead woman's best characteristics; the image of Tonya in mourning; several observations in the street on the way back from the cemetery; the washed laundry in the place where one night long ago a blizzard had howled and he had wept as a little boy.

Part Four

IMMINENT INEVITABILITIES

I

Lara lay half delirious in the bedroom on Felitsata Semyonovna's bed. Around her the Sventitskys, Dr Drokov, the servants were whispering.

The Sventitskys' empty house was sunk in darkness, and only in the middle of the long suite of rooms, in a small sitting room, was there a dim wall lamp burning, casting its light up and down the length of this single extended hallway.

Through it, not like a guest, but as if he were in his own home, Viktor Ippolitovich paced rapidly with angry and resolute steps. Now he looked into the bedroom to ask what was going on there, now he set off for the opposite end of the house and, going past the Christmas tree with its strings of silver beads, came to the dining room, where the table was laden with untouched food and the green wineglasses tinkled whenever a carriage drove by outside the window or a little mouse darted over the tablecloth among the dishes.

Komarovsky stormed and raged. Contradictory feelings crowded in his breast. What scandal and indecency! He was furious. His position was threatened. The incident might undermine his reputation. He had at all costs to forestall, to cut short any gossip before it was too late, and if the news had already spread, to hush up, to stifle the rumours at their source. Besides that, he again experienced how irresistible this desperate, crazy girl was. You could see at once that she was not like everyone else. There had always been something extraordinary about her. Yet how painfully and, apparently, irreparably he had mutilated her life! How she thrashes about, how she rises up and rebels all the time, striving to remake her fate in her own way and begin to exist over again!

He has to help her from all points of view, perhaps to rent a room for her, but in any case not to touch her; on the contrary, to withdraw completely, to step aside, so as to cast no shadow, otherwise, being what she is, she might just pull something else for all he knows.

And there's so much trouble ahead! You don't get patted on the head for such things. The law never naps. It's still night and less than two hours since the incident took place, but the police had already come twice, and Komarovsky had gone to the kitchen to have a talk with the police officer and settle it all.

And the further it goes, the more complicated it will get. They'll demand proof that Lara was aiming at him and not at Kornakov. But things won't end there. Part of the responsibility will be taken off Lara, but she will be liable to prosecution for the rest.

Naturally, he will do everything in his power to prevent that, and if proceedings are started, he will obtain findings from psychiatric experts that Lara was not answerable at the moment of the shooting, and have the case dropped.

After these thoughts Komarovsky began to calm down. The night was over. Streaks of light began to dart from room to room, peeking under the tables and sofas like thieves or pawnshop appraisers.

Having stopped at the bedroom and learned that Lara was no better, Komarovsky left the Sventitskys' and went to see a lady of his acquaintance, Rufina Onisimovna Voit-Voitkovskaya, a lawyer and the wife of a political émigré. Her eight-room apartment now exceeded her needs and was beyond her means. She rented out two rooms. One of them had recently been vacated, and Komarovsky took it for Lara. A few hours later Lara was transported there with a high temperature and half-conscious. She had brain fever.

2

Rufina Onisimovna was a progressive woman, the enemy of prejudice, the well-wisher, as she thought and expressed it, of all that was 'positive and viable' around her.

On her chest of drawers lay a copy of the Erfurt Programme with a dedication by the author. One of the photographs pinned to the wall showed her husband, 'my good Voit', at a popular fairground in Switzerland together with Plekhanov.[1] They were both wearing lustrine jackets and panama hats.

Rufina Onisimovna disliked her sick lodger at first glance. She considered Lara an inveterate malingerer. Lara's fits of delirium seemed a pure sham to

Rufina Onisimovna. She was ready to swear that Lara was playing the mad Gretchen in prison.[2]

Rufina Onisimovna expressed her contempt for Lara by a heightened animation. She slammed doors and sang loudly, rushed like a whirlwind around her part of the apartment, and spent whole days airing out the rooms.

Her apartment was on the top floor of a big house on the Arbat. The windows of this floor, starting with the winter solstice, were filled to overflowing with light blue sky, wide as a river in flood. For half the winter the apartment was full of signs of the coming spring, its harbingers.

A warm breeze from the south blew through the vent windows, locomotives howled rendingly in the train stations, and the ailing Lara, lying in bed, gave herself at leisure to distant memories.

Very often she remembered the first evening of their arrival in Moscow from the Urals, seven or eight years ago, in her unforgettable childhood.

They rode in a hackney cab through semi-dark lanes across the whole of Moscow, from the train station to the hotel. The street lamps, approaching and withdrawing, cast the shadow of their hunched cabby on the walls of the buildings. The shadow grew, grew, reached unnatural dimensions, covered the pavement and the roofs, then dropped away. And everything began again.

In the darkness overhead the forty-times-forty Moscow churches rang their bells, on the ground horse-drawn trams drove around clanging, but the gaudy shop windows and lights also deafened Lara, as if they, too, gave out a sound of their own, like the bells and wheels.

In the hotel room, she was stunned by an unbelievably huge watermelon on the table, Komarovsky's welcoming gift in their new lodgings. The watermelon seemed to Lara a symbol of Komarovsky's imperiousness and of his wealth. When Viktor Ippolitovich, with a stroke of the knife, split in two the loudly crunching, dark green, round marvel, with its ice-cold, sugary insides, Lara's breath was taken away from fear, but she did not dare refuse. She forced herself to swallow the pink, fragrant pieces, which stuck in her throat from agitation.

And this timidity before the costly food and the night-time capital was then repeated in her timidity before Komarovsky – the main solution to all that came after. But now he was unrecognisable. He demanded nothing, gave no reminders of himself, and did not even appear. And, keeping his distance, constantly offered his help in the noblest way.

Kologrivov's visit was quite another matter. Lara was very glad to see Lavrenty Mikhailovich. Not because he was so tall and stately, but owing to the liveliness and talent he exuded, the guest took up half the room with himself, his sparkling eyes, and his intelligent smile. The room became crowded.

He sat by Lara's bed rubbing his hands. When he was summoned to the council of ministers in Petersburg, he talked with the old dignitaries as if they were prankish schoolboys. But here before him lay a recent part of his domestic hearth, something like his own daughter, with whom, as with everyone at home, he exchanged glances and remarks only in passing and fleetingly (this constituted the distinctive charm of the brief, expressive communications, both sides knew that). He could not treat Lara gravely and indifferently, like a grown-up. He did not know how to talk with her so as not to offend her, and so he said, smiling to her, as to a child:

'What's this you're up to, my dearest? Who needs these melodramas?' He fell silent and started examining the damp spots on the ceiling and wallpaper. Then, shaking his head reproachfully, he went on: 'An exhibition is opening in Düsseldorf, an international one – of painting, sculpture, and gardening. I'm going. Your place is a bit damp. How long do you intend to hang between heaven and earth? There's not much elbow room here, God knows. This Voitessa, just between us, is perfect trash. I know her. Move. Enough lolling about. You've been sick and there's an end to it. Time to get up. Move to another room, go back to your studies, finish school. There's an artist I know. He's going to Turkestan for two years. His studio is divided up by partitions, and, strictly speaking, it's a whole little apartment. It seems he's prepared to leave it, together with the furnishings, in good hands. Would you like me to arrange it? And there's also this. Let me talk business. I've long been meaning, it's my sacred duty . . . Since Lipa . . . Here's a small sum, a bonus for her graduation . . . No, let me, let me . . . No, I beg you, don't be stubborn . . . No, excuse me, please.'

And, on leaving, he forced her, despite her objections, tears, and even something like a scuffle, to accept from him a bank cheque for ten thousand.

On recovering, Lara moved to the new hearth so praised by Kologrivov. The place was right next to the Smolensk market. The apartment was on the upper floor of a small, two-storey stone building of old construction. The ground floor was used as a warehouse. The inhabitants were draymen. The inner courtyard was paved with cobbles and always covered with spilled oats and scattered hay. Pigeons strutted about, cooing. Their noisy flock would flutter up from the ground no higher than Lara's window when a pack of rats scurried along the stone gutter in the yard.

3

There was much grief to do with Pasha. While Lara was seriously ill, they would not let him see her. What must he have felt? Lara had wanted to kill a man who, in Pasha's understanding, was indifferent to her, and had then ended up under the patronage of that same man, the victim of her unsuccessful murder. And all that after their memorable conversation on a Christmas night, with the burning candle! Had it not been for this man, Lara would have been arrested and tried. He had warded off the punishment that threatened her. Thanks to him, she had remained at school, safe and sound. Pasha was tormented and perplexed.

When she was better, Lara invited Pasha to come to her. She said:

'I'm bad. You don't know me; some day I'll tell you. It's hard for me to speak, you see, I'm choking with tears, but drop me, forget me, I'm not worthy of you.'

Heart-rending scenes followed, one more unbearable than the other. Voitkovskaya – because this happened while Lara was still living on the Arbat – Voitkovskaya, seeing the tearful Pasha, rushed from the corridor to her side, threw herself on the sofa, and laughed herself sick, repeating: 'Ah, I can't stand it, I can't stand it! No, I must say, that's really . . . Ha, ha, ha! A mighty man! Ha, ha, ha! Eruslan Lazarevich!'[3]

To rid Pasha of this defiling attachment, to tear it out by the root and put an end to his suffering, Lara announced to Pasha that she flatly refused him, because she did not love him, but she sobbed so much as she uttered this renunciation that it was impossible to believe her. Pasha suspected her of all the deadly sins, did not believe a single word of hers, was ready to curse and hate her, and loved her devilishly, and was jealous of her thoughts, of the mug she drank from, and of the pillow she lay on. So as not to lose their minds, they had to act resolutely and quickly. They decided to get married without delay, even before the end of examinations. The plan was to marry on the first Sunday after Easter. The marriage was postponed again at Lara's request.

They were married on the Day of the Holy Spirit, the Monday after the feast of Pentecost, when there was no doubt of their successful graduation. It was all organised by Liudmila Kapitonovna Chepurko, the mother of Tusya Chepurko, Lara's classmate, who graduated with her. Liudmila Kapitonovna was a beautiful woman with a high bosom and a low voice, a good singer, and terribly inventive. On top of the actual superstitions and beliefs known to her, she spontaneously invented a multitude of her own.

It was terribly hot in town when Lara was 'led under the golden crown', as Liudmila Kapitonovna murmured to herself in the bass voice of the Gypsy Panina,[4] as she dressed Lara before setting off. The gilded cupolas of the churches and the fresh sand of the walks were piercingly yellow. The dusty birch greens cut the day before for Pentecost hung downcast on the church fences, rolled up in little tubes and as if scorched. It was hard to breathe, and everything rippled before one's eyes from the sunshine. And it was as if thousands of weddings were being celebrated round about, because all the girls had their hair in curls and were dressed in white like brides, and all the young men, on the occasion of the feast, had their hair pomaded and were wearing tight-fitting two-piece suits. And everyone was excited, and everyone was hot.

Lagodina, the mother of another of Lara's classmates, threw a handful of silver coins under Lara's feet as she stepped onto the rug, to signify future wealth, and Liudmila Kapitonovna, with the same purpose, advised Lara, when she was standing under the crown, not to cross herself with her bare arm sticking out, but to half cover it with gauze or lace. Then she told Lara to hold the candle high and she would have the upper hand in the house. But, sacrificing her future in favour of Pasha's, Lara held the candle as low as possible, though all in vain, for no matter how she tried, it always came out that her candle was higher than his.

From the church they went straight to a party in the artist's studio, which was also the Antipovs' housewarming. The guests shouted: 'Bitter, we can't drink it!' And in reply from the other end they roared in unison: 'Make it sweeter!' And the newlyweds smiled bashfully and kissed. In their honour, Liudmila Kapitonovna sang 'The Vineyard' with its double refrain, 'God grant you love and concord', and the song 'Be undone, thick braid, fall free, golden hair'.

When everyone went home and they were left alone, Pasha felt ill at ease in the suddenly fallen silence. Across the yard from Lara's window there was a lighted street lamp, and no matter how Lara arranged the curtains a strip of light, narrow as the edge of a board, came through the space between the two panels. This bright strip bothered Pasha, as if someone were spying on them. Pasha discovered with horror that he was more concerned with this street lamp than with himself, Lara, and his love for her.

In the course of that night, which lasted an eternity, the recent student Antipov, 'Stepanida' and 'Fair Maiden' as his comrades called him, visited the heights of bliss and the depths of despair. His suspicious surmises alternated with Lara's confessions. He asked and his heart sank after each answer from Lara, as if he were falling into an abyss. His much-wounded imagination could not keep up with the new revelations.

They talked till morning. In Antipov's life there was no change more striking and sudden than that night. In the morning he got up a different man, almost astonished that he still had the same name.

4

Ten days later their friends organised a farewell party in that same room. Pasha and Lara had both graduated, both equally brilliantly, both had offers of jobs in the same town in the Urals, and they were to leave for there the next morning.

Again there was drinking, singing, and noise, only now it was just young people, without their elders.

Behind the partition that separated the living quarters from the large studio, where the guests gathered, stood Lara's big wicker hamper and a medium-sized one, a suitcase, and a crate of dishes. In the corner lay several sacks. They had a lot of things. Part of them would leave the next morning by slow freight. Almost everything had been packed, but not quite. The crate and the hampers stood open, not filled to the top. From time to time Lara remembered something, took the forgotten thing behind the partition and, putting it in a hamper, evened out the unevenness.

Pasha was already at home with the guests when Lara, who had gone to her school's office to get her birth certificate and some papers, came back accompanied by the yard porter with a bast mat and a big coil of stout, thick rope to tie up their luggage tomorrow. Lara dismissed the porter and, making the round of the guests, greeted some with a handshake and kissed others, and then went behind the partition to change. When she came out after changing, everyone applauded, broke into chatter, started taking their seats, and the noise began, just as some days ago at the wedding. The most enterprising took to pouring vodka for their neighbours, many hands, armed with forks, reached to the centre of the table for bread and to plates of food and hors d'oeuvres. They speechified, grunted after wetting their gullets, and cracked jokes. Some quickly became drunk.

'I'm dead tired,' said Lara, sitting beside her husband. 'Did you manage to do everything you wanted?'

'Yes.'

'And even so I'm feeling remarkably well. I'm happy. And you?'

'Me, too. I feel good. But that's a long story.'

As an exception, Komarovsky was admitted to the young people's party. At the end of the evening, he wanted to say that he would be orphaned after his young friends' departure, that Moscow would become a desert for him, a Sahara, but he was so deeply moved that he sobbed and had to repeat the phrase interrupted by his agitation. He asked the Antipovs for permission to correspond with them and visit them in Yuriatin, their new place of residence, if he could not bear the separation.

'That is totally unnecessary,' Lara retorted loudly and carelessly. 'And generally it's all pointless – correspondence, the Sahara, and all that. And don't even think of visiting. With God's help you'll survive without us, we're not such a rarity – right, Pasha? Maybe you'll find somebody to replace your young friends.'

And totally forgetting whom she was talking with and about what, Lara remembered something and, hastily getting up, went behind the partition to the kitchen. There she dismantled the meat grinder and began stuffing the parts into the corners of the crate of dishes, layering them with tufts of straw. In the process she almost pricked her hand on a sharp splinter split from the edge.

While busy with that, she lost sight of the fact that she had guests, ceased to hear them, but they suddenly reminded her of themselves with a particularly loud burst of chatter behind the partition, and then Lara reflected on the diligence with which drunk people always like to imitate drunk people, and with all the more giftless and amateurish deliberateness the drunker they are.

At that moment quite another, special noise attracted her attention to the yard outside the open window. Lara drew the curtain and leaned out.

A hobbled horse was moving about the courtyard in halting leaps. It was an unknown horse and must have wandered into the yard by mistake. It was already completely light, but still long before sunrise. The sleeping and as if totally deserted city was sunk in the greyish purple coolness of early morning. Lara closed her eyes. God knows to what country remoteness and enchantment she was transported by this distinctive and quite incomparable stamping of shod horse hooves.

There was a ring from the stairway. Lara pricked up her ears. Someone left the table and went to open the door. It was Nadya! Lara rushed to meet her. Nadya had come straight from the train, fresh, bewitching, and as if all fragrant with Duplyanka lilies of the valley. The two friends stood there unable to speak a word, and only sobbed, embracing and all but choking each other.

Nadya brought Lara congratulations and wishes for a good journey from the whole household and a precious gift from her parents. She took from her bag a case wrapped in paper, unwrapped it, and, unclasping the lid, handed Lara a necklace of rare beauty.

There were ohs and ahs. One of the drunken guests, now somewhat sobered up, said:

'A pink jacinth. Yes, yes, pink, if you can believe it. A stone not inferior to the diamond.'

But Nadya insisted that they were yellow sapphires.

Seating her next to herself and giving her something to eat, Lara put the necklace near her place and could not tear her eyes from it. The stones, gathered into a little pile on the violet cushion of the case, burned iridescently, looking now like drops of moisture running together, now like a cluster of small grapes.

Some of those at the table had meanwhile managed to come to their senses. They again downed a glass to keep Nadya company. Nadya quickly got drunk.

The house soon turned into a sleeping kingdom. Most of the guests, anticipating the next day's farewell at the station, stayed for the night. Half of them had long been snoring in various corners. Lara herself did not remember how she wound up fully dressed on the sofa beside the already sleeping Ira Lagodina.

Lara was awakened by a loud conversation just at her ear. They were the voices of some strangers who had come into the courtyard looking for the stray horse. Lara opened her eyes and was surprised. 'How tireless this Pasha is, really, standing like a milepost in the middle of the room and endlessly poking about.' Just then the supposed Pasha turned his face to her, and she saw that it was not Pasha at all, but some pockmarked horror with a scar cutting across his face from temple to chin. Then she realised that a thief, a robber, had got into her apartment and wanted to shout, but it turned out that she could not utter a sound. Suddenly she remembered the necklace and, raising herself stealthily on her elbow, looked furtively at the dinner table.

The necklace lay in its place amidst the bread crumbs and gnawed caramels, and the slow-witted malefactor did not notice it in the heap of leftovers, but only rummaged in the hamper of linens and disturbed the order of Lara's packing. The tipsy and half-asleep Lara, dimly aware of the situation, felt especially grieved about her work. In indignation, she again wanted to shout and again was unable to open her mouth and move her tongue. Then she gave Ira Lagodina, who was sleeping beside her, a strong nudge of the knee in the pit of the stomach, and when she cried out from pain in a voice not her own, Lara shouted along with her. The thief dropped the bundle of stolen things and hurtled headlong out of the room. Some of the men jumped up, barely understanding what was happening, and rushed after him, but the robber's trail was already cold.

The commotion that had taken place and the collective discussion of it served as a signal for everyone to get up. The last traces of Lara's tipsiness vanished. Deaf to their entreaties to let them doze and lie about a little longer, Lara made all the sleepers get up, quickly gave them coffee, and sent them home until they were to meet again in the station at the moment of the train's departure.

When they were all gone, the work went at a boil. With a quickness peculiar to her, Lara rushed from bundle to bundle, stuffing in pillows, tightening straps, and only begging Pasha and the porter's wife not to hinder her by helping.

Everything got done properly and on time. The Antipovs were not late. The train set off smoothly, as if imitating the movement of the hats waved to them in farewell. When the waving ceased and from afar came a triple roaring of something (probably 'hurrah'), the train picked up speed.

5

For the third day there was foul weather. It was the second autumn of the war. After the successes of the first year, the failures began. Brusilov's Eighth Army, concentrated in the Carpathians, ready to descend from the passes and invade Hungary, was withdrawing instead, pulled back by a general retreat. We were evacuating Galicia, occupied during the first months of military action.[5]

Dr Zhivago, who was formerly known as Yura, but whom people one after another now more often called by his name and patronymic, stood in the corridor of the maternity ward of the gynaecological clinic, facing the door through which he had just brought his wife, Antonina Alexandrovna. He had taken his leave and was waiting for the midwife, so as to arrange with her how to inform him in case of need and how he could get in touch with her about Tonya's health.

He had no time, he was hurrying to his own hospital, and before that had to make house calls on two patients, and here he was wasting precious moments gazing out of the window at the oblique hatching of the rain, broken and deflected by a gusty autumnal wind, as wheat in a field is blown over and tangled by a storm.

It was not very dark yet. Yuri Andreevich's eyes made out the backyard of the clinic, the glassed-in terraces of the mansions on Devichye Field, the line of the electric tramway that led to the rear entrance of one of the hospital buildings.

The rain poured down most disconsolately, not intensifying and not letting up, despite the fury of the wind, which seemed aggravated by the imperturbability of the water being dashed on the earth. Gusts of wind tore at the shoots of the wild grape vine that twined around one of the terraces. The wind seemed to want to tear up the whole plant, raised it into the air, shook it about, and threw it down disdainfully like a tattered rag.

A motorised wagon with two trailers came past the terrace to the clinic. Wounded men were taken out of it.

In the Moscow hospitals, filled to the utmost, especially after the Lutsk operation,[6] the wounded were now being put on the landings and in the corridors. The general overcrowding of the city's hospitals began to tell on the situation in the women's sections.

Yuri Andreevich turned his back to the window and yawned from fatigue. He had nothing to think about. Suddenly he remembered. In the surgical section of the Krestovozdvizhensky Hospital,[7] where he worked, a woman patient had died a couple of days ago. Yuri Andreevich had insisted that she had echinococcus of the liver. Everyone had disagreed with him. Today there would be an autopsy. The autopsy would establish the truth. But the prosector of their clinic was a hardened drunkard. God knows how he would go about it.

It quickly grew dark. It was now impossible to see anything outside the window. As if by the stroke of a magic wand, electricity lit up in all the windows.

From Tonya's room, through a small vestibule that separated the ward from the corridor, the head doctor of the section came out, a mastodon of a gynaecologist, who always responded to all questions by raising his eyes to the ceiling and shrugging his shoulders. These gestures of his mimic language meant that, however great the successes of knowledge, there are riddles, friend Horatio,[8] before which science folds.

He walked past Yuri Andreevich, bowing to him with a smile, performed several swimming movements with the fat palms of his plump hands, implying that one had to wait and be humble, and went down the corridor to smoke in the waiting room.

Then the assistant of the reticent gynaecologist came out to Yuri Andreevich, in her garrulousness the total opposite of her superior.

'If I were you, I'd go home. I'll phone you tomorrow at the Krestovozdvizhensky. It will hardly begin before then. I'm sure the delivery will be natural, without artificial interference. But, on the other hand, the somewhat narrow pelvis, the occipito-posterior position of the foetus, the absence of pain, and the insignificance of the contractions are cause for some apprehension. However, it's too early to tell. It all depends on how she responds to the contractions once the delivery begins. And that the future will show.'

The next day, in answer to his telephone call, the hospital porter who took the phone told him not to hang up, went to find out, left him hanging for some ten minutes, and brought the following information in a crude and incompetent form: 'They told me to tell you, tell him, they said, you brought your wife too early, you have to take her back.' Furious, Yuri Andreevich demanded that someone better informed take the phone. 'Symptoms can be deceptive,' a nurse told him. 'The doctor shouldn't be alarmed, he'll have to wait a day or two.'

On the third day he learned that the delivery had begun during the night, the water had broken at dawn, and strong contractions had continued uninterruptedly since morning.

He rushed headlong to the clinic, and as he walked down the corridor, he heard, through the accidentally half-open door, Tonya's screams, like the screams of accident victims with severed limbs when they are pulled from under the wheels of a train.

He was not allowed to go to her. Biting his bent finger till it bled, he went to the window, outside which oblique rain poured down, the same as yesterday and the day before.

A hospital nurse came out of the ward. The squealing of a newborn could be heard from there.

'Safe, safe,' Yuri Andreevich repeated joyfully to himself.

'A little son. A boy. Congratulations on the successful delivery,' the nurse said in a singsong voice. 'You can't go in now. We'll show him to you in due time. Then you'll have to loosen your purse strings for the new mother. She suffered all right. It's her first. They always suffer with the first one.'

'Safe, safe,' Yuri Andreevich rejoiced, not understanding what the nurse was saying and that with her words she was including him as a participant in what had happened, though what did he have to do with it? Father, son – he saw no pride in this gratuitously obtained fatherhood, he felt nothing at this sonhood fallen from the sky. It all lay outside his consciousness. The main thing was Tonya, Tonya who had been exposed to mortal danger and had happily escaped it.

He had a patient who lived not far from the clinic. He went to see him and came back in half an hour. Both doors, from the corridor to the vestibule, and further on, from the vestibule to the ward, were again slightly open. Himself not knowing what he was doing, Yuri Andreevich slipped into the vestibule.

Spreading his arms, the mastodon-gynaecologist in his white smock rose up before him as if from under the earth.

'Where are you going?' he stopped him in a breathless whisper, so that the new mother would not hear him. 'Are you out of your mind? Lesions, blood, antiseptics, not to mention the psychological shock. A good one you are! And a doctor at that.'

'But I didn't . . . I only wanted a little peek. From here. Through the chink.'

'Ah, that's a different matter. All right, then. But don't you . . . ! Watch out! If she sees you, you're dead, I won't leave an ounce of life in you!'

In the ward, their backs to the door, stood two women in white smocks, the midwife and the nurse. On the nurse's hand squirmed a squealing and tender human offspring, contracting and stretching like a piece of dark red rubber. The midwife was putting a ligature on the umbilical cord, to separate the baby from the placenta. Tonya lay in the middle of the ward on a surgical bed with an adjustable mattress. She lay rather high. Yuri Andreevich, who in his excitement exaggerated everything, thought she was lying approximately on the level of those desks one can write at standing up.

Raised higher towards the ceiling than happens with ordinary mortals, Tonya was floating in the vapours of what she had suffered, she was as if steaming from exhaustion. She rose up in the middle of the ward, as a bark just moored and unloaded rides high in a bay, a bark that crosses the sea of death to the land of life with new souls, migrating here from no one knows where. She had just carried out the landing of one of these souls and now stood at anchor, resting with all the emptiness of her lightened hull. Along with her rested her broken and toil-worn rigging and planking, and her forgetfulness, her extinguished memory of where she had recently been, what she had crossed, and how she had moored.

And just as no one knew the geography of the country under whose flag she had dropped anchor, so no one knew in what language to address her.

At work they all vied with each other in congratulating him. 'How quickly they found out!' Yuri Andreevich thought in surprise.

He went to the interns' room, which was known as the pot-house and the garbage dump, because, owing to the crowdedness of the overburdened hospital, people now took their coats off there, came from outside in galoshes, forgot all sorts of things brought from elsewhere, littered it with cigarette butts and paper.

By the window of the interns' room stood the bloated prosector, his arms raised, looking over his spectacles and examining against the light some cloudy liquid in a flask.

'Congratulations,' he said, continuing to look in the same direction and not even deigning to glance at Yuri Andreevich.

'Thank you. I'm touched.'

'No need to thank me, I had nothing to do with it. Pichuzhkin did the autopsy. But everybody's amazed. Echinococcus. There, they say, is a diagnostician! It's all they talk about.'

Just then the head doctor of the clinic came in. He greeted the two men and said:

'Devil knows what this is. A public square, not an interns' room, it's outrageous! Ah, yes, Zhivago, imagine – it was echinococcus! We were wrong. Congratulations. And another thing – rather unpleasant. They've reviewed your category again. This time we won't be able to keep you from it. There's a terrible lack of medical personnel at the front. You'll be getting a whiff of powder.'

6

Beyond all expectations, the Antipovs settled very well in Yuriatin. There was a good memory of the Guichards there. For Lara this lightened the difficulties attendant upon getting installed in a new place.

Lara was immersed in work and cares. The house and their little three-year-old Katenka fell to her. No matter how red-haired Marfutka, the Antipovs' maid, tried, her help was not enough. Larissa Fyodorovna entered into all of Pavel Pavlovich's affairs. She herself taught in the girls' high school. She worked without respite and was happy. This was precisely the life she had dreamed of.

She liked it in Yuriatin. It was her native town. It stood on the big river Rynva, navigable in its middle and lower parts, and also on one of the Ural railway lines.

The approach of winter in Yuriatin was betokened by boat owners transporting their boats from the river to town on carts. There they conveyed them to their own courtyards, where the boats wintered over until spring under the open sky. The overturned boats, showing white on the ground at the far end of the yards, signified in Yuriatin the same thing as the autumn migration of cranes or the first snow in other places.

Such a boat, under which Katenka played as under the domed roof of a garden gazebo, lay with its white bottom up in the courtyard of the house the Antipovs rented.

Larissa Fyodorovna liked the ways of the remote place, the local intelligentsia with their long northern o, their felt boots and warm grey flannel jackets, their naïve trustfulness. She was drawn to the earth and to simple people.

Strangely, it was Pavel Pavlovich, the son of a Moscow railway worker, who turned out to be an incorrigible capital dweller. His attitude towards the people of Yuriatin was much more severe than his wife's. He was annoyed by their wildness and ignorance.

Now in retrospect it became clear that he had an extraordinary ability to acquire and retain knowledge drawn from cursory reading. Even before, partly with Lara's help, he had read a great deal. During these years of provincial solitude, he read so much that now even Lara seemed insufficiently informed to him. He was head and shoulders above the pedagogical milieu of his colleagues and complained that he felt stifled among them. In this time of war, their humdrum patriotism, official and slightly jingoist, did not correspond to the more complex forms of the same feeling that Antipov entertained.

Pavel Pavlovich had graduated in classics. He taught Latin and ancient history in the high school. But suddenly the almost extinguished passion for mathematics, physics, and the exact sciences awakened in him, the former progressive school student. By self-education he acquired a command of all these disciplines at a university level. He dreamed of passing examinations in them at the first opportunity in the district capital, of reorientating himself to some mathematical specialisation, and being transferred with his family to Petersburg. Arduous studying at night undermined Pavel Pavlovich's health. He began to suffer from insomnia.

His relations with his wife were good but lacking in simplicity. She overwhelmed him with her kindness and care, and he did not allow himself to criticise her. He was afraid that his most innocent observation might sound to her like some imaginary, hidden reproach, for instance, for being above him socially, or for having belonged to another before him. The fear that she might suspect him of some unjustly offensive absurdity introduced an artificiality into their life. They tried to outdo each other in nobility and that complicated everything.

The Antipovs had guests – several teachers, Pavel Pavlovich's colleagues, the headmistress of Lara's high school, a member of the court of arbitration in which Pavel Pavlovich had once acted as a conciliator, and others. From Pavel Pavlovich's point of view, every man and woman of them was an utter fool. He was amazed at Lara, who was amiable with them all, and did not believe that she could sincerely like anyone there.

When the guests left, Lara spent a long time airing out and sweeping the rooms and washing dishes in the kitchen with Marfutka. Then, having made sure that Katenka was well tucked in and Pavel was asleep, she quickly undressed, put out the light, and lay down next to her husband with the naturalness of a child taken into its mother's bed.

But Antipov was pretending to be asleep – he was not. He was having a fit of the insomnia that had recently become usual with him. He knew he was going to lie sleepless like that for another three or four hours. To walk himself to sleep and get rid of the tobacco smoke left by the guests, he quietly got up and, in his hat and fur coat over nothing but his underwear, went outside.

It was a clear autumn night with frost. Fragile sheets of ice crunched loudly under Antipov's feet. The starry night, like a flame of burning alcohol, cast its wavering pale blue glow over the black earth with its clods of frozen mud.

The house in which the Antipovs lived was on the opposite side of town from the docks. It was the last house on the street. Beyond it the fields began. They were cut across by the railway. Near the line stood a guardhouse. There was a level crossing over the rails.

Antipov sat down on the overturned boat and looked at the stars. Thoughts he had become used to in recent years seized him with alarming force. He imagined that sooner or later he would have to think them through to the end and that it would be better to do it now.

This can't go on any longer, he thought. But it all could have been foreseen earlier; he had noticed it too late. Why had she allowed him as a child to admire her so much? Why had she done whatever she wanted with him? Why had he not been wise enough to renounce her in time, when she herself had insisted on it in the winter before their marriage? Doesn't he understand that she loved not him but her noble task in relation to him, her exploit personified? What is there in common between this inspired and praiseworthy mission and real family life? Worst of all is that he loves her to this day as strongly as ever. She is maddeningly beautiful. But maybe what he feels is also not love, but a grateful bewilderment before her beauty and magnanimity? Pah, just try sorting it out! Here the devil himself would break a leg.

What's to be done in that case? Free Lara and Katenka from this sham? That's even more important than to free himself. Yes, but how? Divorce? Drown himself? 'Pah, how vile!' He became indignant. 'I'll never go and do such a thing! Then why mention these spectacular abominations even to myself?'

He looked at the stars as if asking their advice. They glimmered, densely and sparsely, big and small, blue and iridescent. Suddenly, eclipsing their glimmer, the courtyard with the house, the boat, and Antipov sitting on it were lit up by a sharp, darting light, as if someone were running from the field to the gate waving a burning torch. It was a military train, throwing puffs of yellow, flame-shot smoke into the sky, going through the crossing to the west, as countless numbers had done day and night for the last year.

Pavel Pavlovich smiled, got up from the boat, and went to bed. The desired way out had been found.

7

Larissa Fyodorovna was stunned and at first did not believe her ears when she learned of Pasha's decision. 'Absurd. Another whim,' she thought. 'Pay no attention, and he'll forget all about it himself.'

But it turned out that her husband's preparations had already begun two weeks ago, the papers were in the recruiting office, there was a replacement at school, and from Omsk notification had come of his admission to the military school there. The time of his departure was near.

Lara howled like a peasant woman and, seizing Antipov's hands, fell at his feet.

'Pasha, Pashenka,' she cried, 'why are you leaving me and Katenka? Don't do it! Don't! It's not too late. I'll straighten it all out. And you haven't even been seen properly by a doctor. With your heart. You're ashamed? And aren't you ashamed to sacrifice your family to some sort of madness? As a volunteer! All your life you've made fun of banal Rodka, and suddenly you're envious! You want to rattle a sabre, to play the officer. What's wrong with you, Pasha, I don't recognise you! You're like somebody else! What's got into you? Kindly tell me, tell me honestly, for Christ's sake, without ready-made phrases, is this what Russia needs?'

Suddenly she understood that this was not the point at all. Unable to make sense of the particulars, she grasped the main thing. She perceived that Patulya was mistaken about her attitude towards him. He did not appreciate the maternal feeling that she had mixed all her life with her tenderness towards him, and he did not perceive that such love was greater than ordinary woman's love.

She bit her lip, all shrunken inwardly, as if she had been beaten, and, saying nothing and silently swallowing her tears, set about preparing her husband for the road.

When he left, it seemed to her that the whole town became silent and that there was even a smaller number of crows flying in the sky. 'Mistress, mistress,' Marfutka called out to her unsuccessfully. 'Mama, mama,' Katenka prattled endlessly, tugging at her sleeve. This was the most serious defeat in her life. Her best, her brightest hopes had collapsed.

Through his letters from Siberia, Lara knew all about her husband. Things soon became clearer to him. He missed his wife and daughter very much. In a few months, Pavel Pavlovich graduated early as a second lieutenant and was just as unexpectedly assigned to active duty. He travelled with the utmost urgency far from Yuriatin and in Moscow had no time to see anyone.

His letters from the front began to come, more lively and not so sad as from the school in Omsk. Antipov wanted to distinguish himself, so that in reward for some military exploit or as the result of a slight wound he could ask for leave to see his family. The possibility of promotion presented itself. Following a recently accomplished breakthrough, which was later named for Brusilov, the army went on the offensive.[9] Letters from Antipov ceased. At first that did not worry Lara. She explained Pasha's silence by the unfolding military action and the impossibility of writing on the march.

In the autumn the army's advance came to a halt. The troops dug themselves in. But there was still no news from Antipov. Larissa Fyodorovna began to worry and made enquiries, first in Yuriatin and then by mail to Moscow and to the front, to the old field address of Pasha's unit. No one knew anything, no reply came from anywhere.

Like many lady benefactresses in the district, from the beginning of the war Larissa Fyodorovna had helped as much as she could in the hospital set up in the community clinic of Yuriatin.

Now she began seriously to study the basics of medicine and passed an examination at the clinic to qualify as a nurse.

In that quality she asked for a six-month leave from her work at the school, left Marfutka in charge of the apartment in Yuriatin, and, taking Katenka with her, went to Moscow. There she installed her daughter with Lipochka, whose husband, the German subject Friesendank, along with other civilian prisoners, was interned in Ufa.

Convinced of the uselessness of her search from afar, Larissa Fyodorovna decided to transfer it to the scene of recent events. With that aim, she went to work as a nurse on a hospital train that was going through the town of Lisko to Mezo-Laborszh on the Hungarian border. That was the name of the place from which Pasha had written her his last letter.

8

A train-bathhouse, fitted out on donations from St Tatiana's committee for aid to the wounded,[10] arrived in staff headquarters at the front. In the first-class carriage of the long train composed of short, ugly freight cars, visitors arrived, activists from Moscow with gifts for the soldiers and officers. Among them was Gordon. He had learned that the division infirmary in which, according to his information, his childhood friend Zhivago worked, was located in a nearby village.

Gordon obtained the necessary permission to circulate in the front-line zone, and, pass in hand, went to visit his friend in a wagon that was headed in that direction.

The driver, a Belorussian or Lithuanian, spoke Russian poorly. The fear known as spymania had reduced all speech to a single formal, predictable pattern. The display of good intentions in discourse was not conducive to conversation. Passenger and driver went the greater part of the way in silence.

At headquarters, where they were used to moving whole armies and measuring distances by hundred-mile marches, they assured him that the village was somewhere nearby, around twelve or fifteen miles away. In reality it turned out to be more than sixty.

For the whole way, along the horizon to the left of the direction they were moving in, there was an unfriendly growling and rumbling. Gordon had never in his life been witness to an earthquake. But he reasoned correctly that the sullen and peevish grumbling of enemy artillery, barely distinguishable in the distance, was most comparable to underground tremors and rumblings of a volcanic origin. Towards evening, the lower part of the sky in that direction flushed with a rosy, quivering fire, which did not go out until morning.

The driver took Gordon past ruined villages. Some of them had been abandoned by their inhabitants. In others, people huddled in cellars deep underground. The villages had become heaps of rubble and broken brick, which stretched along the same lines as the houses once had done. These burned-down settlements could be surveyed at a glance from end to end, like barren wastes. On their surface, old women rummaged about, each in her own burnt debris, digging up something from the ashes and hiding it away each time, imagining they were hidden from strangers' eyes, as if the former walls were still around them. They met and followed Gordon with their gaze, as if asking if the world would soon come to its senses and return to a life of peace and order.

During the night the travellers came upon a patrol. They were told to turn off the main road, go back, and skirt this area by a roundabout country road. The driver did not know the new way. They spent some two hours senselessly wandering about. Before dawn the traveller and his driver arrived at a settlement that bore the required name. No one there had heard anything about a field hospital. It soon became clear that there were two villages of the same name in the area, this one and the one they were looking for. In the morning they reached their goal. As they drove along the outskirts, which gave off a smell of medicinal chamomile and iodoform, he thought he would not stay overnight with Zhivago, but, after spending the day in his company, would head back in the evening to the railway station and the comrades he had left. Circumstances kept him there for more than a week.

9

In those days the front began to stir. Sudden changes were going on there. To the south of the place where Gordon ended up, one of our combined units, in a successful attack of its separate constituent parts, broke through the fortified positions of the enemy. Developing its strike, the attacking group kept cutting deeper into their disposition. After it followed auxiliary units, widening the breach. Gradually falling behind, they became separated from the head group. This led to its being captured. In these circumstances, Second Lieutenant Antipov was taken prisoner, forced into it by the surrender of his platoon.

False rumours went around about him. He was considered dead and buried under the earth in a shell crater. This was repeated from the words of his acquaintance Galiullin, a lieutenant serving in the same regiment, who supposedly saw him die through his binoculars from an observation post, when Antipov was leading his men in an attack.

Before Galiullin's eyes was the habitual spectacle of a unit attacking. They were supposed to advance quickly, almost at a run, across the space that separated the two armies, an autumn field overgrown with dry wormwood swaying in the wind and prickly thistles motionlessly sticking up. By the boldness of their courage, the attackers were either to entice the Austrians lodged in the opposite trenches to come and meet their bayonets or to shower them with grenades and destroy them. To the running men the field seemed endless. The ground yielded under their feet like a shifting swamp. First ahead, then mixing with them, ran their lieutenant, brandishing his revolver over his head and shouting 'Hurrah!' with his mouth ripped open from ear to ear, though neither he nor the soldiers running around him could hear it. At regular intervals the running men fell to the ground, got to their feet all at once, and with renewed shouting ran on further. Each time, together with them, but quite differently from them, individual men who had been hit fell full length, like tall trees cut down, and did not get up again.

'They're overshooting. Phone the battery,' the alarmed Galiullin said to the artillery officer standing next to him. 'No, wait. They're right to shift the aim deeper in.'

Just then the attackers moved in close to the enemy. The artillery fire stopped. In the ensuing silence, the hearts of the men standing at the observation post pounded hard and fast, as if they were in Antipov's place and, like him, having led men to the edge of the Austrian trench, in the next moment had to display prodigies of resourcefulness and courage. Just then two sixteen-inch German shells exploded ahead of them, one after the other. Black columns of earth and smoke concealed all that followed. 'Yeh Allah! That's it! The bazaar's over!' Galiullin whispered with pale lips, considering the lieutenant and his soldiers lost. A third shell landed just next to the observation post. Bending low to the ground, they all hurried away from it.

Galiullin had slept in the same dugout with Antipov. When the regiment became reconciled with the thought that he had been killed and would not come back, Galiullin, who had known Antipov well, was put in charge of his belongings, with a view to handing them over in the future to his wife, of whom many photographs were found among Antipov's things.

A former second lieutenant from the volunteers, the mechanic Galiullin, son of the yard porter Gimazetdin from Tiverzin's courtyard and in the distant past an apprentice to a locksmith, beaten by his master Khudoleev, owed his advancement to his former tormentor.

Having been made a second lieutenant, Galiullin, no one knew how and without his own will, wound up in a warm and cushy billet in one of the garrisons far in the rear. There he had command of a detachment of semi-invalids, whom equally decrepit veterans instructed in the mornings in a drill they had long forgotten. Besides that, Galiullin checked whether sentinels had been correctly placed at the supply depots. It was a carefree life – nothing more was required of him. Then suddenly, along with reinforcements consisting of militiamen from earlier drafts and coming from Moscow to be under his command, arrived Pyotr Khudoleev, who was all too well-known to him.

'Ah, an old acquaintance!' Galiullin said, smiling darkly.

'Yes, sir,' replied Khudoleev, standing to attention and saluting.

It could not end so simply. At the very first negligence in drill, the lieutenant yelled at the lower-ranking man, and when it seemed to him that the soldier was not looking him straight in the eye, but somehow vaguely to the side, he punched him in the teeth and put him in the guardhouse for two days on bread and water.

Now Galiullin's every move smacked of revenge for past things. To settle accounts like this, under the discipline of the rod, was too unsporting and ignoble a game. What was to be done? It was impossible for the two of them to remain in the same place any longer. But where and on what pretext could an officer transfer a soldier from his assigned unit, unless he sent him to a disciplinary one? On the other hand, what grounds could Galiullin think up for requesting his own transfer? Justifying himself by the boredom and uselessness of garrison duty, Galiullin asked to be sent to the front. This earned him a good reputation, and when, in the next action, he displayed his other qualities, it became clear that he was an excellent officer, and he was quickly promoted to first lieutenant.

Galiullin had known Antipov since the time at Tiverzin's. In 1905, when Pasha Antipov had lived for half a year with the Tiverzins, Yusupka had gone to see him and play with him on Sundays. He had seen Lara there once or twice then. After that he had heard nothing about them. When Pavel Pavlovich left Yuriatin and landed in their regiment, Galiullin was struck by the change that had come over his old friend. The bashful, laughter-prone, prissy prankster, who looked like a girl, had turned into a nervous, all-knowing, scornful hypochondriac. He was intelligent, very brave, taciturn, and sarcastic. At times, looking at him, Galiullin was ready to swear that he could see in Antipov's heavy gaze, as in the depths of a window, some second person, a thought firmly embedded in him, a longing for his daughter or the face of his wife. Antipov seemed bewitched, as in a fairy tale. And now he was no more, and in Galiullin's hands there remained Antipov's papers and photographs and the mystery of his transformation.

Sooner or later Lara's enquiries had to reach Galiullin. He was preparing to answer her. But it was a hot time. He felt unable to give her a proper answer. He wanted to prepare her for the coming blow. And so he kept postponing a long, detailed letter to her, until he heard that she herself was somewhere at the front, as a nurse. And now he did not know where to address a letter to her.

10

'Well? Will there be horses today?' Gordon would ask Dr Zhivago when he came home in the afternoon to the Galician cottage they were living in.

'Horses, hah! And where will you go, if there's no way forward or back? There's terrible confusion all around. Nobody understands anything. In the south, we've encircled the Germans or broken through them in several places, and they say that in the process several of our scattered units got into a pocket, and in the north, the Germans have crossed the Sventa, which was considered impassable at that point. It's their cavalry, up to a corps in number. They're damaging railways, destroying depots, and, in my opinion, encircling us. Do you get the picture? And you say horses. Well, look lively, Karpenko, set the table and get a move on. What are we having today? Ah, calves' feet. Splendid.'

The medical unit with the hospital and all its dependencies was scattered through the village, which by a miracle had gone unscathed. Its houses, with gleaming western-style, narrow, many-paned windows from wall to wall, were preserved to the last one.

It was Indian summer, the last days of a hot, golden autumn. During the day, the doctors and officers opened the windows, killed the flies that crawled in black swarms over the windowsills and low, white-papered ceilings, and, unbuttoning their tunics and field shirts, dripping with sweat, burned their tongues on hot cabbage soup or tea, and in the evenings squatted in front of the open stove, blowing on the dying coals under the damp firewood that refused to burn, and, their eyes tearful from the smoke, cursed their orderlies, who did not know how to heat a stove in human fashion.

It was a quiet night. Gordon and Zhivago lay facing each other on benches against the two opposite walls. Between them was the dinner table and a long, narrow window stretching from wall to wall. The room was overheated and filled with tobacco smoke. They opened the two end casements and breathed in the autumnal freshness of the night, which covered the glass with sweat.

As usual, they were talking, just as they had all those days and nights. As always, there was a pink glow on the horizon in the direction of the front, and when, into the steady growl of gunfire, which never ceased for a moment, there fell deeper, separately distinct and weighty blows, which seemed to shift the ground in the distance slightly to one side, Zhivago broke off the conversation out of respect for the sound, held the pause, and said: 'That's Bertha, a German sixteen-incher, there's a ton of weight in the little thing,' and then went on with the conversation, forgetting what they had been talking about.

'What's that smell all the time in the village?' asked Gordon. 'I noticed it the first day. Such a sickly sweet, cloying smell. Like mice.'

'Ah, I know what you mean. It's hemp. There are a lot of hemp fields here. Hemp by itself gives off an oppressive and obnoxious smell of carrion. Besides, in a zone of military action, when men are killed in a hemp field, they go unnoticed for a long time and begin to rot. There's a putrid smell all over the place, it's only natural. Another Bertha. Hear it?'

In the course of those days they discussed everything in the world. Gordon knew his friend's thoughts about the war and the spirit of the time. Yuri

Andreevich told him how hard it was to get used to the bloody logic of mutual destruction, to the sight of the wounded, especially to the horrors of some modern wounds, to the mutilated survivors that present-day technology turned into hunks of disfigured flesh.

Each day Gordon landed somewhere as he accompanied Zhivago, and thanks to him he saw something. He was, of course, aware of the immorality of gazing idly at other men's courage and at how some, with an inhuman effort of will, overcame the fear of death, with great sacrifice and at great risk. But an inactive and inconsequential sighing over it seemed to him in no way more moral. He considered that you ought to behave honestly and naturally according to the situation life puts you in.

That one can faint at the sight of the wounded he proved to himself when he went to a mobile Red Cross unit that was working to the west of them at a first-aid field station almost on the front line.

They came to the edge of a big wood half cut down by artillery fire. Smashed and twisted gun carriages lay upside down among the broken and trampled underbrush. A riding horse was tied to a tree. Further in was the wooden house of the forest service with half its roof blown off. The first-aid station was set up in the forestry office and in two big grey tents across the road from it, in the middle of the wood.

'I shouldn't have brought you here,' said Zhivago. 'Our trenches are very close by, a mile or so, and our batteries are over there behind the wood. Do you hear what's going on? Don't play the hero, please – I won't believe you. Your heart's in your boots right now, and that's only natural. The situation may change any moment. Shells will start flying here.'

On the ground by the forest road, spreading their legs in heavy boots, dusty and weary young soldiers lay on their stomachs or backs, their field shirts soaked with sweat on their chests and shoulder blades – the survivors of a greatly diminished detachment. They had been taken out of a battle that had been going on for four days and sent to the rear for a brief respite. The soldiers lay as if made of stone, they had no strength to smile or curse, and not one of them turned his head when from the road deep in the wood came the rumble of several quickly approaching carts. These were springless machine-gun carts coming at a trot, bouncing up and down, breaking the bones and spilling the guts of the wretched wounded men they were bringing to the dressing station, where they would be given first aid, bandaged up, and, in certain especially urgent cases, hastily operated on. Half an hour earlier, during a brief lull in the firing, they had been carried off the field beyond the trenches in appalling numbers. A good half of them were unconscious.

When they drew up to the porch of the office, orderlies came down with stretchers and started unloading the carts. Holding the lower flaps with her hands, a nurse peeked out of one of the tents. It was not her shift. She was free. In the wood behind the tent, two men were yelling loudly at each other. The fresh, tall wood resounded with the echoes of their argument, but the words could not be heard. When the wounded were brought, the arguers came out to the road and went towards the office. A hot-headed little officer was shouting at a doctor from the mobile unit, trying to find out from him where they had moved the artillery park formerly stationed there in the wood. The doctor knew nothing, it was not his concern. He begged the officer to leave him alone and not shout, because wounded men had been brought and he had work to do, but the little officer would not calm down and berated the Red Cross, and the artillery department, and everybody in the world. Zhivago went up to the doctor. They greeted each other and went to the forestry house. The officer, still cursing loudly with a slight Tartar accent, untied the horse from the tree, jumped onto it, and galloped down the road into the wood. And the nurse went on looking, looking . . .

Suddenly her face became distorted with horror.

'What are you doing? You're out of your minds!' she cried to two lightly wounded men, who, with no external help, were walking between the stretchers to the dressing station, and, running out of the tent, she rushed towards them.

An unfortunate man, especially horribly and hideously mutilated, was being carried on a stretcher. The bottom of an exploded shell, which had split his face open, turning his tongue and teeth into a bloody gruel, but without killing him, was lodged between his jawbones in place of his torn-out cheek. In a thin little voice, resembling nothing human, the mangled man kept uttering short, broken moans, which no one could fail to understand as a plea to finish him off quickly and end his inconceivably prolonged suffering.

The nurse imagined that, under the influence of his moaning, the lightly wounded men walking beside him were about to pull this horrible iron splinter out of his cheek with their bare hands.

'No, you can't do that! A surgeon will do it with special instruments. If it gets that far. (God, God, take him, don't make me doubt Your existence!)'

The next moment, as he was being carried up the porch, the mutilated man cried out, shuddered all over, and gave up the ghost.

The mutilated man who had just died was Reserve Private Gimazetdin; the officer shouting in the wood was his son, Lieutenant Galiullin; the nurse was Lara; Gordon and Zhivago were the witnesses. They were all there, all side by side, and some did not recognise each other, while others had never known each other, and some things remained forever unascertained, while others waited till the next occasion, till a new meeting, to be revealed.

I I

In this sector the villages had been preserved in some miraculous way. They made up an inexplicably intact island in the midst of a sea of destruction. Gordon and Zhivago were returning home in the evening. The sun was setting. In one of the villages they rode past, a young Cossack, to the unanimous guffawing of those around him, was making an old grey-bearded Jew in a long overcoat catch a five-kopeck copper coin he tossed in the air. The old man invariably failed to catch it. The coin, falling through his pathetically spread hands, fell in the mud. The old man bent down to pick it up, the Cossack slapped his behind, those standing around held their sides and moaned with laughter. This constituted the whole amusement. So far it was inoffensive, but no one could guarantee that it would not take a more serious turn. His old woman would come running from a cottage across the road, shouting and reaching her arms out to him, and each time would disappear again in fright. Two little girls looked at their grandfather through the window and wept.

The driver, who found it all killingly funny, slowed the horses' pace to give the gentlemen time to amuse themselves. But Zhivago, calling the Cossack over, reprimanded him and told him to stop the mockery.

'Yes, sir,' the man said readily. 'We didn't mean nothing, it was just for laughs.'

For the rest of the way Zhivago and Gordon were silent.

'It's terrible,' Yuri Andreevich began, when their own village came in sight. 'You can hardly imagine what a cup of suffering the unfortunate Jewish populace has drunk during this war. It's being conducted right within the pale of their forced settlement. And for all they've endured, for the sufferings, the taxes, and the ruin, they have the added reward of pogroms, taunts, and the accusation that these people lack patriotism. But where are they to get it, when they enjoy all rights with the enemy, and with us they're only subjected to persecution? The very hatred of them, the basis of it, is contradictory. What vexes people is just what should touch them and win them over. Their poverty and overcrowding, their weakness and inability to fend off blows. Incomprehensible. There's something fateful in it.'

Gordon made no reply.

12

And here again they were lying on two sides of the long, narrow window, it was night, and they were talking.

Zhivago was telling Gordon how he had seen the sovereign at the front. He told it well.

It was his first spring at the front. The headquarters of the unit to which he had been attached was in the Carpathians, in a hollow, the entrance to which, from the Hungarian valley, was blocked by that army unit.

At the bottom of the hollow there was a railway station. Zhivago described to Gordon the external appearance of the place, the mountains overgrown with mighty firs and pines, with white tufts of clouds caught among them, and the stone cliffs of grey slate and graphite, which showed through the forest like worn spots in thick fur. It was a damp, dark April morning, grey as that slate, locked in by the heights on all sides and therefore still and stuffy. Steaming hot. Steam hung over the hollow, and everything fumed, everything drew upwards in streams of smoke, engine smoke from the station, grey steam from the meadows, grey mountains, dark forests, dark clouds.

In those days the sovereign was making the rounds of Galicia. Suddenly it became known that he would visit the unit stationed here, of which he was the honorary colonel.

He might come at any moment. An honour guard was stationed on the platform to meet him. An hour or two of wearisome waiting followed. Then quickly, one after another, two trains came with the suite. Shortly afterwards the tsar's train arrived.

Accompanied by the grand duke Nikolai Nikolaevich, the sovereign inspected the lined-up grenadiers. With every syllable of his quiet greeting he raised up bursts and splashes of thunderously rolling hurrahs, like water dancing in swaying buckets.

The embarrassed and smiling sovereign gave the impression of a man older and more gone to seed than he appeared on rubles and medals. He had a listless, slightly puffy face. He kept casting guilty sidelong glances at Nikolai Nikolaevich, not knowing what was required of him in the given circumstances, and Nikolai Nikolaevich, respectfully bending towards his ear, not even with words but with the movement of an eyebrow or a shoulder, helped him out of his difficulty.

The tsar was pitiable on that grey and warm mountain morning, and it was eerie to think that such timorous reserve and shyness could be the essence of an oppressor, that this weakness could punish and pardon, bind and loose.

'He should have pronounced something on the order of "I, my sword, and my people", like Wilhelm,[11] or something in that spirit. But certainly about the people, that's indispensable. But, you understand, he was natural in a Russian way and tragically above such banality. In Russia this theatricality is unthinkable. Because it is theatricality, isn't it? I can understand that there were still such peoples in Caesar's time, some sort of Gauls, or Suevians, or Illyrians. But from then on it's only been a fiction, existing so that tsars and activists and kings could make speeches about it: "The people, my people."

'Now the front is flooded with correspondents and journalists. They note down "observations", the utterances of popular wisdom, make the rounds of the wounded, construct a new theory of the people's soul. It's a sort of new Dahl,[12] just as contrived, a linguistic graphomania of verbal incontinence. That's one type. But there's another. Clipped speech, "jottings and sketches", scepticism, misanthropy. For instance, in one of them (I read it myself), there are such sentences as: "A grey day, like yesterday. Rain and slush since morning. I look through the window at the road. Prisoners strung out in an endless line. Wounded being transported. A cannon fires. It fires again, today as yesterday, tomorrow as today, and so on every day and every hour . . ." Just look, how perceptive and witty! Though why is he offended at the cannon? What a strange pretension, to demand diversity from a cannon! Instead of the cannon, why isn't he astonished at himself, firing off lists, commas, phrases, day in and day out, why doesn't he stop this barrage of journalistic philanthropy, as hasty as a hopping flea? How is it he doesn't understand that it's he, not the cannon, who should be new and not repeat himself, that the accumulation of a great quantity of senselessness in a notebook will never arrive at any sense, that facts don't exist until a man puts something of his own into them, some share of whimsical human genius, something of the fantastic.'

'Strikingly true,' Gordon interrupted him. 'Now I'll answer you concerning the scene we witnessed today. That Cossack mocking the poor patriarch, along with thousands of cases like it, is, of course, an example of the most elementary baseness, which should occasion, not philosophising, but a punch in the nose, that's clear. But to the question of the Jews as a whole, philosophy is applicable, and then it turns its unexpected side to us. But here I'm not telling you anything new. All these thoughts, in me as in you, come from your uncle.

' "What is a people?" you ask. Must we make a fuss over it, and doesn't he do more for it who, without thinking of it, by the very beauty and triumph of his deeds, raises it to universality and, having glorified it, makes it eternal? Well, of course, of course. And what kind of peoples can we talk about in Christian times? They're not simple peoples, but converted, transformed peoples, and the whole point is precisely in the transformation, not in faithfulness to old principles. Let's remember the Gospel. What did it say on this subject? First, it wasn't an assertion: this is so and that is so. It was a naïve and timid suggestion. The suggestion was: Do you want to exist in a new way, as never before, do you want the blessedness of the spirit? And everyone accepted the suggestion, caught up for millennia.

'When it said that in the Kingdom of God there are no Greeks and Jews, did it merely mean to say that everyone is equal before God?[13] No, there was no need for that; the Greek philosophers, the Roman moralists, the prophets of the Old Testament knew that before. But it said: in that new way of existence and new form of communion, conceived in the heart and known as the Kingdom of God, there are no peoples, there are persons.

'You just said that a fact is senseless unless one puts sense into it. Christianity, the mystery of the person, is precisely what needs to be put into the fact for it to acquire meaning for man.

'And we talked about average figures, who have nothing to say to life and the world as a whole, about second-rate forces interested in narrowness, in having the talk always be about some people or other, preferably a small one, that should suffer, so that it's possible to sit and talk endlessly and thrive on their own pity. Jewry is fully and completely the victim of this element. Its own notion of itself as a people laid upon it the deadening necessity of being and remaining a people and only that over the centuries, during which, by a power that had once come from its own midst, the whole world was delivered from this humiliating task. How astounding it is! How could it have happened? This festivity, this deliverance from the bedevilment of mediocrity, this soaring above the dull-witted workaday world – all this was born on their soil, spoke their language, and belonged to their tribe. And they saw and heard it and let it slip. How could they have let a spirit of such all-absorbing beauty and power leave them, how could they think that next to its triumph and reign they would remain as the empty shell this miracle had once cast off? To whose profit is this voluntary martyrdom, who needs these centuries of the mockery and bloodletting of so many utterly blameless old men, women, and children, so fine and so capable of good and of the heart's communion! Why are the people-loving writers of all peoples so lazy and giftless? Why do the rulers of this people's minds never go beyond the two easily accessible forms of world sorrow and ironising wisdom? Why, faced with the risk of exploding from the irrevocability of their duty, as a steam boiler explodes from pressure, did they not disband this troop that fights and gets beaten nobody knows what for? Why didn't they say: "Come to your senses. Enough. There's no need for more. Don't call yourselves by the old name. Don't cling together, disperse. Be with everyone. You are the first and best Christians in the world. You are precisely that which you have been set against by the worst and weakest among you." '

13

The next day, coming to dinner, Zhivago said:

'So you couldn't wait to leave, and now you've called it down on us. I can't say, "You're in luck," because what kind of luck is it that we're pressed back or beaten again? The way east is free, and we're being squeezed from the west. All army medical units are ordered to pack up. Tomorrow or the day after, we'll be on our way. Where – nobody knows. And of course Mikhail Grigorievich's laundry hasn't been washed, has it, Karpenko. The eternal story. It's that woman, that woman . . . but ask him what woman, he doesn't know himself, the blockhead.'

He did not listen to what his medical orderly spun out to justify himself, and paid no attention to Gordon, who was upset that he had been wearing Zhivago's linen and was leaving in his shirt. Zhivago went on.

'Ah, this camp life, these Gypsy wanderings. When we moved in here, none of it was to my liking – the stove was in the wrong place, the ceiling was low, it was dirty and stuffy. And now for the life of me I can't remember where we were stationed before this. And it seems I could spend all my life here, looking at the stove in the corner, with sun on the tiles and the shadow of a roadside tree moving over it.'

They began unhurriedly to pack.

During the night they were awakened by noise and shouts, gunshots and running feet. There was a sinister glow over the village. Shadows flitted past the windows. The owners of the house woke up and began stirring behind the wall.

'Run out, Karpenko, ask what's the cause of this bedlam,' said Yuri Andreevich.

Soon everything became known. Zhivago himself dressed hastily and went to the hospital to verify the rumours, which proved correct. The Germans had broken the resistance in this sector. The line of defence had moved closer to the village and kept getting closer. The village was under fire. The hospital and offices were quickly removed, without waiting for the order to evacuate. Everything was supposed to be finished before dawn.

'You'll go with the first echelon. The carriage is leaving now, but I told them to wait for you. Well, goodbye. I'll come with you and see that you get seated.'

They were running to the other end of the village, where the detachment was formed up. Running past the houses, they bent down and hid behind their projecting parts. Bullets hummed and whined in the street. From intersections with roads leading to the fields, they could see shrapnel exploding over them in umbrellas of flame.

'And what about you?' Gordon asked as they ran.

'I'll come later. I must go home and get my things. I'll be in the second party.'

They said goodbye at the village gate. The carriage and the several carts that made up the train set off, driving into each other and gradually forming a line. Yuri Andreevich waved to his departing friend. The flames of a burning barn lit them up.

Again trying to stay close to the cottages, under cover of their corners, Yuri Andreevich quickly headed back to his place. Two houses before his own porch, he was knocked off his feet by the blast of an explosion and wounded by a shrapnel bullet. Yuri Andreevich fell in the middle of the road, covered with blood, and lost consciousness.

14

The hospital in the rear was lost in one of the little towns in the western territory, on a railway line, near general headquarters. Warm days set in at the end of February. In the ward for convalescent officers, at the request of Yuri Andreevich, who was a patient there, the window next to his bed had been opened.

Dinnertime was approaching. The patients filled the remaining time however they could. They had been told that a new nurse had come to the hospital and would make her rounds for the first time that day. Lying across from Yuri Andreevich, Galiullin was looking through the just-arrived editions of *Speech* and *The Russian Word* and exclaiming indignantly at the blanks in the print left by the censors. Yuri Andreevich was reading letters from Tonya, a number of which had accumulated and were delivered all at once by the field post. The wind stirred the pages of the letters and newspapers. Light footsteps were heard. Yuri Andreevich raised his eyes from a letter. Lara came into the ward.

Yuri Andreevich and the lieutenant each recognised her on his own, without knowing about the other. She did not know either of them. She said:

'Good afternoon. Why is the window open? Aren't you cold?' – and she went up to Galiullin. 'What's your complaint?' she asked and took his wrist to count the pulse, but at the same moment she let go of it and sat down on a chair by his cot, perplexed.

'How unexpected, Larissa Fyodorovna,' said Galiullin. 'I served in the same regiment as your husband and knew Pavel Pavlovich. I have his belongings ready for you.'

'It can't be, it can't be,' she repeated. 'What an amazing chance. So you knew him? Tell me quickly, how did it all happen? So he died buried under the earth? Don't conceal anything, don't be afraid. I know everything.'

Galiullin did not have the heart to confirm her information, which was based on rumours. He decided to lie in order to calm her.

'Antipov was taken prisoner,' he said. 'He got too far ahead with his unit during an attack and found himself alone. They surrounded him. He was forced to surrender.'

But Lara did not believe Galiullin. The stunning suddenness of the conversation agitated her. She could not hold back the rising tears and did not want to cry in front of strangers. She got up quickly and left the ward, to regain her composure in the corridor.

After a moment she came back, outwardly calm. She deliberately did not look at Galiullin in the corner, so as not to start crying again. Going straight to Yuri Andreevich's bed, she said absent-mindedly and by rote:

'Good afternoon. What's your complaint?'

Yuri Andreevich had observed her agitation and tears, wanted to ask her what was the matter, wanted to tell her how he had seen her twice in his life, as a schoolboy and as a university student, but he thought it would come out as too familiar and she would misunderstand him. Then he suddenly remembered the dead Anna Ivanovna in her coffin and Tonya's cries that time in Sivtsev Vrazhek, restrained himself, and, instead of all that, said:

'Thank you. I'm a doctor myself, and I treat myself on my own. I have no need of anything.'

'Why is he offended with me?' Lara thought and looked in surprise at this snub-nosed, in no way remarkable stranger.

For several days there was changing, unstable weather, with a warm, endlessly muttering wind in the nights, which smelled of wet earth.

And all those days strange information came from headquarters, alarming rumours arrived from home, from inside the country. Telegraph connections with Petersburg kept being interrupted. Everywhere, at every corner, political conversations went on.

Each time she was on duty, the nurse Antipova made two rounds, in the morning and in the evening, and exchanged inconsequential remarks with patients in other wards, with Galiullin and Yuri Andreevich. 'A strange, curious man,' she thought. 'Young and unfriendly. Snub-nosed, and you couldn't call him very handsome. But intelligent in the best sense of the word, with an alive, winning mind. But that's not the point. The point is that I must quickly finish my obligations here and get transferred to Moscow, closer to Katenka. And in Moscow I must apply to be discharged as a nurse and go back home to Yuriatin, to my work at the school. It's all clear about poor Patulechka, there's no hope, and so there's no more need to stay on as a heroine of the battlefield, the whole thing was cooked up for the sake of finding him.'

How is it there with Katenka now? Poor little orphan (here she began to cry). Some very sharp changes have been noticeable recently. Not long ago there was a sacred duty to the motherland, military valour, lofty social feelings. But the war is lost, that's the main calamity, and all the rest comes from that, everything is dethroned, nothing is sacred.

Suddenly everything has changed, the tone, the air; you don't know how to think or whom to listen to. As if you've been led all your life like a little child, and suddenly you're let out – go, learn to walk by yourself. And there's no one around, no family, no authority. Then you'd like to trust the main thing, the force of life, or beauty, or truth, so that it's they and not the overturned human principles that guide you, fully and without regret, more fully than it used to be in that peaceful, habitual life that has gone down and been abolished. But in her case – Lara would catch herself in time – this purpose, this unconditional thing will be Katenka. Now, without Patulechka, Lara is only a mother and will give all her forces to Katenka, the poor little orphan.

Yuri Andreevich learned from a letter that Gordon and Dudorov had released his book without his permission, that it had been praised and a great literary future was prophesied for him, and that it was very interesting and alarming in Moscow now, the latent vexation of the lower classes was growing, we were on the eve of something important, serious political events were approaching.

It was late at night. Yuri Andreevich was overcome by a terrible sleepiness. He dozed off intermittently and fancied that, after the day's excitement, he could not fall asleep, that he was not asleep. Outside the window, the sleepy, sleepily breathing wind kept yawning and tossing. The wind wept and prattled: 'Tonya, Shurochka, how I miss you, how I want to be home, at work!' And to the muttering of the wind, Yuri Andreevich slept, woke up, and fell asleep in a quick succession of happiness and suffering, impetuous and alarming, like this changing weather, like this unstable night.

Lara thought: 'He showed so much care, preserving this memory, these poor things of Patulechka's, and I'm such a pig, I didn't even ask who he is or where he's from.'

During the next morning's round, to make up for her omission and smooth over the traces of her ingratitude, she asked Galiullin about it all and kept saying 'oh' and 'ah'.

'Lord, holy is Thy will! Twenty-eight Brestskaya Street, the Tiverzins, the revolutionary winter of 1905! Yusupka? No, I didn't know Yusupka, or I don't remember, forgive me. But that year, that year and that courtyard! It's true, there really was such a courtyard and such a year!' Oh, how vividly she suddenly felt it all again! And the shooting then, and (God, how did it go?) 'Christ's opinion!' Oh, how strongly, how keenly you feel as a child, for the first time! 'Forgive me, forgive me, what is your name, Lieutenant? Yes, yes, you already told me once. Thank you, oh, how I thank you, Osip Gimazetdinovich, what memories, what thoughts you've awakened in me!'

All day she went about with 'that courtyard' in her soul, and kept sighing and reflecting almost aloud.

Just think, twenty-eight Brestskaya! And now there's shooting again, but so much more terrible! This is no 'the boys are shooting' for you. The boys have grown up, and they're all here, as soldiers, all simple people from those courtyards and from villages like this one. Amazing! Amazing!

Rapping with their canes and crutches, invalids and non-bedridden patients from other wards came, ran, and hobbled into the room, and started shouting at the same time:

'An event of extraordinary importance. Disorder in the streets of Petersburg. The troops of the Petersburg garrison have gone over to the side of the insurgents. Revolution.'

Part Five

1

The little town was called Meliuzeevo. It was in the black earth region.[1] Over its roofs, like a swarm of locusts, hung the black dust raised by the troops and wagon trains that kept pouring through it. They moved from morning to evening in both directions, from the war and to the war, and it was impossible to say exactly whether it was still going on or was already over.

Each day, endlessly, like mushrooms, new functions sprang up. And they were elected to them all. Himself, Lieutenant Galiullin, and the nurse Antipova, and a few more persons from their group, all of them inhabitants of big cities, well-informed and worldly-wise people.

They filled posts in the town government, served as commissars in minor jobs in the army and in medical units, and looked upon these succeeding occupations as an outdoor amusement, like a game of tag. But more and more often they wanted to leave this tag and go home to their permanent occupations.

Work often and actively threw Zhivago and Antipova together.

2

In the rain, the black dust in the town turned to a dark brown slush of a coffee colour, which covered its mostly unpaved streets.

It was not a big town. From any place in it, at each turn, the gloomy steppe, the dark sky, the vast expanses of the war, the vast expanses of the revolution opened out.

Yuri Andreevich wrote to his wife:

'The disorganisation and anarchy in the army continue. Measures are being taken to improve the discipline and martial spirit of the soldiers. I made a tour of the units stationed nearby.

'Finally, instead of a postscript, though I might have written you about this much earlier – I work here alongside a certain Antipova, a nurse from Moscow, born in the Urals.

'Do you remember, at the Christmas party on the dreadful night of your mother's death, a girl shot at a prosecutor? It seems she was tried later. As I recall, I told you then that Misha and I had seen this girl when she was still in high school, in some trashy hotel rooms we had gone to with your father, for what purpose I don't remember, at night, in the freezing cold, during an armed uprising on Presnya, as it now seems to me. That girl is Antipova.

'I have tried several times to go home. But it is not so simple. What mainly keeps us here is not the work, which we could turn over to others without any harm. The difficulties are presented by the trip itself. The trains either don't run at all or come so full that it is impossible to get on them.

'However, to be sure, it cannot go on like this endlessly, and therefore several people who have recovered or have left the service or been discharged, including myself, Galiullin, and Antipova, have decided at all costs to leave starting next week, and, to make taking the train easier, to leave separately on different days.

'I may arrive any day now like a bolt from the blue. However, I will try to send you a telegram.'

But even before his departure, Yuri Andreevich had time to receive a reply from Antonina Alexandrovna.

In her letter, in which the construction of the sentences was broken by sobs, and tearstains and inkblots served as periods, Antonina Alexandrovna insisted that her husband should not return to Moscow, but go straight on to the Urals after that wonderful nurse, who journeys through life accompanied by such portents and coincidences, with which her, Tonya's, modest path in life could not be compared.

'Don't worry about Sashenka and his future,' she wrote. 'You will not have to be ashamed for him. I promise to bring him up by those same principles that you saw an example of as a child in our home.'

'You're out of your mind, Tonya,' Yuri Andreevich rushed to reply. 'What suspicions! Don't you know, or don't you know well enough, that you, the thought of you, and faithfulness to you and our home saved me from death and all sorts of destruction during these two horrible and devastating years of war? Anyhow, there's no need for words. Soon we'll see each other, our former life will begin again, everything will become clear.

'But that you could reply to me like that frightens me in another way. If I gave you cause for such a reply, maybe I am indeed behaving ambiguously, and am therefore also to blame before this woman for misleading her, and will have to apologise to her. I will do so as soon as she comes back from making the round of several nearby villages. The zemstvo, which previously existed only in provinces and districts, is now being introduced on a lower level, in village neighbourhoods. Antipova went to help her acquaintance, a woman who works as an instructor in these legislative innovations.

'It is remarkable that, living in the same house with Antipova, I am unaware to this day of where her room is, and I've never been interested in finding out.'

3

Two main roads went east and west from Meliuzeevo. One, a forest dirt road, led to Zybushino, a grain trading post, administratively subordinate to Meliuzeevo, but far ahead of it in all respects. The other, paved with gravel, was laid across swampy meadows that dried up in the summer and went to Biriuchi, a railway junction not far from Meliuzeevo.

That June in Zybushino the independent republic of Zybushino, which lasted for two weeks, was proclaimed by the local miller Blazheiko.

The republic was supported by deserters from the 212th infantry regiment, who, weapons in hand, abandoned their positions and came through Biriuchi to Zybushino at the moment of the coup.

The republic did not recognise the authority of the Provisional Government[2] and separated itself from the rest of Russia. The sectarian Blazheiko, who as a young man had corresponded with Tolstoy, proclaimed a new thousand-year kingdom in Zybushino, communalised labour and property, and renamed the local administration an apostolate.

Zybushino had always been a source of legends and exaggerations. It stood in the deep forest, was mentioned in documents from the Time of Troubles,[3] and in later times its environs swarmed with robbers. The prosperity of its merchants and the fantastic fertility of its soil were on everyone's lips. Some of the beliefs, customs, and peculiarities of speech that distinguished this western sector of the front line came precisely from Zybushino.

Now the same sort of tall tales were told about Blazheiko's chief assistant. It was maintained that he was deaf and dumb from birth, acquired the gift of speech under inspiration, and lost it again when the illumination expired.

In July the Zybushino republic fell. A unit loyal to the Provisional Government entered the place. The deserters were driven out of Zybushino and withdrew to Biriuchi.

There, beyond the tracks, for a few miles around, stood a cleared forest, with stumps sticking up overgrown with wild strawberry, stacks of old, undelivered firewood, half of which had been stolen, and the dilapidated mud huts of the seasonal woodcutters who had once worked there. It was here that the deserters lodged themselves.

4

The hospital in which the doctor had been a patient, and had then worked, and which he was now preparing to leave, was housed in the mansion of the countess Zhabrinskaya, which the owner had donated for the care of the wounded at the beginning of the war.

The two-storey mansion occupied one of the best locations in Meliuzeevo. It stood at the intersection of the main street with the central square of the town, the so-called 'platz', on which soldiers formerly performed their drills and meetings now took place in the evenings.

Its position at the intersection gave the mansion good views on several sides. Besides the main street and the square, one could see the next-door neighbours' yard – a poor provincial property, in no way different from a villager's. One could also see the countess's old garden behind the back wall of the house.

The mansion had never had any independent value for Countess Zhabrinskaya. Razdolnoe, a large estate in the district, belonged to her, and the house in town served only as a pied-à-terre for business visits, and also as a gathering place for guests who came to the estate from all sides in the summer.

Now there was a hospital in the house, and the owner had been arrested in Petersburg, her place of permanent residence.

Of the former staff, two curious women remained in the mansion, Mademoiselle Fleury, the old governess of the countess's daughters (now married), and the countess's former first cook, Ustinya.

The grey-haired and ruddy-cheeked old woman, Mademoiselle Fleury, shuffling her slippers, in a loose, shabby jacket, slovenly and dishevelled, strolled about the whole hospital, where she was now on familiar terms with everyone, as once with the Zhabrinsky family, and told something or other in broken language, swallowing the endings of the Russian words in French fashion. She struck a pose, swung her arms, and at the end of her babble burst into hoarse laughter, which turned into a prolonged, irrepressible coughing.

Mademoiselle knew all about the nurse Antipova. It seemed to her that the doctor and the nurse simply must like each other. Yielding to the passion for matchmaking deeply rooted in the Latin nature, Mademoiselle was glad when she found them together, shook her finger at them meaningfully, and winked mischievously. Antipova was perplexed, the doctor was angry, but Mademoiselle, like all eccentrics, greatly valued her delusions and would not part with them for anything.

Ustinya presented a still more curious nature. She was a woman of a figure tapering awkwardly upward, which gave her the look of a brooding hen. Ustinya was dry and sober to the point of venom, but with that rationality she combined an unbridled fantasy with regard to superstitions.

Ustinya knew a great many folk charms, and never stepped out without putting a spell against fire on the stove and whispering over the keyhole to keep the unclean spirit from slipping in while she was gone. She was a native of Zybushino. They said she was the daughter of the local sorcerer.

Ustinya could be silent for years, but once the first fit came and she burst out, there was no stopping her. Her passion was standing up for justice.

After the fall of the Zybushino republic, the executive committee of Meliuzeevo launched a campaign against the anarchic tendencies coming from there. Every evening on the platz peaceful and poorly attended meetings sprang up of themselves, to which the unoccupied Meliuzeevans would trickle in, as in past times they used to sit together in summer under the open sky by the gates of the fire station. The Meliuzeevo cultural committee encouraged these meetings and sent their own or visiting activists to them in the quality of guides for the discussion. They considered the talking deaf-mute the most crying absurdity of all the tales told about Zybushino, and referred to him especially often in their exposures. But the small artisans of Meliuzeevo, the soldiers' wives, and the former servants of the nobility were of a different opinion. The talking deaf-mute did not seem to them the height of nonsense. They defended him.

Among the disjointed cries coming from the crowd in his defence, Ustinya's voice was often heard. At first she did not dare to come forward; womanly modesty held her back. But, gradually plucking up courage, she began ever more boldly to attack the orators, whose opinions were not favoured in Meliuzeevo. Thus inconspicuously she became a real speaker from the rostrum.

Through the open windows of the mansion, the monotonous hum of voices on the square could be heard, and on especially quiet evenings even fragments of some of the speeches. Often, when Ustinya spoke, Mademoiselle would run into the room, insist that those present listen, and, distorting the words, imitate her good-naturedly:

'Raspou! Raspou! Sar's diamon! Zybush! Deaf-mute! Trease! Trease!'[4]

Mademoiselle was secretly proud of this sharp-tongued virago. The two women had a tender attachment to each other and grumbled at each other endlessly.

5

Yuri Andreevich was gradually preparing for departure, went to homes and offices where he had to say goodbye to someone, and obtained the necessary papers.

Just then a new commissar of that sector of the front stopped in town on his way to the army. The storey went that he was still nothing but a boy.

Those were days of preparation for a major new offensive. There was an effort to achieve a change of morale in the mass of soldiers. The troops were tightened up. Military-revolutionary courts were established, and the recently abolished death penalty was reinstated.[5]

Before departure the doctor had to register with the commandant, whose duties in Meliuzeevo were fulfilled by the military superior – 'the district', as he was known for short.

Ordinarily there was jostling in his quarters. There was not room enough for the babel in the front hall and the yard, and it filled half the street in front of the office windows. It was impossible to push through to the desks. In the noise of hundreds of people, no one understood anything.

On that day there was no reception. In the empty and quiet offices, the clerks, displeased by the ever more complicated procedures, wrote silently, exchanging ironic glances. From the chief's office came merry voices, as if, having unbuttoned their tunics, they were taking some cool refreshment.

Galiullin came out to the common room, saw Zhivago, and, with a movement of the whole torso, as if preparing to break into a run, invited the doctor to share in the animation that reigned inside.

The doctor had to go to the office anyway for the superior's signature. He found everything there in the most artistic disorder.

The village sensation and hero of the day, the new commissar, instead of proceeding to his appointed goal, turned up there, in the office, which had no relation to the vital sections of headquarters or operative questions, turned up before the administrators of the military paper kingdom, stood before them, and held forth.

'And here is another of our stars,' said the district, introducing the doctor to the commissar, who did not even glance at him, totally absorbed in himself, while the district, changing his pose only in order to sign the paper the doctor held out to him, assumed it again and, with a courteous movement of the hand, showed Zhivago to the low, soft pouffe that stood in the middle of the room.

Of all those present, only the doctor settled himself in the study like a human being. The others sat one more oddly and casually than the other. The district, his head propped on his hand, reclined Pechorin-like[6] at the desk; facing him, his assistant heaped himself up on a bolster of the couch, tucking his legs under as if riding sidesaddle. Galiullin sat astride a reversed chair, embracing the back and laying his head on it, while the young commissar first swung himself up by the arms into the embrasure of the windowsill, then jumped down from it, and, like a spinning top, never for a moment falling silent and moving all the time, paced the office with small, rapid steps. He talked non-stop. The subject was the Biriuchi deserters.

The rumours about the commissar proved true. He was thin and slender, a still quite unfledged youth, who burned like a little candle with the loftiest ideals. He was said to be from a good family, maybe even the son of a senator, and in February had been one of the first to lead his company to the State Duma.[7] His last name was Gintze or Gintz; they pronounced it unclearly when he and the doctor were introduced. The commissar had a correct Petersburg enunciation, as distinct as could be, with a slight hint of the Baltic.

He wore a very tight field jacket. He was probably embarrassed at being so young, and, in order to seem older, he made a wry, peevish face and put on an affected stoop. For that he thrust his hands deep into the pockets of his riding breeches and hunched his shoulders in their new, stiff epaulettes, which in fact gave his figure a simplified cavalryman's look, so that it could have been drawn from shoulders to feet in two lines converging downwards.

'There's a Cossack regiment stationed on the railway line several stops from here. Red, devoted. Call them in, the rebels will be surrounded, and that will be the end of it. The commander of the corps insists they should be speedily disarmed,' the district informed the commissar.

'Cossacks? Never!' the commissar flared up. 'That's some sort of 1905, some pre-revolutionary reminiscence! Here we're at opposite poles from you, here your generals have outsmarted themselves!'

'Nothing's been done yet. It's all just a plan, a suggestion.'

'We have an agreement with the military command not to interfere in operational instructions. I don't cancel the Cossacks. Let it be. But I for my part will undertake the steps prompted by good sense. Do they have a bivouac there?'

'Hard to say. A camp, in any case. Fortified.'

'Excellent. I want to go to them. Show me this menace, these forest bandits. They may be rebels, even deserters, but they're the people, gentlemen, that's what you forget. And the people are children, you must know that, you must know their psychology. Here a special approach is needed. You must know how to touch their best, most sensitive strings, so that they begin to sound. I'll go to them in their clearing and have a heart-to-heart talk with them. You'll see in what exemplary order they return to their abandoned positions. Want to bet? You don't believe me?'

'It's doubtful. But God grant it.'

'I'll tell them: "Brothers, look at me. See how I, an only son, the hope of the family, with no regrets, sacrificed my name, my position, my parents' love, in order to gain freedom for you, the like of which no other people in the world enjoys. I did it, and so did many young men, to say nothing of the old guard of our glorious predecessors, of the hard-labour populists and the People's Will Schlüsselburgers.[8] Were we doing it for ourselves? Did we need that? You're no longer rank-and-file soldiers as before, but warriors of the world's first revolutionary army. Ask yourselves honestly, are you worthy of that lofty title? At a time when your motherland, bleeding profusely, makes a last effort to shake off the enemy that has twined around her like a hydra, you let yourselves be stupefied by a gang of obscure adventurers and turned into irresponsible riff-raff, a mob of unbridled scoundrels, glutted with freedom, for whom whatever they're given is always too little, just like that pig – sit him at a table and he'll put his feet on it" – oh, I'll get to them, I'll shame them!'

'No, no, it's risky,' the district tried to object, furtively exchanging meaningful glances with his assistant.

Galiullin tried to talk the commissar out of his insane plan. He knew the daredevils of the 212th from the division their regiment belonged to, in which he had once served himself. But the commissar would not listen to him.

Yuri Andreevich kept trying all the while to get up and leave. The commissar's naïveté embarrassed him. But the sly knowingness of the district and his assistant, two jeering and underhanded finaglers, was not much better. The foolishness and the craftiness were worthy of each other. And all of it – superfluous, non-existent, lacklustre, which life itself so longs to avoid – spewed out in a torrent of words.

Oh, how one wants sometimes to go from such giftlessly high-flown, cheerless human wordiness into the seeming silence of nature, into the arduous soundlessness of long, persistent labour, into the wordlessness of deep sleep, of true music, and of a quiet, heartfelt touch grown mute from fullness of soul!

The doctor remembered that he still faced a talk with Antipova, unpleasant in any case. He was glad of the necessity to see her, even at that price. But it was unlikely that she had come back yet. Taking advantage of the first appropriate moment, the doctor got up and inconspicuously left the office.

6

As it happened, she was already at home. The doctor was informed of her arrival by Mademoiselle, who added that Larissa Fyodorovna had come back tired, quickly eaten supper, and gone to her room, asking not to be disturbed.

'But knock at her door,' Mademoiselle advised. 'She's probably not asleep yet.'

'And how do I find her?' asked the doctor, causing unutterable astonishment in Mademoiselle with the question.

It turned out that Antipova was lodged at the end of the upstairs corridor, next to the rooms where all of Zhabrinskaya's belongings were locked away, and where the doctor had never been.

Meanwhile it was quickly getting dark. The streets contracted. Houses and fences huddled together in the evening darkness. From the depths of the courtyards, trees came up to the windows, to the light of the burning lamps. It was a hot and sultry night. Every movement made one break into a sweat. Strips of kerosene light, falling into the yard, ran down the tree trunks in streams of dirty perspiration.

At the last step, the doctor stopped. He thought that even to knock at the door of a person tired out from travelling was awkward and importunate. It would be better to put off the talk until the next day. In distraction, which always accompanies a change of mind, he walked to the other end of the corridor. There was a window there that gave onto the neighbouring courtyard. The doctor leaned out.

The night was filled with soft, mysterious sounds. Close by in the corridor, water was dripping from a washstand, measuredly, with pauses. There was whispering somewhere behind a window. Somewhere, where the kitchen garden began, beds of cucumbers were being watered, water was being poured from one bucket into another, with a clink of the chain drawing it from the well.

It smelled of all the flowers in the world at once, as if the earth had lain unconscious during the day and was now coming to consciousness through all these scents. And from the countess's centuries-old garden, so littered with windfallen twigs and branches that it had become impassable, there drifted, as tall as the trees, enormous as the wall of a big house, the dusty, thickety fragrance of an old linden coming into bloom.

Shouts came from the street beyond the fence to the right. A soldier on leave was acting up there, doors slammed, snippets of some song beat their wings.

Beyond the crow's nests of the countess's garden appeared a blackish purple moon of monstrous dimensions. At first it looked like the brick steam mill in Zybushino; then it turned yellow like the Biriuchi railway pump house.

And below, in the courtyard under the window, the scent of showy four o'clocks mingled with the sweet smell of fresh hay, like tea with flowers. Earlier a cow, bought in a far-off village, had been brought here. She had been led all day, was tired, missed the herd she had left, and refused to take food from the hands of her new mistress, whom she had not yet grown used to.

'Now, now, don't be naughty, Bossie, I'll teach you to butt, you devil,' the mistress admonished her in a whisper, but the cow either tossed her head angrily or stretched her neck and mooed rendingly and pitifully, while beyond the black sheds of Meliuzeevo the stars twinkled, and from them to the cow stretched threads of invisible compassion, as if they were the cattle yards of other worlds, where she was pitied.

Everything around fermented, grew, and rose on the magic yeast of being. The rapture of life, like a gentle wind, went in a broad wave, not noticing where, over the earth and the town, through walls and fences, through wood and flesh, seizing everything with trembling on its way. To stifle the effect of this current, the doctor went to the platz to listen to the talk at the meeting.

<h1 style="text-align:center">7</h1>

The moon was already high in the sky. Everything was flooded by its light, thick as spilled white lead.

By the porches of the official stone buildings with columns that surrounded the square, their wide shadows lay on the ground like black carpets.

The meeting was taking place on the opposite side of the square. If one wished, one could listen and make out everything that was being said across the platz. But it was the magnificence of the spectacle that fascinated the doctor. He sat down on a bench by the gates of the fire brigade, without paying attention to the voices heard across the street, and began to look around.

From all sides, obscure little streets flowed into the square. Deep down them one could see decrepit, lopsided little houses. The mud was as impassable in these little streets as in a village. From the mud long fences of woven willow withes stuck up, looking like nets thrown into a pond or baskets for catching crayfish.

In the little houses, the glass in the frames of the open windows gleamed weak-sightedly. From the front gardens, sweaty, fair-haired corn reached into the rooms, its silks and tassels gleaming as if they were oiled. From behind the sagging wattle fences, pale, lean mallows gazed solitarily into the distance, looking like farm women whom the heat had driven out of the stuffy cottages in their nightshirts for a breath of fresh air.

The moonlit night was astounding, like mercy or the gift of clairvoyance, and suddenly, into the silence of this bright, scintillating fairy tale, the measured, clipped sounds of someone's voice, familiar, as if just heard, began to fall. The voice was beautiful, fervent, and breathed conviction. The doctor listened and at once recognised who it was. It was the commissar Gintz. He was speaking on the square.

The local powers had probably asked him to support them with his authority, and he, with great feeling, was reproaching the Meliuzeevans for being disorganised, for succumbing too easily to the corrupting influence of the Bolsheviks, the real perpetrators, he insisted, of the Zybushino events. In the same spirit as he had spoken at the military superior's, he reminded them of the cruel and powerful enemy and the hour of trial that had struck for the motherland. Midway through his speech, he began to be interrupted.

Requests not to interrupt the speaker alternated with shouts of disagreement. The expressions of protest became louder and more frequent. Someone who accompanied Gintz and for the moment took upon himself the task of chairman shouted that remarks from the audience were not allowed and called for order. Some demanded that a citizeness from the crowd be given the floor, others hissed and asked them not to interfere.

A woman was making her way through the crowd towards the upside-down box that served as a platform. She had no intention of getting onto the box, but having squeezed her way there, she stood beside it. The woman was known. Silence fell. The woman held the attention of the crowding people. It was Ustinya.

'Zybushino, you were saying, comrade commissar, and then concerning eyes, you were saying, we must have eyes and not fall into deception, and yet you yourself, I listened to you, only know how to carp at us with your Bolsheviks and Mensheviks – Bolsheviks and Mensheviks, that's all we hear from you.[9] But that there'll be no more war and everything will be like between brothers, that's called God's way and not the Mensheviks', and that the mills and factories go to the poor, that again is not the Bolsheviks, but human pity. And the deaf-mute gets thrown in our faces without you, I'm sick of hearing it. What is he to you, really! Have you got something against him? That he went around mute all the time, and then suddenly up and spoke without asking anybody? Never saw the like, eh? Well, there's been even better! That famous she-ass, for instance. "Balaam, Balaam," she says, "I ask you honestly, don't go there, you'll be sorry."[10] Well, sure enough, he didn't listen and went. Like you saying, "A deaf-mute." He thinks, "Why listen to her – she's an ass, an animal." He scorned the brute. And how he repented later. But you surely know how it ended.'

'How?' someone in the public became curious.

'All right!' barked Ustinya. 'Ask me no questions, I'll tell you no lies.'

'No, that's no good. Tell us how.' The same voice would not quiet down.

'How, how – you stick like a thistle! He turned into a pillar of salt.'

'Nice try, dearie! That was Lot. Lot's wife,'[11] shouts rang out. Everyone laughed. The chairman called the assembly to order. The doctor went to bed.

                                    8

The next day he saw Antipova. He found her in the butler's pantry. Before Larissa Fyodorovna lay a pile of laundry. She was ironing.

The pantry was one of the back rooms on the upper floor, and it gave onto the garden. In it samovars were prepared, food delivered on the dumb-waiter from the kitchen was put on plates, dirty dishes were sent down to be washed. In the pantry the material accounts of the hospital were kept. In it dishes and linen were checked against the lists, people rested during their time off and arranged meetings with each other.

The windows on the garden were open. The pantry smelled of linden blossoms, the caraway bitterness of dry twigs, as in old parks, and slightly of coal gas from the two irons, which Larissa Fyodorovna used alternately, putting now one, now the other into the ventilation pipe to fire them up again.

'Why didn't you knock on my door yesterday? Mademoiselle told me.

Anyhow, you did the right thing. I was already in bed and couldn't have let you in. Well, hello. Be careful, don't get yourself dirty. There's coal spilled here.'

'You're obviously ironing for the whole hospital?'

'No, a lot of it is mine. So you've been teasing me that I'll never get out of here. But this time I'm serious. See, I'm getting ready, packing. I'll pack up – and be off. I to the Urals, and you to Moscow. And then one day they'll ask Yuri Andreevich: "Have you ever heard of the little town of Meliuzeevo?" "Not that I recall." "And who is this Antipova?" "I have no idea."'

'Well, that's unlikely. How was your trip around the rural areas? Is it nice in the country?'

'I can't put it in a couple of words. How quickly the irons get cold! Give me a new one, please, if you don't mind. There, sticking in the ventilation pipe. And this one goes back into the pipe. So. Thank you. Villages differ. It all depends on the inhabitants. In some the people are hard-working, industrious. There it's all right. But in others there must be nothing but drunkards. There it's desolation. It's frightening to look at.'

'Don't be silly. What drunkards? A lot you understand. There's simply nobody there, the men have all been taken as soldiers. Well, all right. And how is the zemstvo, the new revolutionary one?'

'You're not right about the drunkards, I disagree with you. And the zemstvo? There will be a long torment with the zemstvo. The instructions are inapplicable, there's nobody to work with in the rural areas. At the moment all the peasants are interested in is the land question.[12] I went to Razdolnoe. What beauty! You should go there. In the spring there was a bit of burning and looting. A barn burned down, the fruit trees got charred, part of the façade is damaged by soot. I didn't get to Zybushino, didn't have time. But everywhere they assure you that the deaf-mute isn't made up. They describe his appearance. They say he's young, educated.'

'Last night Ustinya laid herself out for him on the platz.'

'I only just came back, and again there was a whole cartload of junk from Razdolnoe. I've begged them so many times to leave us in peace. As if we don't have enough of our own! And this morning guards came from the commandant's with a note from the district. They desperately need the countess's silver tea service and crystal. Just for one evening, to be returned. We know their "to be returned". Half of the things will be missing. For a party, they say. Some sort of visitor.'

'Ah, I can guess who. A new front-line commissar has come. I saw him by chance. He's preparing to take on the deserters, surround them and disarm them. The commissar is still quite green, an infant in practical matters. The locals suggest using Cossacks, but he thinks he can take them with tears. He says the people are children, and so on, and he thinks it's all children's games. Galiullin begs him, says don't awaken the sleeping beast, leave it to us, but you can't argue with such a man once something's lodged in his head. Listen. Leave your irons for a moment and listen. There's going to be an unimaginable scramble here soon. It's not in our power to prevent it. How I wish you'd be gone before the mess begins!'

'Nothing will happen. You're exaggerating. Besides, I am leaving. But it can't be just like that: snip-snap and good luck to you. I have to turn over the inventory with a list, otherwise it will look as if I've stolen something. And who am I to turn it over to? That's the question. I've suffered so much with this inventory, and the only reward is reproaches. I registered Zhabrinsky's property as the hospital's, because that was the sense of the decree. And now it comes out that I did it as a pretence, in order to keep things for the owner. How vile!'

'Ah, spit on the rugs and china, let it all perish. As if there was anything to be upset about! Yes, yes, it's vexing in the highest degree that we didn't see each other yesterday. I was so inspired! I'd have explained all of heavenly mechanics for you, and answered all the accursed questions![13] No, no joking, I really was longing to speak myself out. To tell about my wife, my son, my life. Devil take it, can't a grown-up man talk with a grown-up woman without the immediate suspicion that there's something "behind" it? Brr! To the devil with all these fronts and behinds!

'Iron, iron, please – I mean, iron the laundry and pay no attention to me, and I'll talk. I'll talk for a long time.

'Just think what a time it is now! And you and I are living in these days! Only once in eternity do such unprecedented things happen. Think: the roof over the whole of Russia has been torn off, and we and all the people find ourselves under the open sky. And there's nobody to spy on us. Freedom! Real, not just in words and demands, but fallen from the sky, beyond all expectation. Freedom by inadvertence, by misunderstanding.

'And how perplexedly enormous everyone is! Have you noticed? As if each of them is crushed by himself, by the revelation of his own heroic might.

'No, go on ironing. Keep still. You're not bored? I'll change the iron for you.

'I watched a meeting last night. An astounding spectacle. Mother Russia has begun to move, she won't stay put, she walks and never tires of walking, she talks and can't talk enough. And it's not as if only people are talking. Stars and trees come together and converse, night flowers philosophise, and stone buildings hold meetings. Something gospel-like, isn't it? As in the time of the apostles. Remember, in Paul? "Speak in tongues and prophesy. Pray for the gift of interpretation.""[14]

'About the meetings of the trees and stars I understand. I know what you want to say. The same has happened to me.'

'The war did half of it, the rest was completed by the revolution. The war was an artificial interruption of life, as if existence could be postponed for a time (how absurd!). The revolution broke out involuntarily, like breath held for too long. Everyone revived, was reborn, in everyone there are transformations, upheavals. You might say that everyone went through two revolutions, one his own, personal, the other general. It seems to me that socialism is a sea into which all these personal, separate revolutions should flow, the sea of life, the sea of originality. The sea of life, I said, the life that can be seen in paintings, life touched by genius, life creatively enriched. But now people have decided to test it, not in books, but in themselves, not in abstraction, but in practice.'

The unexpected tremor in his voice betrayed the doctor's incipient agitation. Interrupting her ironing for a moment, Larissa Fyodorovna gave him a serious and surprised look. He became confused and forgot what he was talking about. After a short pause, he began to talk again. Rushing headlong, he poured out God knows what. He said:

'In these days one longs so much to live honestly and productively! One wants so much to be part of the general inspiration! And then, amidst the joy that grips everyone, I meet your mysteriously mirthless gaze, wandering no one knows where, in some far-off kingdom, in some far-off land. What wouldn't I give for it not to be there, for it to be written on your face that you are pleased with your fate and need nothing from anyone. So that somebody close to you, your friend or husband (best if he were a military man), would take me by the hand and ask me not to worry about your lot and not to burden you with my attention. And I would tear my hand free, swing, and . . . Ah, I've forgotten myself! Forgive me, please.'

The doctor's voice failed him again. He waved his hand and with the feeling of an irreparable blunder got up and went to the window. He stood with his back to the room, propped his cheek in his hand, leaning his elbow on the windowsill, and, in search of pacification, directed his absent-minded, unseeing gaze into the depths of the garden shrouded in darkness.

Going around the ironing board that rested on the table and on the edge of the other window, Larissa Fyodorovna stopped a few steps away from the doctor, behind him, in the middle of the room.

'Ah, how I've always been afraid of this!' she said softly, as if to herself.

'What a fatal error! Stop, Yuri Andreevich, you mustn't. Ah, look what I've done because of you!' she exclaimed loudly and ran to the board, where a thin stream of acrid smoke was rising from a blouse burned through under the iron forgotten on it. 'Yuri Andreevich,' she went on, banging the iron down angrily on the burner. 'Yuri Andreevich, be a good boy, go to Mademoiselle for a moment, drink some water, dearest, and come back here the way I'm used to you and would like to see you. Do you hear, Yuri Andreevich? I know you can do it. Please, I beg you.'

Such talks between them were not repeated again. A week later Larissa Fyodorovna left.

9

A short time later Zhivago began to prepare for the road. The night before his departure, there was a terrible storm in Meliuzeevo.

The noise of the hurricane merged with the noise of the downpour, which now fell vertically on the roofs, now, under the pressure of the shifting wind, moved down the street, its lashing torrents as if winning step by step.

Peals of thunder followed one another without pause, becoming one uniform rumbling. Frequent flashes of lightning showed the street running away into the distance, with trees bending over and running in the same direction.

During the night, Mademoiselle Fleury was awakened by an anxious knocking at the front door. Frightened, she sat up in bed and listened. The knocking did not stop.

Can it be that in the whole hospital not a soul will be found to come out and open the door, she thought, and that she alone, a wretched old woman, must do it all for them, only because nature had made her honest and endowed her with a sense of duty?

Well, all right, the Zhabrinskys were rich people, aristocrats. But the hospital is theirs, the people's. Why did they abandon it? It would be curious to know, for instance, where the orderlies have vanished to. Everybody's scattered, there are no directors, no nurses, no doctors. And there are still wounded in the house, two with amputated legs upstairs in the surgical section, where the drawing room used to be, and the storeroom downstairs, next to the laundry, is full of dysentery cases. And that she-devil Ustinya has gone visiting somewhere. The foolish woman could see the storm gathering, why the deuce did she have to go? Now she's got a good excuse for staying the night.

Well, they've stopped, thank God, they've quieted down. They saw no one will open and they waved their hand and left. What the devil are they doing out in such weather? But maybe it's Ustinya? No, she has her own key. My God, how frightening, they're knocking again!

But, all the same, what swinishness! I suppose you can't expect anything from Zhivago. He's leaving tomorrow, and in his thoughts he's already in Moscow or on his way. But what about Galiullin? How can he snore away or lie quiet, hearing such knocking, and count on her, a weak and defence-less old woman, to get up in the end and go to open the door to some unknown person, on this dreadful night, in this dreadful country?

'Galiullin!' She suddenly caught herself. 'What Galiullin?' No, only half-awake could such an absurdity occur to her! What Galiullin, if even his tracks are cold? Didn't she herself, together with Zhivago, hide him and change him into civilian clothes, and then explain about the roads and vil-lages in the area, so he'd know where to escape to, when that dreadful lynching took place at the station and they killed Commissar Gintz, and chased Galiullin from Biriuchi as far as Meliuzeevo, shooting after him and searching for him all over town? Galiullin!

If those fellows hadn't come rolling in, there'd be no stone left upon stone in the town. An armoured division happened to be passing through. They stood up for the inhabitants and curbed the scoundrels.

The thunderstorm was weakening, moving away. The thunderclaps came from a distance, more rare and muffled. The rain stopped intermittently, but water continued to trickle down with a soft splashing from the leaves and gutters. Soundless glimmers of lightning came into Mademoiselle's room, lit it up, and lingered there for an extra moment, as if searching for something.

Suddenly the knocking at the door, which had ceased for a long time, started again. Someone needed help and was knocking desperately and rap-idly. The wind picked up again. More rain poured down.

'One moment!' Mademoiselle cried out, not knowing to whom, and frightened herself with her own voice.

An unexpected surmise dawned on her. Lowering her feet from the bed and putting on her slippers, she threw her dressing gown over her and ran to awaken Zhivago, so as not to feel so frightened alone. But he, too, had heard the knocking and was himself coming down to meet her with a can-dle. They had made the same assumptions.

'Zhivagó, Zhivagó! There's knocking at the outside door, I'm afraid to open it by myself,' she cried in French, and added in Russian: ' 'Ave a luke. Ees Lar or Lieutenant Gaioul.'

Yuri Andreevich had also been awakened by the knocking, and thought that it must be someone they knew, either Galiullin, hindered by something and coming back to the refuge where he could hide, or the nurse Antipova, forced by some difficulties to turn back from her journey.

In the front hall, the doctor handed Mademoiselle the candle, while he turned the key in the door and unbolted it. A gust of wind tore the door from his hand, blew out the candle, and showered them both with a cold spray of rain from outside.

'Who's there? Who's there? Is anybody there?' Mademoiselle and the doctor called out in turn into the darkness, but nobody answered. Suddenly they heard the former knocking in another place, from the back entrance, or, as it now seemed to them, at the window to the garden.

'It's evidently the wind,' said the doctor. 'But for the sake of a clear conscience, go to the back door anyway, to make sure, and I'll wait here, so that we don't cross each other, if it really is someone, and not from some other cause.'

Mademoiselle went off into the depths of the house, and the doctor went outside under the roof of the porch. His eyes, growing accustomed to the darkness, made out signs of the coming dawn.

Over the town, like halfwits, clouds raced swiftly, as if escaping pursuit. Their tatters flew so low that they almost caught in the trees leaning in the same direction, so that it looked as if someone were sweeping the sky with them, as if with bending besoms. Rain lashed at the wooden wall of the house, turning it from grey to black.

'Well?' the doctor asked Mademoiselle when she came back.

'You're right. There's nobody.' And she told him that she had gone around the whole house. In the butler's pantry a window had been broken by a piece of a linden branch that struck the glass, and there were huge puddles on the floor, and it was the same in the room Lara had left behind, a sea, a veritable sea, a whole ocean.

'And here's a shutter torn loose and beating against the window frame. You see? That's the whole explanation.'

They talked a little more, locked the door, and went their ways to bed, both sorry that the alarm had proved false.

They had been certain that they would open the front door and the woman they knew so well would come in, wet to the skin and freezing, and they would bombard her with questions while she shook herself off. And then, having changed her clothes, she would come to dry herself by the lingering heat of the stove in the kitchen and would tell them about her countless misadventures, smoothing her hair and laughing.

They were so certain of it that, when they locked the door, the traces of their certainty remained by the corner of the house outside, in the form of the woman's watermark or image, which continued to appear to them from around the turning.

10

The one considered to be indirectly responsible for the soldiers' riot at the station was the Biriuchi telegraphist Kolya Frolenko.

Kolya was the son of a well-known Meliuzeevo watchmaker. He had been known in Meliuzeevo from the cradle. As a boy, he had visited someone among the Razdolnoe house staff and, under the surveillance of Mademoiselle, had played with her two charges, the countess's daughters. Mademoiselle knew Kolya well. It was then that he had begun to understand a little French.

People in Meliuzeevo were used to seeing Kolya lightly dressed in any weather, without a hat, in canvas summer shoes, on a bicycle. Letting go of the handlebars, his body thrown back and his arms crossed on his chest, he rolled down the main street and around town and glanced at the poles and wires, checking the state of the network.

Some houses in town were connected with the station through a branch line of the railway telephone. The management of this line was in Kolya's hands at the station control room.

There he was up to his ears in work: the railway telegraph, the telephone, and occasionally, in moments of the station chief Povarikhin's brief absences, the signals and the block system, the apparatus for which was also in the control room.

The necessity of keeping an eye on the operation of several mechanisms at once made Kolya develop a special manner of speaking, obscure, abrupt, and full of riddles, to which Kolya resorted when he had no wish to answer someone or get into conversation. The word was that he had made too broad a use of this right on the day of the disorders.

By his omissions he had, in fact, deprived of force all of Galiullin's good intentions in his phone calls from town, and, perhaps against his will, had given a fatal turn to the subsequent events.

Galiullin had asked to speak to the commissar, who was somewhere at the station or nearby, in order to tell him that he would soon come to join him at the clearing and to ask that he wait for him and undertake nothing without him. Kolya had refused Galiullin's request to call Gintz to the phone, on the pretext that he had the line busy transmitting signals to the train approaching Biriuchi, while he himself was at the same time trying by

hook or by crook to hold the train, which was bringing the summoned Cossacks to Biriuchi, at the previous junction.

When the troop train arrived after all, Kolya could not hide his dis-
pleasure.

The engine slowly crept under the dark roof of the platform and stopped
just in front of the huge window of the control room. Kolya opened wide
the heavy railway station curtains of dark blue broadcloth with railway
monograms woven into the borders. On the stone windowsill stood a huge
carafe of water and a thick, simply cut glass on a big tray. Kolya poured
water into the glass, took several gulps, and looked out of the window.

The engineer noticed Kolya and gave him a friendly nod from the cab.
'Ooh, you stinking trash, you wood louse!' Kolya thought with hatred,
stuck his tongue out at the engineer, and shook his fist at him. The engineer
not only understood Kolya's miming, but, by shrugging his shoulders and
turning his head in the direction of the carriages, was able to convey: 'What
can I do? Try it yourself. He's in charge.' 'You're trash and filth all the same,'
Kolya mimed back.

They began leading the horses out of the freight cars. They balked, refusing to move. The hollow thud of hooves on the wooden gangways changed
to the clanging of horseshoes against the stone of the platform. The rearing
horses were led across several lines of tracks.

They ended up by two rows of discarded carriages on two pairs of rusty
rails overgrown with grass. The degradation of the wood, stripped of
paint by the rain and rotted by worms and dampness, had restored to
these broken-down carriages their original kinship with the damp forest
that began on the other side of the tracks, with the tinder fungus that ailed
the birches, with the clouds piling up over it.

At the edge of the forest, the Cossacks mounted up on command and
rode to the clearing.

The mutineers of the 212th were surrounded. Horsemen always look
taller and more imposing among trees than in the open. They impressed the
soldiers, though they had rifles in their dugouts. The Cossacks drew their
sabres.

Inside the ring of horses, Gintz jumped onto a pile of stacked and levelled
firewood and addressed a speech to the surrounded soldiers.

Again, as was usual with him, he spoke of military duty, the importance
of the motherland, and many other lofty subjects. His notions met with no
sympathy here. The mob was too numerous. It consisted of men who had
suffered much during the war, had become coarse and weary. The words
Gintz uttered had long since stuck in their ears. Four months of ingratiation

from the right and the left had corrupted this crowd. The simple folk who made it up gave a cool reception to the orator's non-Russian name and Baltic accent.

Gintz felt that he was speaking too long, and was vexed with himself, but thought he was doing it for the sake of greater accessibility to his listeners, who, instead of gratitude, paid him back with expressions of indifference and hostile boredom. Becoming more and more annoyed, he decided to address his audience in stiffer terms and make use of the threats he was keeping in reserve. Not hearing the rising murmur, he reminded the soldiers that revolutionary courts-martial had been introduced and were functioning, and demanded on pain of death that they lay down their weapons and hand over the instigators. If they did not do so, Gintz said, it would prove that they were lowdown traitors, irresponsible riff-raff, conceited boors. These people were no longer accustomed to such a tone.

A roar of hundreds of voices arose. 'You've had your say. Enough. All right,' some cried in bass voices and almost without malice. But there were hysterical outcries from the trebles overstrained with hatred. They were listened to. They shouted:

'Do you hear how he lays it on, comrades? Just like the old days! They haven't shed their officer's habits! So we're the traitors! And where do you come from, Your Honour? Why dance around him? You can see, can't you, he's a German, an infiltrator. Hey, blue blood, show us your papers! And what are you pacifiers gaping at? Here we are, put the ropes on us, eat us up!'

But the Cossacks also had less and less liking for Gintz's unfortunate speech. 'It's all boors and swine. The little squire!' they exchanged in whispers. First singly, then in greater numbers, they began to sheath their sabres. One after another they got off their horses. When enough of them had dismounted, they moved in disorder towards the centre of the clearing to meet the 212th. Everything became confused. Fraternisation began.

'You'd better quietly disappear somehow,' the worried Cossack officers said to Gintz. 'Your car is near the junction. We'll send word that it should be brought closer. Get away quickly.'

Gintz did so, but since he found it undignified to sneak off, he headed for the station without the necessary caution, almost openly. He walked in terrible agitation, forcing himself out of pride to go calmly and unhurriedly.

It was not far to the station; the forest was just next to it. At the edge, already within sight of the tracks, he looked back for the first time. Behind him walked soldiers with guns. 'What do they want?' thought Gintz and quickened his pace.

His pursuers did the same. The distance between him and the chase did not change. The double wall of broken-down carriages appeared ahead. Once behind them, Gintz broke into a run. The train that had delivered the Cossacks had been taken to the depot. The tracks were clear. Gintz crossed them at a run.

He made a running leap onto the high platform. At that moment the soldiers chasing him ran from behind the broken-down carriages. Povarikhin and Kolya shouted something to Gintz and made signs for him to come inside the station, where they could save him.

But again the sense of honour bred over generations, urban, sacrificial, and inapplicable here, barred his way to safety. By an inhuman effort of will, he tried to control the trembling of his runaway heart. 'I must call out to them: "Brothers, come to your senses, what kind of spy am I?"' he thought. 'Something sobering, heartfelt, that will stop them.'

In recent months the sense of heroic deeds, of the soul's outcry, had unconsciously become connected with rostrums and tribunes, with chairs that one could jump up on and hurl some call, something fiery, to the throng.

By the door of the station, under the signal bell, stood a tall firefighting barrel. It was tightly covered. Gintz jumped onto the lid and addressed to the approaching men several soul-wrenching words, inhuman and incoherent. The insane boldness of his address, two steps from the thrown-open doors of the station, where he could so easily have run, stunned them and rooted them to the spot. The soldiers lowered their guns.

But Gintz stepped on the edge of the lid and turned it under. One of his legs went into the water, the other hung down the side of the barrel. He wound up sitting astride the edge.

The soldiers met this clumsiness with an explosion of guffaws and the first one killed the unfortunate man with a point-blank shot in the neck, while the others rushed to stab the dead body with their bayonets.

11

Mademoiselle called Kolya on the telephone and told him to settle the doctor comfortably on the train, threatening him otherwise with disclosures that he would find unpleasant.

While answering Mademoiselle, Kolya was as usual conducting some other telephone conversation and, judging by the decimals that peppered his speech, was telegraphing something in ciphers to a third place.

'Pskov, north line, do you hear me? What rebels? What hand? What is it,

Mam'selle? Nonsense, mumbo jumbo. Get off, hang up the phone, you're bothering me. Pskov, north line, Pskov. Thirty-six comma zero zero fifteen. Ah, curse it all, the tape broke off! What? What? I don't hear. Is that you again, Mam'selle? I told you in plain Russian, it's impossible, I can't. Ask Povarikhin. Nonsense, mumbo jumbo. Thirty-six . . . ah, the devil . . . Get off, don't bother me, Mam'selle.'

And Mademoiselle was saying:

'Don't throw dust in my eye, mumbo jumbo, Pskov, Pskov, mumbo jumbo, I see right through you and back again, you put the doctor in carriage tomorrow, and I won't more speak with any murderer and little Judas-traitor.'

12

It was sultry when Yuri Andreevich left. A thunderstorm was gathering, as two days earlier.

The clay huts and geese in the settlement around the station, all scattered with spat-out husks of sunflower seeds, sat white and frightened under the immobile gaze of the black, menacing sky.

Bordering the station building was a wide clearing that stretched far to both sides. The grass on it was trampled down, and it was entirely covered by an immense crowd of people, who had spent weeks waiting for trains in the various directions each needed.

There were old men in the crowd, dressed in coarse grey kaftans, who went from group to group under the scorching sun gathering rumours and information. Silent adolescents around fourteen years old lay on their sides, propped on an elbow with a leafless switch in their hands, as if tending cattle. Their younger brothers and sisters darted underfoot, their shirts pulling up, exposing their pink bottoms. Their mothers sat on the ground, their tightly joined legs stretched out, with nursing babies swaddled crookedly under their brown homespun coats.

'They all scattered like sheep when the shooting began. Didn't like it at all!' the stationmaster Povarikhin was saying with hostility as he and the doctor zigzagged their way among the rows of bodies lying next to each other outside the doors and inside on the floor of the station.

'The lawn was suddenly empty! We could see the ground again. What a joy! For four months we hadn't seen it under this Gypsy camp – forgot what it looked like. Here's where he lay. Amazing thing, I've seen all sorts of horrors during the war, it's time I got used to them. But here I was seized by such pity! Above all – the senselessness. For what? What harm had he done them? Can they be human beings? They say he was the family favourite. And now to the right, here, here, this way, please, to my office. Don't even think of getting on this train, you'll be crushed to death. I'll put you on another one, a local one. We're making it up ourselves, it's going to be formed right now. Only not a word till you get on, not to anyone! If you let it slip, they'll tear it apart even before it's coupled. You'll have to change in Sukhinichi during the night.'

13

When the secret train was formed and started backing into the station from behind the depot, all the people crowded on the lawn rushed to intercept the slowly moving carriages. People came rolling off the hillocks like peas and ran up the embankment. Pushing each other aside, they leaped onto the buffers and footboards in motion, while others climbed through the windows and onto the roofs of the carriages. The still-moving train was filled up in no time, and when it reached the platform it was jam packed and hung from top to bottom with passengers.

By a miracle, the doctor squeezed himself onto a rear platform and then, in a still more incomprehensible way, penetrated into the corridor of the carriage.

And in the corridor he remained throughout the entire trip, and got to Sukhinichi sitting on his things on the floor.

The storm clouds had long since dispersed. Over the fields flooded by the burning rays of the sun, the ceaseless chirring of grasshoppers rolled from end to end, drowning out the noise of the train's movement.

The passengers standing at the windows blocked the light for all the others. They cast long shadows, folded double and triple on the floor, the benches, the partitions. The shadows did not fit into the carriage. They were pushed out of the windows opposite and ran skipping along the other side of the embankment, together with the shadow of the whole rolling train.

All around people jabbered, bawled songs, cursed, and played cards. At the stops, the bedlam inside was joined by the noise of the crowd besieging the train from outside. The din of voices reached the deafening level of a sea storm. And, as at sea, in the middle of a stop there would suddenly fall an inexplicable silence. One could hear hurried steps on the platform along the whole length of the train, scurrying about and arguing by the baggage car, separate words spoken by people seeing someone off in the distance, the quiet clucking of hens, and the rustling of trees in the station's front garden.

Then, like a telegram received on the way, or like greetings from Meliuzeevo, a fragrance floated through the window, familiar, as if addressed to Yuri Andreevich. It manifested itself with quiet superiority somewhere to one side and came from a height unusual for wild or garden flowers.

The doctor could not get to the window owing to the crush. But even without looking, he could see those trees in his imagination. They probably grew quite nearby, calmly reaching towards the roofs of the carriages with their spreading branches, the foliage dusty from railroad commotion and thick as night, finely sprinkled with the waxy little stars of glimmering flower clusters.

This was repeated for the whole way. Everywhere there were noisy crowds. Everywhere there were blossoming lindens.

The ubiquitous wafting of this smell seemed to precede the northbound train, like a rumour spread to all junctions, watch houses, and little stations, which the travellers found everywhere, already established and confirmed.

14

At night in Sukhinichi an obliging porter of the old stamp took the doctor to some unlit tracks and put him through the rear door of a second-class carriage of some train that had just arrived and did not figure on the schedule.

The porter had no sooner opened the rear door with a pass key and thrown the doctor's things onto the platform, than he had to face a brief fight with the conductor, who immediately wanted to get rid of them, but, mollified by Yuri Andreevich, he effaced himself and vanished into thin air.

The mysterious train was of special purpose and went rather quickly, with brief stops and some sort of guard. The carriages were quite vacant.

The compartment Zhivago entered was brightly lit by a guttering candle on a little table, its flame wavering in the stream of air from a half-lowered window.

The candle belonged to the sole passenger in the compartment. He was a fair-haired youth, probably very tall, judging by his long arms and legs. They flexed extremely freely at the joints, like poorly fastened component parts of folding objects. The young man was sitting on the seat by the window, leaning back casually. When Zhivago appeared, he politely rose and changed his half-reclining position to a more appropriate sitting one.

Under his seat lay something like a floor rag. Suddenly the end of the rag moved and a flop-eared hound bustled herself up and came out. She sniffed Yuri Andreevich, looked him over, and started running from corner to corner of the compartment, her legs flexing as freely as her lanky master's when he crossed them. Soon, at the latter's command, she bustled herself back under the seat and assumed her former look of a crumpled floor-polishing cloth.

Only then did Yuri Andreevich notice a double-barrelled shotgun in a case, a leather cartridge belt, and a game bag tightly stuffed with shot birds, hanging on hooks in the compartment.

The young man was a hunter.

He was distinguished by an extreme garrulousness and with an amiable smile hastened to get into conversation with the doctor. As he did so he looked the doctor in the mouth all the while, not figuratively but in the most direct sense.

The young man turned out to have an unpleasantly high voice, at its highest verging on a metallic falsetto. Another oddity: by all tokens a Russian, he pronounced one vowel, namely the *u*, in a most peculiar way. He softened it like the French *u* or the German *ü*. Moreover, this defective *u* was very hard for him to get out; he articulated its sound more loudly than all the others, straining terribly, with a slight shriek. Almost at the very beginning, he took Yuri Andreevich aback with the following phrase:

'Only yesterday morning I was shüting wüdcock.'

At moments, when he obviously watched himself more carefully, he overcame this irregularity, but he had only to forget himself and it would creep in again.

'What is this bedevilment?' thought Zhivago. 'It's something familiar, I've read about it. As a doctor, I ought to know, but it's skipped my mind. Some phenomenon of the brain that provokes a speech defect. But this mewling is so funny, it's hard to remain serious. Conversation is utterly impossible. I'd better climb up and get into bed.'

And so the doctor did. When he began to settle himself on the upper berth, the young man asked if he should put out the candle, which might bother Yuri Andreevich. The doctor gratefully accepted the offer. His neighbour put out the light. It became dark.

The window in the compartment was half lowered.

'Shouldn't we close the window?' asked Yuri Andreevich. 'Aren't you afraid of thieves?'

His neighbour made no reply. Yuri Andreevich repeated the question very loudly, but again the man did not respond.

Then Yuri Andreevich lit a match so as to see what his neighbour was up to, whether he had left the compartment in such a brief space of time, or was asleep, which would be still more incredible.

But no, he was sitting open-eyed in his place and smiled when the doctor hung his head down.

The match went out. Yuri Andreevich lit another and by its light repeated for the third time what he wished to ascertain.

'Do as you think best,' the hunter answered at once. 'I've got nothing worth stealing. However, it would be better not to close it. It's stuffy.'

'Fancy that,' thought Zhivago. 'The strange fellow's apparently used to talking only in full light. And how clearly he pronounced it all just now, without his irregularities! Inconceivable to the mind!'

15

The doctor felt broken by the events of the past week, the agitation before departure, the preparations for the road, and boarding the train in the morning. He thought he would fall asleep the moment he stretched out in a comfortable place. Not so. Excessive exhaustion made him sleepless. He dozed off only towards morning.

Chaotic as was the whirlwind of thoughts swarming in his head during those long hours, there were, essentially speaking, two spheres of them, two persistent balls, which kept winding up and then unwinding.

One sphere consisted of thoughts of Tonya, home, and the former smooth-running life, in which everything down to the smallest details was clothed in poetry and imbued with warmth and purity. The doctor worried about that life and wished it to be preserved intact, and, flying through the night on the speeding train, he longed impatiently to be back in that life after more than two years of separation.

Faithfulness to the revolution and admiration for it also belonged to that sphere. This was the revolution in the sense in which it was taken by the middle classes, and in that understanding imparted to it by the student youth of the year 1905, who worshipped Blok.

To that sphere, intimate and habitual, also belonged those signs of the new, those promises and presages, which had appeared on the horizon before the war, between the years 1912 and 1914, in Russian thought, Russian art, and Russian destiny, the destiny of all Russia and of himself, Zhivago.

After the war, he wanted to go back to that spirit, to its renewal and continuation, just as he longed to be back home after his absence.

The new was likewise the subject of his thoughts in the second sphere, but how differently, how distinctly new! This was not his own habitual new, prepared for by the old, but a spontaneous, irrevocable new, prescribed by reality, sudden as a shock.

To this new belonged the war, its blood and horrors, its homelessness and savagery. To this new belonged the trials and the wisdom of life taught by the war. To this new belonged the remote towns the war brought you to and the people you ran into. To this new belonged the revolution, not as idealised by university intellectuals in 1905, but this present-day one, born of the war, bloody, a soldiers' revolution, reckless of everything, led by connoisseurs of this element, the Bolsheviks.

To this new belonged the nurse Antipova, flung God knows where by the war, with a life completely unknown to him, who reproached no one for anything and was almost plaintive in her muteness, mysterious in her laconism, and so strong in her silence. To this new belonged Yuri Andreevich's honest trying with all his might not to love her, just as he had tried all his life to treat all people with love, not to mention his family and close friends.

The train raced along at full steam. The head wind coming through the lowered window tousled and blew dust in Yuri Andreevich's hair. During the stops at night the same thing went on as during the day, the crowds raged and the lindens rustled.

Sometimes out of the depths of the night carts and gigs rolled up with a clatter to the station. Voices and the rumbling of wheels mixed with the sound of the trees.

In those moments one seemed to understand what made these night shadows rustle and bend to each other and what they whispered together, barely stirring their sleep-laden leaves, as if with thick, lisping tongues. It was the same thing Yuri Andreevich thought about as he stirred on his upper berth: the news of Russia gripped by ever-widening disturbances, the news of the revolution, the news of her fatal and difficult hour, of her probable ultimate grandeur.

<h1 style="text-align:center">16</h1>

The next day the doctor woke up late. It was past eleven. 'Marquise, Marquise!' his neighbour was restraining his growling dog in a half whisper. To Yuri Andreevich's surprise, he and the hunter remained alone in the compartment; no one had joined them on the way. The names of the stations were now familiar from childhood. The train had left the province of Kaluga and cut deep into Moscow province.

Having performed his travelling ablutions in pre-war comfort, the doctor returned to the compartment for breakfast, offered him by his curious companion. Now Yuri Andreevich had a better look at him.

The distinctive features of this personage were extreme garrulousness and mobility. The stranger liked to talk, and the main thing for him was not communication and the exchange of thoughts, but the activity of speech itself, the pronouncing of words and the uttering of sounds. While talking, he bounced up and down on the seat as if on springs, guffawed deafeningly and causelessly, rubbed his hands briskly with pleasure, and when this proved insufficient to express his delight, slapped his knees with his palms, laughing to the point of tears.

The conversation resumed with all the previous day's oddities. The stranger was astonishingly inconsistent. Now he would make confessions to which no one had prompted him; now, without batting an eye, he would leave the most innocent questions unanswered.

He poured out a whole heap of the most fantastic and incoherent information about himself. Sad to say, he probably fibbed a little. He was undoubtedly aiming at the effect of the extremity of his views and the denial of all that was generally accepted.

It was all reminiscent of something long familiar. The nihilists of the last century had talked in the spirit of such radicalism, and some of Dostoevsky's heroes a little later, and then still quite recently their direct continuation, that is, the whole of educated provincial Russia, often going ahead of the capitals, thanks to a thoroughness preserved in the backwoods, which in the capitals had become dated and unfashionable.

The young man told him that he was the nephew of a well-known revolutionary, while his parents, on the contrary, were incorrigible reactionaries – mastodons, as he put it. They had a decent estate in one of the areas near the front. It was there that the young man had grown up. His parents had been at daggers drawn with his uncle all their lives, but the young man felt no rancour and now his influence had spared them many an unpleasantness.

He himself, in his convictions, had taken after his uncle, the garrulous subject informed him – extremist and maximalist in everything: in questions of life, politics, and art. Again there was a whiff of Petenka Verkhovensky, not in the leftist sense, but in the sense of depravity and hollow verbiage. 'Next he'll recommend himself as a Futurist,' thought Yuri Andreevich, and indeed the talk turned to the Futurists.[15] 'And next he'll start talking about sports,' the doctor went on second-guessing, 'horse races or skating rinks or French wrestling'. And in fact the conversation turned to hunting.

The young man said that he had just been hunting in his native region, and boasted that he was an excellent shot, and if it were not for his physical defect, which kept him from being a soldier, he would have distinguished himself in war by his marksmanship.

Catching Zhivago's questioning glance, he exclaimed:

'What? You mean you haven't noticed anything? I thought you'd guessed about my deficiency.'

And he took two cards from his pocket and gave them to Yuri Andreevich. One was his visiting card. He had a double last name. He was Maxim Aristarkhovich Klintsov-Pogorevshikh – or just Pogorevshikh, as he asked to be called in honour of his uncle, who called himself precisely by that name.

The other card had on it a table divided into squares showing pictures of variously joined hands with their fingers composed in various ways. It was sign language for deaf-mutes. Suddenly everything became clear.

Pogorevshikh was a phenomenally gifted pupil of either Hartmann's or Ostrogradsky's school, that is, a deaf-mute who had learned with incredible perfection to speak not from hearing, but from looking at the throat muscles of his teacher, and who understood his interlocutor's speech in the same way.

Then, putting together in his mind where he was from and in what parts he had been hunting, the doctor asked:

'Forgive my indiscretion, and you needn't answer – but, tell me, did you have anything to do with the Zybushino republic and its creation?'

'But how do you . . . Excuse me . . . So you knew Blazheiko? . . . I did have, I did! Of course I did!' Pogorevshikh rattled out joyfully, laughing, swaying his whole body from side to side, and slapping himself furiously on the knees. And the phantasmagoria went on again.

Pogorevshikh said that Blazheiko had been a pretext for him and Zybushino an indifferent point for applying his own ideas. It was hard for Yuri Andreevich to follow his exposition of them. Pogorevshikh's philosophy consisted half of the theses of anarchism and half of sheer hunter's humbug.

In the imperturbable tone of an oracle, Pogorevshikh predicted ruinous shocks in the nearest future. Yuri Andreevich inwardly agreed that they might be inevitable, but the authoritative calm with which this unpleasant boy mouthed his predictions exasperated him.

'Wait a minute, wait a minute,' he objected timorously. 'That all may be so. But in my opinion it's not the time for such risky experiments, in the midst of our chaos and breakdown, in the face of enemy pressure. The country must be allowed to come to its senses and catch its breath after one upheaval, before venturing upon another. We must wait for some calm and order, however relative.'

'That's naïve,' said Pogorevshikh. 'What you call breakdown is as normal a phenomenon as your much-praised and beloved order. Such destruction is a natural and preliminary part of a vaster constructive project. Society has not yet broken down enough. It must fall apart completely, and then the real revolutionary power will piece it back together on totally different principles.'

Yuri Andreevich felt ill at ease. He went out to the corridor.

The train, gathering speed, raced through the Moscow outskirts. Every moment, birch groves with dachas standing close together ran up to the windows and went racing by. Narrow, roofless platforms flew past, with summer residents, men and women, standing on them, who flew far off to one side in the cloud of dust raised by the train and twirled around as on a carousel. The train gave whistle after whistle, and the empty, pipelike, hollow forest echo breathlessly carried its whistles far away.

Suddenly, for the first time in all those days, Yuri Andreevich understood with full clarity where he was, what was happening to him, and what would meet him in a little more than an hour or two.

Three years of changes, uncertainty, marches, war, revolution, shocks, shootings, scenes of destruction, scenes of death, blown-up bridges, ruins, fires – all that suddenly turned into a vast empty place, devoid of content. The first true event after the long interruption was this giddy train ride towards his home, which was intact and still existed in the world, and where every little stone was dear to him. This was what life was, this was what experience was, this was what the seekers of adventure were after, this was what art had in view – coming to your dear ones, returning to yourself, the renewing of existence.

The woods ended. The train burst from leafy thickets into freedom. A sloped clearing went off into the distance on a wide hillock rising from a ravine. It was entirely covered lengthwise with rows of dark green potato plants. At the top of the clearing, at the end of the potato field, glass frames pulled from hothouses lay on the ground. Facing the clearing, behind the tail of the moving train, taking up half the sky, stood an enormous black-purple cloud. The rays of sun breaking from behind it spread wheel-like in all directions, catching at the hothouse frames on their way, flashing on their glass with an unbearable brilliance.

Suddenly out of the cloud a heavy mushroom rain[16] poured down obliquely, sparkling in the sun. It fell in hasty drops at the same tempo as the speeding train clacked its wheels and rattled its bolts, as if trying to catch up with it or afraid of lagging behind.

The doctor had barely turned his attention to that, when the cathedral of Christ the Saviour appeared from beyond the hill, and the next moment – the cupolas, the roofs, the houses and chimneys of the whole city.

'Moscow,' he said, returning to the compartment. 'Time to get ready.'

Pogorevshikh jumped up, began rummaging in his game bag, and chose one of the larger ducks.

'Take it,' he said. 'In remembrance. I've spent the whole day in such pleasant company.'

No matter how the doctor protested, nothing worked.

'Well, all right,' he was forced to accept, 'I'll take it from you as a present for my wife.'

'For your wife! For your wife! A present for your wife!' Pogorevshikh joyfully repeated, as if hearing the word for the first time, and he began to twitch all over and laughed so much that Marquise came leaping out to share in his joy.

The train was approaching the platform. It became dark as night in the carriage. The deaf-mute handed the doctor a wild drake wrapped in a scrap of some printed proclamation.

Part Six

THE MOSCOW ENCAMPMENT

I

On the way, as a result of sitting motionless in a narrow compartment, it had seemed that only the train was moving, while time stood still, and that it was as yet only noon.

But night was already falling when the cab bringing the doctor and his things emerged with difficulty, at a walk, from the numberless multitude of people crowding around the Smolensky market.

It may have been so, or it may have been that layers of experience from later years were added to the doctor's impression of that time, but afterwards, in his memory, it seemed to him that even then people bunched together only out of habit, and there was no reason for them to crowd around, because the awnings of the empty stands were lowered and not even fastened with padlocks, and there was nothing to sell on the filthy square, which was no longer swept of dirt and refuse.

And it seemed to him that even then he had seen thin, decently dressed old women and men huddled on the pavements, standing as a mute reproach to passers-by, silently offering to sell something that no one took and no one had need of: artificial flowers, round spirit lamps for boiling coffee, with glass lid and whistle, evening gowns of black gauze, the uniforms of abolished departments.

A public of a simpler sort traded in more essential things: the prickly, quickly stale crusts of rationed black bread; the dirty, wet ends of sugar-loaves; and two-ounce packets of shag tobacco cut in half through the wrapper.

And all over the market some sort of mysterious junk circulated, increasing in price as it passed through everyone's hands.

The cab turned into one of the lanes adjacent to the square. The sun was setting behind them and hit them in the back. In front of them rumbled a drayman on his bouncing, empty cart. He raised pillars of dust that burned like bronze in the rays of the setting sun.

They finally managed to get ahead of the drayman who was blocking their way. They drove faster. The doctor was struck by the piles of old newspapers and posters torn from the houses and fences scattered everywhere on the streets and pavements. The wind dragged them to one side, and the hooves, wheels, and feet of those driving and walking to the other.

Soon, after several intersections, his own house appeared at the corner of two lanes. The cab stopped.

Yuri Andreevich's breath was taken away and his heart began to beat loudly, when, getting down from the droshky, he went to the front door and rang. The bell had no effect. Yuri Andreevich rang again. When nothing came of this attempt either, he began, with increasing alarm, to ring again and again at short intervals. Only at the fourth time was there a rattle of the hook and the chain inside, and, along with the front door moving aside, he saw Antonina Alexandrovna holding it wide open. The unexpectedness left them both dumbfounded for the first moment, and they did not hear themselves cry out. But as Antonina Alexandrovna's arm holding the door wide open presented half of a wide-open embrace, this brought them out of their dumbfoundedness, and they threw themselves madly onto each other's necks. A moment later they both began talking at once, interrupting each other.

'First of all, is everyone well?'

'Yes, yes, don't worry. Everything's all right. I wrote foolish things to you. Forgive me. But we'll have to talk. Why didn't you send a telegram? Markel will carry your things. Ah, I understand, you got alarmed because it wasn't Egorovna who opened the door? Egorovna's in the country.'

'And you've lost weight. But so young and slender! I'll go and dismiss the cabby.'

'Egorovna went to get flour. The rest have been let go. Now there's only one new girl, you don't know her, Nyusha, to take care of Sashenka, and no one else. Everyone's been told you'd be coming, they're all impatient. Gordon, Dudorov, everyone.'

'How's Sashenka?'

'He's all right, thank God. He just woke up. If you hadn't just come from the road, we could go to him now.'

'Is papa home?'

'Didn't we write to you? He's at the district duma from morning till late

at night. As chairman. Yes, imagine. Did you pay the cabby? Markel!
Markel!'

They were standing with the wicker hamper and suitcase in the middle of
the pavement, blocking the way, and the passers-by, going around them,
looked them up and down and gaped for a long time at the departing cab
and the wide-open front door, waiting to see what would happen next.

Meanwhile Markel, in a waistcoat over a calico shirt, with his porter's
cap in his hand, came running from the gateway to his young masters,
shouting as he ran:

'Heavens above, can it be Yurochka? Well, of course! Here he is, our little
falcon! Yuri Andreevich, light of our lives, you haven't forgotten us who
pray for you, you've kindly come to visit your own fireside! And what do
you all want? Eh? What's there to see?' he snarled at the curious ones.
'Move on, my worthies. Bugging your eyes out!'

'Hello, Markel, let me embrace you. Do put your cap on, you funny man.
What's the good news? How are your wife and daughters?'

'They're doing all right. Growing apace. Thanks be for that. As for news
– while you've been about your mighty deeds there, you see, we haven't let
things slide either. We've got such pot-housing and bedlant going on, it
makes the devils sick, brother, can't figure out what's what! Streets not
swept, houses and roofs not repaired, bellies clean as in Lent, without
annexates and contributses.'[1]

'I'll complain about you to Yuri Andreevich, Markel. He's always like
this, Yurochka. I can't bear his stupid tone. And of course he's trying hard
for your sake, thinking to please you. But meanwhile he keeps his own
counsel. Enough, enough, Markel, don't justify yourself. You're a shady
person, Markel. It's time you got smart. Seems you don't live with grain
dealers.'

When Markel had taken the things to the entryway and slammed the
front door, he went on softly and confidingly:

'Antonina Alexandrovna's cross with me, I could hear just now. And
it's always like that. You, Markel, she says, are all black inside, same as
soot in the chimney. Now, she says, not just some little child, now maybe
even pugs or lapdogs are learning a bit of sense. There's no disputing that,
of course, only, Yurochka, maybe it's true, maybe it's not, but there's
knowing people saw a book, some Mason cometh, a hundred and forty
years it lay under a stone, and now such is my opinion, we've been sold,
Yurochka, sold for a penny, for a copper penny, for a whiff of tobacco.
Look, Antonina Alexandrovna won't let me say a word, see, she's waving
me away again.'

'What else can I do? Well, all right. Put the things down and, thank you, you can go, Markel. If need be, Yuri Andreevich will send for you again.'

2

'Alone at last, and good riddance. Trust him, go ahead. It's sheer clowning. With others he keeps playing the little fool, but in secret he's got his knife sharpened just in case. Though he hasn't decided for whom yet, poor orphan.'

'No, you're going too far! I think he's simply drunk, and so he plays the buffoon, that's all.'

'And tell me, when is he ever sober? Ah, to hell with him, really. My fear is that Sashenka may fall asleep again. If it weren't for that typhus on the railways . . . Do you have lice?'

'I don't think so. I travelled in comfort, like before the war. Though maybe I should wash a little? Slapdash, anyhow. And later more thoroughly. But where are you going? Why not through the drawing room? Do you go upstairs another way now?'

'Ah, yes! You don't know anything. Papa and I thought and thought, and gave part of the downstairs to the Agricultural Academy. Otherwise in winter we won't be able to heat it ourselves. And there's more than enough room upstairs as well. We offered it to them. So far they haven't accepted. They have all sorts of scientific rooms here, herbariums, seed collections. If only they don't attract rats. It's grain, after all. But so far they've kept the rooms neat. It's now known as living space. This way, this way. How slow-witted you are! Around by the back stairs. Understand? Follow me, I'll show you.'

'You did very well to give up the rooms. I worked in a hospital that was also stationed in a manor house. Endless suites, parquet intact in some places. Palm trees in tubs spread their fingers over the cots at night like phantoms. Seasoned soldiers, wounded in battle, would get frightened and cry out on waking up. Not quite normal ones, though – shell-shocked. The palm trees had to be taken away. I mean to say that there was, in fact, something unhealthy in the life of well-to-do people. No end of superfluity. Superfluous furniture and superfluous rooms in the houses, superfluous refinement of feelings, superfluous expressions. You did very well to make room. But it's not enough. We must do more.'

'What have you got sticking out of that package? A bird's beak, a duck's head. How beautiful! A wild drake! Where did you get it? I can't believe my eyes! These days it's a whole fortune!'

'It was given to me on the train. A long story, I'll tell you later. What's your advice, shall I unwrap it and leave it in the kitchen?'

'Yes, of course. I'll send Nyusha now to pluck it and gut it. There are predictions of all sorts of horrors towards winter – hunger, cold.'

'Yes, there's talk about it everywhere. Just now I was looking out of the window of the train and thinking. What can be higher than peace in the family and work? The rest isn't in our power. It's apparently true that there are misfortunes in store for many people. Some think of saving themselves in the south, in the Caucasus, of trying to get somewhere further away. That's not in my rule book. A grown-up man must grit his teeth and share the fate of his native land. In my opinion, that's obvious. You are a different matter. How I'd like to protect you from calamities, to send you to some safer place, to Finland or somewhere. But if we stand for half an hour on each step like this, we'll never get upstairs.'

'Wait. Listen. There's news. And what news! I forgot. Nikolai Nikolaevich has come.'

'What Nikolai Nikolaevich?'

'Uncle Kolya.'

'Tonya! It can't be! How on earth?'

'Well, so it is. From Switzerland. In a roundabout way by London. Through Finland.'

'Tonya! You're not joking? Have you seen him? Where is he? Can't we get him here at once, this minute?'

'Such impatience! He's outside the city in someone's dacha. Promised to come back the day after tomorrow. He's very changed, you'll be disappointed. Got stuck and Bolshevised passing through Petersburg. Papa argues with him till he's hoarse. But why, indeed, do we stop at every step? Come on. So you've also heard that there's nothing good coming, only difficulties, dangers, uncertainty?'

'I think so myself. Well, what then. We'll fight. It's not necessarily the end for everybody. Let's see how others do.'

'They say we'll be without firewood, without water, without light. Money will be abolished. There will be no supplies. And again we've stopped. Come on. Listen. They praise the flat cast-iron stoves from a workshop on the Arbat. You can cook supper on a fire of newspapers. I've got the address. We should buy one before they're all snapped up.'

'Right. Let's buy one. Smart girl, Tonya! But Uncle Kolya, Uncle Kolya! Just think! I can't get over it!'

'Here is my plan. We'll choose some out-of-the-way corner upstairs and live there with papa, Sashenka, and Nyusha, say in two or three rooms, connecting, of course, somewhere at the end of the floor, and give up the rest of the house completely. Close ourselves in, as if from the street. We'll put one of those cast-iron stoves in the middle room, with a pipe through the window. The laundry, the cooking, dinners, receiving guests, will all be done there, to justify the heating, and, who knows, maybe, God willing, we'll survive the winter.'

'What else? Of course we'll survive. Beyond any doubt. You've thought it out excellently. Good girl. And you know what? Let's celebrate our acceptance of your plan. We'll roast my duck and invite Uncle Kolya to the housewarming.'

'Splendid. And I'll ask Gordon to bring some alcohol. He gets it from some laboratory. And now look. Here's the room I was talking about. Here's what I've chosen. Do you approve? Put the suitcase down and go back for the wicker hamper. Besides uncle and Gordon, we can also invite Innokenty and Shura Schlesinger. You don't object? You haven't forgotten where our bathroom is? Spray yourself with something disinfecting. And I'll go to Sashenka, send Nyusha downstairs, and when I can, I'll call you.'

3

The main news for him in Moscow was this boy. Sashenka had only just been born when Yuri Andreevich was called up. What did he know about his son?

Once, when he was already mobilised, Yuri Andreevich came to the clinic to visit Tonya before his departure. He came at the moment when the babies were being fed. They would not let him see her.

He sat down to wait in the anteroom. Just then the far-off children's corridor, which went at right angles to the delivery corridor, and along which the mothers' rooms were located, was filled with a weeping chorus of ten or fifteen infant voices, and the nurses, so as not to expose the swaddled newborn babies to the cold, hurriedly began carrying them under their arms, two at a time, like big shopping parcels, to their mothers to be fed.

'Wah, wah,' the babies squealed on one note, almost without feeling, as if performing a duty, and only one voice stood out from this unison. The infant also cried 'wah, wah', and also without a trace of suffering, but, as it seemed, not by obligation, but with some sort of bass-voiced, deliberate, sullen hostility.

Yuri Andreevich had already decided then to call his son Alexander, in honour of his father-in-law. For no apparent reason he imagined that it was his boy who was crying like that, because it was a weeping with a physiognomy, already containing the future character and destiny of the person, a weeping with a tone colour that included in itself the name of the boy, the name Alexander, as Yuri Andreevich imagined.

Yuri Andreevich was not mistaken. As it turned out later, that had indeed been Sashenka crying. That was the first thing he knew about his son.

His next acquaintance with him Yuri Andreevich drew from photographs, in letters sent to him at the front. In them a merry, chubby, pretty boy with a big head and pursed lips stood bow-legged on a spread-out blanket and, raising both arms, seemed to be doing a squatting dance. He was one year old then, he was learning to walk; now he was almost two and was beginning to talk.

Yuri Andreevich picked the suitcase up from the floor, undid the straps, and laid it on a card table by the window. What room was this before? The doctor did not recognise it. Tonya must have taken the furniture out or hung some new wallpaper in it.

The doctor opened the suitcase in order to take out his shaving kit. A bright full moon appeared between the columns of the church bell tower that rose up just opposite the window. When its light fell into the suitcase on the linen, books, and toilet articles lying on top, the room lit up somehow differently, and the doctor recognised it.

It was a vacated storeroom of the late Anna Ivanovna. In former times, she used to pile broken tables and chairs and unnecessary old waste paper in it. Here was her family archive; here, too, were the trunks in which winter things were put away for the summer. When the late woman was alive, every corner of the room was heaped up to the ceiling, and ordinarily no one was allowed into it. But for big holidays, on days of crowded children's gatherings, when they were allowed to horse around and run all over the upper floor, this room, too, was unlocked, and they played robbers in it, hid under the tables, painted their faces with burnt cork, and dressed up in costumes.

For some time the doctor stood recalling all this, and then he went down to the entryway for the wicker hamper he had left there.

Downstairs in the kitchen, Nyusha, a timid and bashful girl, squatting down, was plucking the duck over a spread-out newspaper in front of the stove. At the sight of Yuri Andreevich with a heavy thing in his hands, she turned bright red, straightened up in a supple movement, shaking off the feathers stuck to her apron, and, having greeted him, offered her help. But the doctor thanked her and said he would carry the hamper himself.

He had just entered Anna Ivanovna's former storeroom, when, from two or three rooms away, his wife called to him:

'You can come, Yura!'

He went to Sashenka.

The present nursery was situated in his and Tonya's former schoolroom. The boy in the little bed turned out to be not at all as pretty as the photos portrayed him, but on the other hand he was the very image of Yuri Andreevich's mother, the late Marya Nikolaevna Zhivago, a striking copy of her, resembling her more than any of the surviving portraits.

'This is papa, this is your papa, wave to papa,' Antonina Alexandrovna kept saying, as she lowered the side of the bed so that the father could more easily embrace the boy and pick him up.

Sashenka allowed the unfamiliar and unshaven man, who probably frightened and repelled him, to come close, and when he bent down, abruptly stood up, clutched his mother's blouse, swung and angrily slapped him in the face. His own boldness so terrified Sashenka that he immediately threw himself onto his mother's breast, buried his face in her dress, and burst into bitter, inconsolable child's tears.

'Pooh, pooh,' Antonina Alexandrovna chided him. 'You mustn't do that, Sashenka. Papa will think Sasha bad, Sasha no-no. Show papa how you kiss. Kiss him. Don't cry, you mustn't cry, what is it, silly?'

'Leave him alone, Tonya,' the doctor asked. 'Don't torment him, and don't be upset yourself. I know what kind of foolishness gets into your head. That it's not by chance, that it's a bad sign. It's all such nonsense. And so natural. The boy's never seen me. Tomorrow he'll get used to me, there'll be no tearing him away from me.'

But he himself left the room quite downcast, with a sense of foreboding.

4

In the course of the next few days it became clear how alone he was. He did not blame anyone for that. Evidently he himself had wanted it and achieved it.

His friends had become strangely dull and colourless. None of them had held on to his own world, his own opinion. They were much brighter in his memories. Apparently he had overestimated them earlier.

As long as the order of things had allowed the well-to-do to be whimsical and eccentric at the expense of the deprived, how easy it had been to mistake for a real face and originality that whimsicality and the right to idleness which the minority enjoyed while the majority suffered!

But as soon as the lower strata arose and the privileges of the upper strata were abolished, how quickly everyone faded, how unregretfully they parted with independent thinking, which none of them, evidently, had ever had!

Now the only people who were close to Yuri Andreevich were those without phrases and pathos – his wife and father-in-law, and two or three fellow doctors, humble toilers, ordinary workmen.

The evening with the duck and the alcohol had taken place in its time, as planned, on the second or third day after his arrival, once he had had time to see everyone invited, so that it was not their first meeting.

The fat duck was an unheard-of luxury in those already hungry times, but there was no bread to go with it, and that made the magnificence of the food pointless, so that it was even irritating.

Gordon brought the alcohol in a pharmaceutical bottle with a ground-glass stopper. Alcohol was a favourite medium of exchange for black marketeers. Antonina Alexandrovna did not let the bottle out of her hands and diluted the alcohol in small quantities, as it was needed, by inspiration, making it now too strong, now too weak. It turned out that an uneven drunkenness from changing concentrations was much worse than from a strong but consistent one. That, too, was annoying.

The saddest thing of all was that their party represented a deviation from the conditions of the time. It was impossible to imagine that in the houses across the lane people were eating and drinking in the same way at such an hour. Beyond the window lay mute, dark, hungry Moscow. Her food stores were empty, and people had even forgotten to think of such things as game and vodka.

And thus it turned out that the only true life is one that resembles the life around us and drowns in it without leaving a trace, that isolated happiness is not happiness, so that a duck and alcohol, when they seem to be the only ones in town, are even not alcohol and a duck at all. That was the most distressing thing.

The guests also brought on joyless reflections. Gordon had been fine as long as he had thought heavily and explained things morosely and incoherently. He had been Yuri Andreevich's best friend. He had been liked in high school.

But now he had come to dislike himself and had begun to introduce unfortunate corrections in his moral image. He bucked himself up, played the merry fellow, told stories all the time with a pretence to wit, and often said 'How entertaining' and 'How amusing' – words not in his vocabulary, because Gordon had never understood life as a diversion.

Before Dudorov's arrival he told a funny – as it seemed to him – story about Dudorov's marriage, which circulated among friends. Yuri Andreevich did not know it.

It turned out that Dudorov had been married for about a year, and then separated from his wife. The unlikely salt of the adventure consisted in the following.

Dudorov had been drafted into the army by mistake. While he served and waited for the misunderstanding to be clarified, he was most often on punishment duty for gawkishness and for not saluting officers in the street. Long after he was discharged, his arm would jerk up at the sight of an officer, and he went around as if dazzled, seeing epaulettes everywhere.

In that period, he did everything out of place, committed various blunders and false steps. Precisely at that time he supposedly made the acquaintance, on a Volga landing, of two girls, sisters, who were waiting for the same boat, and, as if absent-mindedly, owing to the multitude of officers flashing about, with vestiges of his soldierly saluting still alive, not watching himself, he fell in love by oversight and hastily made the younger sister a proposal. 'Amusing, isn't it?' asked Gordon. But he had to cut short his description. The voice of the story's hero was heard outside the door. Dudorov came into the room.

With him the opposite change had taken place. The former unstable and extravagant featherbrain had turned into a concentrated scholar.

When he was expelled from school in his youth for participating in the preparation of a political escape, he spent some time wandering through various art schools, but in the end washed up on the classical shore. Dudorov finished university later than his peers, during wartime, and was kept on in two departments, Russian and general history. For the first he was writing something about the land policy of Ivan the Terrible, for the second some research about Saint-Just.[2]

He now reasoned about everything amiably, in a low voice, as if he had a cold, staring dreamily at one spot, and not raising or lowering his eyes, as one reads a lecture.

By the end of the evening, when Shura Schlesinger burst in with her attacks, and everyone, heated up enough without that, was shouting simultaneously, Innokenty, whom Yuri Andreevich had addressed formally since their schooldays, asked him several times:

'Have you read *War and Peace* and *The Backbone Flute*?'[3]

Yuri Andreevich had long since told him what he thought on the subject, but Dudorov had not heard him because of the rousing general argument, and therefore, a little later, he asked once more:

'Have you read *The Backbone Flute* and *Man*?'

'But I answered you, Innokenty. It's your fault if you didn't hear me. Well, have it your way. I'll say it again. I've always liked Mayakovsky. It's some sort of continuation of Dostoevsky. Or, more rightly, it's lyric verse written by one of his young, rebellious characters, like Ippolit, Raskolnikov, or the hero of *The Adolescent*.[4] Such all-devouring force of talent! How it's said once and for all, implacably and straight out! And above all, with what bold sweep it's all flung in the face of society and somewhere further out into space!'

But the big hit of the evening was certainly the uncle. Antonina Alexandrovna was mistaken in saying that Nikolai Nikolaevich was at a dacha. He came back on the day of his nephew's arrival and was in town. Yuri Andreevich had already seen him two or three times and had managed to talk a lot with him, to laugh a lot, to 'oh' and 'ah' a lot.

Their first meeting took place in the evening of a grey, overcast day. Light rain drizzled down in a fine watery dust. Yuri Andreevich came to Nikolai Nikolaevich's hotel room. Hotels were already accepting people only at the insistence of the city authorities. But Nikolai Nikolaevich was known everywhere. He still had his old connections.

The hotel gave the impression of a madhouse abandoned by its fleeing administration. Emptiness, chaos, the rule of chance on the stairways and corridors.

Into the big window of the untidied room gazed the vast, peopleless square of those mad days, somehow frightening, as if it had been dreamed of in sleep at night, and was not in fact lying before their eyes under the hotel window.

It was an astounding, unforgettable, portentous meeting! The idol of his childhood, the ruler of his youthful thoughts, stood before him again, alive, in the flesh.

Grey hair was very becoming to Nikolai Nikolaevich. His loose foreign suit fitted him well. He was still very young for his age and handsome to look at.

Of course, he lost much next to the enormity of what was going on. Events overshadowed him. But it had never occurred to Yuri Andreevich to measure him with such a measure.

He was surprised by Nikolai Nikolaevich's calmness, by the cool, bantering tone in which he talked on political themes. His social bearing exceeded Russian possibilities of the day. This feature bespoke a newcomer. It struck the eye, seemed old-fashioned, and caused a certain awkwardness.

Ah, it was not at all that, not that which filled the first hours of their meeting, made them throw themselves into each other's arms, weep, and, breathless with excitement, interrupt the rush and fervour of their initial conversation with frequent pauses.

This was a meeting of two creative characters, bound by family ties, and, though the past arose and began to live a second life, memories came in a flood, and circumstances surfaced that had occurred during their time of separation; still, as soon as the talk turned to what was most important, to things known to people of a creative cast, all ties disappeared except that single one, there was neither uncle nor nephew, nor any difference in age, and there remained only the closeness of element to element, energy to energy, principle to principle.

Over the last decade, Nikolai Nikolaevich had had no occasion to speak of the fascination of authorship and the essence of the creative vocation in such conformity with his own thoughts and so deservedly apropos as now. On the other hand, Yuri Andreevich had never happened to hear opinions that were so perceptively apt and so inspiringly captivating as this analysis.

The two men constantly exclaimed and rushed about the room, clutching their heads from the faultlessness of each other's conjectures, or went to the window and silently drummed on the glass with their fingers, amazed at the proofs of mutual understanding.

So it was at their first meeting, but later the doctor saw Nikolai Nikolaevich several times in company, and among people he was different, unrecognisable.

He was aware of being a visitor in Moscow and had no wish to part with that awareness. Whether he considered Petersburg or some other place his home remained unclear. He was flattered by the role of political fine talker and society charmer. He may have imagined that political salons would be opened in Moscow as in Paris at Mme Roland's before the Convention.[5]

He called on his lady friends, hospitable dwellers in quiet Moscow lanes, and most sweetly mocked them and their husbands for their halfway thinking and backwardness, for the habit of judging everything by their own parochial standards. And he now flaunted his newspaper erudition, just as he once had with the Apocrypha and Orphic texts.

It was said that he had left a new young passion behind in Switzerland, half-finished business, a half-written book, and that he would merely dip himself into the stormy whirlpool of the fatherland, and then, if he came up unharmed, would flit off to his Alps again and be seen no more.

He was for the Bolsheviks and often mentioned two left SR names[6] as being of one mind with him: the journalist writing under the pseudonym of Miroshka Pomor, and the essayist Sylvia Coterie.

Alexander Alexandrovich grumblingly reproached him:

'It's simply dreadful how low you've sunk, Nikolai Nikolaevich! These Miroshkas of yours. What a pit! And then you've got this Lydia Could-be.'

'Coterie,' Nikolai Nikolaevich corrected. 'And it's Sylvia.'

'Well, it's all the same. Could-be or Potpourri, we won't stick at words.'

'Sorry, but all the same it's Coterie,' Nikolai Nikolaevich patiently insisted. He and Alexander Alexandrovich exchanged such speeches as:

'What are we arguing about? It's simply a shame to have to demonstrate such truths. It's like ABC. The main mass of people have led an unthinkable existence for centuries. Take any history book. Whatever it's called, feudalism, or serfdom, or capitalism and factory industry, the unnaturalness and injustice of such an order have long been noted, and the revolution has long been prepared that will lead the people towards the light and put everything in its place.

'You know that a partial renovation of the old is unsuitable here, what's needed is to break it radically. Maybe that will cause the building to collapse. Well, what of it? Just because it's frightening, it doesn't mean that it won't happen. It's a question of time. How can you argue against that?'

'Eh, that's not the point. I'm not talking about that, am I?' Alexander Alexandrovich would get angry and the argument would flare up.

'Your Potpourris and Miroshkas are people without conscience. They say one thing and do another. And then, too, where's the logic here? There's no coherence. No, wait, I'll show you right now.'

And he would start looking for some magazine with a contrary article, pulling open his desk drawers and slamming them shut, and rousing his eloquence with this noisy fussing about.

Alexander Alexandrovich liked to be hampered by something when he talked, so that the impediment would justify his mumbling pauses, his hems and haws. Loquaciousness would come over him while he was searching for something he had lost, for instance, when he was looking for his second galosh in the semi-darkness of the front hall, or when he was standing on the bathroom threshold with a towel over his shoulder, or as he was passing a heavy platter across the table, or while he was pouring glasses of wine for his guests.

Yuri Andreevich listened to his father-in-law with delight. He adored the old Moscow singsong speech he knew so well, with the Gromekos' soft, slightly guttural *r*s, like a cat's purring.

Alexander Alexandrovich's upper lip with its trim little moustache protruded slightly over the lower one. The bow tie stood out on his chest in the same way. There was something in common between the lip and the tie, and it lent Alexander Alexandrovich a certain touching, trustfully childish quality.

Late at night, just before the guests' departure, Shura Schlesinger appeared. She came straight from some meeting, in a jacket and worker's visored cap, walked into the room with resolute strides, shook everyone's hand in turn, and in the same motion abandoned herself to reproaches and accusations.

'Hello, Tonya. Hello, Sanechka. Anyhow it's swinishness, you must agree. I hear from everywhere, he's here, the whole of Moscow is talking about it, and I'm the last to learn it from you. Well, to hell with you. Obviously, I don't deserve it. Where is he, the long-awaited one? Let me through. You're standing around him like a wall. Well, hello! Good for you, good for you. I've read it. I don't understand a thing, but it's brilliant. You can see it straight off. Hello, Nikolai Nikolaevich. I'll come back to you at once, Yurochka. I must have a big, special talk with you. Hello, young people. Ah, Gogochka, you're here, too? Goosey Goosey Gander, whither do you wander?'

The last exclamation referred to the Gromekos' distant relation Gogochka, a zealous admirer of all the rising powers, who for being silly and laughter-prone was known as Goosey, and for being tall and skinny – the Tapeworm.

'So you're all eating and drinking here? I'll catch up with you right away. Ah, ladies and gentlemen! You know nothing, you suspect nothing! What's going on in the world! Such things are happening! Go to some real local meeting with non-fictional workers, with non-fictional soldiers, not out of books. Try to make a peep there about war to a victorious conclusion. You'll get your victorious conclusion![7] I was just listening to a sailor! Yurochka, you'd go out of your mind! Such passion! Such integrity!'

Shura Schlesinger was interrupted. They all shouted with no rhyme or reason. She sat down beside Yuri Andreevich, took him by the hand, and, bringing her face close to his, so as to outshout the others, shouted without raising or lowering her voice, as through a speaking trumpet:

'Come with me some day, Yurochka. I'll show you the people. You must, you must touch the earth, remember, like Antaeus. Why are you goggling your eyes? It seems I surprise you? I'm an old warhorse, an old Bestuzhevist,[8] didn't you know, Yurochka? I've known preliminary detention, I've fought at the barricades. Of course! What did you think? Oh, we don't know the people! I've come straight from there, from the thick of them. I'm setting up a library for them.'

She had already taken a drop and was obviously getting tipsy. But Yuri

Andreevich also had a clamour in his head. He did not notice how Shura Schlesinger turned up at one end of the room and he at the other, at the head of the table. He was standing and, by all tokens, beyond his own expectations, speaking. He did not obtain silence all at once.

'Ladies and gentlemen . . . I want . . . Misha! Gogochka! . . . But what else can I do, Tonya, when they don't listen? Ladies and gentlemen, allow me to say a couple of words. Something unheard-of, something unprecedented is approaching. Before it overtakes us, here is my wish for you. When it comes, God grant that we do not lose each other and do not lose our souls. Gogochka, you can shout hurrah afterwards. I haven't finished. Stop talking in the corners and listen carefully.

'By the third year of the war a conviction has been formed in the people that sooner or later the boundary between the front and the rear will be effaced, the sea of blood will come to everyone and flood those who sat it out and entrenched themselves. That flood is the revolution.

'In the course of it, it might seem to you, as to us at the war, that life has ceased, everything personal is over, nothing happens in the world any more except killing and dying, and if we survive till there are notes and memoirs of this time, and we read those recollections, we will realise that in these five or ten years we have lived through more than some do in a whole century.

'I don't know if the people themselves will rise and move like a wall, or if everything will be done in their name. An event of such enormity does not call for dramatic proofs. I'll believe it without that. It's petty to rummage around for the causes of cyclopean events. They don't have any. Domestic squabbles have their genesis, and after so much pulling each other's hair and smashing of dishes, no one can figure out who first began it. But everything truly great is without beginning, like the universe. It does not emerge, but is suddenly there, as if it always existed or fell from the sky.

'I also think that Russia is destined to become the first realm of socialism since the existence of the world. When that happens, it will stun us for a long time, and, coming to our senses, we will no longer get back the memory we have lost. We will forget part of the past and will not seek explanations for the unprecedented. The new order will stand around us, with the accustomedness of the forest on the horizon or the clouds over our heads. It will surround us everywhere. There will be nothing else.'

He said something more and by then had sobered up completely. But, as before, he did not hear very well what was being said around him, and his answers were beside the point. He saw manifestations of general love for him, but was unable to drive away the sorrow that made him not himself. And so he said:

'Thank you, thank you. I see your feelings. I don't deserve them. But you shouldn't love so sparingly and hurriedly, as if fearing you'll have to love more strongly later.'

They all laughed and applauded, taking it for a deliberate witticism, while he did not know where to escape from the sense of impending misfortune, from the awareness of his powerlessness over the future, despite all his thirst for the good and capacity for happiness.

The guests were leaving. They all had long faces from fatigue. Yawning opened and closed their jaws, making them look like horses.

As they were saying goodbye, they drew the window curtain aside. Threw open the window. A yellowish dawn appeared, a wet sky covered with dirty, sallow clouds.

'There must have been a thunderstorm while we were blathering,' somebody said.

'I got caught in the rain on my way here. Barely made it,' confirmed Shura Schlesinger.

In the deserted and still-dark lane they could hear the sound of drops dripping from the trees, alternating with the insistent chirping of drenched sparrows.

There was a roll of thunder, like a plough drawing a furrow across the whole of the sky, and everything grew still. But then four resounding, belated booms rang out, like big potatoes dumped from a shovelful of loose soil in autumn.

The thunder cleared the space inside the dusty, smoke-filled room. Suddenly, like electrical elements, the component parts of existence became tangible – water and air, the desire for joy, earth, and sky.

The lane became filled with the voices of the departing guests. They went on loudly discussing something outside, exactly as they had just been wrangling about it in the house. The voices moved off, gradually dying down and dying out.

'So late,' said Yuri Andreevich. 'Let's go to bed. Of all the people in the world, I love only you and papa.'

5

August passed, September was coming to an end. The unavoidable was imminent. Winter was drawing near, and so, in the human world, was the foreordained, like winter's swoon, which hung in the air and was on everyone's lips.

They had to prepare for the cold, stock up on food, firewood. But in the days of the triumph of materialism, matter turned into a concept, food and firewood were replaced by the provision and fuel question.

People in the cities were helpless as children in the face of the approaching unknown, which overturned all established habits in its way and left devastation behind it, though it was itself a child of the city and the creation of city dwellers.

All around there was self-deception, empty verbiage. Humdrum life still limped, floundered, hobbled bow-legged somewhere out of old habit. But the doctor saw life unvarnished. Its condemnation could not be concealed from him. He considered himself and his milieu doomed. They faced ordeals, perhaps even death. The numbered days they had left melted away before his eyes.

He would have gone out of his mind, if it had not been for everyday trifles, labours, and cares. His wife, his child, the need to earn money, were his salvation – the essential, the humble, the daily round, going to work, visiting patients.

He realised that he was a pygmy before the monstrous hulk of the future; he feared it, he loved this future and was secretly proud of it, and for the last time, as if in farewell, with the greedy eyes of inspiration, he gazed at the clouds and trees, at the people walking down the street, at the big Russian city trying to weather misfortune, and was ready to sacrifice himself to make things better, and could do nothing.

The sky and the passers-by he most often saw from the middle of the street, when crossing the Arbat by the pharmacy of the Russian Medical Society, at the corner of Starokoniushenny Lane.

He went back to work at his old hospital. By old memory it was still called Krestovozdvizhensky, though the community of that name had been disbanded. But they had not yet invented a new name for it at the hospital.

Differentiations had already begun there. To the moderates, whose dull-wittedness provoked the doctor's indignation, he seemed dangerous; to politically advanced people, he seemed insufficiently red. Thus he found himself neither here nor there, having left one bank and not reached the other.

In the hospital, besides his immediate duties, the director charged him with looking after the general statistical accounting. How many forms, questionnaires, and blanks he had to go over, how many orders he had to fill out! Mortality rates, sick rates, the property status of the employees, the level of their civic consciousness and participation in elections, the unsatisfiable needs for fuel, provisions, medications – the central office of statistics was interested in all of it, and answers had to be provided for it all.

The doctor busied himself with all this at his old desk by the window of the interns' room. Stacks of ruled paper of various forms and patterns lay before him, pushed to one side. Sometimes by snatches, besides periodic notes for his medical work, he wrote here his *Playing at People,* a gloomy diary or journal of those days, consisting of prose, verse, and miscellanea, suggested by the awareness that half of the people had stopped being themselves and were acting out who knows what.

The bright, sunny interns' room with its white-painted walls was flooded with the cream-coloured sunlight of golden autumn, which distinguishes the days following the Dormition,[9] when the first morning frosts set in, and winter chickadees and magpies flit among the motley and bright colours of the thinning woods. On such days the sky rises to its utmost height and a dark blue, icy clarity breathes from the north through the transparent column of air between it and the earth. The visibility and audibility of everything in the world are enhanced. Distances transmit sounds in a frozen ringing, distinctly and separately. What is far away becomes clear, as if opening out a view through all of life for many years ahead. This rarefaction would be impossible to bear if it were not so short-termed and did not come at the end of a short autumn day on the threshold of early twilight.

Such light bathed the interns' room, the light of the early-setting autumn sun, juicy, glassy, and watery, like a ripe golden apple.

The doctor sat at the desk, dipping his pen in the ink, pondering and writing, and some quiet birds flew close by the big windows, casting soundless shadows into the room, over the doctor's moving hands, the table with its ruled paper, the floor and walls, and just as soundlessly disappeared.

'The maple's losing its leaves,' said the prosector, coming in. Once a stout man, his skin had become baggy from loss of weight. 'The rain poured down on it, the wind tore at it, and they couldn't defeat it. But see what one morning frost has done!'

The doctor raised his head. Indeed, the mysterious birds flitting past the window turned out to be the wine and flame leaves of the maple, which flew off, floated smoothly through the air, and, like convex orange stars, settled away from the tree on the grass of the hospital lawn.

'Have you sealed the windows?' asked the prosector.

'No,' said Yuri Andreevich, and he went on writing.

'Why not? It's time.'

Yuri Andreevich did not reply, absorbed in writing.

'Eh, no Tarasiuk,' the prosector went on. 'He was solid gold. Could mend boots. And watches. And do everything. And supply anything in the world. It's time to seal them. Have to do it yourself.'

'There's no putty.'

'Make some. Here's the recipe.' And the prosector explained how to pre-pare putty from linseed oil and chalk. 'Well, forget it. I'm bothering you.'

He went to the other window and busied himself with his vials and preparations. It was getting dark. After a minute, he said:

'You'll ruin your eyes. It's dark. And they won't give us any light. Let's go home.'

'I'll work a little longer. Twenty minutes or so.'

'His wife's here as a nurse's aide.'

'Whose?'

'Tarasiuk's.'

'I know.'

'But where he is, nobody knows. He roams the wide earth. Came to visit a couple of times in the summer. Stopped by the hospital. Now he's somewhere in the country. Founding the new life. He's one of those Bol-shevik soldiers you meet on the boulevards and on trains. And do you want to know the answer? To Tarasiuk's riddle, for instance? Listen. He's a jack-of-all-trades. Can't do a bad piece of work. Whatever he turns his hand to goes without a hitch. The same thing happened to him in the war. He studied it like any other trade. Turned out to be a crack shot. In the trenches, at a listening post. His eye, his hand – first class! He got all his decorations, not for bravery, but for never missing. Well. Every job becomes a passion for him. He fell in love with military things. He sees that a weapon is power, that he can use it. He wanted to become power himself. An armed man is no longer simply a man. In the old days his kind went from the sharpshooters to the robbers. Try taking his rifle from him now. And suddenly there comes the call: "Bayonets, about face!" and so on. And he about-faced. That's the whole story for you. And the whole of Marxism.'

'And the most genuine besides, straight from life. What do you think?'

The prosector stepped over to his window, pottered a little with his vials. Then asked:

'Well, how's the stove man?'

'Thanks for recommending him. A very interesting man. We spent around an hour talking about Hegel and Benedetto Croce.'[10]

'Well, what else! He has a doctorate in philosophy from Heidelberg Uni-versity. And the stove?'

'Don't talk about it.'

'Smokes?'

'Nothing but trouble.'

'He installed the pipe wrong. He should have built it into the Dutch stove, but he probably stuck it through the vent window.'

'No, he set it into the stove. But it smokes.'

'That means he didn't find the smokestack and put it through the ventilation duct. Or into the airway. Eh, no Tarasiuk! But be patient. Moscow wasn't built in a day. Using a stove isn't like playing the piano. It takes learning. Laid in firewood?'

'Where can I get it?'

'I'll send you the churchwarden. He's a firewood thief. Takes fences apart for fuel. But I warn you. You've got to haggle. He asks a lot. Or there's the exterminator woman.'

They went down to the porter's lodge, put their coats on, went out.

'Why the exterminator?' asked the doctor. 'We don't have bedbugs.'

'What have bedbugs got to do with it? I'm talking apples and you're talking oranges. Not bedbugs, but firewood. The woman's set it all up on a commercial footing. Buys up houses and framing for firewood. A serious supplier. Watch out, don't stumble, it's really dark. Once I could have gone through this neighbourhood blindfolded. I knew every little stone. I was born in Prechistenka. But they started taking down the fences, and even with open eyes I don't recognise anything, like in a foreign city. What little corners they've uncovered, though! Little Empire houses in the bushes, round garden tables, half-rotten benches. The other day I walked past a little vacant plot like that, at the intersection of three lanes. I see a hundred-year-old woman poking the ground with her stick. "God help you, granny," I say. "Digging worms for fishing?" As a joke, of course. And she says very seriously: "No, dearie – champignons." And it's true, the city's getting to be the same as a forest. Smells of rotten leaves, mushrooms.'

'I know that place. It's between Serebryany and Molchanovka, isn't it? Unexpected things keep happening to me when I pass it. Either I meet somebody I haven't seen for twenty years, or I find something. And they say there have been robberies at the corner. Well, no wonder. It's a crossroads. There's a whole network of passages to thieves' dens that are still there around the Smolensky market. You're robbed, stripped, and, poof, go and chase the wind.'

'And the street lights shine so weakly. It's not for nothing they call a black eye a shiner. You're bound to get one.'

6

Indeed, all sorts of chance things happened to the doctor at the above-mentioned place. Late in the autumn, not long before the October fighting,[11] on a dark, cold evening, at that corner, he ran into a man lying unconscious across the pavement. The man lay with his arms spread, his head leaning on a hitching post, and his legs hanging into the roadway. Every now and then he moaned weakly. In response to the loud questions of the doctor, who was trying to bring him back to consciousness, he murmured something incoherent and again passed out for a time. His head was bruised and bloody, but on cursory examination, the bones of the skull turned out to be intact. The fallen man was undoubtedly the victim of an armed robbery. 'Briefcase. Briefcase,' he whispered two or three times.

Using the telephone of a pharmacy nearby on the Arbat, the doctor sent for an old cabby attached to the Krestovozdvizhensky Hospital and took the unknown man there.

The victim turned out to be a prominent politician. The doctor treated him and in his person acquired a protector for long years to come, who saved him in that time filled with suspicion and distrust from many misunderstandings.

7

It was Sunday. The doctor was free. He did not have to go to work. In their house in Sivtsev, they had already settled in three rooms for the winter, as Antonina Alexandrovna had proposed.

It was a cold, windy day with low snow clouds, dark, very dark.

They lit the stove in the morning. It began to smoke. Antonina Alexandrovna, who knew nothing about stoves, gave confused and harmful advice to Nyusha, who was struggling with the damp wood that refused to burn. The doctor, seeing it and understanding what needed to be done, tried to intervene, but his wife gently took him by the shoulders and sent him away with the words:

'Go to your room. You have a habit of butting in with your advice, when my head's in a whirl without that and everything's jumbled up. How can you not understand that your remarks only pour oil on the fire.'

'Oh, Tonechka, that would be excellent – oil! The stove would blaze up in an instant. The trouble is that I don't see either oil or fire.'

'This is no time for puns. There are moments, you understand, when they simply won't do.'

The failure with the stove ruined their Sunday plans. They had all hoped to finish the necessary tasks before dark and be free by evening, but now that was out of the question. Dinner had to be put off, as did someone's wish to wash their hair with hot water, and other such intentions.

Soon it became so smoky that it was impossible to breathe. A strong wind blew the smoke back into the room. A cloud of black soot hung in it like a fairy-tale monster in the midst of a dense pine forest.

Yuri Andreevich drove them all to the other rooms and opened the vent window. He took half the wood out of the stove and made space among the rest for little chips and birch-bark kindling.

Fresh air burst through the vent window. The curtain swayed and billowed up. A few papers flew off the desk. The wind slammed some far-off door and, whirling in all the corners, began, like a cat after a mouse, to chase what was left of the smoke.

The wood caught fire, blazed up, and began to crackle. The little stove choked on the flames. Red-hot circles glowed on its iron body like the rosy spots on a consumptive's cheeks. The smoke in the room thinned out and then disappeared altogether.

The room became brighter. The windows, which Yuri Andreevich had recently sealed on the prosector's instructions, began to weep. The putty gave off a wave of warm, greasy smell. The firewood sawed into small pieces and drying around the stove also gave off a smell: of bitter, throat-chafing, tarry fir bark, and damp, fresh aspen, fragrant as toilet water.

Just then, as impetuously as the wind through the vent, Nikolai Nikolaevich burst into the room with news:

'There's fighting in the streets. Military action is going on between the junkers who support the Provisional Government and the garrison soldiers who are for the Bolsheviks. There are skirmishes at almost every step, there's no counting the centres of the uprising. I fell into scraps two or three times on my way here, once at the corner of Bolshaya Dmitrovka, and again by the Nikitsky Gate. There's no direct route any more, you have to go roundabout. Hurry, Yura! Get dressed and let's go. You've got to see this. It's history. It happens once in a lifetime.'

But he himself went on babbling for about two hours, then they sat down to dinner, and when he got ready to go home and was dragging Yuri Andreevich with him, Gordon's arrival prevented them. He came flying in just as Nikolai Nikolaevich had done, with the same news.

But meanwhile events had moved ahead. There were new details. Gordon spoke about the intensified gunfire and the killing of passers-by, accidentally struck by stray bullets. According to his words, traffic in the city had come to a standstill. By a miracle, he had got through to their lane, but the way back had closed behind him.

Nikolai Nikolaevich would not listen and tried to poke his nose outside, but came back after a minute. He said you could not go out into the lane, that there were bullets whistling through it, knocking bits of brick and plaster off the corners. There was not a soul in the streets; communication by the pavements was broken.

During those days Sashenka caught a cold.

'I've told you a hundred times not to put the child near the hot stove,' Yuri Andreevich said angrily. 'Overheating is forty times more harmful than cold.'

Sashenka had a sore throat and developed a high fever. His distinctive quality was a supernatural, mystical fear of nausea and vomiting, the approach of which he imagined every moment.

Pushing aside Yuri Andreevich's hand with the laryngoscope, he would not let him put it down his throat, closed his mouth, shouted and choked. No persuading or threatening worked. Suddenly by inadvertence Sashenka yawned widely and sweetly, and the doctor profited from the moment, with a lightning movement put the spoon into his son's mouth, pressed his tongue down, and managed to get a glimpse of Sashenka's raspberry-coloured throat and swollen tonsils covered with white spots. Yuri Andreevich was alarmed by the look of them.

A little later, by way of a similar sleight of hand, the doctor managed to take a smear from Sashenka's throat. Alexander Alexandrovich had his own microscope. Yuri Andreevich took it and carried out a makeshift analysis. Luckily, it was not diphtheria.

But on the third night, Sashenka had an attack of false croup. He was burning up and suffocating. Yuri Andreevich could not look at the poor child, powerless as he was to save him from suffering. Antonina Alexandrovna thought the boy was dying. They took him in their arms, carried him about the room, and he became better.

They had to get milk, mineral water, or soda for him to drink. But it was the height of the street fighting. The gunfire, as well as artillery fire, did not cease for a minute. Even if Yuri Andreevich were to risk his life and venture to make his way through the limits of the area criss-crossed by shooting, beyond the line of fire he would also not find any life, because it had come to a standstill throughout the city until the situation finally defined itself.

But it was already clear. Rumours came from all sides that the workers were gaining the upper hand. There was still resistance from isolated groups of junkers, which were cut off from each other and had lost touch with their commanders.

The Sivtsev neighbourhood was within the circle of action of the units of soldiers pressing towards the centre from the Dorogomilovo Gate. The soldiers from the German front and adolescent workers sitting in a trench dug in the lane already knew the inhabitants of the nearby houses and exchanged neighbourly jokes with them when they peeked through the gates or came outside. Circulation in that part of the city was being restored.

Then Gordon and Nikolai Nikolaevich, who had been stuck at the Zhivagos' for three days, left their captivity. Yuri Andreevich was glad of their presence during the difficult days of Sashenka's illness, and Antonina Alexandrovna forgave them the muddle they introduced on top of the general disorder. But in gratitude for the hospitality, both had considered it their duty to entertain the hosts with endless talk, and Yuri Andreevich was so tired of that three-day pouring from empty into void that he was happy to part with them.

8

There was information that they had reached home safely, but precisely this test showed that the talk of a general cessation of hostilities was premature. Military action still went on in various places, it was impossible to cross through various neighbourhoods, and the doctor was still unable to get to his hospital, which he had begun to miss and where his *Playing at People* and scientific writings lay in a drawer in the interns' room.

Only within separate neighbourhoods did people go out in the mornings a short distance from home to buy bread, stopping people carrying milk in bottles and crowding around them, asking where they had got it.

Occasionally the shooting resumed all over the city, scattering the public again. Everyone suspected that some sort of negotiations were going on between the sides, the successful or unsuccessful course of which was reflected in the intensifying or weakening of the shrapnel fire.

Once at the end of the old October, around ten o'clock in the evening, Yuri Andreevich was walking quickly down the street, going with no particular need to see a colleague who lived nearby. Those parts, usually lively, were now deserted. He met almost no one.

Yuri Andreevich walked quickly. The first thin snow was dusting down, with a strong and ever-strengthening wind that transformed it before Yuri Andreevich's eyes into a snowstorm.

Yuri Andreevich was turning from one lane into another and had already lost count of the turns he had made, when the snow suddenly poured down very thickly and a blizzard set in, the kind of blizzard that skims shriekingly over the ground in an open field, and in the city thrashes about in a blind alley like a lost person.

Something similar was taking place in the moral world and in the physical, nearby and far away, on the ground and in the air. Somewhere, in little islands, the last volleys of the broken resistance rang out. Somewhere on the horizon, the weak glow of extinguished fires swelled and popped like bubbles. And the same rings and funnels, driven and whirled by the blizzard, smoked under Yuri Andreevich's feet on the wet streets and pavements.

At one intersection he was overtaken by a paper boy running past with the shout 'Latest news!' and carrying a big bundle of freshly printed sheets under his arm.

'Keep the change,' said the doctor. The boy barely managed to separate the damp page stuck to the bundle, thrust it into the doctor's hands, and vanished into the blizzard as instantly as he had emerged from it.

The doctor went over to a street lamp burning two steps away to look through the headlines at once, without putting it off.

The special issue, printed on one side only, contained an official communiqué from Petersburg about the forming of the Soviet of People's Commissars, the establishment of Soviet power in Russia, and the introduction of the dictatorship of the proletariat. Then came the first decrees of the new power and the publication of various news items transmitted by telegraph and telephone.

The blizzard lashed at the doctor's eyes and covered the printed lines of the newspaper with grey and rustling granular snow. But that did not hinder his reading. The grandeur and eternity of the moment astounded him and would not let him come to his senses.

Still, in order to finish reading the communiqué, he began to look around in search of some lighted place sheltered from the snow. It turned out that he had again ended up at his charmed intersection and was standing at the corner of Serebryany and Molchanovka, outside a tall five-storey house with a glassed-in porch and a spacious, electric-lit entrance.

The doctor went in and, standing under an electric light in the front hall, became absorbed in the telegrams.

Above his head came the sound of footsteps. Someone was coming down the stairs, stopping frequently as if in some hesitation. Indeed, the descending person suddenly changed his mind, turned, and ran back upstairs. Somewhere a door was opened, and two voices poured out in a wave, made so formless by the echo that it was impossible to tell whether they were men's or women's. After that the door slammed and the person who had been coming down earlier now started running down much more resolutely.

Yuri Andreevich, who was completely absorbed in his reading, had his eyes lowered to the newspaper. He did not intend to raise them and examine a stranger. But having run all the way down, the latter stopped running. Yuri Andreevich raised his head and looked at him.

Before him stood an adolescent of about eighteen, in a stiff coat of reindeer hide with the fur side out, as they wear them in Siberia, and a hat of the same fur. The boy had a swarthy face with narrow Kirghiz eyes. There was something aristocratic in his face, that fleeting spark, that hidden fineness that seems brought from far away and occurs in people with complex, mixed blood.

The boy was obviously in error, taking Yuri Andreevich for someone else. He looked at the doctor with shy perplexity, as if he knew who he was and simply could not make up his mind to speak. To put an end to this misunderstanding, Yuri Andreevich looked him up and down with a cold gaze, fending off any urge to approach.

The boy became embarrassed and went to the exit without a word. There, glancing back once more, he opened the heavy, shaky door and went out, slamming it with a bang.

About ten minutes later, Yuri Andreevich went out after him. He forgot about the boy and about the colleague he was going to see. He was full of what he had read and headed for home. On his way another circumstance, a mundane trifle, which in those days had immeasurable importance, attracted and absorbed his attention.

A short distance from his house, in the darkness, he stumbled upon a huge heap of boards and logs, dumped across his way on the pavement by the edge of the road. Here in the lane there was some institution to which a supply of government fuel had probably been delivered in the form of some dismantled log house from the outskirts. There had not been enough room in the courtyard and so they had also cluttered up the street in front of it. The pile was being guarded by a sentry with a rifle, who paced the yard and from time to time came out into the lane.

Without thinking twice, Yuri Andreevich seized a moment when the sentry turned into the yard and the blizzard whirled an especially thick cloud of snow up in the air. He went around the heap of beams to the side where it was dark and the light of the street lamp did not fall, and, moving it from side to side, slowly freed a heavy log that was lying on the very bottom. Pulling it from under the pile with difficulty and heaving it onto his shoulder, he stopped feeling its weight (one's own burden is not heavy), and stealthily, keeping to the shadows of the walls, lugged it home to Sivtsev.

It was timely, the firewood was running out at home. The log was sawed up and split into a pile of small chunks. Yuri Andreevich squatted down to start the stove. He sat silently in front of the trembling and rattling doors. Alexander Alexandrovich rolled the armchair up to the stove and sat in it, warming himself. Yuri Andreevich took the newspaper out of the side pocket of his jacket and handed it to his father-in-law, saying:

'Seen this? Have a look. Read it.'

Still squatting down and stirring the wood in the stove with a small poker, Yuri Andreevich talked to himself out loud.

'What magnificent surgery! To take and at one stroke artistically cut out the old, stinking sores! Simply, without beating around the bush, to sentence age-old injustice, which was used to having people bow and scrape and curtsey before it.

'The fact that it was so fearlessly carried out has something nationally intimate, long familiar about it. Something of Pushkin's unconditional luminosity, of Tolstoy's unswerving faithfulness to facts.'

'Pushkin? What did you say? Wait. I'll finish right now. I can't both read and listen,' Alexander Alexandrovich interrupted his son-in-law, mistakenly taking as addressed to him the monologue Yuri Andreevich was speaking to himself under his breath.

'Above all, where does the genius lie? If anyone were given the task of creating a new world, of beginning a new chronology, he would surely need to have a corresponding space cleared for him first. He would wait first of all for the old times to end, before he set about building the new, he would need a round number, a new paragraph, a blank page.

'But now, take it and like it. This unprecedented thing, this miracle of history, this revelation comes bang in the very thick of the ongoing everydayness, with no heed to its course. It begins not from the beginning but from the middle, without choosing the dates beforehand, on the first weekday to come along, at the very peak of tramways plying the city. That's real genius. Only what is greatest can be so inappropriate and untimely.'

9

Winter came, precisely as had been predicted. It was not yet as scary as the two that followed it, but was already of their kind, dark, hungry, and cold, all a breaking up of the habitual and a rebuilding of the foundations of existence, all an inhuman effort to hold on to life as it slipped away.

There were three of them in a row, these dreadful winters, one after another, and not all that now seems to have happened in the year of 1917 to 1918 actually happened then, but may have taken place later. These successive winters merged together and it was hard to tell one from another.

The old life and the new order did not yet coincide. There was no sharp hostility between them, as a year later in the time of the civil war,[12] but there was insufficient connection. They were two sides, standing apart, one facing the other, and not overlapping each other.

Administrative re-elections were held everywhere: in house committees, in organisations, at work, in public service institutions. Their make-up was changing. Commissars with unlimited power were appointed everywhere, people of iron will, in black leather jackets, armed with means of intimidation and with revolvers, who rarely shaved and still more rarely slept.

They were well acquainted with the petty bourgeois breed, the average holder of small government bonds, the grovelling conformist, and never spared him, talking to him with a Mephistophelean smirk, as with a pilferer caught in the act.

These people controlled everything as the programme dictated, and enterprise after enterprise, association after association became Bolshevik.

The Krestovozdvizhensky Hospital was now called the Second Reformed. Changes took place in it. Some of the personnel were fired, but many left on their own, finding the job unprofitable. These were well-paid doctors with a fashionable practice, darlings of society, phrase mongers and fine talkers. They did not fail to present their leaving out of mercenary considerations as a demonstration from civic motives, and they began to behave slightingly towards those who stayed, all but to boycott them. Zhivago was one of those scorned ones who stayed.

In the evenings the following conversations would take place between husband and wife:

'Don't forget to go to the basement of the Medical Society on Wednesday for frozen potatoes. There are two sacks there. I'll find out exactly what time I'll be free, so that I can help you. We must do it together on a sled.'

'All right. There's no rush, Yurochka. You should go to bed quickly. It's late. The chores won't all get done anyway. You need rest.'

'There's a widespread epidemic. General exhaustion weakens resistance. It's frightening to look at you and papa. Something must be done. Yes, but what precisely? We're not cautious enough. We must be more careful. Listen. Are you asleep?'

'No.'

'I'm not afraid for myself, I'm sturdy enough, but if, contrary to all expectation, I should come down with something, please don't be silly and keep me at home. Take me to the hospital instantly.'

'What are you saying, Yurochka! God help you. Why croak of doom?'

'Remember, there are neither honest people nor friends any more. Still less anyone knowledgeable. If something happens, trust only Pichuzhkin. If he himself stays in one piece, of course. Are you asleep?'

'No.'

'The devils, they went where the rations are better, and now it turns out it was civic feelings, principles. We meet, and they barely shake hands. "You work with them?" And they raise their eyebrows. "Yes," I say, "and don't take it amiss, but I'm proud of our privations, and I respect the people who honour us by subjecting us to these privations."'

10

For a long period the invariable food of the majority was boiled millet and fish soup made from herring heads. The bodies of the herring were fried as a second course. People ate unground rye and wheat. They boiled the grain into a porridge.

A professor's wife whom Antonina Alexandrovna knew taught her to bake boiled dough bread on the bottom of a Dutch heating stove, partly for sale, so that the extra and the income from it would justify using the tile stove as in the old days. This would enable them to give up the tormenting iron stove, which smoked, heated poorly, and did not retain its warmth at all.

Antonina Alexandrovna baked very good bread, but nothing came of her commerce. She had to sacrifice her unrealisable plans and bring the dismissed little stove back into action. The Zhivagos lived in want.

One morning Yuri Andreevich left for work as usual. There were two pieces of wood left in the house. Putting on a little winter coat, in which she shivered from weakness even in warm weather, Antonina Alexandrovna went out 'for booty'.

She spent about half an hour wandering the nearby lanes, where muzhiks sometimes turned up from their suburban villages with vegetables and potatoes. You had to catch them. Peasants carrying loads were arrested.

She soon came upon the goal of her search. A stalwart young fellow in a peasant coat, walking in company with Antonina Alexandrovna beside a light, toylike sleigh, warily led it around the corner to the Gromekos' courtyard.

In the bast body of the sleigh, under a mat, lay a small heap of birch rounds, no thicker than the old-fashioned banisters in photographs from the last century. Antonina Alexandrovna knew what they were worth – birch in name only, it was stuff of the worst sort, freshly cut, unsuitable for heating. But there was no choice, she could not argue.

The young peasant made five or six trips upstairs carrying the wretched logs, and in exchange dragged Antonina Alexandrovna's small mirrored wardrobe downstairs and loaded it on the sleigh as a present for his young wife. In passing, as they made future arrangements about potatoes, he asked the price of the piano standing by the door.

On his return, Yuri Andreevich did not discuss his wife's purchase. To chop the given-away wardrobe to splinters would have been more profitable and expedient, but they could not have brought themselves to do it.

'Did you see the note on the desk?' asked his wife.

'From the head of the hospital? They spoke to me, I know about it. It's a call to a sick woman. I'll certainly go. I'll just rest a little and go. It's quite far. Somewhere by the Triumphal Arch. I wrote down the address.'

'They're offering a strange honorarium. Did you see? Read it anyway. A bottle of German cognac or a pair of lady's stockings for the visit. Some enticement! Who can it be? Bad tone, and total ignorance of our present-day life. Nouveaux riches of some sort.'

'Yes, a state purveyor.'

Along with concessionaires and authorised agents, this title was used to designate small private entrepreneurs, for whom the state authorities, having abolished private trade, made small allowances at moments of economic crisis, concluding contracts and deals with them for various provisions.

Their number did not include the fallen heads of old firms, proprietors on a grand scale. They never recovered from the blow they received. Into this category fell the ephemeral dealers, stirred up from the bottom by war and revolution, new and alien people without roots.

After drinking boiled water with saccharine, whitened by milk, the doctor went to the sick woman.

The pavements and roadways were buried under deep snow, which covered the streets from one row of houses to the other. In places the covering of snow reached the ground-floor windows. Across the whole width of this space moved silent, half-alive shadows, lugging some sort of meagre provisions on their backs or pulling them on sleds. Almost no one drove.

On houses here and there old signboards still remained. The grocery shops and cooperatives placed under them, with no relation to their content, stood locked, their windows barred or boarded up, and empty.

They were locked and empty not only owing to the lack of goods, but because the reorganisation of all sides of life, embracing trade as well, was still being carried out in the most general terms, and these boarded-up shops, as minute particulars, had not yet been touched by it.

11

The house that the doctor had been called to turned out to be at the end of Brestskaya Street, near the Tver Gate.

It was a barracklike brick building of antediluvian construction, with an inner courtyard and wooden galleries running in three tiers round the inside walls of the structure.

The tenants were holding a previously arranged general meeting with the participation of a woman representative of the district soviet, when a military commission suddenly appeared on a round to inspect permits to keep arms and confiscate those without permit. The leader of the round asked the delegate not to leave, assuring her that the search would not take much time, the tenants who had been checked would gradually come back, and the interrupted meeting would soon be able to resume.

The round was nearing its end, and the turn had just come for the apartment where the doctor was awaited when he came to the gate of the house. A soldier with a rifle on a string, who was standing guard by one of the stairways leading to the galleries, flatly refused to let Yuri Andreevich pass, but the commander of the detachment interfered in their dispute. He said the doctor should not be hindered and agreed to hold up the search until he had examined the sick woman.

The doctor was met by the owner of the apartment, a courteous young man with a dull, swarthy complexion and dark, melancholy eyes. He was upset by many circumstances: his wife's illness, the impending search, and the supernatural respect he nursed for medicine and its representatives.

To spare the doctor work and time, the owner tried to speak as briefly as he could, but precisely this haste made his speech long and confused.

The apartment, with a mixture of luxury and cheapness, was furnished with things bought slapdash with the aim of investing money in something stable. Furniture in incomplete sets was supplemented by single objects that were missing a second to make up the pair.

The owner of the apartment thought his wife had some sort of nervous ailment from fright. With many irrelevant digressions, he told how they had bought for next to nothing an old, broken clock with musical chimes, which had not worked for a long time. They had bought it only as a curiosity of clock-making craftsmanship, as a rarity (the sick woman's husband took the doctor to the next room to show it to him). They even doubted it could be fixed. And suddenly the clock, which had not been wound for years, started up by itself, started up, rang out an intricate minuet on its little bells, and stopped. His wife was terrified, the young man said, decided that her last hour had struck, and now she lies there, raves, doesn't eat, doesn't drink, doesn't recognise him.

'So you think it's nervous shock?' Yuri Andreevich asked with doubt in his voice. 'Take me to the patient.'

They went into the next room with its porcelain chandelier and two mahogany bed tables on either side of a wide double bed. At the edge of it, the blanket pulled up over her chin, lay a small woman with big, dark eyes. Seeing the men coming in, she waved them away, freeing an arm from under the blanket, on which the wide sleeve of a peignoir slid up to the armpit. She did not recognise her husband and, as if there were no one in the room, started singing in a soft voice the beginning of a sad little song, which moved her so much that she burst into tears and, sobbing like a child, began asking to be taken home somewhere. The doctor tried to approach her from different sides, but she resisted examination and each time turned her back on him.

'She does need to be examined,' said Yuri Andreevich. 'But, all the same, I can see quite clearly. It's typhus, and a very grave form of it at that. She's suffering greatly, poor thing. I'd advise putting her in the hospital. It's not a matter of comfort, which you could provide for her, but of constant medical attention, which is necessary during the first weeks of the illness. Can you find some sort of transportation, hire a cab or at least a cart, to take the patient, making sure that she's well wrapped up beforehand? I'll write an order for you.'

'I can. I'll try. But wait. Can it really be typhus? How terrible!'

'Unfortunately.'

'I'm afraid to lose her if I let her go from here. Isn't there some way you could treat her at home, visiting her as often as possible? I'll pay whatever fee you like.'

'I've already explained to you. The important thing is that she have constant attention. Listen. I'm giving you good advice. Dig up a cab somewhere, and I'll write out an accompanying note for her. It would be best to do it through your house committee. The order will have to have the house seal, and there will be some other formalities.'

12

Having gone through the interrogation and search, the tenants returned one after another, in warm shawls and coats, to the unheated quarters of the former egg storage, now occupied by the house committee.

At one end of the room stood an office desk and several chairs, though not enough to seat so many people. Therefore, in addition to them, long, empty egg crates, turned upside down, were placed around them like benches. A mountain of such crates was piled up to the ceiling at the other end of the room. There in a corner was a swept-up heap of frozen wood shavings stuck together in lumps by the spilt insides of broken eggs. Rats noisily messed about in this heap, occasionally running out to the open space of the stone floor and hiding again in the shavings.

Each time this happened, a loud and fat-bloated woman jumped up on one of the crates with a shriek. She pulled up the corner of her skirt with coquettishly splayed fingers, rapidly stamped her feet in fashionable ladies' high boots, and in a deliberately hoarse voice, affecting drunkenness, shouted:

'Olka, Olka, you've got rats running around here. Ooh, away, you vile thing! Aha, he understands, the scum! He's angry. Ay-yay-yay, he's climbing up the crate! Don't let him get under my skirt! Oh, I'm afraid, I'm afraid! Turn your heads, gentlemen. Sorry, I forgot, you're not gentlemen now, you're comrade citizens.'

The noisy female was wearing an unbuttoned astrakhan sack. Under it her double chin, ample bosom, and belly in a tight silk dress undulated in three layers, like quivering custard. Clearly, she had once passed for a lioness among third-rate shopkeepers and their clerks. She could barely open the slits of her piglike eyes with their swollen eyelids. In time immemorial some rival had thrown a vial of acid at her, but had missed, and only two or three drops had etched light traces on her left cheek and the left corner of her mouth, almost seductive in their inconspicuousness.

'Don't yell, Khrapugina. It's simply impossible to work,' said the woman at the desk, the representative of the district soviet, elected to chair the meeting.

She was well-known from long ago to the old-timers of the house, and she knew them well herself. Before the start of the meeting, she had an unofficial, half-whispered conversation with Fatima, the old caretaker of the house, who had once been cooped up with her husband and children in the dirty basement, but now had moved with her daughter to two bright rooms on the second floor.

'Well, how are things, Fatima?' asked the chairwoman.

Fatima complained that managing such a big and densely populated house was too much for her alone, and there was no help from anywhere, because nobody observed the obligations of tidying the courtyard and the street, which were distributed by apartment.

'Don't worry, Fatima, we'll blunt their horns, I assure you. What kind of committee is that? Is it conceivable? Hidden criminal elements, dubious morals living without registration. We'll give them the boot and elect another one. I'll get you made house manager, only don't start kicking.'

The caretaker begged the chairwoman not to do that, but the latter was not even listening. She looked around the room, found that enough people had gathered, called for silence, and opened the meeting with a short introductory speech. After condemning the inactivity of the former house committee, she proposed the nominating of candidates for the election of a new one and went on to other questions. On finishing that, she said incidentally:

'Well, so that's that, comrades. Let's speak frankly. Your building's roomy, suitable for a hostel. It happens, when delegates come for a conference, there's nowhere to put people up. It has been decided to place the building at the disposal of the district soviet as a house for visitors and give it the name of Comrade Tiverzin, who lived in this house before his exile, which is a well-known fact. Do you have any objections? Now to the schedule for vacating the house. It's not an urgent measure, you still have a year's time. Working people will be relocated to lodgings provided for them, non-workers are put on notice that they must find their own, and are given a term of twelve months.'

'But who here is a non-worker? We have no non-workers! We're all workers,' came cries from all sides, and one strained voice especially: 'That's great-power chauvinism! All nationalities are equal now! I know what you're hinting at!'

'Not all at once! I simply don't know who to answer. What nationalities? What have nationalities got to do with it, Citizen Valdyrkin? For instance, Khrapugina's no nationality, but she'll also be evicted.'

'Evicted! We'll see how you evict me. Flattened old couch! Ten-jobs!' Khrapugina shouted out the senseless nicknames she gave to the woman delegate in the heat of the quarrel.

'What a viper! What a hellcat! You have no shame!' The caretaker became indignant.

'Don't mix into it, Fatima, I can stand up for myself. Stop, Khrapugina. Reach you a hand, and you bite it off. Shut up, I said, or I'll turn you over to the organs immediately and not wait till they pick you up for making moonshine and running a dive.'

The noise reached the limit. No one was given a chance to speak. Just then the doctor came into the storeroom. He asked the first man he ran into by the door to point out someone from the house committee. The man put his hands to his mouth like a megaphone and, above the noise and racket, shouted syllable by syllable:

'Ga-li-ul-li-na! Come here. Somebody's asking for you.'

The doctor could not believe his ears. A thin, slightly stooping woman, the caretaker, came over. The doctor was struck by the resemblance of mother and son. But he did not yet give himself away. He said:

'One of your tenants here has come down with typhus' (he gave the woman's name). 'Precautions must be taken to keep the infection from spreading. Besides, the sick woman will have to be taken to the hospital. I'll write out a document, which the house committee will have to certify. How and where can I do it?'

The caretaker understood the question as referring to transporting the sick woman, not to writing out the accompanying document.

'A droshky will come from the district soviet to pick up Comrade Demina,' said Galiullina. 'Comrade Demina's a kind person, I'll tell her, she'll give it up to you. Don't worry, comrade doctor, we'll transport your sick woman.'

'Oh, I didn't mean that! I just need a corner where I can write out an order. But if there'll be a droshky . . . Excuse me, but are you the mother of Lieutenant Galiullin, Osip Gimazetdinovich? I served with him at the front.'

The caretaker shuddered all over and turned pale. Seizing the doctor's hand, she said:

'Let's step outside. We can talk in the courtyard.'

As soon as they crossed the threshold, she began hurriedly:

'Shh. God forbid anyone hears. Don't ruin me. Yusupka's gone bad. Judge for yourself, who is Yusupka? Yusupka was an apprentice, a workman. Yusup should understand, simple people are much better off now, a blind man can see that, there's nothing to talk about. I don't know what you think, maybe you can do it, but for Yusupka it's wrong, God won't forgive it. Yusup's father died a soldier, killed, and how – no face left, no arms, no legs.'

She was unable to go on speaking and, waving her hand, waited for her agitation to subside. Then she continued:

'Let's go. I'll arrange the droshky for you now. I know who you are. He was here for two days, he told me. He said you know Lara Guisharova. She was a nice girl. She came here to see us, I remember. But who knows what she's like now. Can it be that the masters go against the masters? But for Yusupka it's wrong. Let's go and ask for the droshky. Comrade Demina will let us have it. And do you know who Comrade Demina is? Olya Demina, who used to work as a seamstress for Lara Guisharova's mother. That's who she is. Also from here. From this house. Let's go.'

13

It was already growing quite dark. Night lay all around. Only the white circle of light from Demina's pocket flashlight leaped some five steps ahead of them from one snowdrift to another, and confused more than lit up the way for the walkers. Night lay all around, and the house stayed behind, where so many people had known her, where she used to come as a girl, where, as the story went, her future husband, Antipov, was brought up as a boy.

Demina addressed him with patronising jocularity:

'Will you really get further without the flashlight? Eh? Otherwise I'll give it to you, comrade doctor. Yes. Once I was badly smitten with her, I loved her to distraction, when we were girls. They had a sewing establishment here, a workshop. I lived with them as an apprentice. I saw her this year. Passing through. She was passing through Moscow. I say to her, where are you going, fool? Stay here. We'll live together, you'll find work. No way! She doesn't want to. That's her business. She married Pashka with her head, not her heart, and since then she's been a bit off. She left.'

'What do you think of her?'

'Careful. It's slippery here. How many times have I told them not to pour slops in front of the door – like sand against the wind. What do I think of her? What do you mean, think? What's there to think? I have no time. Here's where I live. I concealed it from her: her brother, who was in the army, has likely been shot. But her mother, my former boss, I'll probably save, I'm interceding for her. Well, I go in here, goodbye.'

And so they parted. The beam of Demina's flashlight poked into the narrow stone stairway and ran ahead, lighting the soiled walls of the dirty way up, and darkness surrounded the doctor. To the right lay Sadovaya-Triumphalnaya Street, to the left Sadovaya-Karetnaya. In the black distance over the black snow, these were no longer streets in the ordinary sense of the word, but like two forest clearings in the dense taiga of stretched-out stone buildings, as in the impassable thickets of the Urals or Siberia.

At home there was light, warmth.

'Why so late?' asked Antonina Alexandrovna, and, not letting him reply, she went on:

'A curious thing happened while you were gone. An inexplicable oddity. I forgot to tell you. Yesterday papa broke the alarm clock and was in despair. The last clock in the house. He tried to repair it, poked at it, poked, with no result. The clockmaker at the corner asked three pounds of bread – an unheard-of price. What to do? Papa was completely downcast. And suddenly, imagine, an hour ago comes a piercing, deafening ring. The alarm clock! You see, it upped and started!'

'So my typhus hour has struck,' joked Yuri Andreevich, and he told his family about the sick woman and her chimes.

14

But he came down with typhus much later. In the meantime, the distress of the Zhivago family reached the limit. They were in want and were perishing. Yuri Andreevich sought out the party man he had once saved, the robbery victim. He did all he could for the doctor. However, the civil war had begun. His protector was travelling all the time. Besides, in accordance with his convictions, the man considered the hardships of the time natural and concealed the fact that he himself was starving.

Yuri Andreevich tried turning to the purveyor by the Tver Gate. But in the months that had passed, even his tracks had grown cold, and of his wife, who had recovered, there was nothing to be heard. The complement of tenants in the house had changed. Demina was at the front, the manager Galiullina was not there when Yuri Andreevich came.

Once by means of a coupon he received firewood at the official price, but had to transport it from the Vindava Station. He accompanied the driver and his nag, hauling this unexpected wealth down the endless Meshchanskaya Street. Suddenly the doctor noticed that Meshchanskaya had ceased somehow to be Meshchanskaya, that he was reeling and his legs would not support him. He realised that he was in for it, things were bad, and it was typhus. The driver picked up the fallen man. The doctor did not remember how they brought him home, somehow placed on top of the firewood.

15

He was delirious for two weeks with some breaks. He dreamed that Tonya put the two Sadovaya streets on his desk, Sadovaya-Karetnaya to the left and Sadovaya-Triumphalnaya to the right, and moved his desk lamp close to them, hot, searching, orange. The streets became light. He could work. And now he is writing.

He is writing heatedly and with extraordinary success something he had always wanted to write and should long ago have written, but never could, and now it is coming out well. And only occasionally is he hindered by a boy with narrow Kirghiz eyes, in an unbuttoned reindeer coat like they wear in Siberia or the Urals.

It is perfectly clear that this boy is the spirit of his death, or, to put it simply, is his death. But how can he be death, when he is helping him to write a poem, can there be any benefit from death, can there be any help from death?

He is writing a poem not about the Resurrection and not about the Entombment, but about the days that passed between the one and the other. He is writing the poem 'Disarray'.

He had always wanted to describe how, in the course of three days, a storm of black, wormy earth besieges, assaults the immortal incarnation of love, hurling itself at him with its clods and lumps, just as the breaking waves of the sea come rushing at the coast and bury it. How for three days the black earthy storm rages, advances, and recedes.

And two rhymed lines kept pursuing him: 'Glad to take up' and 'Have to wake up'.

Hell, and decay, and decomposition, and death are glad to take up, and yet, together with them, spring, and Mary Magdalene,[13] and life are also glad to take up. And – have to wake up. He has to wake up and rise. He has to resurrect.

16

He began to recover. At first, blissfully, he sought no connections between things, he admitted everything, remembered nothing, was surprised at nothing. His wife fed him white bread and butter, gave him tea with sugar, made him coffee. He forgot that this was impossible now and was glad of the tasty food, as of poetry and fairy tales, which were lawful and admissible in convalescence. But when he began to reflect for the first time, he asked his wife:

'Where did you get it?'

'All from your Granya.'

'What Granya?'

'Granya Zhivago.'

'Granya Zhivago?'

'Why, yes, your brother Evgraf, from Omsk. Your half-brother. While you were lying unconscious, he kept visiting us.'

'In a reindeer coat?'

'Yes, yes. So you noticed him through your unconsciousness? He ran into you on the stairs of some house, I know, he told me. He knew it was you and wanted to introduce himself, but you put a scare into him! He adores you, can't read enough of you. He digs up such things! Rice, raisins, sugar! He's gone back to his parts. And he's calling us there. He's so strange, mysterious. I think he has some sort of love affair with the authorities. He says we should leave the big city for a year or two, "to sit on the earth". I asked his advice about the Krügers' place. He strongly recommends it. So that we could have a kitchen garden and a forest nearby. We can't just perish so obediently, like sheep.'

In April of that year the whole Zhivago family set out for the far-off Urals, to the former estate of Varykino near the town of Yuriatin.

Part Seven

ON THE WAY

I

The last days of March came, days of the first warmth, false harbingers of spring, after which each year an intense cold spell sets in.

In the Gromeko house hurried preparations were being made for the journey. To the numerous inhabitants, whose density in the house was now greater than that of sparrows in the street, this bustle was explained as a general cleaning before Easter.

Yuri Andreevich was against the trip. He did not interfere with the preparations, because he considered the undertaking unfeasible and hoped that at the decisive moment it would fall through. But the thing moved ahead and was near completion. The time came to talk seriously.

He once again expressed his doubts to his wife and father-in-law at a family council especially organised for that purpose.

'So you think I'm not right, and, consequently, we're going?' he concluded his objections. His wife took the floor:

'You say, weather it out for a year or two, during that time new land regulations will be established, it will be possible to ask for a piece of land near Moscow and start a kitchen garden. But how to survive in the meantime, you don't suggest. Yet that is the most interesting thing, that is precisely what it would be desirable to hear.'

'Absolute raving,' Alexander Alexandrovich supported his daughter.

'Very well, I surrender,' Yuri Andreevich agreed. 'The only thing that pulls me up short is the total uncertainty. We set out, eyes shut, for we don't know where, not having the least notion of the place. Of three persons who lived in Varykino, two, mama and grandmother, are no longer alive, and the third, Grandfather Krüger, if he's alive, is being held hostage and behind bars.

'In the last year of the war, he did something with the forests and facto-ries, sold them for the sake of appearances to some straw man, or to some bank, or signed them away conditionally to someone. What do we know about that deal? Whose land is it now – that is, not in the sense of property, I don't care, but who is responsible for it? What department? Are they cut-ting the forest? Are the factories working? Finally, who is in power there, and who will be by the time we get there?

'For you, the safety anchor is Mikulitsyn, whose name you like so much to repeat. But who told you that the old manager is still alive and still in Varykino? And what do we know about him, except that grandfather had difficulty pronouncing his name, which is why we remember it?

'But why argue? You're set on going. I'm with you. We must find out how it's done now. There's no point in putting it off.'

2

Yuri Andreevich went to the Yaroslavsky train station to make enquiries about it.

The flow of departing people was contained by a boardwalk with handrails laid across the halls, on the stone floors of which lay people in grey overcoats, who tossed and turned, coughed and spat, and when they talked to each other, each time it was incongruously loudly, not taking into account the force with which their voices resounded under the echoing vaults.

For the most part they were patients who had been sick with typhus. In view of the overcrowding of the hospitals, they were discharged the day after the crisis. As a doctor, Yuri Andreevich had run into such necessity himself, but he did not know that these unfortunates were so many and that the train stations served them as shelters.

'Get sent on an official mission,' a porter in a white apron told him. 'You have to come and check every day. Trains are a rarity now, a matter of chance. And of course it goes without saying . . .' (the porter rubbed his thumb against his first two fingers). 'Some flour or whatever. To grease the skids. Well, and this here . . .' (he upended an invisible shot glass) '. . . is a most sacred thing.'

3

Around that time Alexander Alexandrovich was invited to the Supreme Council of National Economy for several special consultations, and Yuri

Andreevich to a gravely ill member of the government. Both were remuner-
ated in the best form of that time – coupons to the first closed distribution
centre then established.[1]

It was located in some garrison warehouse by the St Simon monastery.
The doctor and his father-in-law crossed two inner courtyards, the church's
and the garrison's, and straight from ground level, with no threshold,
entered under the stone vault of a deep, gradually descending cellar. Its
widening far end was partitioned crosswise by a long counter, at which a
calm, unhurried storekeeper weighed and handed over provisions, occasionally going back to the storeroom for something, and crossing out items
on a list with a broad stroke of the pencil as he handed them over.

There were few customers.

'Your bags,' the storekeeper said to the professor and the doctor, glancing
fleetingly at their invoices. The two men's eyes popped out as flour, grain,
macaroni, and sugar poured into the covers for little ladies' cushions and the
bigger pillowcases they held open, along with lard, soap, and matches, and
also a piece each of something wrapped in paper, which later, at home,
turned out to be Caucasian cheese.

Son-in-law and father-in-law hastened to tie the multitude of small bundles into two big knapsacks as quickly as they could, so that their ungrate-
ful pottering would not offend the eyes of the storekeeper, who had
overwhelmed them with his magnanimity.

They came out of the cellar into the open air drunk not with animal joy,
but with the consciousness that they, too, were not living in this world for
nothing, that they were not just blowing smoke, and at home they would
deserve the praise and recognition of the young mistress of the house,
Tonya.

4

While the men disappeared into various institutions, soliciting missions and
permanent residency papers for the rooms they were leaving, Antonina
Alexandrovna was busy selecting things to be packed.

She walked anxiously about the three rooms of the house now assigned
to the Gromeko family, and endlessly weighed each little trifle in her hand
before placing it in the general pile of things destined to be packed.

Only an insignificant portion of their belongings went as the travellers'
personal luggage; the rest was kept in reserve as a means of exchange, necessary for the journey and on their arrival in the place.

Spring air came through the open vent window, tasting of a freshly bitten

French loaf. Outside, cocks crowed and the voices of playing children were heard. The more they aired the room, the clearer became the smell of camphor, given off by the winter stuff removed from the trunks.

Concerning what ought to be taken and what renounced, there existed a whole theory worked out by those who had left earlier, whose observations had spread in the circle of their acquaintances who stayed behind.

These precepts, shaped into brief, indisputable instructions, were lodged with such distinctness in Antonina Alexandrovna's head that she fancied she heard them from outside, together with the chirping of the sparrows and the noise of the playing children, as if some secret voice from the street were prompting her.

'Cloth, cloth,' said these considerations, 'best of all in lengths, but there are inspections along the way, and it's dangerous. Cut pieces quickly tacked together are more prudent. Fabric in general, textiles, clothes are acceptable, preferably outer wear, not too worn. As little rubbish as possible, no heavy things. Given the frequent need to carry it all yourselves, forget about hampers and trunks. After sorting them a hundred times, tie a few things into bundles light enough for a woman or a child. Salt and tobacco are expedient, as practice has shown, though the risk is considerable. Money in kerenki.[2] Documents are hardest of all.' And so on and so forth.

5

On the eve of departure a snowstorm arose. The wind swept grey clouds of spinning snowflakes up into the sky, and they came back to earth in a white whirl, flew into the depths of the dark street, and spread a white shroud over it.

Everything in the house was packed. The supervision of the rooms and the belongings remaining in them was entrusted to an elderly married couple, Egorovna's Moscow relations, whom Antonina Alexandrovna had met the preceding winter, when she arranged through them to exchange old things, clothes and unneeded furniture, for firewood and potatoes.

It was impossible to rely on Markel. At the police station, which he chose as his political club, he did not complain that the former house owners, the Gromekos, sucked his blood, but he reproached them after the fact for keeping him in the darkness of ignorance, deliberately concealing from him that the world descended from the apes.

Antonina Alexandrovna took this couple, Egorovna's relations, a former commercial employee and his wife, around the rooms for a last time, showed them which keys fitted which locks and what had been put where, unlocked and locked the doors of the cupboards together with them, taught them everything and explained everything.

The tables and chairs in the rooms were pushed up against the walls, the bundles for the journey were dragged to one side, the curtains were taken down from all the windows. The snowstorm, more unhindered than in the setting of winter cosiness, peeped through the bared windows into the empty rooms. It reminded each of them of something. For Yuri Andreevich it was his childhood and his mother's death; for Antonina Alexandrovna and Alexander Alexandrovich, it was the death and funeral of Anna Ivanovna. It kept seeming to them that this was their last night in the house, which they would never see again. In that respect they were mistaken, but under the influence of the delusion, which they did not confide to each other, so as not to upset each other, they each went over the life they had spent under that roof and fought back the tears that kept coming to their eyes.

That did not prevent Antonina Alexandrovna from observing social conventions in front of strangers. She kept up an incessant conversation with the woman to whose supervision she was entrusting everything. Antonina Alexandrovna exaggerated the significance of the service rendered her. So as not to repay the favour with black ingratitude, she apologised every other minute, went to the next room, and came back with a present for this person of a scarf, or a little blouse, or a length of cotton or gauze. And all the materials were dark with white checks or polka dots, just as the dark, snowy outside was speckled with white, looking through the bare, curtainless windows on that farewell evening.

6

They were leaving for the station early in the morning. The inhabitants of the house were not up yet at that hour. The tenant Zevorotkina, the usual ringleader of all concerted actions, together now and heave-ho, ran around to the sleeping lodgers, knocking on their doors and shouting: 'Attention, comrades! It's goodbye time! Look lively, look lively! The former Garumekovs are leaving.'

They came pouring out to the hall and porch of the back entrance (the front entrance was now boarded up year-round) and covered its steps like an amphitheatre, as if preparing for a group photograph.

The yawning tenants stooped so that the skimpy coats thrown over their shoulders would not fall off, hunched up, and shifted their chilled bare feet hastily thrust into loose felt boots.

Markel had contrived to get plastered on something lethal in that

alcohol-less time, and kept toppling against the banisters, which threatened
to break under him. He volunteered to carry the things to the station and was
offended that his help was rejected. They had a hard time getting rid of him.

It was still dark outside. In the windless air, the snow fell more thickly
than the evening before. Big, shaggy flakes floated down lazily and, nearing
the ground, seemed to tarry longer, as if hesitating whether to lie down on it
or not.

When they came out from their lane to the Arbat, it was a little lighter.
Falling snow veiled everything down to the ground with its white, billowing
curtain, the hanging fringe of which tangled under the walkers' feet, so that
the sensation of movement was lost and it seemed to them that they were
marching in place.

There was not a soul in the street. The travellers from Sivtsev met no one
on their way. Soon they were overtaken by an empty cab, the cabby all covered with snow as if he had been dragged through batter, driving a snow-
blanched nag, and for a fabulous sum in those years, amounting to less than
a kopeck, took all of them and their things into the droshky, except for Yuri
Andreevich, who at his own request, light, without luggage, was allowed to
go to the station on foot.

<h2 style="text-align:center">7</h2>

At the station, Antonina Alexandrovna and her father were already standing in a numberless line, squeezed between the barriers of wooden fences.
Boarding was now done not from the platforms, but a good half mile down
the tracks, by the exit semaphore, because there were not enough hands to
clean the approach to the platforms, half of the station area was covered
with ice and refuse, and the trains could not get that far.

Nyusha and Shurochka were not in the crowd with the mother and
grandfather. They strolled freely under the enormous overhanging roof of
the entrance, only rarely coming to see if it was time to join the adults. They
smelled strongly of kerosene, which had been heavily applied to their
ankles, wrists, and necks as protection against typhus lice.

Seeing her husband approaching, Antonina Alexandrovna beckoned to
him with her hand, but, not letting him come nearer, she called out from a
distance to tell him at which window mandates for official missions were
stamped. He went there.

'Show me what kind of seals they gave you,' she asked when he came
back. The doctor handed her a wad of folded papers over the barrier.

'That's a travel warrant for the delegates' coach,' Antonina Alexandrovna's neighbour said behind her, making out over her shoulder the stamp on the document. The neighbour in front, one of those formalist legalists who in every circumstance know all the rules in the world, explained in more detail:

'With that seal you have the right to demand seats in a first-class, in other words, in a passenger coach, if there are any on the train.'

The case was subjected to discussion by the whole line. Voices arose:

'Go find any first-class coaches. That'd be too fat. Nowadays you can say thank you if you get a seat on a freight car buffer.'

'Don't listen to them, you're on official business. Here, I'll explain to you. At the present time separate trains have been cancelled, and there's one combined one, which is for the military, and for convicts, and for cattle, and for people. The tongue can say whatever it likes – it's pliable. But instead of confusing somebody with talk, you ought to explain so he'll understand.'

'So you've explained. What a smart one we've got here. A warrant for the delegates' coach is only half the matter. Take a look at them first, and then talk. What are you going to do with such striking faces in the delegates' coach? The delegates' coach is full of our likes. The sailor's got a sharp eye, and he's got a pistol on a cord. He sees straight off – propertied class, and what's more a doctor, from the former masters. The sailor grabs his pistol and swats him like a fly.'

It is not known where the sympathy for the doctor and his family would have led, had it not been for a new circumstance.

People in the crowd had for some time been casting glances through the thick plate glass of the wide station windows. The long roofs of the platform, stretching into the distance, removed to the last degree the spectacle of the snow falling on the tracks. At such a distance, it seemed that the snowflakes hung in the air almost without moving, slowly sinking into it the way soggy bread crumbs fed to fish sink into the water.

People in groups and singly had long been going off into that depth. While they were few in number, these figures, indistinct through the quivering net of the snow, had been taken for railway workers walking over the ties in the line of duty. But now a whole throng of them came along. In the depths they were heading for, an engine began to smoke.

'Open the doors, you crooks!' people shouted in the line. The crowd heaved and surged towards the doors. The ones at the back pushed those in front.

'Look what's going on! Here we're barred by the wall, and there they cut ahead without lining up. The coaches will be crammed full, and we stand here like sheep! Open up, you devils, or we'll break it down! Hey, boys, all together, heave!'

'The fools don't know who they're envying,' the all-knowing legalist said. 'They've been mobilised, drafted as labour conscripts from Petrograd.[3] They were sent first to Vologda, to the northern front, and now they're being driven to the eastern front. Not of their own will. Under escort. To dig trenches.'

8

They had already been travelling for three days, but had not gone far from Moscow. The landscape along the way was wintry: the tracks, the fields, the forests, the roofs of the villages – everything lay under snow.

The Zhivago family had found themselves by luck on the left corner of the upper front bunk, by a dim, elongated window just under the ceiling, where they settled in a family circle, not breaking up their company.

Antonina Alexandrovna was travelling in a freight car for the first time. When they were getting on the train in Moscow, Yuri Andreevich had lifted the women up to the level of the coach floor, along the edge of which rolled a heavy sliding door. Further on, the women got the knack of it and climbed into the coach by themselves.

At first the coaches had seemed to Antonina Alexandrovna like cattle sheds on wheels. These pens, in her opinion, were bound to fall apart at the first jolt or shake. But it was already the third day that they were being thrown forward or back or sideways on turns or as the momentum changed, and the third day that the axles went on knocking rapidly under the floor, like the sticks of a wind-up toy drum, and the trip went very well, and Antonina Alexandrovna's apprehensions proved unjustified.

The long train, consisting of twenty-three coaches (the Zhivagos were in the fourteenth), stretched only some one part of itself – the head, the tail, the middle – along the short platforms of the stations.

The front ones were for the military, in the middle rode the free public, at the end those mobilised by labour conscription.

There were about five hundred passengers of this category, people of all ages and the most diverse ranks and occupations.

The eight coaches that this public occupied presented a motley spectacle. Alongside well-dressed rich people, Petersburg stockbrokers and lawyers, one could see – also recognised as belonging to the class of exploiters – cab-drivers, floor polishers, bathhouse attendants, Tartar junkmen, runaway madmen from disbanded asylums, small shopkeepers, and monks.

The first sat around the red-hot stoves without their jackets, on short, round blocks stood upright, telling each other something and laughing loudly. They were people with connections. They were not dejected. At home influential relations were interceding for them. In any case, they could buy themselves off further along the way.

The second, wearing boots and unbuttoned kaftans, or long, loose shirts over their pants and going barefoot, bearded or beardless, stood by the slid-open doors of the stuffy coaches, holding on to the doorposts and the bars across the opening, looked sullenly at the area by the wayside and its inhabitants, and talked to no one. They did not have the necessary acquaintances. They had nothing to hope for.

Not all these people were placed in the coaches authorised for them. A portion had been tucked into the middle of the train, mixed with the free public. There were people of that sort in the fourteenth coach.

9

Usually, when the train approached some station, Antonina Alexandrovna, who was lying on the upper level, raised herself to the uncomfortable position she was forced into by the low ceiling, which prevented her from straightening up, hung her head over the side, and, through the chink of the slightly opened door, determined whether the place presented any interest from the point of view of barter and whether it was worthwhile getting down from the bunk and going outside.

And so it was now. The slowing pace of the train brought her out of her drowsiness. The multitude of switches over which the freight car jolted with increasingly loud bumps spoke for the importance of the station and the length of the forthcoming stop.

Antonina Alexandrovna sat bent over, rubbed her eyes, smoothed her hair, and, thrusting her hand into the knapsack, rummaged around and pulled out a towel embroidered with roosters, little figures, yokes, and wheels.

Just then the doctor woke up, jumped down from the berth first, and helped his wife climb down to the floor.

Meanwhile, past the open door of the coach, following the switchmen's boxes and lamp posts, there already floated the trees of the station, weighed down by whole layers of snow, which looked like a welcome offering for the train, and the first to jump down from the still quickly moving train onto the pristine snow of the platform were the sailors, who, to get ahead of everyone, went running around the station building, where, in the shelter of the side wall, women selling forbidden food usually hid.

The sailors' black uniforms, the flying ribbons of their peakless caps, and their bell-bottomed trousers lent a dash and impetuosity to their steps and made everyone give way before them, as before downhill skiers or skaters racing at top speed.

Around the corner of the station, hiding behind one another and as nervous as if they were telling fortunes, peasant women from the nearby villages lined up with cucumbers, cottage cheese, boiled beef, and rye cheesecakes, which, under the quilted covers they were brought in, kept their aroma and warmth even in the cold. The women and girls, in kerchiefs tucked under their winter jackets, blushed like poppies at some of the sailors' jokes, and at the same time feared them worse than fire, because it was mostly of sailors that all sorts of detachments were formed for combating speculation and forbidden free trade.

The peasant women's confusion did not last long. The train was coming to a stop. Other passengers were arriving. The public intermingled. Trade became brisk.

Antonina Alexandrovna was making the rounds of the women, the towel thrown over her shoulder, looking as if she were going behind the station to wash with snow. She had already been called to from the lines several times:

'Hey, you, city girl, what are you asking for the towel?'

But Antonina Alexandrovna, without stopping, walked on further with her husband.

At the end of the line stood a woman in a black kerchief with free crimson designs. She noticed the embroidered towel. Her bold eyes lit up. She glanced sideways, made sure that danger did not threaten from anywhere, quickly went up close to Antonina Alexandrovna, and, throwing back the cover of her goods, whispered in a heated patter:

'Looky here. Ever seen the like? Aren't you tempted? Well, don't think too long – it'll be snapped up. Give me the towel for the halfy.'

Antonina Alexandrovna did not catch the last word. She thought the woman had said something about a calf.

'What's that, my dear?'

By a halfy the peasant woman meant half a hare, split in two and roasted from head to tail, which she was holding in her hands. She repeated:

'I said give me the towel for a halfy. Why are you looking at me? It's not dog meat. My husband's a hunter. It's a hare, a hare.'

The exchange was made. Each side thought she had made a great gain and the opposite side was as great a loser. Antonina Alexandrovna was ashamed to have fleeced the poor woman so dishonestly. But the woman, pleased with the deal, hastened to put sin behind her and, calling the woman next to her, who was all traded out, strode home with her down a narrow path trampled in the snow, which led to somewhere far away.

Just then there was a commotion in the crowd. Somewhere an old woman shouted:

'Where are you off to, young sir? And the money? When did you give it to me, you shameless liar? Ah, you greedy gut, I shout at him, and he walks off and doesn't look back. Stop, I said, stop, mister comrade! Help! Thief! Robbery! There he is, there, hold him!'

'Which one?'

'Him walking there, with the shaved mug, laughing.'

'The one with a hole on his elbow?'

'Yes, yes. Hold him, the heathen!'

'The one with the patched sleeve?'

'Yes, yes. Ah, dear God, I've been robbed!'

'What's the story here?'

'He was buying pies and milk from this old woman, stuffed himself full, and pffft! She's here, howling her head off.'

'It can't be left like that. He's got to be caught.'

'Go on, catch him. He's all belts and cartridges. He'll do the catching.'

10

In freight car 14 there were several men rounded up for the labour army. They were guarded by the convoy soldier Voroniuk. Three of them stood out for different reasons. They were: Prokhor Kharitonovich Pritulyev, known as 'casheteer' in the coach, a former cashier in a state wine shop in Petrograd; the sixteen-year-old Vasya Brykin, a boy from a hardware store; and the grey-haired revolutionary cooperator Kostoed-Amursky, who had been in all the forced labour camps of the old times and had opened a new series of them in the new time.

These recruits were all strangers to each other, picked up here and there, and gradually got to know each other during the trip. From their conversations it was learned that the cashier Pritulyev and the shopkeeper's apprentice Vasya Brykin were fellow countrymen, both from Vyatka, and moreover were both born in places that the train was supposed to pass through some time or other.

The tradesman Pritulyev from Malmyzh was a squat man with a brush cut, pockmarked and ugly. His grey jacket, black from sweat under the armpits, fitted him tightly, like the upper part of a sarafan on the fleshy bust of a woman. He was silent as a block of wood and, brooding about something for hours, picked the warts on his freckled hands until they bled and began to fester.

A year back he had been walking down Nevsky Prospect in the autumn and at the corner of Liteiny had happened upon a street round-up. They had asked for his documents. He turned out to be the holder of a ration card of the fourth category, prescribed for non-labouring elements, with which he had never obtained anything. He had been picked up by that token and, together with many others arrested in the street on the same grounds, had been sent to barracks under guard. The party assembled in that way, on the example of one previously put together, which was now digging trenches at the Arkhangelsk front, was first supposed to be moved to Vologda, but was turned back halfway and sent through Moscow to the eastern front.

Pritulyev had a wife in Luga, where he had been working in the pre-war years, before his job in Petersburg. Having learned of his misfortune by hearsay, his wife rushed to look for him in Vologda, to deliver him from the labour army. But the path of the detachment differed from that of her search. Her efforts came to naught. Everything was confused.

In Petersburg, Pritulyev had cohabited with Pelageya Nilovna Tyagunova. He was stopped at the corner of Nevsky just at the moment when he had taken leave of her and was going another way on business, and in the distance, among the passers-by flashing along Liteiny, he could still see her back, which soon disappeared.

This Tyagunova, a full-bodied, stately tradeswoman with beautiful hands and a thick plait, which, with a deep sigh, she kept tossing now over one shoulder, now over the other, onto her breast, accompanied Pritulyev on the troop train of her own free will.

It was not clear what good the women who clung to Pritulyev found in such a block of wood as he. Besides Tyagunova, in another coach of the train, several coaches closer to the engine, rode another acquaintance of Pritulyev, the tow-headed and skinny girl Ogryzkova, to whom Tyagunova gave the abusive titles of 'the nostril' and 'the syringe', among other insulting nicknames.

The rivals were at daggers drawn and avoided each other's eye. Ogryzkova never showed herself in their coach. It was a mystery where she managed to see the object of her adoration. Perhaps she was content to contemplate him from afar, at the general loading of wood and coal by the forces of all the passengers.

11

Vasya's story was something else again. His father had been killed in the war. His mother had sent Vasya from the village to apprentice with his uncle in Petrograd.

That winter the uncle, who owned a hardware store in the Apraksin Arcade, was summoned to the soviet for explanations. He went through the wrong door and, instead of the room indicated on the summons, landed in the one next to it. By chance it was the anteroom of the commission for labour conscription. There were a great many people there, appearing in that section on subpoena. When enough of them had accumulated, Red Army soldiers came, surrounded them, and took them for the night to the Semyonovsky barracks, and in the morning dispatched them to the station, to be put on the train to Vologda.

The news of the detention of so great a number of inhabitants spread through the city. The next day a host of relations came to bid farewell to their dear ones at the station. Among them were Vasya and his aunt, who came to see the uncle off.

At the station the uncle started begging the sentry to let him out for a minute to see his wife. This sentry was Voroniuk, who was now escorting the group in freight car 14. Voroniuk refused to let the uncle out without a sure guarantee that he would come back. The uncle and aunt offered to leave their nephew under guard as such a guarantee. Voroniuk agreed. Vasya was taken inside the fence, the uncle was taken outside. The uncle and aunt never came back.

When the hoax was discovered, Vasya, who had not suspected any fraud, burst into tears. He fell at Voroniuk's feet and kissed his hands, begging him to let him go, but nothing helped. The convoy guard was implacable, not out of cruelty of character. This was a troubled time, the order was strict. The convoy guard was answerable with his life for the number entrusted to his charge, which was established by roll-call. That was how Vasya ended up in the labour army.

The cooperator Kostoed-Amursky, who enjoyed the respect of all the jailers under both the tsar and the present government, and who was always on a personal footing with them, more than once drew the attention of the head of the convoy to Vasya's intolerable situation. The man acknowledged that it was indeed a blatant error, but that formal difficulties did not allow for touching upon this tangle during the journey, and he hoped to disentangle it once they arrived.

Vasya was a pretty young boy with regular features, like portrayals of the tsar's bodyguards and God's angels on popular prints. He was unusually pure and unspoiled. His favourite amusement was to sit on the floor at the feet of the adults, clasping his knees with both arms and throwing his head back, and listen to their talk and stories. The content of it could be reconstructed from the play of the facial muscles with which he held back the tears that were about to flow or fought with the laughter that was choking him. The subject of the conversation was reflected in the impressionable boy's face as in a mirror.

12

The cooperator Kostoed was sitting up above as a guest of the Zhivagos and sucking with a whistle on the shoulder of hare they had offered him. He feared draughts and chills. 'How it blows! Where's it coming from?' he asked and kept changing his place, seeking a sheltered spot. At last he settled himself so that he felt no cold wind and said: 'Now it's good,' finished gnawing the shoulder, licked his fingers, wiped them with a handkerchief, and, having thanked his hosts, observed:

'It's coming from the window. You should stop it up. However, let's get back to the subject of the argument. You're wrong, doctor. Roasted hare is a splendid thing. But, forgive me, to conclude from it that the countryside is flourishing is bold, to say the least. It's a very risky leap.'

'Oh, come now!' Yuri Andreevich objected. 'Look at these stations. The trees haven't been cut down. The fences are intact. And the markets! The peasant women! Just think, how satisfying! There's life somewhere. Somebody's glad. Not everybody groans. That justifies everything.'

'It would be good if it were so. But it's not. Where did you get all that? Go fifty miles from the railway. There are ceaseless peasant revolts everywhere. Against whom, you ask? Against the Whites and against the Reds, depending on who's in power. You say, aha, the muzhik is the enemy of all order, he doesn't know what he wants himself. Excuse me, but it's too early to be triumphant. He knows it better than you, but what he wants is not at all what you and I want.

'When the revolution woke him up, he decided that his age-old dream was coming true, of life on his own, of anarchic farmstead existence by the labour of his own hands, with no dependence and no obligation to anyone at all. But, from the vise grip of the old, overthrown state, he's fallen under the still heavier press of the revolutionary superstate. And now the countryside is thrashing about and finds no peace anywhere. And you say the peasants are flourishing. You know nothing, my dear man, and, as far as I can see, you don't want to know.'

'Well, so, it's true I don't want to. Perfectly right. Ah, go on! Why should I know everything and lay myself out for everything? The times take no account of me and impose whatever they like on me. So allow me to ignore the facts. You say my words don't agree with reality. But is there any reality

in Russia now? In my opinion, it's been so intimidated that it has gone into
hiding. I want to believe that the countryside has benefitted and is prosper-
ing. If that, too, is a delusion, what am I to do, then? What am I to live by,
whom am I to obey? And I have to live, I'm a family man.'

Yuri Andreevich waved his hand and, leaving it to Alexander Alexandrovich to bring the argument with Kostoed to an end, moved closer to the
edge of the berth and, hanging his head over, began to look at what was
happening below.

A general conversation was going on there between Pritulyev, Voroniuk,
Tyagunova, and Vasya. Seeing that they were nearing their native places,
Pritulyev recalled how they were connected, what station you had to get to,
where to get off, how to move further on, afoot or with horses, and Vasya,
at the mention of familiar villages or hamlets, jumped with lit-up eyes and
delightedly repeated their names, because listing them sounded to him like
an enchanting fairy tale.

'You get off at Dry Ford?' he asked breathlessly. 'Well, of course! That's
our junction! Our station! And then most likely you go down to Buiskoe?'

'Then down the Buiskoe road.'

'That's what I said – Buiskoe. The village of Buiskoe. As if I don't know!
That's our turn-off. To get from there to us you keep bearing to the right, to
the right. Towards Veretenniki. And to you, Uncle Kharitonych, it must be
to the left, away from the river? You've heard of the river Pelga? Well, so!
That's our river! And to us you go by the bank, by the bank. And on that
same river, a bit higher up the Pelga, our village! Our Veretenniki. Right up
on the cliff! The bank's ste-e-ep! We call it "the counter". When you're
standing on top, it's scary to look down, it's so steep. For fear of falling. By
God, it's true. They cut stone there. For millstones. And my mama's there in
Veretenniki. And two little sisters. My sister Alenka. And Arishka, my other
sister. My mama, Auntie Palasha, Pelageya Nilovna, she's like you, I'd say,
young, fair. Uncle Voroniuk! Uncle Voroniuk! I beg you, in Christ's name . . .
Uncle Voroniuk!'

'Well, what? What are you saying it over and over for, like a cuckoo bird?
"Uncle Voroniuk! Uncle Voroniuk!" Don't I know I'm not an aunt? What
do you want, what do you need? Want me to let you slip away? Is
that what you're saying? You clear off, and I go to the wall for it, and
amen?'

Pelageya Tyagunova absent-mindedly gazed off somewhere to the side
and said nothing. She stroked Vasya's head and, thinking about something,
fingered his blond hair. Every once in a while she nodded her head and made
signs to the boy with her eyes and her smiles, the meaning of which was that

he should not be silly and talk to Voroniuk out loud about such things. Just wait, she meant, everything will take care of itself, don't worry.

13

When they left the Central Russian region and made their way east, unexpected things came thick and fast. They began to cross troubled areas, districts ruled by armed bands, places where uprisings had recently been quelled.

Stops in the middle of the fields, inspections of the coaches by anti-profiteering units, searches of luggage, verifications of papers became more frequent.

Once the train got stuck somewhere during the night. No one looked into the coaches, no one was awakened. Wondering if there had been an accident, Yuri Andreevich jumped down from the freight car.

It was a dark night. For no apparent reason, the train was standing at some chance milepost on an ordinary, fir-lined stretch of track in the middle of a field. Yuri Andreevich's neighbours, who had jumped down earlier and were dawdling around in front of the freight car, told him that, according to their information, nothing had happened, but it seemed the engineer himself had stopped the train under the pretext that it was a dangerous place and, until the good condition of the tracks was verified by handcar, he refused to take the train any further. It was said that representatives of the passengers had been sent to entreat him and, in case of necessity, to grease his palm. According to rumour, the sailors were mixing into it. They would bring him round.

While this was being explained to Yuri Andreevich, the snowy smoothness down the tracks near the engine kept being lit up by flashes of fire from the smokestack and the vent under the engine's firebox, like the breathing reflections of a bonfire. Suddenly one of these tongues brightly lit up a piece of the snowy field, the engine, and a few black figures running along the edge of the engine's chassis.

Ahead of them, apparently, flashed the engineer. Having reached the end of the footboard, he leaped up and, flying over the buffer bar, disappeared from sight. The sailors pursuing him made the same movements. They, too, ran to the end of the grid, leaped, flashed in the air, and vanished from sight.

Drawn by what they had seen, Yuri Andreevich and a few of the curious walked towards the engine.

In the free part of the line ahead of the train, the following sight presented itself to them. To one side of the tracks, the vanished engineer stuck halfway out of the untouched snow. Like beaters around their game, the sailors surrounded him in a semicircle, buried, like him, waist-deep in the snow.

The engineer shouted:

'Thanks a lot, you stormy petrels![4] I've lived to see it! Coming with a revolver against your brother, a worker! Why did I say the train would go no further? Comrade passengers, be my witnesses, what sort of country this is. Anybody who wants to hangs around, unscrewing nuts. Up yours and your mother's, what's that to me? Devil stick you in the ribs, I'm not talking about me, I'm talking about you, so they don't pull some job on you. And see what I get for my cares. Well, so shoot me, mine layers! Comrade passengers, be my witnesses, I'm right here – I'm not hiding.'

Various voices were heard from the group on the railway embankment. Some exclaimed, taken aback:

'What's with you? . . . Forget it . . . As if we . . . Who'd let them? They're just . . . To put a scare . . .'

Others loudly egged him on:

'That's right, Gavrilka! Don't give up, old Steam-traction!'

A sailor, who was the first to free himself from the snow and turned out to be a red-haired giant with such an enormous head that it made his face look flat, quietly turned to the crowd and in a soft bass, with Ukrainianisms like Voroniuk, spoke a few words, funny for their perfect calm in those extraordinary night circumstances:

'Beg pardon, but what's all this hullabaloo? You're like to get sick in this wind, citizens. Go back to your coaches out of the cold!'

When the crowd began to disperse, gradually returning to their freight cars, the red-haired sailor went up to the engineer, who had not quite come to his senses yet, and said:

'Enough throwing hysterics, comrade engineer. Leave that hole. Let's get going.'

14

The next day, at a quiet pace, with slowdowns every moment, fearing to run off the slightly snow-powdered and unswept rails, the train stopped at a life-forsaken waste, in which they could not immediately recognise the remains of a station destroyed by fire. On its sooty façade the inscription 'Nizhni Kelmes' could be made out.

It was not only the train station that kept the traces of a fire. Behind the station a deserted and snow-covered village could be seen, which had obviously shared its sorry fate.

The end house of the village was charred, the one next to it had several beams knocked loose at the corner and turned butt end in; everywhere in the street lay pieces of broken sledges, fallen-down fences, torn sheet metal, smashed household crockery. The snow, dirty with ashes and soot, had bare black patches showing through it, and was spread with frozen swill and charred logs, traces of the fire and its extinguishing.

The depopulation of the village and the station was incomplete. There were individual living souls in it here and there.

'Did the whole village burn down?' the train master asked sympathetically, jumping down onto the platform, when the stationmaster came out from behind the ruins to meet him.

'Greetings. Glad you've arrived safely. Burn we did, but it's something worse than a fire.'

'I don't understand.'

'Better not go into it.'

'You mean Strelnikov?'

'Himself.'

'What did you do wrong?'

'It wasn't us. The railroad was just tacked on. It was our neighbours. We got it at the same time. See that village over there? They're the culprits. The village of Nizhni Kelmes of the Ust-Nemda district. It's all because of them.'

'And what did they do?'

'Nearly all the seven deadly sins. They disbanded their poor peasants' committee, that's one for you; they opposed the decree on supplying horses to the Red Army – and, notice, they're all Tartars, horse people, that's two; and they didn't obey the order about the mobilisation, that's three – so you can see.'

'Yes, yes. It's all clear, then. And for that they got it from the artillery?'

'Precisely.'

'From an armoured train?'

'Naturally.'

'Regrettable. Deserving of pity. However, it's none of our business.'

'Besides, it's a thing of the past. But my news won't gladden you any. You'll be staying here for a day or two.'

'Stop joking. I'm not here for just anything at all: I've got draft reinforcements for the front. I'm not used to standing around.'

'This is no joke. It's a snowdrift, you'll see for yourself. A blizzard raged for a week along this whole section. Buried it. And there's nobody to shovel. Half the village has run away. I've set the rest to work, but they don't manage.'

'Ah, confound you all! I'm finished, finished! Well, what to do now?'

'We'll clear it somehow and you'll go on.'

'Big drifts?'

'Not very, I wouldn't say. For stretches. The blizzard went slantwise, at an angle to the tracks. The hardest part's in the middle. There's a mile and a half of hollow. We'll really suffer there. The place is packed solid. But further on it's not bad, taiga – the forest sheltered it. The same before the hollow, there's an open stretch, nothing terrible. The wind blew it away.'

'Ah, devil take you all! What a nightmare! I'll get the whole train on their feet, they can all help.'

'I thought the same thing.'

'Only don't touch the sailors and the Red Army soldiers. There's a whole trainload of labour conscripts. Along with freely travelling people, it's as much as seven hundred.'

'That's more than enough. As soon as the shovels are delivered, we'll set them to it. There aren't enough shovels. We've sent to the neighbouring villages. There'll be some.'

'God, what a disaster! Do you think we'll manage?'

'Sure. Pull together, they say, and you take cities. It's the railway. An artery. For pity's sake.'

15

Clearing the line took three days. All the Zhivagos, including Nyusha, took an active part in it. This was the best time of their trip.

The country had something reserved, not fully told, about it. It gave off a breath of Pugachevism, in Pushkin's perception of it, of Asiatic, Aksakovian description.[5]

The mysteriousness of the corner was completed by the destruction and by the reticence of the few remaining inhabitants, who were frightened, avoided the passengers on the train, and did not communicate with each other for fear of denunciations.

People were led out to work by categories, not all kinds simultaneously. The work area was cordoned off by the guards.

The line was cleared from both ends at once, by separate brigades set up in different places. Between the freed sections there remained to the very end piles of untouched snow, which separated the adjacent groups from each other. These piles were removed only at the last moment, once the clearing had been completed over the whole required stretch.

Clear, frosty days set in. They spent them in the open air, returning to the coach only for the night. They worked in short shifts, which caused no fatigue, because there were too many workers and not enough shovels. The untiring work afforded nothing but pleasure.

The place where the Zhivagos went to dig was open, picturesque. The country at this point first descended to the east of the tracks, and then went up in an undulating slope as far as the horizon.

On a hill stood a solitary house, exposed on all sides. It was surrounded by a garden, which probably bushed out in the summer, but now its spare, frost-covered tracery did not protect the building.

The shroud of snow levelled and rounded everything. But, judging by the main irregularities of the slope, which it was unable to conceal with its drifts, in spring a brook, flowing into the pipe of the viaduct under the railway, probably ran from above down the meandering gully, now thickly covered by the deep snow, like a child hiding its head under the heap of a down coverlet.

Was anyone living in the house, or was it standing empty and falling to ruin, set down on a list by the local or district land committee? Where were its former inhabitants, and what had happened to them? Had they escaped abroad? Had they perished at the hands of the peasants? Or, having earned a good name, had they settled in the district town as educated experts? Had Strelnikov spared them, if they stayed until recently, or had they been included in his summary justice along with the kulaks?[6]

The house on the hill piqued his curiosity and kept mournfully silent. But questions were not asked then, and no one answered them. And the sun lit up the snowy smoothness with a blinding white brilliance. How regular were the pieces the shovel cut from it! What dry, diamond-like sparkles spilled from the cuts! How it reminded him of the far-off days of childhood, when, in a light-coloured hood trimmed with braid and a lambskin coat with hooks tightly sewn into the black, curly wool, little Yura had cut pyramids and cubes, cream cakes, fortresses, and cave dwellings from the snow in the courtyard, which was just as blinding. Ah, how tasty it was to live in the world then, how delightful and delicious everything around him was!

But even this three-day life in the open air produced an impression of satiety. And not without reason. In the evening the workers were allotted hot, freshly baked white bread, brought from no one knew where, on no one knew whose orders. The bread had a delicious glazed crust that was cracked on the sides, and a thick, superbly browned bottom crust with little bits of coal baked into it.

16

They came to love the ruins of the station, as one can grow attached to a temporary shelter during an excursion in the snowy mountains. They kept the memory of its situation, the external appearance of the buildings, certain details of the damage.

They returned to the station in the evening, when the sun was setting. As if out of faithfulness to the past, it continued to set in the same place, behind the old birch that grew just by the telegraphist's office window.

The outer wall at that place had collapsed inward and blocked up the room. But the cave-in had not harmed the back corner of the room, facing an intact window. There everything was preserved: the coffee-coloured wallpaper, the tile stove with a round vent under a brass cover on a chain, and a list of the inventory in a black frame on the wall.

Having sunk to the ground, the sun, just as before the disaster, reached the tiles of the stove, lit up the coffee-coloured wallpaper with a russet heat, and hung the shadows of birch branches on the wall like a woman's shawl.

In another part of the building, there was a boarded-up door to a waiting room with an inscription of the following content, done probably in the first days of the February revolution or shortly before it:

'In view of medications and bandaging supplies, our respected patients are asked not to worry temporarily. For the reason observed, I am sealing the door, of which I hereby give notice. Senior medical assistant of Ust-Nemda so-and-so.'

When the last snow, which had been left in mounds between the cleared sections, was shovelled away, the whole railway opened out and became visible, straight, like an arrow flying off into the distance. Along the sides of it lay white heaps of cleared snow, bordered for the entire length by two walls of black pine forest.

As far as the eye could see, groups of people with shovels stood in various places along the rails. They were seeing each other in full muster for the first time and were surprised at their great numbers.

17

It became known that the train would leave in a few hours, even though it was late and night was approaching. Before its departure, Yuri Andreevich and Antonina Alexandrovna went for the last time to admire the beauty of the cleared line. There was no one on the tracks now. The doctor and his wife stood for a while, looked into the distance, exchanged two or three remarks, and turned back to their freight car.

On the way back they heard the angry, raucous cries of two quarrelling women. They recognised them at once as the voices of Ogryzkova and Tyagunova. The two women were walking in the same direction as the doctor and his wife, from the head to the tail of the train, but along the opposite side of it, facing the station, while Yuri Andreevich and Antonina Alexandrovna were walking on the forest side. Between the two pairs, concealing them from each other, stretched the unbroken wall of coaches. The women almost never came abreast of the doctor and Antonina Alexandrovna, but either got way ahead of them or lagged far behind.

Both were in great agitation. Their strength failed them every moment. As they went, their legs probably either sank deep in the snow or gave way under them, judging by their voices, which, owing to the unevenness of their gait, now rose to a shout, now fell to a whisper. Evidently, Tyagunova was chasing Ogryzkova and, overtaking her, may have brought her fists into play. She showered her rival with choice abuse, which, on the melodious lips of such a peahen and grande dame sounded a hundred times more shameless than coarse and unmusical male abuse.

'Ah, you whore, ah, you slattern,' shouted Tyagunova. 'You can't take a step but she's there, swishing her skirts on the floor, goggling her eyes! So my oaf's not enough for you, you bitch, you've got to gawk at a child's soul, spreading your tail, you've got to corrupt a young one.'

'So it means you're Vasenka's lawful one, too?'

'I'll show you who's lawful, you gob, you plague! You won't escape me alive, don't lead me into sin!'

'Hey, hey, stop swinging! Keep your hands to yourself, hellcat! What do you want from me?'

'I want you to drop dead, you lousy trollop, mangy she-cat, shameless eyes!'

'There's no talking about me. Sure, I'm a bitch and a she-cat, everybody knows that. But you, you've got you a title. Born in a ditch, married in a gateway, made pregnant by a rat, gave birth to a hedgehog . . . Help, help, good people! Aie, aie, she'll do me to death, the murderous hag! Aie, save a poor girl, protect an orphan . . .'

'Quick, let's go. I can't listen, it's disgusting,' Antonina Alexandrovna began hurrying her husband. 'It won't end well.'

18

Suddenly everything changed, the place and the weather. The plain ended, the road went between mountains, through hills and high country. The north wind that had blown all the time recently ceased. Warmth breathed from the south, as from a stove.

The forests here grew in terraces on the hillsides. When the path of the railway crossed them, the train first had to go up steeply, then change in the middle to a sloping descent. The train crept groaning into the dense forest and barely dragged itself along, like an old forester on foot leading a crowd of passengers who look around on all sides and observe everything.

But there was nothing to look at yet. In the depths of the forest there were sleep and peace, as in winter. Only rarely did some bushes and trees, with a rustle, free their lower branches from the gradually subsiding snow, as if taking off a yoke or unbuttoning a collar.

Yuri Andreevich was overcome by sleepiness. All those days he lay on his upper berth, slept, woke up, reflected, and listened. But as yet there was nothing to listen to.

19

While Yuri Andreevich slept his fill, spring thawed and melted all the masses of snow that had fallen on Moscow the day of their departure and had gone on falling throughout the journey; all the snow that they had spent three days digging and shovelling in Ust-Nemda and that lay in immense and thick layers over thousand-mile expanses.

At first the snow melted from inside, quietly and secretively. But when the Herculean labours were half done, it became impossible to conceal them any longer. The miracle came to light. Water ran from under the shifted shroud of snow and set up a clamour. Impassable forest thickets roused themselves. Everything in them awoke.

The water had room for a spree. It rushed down the cliffs, overflowed the ponds, flooded vast areas. The forest was soon filled with its noise, steam, and haze. Streams snaked their way through the thickets, getting mired down and sinking into the snow that cramped their movement, flowed hissing over the flat places, and dropped down, scattering in a watery spray. The earth could not absorb any more moisture. From a dizzying height, almost from the clouds, it was drunk up by the roots of age-old firs, at whose feet it was churned into puffs of brownish white foam, drying like beer foam on a drinker's lips.

The intoxication of spring went to the sky's head, and it grew bleary from fumes and covered itself with clouds. Low, feltlike clouds with drooping edges drifted over the forest, and warm cloudbursts, smelling of dirt and sweat, poured down through them, washing the last pieces of pierced, black, icy armour from the earth.

Yuri Andreevich woke up, pulled himself over to the square window, from which the frame had been removed, propped himself on his elbow, and began to listen.

20

With the approach of the mining region, the country became more populated, the stages shorter, the stations more frequent. The passengers changed less rarely. More people got on and off at small intermediate stops. Those who were travelling for shorter distances did not settle for long and did not go to sleep, but found places at night somewhere by the doors in the middle of the freight car, talked among themselves in low voices about local affairs, comprehensible only to them, and got off at the next junction or way station.

From some remarks dropped by the local public, who had replaced each other in the freight car over the past three days, Yuri Andreevich concluded that the Whites were gaining the upper hand in the north and either had taken or were about to take Yuriatin. Besides, if his hearing had not deceived him and it was not some namesake of his comrade in the Meliuzeevo hospital, the White forces in that direction were under the command of Galiullin, who was well-known to Yuri Andreevich.

Yuri Andreevich did not say a word to his family about this talk, so as not to upset them uselessly while the rumours remained unconfirmed.

21

Yuri Andreevich woke up at the beginning of the night from a vague feeling of happiness welling up in him, which was so strong that it roused him. The train was standing at some night stop. The station was surrounded by the glassy twilight of a white night. This bright darkness was saturated with something subtle and powerful. It bore witness to the vastness and openness of the place. It suggested that the junction was situated on a height with a wide and free horizon.

On the platform, talking softly, shadows went past the freight car with inaudible steps. That also touched Yuri Andreevich. He perceived in the careful steps and voices a respect for the hour of night and a concern for the sleepers on the train as might have been in the old days, before the war.

The doctor was mistaken. There was the same hubbub and stamping of boots on the platform as everywhere else. But there was a waterfall in the vicinity. Its breathing out of freshness and freedom extended the limits of the white night. It had filled the doctor with a feeling of happiness in his sleep. The constant, never ceasing noise of its falling water reigned over all the sounds at the junction and imparted to them a deceptive semblance of silence.

Not divining its presence, but lulled by the mysterious resilience of the air of the place, the doctor fell fast asleep again.

Two men were talking below in the freight car. One asked the other:

'Well, so, have you calmed them down? Twisted their tails?'

'The shopkeepers, you mean?'

'Yes, the grain dealers.'

'We've pacified them. Like silk now. We knocked off a few as an example, and the rest got quiet. We collected a contribution.'

'How much did you take from the area?'

'Forty thousand.'

'You're kidding!'

'Why should I kid you?'

'Holy cow, forty thousand!'

'Forty thousand bushels.'

'Well, there's no flies on you! Good boys, good boys!'

'Forty thousand milled fine.'

'I suppose it's no wonder. This area's first class. Heart of the meal trade. Here along the Rynva and up to Yuriatin, village after village, it's landings, grain depots. The Sherstobitov brothers, Perekatchikov and sons, wholesaler after wholesaler!'

'Don't shout. You'll wake people up.'

'All right.'

The speaker yawned. The other suggested:

'How about a little snooze? Looks like we'll be starting.'

Just then a deafening noise came rolling from behind, swiftly growing, covering the roar of the waterfall, and an old-fashioned express train raced at full steam down the second track of the junction past their train, which stood without moving, hooted, roared, and, blinking its lights for the last time, vanished into the distance without a trace.

The conversation below resumed.

'Well, that's it now. We'll sit it out.'

'It won't be soon now.'

'Must be Strelnikov. Armoured, special purpose.'

'It's him, then.'

'When it comes to counter-revolutionists, he's ferocious.'

'It's him racing against Galeev.'

'Who's that?'

'The ataman Galeev. They say he's standing with his Czechs covering Yuriatin. Seized control of the landings, blast him, and he's holding them. The ataman Galeev.'[7]

'Prince Galileev, maybe. I forget.'

'There's no such prince. Must be Ali Kurban. You got mixed up.'

'Kurban, maybe.'

'That's another story.'

22

Towards morning Yuri Andreevich woke up a second time. Again he had dreamed something pleasant. The feeling of bliss and liberation that had filled him did not end. Again the train was standing, maybe at a new station, or maybe at the old one. Again there was the noise of a waterfall, most likely the same one, but possibly another.

Yuri Andreevich began to fall asleep at once and through his dozing fancied running feet and turmoil. Kostoed grappled with the head of the convoy, and the two shouted at each other. Outside it was still better than before. There was a breath of something new that had not been there earlier. Something magical, something springlike, black-and-white, flimsy, loose, like the coming of a snowstorm in May, when the wet, melting flakes on the ground make it not white but blacker still. Something transparent, black-and-white, strong scented. 'Bird cherry!' Yuri Andreevich guessed in his sleep.

23

In the morning Antonina Alexandrovna said:

'Still, you're an amazing man, Yura. A tissue of contradictions. Sometimes a fly flies by, you wake up and can't close your eyes till morning, and here there's noise, arguments, commotion, and you can't manage to wake up. During the night the cashier Pritulyev and Vasya Brykin ran off. Yes, just think! And Tyagunova and Ogryzkova. Wait, that's still not all. And Voroniuk. Yes, yes, ran off, ran off. Yes, imagine. Now listen. How they got away, together or separately, and in what order, is an absolute mystery. Well, let's allow that this Voroniuk, naturally, decided to save himself from the responsibility on finding that the others had escaped. But the others? Did they all vanish of their own free will, or was one of them forcibly eliminated? For instance, suspicion falls on the women. But who killed whom, Tyagunova Ogryzkova or Ogryzkova Tyagunova, nobody knows. The head of the convoy runs from one end of the train to the other. "How dare you give the whistle for departure," he shouts. "In the name of the law, I demand that you hold the train until the escapees are caught." But the train master doesn't yield. "You're out of your mind," he says. "I've got draft reinforcements for the front, an urgent first priority. I should wait for your lousy crew! What a thing to come up with!" And both of them, you understand, fall on Kostoed with reproaches. How is it that he, a cooperator, a man of understanding, was right there and didn't keep the soldier, a benighted, unconscious being, from the fatal step. "And you a populist," they say. Well, Kostoed, of course, doesn't let it go at that. "Interesting!" he says. "So according to you a prisoner should look after a convoy soldier? Yes, sure, when a hen crows like a cock!" I nudged you in the side and shoulder. "Yura," I shout, "wake up, an escape!" Forget it! Cannon shots wouldn't have roused you . . . But forgive me, of that later. And meanwhile . . . No, I can't . . . Papa, Yura, look, how enchanting!'

Beyond the opening of the window, by which they lay with their heads thrust forward, spread a flooded area with no beginning or end. Somewhere a river had overflowed, and the waters of its side branch had come up close to the railway embankment. In foreshortening, brought about by looking from the height of the berth, it seemed as if the smoothly rolling train was gliding right over the water.

Its glassy smoothness was covered in a very few places by a ferrous blueness. Over the rest of the surface, the hot morning drove mirrory, oily patches of light, like a cook smearing the crust of a hot pie with a feather dipped in oil.

In this seemingly boundless backwater, along with meadows, hollows, and bushes, the pillars of white clouds were drowned, their piles reaching to the bottom.

Somewhere in the middle of the backwater a narrow strip of land was visible, with double trees suspended upwards and downwards between sky and earth.

'Ducks! A brood!' cried Alexander Alexandrovich, looking in that direction. 'Where?'

'By the island. Not there. To the right, to the right. Ah, damn, they flew away, got frightened.'

'Ah, yes, I see. There's something I must talk with you about, Alexander Alexandrovich. Some other time. But our labour army and the ladies did well to get away. And it was peaceful, I think, without doing anybody harm. They simply ran off, the way water runs.'

24

The northern white night was ending. Everything was visible, but stood as if not believing itself, like something made up: mountain, copse, and precipice.

The copse had barely begun to turn green. In it several bird cherry bushes were blooming. The copse grew under the sheer of the mountain, on a narrow ledge that also broke off some distance away.

Nearby was a waterfall. It could not be seen from everywhere, but only from the other side of the copse, at the edge of the precipice. Vasya got tired going there to gaze at the waterfall for the experience of terror and admiration.

There was nothing around equal to the waterfall, nothing to match it. It was fearsome in this singularity, which turned it into something endowed with life and consciousness, into a fairy-tale dragon or giant serpent of those parts, who exacted tribute from the people and devastated the countryside.

Halfway down, the waterfall struck a protruding jag of rock and divided in two. The upper column of water was almost motionless, but in the two lower ones a barely perceptible movement from side to side never ceased for a moment, as if the waterfall kept slipping and straightening up, slipping and straightening up, and however often it lurched, it always kept its feet.

Vasya, spreading his sheepskin under him, lay down at the edge of the copse. When the dawn became more noticeable, a big, heavy-winged bird flew down from the mountain, glided in a smooth circle around the copse, and alighted at the top of a silver fir near the spot where Vasya lay. He raised his head, looked at the blue throat and blue-grey breast of the roller, and, spellbound, whispered aloud its Urals name: 'Ronzha.' Then he got up, took the sheepskin from the ground, threw it on, and, crossing the clearing, came over to his companion. He said to her:

'Come on, auntie. See, you're chilled, your teeth are chattering. Well, what are you staring at like you're so scared? I'm talking human speech to you, we've got to go. Enter into the situation, we've got to keep to the villages. In a village they won't harm their own kind, they'll hide us. We haven't eaten for two days, we'll starve to death like this. Uncle Voroniuk must have raised hell looking for us. We've got to get out of here, Auntie Palasha, clear off, to put it simply. You're such a pain to me, auntie, you haven't said a word the whole day! Grief's got your tongue, by God. What are you pining over? There was no wrong in you pushing Auntie Katya, Katya Ogryzkova, off the train. You just brushed against her with your side, I saw it myself. She got up from the grass unhurt, got up and ran. And the same with Uncle Prokhor, Prokhor Kharitonych. They're catching up with us, we'll be together again, don't you think? The main thing is you mustn't grieve, then your tongue'll start working again.'

Tyagunova got up from the ground and, giving Vasya her hand, said softly:

'Come on, dovey.'

25

Creaking all over, the coaches went uphill along the high embankment. Under it grew a mixed young forest, the tops of which did not reach its level. Below were meadows from which the water had just receded. The grass, mixed with sand, was covered with logs for ties, which lay randomly in all directions. They had probably been prepared for rafting at some nearby coppice, and had been washed away and carried here by the high water.

The young forest below the embankment was still almost bare, as in winter. Only in the buds, which were spattered all over it like drops of wax, was something superfluous setting in, some disorder, a sort of dirt or swelling, and this superfluous thing, this disorder and dirt, was life, enveloping the first opening trees of the forest in the green flame of foliage.

Here and there birches stood straight as martyrs, pierced by the cogs and arrows of twin, just unfolded leaves. What they smelled of could be told by eye. They smelled of the same thing they shone with. They smelled of wood spirit, from which varnish is made.

Soon the railway came up to the place from which the logs might have been washed. At a turn in the forest, a clearing appeared, strewn with sawdust and chips, with a heap of twenty-foot logs in the middle. The engineer braked by the cutting area. The train shuddered and stopped in the position it assumed, slightly inclined on the high arc of a big curve.

The engine gave several short, barking whistles and someone shouted something. The passengers knew even without the signals: the engineer had stopped the train to take on fuel.

The doors of the freight cars slid open. Out onto the tracks poured the goodly population of a small town, excluding the mobilised men from the front cars, who were always exempt from deckhands' work and did not take part in it now.

The pile of stove wood in the clearing was not enough to load the tender. In addition they were required to cut up a certain number of the twenty-foot logs.

The engine team had saws in its outfit. They were handed out among volunteers, who broke up into pairs. The professor and his son-in-law also received a saw.

From the open doors of the military freight cars, merry mugs stuck out. Adolescents who had never been under fire, naval cadets from the senior classes, mistakenly intruded into the wagon, as it seemed, among stern workers, family men, who had also never smelled powder and had only just finished military training, deliberately made a noise and played the fool with the older sailors, so as not to start thinking. Everyone felt that the hour of trial was at hand.

The jokers accompanied the sawyers, men and women, with loud banter:

'Hey, grandpa! Tell them – I'm a nursling, my mama hasn't weaned me, I can't do physical labour. Hey, Mavra, see you don't saw your skirt off, it'll be draughty! Hey, girl, don't go to the forest, better marry me instead!'

26

In the forest there were several sawhorses made from stakes tied crosswise, their ends driven into the ground. One turned out to be free. Yuri Andreevich and Alexander Alexandrovich set themselves to sawing on it.

It was that time of spring when the earth comes out from under the snow looking almost the same as when it went under the snow six months earlier. The forest exuded dampness and was all littered with last year's leaves, like an untidied room in which people had torn up receipts, letters, and notices for many years of their lives and had had no time to sweep them away.

'Not so fast, you'll get tired,' the doctor said to Alexander Alexandrovich, making the saw go more slowly and measuredly, and suggested that they rest.

The forest was filled with the hoarse ringing of other saws going back and forth, now all in rhythm, now discordantly. Somewhere far, far away the first nightingale was testing its strength. A blackbird whistled at still longer intervals, as if blowing through a clogged flute. Even the steam from the engine's piston rose into the sky with a singsong burble, as if it were milk coming to the boil over a spirit lamp in a nursery.

'You wanted to talk about something,' Alexander Alexandrovich reminded the doctor. 'You haven't forgotten? It was like this: we were passing a flooded field, ducks were flying, you fell to thinking and said: "I must talk with you."'

'Ah, yes. I don't know how to put it briefly. You see, we're going ever deeper . . . The whole region here is in ferment. We'll arrive soon. It's not known what we'll find at our destination. Just in case, we must come to an agreement. I'm not talking about convictions. It would be absurd to find them out or establish them in a five-minute talk in a spring forest. We know each other well. The three of us – you, I, and Tonya – along with many others in our time, make up a single world, differing from each other only in the degree of our comprehension. I'm not talking about that. That's an ABC. I'm talking about something else. We must agree beforehand on how to behave under certain circumstances, so as not to blush for each other and not to put the stain of disgrace on each other.'

'Enough. I understand. I like the way you pose the question. You've found precisely the necessary words. Here's what I'll tell you. Do you remember the night when you brought the leaflet with the first decrees, in winter, during a blizzard? Do you remember how incredibly unconditional it was? That straightforwardness was winning. But these things live in their original purity only in the heads of their creators, and then only on the first day of their proclamation. The very next day the Jesuitism of politics turns them inside out. What can I say to you? This philosophy is alien to me. This power is against us. They didn't ask me to consent to this break-up. But they trusted me, and my actions, even if I was forced into them, placed me under obligation.

'Tonya asks if we'll come in time to start a vegetable garden, if we'll miss the time for planting. What can I answer? I don't know the local soil. What are the climatic conditions? The summer's too short. Does anything at all ripen here?

'Yes, but can we be going such a distance to take up gardening? Even the old saying, "Why walk a mile for a pint of beer," is impossible here, because there are, unfortunately, two or three thousand of those miles. No, frankly speaking, we're dragging ourselves so far with a totally different purpose. We're going to try to vegetate in the contemporary way and somehow get in on squandering grandfather's former forests, machinery, and inventory. Not on restoring his property, but on wasting it, on the socialised blowing of thousands in order to exist on a kopeck, and like everybody else, to be sure, in a contemporary, incomprehensibly chaotic form. Shower me with gold, I still wouldn't take the factory on the old basis even as a gift. It would be as wild as starting to run around naked or forgetting how to read and write. No, the history of property in Russia is over. And personally, we Gromekos already lost the passion for money grubbing in the previous generation.'

27

It was so hot and stuffy that it was impossible to sleep. The doctor's head was bathed in sweat on the sweat-soaked pillow.

He carefully got down from the edge of the berth and quietly, so as not to waken anyone, slid the car door aside.

Dampness breathed in his face, sticky, as when your face runs into a spiderweb in a cellar. 'Mist,' he guessed. 'Mist. The day will probably be sultry, scorching. That's why it's so hard to breathe and there's such an oppressive heaviness on the heart.'

Before getting down on the tracks, the doctor stood for a while in the doorway, listening all around.

The train was standing in some very big station of the junction category. Besides the silence and the mist, the cars were immersed in some sort of non-being and neglect, as if they had been forgotten – a sign that the train was standing in the very back of the yard, and that between it and the far-off station building there was a great distance, occupied by an endless network of tracks.

Two sorts of sounds rang out faintly in the distance.

Behind, where they had come from, could be heard a measured slapping, as if laundry were being rinsed or the wind were flapping the wet cloth of a flag against the wood of a flagpole.

From ahead came a low rumble, which made the doctor, who had been at war, shudder and strain his ears.

'Long-range cannon,' he decided, listening to the even, calmly rolling noise on a low, restrained note.

'That's it. We've come right to the front,' the doctor thought, shook his head, and jumped down from the coach to the ground.

He went several steps forward. After the next two coaches, the train ended. It stood without an engine, which had gone somewhere with the detached front coaches.

'That's why they showed such bravado yesterday,' thought the doctor. 'They clearly felt that, once they arrived, they'd be thrown right into the fire on the spot.'

He went around the end of the train, intending to cross the tracks and find the way to the station. At the corner of the coach, a sentry with a rifle surged up as if out of the ground. He snapped softly:

'Where are you going? Your pass!'

'What station is this?'

'No station. Who are you?'

'I'm a doctor from Moscow. Travelling with my family on this train. Here are my papers.'

'Your papers are crap. Think I'm fool enough to go reading in the dark and ruin my eyes? There's mist, see? I can tell what kind of doctor you are a mile away without any papers. That's your doctors there, banging away from twelve-inchers. You really ought to be knocked off, but it's too early. Back with you, while you're still in one piece.'

'I'm being taken for someone else,' thought the doctor. To get into an argument with the sentry was meaningless. It truly was better to withdraw before it was too late. The doctor turned in the opposite direction.

The cannon fire behind his back died down. That direction was the east. There in the haze of the mist the sun rose and peeped dimly between the scraps of floating murk, the way naked people in a bathhouse flash through clouds of soapy steam.

The doctor walked along the coaches of the train. He passed them all and went on walking further. With each step, his feet sank ever deeper into the loose sand.

The sounds of measured slapping came closer. The ground sloped down. After a few steps the doctor stopped in front of outlines that the mist endowed with incongruously large dimensions. Another step, and the sterns of boats pulled up onto the bank emerged from the murk. He was standing on the bank of a wide river, its lazy ripples slowly and wearily lapping against the sides of fishermen's boats and the planks of the docks on shore.

'Who gave you permission to hang around here?' another sentry asked, detaching himself from the bank.

'What river is this?' the doctor shot back against his own will, though with all the forces of his soul he was determined not to ask anything after his recent experience.

Instead of an answer, the sentry put a whistle between his teeth, but he had no time to use it. The first sentry, whom he had intended to summon by his whistling, and who, as it turned out, had been inconspicuously following behind Yuri Andreevich, came up to his comrade himself. The two began to talk.

'Nothing to think about here. You can tell the bird by its flight. "What station is this? What river is this?" Thought he'd distract our attention by it. What do you think – straight to the jetty, or to the coach first?'

'To the coach, I suppose. Whatever the chief says. Your identity papers,' barked the second sentry, and he grabbed the wad of papers the doctor handed him.

'Keep an eye on him,' he said to some unknown person, and together with the first sentry, he went down the tracks towards the station.

Then, to clarify the situation, a man lying on the sand, evidently a fisherman, grunted and stirred:

'Lucky for you they want to take you to the man himself. It may be your salvation. Only don't blame them. It's their duty. The time of the people. Maybe it's for the best. But meanwhile, don't say anything. You see, they mistook you for somebody. They've been hunting and hunting for some man. So they thought it was you. Here he is, they think, the enemy of the workers' power – we've caught him. A mistake. In case of something, you should insist on seeing the chief. Don't let these two have you. These class-conscious ones are a disaster, God help us. It wouldn't cost them a cent to do you in. They'll say, "Let's go," but don't go. You say, "I want to see the chief."'

From the fisherman Yuri Andreevich learned that the river he was standing beside was the famous navigable river Rynva, that the station by the river was Razvilye, the riverside factory suburb of the city of Yuriatin. He learned that Yuriatin itself, which lay a mile or two further up, kept being fought over, and now seemed finally to have been won away from the Whites. The fisherman told him that there had been disorders in Razvilye as well, and they also seemed to have been put down, and there reigned such silence all around, because the area adjacent to the station had been cleared of civilian inhabitants and surrounded by a strict cordon. He learned, finally, that among the trains standing on the tracks with various military institutions housed in them, there was the special train of the regional army commissar Strelnikov, to whose coach the doctor's papers were taken.

From there a new sentry came after some time to fetch the doctor, one unlike his predecessors in that he dragged his rifle butt on the ground or set it down in front of him, as if carrying a drunken friend under the arm, who otherwise would have fallen down. He led the doctor to the army commissar's coach.

28

In one of the two saloon coaches, connected by a leather passageway, which the sentry, having given the guard the password, climbed into with the doctor, laughter and movement could be heard, which instantly ceased on their appearance.

The sentry led the doctor down a narrow corridor to the wide middle section. Here there was silence and order. In the clean, comfortable room, neat, well-dressed people were working. The doctor had quite a different picture of the headquarters of the non-party military specialist who in a short period of time had become the glory and terror of the whole region.

But the centre of his activity was probably not here, but somewhere ahead, at front-line headquarters, closer to the scene of military activity, while here were his personal quarters, his small home office, and his mobile camp bed.

That was why it was quiet here, like the corridors of hot sea baths, laid with cork and rugs on which attendants in soft shoes step inaudibly.

The middle section of the coach was a former dining room, carpeted over and turned into a dispatch room. There were several desks in it.

'One moment,' said a young officer who was sitting closest to the entrance. After that everyone at the desks thought it their right to forget about the doctor and stop paying attention to him. The same officer dismissed the sentry with an absent-minded nod, and the man withdrew, the butt of his rifle clanking against the metal crossbars of the corridor.

The doctor saw his papers from the threshold. They lay on the edge of the last desk, in front of a more elderly officer of the old colonel type. He was some sort of military statistician. Humming something under his breath, he glanced at reference books, scrutinised army maps, compared, juxtaposed, cut out, and glued in something. He passed his gaze over all the windows in the room, one after the other, and said: 'It's going to be hot today,' as if he had drawn this conclusion from surveying all the windows, and it was not equally clear from each of them.

A military technician was crawling over the floor among the desks, fixing some broken wires. When he crawled under the young officer's desk, the man got up so as not to hinder him. Next to him a girl, a copying clerk, in a man's khaki jacket, was struggling over a broken typewriter. The carriage had gone too far to the side and got stuck in the frame. The young officer stood behind her stool and, together with her, studied the cause of the breakage from above. The military technician crawled over to the typist and examined the lever and gears from below. Getting up from his place, the commander of the colonel type went over to them. Everyone became occupied with the typewriter.

This reassured the doctor. It was impossible to suppose that people better initiated than he into his probable destiny would give themselves so lightheartedly to trifles in the presence of a doomed man.

'Though who knows about them?' he thought. 'Where does their serenity come from? Beside them cannons boom, people are killed, and they make a forecast of a hot day, not in the sense of hot fighting, but of hot weather. Or have they seen so much that everything has gone dull in them?'

And, having nothing else to do, he began looking from his place across the entire room through the windows opposite.

29

In front of the train on this side stretched the rest of the tracks, and the Razvilye station could be seen on a hill in the suburb of the same name.

An unpainted wooden stairway with three landings led from the tracks up to the station.

The railway tracks on this side seemed to be a great engine graveyard. Old locomotives without tenders, with smokestacks shaped like cups or boot tops, stood turned stack to stack amidst piles of scrapped coaches.

The engine graveyard below and the graveyard of the suburb, the crumpled iron on the tracks and the rusty roofs and signboards of the city's outskirts, merged into one spectacle of abandonment and decrepitude under the white sky scalded by the early morning heat.

In Moscow, Yuri Andreevich forgot how many signboards there were in cities and what a great portion of the façades they occupied. The local signboards reminded him of it. Half of them were written in such big letters that they could be read from the train. They came down so low over the crooked little windows of the lopsided one-storey buildings that the squatty houses disappeared under them, like peasant boys' heads with their fathers' caps pulled down over them.

By that time the mist had dispersed completely. Traces of it remained only on the left side of the sky, far to the east. But now they, too, stirred, moved, and parted like a theatre curtain.

There, some two miles from Razvilye, on a hill higher than the suburbs, appeared a large city, a district or provincial capital. The sun lent its colours a yellowish tinge, the distance simplified its lines. It clung to the elevation in tiers, like Mount Athos or a hermits' skete in a cheap print, house above house, street above street, with a big cathedral in the middle on its crown.

'Yuriatin!' the doctor realised with emotion. 'The subject of the late Anna Ivanovna's memories and of the nurse Antipova's frequent remarks! How many times did I hear the name of the city from them, and it's in such circumstances that I'm seeing it for the first time!'

At that moment the attention of the military bent over the typewriter was attracted by something outside the window. They turned their heads there. The doctor also followed their gaze.

Several captured or arrested men were being led up the stairs to the station, among them a high school boy who was wounded in the head. He had been bandaged somewhere, but blood seeped from under the bandage, and he smeared it with his hand over his sunburnt, sweaty face.

The student, between two Red Army men who wound up the procession, caught one's attention not only by the resolution that his handsome face breathed, but by the pity evoked by such a young rebel. He and his two escorts attracted one's gaze by the senselessness of their actions. They constantly did the opposite of what they should.

The cap kept falling off the student's bandaged head. Instead of taking it off and carrying it in his hand, he would straighten it and pull it down further, to the detriment of his dressed wound, and the two Red Army men readily helped him.

In this absurdity, contrary to common sense, there was something symbolic. And, yielding to its significance, the doctor also wanted to run out to the landing and stop the student with a ready phrase that was bursting from him. He wanted to cry out both to the boy and to the people in the coach that salvation lay not in faithfulness to forms, but in liberation from them.

The doctor shifted his gaze aside. In the middle of the room stood Strelnikov, who had just come in with straight, impetuous strides.

How could he, the doctor, amidst such a host of indefinite acquaintances, not have known up to now such definiteness as this man? How had life not thrown them together? How had their paths not crossed?

For some unknown reason it became clear at once that this man represented the consummate manifestation of will. He was to such a degree what he wanted to be that everything on him and in him inevitably seemed exemplary: his proportionately constructed and handsomely placed head, and the impetuousness of his stride, and his long legs in high boots, which may have been dirty but seemed polished, and his grey flannel tunic, which may have been wrinkled but gave the impression of ironed linen.

Thus acted the presence of giftedness, natural, knowing no strain, feeling itself in the saddle in any situation of earthly existence.

This man must have possessed some gift, not necessarily an original one. The gift that showed in all his movements might be the gift of imitation. They all imitated someone then. The glorious heroes of history. Figures seen at the front or in the days of disturbances in the cities and who struck the imagination. The most acknowledged authorities among the people. Comrades who came to the fore. Or simply each other.

Out of courtesy, he did not show that the presence of a stranger surprised or embarrassed him. On the contrary, he addressed everyone with such an air as if he included the doctor, too, in their company. He said:

'Congratulations. We've driven them off. This seems like a war game, and not the real thing, because they're Russians as we are, only with a folly in them that they don't want to part with and that we'll have to knock out of them by force. Their commander used to be my friend. He's of still more proletarian origin than I am. We grew up in the same courtyard. He did a lot for me in my life, I'm obliged to him. But I'm glad I've thrust him back across the river and maybe further. Repair the connection quickly, Guryan. We can't go on with just messengers and the telegraph. Have you noticed how hot it is? I slept for an hour and a half even so. Ah, yes . . .' he recalled and turned to the doctor. He remembered the cause of his waking up. He had been awakened by some nonsense, by force of which this detainee was standing here.

'This one?' thought Strelnikov, measuring the doctor from head to foot with a searching look. 'No resemblance. What fools!' He laughed and said to Yuri Andreevich:

'I beg your pardon, comrade. You've been taken for someone else. My sentries got it wrong. You're free. Where's the comrade's work book? Ah, here are your papers. Excuse my indiscretion, I'll allow myself a passing glance. Zhivago . . . Zhivago . . . Doctor Zhivago . . . Something to do with Moscow . . . You know, all the same let's go to my place for a minute. This is the secretariat, and my coach is the next one. If you please. I won't keep you long.'

30

Who was this man, though? It was astonishing that a non-party man, whom no one knew, because, though born in Moscow, he had left after finishing the university to teach in the provinces, then had been held prisoner for a long time during the war, had been missing until recently and presumed dead, could advance to such posts and hold on to them.

The progressive railway worker Tiverzin, in whose family Strelnikov had been brought up as a boy, had recommended him and vouched for him. The people upon whom appointments depended at that time trusted him. In days of excessive pathos and the most extreme views, Strelnikov's revolutionism, which stopped at nothing, stood out by its genuineness, its fanaticism, not borrowed from another man's singing, but prepared by the whole of his life and not accidentally.

Strelnikov had justified the trust put in him.

His service record in the recent period included the affairs at Ust-Nemda and Nizhni Kelmes, the affair of the Gubasovo peasants, who had shown armed resistance to a supply detachment, and the affair of the robbery of a supply train by the fourteenth infantry regiment at the Medvezhaya Poima station. In his service book was the affair of the Razinsky regiment, who raised a rebellion in the town of Turkatuy and, arms in hand, went over to the side of the White Guard, and the affair of a soldiers' riot at the river wharf of Chirkin Us, with its murder of a commander who remained loyal to Soviet power.

In all these places, he appeared like a bolt from the blue, judged, sentenced, carried out the sentences, quickly, severely, dauntlessly.

His travelling about on the train had put an end to the general desertion in the area. The revision of the recruiting organisations changed everything. The Red Army levy went successfully. The selection committees got to work feverishly.

Finally, in recent days, when the Whites began pushing from the north and the situation was acknowledged as threatening, Strelnikov was charged with new tasks, essentially military, strategic and operational. The results of his intervention were not slow in telling.

Strelnikov knew that rumour had nicknamed him Rasstrelnikov, 'the Executioner'. He calmly took it in stride, he feared nothing.

He was a native of Moscow and the son of a worker who had taken part in the revolution of 1905 and had suffered for it. He himself had kept away from the revolutionary movement in those years because of his youth, and in the following years, when he was studying at the university, because young people from a poor milieu, when they got to do advanced studies, valued it more and studied more assiduously than the children of the rich. The ferment among the well-to-do students had not touched him. He had left the university with a vast amount of knowledge. He had, by his own efforts, supplemented his historico-philological education with a mathematical one.

By law he was not obliged to go into the army, but he had gone to war as a volunteer, had been taken prisoner as a lieutenant, and at the end of the year 1917 had escaped, on learning that there was revolution in Russia.

Two features, two passions, distinguished him.

He thought with outstanding clarity and correctness. And he possessed a rare degree of moral purity and fairness, was a man of warm and noble feelings.

But for the activity of a scientist laying out new paths, his mind lacked the gift of unexpectedness, that power which, with unforeseen discoveries, disrupts the fruitless harmony of empty foresight.

And for doing good, he, a man of principle, lacked the unprincipledness of the heart, which knows no general cases, but only particular ones, and which is great in doing small things.

From an early age Strelnikov had striven for the highest and brightest. He considered life an enormous arena in which people, honourably observing the rules, compete in the attainment of perfection.

When it turned out that this was not so, it never entered his head that he was wrong in simplifying the world order. Having driven the offence inside for a long time, he began to cherish the thought of one day becoming an arbiter between life and the dark principles that distort it, of stepping forth to its defence and avenging it.

Disappointment embittered him. The revolution armed him.

31

'Zhivago, Zhivago,' Strelnikov went on repeating to himself in his coach, to which they had passed. 'From merchants. Or the nobility. Well, yes: a doctor from Moscow. To Varykino. Strange. From Moscow and suddenly to such a godforsaken hole.'

'Precisely with that purpose. In search of quiet. In a remote corner, in the unknown.'

'How poetic. Varykino? I know the area. Krüger's former factories. His little relatives, by any chance? His heirs?'

'Why this mocking tone? What have "heirs" got to do with it? Though, in fact, my wife . . .'

'Aha, you see. Pining for the Whites? I must disappoint you. It's too late. The area's been cleared.'

'You go on jeering?'

'And then – a doctor. An army doctor. And it's a time of war. Just my line. A deserter. The Greens[8] also seclude themselves in the forests. Seeking quiet. What grounds?'

'Twice wounded and discharged as unfit.'

'Now you're going to present a letter from the People's Commissariat of Education or the People's Commissariat of Health, recommending you as "a completely Soviet man", as a "sympathiser", and attesting to your "loyalty". We're now having the Last Judgement on earth, my dear sir, we have apocalyptic beings with swords and winged beasts, and not fully sympathising and loyal doctors. However, I've told you that you're free,

and I won't go back on my word. But only this time. I have a presentiment
that we'll meet again, and then, watch out, the talk will be different.'

The threat and the challenge did not disturb Yuri Andreevich. He said:

'I know everything you think about me. For your part, you're absolutely
right. But the argument you want to draw me into is one I have mentally
conducted all my life with an imaginary accuser, and I should think I've had
time to come to some conclusion. It can't be put in a couple of words. Allow
me to leave without explaining, if I am indeed free, and if not – dispose of
me. I have no need to justify myself before you.'

They were interrupted by the buzzing of the telephone. The connection
was restored.

'Thank you, Guryan,' said Strelnikov, picking up the receiver and blowing into it several times. 'Send someone to accompany Comrade Zhivago,
my dear boy. So that nothing happens again. And get me Razvilye on the
squawk box, please, the Cheka⁹ transport office in Razvilye.'

Left alone, Strelnikov telephoned the station:

'They've brought in a boy, he pulls his cap over his ears, but his head's
bandaged, it's disgraceful. Yes. Give him medical aid, if necessary. Yes, like
the apple of your eye, you'll answer to me personally. A ration, if it's needed.
Right. And now about business. I'm speaking, I haven't finished. Ah, the
devil, some third person's cut in. Guryan! Guryan! Disconnected.'

'He could be from my primary school class,' he thought, setting aside for
a moment the attempt to finish the talk with the station. 'He grew up and
rebels against us.' Strelnikov mentally counted up the years of his teaching,
and the war, and his captivity, to see if the sum would fit the boy's age. Then,
through the coach window, he began searching the panorama visible on the
horizon for that neighbourhood above the river, at the exit from Yuriatin,
where their lodgings had been. And what if his wife and daughter were still
there? Go to them! Now, this minute! Yes, but is that thinkable? That was
from a completely different life. He must first finish this new one, before
going back to that interrupted one. Some day, some day it would happen.
Yes, but when, when?

Book Two

Part Eight

ARRIVAL

I

The train that had brought the Zhivago family to this place still stood on the back tracks of the station, screened by other trains, but there was a feeling that the connection with Moscow, which had stretched over the whole journey, had broken, had ended that morning.

From here on another territorial zone opened out, a different, provincial world, drawn to a centre of gravity of its own.

The local people knew each other more intimately than in the capital. Though the area around the Yuriatin–Razvilye railway had been cleared of unauthorised persons and cordoned off by Red Army troops, local suburban passengers made their way to the line in some incomprehensible way – 'infiltrated', as they would say now. The coaches were already packed with them, they crowded the doorways of the freight cars, they walked on the tracks alongside the train and stood on the embankments by the entrances to their coaches.

All these people to a man were acquainted with each other, conversed from afar, greeted each other when they came near. They dressed and talked slightly differently than in the capitals, did not eat the same things, had other habits.

It was curious to learn what they lived by, what moral and material resources nourished them, how they struggled with difficulties, how they evaded the laws.

The answer was not slow to appear in the most vivid form.

2

Accompanied by the sentry who dragged his gun on the ground and propped himself up on it as on a staff, the doctor went back to his train.

It was sultry. The sun scorched the rails and the roofs of the coaches. The ground, black with oil, burned with a yellow gleam, as if gilded.

The sentry furrowed the dust with his rifle butt, leaving a trail in the sand behind him. The gun knocked against the ties. The sentry was saying:

'The weather's settled. It's the perfect time for sowing the spring crops – oats, summer wheat, or, say, millet. It's too early for buckwheat. We sow buckwheat on St Akulina's day.[1] We're from Morshansk, in Tambov province, not from here. Eh, comrade doctor! If it wasn't for this civil hydra right now, this plague of counter-revolutionists, would I be lost in foreign parts at a time like this? It's run among us like a black cat, this class war, and see what it does!'

3

'Thanks. I'll do it myself,' Yuri Andreevich declined the offered aid. People bent down from the freight car and stretched their hands out to him to help him get in. He pulled himself up and jumped into the coach, got to his feet, and embraced his wife.

'At last. Well, thank God, thank God it all ended like this,' Antonina Alexandrovna kept saying. 'However, this happy outcome is no news to us.'

'How do you mean, no news?'

'We know everything.'

'From where?'

'The sentries kept telling us. Otherwise how could we have borne the uncertainty? Papa and I nearly lost our minds as it was. There he sleeps, you can't wake him. He collapsed from anxiety as if he were cut down – you can't rouse him. There are new passengers. I'm going to have you meet someone now. But first listen to what they're saying all around. The whole coach congratulates you on your happy deliverance. See what a husband I've got!' She suddenly changed the subject, turned her head, and, over her shoulder, introduced him to one of the newly arrived passengers, squeezed by his neighbours back in the rear of the coach.

'Samdevyatov' was heard from there, a soft hat rose above the mass of people's heads, and the owner of the name began pushing his way towards the doctor through the thick of the bodies pressed against him.

'Samdevyatov' Yuri Andreevich reflected meanwhile. 'Something old Russian, I thought, folk epic, broad bushy beard, peasant tunic, studded

belt. But here's some sort of society for lovers of art, greying curls, moustache, goatee.'

'Well, so, did Strelnikov give you a fright? Confess.'

'No, why? The conversation was serious. In any case, he's a strong, sub-
stantial man.'

'That he is. I have some notion of this person. He's not native to us. He's
yours, a Muscovite. The same as our novelties of recent times. Also yours,
imported from the capital. Our own minds would never have come up with
them.'

'This is Anfim Efimovich, Yurochka – all-knowing, omniscient. He's
heard about you, about your father, knows my grandfather, everybody,
everybody. Get acquainted.' And Antonina Alexandrovna asked in passing,
without expression: 'You probably also know the local teacher Antipova?'
To which Samdevyatov replied just as expressionlessly: 'What do you want
with Antipova?'

Yuri Andreevich heard it and did not enter into the conversation. Antonina Alexandrovna went on:

'Anfim Efimovich is a Bolshevik. Watch out, Yurochka. Keep your ears
pricked up with him.'

'No, really? I'd never have thought it. By the looks of him, it's sooner
something artistic.'

'My father kept an inn. Had seven troikas running around for him. But I
am of higher education. And, in fact, a Social Democrat.'[2]

'Listen to what Anfim Efimovich says, Yurochka. Incidentally, don't be
angry, but your name and patronymic are a tongue twister. Yes, so listen to
what I'm saying, Yurochka. We're really terribly lucky. The city of Yuriatin
isn't taking us. There are fires in the city, and the bridge has been blown up,
we can't get in. The train will be transferred by a connecting track to
another line, and it's just the one we need, Torfyanaya is on it. Just think!
And there's no need to change and drag ourselves across the city with our
luggage from one station to the other. Instead we'll get a good knocking
about before we make it anywhere. We'll manoeuvre for a long time. Anfim
Efimovich explained it all to me.'

4

Antonina Alexandrovna's predictions came true. Hitching and unhitching
its coaches and adding new ones, the train rode endlessly back and forth on
congested lines, along which other trains were also moving, for a long time
obstructing its way out into the open fields.

The city was half lost in the distance, concealed by the slopes of the terrain. Only rarely did the roofs of its houses, the tips of factory chimneys, the crosses of belfries appear over the horizon. One of its suburbs was burning. The smoke of the fire was borne on the wind. Its streaming horse's mane spread all across the sky.

The doctor and Samdevyatov sat on the floor of the coach at the edge, their legs hanging over the doorway. Samdevyatov kept explaining things to Yuri Andreevich, pointing into the distance. At times the rumble of the rolling freight car drowned him out, so that it was impossible to hear anything. Yuri Andreevich asked him to repeat it. Anfim Efimovich put his face close to the doctor's and, straining, shouted what he had said right into his ears.

'That's the Giant picture house on fire. The junkers ensconced themselves there. But they already surrendered earlier. Generally, the battle isn't over yet. Do you see those black dots on the belfry? That's our boys. They're removing the Czechs.'

'I don't see anything. How can you make all that out?'

'And that's Khokhriki burning, the artisans' quarter. And Kolodeevo, where the shopping arcades are, is to the side. Why does that interest me? Our place is in the arcades. It's not a big fire. The centre hasn't been touched yet.'

'Repeat that. I didn't hear.'

'The centre, I said, the city centre. The cathedral, the library. Our family name, Samdevyatov, is San Donato altered in Russian style. We supposedly come from the Demidovs.'³

'Again I couldn't make anything out.'

'I said Samdevyatov is a transformed San Donato. We supposedly come from the Demidovs. The princes Demidov San Donato. Maybe it's just a pack of lies. A family legend. And this spot is called Spirka's Bottom. Dachas, amusements, promenades. Strange name, isn't it?'

Before them stretched a field. It was criss-crossed in various directions by branch lines. Telegraph poles went off across it with seven-mile strides, dropping below the skyline. A wide, paved road wound out its ribbon, rivalling the railways in beauty. First it disappeared beyond the horizon, then momentarily showed the wavy arc of a turn. And vanished again.

'Our famous highway. Laid across the whole of Siberia. Much sung by convicts. Base for the local partisans. Generally, it's not bad here. You'll settle in, get used to it. Come to love our town's curiosities. Our water hydrants. At the intersections. Women's clubs in winter under the open sky.'

'We won't be staying in town. In Varykino.'

'I know. Your wife told me. Never mind. You'll come to town on errands.

I guessed who she was at first sight. The eyes. The nose. The forehead. The image of Krüger. Her grandfather all over. In these parts everybody remembers Krüger.'

Tall, round-sided oil tanks showed red at the ends of the field. Industrial billboards perched on tall posts. One of them, which twice crossed the doctor's eye, had written on it: 'Moreau and Vetchinkin. Seeders. Threshers'.

'It was a solid firm. Produced excellent agricultural implements.'

'I didn't hear. What did you say?'

'The firm, I said. Understand? The firm. Produced agricultural implements. A joint-stock company. My father was a shareholder.'

'You said he kept an inn.'

'An inn's an inn. The one doesn't interfere with the other. And he was no fool, he placed his money in the best enterprises. Invested in the Giant picture house.'

'It seems you're proud of it?'

'Of my father's shrewdness? What else!'

'And what about your social democracy?'

'What's that got to do with it, may I ask? Where is it said that a man who reasons as a Marxist has to be a mush-minded driveller? Marxism is a positive science, a teaching about reality, a philosophy of the historical situation.'

'Marxism and science? To argue about that with a man I hardly know is imprudent, to say the least. But come what may. Marxism has too little control of itself to be a science. Sciences are better balanced. Marxism and objectivity? I don't know of a movement more isolated within itself and further from the facts than Marxism. Each of us is concerned with testing himself by experience, but people in power, for the sake of the fable of their own infallibility, turn away from the truth with all their might. Politics says nothing to me. I don't like people who are indifferent to truth.'

Samdevyatov considered the doctor's words the whimsicalities of a witty eccentric. He merely chuckled and did not contradict him.

Meanwhile the train was being shunted. Each time it reached the exit switch by the semaphore, an elderly switchwoman with a milk jug tied to her belt shifted the knitting she was doing from one hand to the other, bent down, turned the disc of the shunting switch, and made the train back up. While it slowly moved backwards, she straightened up and shook her fist at it.

Samdevyatov took her movement to his own account. 'Who is she doing it to?' he fell to thinking. 'There's something familiar. Isn't she Tuntseva? Looks like her. But what's with me? It's hardly her. She's too old for Glasha.

And what have I got to do with it? There are upheavals in Mother Russia, confusion on the railways, the dear heart's probably having a hard time, and it's my fault, I get a fist shaken at me. Ah, well, devil take her, why should I rack my brains over her!'

Finally, after waving the flag and shouting something to the engineer, the switchwoman let the train pass the semaphore and go freely on its way, and when the fourteenth freight car sped by her, she stuck her tongue out at the babblers on the floor of the coach, who were such an eyesore to her. And again Samdevyatov fell to thinking.

5

When the environs of the burning city, the cylindrical tanks, the telegraph poles and advertisements dropped behind and disappeared and other views came along, woods, hills, between which the windings of the highway frequently appeared, Samdevyatov said:

'Let's get up and go our ways. I get off soon. And you, too, one stop later. Watch out you don't miss it.'

'You must know this area thoroughly?'

'Prodigiously. A hundred miles around. I'm a lawyer. Twenty years of practice. Cases. Travels.'

'And up to the present?'

'What else.'

'What sort of cases can be tried now?'

'Anything you like. Old unfinished deals, operations, unfulfilled obligations – up to the ears, it's terrible.'

'Haven't such relations been abolished?'

'Nominally, of course. But in reality there's a need at the same time for mutually exclusive things. The nationalisation of enterprises, and fuel for the city soviet, and wagon transport for the provincial council of national economy. And along with all that everybody wants to live. Peculiarities of the transitional period, when theory doesn't coincide with practice yet. Here there's a need for quick-witted, resourceful people with my kind of character. Blessed is the man who walketh not, who takes a heap and ignores the lot.[4] And a punch in the nose, and so it goes, as my father used to say. Half the province feeds off me. I'll be coming to see you on the matter of wood supplies. By horse, naturally, once he's on his feet. My last one went lame. If he were healthy, I wouldn't be jolting around on this old junk. It drags along, curse it, an engine in name only. I'll be of use to you when you get to Varykino. I know your Mikulitsyns like the palm of my hand.'

'Do you know the purpose of our trip, our intentions?'

'Approximately. I can guess. I have a notion. Man's eternal longing for the land. The dream of living by the work of your own hands.'

'And so? It seems you don't approve? What do you say?'

'A naïve, idyllic dream. But why not? God help you. But I don't believe in it. Utopian. Home-made.'

'How will Mikulitsyn treat us?'

'He won't let you cross the threshold, he'll drive you out with a broom, and he'll be right. He's got bedlam there even without you, a thousand and one nights, factories idle, workers scattered, not a blessed thing in terms of means of existence, no fodder, and suddenly – oh, joy – the deuce brings you along. If he killed you, I wouldn't blame him.'

'There, you see – you're a Bolshevik and you yourself don't deny that this isn't life, but something unprecedented, phantasmagorical, incongruous.'

'Of course. But it's a historical inevitability. We have to go through it.'

'Why an inevitability?'

'What, are you a little boy, or are you pretending? Did you drop from the moon or something? Gluttons and parasites rode on the backs of starving labourers, drove them to death, and it should have stayed that way? And the other forms of outrage and tyranny? Don't you understand the legitimacy of the people's wrath, their wish to live according to justice, their search for the truth? Or does it seem to you that a radical break could have been achieved in the dumas, by parliamentary ways, and that it can be done without dictatorship?'

'We're talking about different things, and if we were to argue for a hundred years, we wouldn't agree on anything. I used to be in a very revolutionary mood, but now I think that we'll gain nothing by violence. People must be drawn to the good by the good. But that's not the point. Let's go back to Mikulitsyn. If that is most likely what awaits us, why should we go there? We ought to swing round.'

'What nonsense. First of all, are the Mikulitsyns the only light in the window? Second, Mikulitsyn is criminally kind, kind in the extreme. He'll make a noise, get his hackles up, then go soft, give you the shirt off his back, share his last crust of bread with you.' And Samdevyatov told this story.

6

'Twenty-five years ago, Mikulitsyn, a student at the Technological Institute, arrived from Petersburg. He was exiled here under police surveillance. Mikulitsyn arrived, got a job as manager at Krüger's, and married. We had four Tuntsev sisters here, one more than in Chekhov – all the students in Yuriatin courted them – Agrippina, Evdokia, Glafira, and Serafima Severinovna. In a paraphrase of their patronymic, the girls were nicknamed "severyanki", or "northern girls". Mikulitsyn married the eldest severyanka.

'Soon a son was born to the couple. As a worshipper of the idea of freedom, the fool of a father christened the boy with the rare name of Liberius. Liberius – Libka in common parlance – grew up a madcap, showing versatile and outstanding abilities. War broke out. Libka faked the date on his birth certificate and, at the age of fifteen, ran off to the front as a volunteer. Agrafena Severinovna, who was generally sickly, could not bear the blow, took to her bed, never got up again, and died two winters ago, just before the revolution.

'The war ended. Liberius returned. Who is he? A heroic lieutenant with three medals, and, well, of course, a thoroughly propagandised Bolshevik delegate from the front. Have you heard of the Forest Brotherhood?'

'No, sorry.'

'Then there's no sense in telling you. Half the effect is lost. There's no need to go staring out of the coach at the highway. What's it noted for? At the present time, for the partisans. What are the partisans? The chief cadres of the civil war. Two sources went to make up this force. The political organisation that took upon itself the guiding of the revolution, and the low-ranking soldiers, who, after the war was lost, refused to obey the old regime. From the combining of these two things came the partisan army. It's of motley composition. They're mostly middle peasants. But alongside them you'll meet anyone you like. There are poor folk, and defrocked monks, and the sons of kulaks at war with their fathers. There are ideological anarchists, and passportless ragamuffins, and overgrown dunces thrown out of school old enough to get married. There are Austro-German prisoners of war seduced by the promise of freedom and returning home. And so, one of the units of this people's army of many thousands, known as the Forest Brotherhood, is commanded by Comrade Forester, Libka, Liberius Averkievich, the son of Averky Stepanovich Mikulitsyn.'

'What are you saying?'

'Just what you heard. But to continue. After his wife's death, Averky Stepanovich married a second time. His new wife, Elena Proklovna, was a schoolgirl, brought straight from the classroom to the altar. Naïve by nature, but also playing at naïveté out of calculation, a young thing, but already playing at being young. To that end she chirps, twitters, poses as an ingénue, a little fool, a lark of the fields. The moment she sees you, she starts testing you: "In what year was Suvorov born?"[5] "List the cases of the equality of triangles." And she's exultant if you fail and put your foot in it. But you'll be seeing her in a few hours and can check on my description.

"'Himself" has other weaknesses: his pipe, seminary archaisms: "in this wise", "suffer it to be so", "all things whatsoever". His calling was to have been the sea. At the institute, he was in the shipbuilding line. He retained it in his appearance and habits. He's clean-shaven, doesn't take the pipe out of his mouth the whole day, speaks through his teeth, amiably, unhurriedly. The jutting lower jaw of a smoker, cold, grey eyes. Ah, yes, I nearly forgot one detail: an SR, elected from the region to the Constituent Assembly.'[6]

'But that's very important. It means father and son are at daggers drawn? Political enemies?'

'Nominally, of course. Though in reality the taiga doesn't make war on Varykino. But to continue. The other Tuntsev girls, Averky Stepanovich's sisters-in-law, are in Yuriatin to this day. Eternal virgins. Times have changed, and so have the girls.

'The oldest of the remaining ones, Avdotya Severinovna, is the librarian in the city reading room. A sweet, dark-haired girl, bashful in the extreme. Blushes like a peony for no reason at all. The silence in the reading room is sepulchral, tense. She's attacked by a chronic cold, sneezes up to twenty times, is ready to fall through the floor from shame. What are you to do? From nervousness.

'The middle one, Glafira Severinovna, is the blessing among the sisters. A sharp girl, a wonder of a worker. Doesn't scorn any task. The general opinion, with one voice, is that the partisan leader Forester took after this aunt. You see her there in a sewing shop or as a stocking maker. Before you can turn round, she's already a hairdresser. Did you pay attention to the switchwoman at the Yuriatin train station, shaking her fist and stick-ing her tongue out at us? Well, I thought, fancy that, Glafira got herself hired as a watchman on the railroad. But it seems it wasn't her. Too old for Glafira.

'The youngest, Simushka, is the family's cross, its trial. An educated girl, well-read. Studied philosophy, loved poetry. But then, in the years of the revolution, under the influence of the general elation, street proces-sions, speeches from a platform on the square, she got touched in the head, fell into a religious mania. The sisters leave for work, lock the door, and she slips out of the window and goes roaming the streets, gathering the public, preaching the Second Coming, the end of the world. But here I'm talking away and we're coming to my station. Yours is the next one. Get ready.'

When Anfim Efimovich got off the train, Antonina Alexandrovna said:

'I don't know how you look at it, but I think this man was sent to us by fate. It seems to me he'll play some beneficial role in our existence.'

'That may well be, Tonechka. But I'm not glad that you're recognised by your resemblance to your grandfather and that he's so well remembered here. And Strelnikov, too, as soon as I mentioned Varykino, put in caustically: "Varykino? Krüger's factories? His little relatives, by any chance? His heirs?"

'I'm afraid we'll be more visible here than in Moscow, which we fled from in search of inconspicuousness.'

'Of course, there's nothing to be done now. No use crying over spilt milk. But it will be better not to show ourselves, to lie low, to behave more modestly. Generally, I have bad presentiments. Let's wake up the others, pack our things, tie the belts, and prepare to get off.'

7

Antonina Alexandrovna stood on the platform in Torfyanaya counting people and things innumerable times to make sure nothing had been forgotten in the coach. She felt the trampled sand under her feet, and yet the fear of somehow missing the stop did not leave her, and the rumble of the moving train went on sounding in her ears, though her eyes convinced her that it was standing motionless by the platform. This kept her from seeing, hearing, and understanding.

Her companions on the long journey said goodbye to her from above, from the height of the coach. She did not notice them. She did not notice the train leaving and discovered its disappearance only after she noticed the second track, revealed after its departure, with a green field and blue sky beyond it.

The station building was of stone. By its entrance stood two benches, one on each side. The Moscow travellers from Sivtsev were the only passengers to get off at Torfyanaya. They put down their things and sat on one of the benches.

The newcomers were struck by the silence at the station, the emptiness, the tidiness. It seemed unusual to them that there was no crowding around, no swearing. Life was delayed in this out-of-the-way place, it lagged behind history. It had yet to catch up with the savagery of the capital.

The station was hidden in a birch grove. It became dark in the train as it approached it. The moving shadows cast by its barely swaying tops shifted over hands and faces and over the clean, damp yellow sand of the platform. The whistling of birds in the grove suited its freshness. As undisguisedly pure as ignorance, the full sounds echoed throughout the wood and permeated it. The grove was cross-cut by two roads, the railway and the country track, and it curtained both with its flung-out, low-hanging branches, like the ends of wide, floor-length sleeves.

Suddenly Antonina Alexandrovna's eyes and ears were opened. She became aware of everything at once. The ringing bird calls, the purity of the forest solitude, the serenity of the peace all around her. In her mind she had composed a phrase: 'I couldn't believe we would arrive unharmed. You understand, your Strelnikov might play at magnanimity before you and let you go, but telegraph orders here to have us all detained when we got off. I don't believe in their nobility, my dear. It's all only for show.' Instead of these prepared words, she said something different. 'How delightful!' escaped her when she saw the loveliness around her. She could not say any more. Tears began to choke her. She burst into loud sobs.

Hearing her weeping, a little old man, the stationmaster, came out of the building. With rapid little steps he trotted over to the bench, put his hand politely to the visor of his red-topped uniform cap, and asked:

'Perhaps the young lady needs some drops of calmative? From the station medicine chest?'

'It's nothing. Thank you. It will pass.'

'The cares and anxieties of travel. A well-known, widespread thing. Besides, there's this African heat, rare in our latitudes. And, on top of that, the events in Yuriatin.'

'We watched the fire from the train as we passed.'

'So you'd be coming from Russia, if I'm not mistaken?'

'From our White-Stoned Mother.'[7]

'Muscovites? Then no wonder the lady's nerves are upset. They say there's no stone left upon stone?'

'They're exaggerating. But it's true we've seen all kinds of things. This is my daughter, this is my son-in-law. This is their little boy. And this is our young nanny, Nyusha.'

'How do you do. How do you do. Very pleased. I've been partly fore-warned. Anfim Efimovich Samdevyatov rang up on the railway phone from the Sakma junction. Doctor Zhivago and family from Moscow, he says, please render them all possible assistance. So you must be that same doctor?'

'No, this is Doctor Zhivago, my son-in-law, and I'm in a different sector, in agriculture – Gromeko, professor of agronomy.'

'Sorry, my mistake. Forgive me. Very glad to make your acquaintance.'

'So, judging by your words, you know Samdevyatov?'

'Who doesn't know that magician! Our hope and provider. Without him

we'd all have turned our toes up long ago. Yes, he says, render them all possible assistance. Yes, sir, I say. I promised. So you'll have a horse, if need be,
or anything else I can do to help. Where are you headed for?'

'Varykino. Is it far from here?'

'Varykino? That's why I keep thinking who on earth your daughter
reminds me of so much. So you're headed for Varykino! Then everything's
explained. Ivan Ernestovich and I built that road together. I'll get busy and
fit you out. We'll call a man, get hold of a cart. Donat! Donat! Here are the
things, take them to the waiting room meanwhile. And what about a horse?
Run over to the tea room, brother, and ask if there isn't one. Seems like
Vakkh was hanging around here this morning. Ask if he maybe hasn't gone.
Tell them there's four people to be taken to Varykino, with no luggage to
speak of. Newcomers. Look lively. And some fatherly advice for you,
madam. I'm purposely not asking you about the degree of your relation to
Ivan Ernestovich, but be careful on that account. Don't go unbuttoning
yourself to just anybody. Think what times these are.'

At the name of Vakkh, the travellers glanced at each other in amazement.
They still remembered the late Anna Ivanovna's stories about the legendary
blacksmith who forged indestructible iron guts for himself, and other local
tall tales and fables.

8

A lop-eared, white-haired, shaggy old man was driving them behind a
white, just foaled mare. Everything on him was white for different reasons.
His new bast shoes had not yet darkened from wear, and his pants and shirt
had grown faded and bleached with time.

Behind the white mare, kicking up his wobbly, soft-boned legs, ran a
curly-headed foal, black as night, looking like a hand-carved toy.

Sitting at the sides of the cart, which jolted over the potholes in the road,
the travellers clung to the edges so as not to fall. There was peace in their
souls. Their dream was coming true, they were nearing the goal of their
journey. With generous largesse and luxury, the pre-evening hours of the
wonderful, clear day lingered, delayed.

The road went now through forest, now through open clearings. In the
forest, the bumping over snags threw the travellers into a heap, and they
huddled, frowned, pressed close to each other. In the open places, where it
was as if space itself doffed its hat out of fullness of feeling, they straightened
up, settled more freely, shook their heads.

It was mountainous country. The mountains, as always, had their own look, their physiognomy. They stood dark in the distance, mighty, arrogant shadows, silently scrutinising the people in the cart. A comforting rosy light followed the travellers across the field, reassuring them and giving them hope.

They liked everything, were surprised at everything, and most of all at the incessant babble of their whimsical old driver, in which traces of vanished old Russian forms, Tartar layers, and regional peculiarities were mixed with unintelligibilities of his own invention.

When the foal lagged behind, the mare stopped and waited for him. He smoothly overtook her in wavy, splashing leaps. With awkward steps of his long, close-set legs, he came to the cart from the side and, thrusting his tiny head on its long neck behind the shaft, sucked at his mother.

'I still don't understand,' Antonina Alexandrovna shouted to her husband, her teeth chattering from the jolts, spacing out the words so as not to bite off the tip of her tongue at an unforeseen bump. 'Is it possible that this is the same Vakkh mama told us about? Well, you remember, all sorts of balderdash. A blacksmith, his guts hurt in a fight, fashioned new ones for himself. In short, the blacksmith Vakkh Iron Belly. I understand it's all just a tall tale. But can it be a tale about him? Can he be the same one?'

'Of course not. First of all, you say yourself it's just a tall tale, folklore. Second, in mama's time this folklore was already over a hundred years old, as she said. But why so loud? The old man will hear and get offended.'

'He won't hear anything – he's hard of hearing. And if he does hear, he won't make sense of it – he's a bit off.'

'Hey, Fyodor Nefyodych!' the old man urged the mare on, addressing her with a masculine name for no apparent reason, knowing perfectly well, and better than his passengers, that she was a mare. 'What anathematic heat! Like the Hebrew youths in the Persian furnace! Hup, you unpastured devil. I'm talking to you, Mazeppa!'[8]

He would unexpectedly strike up snatches of popular songs composed in the local factories in former times.

> Farewell to the central office,
> Farewell to the pit yard and boss,
> I'm sick to death of the master's bread,
> I've drunk my fill of stagnant water.
> A swan goes swimming by the shore,
> Paddling the water with his feet.
> It isn't wine that makes me tipsy,
> Vanya's been taken for a soldier.

But me, Masha, I'm a bright one,
But me, Masha, I'm no fool.
I'll go off to Selyaba town,
Get hired by the Sentetyurikha.

'Hey, little sod, you've forgotten God! Look, people, at this carrion of a beast! You give her the whip, she gives you the slip. Hup, Fedya-Nefedya, where'll that get ya? This here forest's called the taiga, there's no end to it. There's a force of peasant folk in it, ho, ho! There's the Forest Brotherhood in it. Hey, Fedya-Nefedya, stopped again, you devil, you goblin!'

Suddenly he turned round and, looking point-blank at Antonina Alexandrovna, said:

'What notion's got into you, young'un, think I don't sense where you come from? You're a simple one, ma'am, I must say. Let the earth swallow me up, but I recognise you! That I do! Couldn't believe my blinkers, a live Grigov!' (The old man called eyes 'blinkers' and Krüger 'Grigov'.) 'You wouldn't happen to be his granddaughter? Ain't I got an eye for Grigov? I spent my whole life around him, broke my teeth on him. In all kinds of handiwork, all the jobs. As a pit-prop man, a winch man, a stable man. Hup, shake a leg! She's stopped again, the cripple! Angels in China-land, I'm talking to you, ain't I?

'Here you're asking what Vakkh is he, that blacksmith maybe? You're real simple, ma'am, such a big-eyed lady, but a fool. Your Vakkh, he was Postanogov by name. Postanogov Iron Belly, it's fifty years he's been in the ground, between the boards. And us now, on the contrary, we're Mekhonoshin. Same name, namesakes, but the last name's different – Efim, but not him.'

The old man gradually told his passengers in his own words what they already knew about the Mikulitsyns from Samdevyatov. He called him Mikulich and her Mikulichna. The manager's present wife he called the second-wed, and of 'the little first, the deceased one', he said that she was a honey-woman, a white cherub. When he got on to the partisan leader Liberius and learned that his fame had not yet reached Moscow, that seemed incredible to him:

'You haven't heard? Haven't heard of Comrade Forester? Angels in China-land, what's Moscow got ears for?'

Evening was beginning to fall. The travellers' own shadows, growing ever longer, raced ahead of them. Their way lay across a wide empty expanse. Here and there, sticking up high, grew woody stalks of goosefoot, thistles, loosestrife, in solitary stands, with clusters of flowers at their tips. Lit from below, from the ground, by the rays of the sunset, their outlines rose up ghostly, like motionless mounted sentinels posted thinly across the field.

Far ahead, at the end, the plain came up against the transverse ridge of a rising height. It stood across the road like a wall, at the foot of which a ravine or river could be surmised. As if the sky there were surrounded by a fence, with the country road leading to its gates.

At the top of the rise appeared the elongated form of a white, one-storey house.

'See the lookout on the knob?' Vakkh asked. 'That's your Mikulich and Mikulichna. And under them there's a split, a ravine, it's called Shutma.'

Two gunshots, one after the other, rang out from that direction, generating multiple fragmented echoes.

'What's that? Can it be partisans, grandpa? Shooting at us?'

'Christ be with you. What partizhans? It's Stepanych scarifying wolves in Shutma.'

9

The first meeting of the new arrivals with the hosts took place in the yard of the director's little house. A painful scene, at first silent, then confusedly noisy and incoherent, was played out.

Elena Proklovna was returning to the yard from her evening walk in the forest. The sun's evening rays stretched behind her from tree to tree across the whole forest, almost the same colour as her golden hair. Elena Proklovna was dressed in light summer clothes. She was red-cheeked and was wiping her face, flushed from walking, with a handkerchief. Her open neck was crossed in front by an elastic band, which held the hanging straw hat thrown behind her back.

Her husband was coming home from the opposite direction with a gun, climbing up from the ravine and intending to see at once to the cleaning of the sooty barrels, in view of the defects he had noticed in the discharge.

Suddenly, out of the blue, over the stones of the paved driveway, Vakkh drove up dashingly and loudly with his surprise.

Very soon, having climbed out of the cart with all the rest, Alexander Alexandrovich, falteringly, taking off his hat, then putting it on again, gave the first explanations.

The genuine, unaffected stupefaction of the nonplussed hosts and the unfeigned, sincere embarrassment of the wretched guests, burning with shame, lasted for several moments. The situation was clear without explanations, not only to the participants, Vakkh, Nyusha, and Shurochka. The oppressive feeling communicated itself to the mare and the colt, to the golden rays of the sun, and to the mosquitoes circling around Elena Proklovna and settling on her face and neck.

'I don't understand,' Averky Stepanovich finally broke the silence. 'I don't understand, don't understand a thing and never will. What have we got here, the south, the Whites, the land of plenty? Why did your choice fall precisely on us? Why have you come here, here, why on earth to us?'

'I wonder if you've thought of what a responsibility it is for Averky Stepanovich?'

'Lenochka, don't interrupt. Yes, precisely. She's perfectly right. Have you thought of what a burden it is for me?'

'For God's sake. You haven't understood us. What are we talking about? About a very small thing, a nothing. There's no encroachment on you, on your peace. A corner in some empty, dilapidated building. A spot of land nobody needs, gone to waste, for a vegetable garden. And a load of firewood from the forest when nobody's looking. Is that so much to ask, is it some sort of infringement?'

'Yes, but the world is wide. What have we to do with it? Why is this honour bestowed precisely on us and not on somebody else?'

'We knew about you and hoped you had heard about us. That we're no strangers to you and will not be coming to strangers ourselves.'

'Ah, so it's a matter of Krüger, of you being his relatives? How can you open your mouth and acknowledge such things in our time?'

Averky Stepanovich was a man with regular features, wore his hair thrown back, stepped broadly on his whole foot, and in summer belted his Russian shirt with a tasselled strip of braid. In older times such men went and became river pirates; in modern times they constituted the type of the eternal student, the lesson-giving dreamer.

Averky Stepanovich gave his youth to the liberation movement, the revolution, and only feared that he would not live to see it or that, once it broke out, its moderation would not satisfy his radical and bloody lust. And then it came, overturning all his boldest suppositions, and he, a born and steadfast lover of the workers, who had been among the first to found a factory workers' committee at the 'Mighty Sviatogor' and set up workers' control in it, was left with nothing for his trouble, excluded, in an empty village, deserted by the workers, who here mostly followed the Mensheviks. And now this absurdity, these uninvited last remnants of the Krügers, seemed to him a mockery of fate, a purposely mean trick, and they made the cup of his patience run over.

'No, that's beyond me. Inconceivable. Do you realise what a danger you are to me, what position you put me in? I really must be going out of my mind. I don't understand anything and never will.'

'I wonder if you can conceive of what a volcano we're sitting on here even without you?'

'Wait, Lenochka. My wife is perfectly right. It's no sweet time even without you. A dog's life, a madhouse. Between two fires all the time, and no way out. Some hang it on us that we've got such a red son, a Bolshevik, a people's darling. Others don't like it that I myself was elected to the Constituent Assembly. Nobody's pleased, so just flounder about. And now you. How very merry to go and get shot over you!'

'What are you saying! Come to your senses! For God's sake!'

After a while, exchanging wrath for mercy, Mikulitsyn said:

'Well, we've been yelping in the yard, and enough. We can continue in the house. Of course, I don't see anything good ahead, but these be the dark waters in the clouds, the shadow-scripted murk of secrecy.[9] However, we're not Janissaries, not heathens. We won't drive you into the forest as a meal for Bruin the bear. I think, Lenok, they'll be best off in the palm room, next to the study. And then we'll discuss where they can settle. I think we'll install them in the park. Please come in. Welcome. Bring the things in, Vakkh. Give the newcomers a hand.'

In carrying out the order, Vakkh merely sighed:

'Unwedded Mother! Wanderers have as much stuff. Just little bundles. Not a single sweetcase!'

10

A cold night set in. The newcomers washed. The women got busy turning the room allotted to them into night lodgings. Shurochka, who was unconsciously accustomed to having adults receive his infantile utterances in baby talk with delight, and who therefore, adapting himself to their taste, was pouring out his twaddle animatedly and zealously, felt disconcerted. Today his babble had no success, no one paid any attention to him. He was displeased that the black colt had not been brought into the house, and, when they told him to be quiet, he burst into tears, afraid that, being a bad and unsuitable boy, he would be sent back to the baby shop, from which, as he thought, he had been delivered to his parents when he was born. He loudly voiced his genuine fears to all around him, but his sweet absurdities did not make the usual impression. Constrained by staying in a strange house, the adults moved about more hurriedly than usual and were silently immersed in their cares. Shurochka felt hurt and blubbered, as nannies say. He was given something to eat and, with some trouble, put to bed. At last he fell asleep. Mikulitsyn's Ustinya took Nyusha to her room, to give her supper and initiate her into the mysteries of the house. Antonina Alexandrovna and the men were invited to evening tea.

Alexander Alexandrovich and Yuri Andreevich asked permission to absent themselves for a moment and went out to the porch for a breath of fresh air.

'So many stars!' said Alexander Alexandrovich.

It was dark. Standing two steps apart on the porch, the son- and father-in-law could not see each other. But behind them, from around the corner of the house, the light of a lamp fell from the window into the ravine. In its column, bushes, trees, and some other vague objects showed mistily in the damp air. The bright strip did not take in the conversing men and made the darkness around them still thicker.

'Tomorrow morning we'll have to examine the outbuilding he intends for us, and if it's fit to live in, start repairing it at once. While we're getting that corner in shape, the soil will thaw, the earth will warm up. Then, without losing a moment, we'll get to the garden beds. Between words in the conversation, I thought I heard him promise to help us with seed potatoes. Or did I hear wrong?'

'He promised, he promised. And other seed. I heard it with my own ears. And the corner he's offering us we saw in passing as we crossed the park. You know where? It's the rear of the manor house, drowning in nettles. It's made of wood, but the house itself is stone. I showed you from the cart, remember? I'd dig the beds there. I think it's the remains of a flower garden. It seemed so to me from a distance. Maybe I'm mistaken. The paths will have to be avoided, passed over, but the soil of the old flower beds was probably well manured and rich in humus.'

'We'll see tomorrow. I don't know. The ground is probably terribly overgrown with grass and hard as a rock. The manor must have had a kitchen garden. Maybe the plot's still there and lying fallow. It will all become clear tomorrow. There are probably still morning frosts here. There will certainly be a frost during the night. How fortunate that we're already here, in place. We can congratulate each other on that. It's good here. I like it.'

'Very nice people. He especially. She's a bit affected. She's displeased with herself, there's something in her she doesn't like. Hence this tireless, fussily false garrulousness. As if she's hastening to distract attention from her appearance, to forestall an unfavourable impression. And that she forgets to take her hat off and carries it on her shoulders is not absent-mindedness either. It really becomes her.'

'Anyhow, let's go in. We got stuck out here too long. It's awkward.'

On their way to the lighted dining room, where, at a round table under a hanging lamp, the hosts and Antonina Alexandrovna were sitting by the samovar and drinking tea, the father- and son-in-law passed through the director's dark study.

In it there was a wide, single-pane window across the whole wall, high above the ravine. From the window, as the doctor had managed to notice earlier, while it was still light, the view opened onto the distance far beyond the ravine and the plain across which Vakkh had taken them. By the window stood a planning or drafting table, wide, also across the whole wall. On it a big fowling piece lay lengthwise, leaving empty space to right and left, and thereby emphasising the great width of the table.

Now, passing by the study, Yuri Andreevich again noted enviously the window with its panoramic view, the size and position of the table, and the spaciousness of the well-furnished room, and this was the first thing that escaped him in the form of an exclamation to his host, when he and Alexander Alexandrovich, on entering the dining room, went to the tea table.

'What a wonderful spot you have here. And what an excellent study, conducive to work, inspiring.'

'In a glass or in a cup? And how do you like it, weak or strong?'

'Look, Yurochka, what a stereoscope Averky Stepanovich's son made for himself when he was little.'

'He still hasn't grown up, hasn't settled down, though he wins over district after district for Soviet power from the Komuch.'

'The what?'

'The Komuch.'

'What is that?'

'It's the army of the Siberian government, which is for the restoration of power to the Constituent Assembly.'

'All day we've heard ceaseless praise of your son. You have every right to be proud of him.'

'These are views of the Urals, double, stereoscopic, also made by him and taken by a camera he made himself.'

'Are these biscuits made with saccharine? They're excellent.'

'Oh, come now! Such a backwater and saccharine? Hardly! Real, honest sugar. I put some in your tea from the sugar bowl. Didn't you notice?'

'Yes, in fact. I was looking at the photographs. And it seems the tea is also natural?'

'With flower petals. It goes without saying.'

'From where?'

'The magic tablecloth. An acquaintance. A modern-day activist. Of very leftist convictions. An official representative of the local economic council. He hauls our timber to town, and through acquaintances gets grain, butter, and flour for us. Siverka.' (So she called her Averky.) 'Siverka, move the biscuit plate closer to me. And now I wonder if you can answer, what was the year of Griboedov's death?'[10]

'He was born, I think, in 1795. I don't remember exactly when he was killed.'

'More tea?'

'No, thank you.'

'And now something else. Tell me when and between what countries was the peace of Nimwegen concluded?'

'Don't torment them, Lenochka. Let the people recover from the trip.'

'Now here's what interests me. List for me, please, the kinds of magnifying glasses and what images they produce in each case: actual, inverted, direct, or imaginary.'

'Where did you get such a knowledge of physics?'

'We had an excellent mathematician here in Yuriatin. He taught in two schools, the boys' and ours. How he explained things, oh, how he explained things! Like a god! He'd chew it all and put it in your mouth. Antipov. He was married to a teacher here. The girls lost their minds over him, they were all in love with him. He went to war as a volunteer and never came back. He was killed. It's alleged that our scourge of God and punishment from heaven, Commissar Strelnikov, is Antipov come back to life. A legend, of course. And it's not like him. Who knows, though. Anything's possible. Another little cup?'

Part Nine

VARYKINO

I

In the winter, when there was more time, Yuri Andreevich began to take various kinds of notes. He noted for himself:

'How often during the summer I wanted to say together with Tyutchev:[1]

> What a summer, ah, what a summer!
> In truth it's something magical.
> And how, I ask, was it given to us,
> Just so, for no reason at all?

'What happiness to work for yourself and your family, from dawn to dusk, to construct a shelter, to till the soil for the sake of subsistence, to create your own world like Robinson Crusoe, imitating our Maker in creating the universe, following your own mother in bringing yourself again and again into the world!

'So many thoughts go through your consciousness, you think so much that is new, while your hands are busy with the muscular, corporeal work of digging or carpentry; while you set yourself reasonable, physically solvable tasks, which reward you at their completion with joy and success; while for six hours in a row you trim something with an axe or dig the earth under the open sky, which scorches you with its beneficent breath. And that these thoughts, surmises, and juxtapositions are not set down on paper, but are forgotten in all their passing transience, is not a loss, but a gain. You city recluse, whipping up your sagging nerves and imagination with strong black coffee or tobacco, you don't know the most powerful drug, which consists in unfeigned need and sound health.

'I go no further than what I've said, I do not preach Tolstoyan simplification and return to the earth, I do not invent my own amendment to socialism on agrarian questions. I merely establish the fact and do not erect our accidentally befallen fate into a system. Our example is questionable and not suitable for drawing conclusions. Our housekeeping is of too heterogeneous a composition. We owe only a small part of it – the store of vegetables and potatoes – to the work of our hands. All the rest comes from another source.

'Our use of the land is illegal. It is arbitrarily concealed from the accounting established by the state authorities. Our cutting of wood is theft, not excusable by the fact that we are stealing from the state pocket – formerly Krüger's. We are protected by the connivance of Mikulitsyn, who lives by approximately the same means; we are saved by the distances, by being far from the city, where for now, fortunately, they know nothing of our tricks.

'I have given up medicine and keep quiet about being a doctor, so as not to trammel my freedom. But some good soul from the back of beyond always finds out that a doctor has settled in Varykino, and drags himself from twenty miles away for advice, one with a chicken, another with eggs, another with a bit of butter or something else. No matter how I dodge the honoraria, it's impossible to fend them off, because people don't believe in the effectiveness of unpaid-for, freely given advice. And so my medical practice brings me something. But our main support, and Mikulitsyn's, is Samdevyatov.

'It is inconceivable what opposites this man unites in himself. He is sincerely for the revolution and fully deserves the trust that the Yuriatin City Council has vested in him. With his almighty powers, he could requisition and transport the entire forest of Varykino without even telling us and the Mikulitsyns, and we wouldn't bat an eye. On the other hand, if he wished to steal from the state, he could most calmly pocket whatever and however much he wanted, and nobody would make a peep. He has no one to divide with and no one to butter up. What, then, induces him to look after us, help the Mikulitsyns, and support everybody around, such as, for example, the stationmaster in Torfyanaya? He's on the go all the time, fetching and bringing things, and he analyses and interprets Dostoevsky's *Demons* and the Communist Manifesto[2] with equal enthusiasm, and it seems to me that if he didn't needlessly complicate his life so wastefully and obviously, he would die of boredom.'

2

A little later the doctor noted:

'We're settled in the back part of the old manor house, in the two rooms of the wooden extension, which in Anna Ivanovna's childhood years was intended for the select among Krüger's servants – the live-in seamstress, the housekeeper, and the retired nanny.

'This corner was fairly decrepit. We repaired it rather quickly. With the help of knowledgeable people, we relaid the stove that heats the two rooms in a new way. With the present position of the flue, it gives more heat.

'In this part of the park, the traces of the former layout had disappeared under the new growth that filled everything. Now, in winter, when everything around is dormant and the living does not obscure the dead, the snow-covered outlines of former things stand out more clearly.

'We've been lucky. The autumn happened to be dry and warm. We managed to dig the potatoes before the rain and cold set in. Minus what we owed and returned to the Mikulitsyns, we have up to twenty sacks, and it is all in the main bin of the cellar, covered above, over the floor, with straw and old, torn blankets. Down there, under the floor, we also put two barrels of Tonya's salted cucumbers and another two of cabbage she has pickled. The fresh cabbage is hung from the crossbeams, head to head, tied in pairs. The supply of carrots is buried in dry sand. As is a sufficient amount of harvested black radishes, beets, and turnips, and upstairs in the house there is a quantity of peas and beans. The firewood stored up in the shed will last till spring. I like the warm smell of the underground in winter, which hits your nose with roots, earth, and snow as soon as you lift the trapdoor of the cellar, at an early hour, before the winter dawn, with a weak, ready to go out, barely luminous light in your hand.

'You come out of the shed, day has not broken yet. The door creaks, or you sneeze unexpectedly, or the snow simply crunches under your foot, and from the far-off vegetable patch, where cabbage stumps stick up from under the snow, hares pop up and go pelting off, scrawling tracks that furrow the snow around far and wide. And in the neighbourhood, one after another, the dogs set up a long barking. The last cocks already crowed earlier, they will not start now. And it begins to grow light.

'Besides hare tracks, the vast snowy plain is crossed by lynx tracks, hole after hole, strung neatly on a drawn-out thread. A lynx walks like a cat, one paw in front of the other, covering many miles a night, as people maintain.

'They set snares for them, "sloptsy", as they call them here. Instead of lynxes, poor hares fall into the traps, and are taken out frozen stiff and half covered with snow.

'At first, in spring and summer, it was very hard. We were exhausted. Now, in the winter evenings, we rest. We gather around the lamp, thanks to Anfim, who provides us with kerosene. The women sew or knit, I or

Alexander Alexandrovich reads aloud. The stove is burning, I, as the long-recognised stoker, keep an eye on it, so as to close the damper in time and not lose any heat. If a smouldering log hampers the heating, I take it out all smoky, run outside with it, and throw it far off into the snow. Scattering sparks, it flies through the air like a burning torch, lighting up the edge of the black, sleeping park with its white quadrangles of lawn, lands in a snow-drift, hisses, and goes out.

'We endlessly reread *War and Peace, Evgeny Onegin* and all the poems, we read *The Red and the Black* by Stendhal, *A Tale of Two Cities* by Dickens, and the short stories of Kleist.'

3

Closer to spring, the doctor wrote:

'I think Tonya is expecting. I told her so. She does not share my supposition, but I am sure of it. Until more unquestionable signs appear, I cannot be deceived by the preceding, less perceptible ones.

'A woman's face changes. It cannot be said that she loses her good looks. But her appearance, which before was entirely under her supervision, now escapes her control. She is at the disposal of the future, which will come out of her and is no longer her. This escape of her appearance from under her surveillance wears a look of physical perplexity, in which her face becomes dull, her skin more coarse, and her eyes begin to shine differently, not as she would like, as if she could not manage it all and let it go.

'Tonya and I have never had any distance from each other. But this year of work has brought us closer still. I've noticed how efficient, strong, and untiring she is, how quick-witted in lining up tasks, so that in moving from one to the other she loses as little time as possible.

'It has always seemed to me that every conception is immaculate, that this dogma concerning the Mother of God expresses the general idea of mother-hood.

'On every woman giving birth there lies the same reflection of solitude, of being abandoned, left to her own resources. The man is excluded from things to such a degree now, at this most essential of moments, that it is as if he had never been there and everything had fallen from the sky.

'A woman herself brings her progeny into the world, herself retires with him into the background of existence, where it is more quiet and where she can put the cradle without fear. She herself, in silent humility, nurses him and rears him.

'People ask the Mother of God: "Pray fervently to your Son and your God!" They put fragments of a psalm into her mouth: "And my spirit rejoices in God my Saviour. For He has regarded the low estate of His hand-maiden. For behold, henceforth all generations will call me blessed." She says this about her infant, he will exalt her ("For he who is mighty has done great things for me"), he is her glory.[3] Every woman can say the same. Her god is in her child. Mothers of great people should be familiar with that feeling. But decidedly all mothers are mothers of great people, and it is not their fault that life later disappoints them.'

4

'We endlessly reread *Evgeny Onegin* and the poems. Anfim was here yesterday and brought presents. We regale ourselves, we have light. Endless conversations about art.

'My long-standing thought that art is not the name of a category or sphere that embraces a vast multitude of notions and ramified phenomena, but, on the contrary, is something narrow and concentrated, the designation of a principle that enters into the composition of an artistic work, the name of the force applied or the truth worked out in it. And to me art has never seemed a subject or an aspect of form, but rather a mysterious and hidden part of content. To me it is clear as day, I feel it with my every fibre, but how express and formulate this thought?

'Works speak through many things: themes, situations, plots, heroes. But most of all they speak through the art contained in them. The presence of art in the pages of *Crime and Punishment* is more astounding than Raskolnikov's crime.

'Primitive art, Egyptian, Greek, our own, is surely one and the same art in the course of the millennia and always remains in the singular. It is some thought, some assertion about life, which, in its all-embracing breadth, cannot be broken down into separate words, and when a grain of that force enters into the composition of some more complex mixture, this admixture of art outweighs the significance of all the rest and turns out to be the essence, the soul, and the foundation of what is depicted.'

5

'A slight cold, a cough, and probably a small fever. All day I've been catching my breath somewhere at the level of the throat, as if there is a lump there. Things are bad for me. It's the aorta. The first warnings of heredity from my poor mama's side, a lifelong story of heart ailment. Can it be true? So early? In that case, I'm not long for this world.

'It is a bit fumy in the room. Smells of ironing. Someone's ironing and keeps adding hot, flaming coals from the still-burning stove to the coal iron, which clacks its lid like teeth. It reminds me of something. I can't remember what. A sick man's forgetfulness.

'Overjoyed that Anfim brought some nut-oil soap, they flew into a general laundering, and Shurochka hasn't been looked after for two days. When I write, he gets under the table, sits on the crossbar between the legs, and, imitating Anfim, who takes him for a sleigh ride each time he comes, pretends that he's also driving me in a sledge.

'When I get better, I must go to town to read up on the ethnography of the region and its history. I'm assured there is an excellent town library, put together from several rich donations. I want to write. I must hurry. Before I turn round, spring will be here. Then there will be no bothering with reading and writing.

'My headache keeps getting worse. I didn't sleep well. I had a confused dream, one of those that you forget on the spot when you wake up. The dream left my head, in my consciousness there remained only the cause of my waking up. I was awakened by a woman's voice, which I heard in my sleep, which in my sleep resounded in the air. I remembered its sound and, reproducing it in my memory, mentally went through all the women I know, searching for which of them might be the owner of that chesty, moist voice, soft from heaviness. It did not belong to any. I thought that my excessive habituation to Tonya might stand between us and dull my hearing in relation to her. I tried to forget she was my wife and moved her image further off, to a distance sufficient for clarifying the truth. No, it was not her voice either. So it remained unclarified.

'Incidentally, about dreams. It is an accepted notion that we tend to dream at night of something that has strongly impressed us in the daytime, when we were awake. My observations are the opposite.

'I've noticed more than once that it is precisely things we have barely noticed in the daytime, thoughts not brought to clarity, words spoken without feeling and left without attention, that return at night clothed in flesh and blood, and become the subjects of dreams, as if in compensation for our neglect of them in the daytime.'

6

'A clear, frosty night. Extraordinary brightness and wholeness of the visible. Earth, air, moon, stars, fettered together, riveted by frost. In the park, the distinct shadows of trees lie across the alleys, seeming carved in relief. It seems all the time as if some dark figures are ceaselessly crossing the path in various places. Big stars like blue mica lamps hang in the forest among the branches. The whole sky is strewn with little stars like a summer meadow with chamomile.

'Our evening talks about Pushkin continue. We discussed his lycée poems in the first volume. How much depended on the choice of metre!

'In the poems with long lines, his youthful ambition did not go beyond the limits of Arzamas, the wish not to fall behind his elders, to blow smoke in his uncle's eyes with mythologisms, pomposity, affected depravity and epicureanism, and premature, feigned sober-mindedness.

'But as soon as the young man, after his imitations of Ossian or Parny or the "Reminiscences in Tsarskoe Selo", hit upon the short lines of "The Little Town" or "Epistle to My Sister", or "To My Inkstand" from the later Kishinev period, or upon the rhythms of the "Letter to Yudin", the whole future Pushkin awakened in the adolescent.[4]

'Light and air, the noise of life, things, essences burst from outside into the poem as into a room through an open window. Objects from the external world, everyday objects, nouns, thronging and pressing, took over the lines, ousting the less definite parts of speech. Objects, objects, objects lined up in a rhymed column along the edge of the poem.

'As if this later celebrated Pushkinian tetrameter was a sort of metrical unit of Russian life, its yardstick, as if it was a measure taken from the whole of Russian existence, as when the form of a foot is outlined to make the pattern for a shoe, or when you give the size so as to find a glove to fit your hand.

'So later the rhythms of talking Russia, the chant of her colloquial speech, were expressed metrically in Nekrasov's trimeters and dactylic rhymes.'[5]

7

'How I would like, along with having a job, working the earth, or practising medicine, to nurture something lasting, fundamental, to write some scholarly work or something artistic.

'Everyone is born a Faust, to embrace everything, experience everything, express everything. The fact that Faust was a scientist was seen to by the mistakes of his predecessors and contemporaries. A step forward in science is made by the law of repulsion, with the refutation of reigning errors and false theories.

'That Faust was an artist was seen to by the infectious example of his teachers. A step forward in art is made by the law of attraction, with the imitation, following, and veneration of beloved predecessors.

'What then prevents me from working, treating, and writing? I think it is not privations and wanderings, not instability and frequent change, but the reigning spirit of bombastic phrases so widespread in our day – such as: the dawn of the future, the building of the new world, the lights of mankind. You hear that and at first you think – what breadth of imagination, what wealth! But in reality it is pompous precisely in its lack of talent.

'Only the ordinary is fantastic, once the hand of genius touches it. The best lesson in this respect is Pushkin. What a glorification of honest labour, duty, habitual everyday things! With us "bourgeois" and "philistine" have now come to sound reproachful. That reproof was forestalled by lines from "Genealogy":

> I am a bourgeois, a bourgeois.

'And from "Onegin's Journey":

> My ideal now is a housewife,
> My desire is for peace,
> A pot of soup, and my fine self.[6]

'Of all things Russian I now love most the Russian childlikeness of Pushkin and Chekhov, their shy unconcern with such resounding things as the ultimate goals of mankind and their own salvation. They, too, understood all these things, but such immodesties were far from them – not their business, not on their level! Gogol, Tolstoy, Dostoevsky prepared for death, were anxious, sought meaning, summed things up, but these two till the end were distracted by the current particulars of their artistic calling, and in their succession lived their lives inconspicuously, as one such particular, personal, of no concern to anyone, and now that particular has become common property and, like still unripe apples picked from the tree, is ripening in posterity, filling more and more with sweetness and meaning.'

8

'The first heralds of spring, a thaw. The air smells of pancakes and vodka, as during the week before Lent, when nature herself seems to rhyme with the calendar. Somnolent, the sun in the forest narrows its buttery eyes; somnolent, the forest squints through its needles like eyelashes; the puddles at noontime have a buttery gleam. Nature yawns, stretches herself, rolls over on the other side, and falls asleep again.

'In the seventh chapter of *Evgeny Onegin* – spring, the manor house empty after Onegin's departure, Lensky's grave down by the water, under the hill.

And there the nightingale, spring's lover,
Sings all night long. The wild rose flowers.

'Why "lover"? Generally speaking, the epithet is natural, appropriate. Indeed he is a lover. Besides that, it's needed for the rhyme. But in terms of sound, do we not also have here the epic Nightingale the Robber?[7]
'In the folk epic he is called Nightingale the Robber, son of Odikhmanty. How well it speaks of him!

From him and from his nightingale whistle,
From him and from his wild beast cry,
All the grassy masses shrink and shrivel,
All the sky-blue flowers wither and die,
The dark woods all bow down their heads,
And if there are people, they all lie dead.

'We arrived at Varykino in early spring. Soon everything began to turn green, especially in Shutma, as the ravine under Mikulitsyn's house is called – bird cherry, alder, hazel. Several nights later the nightingales began to trill.
'And again, as if hearing them for the first time, I was amazed at how this song stands out from the calls of all other birds, what a leap, without gradual change, nature performs to the richness and singularity of this trilling. So much variety in changing figures and such force of distinct, far-reaching sound! In Turgenev somewhere[8] there is a description of these whistlings, the wood demon's piping, the larklike drumming. Two turns stood out particularly. The quick, greedy, and luxurious "tiokh, tiokh, tiokh", sometimes with three beats, sometimes countless, in response to which the thicket, all in dew, shook itself, preened itself, flinching as if it had been tickled. And another falling into two syllables, calling out, soul-felt, entreating, like a plea or an exhortation: "A-wake! A-wake! A-wake!"'

9

'Spring. We're getting ready for farmwork. So no more diary. But it has been pleasant to take these notes. I'll have to set them aside till winter.
'The other day, this time indeed during the week before Lent, the season of bad roads, a sick peasant drives his sled into the yard over water and mud. Naturally, I refuse to receive him. "Forgive me, my dear fellow, I've stopped doing that – I have neither a real choice of medicines, nor the necessary

equipment." But there was no getting rid of him. "Help me. My skin's going scant. Have mercy. A bodily ailment."

'What to do? I don't have a heart of stone. I decided to receive him. "Get undressed." I examined him. "You've got lupus." I busy myself with him, glancing sidelong towards the windowsill, at the bottle of carbolic acid. (Good God, don't ask me where I got it, and another thing or two, the most necessary! It's all from Samdevyatov.) I look – another sled drives into the yard, with a new patient, as it seems to me at first. And my brother Evgraf drops as if from the clouds. For a while he is at the disposal of the household, Tonya, Shurochka, Alexander Alexandrovich. Afterwards, when I'm free, I join the others. Questions begin – how, from where? As usual, he dodges, evades, not one direct answer, smiles, wonders, riddles.

'He was our guest for about two weeks, often going by himself to Yuriatin, and suddenly he vanished as if he'd fallen through the earth. During that time I was able to notice that he was still more influential than Samdevyatov, yet his doings and connections were still less explicable. Where does he come from? Where does his power come from? What is he engaged in? Before his disappearance, he promised to lighten our farmwork, so that Tonya would have free time to bring up Shura, and I for medical and literary pursuits. We asked curiously what he intended to do towards that end. Again silence and smiles. But he did not deceive us. There are signs that the conditions of our life will indeed change.

'Astonishing thing! He is my half-brother. He has the same last name. And yet, strictly speaking, I know him least of all.

'This is already the second time that he has irrupted into my life as a good genius, a deliverer who resolves all difficulties. Perhaps the composition of every biography, along with the cast of characters acting in it, also calls for the participation of a mysterious unknown power, an almost symbolic person, appearing to help without being called, and the role of this beneficent and hidden mainspring is played in my life by my brother Evgraf?'

With that the notes of Yuri Andreevich ended. He never continued them.

10

Yuri Andreevich was looking over the books he had ordered in the Yuriatin city reading room. The many-windowed reading room for a hundred persons was set with several rows of long tables, their narrow ends towards the windows. The reading room closed with the coming of darkness. In springtime the city was not lighted in the evening. But Yuri Andreevich never sat until dusk anyway, and did not stay in the city past dinnertime. He would leave the horse that the Mikulitsyns gave him at Samdevyatov's inn, spend the whole morning reading, and at midday return home on horseback to Varykino.

Before these raids on the library, Yuri Andreevich had rarely been to Yuriatin. He had no particular business in the city. He knew it poorly. And when the room gradually filled before his eyes with Yuriatin's citizens, who would seat themselves now far from him, now right next to him, Yuri Andreevich felt as if he was becoming acquainted with the city, standing at one of its populous intersections, and as if what poured into the room were not Yuriatin's readers, but the houses and streets they lived in.

However, the actual Yuriatin, real and not imagined, could be seen through the windows of the room. Near the middle window, the biggest of them, stood a tank of boiled water. Readers, by way of taking a break, went out to the stairway to smoke, surrounded the tank, drank water, pouring what was left into a basin, and crowded by the window, admiring the view of the city.

There were two kinds of readers: old-timers from the local intelligentsia – they were the majority – and those from simple people.

The first, most of whom were women, poorly dressed, neglectful of themselves and gone to seed, had unhealthy, drawn faces, puffy for various reasons – hunger, biliousness, dropsy. These were the habitués of the reading room, personally acquainted with the library workers and feeling themselves at home there.

Those from the people, with beautiful, healthy faces, dressed neatly, festively, came into the room embarrassed and timid, as into church, and made their appearance more noisily than was customary, not from ignorance of the rules, but owing to their wish to enter perfectly noiselessly and their inability to adjust their healthy steps and voices.

Opposite the windows there was a recess in the wall. In this niche, on a podium, separated from the rest of the room by a high counter, the reading room staff, the senior librarian and his two female assistants, were busy with their tasks. One of them, angry, wearing a woollen shawl, constantly took off her pince-nez and then perched it back on her nose, guided, apparently, not by the needs of vision, but by the changes of her inner state. The other, in a black silk blouse, was probably suffering from chest congestion, because she almost never took the handkerchief from her mouth and nose, and talked and breathed into it.

The library staff had the same swollen faces, elongated and puffy, as half the readers, the same slack skin, sallow shot with green, the colour of a pickle covered with grey mould, and the three of them took turns doing one and the same thing, explaining in a whisper to novices the rules for using books, sorting out order slips, handing over books, and receiving the returned ones, and in between worked on putting together some sort of annual report.

And, strangely, by some incomprehensible coupling of ideas, in the faces of the real city outside the window and the imaginary one in the room, and also by some likeness caused by the general deathly puffiness, as if they were all sick with goitre, Yuri Andreevich recalled the displeased switchwoman on the tracks of Yuriatin the morning of their arrival, and the general panorama of the city in the distance, and Samdevyatov beside him on the floor of the coach, and his explanations. And Yuri Andreevich wanted to connect those explanations, given far outside the limits of the place, at a great distance, with everything he now saw close up, in the heart of the picture. But he did not remember Samdevyatov's designations, and nothing came of it.

11

Yuri Andreevich was sitting at the far end of the room, surrounded by books. Before him lay periodicals on local zemstvo statistics and several works on the ethnography of the region. He tried to request two more works on the history of Pugachev, but the librarian in the black silk blouse, whispering through the handkerchief pressed to her lips, observed to him that they did not give out so many books at once into the same hands, and that to obtain the works that interested him, he would have to return some of the reference books and periodicals he had taken.

Therefore Yuri Andreevich began more assiduously and hurriedly to acquaint himself with the as yet unsorted books, so as to select and keep the most necessary out of the pile and exchange the rest for the historical works that interested him. He quickly leafed through the collections and ran his eyes over the tables of contents, undistracted by anything and not looking to either side. The many people in the room did not disturb or divert him. He had studied his neighbours well and saw them with his mental gaze to right and left of him without raising his eyes from the book, with the feeling that their complement would not change before he left, any more than the churches and buildings of the city seen through the window would move from their place.

Meanwhile the sun did not stand still. It moved all the while around the eastern corner of the library. Now it was shining through the windows on the southern side, blinding those who sat close to them and preventing them from reading.

The librarian with a cold came down from her fenced-off elevation and headed for the windows. They had festoon curtains of white fabric, which pleasantly softened the light. The librarian lowered them on all the windows but one. That one, at the end, in the shade, she left uncurtained. Pulling the cord, she opened the vent pane and went into a fit of sneezing.

When she had sneezed for the tenth or twelfth time, Yuri Andreevich guessed that she was Mikulitsyn's sister-in-law, one of the Tuntsevs, of whom Samdevyatov had told him. Along with other readers, Yuri Andreevich raised his head and looked in her direction.

Then he noticed that a change had taken place in the room. At the opposite end a new visitor had been added. Yuri Andreevich recognised Antipova at once. She was sitting with her back turned to the front tables, at one of which the doctor had placed himself, and talking in a low voice with the sick librarian, who stood bending towards Larissa Fyodorovna and exchanged whispers with her. This conversation must have had a beneficial influence on the librarian. She was instantly cured not only of her annoying cold, but also of her nervous apprehension. Casting a warm, grateful glance at Antipova, she took away the handkerchief that she kept pressed to her lips all the time and, putting it in her pocket, went back to her place behind the counter, happy, confident, and smiling.

This scene marked by touching details did not escape some of those present. From all sides of the room, people looked sympathetically at Antipova and also smiled. By these insignificant signs, Yuri Andreevich ascertained how well-known and loved she was in the city.

12

Yuri Andreevich's first intention was to get up and go over to Larissa Fyodorovna. But then the constraint and lack of simplicity, foreign to his nature but established in him in relation to her, got the upper hand. He decided not to bother her, and also not to interrupt his own work. To shield himself from the temptation to look in her direction, he placed the chair sideways to the table, almost back to the readers, and immersed himself in his books, holding one in his hand in front of him and another open on his knees.

However, his thoughts wandered a thousand miles away from the subject of his studies. Outside of any connection with them, he suddenly realised that the voice he had once heard in his sleep on a winter night in Varykino had been Antipova's voice. He was struck by this discovery and, attracting the attention of those around him, he abruptly put his chair back in its former position, so as to see Antipova from where he sat, and began to look at her.

He saw her almost from behind, her back half turned. She was wearing a light-coloured chequered blouse tied with a belt, and was reading eagerly, with self-abandon, as children do, her head slightly inclined towards her right shoulder. Now and then she lapsed into thought, raising her eyes to the ceiling or narrowing them and peering somewhere far ahead of her, and then again, propped on her elbow, her head resting on her hand, in a quick, sweeping movement she pencilled some notes in her notebook.

Yuri Andreevich tested and confirmed his former observations in Meliuzeevo. 'She doesn't want to be admired,' he thought, 'to be beautiful, captivating. She scorns that side of a woman's nature, and it is as if she punishes herself for being so good-looking. And that proud hostility to herself increases her irresistibility tenfold.

'How good is everything she does. She reads as if it were not man's highest activity, but the simplest of things, accessible to animals. As if she were carrying water or peeling potatoes.'

These reflections calmed the doctor. A rare peace descended into his soul. His thoughts stopped scattering and jumping from subject to subject. He smiled involuntarily. Antipova's presence had the same effect on him as on the nervous librarian.

Not bothering about how his chair stood, and fearing no hindrances or distractions, he worked for an hour or an hour and a half still more assiduously and concentratedly than before Antipova's arrival. He went through the tall stack of books in front of him, selected the most necessary ones, and even managed in passing to gulp down the two important articles he came across in them. Deciding to be satisfied with what he had done, he started gathering up the books in order to take them to the librarian's desk. All extraneous considerations, derogatory to his consciousness, abandoned him. With a clear conscience, and with no second thoughts, he decided that his honestly done work had earned him the right to meet with an old and good acquaintance and that he had legitimate grounds for allowing himself this joy. But when he stood up and looked around the reading room, he did not find Antipova; she was no longer there.

On the counter to which the doctor carried his tomes and brochures, the literature returned by Antipova still lay unshelved. It was all manuals on Marxism. She was probably requalifying herself to be a teacher, as before, going through political retraining on her own at home.

Larissa Fyodorovna's catalogue requests lay in the books. The ends of the slips were showing. On them Larissa Fyodorovna's address was written. It could easily be read. Yuri Andreevich wrote it down, surprised by the strangeness of the designation. 'Kupecheskaya Street, opposite the house with figures.'

On the spot, having asked someone, Yuri Andreevich learned that the expression 'house with figures' was as current in Yuriatin as the naming of neighbourhoods by parish churches in Moscow or the name Five Corners in Petersburg.

It was the name of a dark grey, steel-coloured house with caryatids and statues of Greek muses with tambourines, lyres, and masks in their hands, built in the last century by a theatre-loving merchant as his private theatre. The merchant's heirs sold this house to the Merchants' Association, which gave its name to the street on the corner of which the house stood. The whole area around it was named for this house with figures. Now the house with figures accommodated the city's party committee, and the wall of its slanting basement, running obliquely downhill, where theatre and circus posters hung in former times, was now covered with government decrees and resolutions.

13

It was a cold, windy day at the beginning of May. Having wandered around town on errands, and looked into the library for a moment, Yuri Andreevich suddenly cancelled all his plans and went in search of Antipova.

The wind often stopped him on his way, blocking his path by raising clouds of sand and dust. The doctor turned away, squinted his eyes, lowered his head, waiting for the dust to sweep past, and went further on.

Antipova lived at the corner of Kupecheskaya and Novosvalochny Lane, opposite the dark, verging on blue, house with figures, which the doctor now saw for the first time. The house indeed corresponded to its nickname and made a strange, disturbing impression.

The whole top was surrounded by female mythological caryatids half again human size. Between two gusts of wind that hid its façade, the doctor fancied for a moment that the entire female population of the house had come out to the balcony and was leaning over the balustrade looking at him and at Kupecheskaya spread out below.

There were two entrances to Antipova's, the front one from the street and one through the courtyard from the lane. Not knowing about the existence of the first, Yuri Andreevich took the second.

When he turned through the gate from the lane, the wind whirled dirt and litter from the whole yard up into the sky, screening the yard from the doctor. Hens rushed clucking from under his feet behind this black curtain, trying to save themselves from the rooster pursuing them.

When the cloud scattered, the doctor saw Antipova by the well. The whirlwind had surprised her with water already drawn in both buckets and the yoke over her left shoulder. Her head was covered with a kerchief, hastily knotted on her forehead, so as not to get dust in her hair, and she was holding the billowing skirt of her coat to keep it from being lifted by the wind. She started towards the house, carrying the water, but stopped, held back by a new gust of wind, which tore the kerchief from her head, started blowing her hair about, and carried the kerchief towards the far end of the fence, to the still clucking hens.

Yuri Andreevich ran after the kerchief, picked it up, and handed it to the taken-aback Antipova by the well. Ever faithful to her naturalness, she did not betray how amazed and perplexed she was by any exclamation. The only thing that escaped her was:

'Zhivago!'

'Larissa Fyodorovna!'

'By what miracle? By what chance?'

'Put your buckets down. I'll carry them.'

'I never turn back halfway, never abandon what I've started. If you've come to me, let's go.'

'And to whom else?'

'Who knows with you?'

'Anyway, let me take the yoke from your shoulders. I can't stand idle while you work.'

'Work, is it! I won't let you. You'll splash water all over the stairs. Better tell me what wind blew you here. You've been around for more than a year, and still couldn't decide, couldn't find time?'

'How do you know?'

'Word gets around. And I saw you, finally, in the library.'

'Why didn't you call out to me?'

'You won't make me believe you didn't see me yourself.'

Following Larissa Fyodorovna, who was swaying slightly under the swaying buckets, the doctor stepped under the low archway. This was the back entrance to the ground floor. Here, quickly squatting down, Larissa Fyodorovna set the buckets on the dirt floor, freed her shoulders from the yoke, straightened up, and began to wipe her hands with a little handkerchief she took from no one knows where.

'Come, I'll take you, there's an inner passage to the front entrance. It's

light there. You can wait there. And I'll take the water up the back way, tidy
things upstairs a little, change my clothes. See what sort of stairs we've got.
Cast-iron steps with an openwork design. You can see everything through
them from above. It's an old house. It got jolted a bit during the days of the
shelling. There was artillery fire. See, the stones have separated. There are
holes, openings between the bricks. Katenka and I put the key to the apartment into this hole and cover it with a brick when we leave. Keep that in
mind. You may come one day and not find me here, and then you're welcome to open the door, come in, make yourself at home. And meanwhile I'll
come back. It's here now, the key. But I don't need it. I'll go in from the back
and open the door from inside. The one trouble is the rats. Hordes and
hordes, there's no getting rid of them. They jump all over us. The structure's
decrepit, the walls are shaky, there are cracks everywhere. Where I can, I
plug them, I fight. It doesn't do much good. Maybe some day you'll come by
and help me? Together we can bush up the floors and plinths. Hm? Well,
stay on the landing, think about something. I won't let you languish long,
I'll call you soon.'

Waiting to be called, Yuri Andreevich let his eyes wander over the peeling
walls of the entrance and the cast-iron steps of the stairs. He was thinking:
'In the reading room I compared the eagerness of her reading with the passion and ardour of actually doing something, of physical work. And, on the
contrary, she carries water lightly, effortlessly, as if she were reading. She has
this facility in everything. As if she had picked up the momentum for life
way back in her childhood, and now everything is done with that momentum, of itself, with the ease of an ensuing consequence. She has it in the line
of her back when she bends over, and in the smile that parts her lips and
rounds her chin, and in her words and thoughts.'

'Zhivago!' rang out from the doorway of an apartment on the upper
landing. The doctor went upstairs.

14

'Give me your hand and follow me obediently. There will be two rooms here
where it's dark and things are piled to the ceiling. You'll stumble and hurt
yourself.'

'True, it's a sort of labyrinth. I wouldn't find my way. Why's that? Are you
redoing the apartment?'

'Oh, no, not at all. It's somebody else's apartment. I don't even know
whose. We used to have our own, a government one, in the school building.
When the building was taken over by the housing office of the Yuriatin City

Council, they moved me and my daughter into part of this abandoned one. There were leftovers from the former owners. A lot of furniture. I don't need other people's belongings. I put all their things in these two rooms and whitewashed the windows. Don't let go of my hand or you'll get lost. That's it. To the right. Now the jungle's behind us. This is my door. There'll be more light. The threshold. Don't trip.'

When Yuri Andreevich went into the room with his guide, there turned out to be a window in the wall facing the door. The doctor was struck by what he saw through it. The window gave onto the courtyard of the house, onto the backs of the neighbouring houses and the vacant plots by the river. Sheep and goats were grazing on them, sweeping the dust with their long wool as if with the skirts of unbuttoned coats. Besides, there was on them, facing the window, perched on two posts, a billboard familiar to the doctor: 'Moreau and Vetchinkin. Seeders. Threshers'.

Under the influence of seeing the billboard, the doctor began from the first word to describe for Larissa Fyodorovna his arrival in the Urals with his family. He forgot about the rumour that identified Strelnikov with her husband and, without thinking, told her about his encounter with the commissar on the train. This part of the story made a special impression on Larissa Fyodorovna.

'You've seen Strelnikov?!' she asked quickly. 'I won't tell you any more right now. But how portentous! Simply some sort of predestination that you had to meet. I'll explain to you after a while, you'll simply gasp. If I've understood you rightly, he made a favourable impression on you rather than otherwise?'

'Yes, perhaps so. He ought to have repelled me. We passed through the areas of his reprisals and destructions. I expected to meet a brutal soldier or a murderous revolutionary maniac, and found neither the one nor the other. It's good when a man deceives your expectations, when he doesn't correspond to the preconceived notion of him. To belong to a type is the end of a man, his condemnation. If he doesn't fall into any category, if he's not representative, half of what's demanded of him is there. He's free of himself, he has achieved a grain of immortality.'

'They say he's not a party member.'

'Yes, so it seems. What makes him so winning? He's a doomed man. I think he'll end badly. He'll pay for the evil he's brought about. The arbitrariness of the revolutionaries is terrible not because they're villains, but because it's a mechanism out of control, like a machine that's gone off the rails. Strelnikov is as mad as they are, but he went crazy not from books, but from something he lived and suffered through. I don't know his secret, but

I'm certain he has one. His alliance with the Bolsheviks is accidental. As long as they need him, they'll tolerate him, they're going the same way. But the moment that need passes, they'll cast him aside with no regret and trample on him, like so many military specialists before him.'

'You think so?'

'Absolutely.'

'But is there really no salvation for him? In flight, for instance?'

'Where to, Larissa Fyodorovna? That was before, under the tsars. Try doing it now.'

'Too bad. Your story has made me feel sympathy for him. But you've changed. Before, your judgement of the revolution wasn't so sharp, so irritated.'

'That's just the point, Larissa Fyodorovna, that there are limits to everything. There's been time enough for them to arrive at something. But it turns out that for the inspirers of the revolution the turmoil of changes and rearrangements is their only native element, that they won't settle for less than something on a global scale. The building of worlds, transitional periods – for them this is an end in itself. They haven't studied anything else, they don't know how to do anything. And do you know where this bustle of eternal preparations comes from? From the lack of definite, ready abilities, from giftlessness. Man is born to live, not to prepare for life. And life itself, the phenomenon of life, the gift of life, is so thrillingly serious! Why then substitute for it a childish harlequinade of immature inventions, these escapes of Chekhovian schoolboys to America?[9] But enough. Now it's my turn to ask. We were approaching the city on the morning of your coup. Was it a big mess for you then?'

'Oh, what else! Of course. Fires all around. We almost burned down ourselves. The house, I told you, got so shaken! There's still an unexploded shell in the yard by the gate. Looting, bombardment, outrage. As always with a change of power. By then we'd already learned, we were used to it. It wasn't the first time. And what went on under the Whites! Covert killings for personal revenge, extortions, bacchanalias! But I haven't told you the main thing. Our Galiullin! He turned up here as the most important bigwig with the Czechs. Something like a governor-general.'

'I know. I heard. Did you see him?'

'Very often. I saved so many people thanks to him! Hid so many! He has to be given credit. He behaved irreproachably, chivalrously, not like the small fry, all those Cossack chiefs and police officers. But the tone was set then precisely by the small fry, not the decent people. Galiullin helped me in many ways, I'm thankful to him. We're old acquaintances. As a little girl, I often came to the courtyard where he grew up. Railroad workers lived in that house. In my childhood I saw poverty and labour close up. That makes my attitude towards the revolution different from yours. It's closer to me. There's much in it that is dear to me. And suddenly he becomes a colonel, this boy, the yard porter's son. Or even a White general. I come from a civilian milieu and don't know much about ranks. By training I'm a history teacher. Yes, that's how it is, Zhivago. I helped many people. I went to him. We spoke of you. I have connections and protectors in all the governments, and griefs and losses under all regimes. It's only in bad books that living people are divided into two camps and don't communicate. In reality everything's so interwoven! What an incorrigible nonentity one must be to play only one role in life, to occupy only one place in society, to always mean one and the same thing!'

'Ah, so you're here?'

A girl of about eight with two tightly plaited pigtails came into the room. Her narrow, wide-set eyes slanting upwards gave her a mischievous and sly look. She raised them when she laughed. She had already discovered outside the door that her mother had a guest, but, appearing on the threshold, she considered it necessary to show an inadvertent astonishment on her face, curtsied, and turned to the doctor the unblinking, fearless eye of a precociously thoughtful child growing up in solitude.

'Kindly meet my daughter Katenka.'

'You showed me pictures of her in Meliuzeevo. How she's grown and changed!'

'So it turns out you're at home? And I thought you were outside. I didn't hear you come in.'

'I took the key from the hole, and there was a rat this big! I screamed and backed away. I thought I'd die of fear.'

Katenka made the sweetest faces when she talked, rolling her sly eyes and forming her little mouth into a circle, like a fish taken out of the water.

'Well, go to your room. I'll persuade the nice man to stay for dinner, take the kasha from the oven, and call you.'

'Thank you, but I'm forced to decline. Because of my visits to the city, our dinners are served at six. I'm used to not being late, and it's over a three-hour ride, if not all of four. That's why I came early – forgive me – I'll get up and go soon.'

'Just half an hour more.'

'With pleasure.'

15

'And now – frankness for frankness. Strelnikov, whom you told about, is my husband Pasha, Pavel Pavlovich Antipov, whom I went to the front in search of and in whose imaginary death I so rightly refused to believe.'

'I'm not shocked and have been prepared. I've heard that fable and consider it nonsense. That's why I forgot myself to such an extent that I spoke to you so freely and incautiously about him, as if this gossip didn't exist. But these rumours are senseless. I saw the man. How could he be connected with you? What do you have in common?'

'And all the same it's so, Yuri Andreevich. Strelnikov is Antipov, my husband. I agree with the general opinion. Katenka also knows it and is proud of her father. Strelnikov is his assumed name, a pseudonym, as with all revolutionary activists. For certain considerations, he must live and act under a different name.

'He took Yuriatin, poured shells on us, knew that we were here, never once asked if we were alive, so as not to violate his secret. That was his duty, of course. If he had asked us how to act, we would have advised him to do the same. You could also say that my immunity, the acceptable living quarters given me by the city council, and so on, are indirect proofs of his secret caring for us! All the same, you won't persuade me of it. To be right here and resist the temptation to see us! My mind refuses to grasp that, it's beyond my understanding. It's something inaccessible to me – not life, but some Roman civic valour, one of the clever notions of today. But I'm falling under your influence and beginning to sing your tune. I wouldn't want that. You and I are not of one mind. We may understand some elusive, optional thing in the same way. But in matters of broad significance, in philosophy of life, it's better for us to be opponents. But let's get back to Strelnikov. He's in Siberia now, and you're right, information about criticism of him, which chills my heart, has reached me, too. He's in Siberia, at one of our advanced positions, in the process of defeating his courtyard friend and later front-line comrade, poor Galiullin, for whom his name and his marriage to me are no secret, and who, in his priceless delicacy, has never let me feel it, though he storms and rages and goes out of his mind at the mention of Strelnikov. Yes, well, so he's now in Siberia.

'And while he was here (he spent a long time here and lived on the railway, in the carriage of a train, where you saw him), I kept trying to run into him accidentally, unexpectedly. He sometimes went to headquarters, housed where the military command of the Komuch, the army of the Constituent

Assembly, used to be. And – strange trick of fate – the entrance to the headquarters was in the same wing where Galiullin used to receive me when I came to solicit for others. For instance, there was an incident in the cadet corps that made a lot of noise, the cadets began to ambush and shoot objectionable teachers on the pretext of their adherence to Bolshevism. Or when the persecution and slaughter of the Jews began. By the way. If we're city dwellers and people doing intellectual work, half of our acquaintances are from their number. And in such periods of pogroms, when these horrors and abominations begin, we're hounded, not only by indignation, shame, and pity, but by an oppressive feeling of duplicity, that our sympathy is half cerebral, with an unpleasant, insincere aftertaste.

'The people who once delivered mankind from the yoke of paganism, and have now devoted themselves in such great numbers to freeing it from social evil, are powerless to free themselves from themselves, from being faithful to an outlived, antediluvian designation, which has lost its meaning; they cannot rise above themselves and dissolve without a trace among others, whose religious foundations they themselves laid, and who would be so close to them if only they knew them better.

'Persecution and victimisation probably oblige them to adopt this useless and ruinous pose, this shamefaced, self-denying isolation, which brings nothing but calamities, but there is also an inner decrepitude in it, many centuries of historical fatigue. I don't like their ironic self-encouragement, humdrum poverty of notions, timorous imagination. It's as irritating as old people talking about old age and sick people about sickness. Do you agree?'

'I haven't thought about it. I have a friend, a certain Gordon, who is of the same opinion.'

'So I went there to watch for Pasha. In hopes of his coming or going. The governor-general's office used to be in the wing. Now there's a plaque on the door: "Complaints Bureau". Maybe you've seen it? It's the most beautiful place in the city. The square in front of the door is paved with cut stone. Across the square is the city garden. Viburnums, maples, hawthorns. I stood on the pavement in the group of petitioners and waited. Naturally, I didn't try to force my way in, I didn't tell them I was his wife. Anyway, our last names aren't the same. What has the voice of the heart got to do with it? Their rules are completely different. For instance, his own father, Pavel Ferapontovich Antipov, a worker and a former political exile, works in the court here, somewhere quite close by, just down the highway. In the place of his earlier exile. So does his friend Tiverzin. They're members of the revolutionary tribunal. And what do you think? The son doesn't reveal himself to the father either, and the father accepts it as proper, does not get offended. If the son is a cipher, it means nothing doing. They're flint, not people. Principles. Discipline.

'And, finally, if I proved that I was his wife, it's no big deal! What have wives got to do with it? Is it the time for such things? The world proletariat, the remaking of the universe – that's something else, that I understand. But an individual biped of some wifely sort, pah! It's just some last little flea or louse!

'An adjutant went around asking questions. He let a few people in. I didn't tell him my last name, and to the question about my business answered that it was personal. You could tell beforehand that it was a lost cause, a nonsuit. The adjutant shrugged his shoulders and looked at me suspiciously. So I never saw him even once.

'And you think he disdains us, doesn't love us, doesn't remember? Oh, on the contrary! I know him too well! He planned it this way from an excess of feeling! He needs to lay all these military laurels at our feet, so as not to come back empty-handed, but all in glory, a conqueror! To immortalise, to bedazzle us! Like a child!'

Katenka came into the room again. Larissa Fyodorovna took the bewildered little girl in her arms, began to rock her, tickle her, kiss her, and smothered her in her embrace.

16

Yuri Andreevich was returning on horseback from the city to Varykino. He had passed these places countless times. He was used to the road, had grown insensitive to it, did not notice it.

He was nearing the intersection in the forest where a side road to the fishing village of Vassilievskoe, on the Sakma River, branched off from the straight way to Varykino. At the place where they divided stood the third post in the area displaying an agricultural advertisement. Near this crossroads, the doctor was usually overtaken by the sunset. Now, too, night was falling.

It was over two months since, on one of his visits to town, he had not returned home in the evening, but had stayed with Larissa Fyodorovna, and said at home that he had been kept in town on business and had spent the night at Samdevyatov's inn. He had long been on familiar terms with Antipova and called her Lara, though she called him Zhivago. Yuri Andreevich was deceiving Tonya and was concealing ever more grave and inadmissible things from her. This was unheard-of.

He loved Tonya to the point of adoration. The peace of her soul, her tranquillity, were dearer to him than anything in the world. He stood staunchly for her honour, more than her own father or than she herself. In defence of her wounded pride he would have torn the offender to pieces with his own hands. And here that offender was he himself.

At home, in his family circle, he felt like an unexposed criminal. The ignorance of the household, their habitual affability, killed him. In the midst of a general conversation, he would suddenly remember his guilt, freeze, and no longer hear or understand anything around him.

If this happened at the table, the swallowed bite stuck in his throat, he set his spoon aside, pushed the plate away. Tears choked him. 'What's the matter?' Tonya would ask in perplexity. 'You must have found out something bad in the city? Somebody's been sent to prison? Or shot? Tell me. Don't be afraid of upsetting me. You'll feel better.'

Had he betrayed Tonya, had he preferred someone else to her? No, he had not chosen anyone, had not compared. Ideas of 'free love', words like 'the rights and demands of feeling', were foreign to him. To talk and think of such things seemed vulgar to him. In his life he had never gathered any 'flowers of pleasure', had not counted himself among the demigods or supermen, had demanded no special benefits or advantages for himself. He was breaking down under the burden of an unclean conscience.

'What will happen further on?' he sometimes asked himself and, finding no answer, hoped for something unfeasible, for the interference of some unforeseen circumstances that would bring a resolution.

But now it was not so. He had decided to cut this knot by force. He was bringing home a ready solution. He had decided to confess everything to Tonya, to beg her forgiveness, and not to see Lara any more.

True, not everything was smooth here. It remained insufficiently clear, as it now seemed to him, that he was breaking with Lara forever, for all eternity. That morning he had announced to her his wish to reveal everything to Tonya and the impossibility of further meetings, but he now had the feeling that he had said it to her too mildly, not resolutely enough.

Larissa Fyodorovna had not wanted to upset Yuri Andreevich with painful scenes. She understood how much he was suffering even without that. She tried to listen to his news as calmly as possible. Their talk took place in the empty room of the former owners, unused by Larissa Fyodorovna, which gave onto Kupecheskaya. Unfelt, unbeknownst to her, tears flowed down Lara's cheeks, like the rainwater that now poured down the faces of the stone statues opposite, on the house with figures. Sincerely, without affected magnanimity, she repeated quietly: 'Do what's better for you, don't think about me. I'll get over it all.' And she did not know she was crying, and did not wipe her tears.

At the thought that Larissa Fyodorovna had misunderstood him and that he had left her in delusion, with false hopes, he was ready to turn and gallop back to the city, to finish what had been left unsaid, and above all to take leave of her much more ardently and tenderly, in greater accordance with what was to be a real parting for their whole lives, forever. He barely controlled himself and continued on his way.

As the sun went down, the forest became filled with cold and darkness. It began to smell of the leafy dampness of a steamed besom, as on going into a bathhouse. Motionless in the air, like floats on the water, spread hanging swarms of mosquitoes, whining in high-pitched unison, all on one note. Yuri Andreevich swatted countless numbers of them on his forehead and neck, and the resounding slaps of his palm on his sweaty body responded amazingly to the other sounds of his riding: the creaking of the saddle girths, the ponderous thud of hooves glancing, swiping, through the squelching mud, and the dry, popping salvos emitted by the horse's guts. Suddenly, in the distance, where the sunset had got stuck, a nightingale began to trill.

'A-wake! A-wake!' it called and entreated, and it sounded almost like before Easter: 'My soul, my soul! Arise, why are you sleeping!'[10]

Suddenly a very simple thought dawned on Yuri Andreevich. What's the hurry? He would not go back on the word he had given himself. The exposure would be made. But where was it said that it must take place today? Nothing had been declared to Tonya yet. It was not too late to put off the explanation till next time. Meanwhile he would go to the city once more. The conversation with Lara would be brought to an end, with the depth and sincerity that redeem all suffering. Oh, how good! How wonderful! How astonishing that it had not occurred to him before!

The assumption that he would see Antipova once more made Yuri Andreevich mad with joy. His heart began to beat rapidly. He lived it all over in anticipation.

The log-built back streets of the outskirts, the wood-paved pavements. He is going to her. Now, in Novosvalochny, the vacant plots and wooden part of the city will end and the stone part will begin. The little houses of the suburb race by like the pages of a quickly leafed-through book, not when you turn them with your index finger, but when you flip through them all with the soft part of your thumb, making a crackling noise. It takes your breath away! She lives there, at that end. Under the white gap in the rainy sky that has cleared towards evening. How he loves these familiar little houses on the way to her! He could just pick them up from the ground and kiss them all over! These one-eyed mezzanines pulled down over the roofs! The little berries of lights and oil lamps reflected in the puddles! Under that white strip of rainy street sky. There again he will receive from the hands of the Creator the gift of this God-made white loveliness. The door will be opened by a figure wrapped in something dark. And the promise of her intimacy, restrained, cold as the pale night of the north, no one's, belonging to nobody, will come rolling towards him like the first wave of the sea, which you run to in the darkness over the sand of the coast.

Yuri Andreevich dropped the reins, leaned forward in the saddle, embraced his horse's neck, and buried his face in its mane. Taking this tenderness for an appeal to its full strength, the horse went into a gallop.

At a smooth, flying gallop, in the intervals between the rare, barely noticeable contacts of the horse with the earth, which kept tearing away from its hoofs and flying backwards, Yuri Andreevich, besides the beating of his heart, which stormed with joy, also heard some shouts, which he thought he was imagining.

A shot close by deafened him. The doctor raised his head, seized the reins, and pulled at them. The racing horse made several clumsy leaps sideways, backed up, and began to lower his croup, preparing to rear.

Ahead the road divided in two. Beside it the billboard 'Moreau and Vetchinkin. Seeders. Threshers' glowed in the rays of the setting sun. Across the road, barring it, stood three armed horsemen. A high school student in a uniform cap and a jacket criss-crossed with machine-gun cartridge belts, a cavalryman in an officer's greatcoat and a Cossack hat, and a strange fat man, as if dressed for a masquerade, in quilted trousers, a padded jacket, and a broad-brimmed priest's hat pulled down low.

'Don't move, comrade doctor,' the oldest of the three, the cavalryman in the Cossack hat, said evenly and calmly. 'If you obey, we guarantee you complete safety. Otherwise – no hard feelings – we'll shoot you. The medic in our detachment got killed. We mobilise you forcibly as a medical worker. Get off your horse and hand the reins over to our younger comrade. I remind you. At the least thought of escape, we won't stand on ceremony.'

'Are you the Mikulitsyns' son Liberius, Comrade Forester?'

'No, I'm his chief liaison officer, Kamennodvorsky.'

Part Ten

ON THE HIGH ROAD

I

There stood towns, villages, settlements. The town of Krestovozdvizhensk, the Cossack settlement of Omelchino, Pazhinsk, Tysiatskoe, the hamlet of Yaglinskoe, the township of Zvonarskaya, the settlement of Volnoe, Gurtovshchiki, the Kezhemskaya farmstead, the settlement of Kazeevo, the township of Kuteiny Posad, the village of Maly Ermolai.

The highway passed through them – old, very old, the oldest in Siberia, the ancient post road. It cut through towns like bread with the knife of the main street, and flew through villages without looking back, scattering the lined-up cottages far behind it or bending them in the curve or hook of a sudden turn.

Long ago, before the railway came to Khodatskoe, stagecoaches raced down the road. Wagon trains of tea, bread, and wrought iron went one way, and in the other parties of convicts were driven on foot under convoy to the next halting place. They marched in step, their iron chains clanking in unison, lost, desperate men, scary as lightning from the sky. And the forests rustled around them, dark, impenetrable.

The highway lived as one family. Town knew and fraternised with town, village with village. In Khodatskoe, at the railway crossing, there were locomotive repair shops, machine shops servicing the railways; wretches lived miserably, crowded into barracks, fell sick, died. Political prisoners with some technical knowledge, having served their term at hard labour, became foremen here and settled down.

Along all this line, the initial Soviets had long since been overthrown. For some time the power of the Siberian Provisional Government had held out, but now it had been replaced throughout the region by the power of the Supreme Ruler, Kolchak.[1]

2

At one stretch the road went uphill for a long time. The field of vision
opened out ever more widely into the distance. It seemed there would be no
end to the ascent and the increasing view. And just when the horses and
people got tired and stopped to catch their breath, the ascent ended. Ahead
the swift river Kezhma threw itself under a roadway bridge.

Across the river, on a still steeper height, appeared the brick wall of the
Vozdvizhensky Monastery. The road curved around the foot of the monastery
hillside and, after several twists among outlying backyards, made its way into
the town.

There it once more skirted the monastery grounds on the main square,
onto which the green-painted iron gates of the monastery opened. The icon
on the arch of the entrance was half wreathed by a gilt inscription: 'Rejoice,
lifegiving Cross, invincible victory of Orthodoxy.'

It was the departure of winter. Holy Week, the end of the Great Lent.[2]
The snow on the roads was turning black, indicating the start of the thaw,
but on the roofs it was still white and hung there in dense, tall hats.

To the boys who climbed up to the ringers in the Vozdvizhensky bell
tower, the houses below seemed like little boxes or chests clustered together.
Little black men the size of dots went up to the houses. Some could be
recognised from the bell tower by the way they moved. They were reading
the decree of the Supreme Ruler, pasted on the walls, about the conscription
of the next three age groups into the army.

3

Night brought much that was unforeseen. It became warm, unusually so for
the time of year. A fine-beaded rain drizzled down, so airy that it seemed to
diffuse through the air in a misty, watery dust without reaching the earth.
But that was an illusion. Its warm, streaming water was enough to wash the
earth clean of snow and leave it all black now, glistening as if with sweat.

Stunted apple trees, all covered with buds, miraculously sent their
branches from the gardens over the fences into the streets. Drops, tapping
discordantly, fell from them onto the wooden pavements. Their random
drumming resounded all over town.

The puppy Tomik, chained up in the photographers' yard since morning,
barked and whined. Perhaps annoyed by his barking, a crow in the
Galuzins' garden cawed for the whole town to hear.

In the lower part of town, three cartloads of goods were delivered to the merchant Lyubeznov. He refused to accept them, saying it was a mistake and he had never ordered these goods. Pleading the lateness of the hour, the stalwart carters asked him to let them spend the night. The merchant shouted at them, told them to go away, and would not open the gates. Their altercation could also be heard all over town.

At the seventh hour by church time,[3] and by common reckoning at one o'clock in the morning, a wave of soft, dark, and sweet droning separated from the heaviest, barely moving bell of the Vozdvizhenye and floated away, mixing with the dark moisture of the rain. It pushed itself from the bell as a mass of soil washed away by flooding water is torn from the bank and sinks, dissolving in the river.

This was the night of Holy Thursday, the day of the Twelve Gospels.[4] In the depths behind the netlike veil of rain, barely distinguishable little lights, and the foreheads, noses, and faces lit up by them, set out and went floating along. The faithful were going to matins.

A quarter of an hour later, steps were heard coming from the monastery along the boards of the pavement. This was the shopkeeper Galuzina returning home from the just-begun service. She walked irregularly, now hastening, now stopping, a kerchief thrown over her head, her fur coat unbuttoned. She had felt faint in the stuffy church and had gone outside for a breath of air, and now she was ashamed and regretted that she had not stood through the service and for the second year had not gone to communion. But that was not the cause of her grief. During the day she had been upset by the mobilisation order posted everywhere, which concerned her poor, foolish son Teresha. She had tried to drive this unpleasantness from her head, but the white scrap of the announcement showing everywhere in the darkness had reminded her of it.

Her house was around the corner, within arm's reach, but she felt better outside. She wanted to be in the open air, she did not feel like going home to more stuffiness.

She was beset by sad thoughts. If she had undertaken to think them aloud, in order, she would not have had words or time enough before morning. But here in the street these joyless reflections fell upon her in whole lumps, and she could have done with them all in a few moments, in two or three turns from the corner of the monastery to the corner of the square.

The bright feast is at hand, and there's not a living soul in the house, they've all gone off, leaving her alone. What, isn't she alone? Of course she's alone. Her ward, Ksiusha, doesn't count. Who is she, anyway? There's no looking into another's heart. Maybe she's a friend, maybe an enemy, maybe a secret rival. She came as an inheritance from her husband's first marriage, as Vlasushka's adopted daughter. Or maybe not adopted, but illegitimate? And maybe not a daughter at all, but from a completely different opera! Can you climb into a man's soul? Though there's nothing to be said against the girl. Intelligent, beautiful, well-behaved. Way smarter than the little fool Tereshka and her adoptive father.

So here she is alone on the threshold of the Holy Feast, abandoned, they've all flown off this way and that.

Her husband Vlasushka had gone down the high road to make speeches to the new recruits, as a send-off to their feats of arms. The fool would have done better to look after his own son, to protect him from mortal danger.

The son, Teresha, also couldn't help himself and took to his heels on the eve of the great feast. Buzzed off to Kuteiny Posad to some relatives, to have fun, to comfort himself after what he'd gone through. The boy had been expelled from high school. Repeated half the classes and nobody said anything, but in the eighth year they lost patience and threw him out.

Ah, what anguish! Oh, Lord! Why has it turned out so bad? You just lose heart. Everything drops from your hands, you don't want to live! Why has it turned out like this? Is it the force of the revolution? No, ah, no! It's all because of the war. All the flower of manhood got killed, and what was left was worthless, good-for-nothing rot.

A far cry from her father's home – her father the contractor. Her father didn't drink, he was literate, the family lived in plenty. There were two sisters, Polya and Olya. The names went so nicely together, just as the two of them suited each other, a pair of beauties. And the head carpenters who called on their father were distinguished, stately, fine-looking. Then suddenly they took it into their heads – there was no want in the house – took it into their heads to knit scarves out of six kinds of wool. And what then? They turned out to be such knitters, their scarves became famous throughout the district. And everything used to give joy by its richness and shapeliness – church services, dances, people, manners – even though the family was from simple folk, tradesmen, from peasants and workers. And Russia, too, was a young girl, and she had real suitors, real protectors, not like nowadays. Now everything's lost its sheen, there's nothing but the civilian trash of lawyers and Yids, chewing words tirelessly, day and night, choking on words. Vlasushka and his retinue hope to lure the old golden times back with champagne and good wishes. Is that any way to win back a lost love? You've got to overturn stones for that, move mountains, dig up the earth!

4

More than once already, Galuzina had gone as far as the marketplace, the central square of Krestovozdvizhensk. From there her house was to the left. But she changed her mind each time, turned round, and again went deep into the back alleys adjacent to the monastery.

The marketplace was the size of a big field. On market days in former times, peasants had covered it all over with their carts. One end of it lay against the end of Eleninskaya Street. The other end was built up along a curved line with small one- or two-storey houses. They were all used as storage spaces, offices, trading premises, and artisans' workshops.

Here, in quiet times, on a chair by the threshold of his very wide, four-leaf iron door, reading the *Penny Daily,* the woman-hater Briukhanov used to sit, a boorish bear in spectacles and a long-skirted frock coat, a dealer in leather, tar, wheels, horse harness, oats, and hay.

Here, displayed in a dim little window, gathering dust for many years, stood several cardboard boxes of paired wedding candles, decorated with ribbons and little bunches of flowers. Behind the little window, in an empty little room without furniture and with almost no sign of goods, unless one counted several rounds of wax piled one on top of the other, deals in the thousands for mastic, wax, and candles were concluded by no one knew what agents of a candle millionaire who lived no one knew where.

Here, in the middle of the shop-lined street, was the big colonial shop of the Galuzins with its three-window façade. In it the splintery, unpainted floor was swept three times a day with the used leaves of the tea which the shopkeepers and owner drank without moderation all day long. Here the owner's young wife had often and willingly kept the till. Her favourite colour was purple, violet, the colour of especially solemn church vestments, the colour of unopened lilacs, the colour of her best velvet dress, the colour of her wineglasses. The colour of happiness, the colour of memories, the colour of the long-vanished maidenhood of pre-revolutionary Russia also seemed to her to be pale lilac. And she liked keeping the till at the shop, because the violet dusk of the premises, fragrant with starch, sugar, and deep purple blackcurrant sweets in their glass jar, matched her favourite colour.

Here, at the corner, next to the timber yard, stood an old, grey, two-storey wooden house, sagging on four sides like a second-hand coach. It consisted of four apartments. There were two entrances to them, at either end of the façade. The left half of the ground floor was occupied by Zalkind's pharmacy, the right by a notary's office. Over the pharmacy lived old Shmulevich, a ladies' tailor, with his numerous family. Across from the tailor, over the notary, huddled many tenants, whose professions were announced on the signs and plaques that covered the whole front door. Here watches were repaired and a cobbler took in orders. Here the partners Zhuk and Shtrodakh kept a photography studio, here were the premises of the engraver Kaminsky.

In view of the crowdedness of the overfilled apartment, the photographers' young assistants, the retoucher Senya Magidson and the student Blazhein, built themselves a sort of labouratory in the yard, in the front office of the woodshed. They were apparently busy there now, judging by the angry eye of the developing lamp blinking nearsightedly in the little window of the office. It was under this window that the little dog Tomka was chained up, yelping for the whole of Eleninskaya Street to hear.

'The whole kahal's bunched up in there,' thought Galuzina, walking past the grey house. 'A den of misery and filth.' But she decided at once that Vlas Pakhomovich was wrong in his Judaeophobia. These people aren't such big wheels as to mean anything in the destiny of the state. However, if you ask old Shmulevich why the trouble and disorder, he'll cringe, pull a twisted mug, and say with a grin: 'That's Leibochka's little tricks.'[5]

Ah, but what, what is she thinking about, what is her head stuffed with? Is that really the point? Is that where the trouble is? The trouble is the cities. Russia doesn't stand on them. People got seduced by education, trailed after the city folk, and couldn't pull it off. Left their own shore and never reached the other.

Or maybe, on the contrary, the whole trouble is ignorance. A learned man can see through a stone wall, he figures everything out beforehand. And we go looking for our hat when our head's been cut off. Like in a dark forest. I suppose they're not having a sweet time of it either, the educated ones. Lack of bread drives them from the cities. Well, just try sorting it out. The devil himself would break a leg.

But even so, aren't our country relations something else again? The Selitvins, the Shelaburins, Pamphil Palykh, the brothers Nestor and Pankrat Modykh? Their own masters, their own heads, good farmers. New farmsteads along the high road, admirable. Each has some forty acres sown, plus horses, sheep, cows, pigs. Enough grain stocked up for three years ahead. The inventory – a feast for the eyes. Harvesting machines. Kolchak fawns on them, invites them to him, commissars entice them to the forest militia. They came back from the war covered with medals and were snapped up at once as instructors. With epaulettes, or without. If you're a man with know-how, you're in demand everywhere. You won't perish.

But it's time to go home. It's simply improper for a woman to walk about for so long. It would be all right in my own garden. But it's all soggy there, you could sink into the mud. Seems I feel a bit better.

And having got definitively entangled in her reasoning and lost the thread, Galuzina came to her house. But before crossing the threshold, she lingered for a moment in front of the porch, her mental gaze taking in many different things.

She remembered the present-day ringleaders in Khodatskoe, of whom she had a good notion, political exiles from the capitals, Tiverzin, Antipov, the anarchist Vdovichenko, called the Black Banner, the local locksmith Gorshenia the Rabid. These were all people who kept their own counsel. They had caused a lot of trouble in their day; they're sure to be plotting and preparing something again. They couldn't do without it. Their lives had been spent with machines, and they themselves are merciless, cold, like machines. They go around in short jackets with sweaters under them, smoke cigarettes in bone holders so as not to pick up an infection, drink boiled water. Vlasushka won't get anywhere with them, they'll turn everything round, they'll always have it their way.

And she fell to thinking about herself. She knew that she was a nice and original woman, well-preserved and intelligent, a not-bad person. Not one of these qualities met with recognition in this godforsaken hole, or anywhere else, maybe. And the indecent couplets about foolish Sentetyurikha, known all over the Trans-Urals, of which only the first two lines could be quoted:

> Sentetyurikha sold her cart
> And bought herself a balalaika,

because further on they turned scabrous, were sung in Krestovozdvizhensk, she suspected, with a hint at her.

And, sighing bitterly, she went into the house.

5

Not stopping in the front hall, she went in her fur coat to the bedroom. The windows of the room gave onto the garden. Now, at night, the heaped-up shadows in front of the windows inside and beyond the windows outside almost repeated each other. The hanging sacks of the draped window curtains were almost like the hanging sacks of the trees in the yard, bare and black, with vague outlines. The taffeta darkness of this night at the end of winter was being warmed in the garden by the black violet heat of approaching spring breaking through the ground. Inside the room approximately the same combination was made up by two similar elements, and the dusty stuffiness of the poorly beaten curtains was softened and brightened by the deep violet heat of the coming feast.

The Holy Virgin on the icon freed her narrow, upturned, swarthy palms from the silver casing. She was holding in them, as it were, the first and last letters of her Byzantine title: *Meter Theou,* the Mother of God. Enclosed in a golden lamp holder, the icon lamp of garnet-coloured glass, dark as an inkwell, cast on the bedroom rug a star-shaped glimmer, broken up by the lacy edge of the cup.

Throwing off her kerchief and fur coat, Galuzina turned awkwardly, and again felt a stitch in her side and a throb in her shoulder blade. She cried out, frightened, and began to murmur: 'Great Intercessor for those in sorrow, most pure Virgin, Swift Defender, Protectress of the world' – and burst into tears. Then, after waiting for the pain to subside, she began to undress. The hooks behind the collar and on the back slipped from her fingers and hid in the wrinkles of the smoke-coloured fabric. She had trouble feeling for them.

Her ward, Ksiusha, came into the room, awakened by her arrival.

'Why are you in the dark, mama? Would you like me to bring you a lamp?'

'Don't bother. I can see like this.'

'Mama dear, Olga Nilovna, let me undo it. You needn't suffer.'

'My fingers don't obey me, I could just cry. The mangy Yid didn't have brains enough to sew the hooks on like a human being, the blind bat. I'd like to rip it off all the way down and shove the whole flap in his mug.'

'They sang well in the Vozdvizhenye. A quiet night. It carried here through the air.'

'The singing was good. But I feel bad, my dear. I've got stitches here and here. Everywhere. That's the misery of it. I don't know what to do.'

'The homeopath Stydobsky used to help you.'

'His advice was always impossible to follow. A horse doctor your homeopath turned out to be. Neither fish nor fowl. That's the first thing. And second, he's gone away. Gone away, gone away. And not him alone. Before the feast everybody went rushing out of the city. Are they expecting an earthquake or something?'

'Well, then that captured Hungarian doctor's treatment did you good.'

'More poppycock with sugar on top. I'm telling you, there's nobody left, everybody's scattered. Kerenyi Lajos and the other Magyars wound up behind the demarcation line. They forced the dear fellow into service. Took him into the Red Army.'

'Anyhow, you're overanxious about your health. Neurosis of the heart. A simple folk charm can work wonders here. Remember, the army wife whispered it away for you quite successfully. Like it was never there. What's her name, that army wife? I forget.'

'No, you decidedly consider me an ignorant fool. You sing "Sentetyurikha" about me behind my back, for all I know.'

'God forbid! It's sinful to say such things, mama. Better remind me of the army wife's name. It's on the tip of my tongue. I won't have any peace until I remember it.'

'She's got more names than skirts. I don't know which one you want. They call her Kubarikha, and Medvedikha, and Zlydarikha.[6] And a dozen more nicknames. She's not around any more. The ball's over, go and look for wind in the clover. They locked up the servant of God in the Kezhem prison. For exterminating a foetus and for some sort of powders. But she, look you, rather than languish behind bars, buggered off from prison to somewhere in the Far East. I'm telling you, everybody's scattered. Vlas Pakhomych, Teresha, Aunt Polya with her yielding heart. The only honest women left in the whole town are you and me – two fools, I'm not joking. And no medical help. If anything happens, it's the end, call and nobody'll hear you. They say there's a celebrity from Moscow in Yuriatin, a professor, the son of a suicide, a Siberian merchant. While I was making up my mind to invite him, they set up twenty Red cordons on the road, there's no room to sneeze. But now about something else. Go to bed, and I'll try to lie down. The student Blazhein has turned your head. No use denying it. You won't hide it anyway, you're red as a lobster. Your wretched student is toiling over prints on a holy night, developing and printing my photographs. They don't sleep themselves and won't let others sleep. Their Tomik barks his head off for the whole town to hear. And the nasty crow is cawing in our apple tree, must be I'm not to sleep all night. Why are you offended, miss touch-me-not? Students are there for the girls to like them.'

6

'Why is the dog carrying on like that? We must go and see what's the matter. He wouldn't bark for nothing. Wait, Lidochka, blast you, shut up for a minute. We've got to clarify the situation. A posse may descend on us any minute. Don't leave, Ustin. And you stay put, Sivobluy. They'll get along without you.'

Not hearing the request to stop and wait a little, the representative from the centre went on wearily in an oratorical patter:

'The bourgeois military power existing in Siberia by its politics of robbery, taxation, violence, executions, and torture should open the eyes of the deluded. It is hostile not only to the working class, but, by the essence of things, to all the labouring peasantry as well. The labouring peasantry of Siberia and the Urals should understand that only in union with the urban proletariat and the soldiers, in union with the Kirghiz and Buryat poor . . .'[7]

Finally he caught the fact that he was being interrupted and stopped, wiping his sweaty face, wearily lowered his puffy eyelids, and closed his eyes.

Those standing near him said in a half whisper:

'Rest a bit. Have a sip of water.'

The anxious partisan leader was told:

'What are you worried about? Everything's all right. The signal lamp is in the window. The lookout, to put it picturesquely, devours space with his eyes. I think we can resume the lecturer's talk. Speak, Comrade Lidochka.'

The interior of the big shed had been freed of firewood. In the cleared space an illegal meeting was going on. The firewood piled to the ceiling served to screen off the meeting, separating this emptied half from the front desk and the entrance. In case of danger, the assembled men were provided with a way down into the basement and an underground exit to the overgrown backyard of the Konstantinovsky Impass beyond the monastery wall.

The speaker, in a black cotton cap that covered his completely bald head, with a matte, pale olive complexion and a black beard up to his ears, suffered from nervous perspiration and sweated profusely all the time. He greedily relighted his unfinished butt in the stream of hot air over the kerosene lamp burning on the table, and bent low to the scraps of paper scattered in front of him. He ran his nearsighted little eyes over them nervously and quickly, as if he were sniffing them, and went on in a dull and weary voice:

'This union of the urban and village poor can be realised only through the soviets. Like it or not, the Siberian peasantry will now strive towards the same thing for which the Siberian workers have long since begun to fight. Their common goal is the overthrow of the autocracy of admirals and atamans, hateful to the people, and the establishment of the power of the peasants' and soldiers' soviets by means of a nationwide armed insurrection. For that, their struggle against the Cossack-officer hirelings of the bourgeoisie, who are armed to the teeth, will have to be conducted as a regular front-line war, persistent and prolonged.'

Again he stopped, wiped his forehead, and closed his eyes. Contrary to the rules, someone stood up, raised his hand, and wished to put in a comment.

The partisan leader, or, more precisely, the commander of the Kezhem formation of the Trans-Ural partisans, was sitting right in front of the speaker's nose in a defiantly casual posture and kept rudely interrupting him, without showing him any respect. It was hard to believe that such a young soldier, almost a boy, was in command of whole armies and formations, and was obeyed and held in awe. He was sitting with his hands and feet covered by the skirts of his cavalry greatcoat. The flung-off top and sleeves of the greatcoat, thrown over the back of the chair, revealed his body in a tunic with dark spots where the lieutenant's epaulettes had been ripped off.

At his sides stood two silent stalwarts of his guard, the same age as he, in white sheepskin sleeveless jackets that had had time to turn grey, with curly lambswool showing at the edges. Their handsome, stony faces showed nothing but blind devotion to their superior and a readiness for anything for his sake. They remained indifferent to the meeting, the questions touched upon at it, the course of the debate, did not speak, and did not smile.

Besides these people, there were another ten or fifteen men in the shed. Some stood, others sat on the floor with their legs stretched out or their knees sticking up, leaning against the wall and its roundly projecting caulked logs.

For the guests of honour, chairs had been provided. They were occupied by three or four workers, former participants in the first revolution, among them the sullen, changed Tiverzin and his friend, old Antipov, who always yessed him. Counted among the divinities at whose feet the revolution laid all its gifts and sacrifices, they sat like silent, stern idols in whom political arrogance had exterminated everything alive and human.

There were other figures worthy of attention in the shed. Not knowing a moment's peace, getting up from the floor and sitting down again, pacing the shed and stopping in the middle of it, was the pillar of Russian anarchism, Vdovichenko the Black Banner, a fat giant with a big head, a big mouth, and a leonine mane, an officer, if not in the last Russo-Turkish War, then at least in the Russo-Japanese War, a dreamer eternally absorbed in his ravings.

By reason of his boundless good nature and gigantic height, which kept him from noticing events of unequal and smaller size, he treated all that was happening with insufficient attention and, misunderstanding everything, took opposite opinions for his own and agreed with everybody.

Next to his place on the floor sat his acquaintance, the forest hunter and trapper Svirid. Though Svirid did not live as a peasant, his earthy, soil-tilling essence showed through the opening of his dark broadcloth shirt, which he bunched up at the collar together with his cross and scraped and drove over his body, scratching his chest. He was a half-Buryat muzhik, amiable and illiterate, with hair that lay in flat strands, sparse moustaches, and a still more sparse beard of a few hairs. His face, puckering all the time in a sympathetic smile, looked aged because of its Mongolian features.

The lecturer, who was travelling around Siberia with military instructions from the Central Committee, wandered in his mind over the vast spaces he was still to cover. He regarded the majority of those present at the meeting with indifference. But, a revolutionary and lover of the people from early on, he looked with adoration at the young general who sat facing him. He not only forgave the boy all his rudeness, which the old man took for the voice of an ingrained, latent revolutionism, but regarded with admiration his casual sallies, as a woman in love may like the insolent unceremoniousness of her lord and master.

The partisan leader was Mikulitsyn's son Liberius; the lecturer from the centre was the former cooperative labourist Kostoed-Amursky, connected in the past with the Social Revolutionaries.[8] Recently he had reconsidered his position, recognised the mistakenness of his platform, offered his repentance in several detailed declarations, and had not only been received into the Communist Party, but soon after joining it had been sent on such a responsible assignment.

Though by no means a military man, he had been entrusted with this assignment out of respect for his revolutionary record, for his ordeals and terms in prison, and also on the assumption that, as a former cooperator, he must be well acquainted with the mood of the peasant masses in rebellion-gripped western Siberia. And in the given matter, this supposed familiarity was more important than military knowledge.

The change of political convictions had made Kostoed unrecognisable. It had altered his appearance, movements, manners. No one remembered that he was ever bald and bearded in former times. But maybe it was all false? The party prescribed strict secrecy for him. His underground nicknames were Berendey and Comrade Lidochka.

When the noise raised by Vdovichenko's untimely announcement of his agreement with the read-out points of the instructions subsided, Kostoed went on:

'With the aim of the fullest possible involvement of the growing movement of the peasant masses, it is necessary to establish connections immediately with all partisan detachments located in the area of the provincial committee.'

Further on, Kostoed spoke of arranging meeting places, passwords, ciphers, and means of communication. Then he again passed on to details.

'Inform the detachments of those points where the White institutions and organisations have supplies of arms, clothing, and food, where they keep large sums of money and the system of their keeping.

'There is need to work out in full detail the questions of the internal organisation of the detachments, of leadership, of military-comradely discipline, of conspiracy, of the connection of the detachments with the outside world, of relations with the local populace, of the military-revolutionary field court, of the tactics of sabotage on enemy territory, such as the destruction of bridges, railway lines, steamboats, barges, stations, workshops and their technical equipment, the telegraph, mines, food supplies.'

Liberius listened, listened, and finally could not bear it. All this seemed like dilettantish nonsense to him, with no relation to reality. He said:

'A beautiful lecture. I'll make a note of it. Obviously, it must all be accepted without objection, so as not to lose the support of the Red Army.'

'Naturally.'

'But, blast it all, what am I to do with your childish little crib, my most excellent Lidochka, when my forces, consisting of three regiments including artillery and cavalry, have long been on the march and are splendidly beating the enemy?'

'What charm! What strength!' thought Kostoed.

Tiverzin interrupted the argument. He did not like Liberius's disrespectful tone. He said:

'Excuse me, comrade lecturer. I'm not sure. I may have written down one of the points of the instructions incorrectly. I'll read it. I want to make certain: "It is highly desirable to involve former front-line troops in the committee, men who were at the front during the revolution and took part in the soldiers' organisations. It is desirable to have one or two non-commissioned officers and a military technician on the committee." Have I written that down correctly, Comrade Kostoed?'

'Yes, correctly. Word for word. Yes.'

'In that case allow me to make the following observation. This point about military specialists disturbs me. We workers who took part in the revolution of 1905 are not used to trusting army men. Counter-revolution always worms its way in with them.'

Voices rang out all around:

'Enough! The resolution! The resolution! It's time to break up. It's late.'

'I agree with the opinion of the majority,' Vdovichenko inserted in a rumbling bass. 'To put it poetically, it's precisely like this. Civil institutions should grow from below, on democratic foundations, the way tree layers are set in the ground and take root. They can't be hammered in from above like fenceposts. That was the mistake of the Jacobin dictatorship, which is why the Convention was crushed by the Thermidorians.'[9]

'It's clear as day,' Svirid supported the friend of his wanderings, 'a little child could understand it. We should have thought earlier, but now it's too late. Now our business is to fight and smash our way through. Groan and bend. Otherwise what is it, you swing and back away? You cooked it, you eat it. You've jumped in the water, don't shout that you're drowning.'

'The resolution! The resolution!' demands came from all sides. There was a little more talk, with less and less observable coherence, with no rhyme or reason, and at dawn the meeting was closed. They went off one by one with all precaution.

7

There was a picturesque place on the highway. Situated on steep banks and separated by the swift river Pazhinka, the town of Kuteiny Posad descending from above and the motley-looking village of Maly Ermolai below almost touched each other. In Kuteiny they were seeing off new recruits taken into the service; in Maly Ermolai, under the chairmanship of Colonel Strese, the selection committee went on with its work, after the Easter break, certifying the young men of the village and some adjacent areas liable to be called up. On the occasion of the levy, there were mounted militia and Cossacks in the village.

It was the third day of the unseasonably late Easter and the unseasonably early spring, quiet and warm. Tables with refreshments for the departing recruits stood outside in Kuteiny, under the open sky, along the edge of the road, so as not to hinder traffic. They were put together not quite in a straight line, and stretched out like a long, irregular gut under white table-cloths that went down to the ground.

The new conscripts were treated to potluck. The main food was leftovers from the Easter table: two smoked hams, several *kulichi,* two or three *paschas.*[10] Down the whole length of the table stood bowls of salted mushrooms, cucumbers, and pickled cabbage, plates of home-made, thickly sliced village bread, wide platters of coloured eggs piled up high. They were mostly pink and light blue.

The grass around the tables was littered with picked-off eggshells – light blue, pink, and, on the inside, white. Light blue and pink were the boys' shirts showing from under their suit jackets. Light blue and pink were the young girls' dresses. Light blue was the sky. Pink were the clouds floating across the sky, as slowly and orderly as if the sky were floating with them.

Pink was the shirt, tied with a silk sash, on Vlas Pakhomovich Galuzin, when he – briskly stamping the heels of his boots and kicking his feet to left and right – ran down the high porch steps of the Pafnutkins' house to the tables – the Pafnutkins' house stood on a little hill above the tables – and began:

'This glass of the people's home brew I drink to you, dear lads, in place of champagne. Many years to you, many years to you departing young men![11] Gentlemen recruits! I wish to congratulate you on many other points and respects. Give me your attention. The way of the cross that stretches like a long road before you is to staunchly defend the motherland from violators who have flooded the motherland's fields with fratricidal blood. The people cherished bloodless discussions of the conquests of the revolution, but the Bolshevik Party being servants of foreign capital, its sacred dream, the Constituent Assembly, is dispersed by the crude force of the bayonet, and blood flows in a defenceless stream. Young departing men! Raise higher the violated honour of Russian arms, as being indebted to our honourable allies, we have covered ourselves in shame, observing, in the wake of the Reds, Germany and Austria again insolently raising their heads. God is with us, dear lads,' Galuzin was still saying, but already shouts of 'Hurrah' and demands that Vlas Pakhomovich be carried in triumph drowned out his words. He put his glass to his lips and began taking small sips of the raw, poorly distilled liquid. The drink did not afford him any pleasure. He was used to grape wines of a more delicate bouquet. But the consciousness of the sacrifice offered to society filled him with a sense of satisfaction.

'Your old man's an eagle. Such a fierce, flaming talker! Like some Miliukov in the Duma.[12] By God,' Goshka Ryabykh, with a half-drunken tongue, amidst the drunken hubbub that had arisen, praised the father of his friend and companion at the table, Terenty Galuzin. 'I tell you true – an eagle. Obviously not for nothing. Wants his tongue to solicit you out of going for a soldier.'

'Come on, Goshka! Shame on you. To think up that "solicit out". I'll get a notice the same day as you, for all his soliciting out. We'll wind up in the same unit. Now they've kicked me out of school, the scum. My mother's crushed. It'll be a good thing if I don't wind up with the volumpeers. Get sent to the ranks. And as for formal speeches, papa really is unbeatable, no disputing it. A master. The main thing is, where'd he get it? It's natural. He has no systematic education.'

'Did you hear about Sanka Pafnutkin?'

'Yes. Is it really so nasty?'

'For life. He'll waste away in the end. It's his own fault. He was warned not to go there. The main thing is who you get tangled up with.'

'What'll happen to him now?'

'A tragedy. He wanted to shoot himself. Today he's being examined by the commission in Ermolai. They'll probably take him. "I'll go to the partisans," he says. "I'll avenge the sores of society."'

'Listen, Goshka. You say it's so nasty. But if you don't go to them, you can get sick with something else.'

'I know what you're getting at. You must be doing it. That's not a sickness, it's a secret vice.'

'I'll punch your face in for such words, Goshka. Don't you dare offend a comrade, you rotten liar!'

'Calm down, I was joking. I wanted to tell you something. I went to Pazhinsk for the Easter meal. In Pazhinsk an itinerant lecturer talked about "The Emancipation of the Person". Very interesting. I liked the thing. I'll damn well sign up with the anarchists. There's a force inside us, he says. Sex and character, he says, that's the awakening of animal electricity. Eh? Quite a wunderkind. But I'm really plastered. And they're shouting all around, jabber-jabber, it's deafening. I can't stand it, Tereshka, be quiet. You son of a bitch, you little mama's boy, shut up, I said.'

'Just tell me this, Goshka. I still don't know all the words about socialism. Saboteur, for instance. What kind of expression is that? What's it about?'

'I'm a real professor in these words, but like I told you, Tereshka, leave off, I'm drunk. A saboteur is somebody who's in the same band as others. Once they say soboater, it means you're in the same boat with them. Get it, blockhead?'

'I also thought it was a swearword. But about electric force, you're right. I decided from an advertisement to order an electric truss from Petersburg. To step up the activity. COD. But then suddenly there's a new upheaval. Trusses are out.'

Terenty did not finish. The din of drunken voices was drowned out by the thundering burst of a nearby explosion. The noise at the table momentarily ceased. A minute later it started up again with still more disorderly force. Some jumped up from their seats. The steadier ones stayed on their feet. Others, staggering, wanted to make off somewhere, but gave way and, collapsing under the table, immediately began to snore. Women shrieked. A commotion began.

Vlas Pakhomovich glanced around, looking for the culprit. At first he thought the bang came from somewhere in Kuteiny, quite near, maybe even very close to the tables. He strained his neck, his face turned purple, he bawled at the top of his lungs:

'What Judas has wormed his way into our ranks to commit outrages? What mother's son is playing with grenades here? Whoever he is, even if he's my own, I'll strangle the vermin! We won't suffer such jokes, citizens! I demand that we make a round-up. Let's surround Kuteiny Posad! Let's catch the provocator! Don't let the son of a bitch escape!'

At first he was listened to. Then attention was distracted by the column of black smoke slowly rising into the sky from the local council building in Maly Ermolai. Everybody ran to the bank to see what was going on there.

Several undressed recruits came running out of the burning Ermolai council building, one completely barefoot and naked, just pulling on his trousers, along with Colonel Strese and the other military who had been carrying out the selective service examination. Mounted Cossacks and militiamen rushed back and forth in the village, swinging their whips and stretching out their bodies and arms on their horses, themselves stretched out like writhing snakes. They were searching for someone, chasing someone. A great many people were running down the road to Kuteiny. In pursuit of the running people came the rapid and anxious ringing of the alarm from the Ermolai bell tower.

Events developed further with terrible swiftness. At dusk, continuing his search, Strese and his Cossacks went up from the village to neighbouring Kuteiny. Surrounding it with patrols, they began searching each house, each farmstead.

By that time half of the merrymakers were done in and, drunk as lords, lay in a deep sleep, resting their heads on the edges of the tables or sprawled on the ground under them. When it became known that the militia had come to the village, it was already dark.

Several lads, fleeing the militia, rushed to the backyards of the village and, urging each other on with kicks and shoves, got under the siding of the first storehouse they came to, which did not reach the ground. In the darkness it was impossible to tell whose it was, but, judging by the smell of fish and kerosene, it must have been the crawl space of the grocery cooperative.

The hiders had nothing on their conscience. It was a mistake for them to conceal themselves. Most of them had done it in haste, drunkenly, foolishly. Some had acquaintances who seemed blameworthy to them and might, as they thought, be the ruin of them. Now everything had been given a political colouring. Mischief and hooliganism were counted as signs of the Black Hundred[13] in Soviet areas; in White Guard areas ruffians were taken for Bolsheviks.

As it turned out, the lads who slipped under the cottage had predecessors. The space between the ground and the storehouse floor was full of people.

Several men from Kuteiny and Ermolai were hiding there. The former were dead drunk. Some were snoring with moaning undertones, grinding their teeth and whining; others were sick and throwing up. It was pitch-dark under the storehouse, stuffy and stinking. Those who crawled in last filled the opening they had come through from inside with earth and stones, so that the hole would not give them away. Soon the snoring and moaning of the drunk ceased entirely. There was total silence. They all slept quietly. Only in one corner was there quiet whispering between the particularly restless ones, the scared-to-death Terenty Galuzin and the Ermolai fistfighter Koska Nekhvalenykh.

'Pipe down, you son of a bitch, you'll be the end of us all, you snotty devil. You hear, Strese's men are on the prowl – sneaking around. They turned at the village gate, they're coming down the row, they'll be here soon. That's them. Freeze, don't breathe, I'll strangle you! Well, you're in luck – they're gone. Passed us by. What devil brought you here? And hiding, too, you blockhead! Who'd lay a finger on you?'

'I heard Goshka shouting, "Take cover, you slob!" So I slipped in.'

'Goshka's another matter. The whole Ryabykh family is being eyed as untrustworthy. They've got relations in Khodatskoe. Artisans, worker stock. Don't twitch like that, you lunkhead, lie quiet. They've crapped and puked all around here. If you move, you'll smear yourself with shit, and me, too. Can't you smell the stench? Why do you think Strese's rushing around the village? He's looking for men from Pazhinsk. Outsiders.'

'How did all this come about, Koska? Where did it begin?'

'Sanka sparked the whole thing off, Sanka Pafnutkin. We're standing naked in line for the examination. Sanka's time came, it's Sanka's turn. He won't undress. Sanka was a bit drunk, he came to the office tipsy. The clerk looks him over. "Get undressed, please," he says. Politely. Addresses Sanka formally. A military clerk. And Sanka answers him rudely: "I won't. I ain't gonna show everybody my private parts." As if he's embarrassed. And he sidles up to the clerk, like he's going to haul off and punch him in the jaw. Yes. And what do you think? Before you could bat an eye, Sanka bends over, grabs the little office desk by the leg, and dumps it and everything on it, the inkstand, the army lists, on the floor! From the boardroom door, Strese shouts: "I won't tolerate excesses. I'll show you your bloodless revolution and disrespect for the law in a government office. Who's the instigator?"

'But Sanka's at the window. "Help!" he shouts. "Grab your clothes! It's all up for us, comrades!" I grabbed my clothes, got dressed on the run, and went over to Sanka. Sanka smashed the window with his fist and, whoop, he's outside, try catching the wind. And me after him. And some others as well. Running our legs off. And there's already hallooing after us, the chase is on. But if you ask me what it was all about? Nobody understands anything.'

'And the bomb?'

'What about the bomb?'

'Who threw the bomb? Well, bomb, grenade, whatever?'

'Lord, you don't think it was us?'

'But who, then?'

'How should I know? Somebody else. He saw the turmoil, thought, I could blow up the council on the sly. They'll think it was other people. Somebody political. There's a lot of politicals from Pazhinsk here. Quiet. Shut up. Voices. You hear, Strese's men are coming back. Well, we're lost. Freeze, I said.'

The voices came closer. Boots creaked, spurs jangled.

'Don't argue. You can't fool me. I'm not that kind. There was definitely talking somewhere,' boomed the domineering, all-distinct Petersburg voice of the colonel.

'You may have imagined it, Your Excellency,' reasoned the village headman of Maly Ermolai, the old fishmonger Otviazhistin. 'And no wonder if there's talking, since it's a village. Not a cemetery. Maybe they were talking somewhere. They're not dumb beasts in the houses. Or maybe a hobgoblin's choking somebody in his sleep . . .'

'Enough! I'll teach you to play the holy fool, pretending you're a poor orphan! Hobgoblin! You've grown too free and easy here! You'll get the international on you with your cleverness, then it'll be too late. Hobgoblin!'

'Good gracious, Your Excellency, mister colonel, sir! What international! They're thick-headed oafs, impenetrable darkness. Stumble over the old prayer books. What do they want with revolution?'

'You all talk that way till the first evidence. Search the premises of the cooperative from top to bottom. Shake all the coffers, look under the counters. Search the adjoining buildings.'

'Yes, Your Excellency.'

'Get Pafnutkin, Ryabykh, Nekhvalenykh, dead or alive. From the ends of the earth. And that Galuzin pup. Never mind that his papa delivers patriotic speeches, he won't fine-talk us. On the contrary. We're not lulled by it. Once a shopkeeper starts orating, it means something's wrong. It's suspicious. It's contrary to nature. There's secret information that there are political exiles hidden in their courtyard in Krestovozdvizhensk, that secret meetings are held. Catch the boy. I haven't decided yet what to do with him, but if something's uncovered, I'll hang him without pity as a lesson to the rest.'

The searchers moved on. When they had gone far enough away, Koska Nekhvalenykh asked Tereshka Galuzin, who was dead with fright:

'Did you hear?'

'Yes,' the boy whispered in a voice not his own.

'For you and me, and Sanka, and Goshka, the only road now is to the forest. I don't say forever. Till they get reasonable. And when they come to their senses, then we'll see. Maybe we'll come back.'

Part Eleven

THE FOREST ARMY

1

It was the second year since Yuri Andreevich fell captive to the partisans. The limits of this bondage were very vague. The place of Yuri Andreevich's imprisonment was not fenced in. He was not guarded, not watched over. The partisan troops were on the move all the time. Yuri Andreevich made the marches with them. The troops did not separate themselves, did not shut themselves off from the rest of the people, through whose settlements and regions they moved. They mixed with them, dissolved in them.

It seemed that this dependence, this captivity, did not exist, that the doctor was free and simply did not know how to take advantage of it. The doctor's dependence, his captivity, in no way differed from other forms of constraint in life, equally invisible and intangible, which also seem like something non-existent, a chimera and a fiction. Despite the absence of fetters, chains, and guards, the doctor was forced to submit to his unfreedom, which looked imaginary.

His three attempts to escape from the partisans ended in capture. They let him off for nothing, but it was playing with fire. He did not repeat them any more.

The partisan chief Liberius Mikulitsyn was indulgent towards him, had him sleep in his tent, liked his company. Yuri Andreevich was burdened by this imposed closeness.

2

This was the period of the almost continuous withdrawal of the partisans towards the east. At times this displacement was part of the general offensive plan for driving Kolchak out of western Siberia. At times, when the

Whites turned the partisans' rear in an attempt to surround them, movement in the same direction was converted into a retreat. For a long time the
doctor could not comprehend these subtleties.

The little towns and villages along the highway, most often parallel to
which, but sometimes along which, the partisans made this withdrawal,
varied between White and Red, depending on changing military fortunes. It
was rarely possible to determine by their outward appearance who was in
power in them.

In moments when the peasant militia passed through these small towns
and villages, the main thing in them became precisely this army filing
through them. The houses on both sides of the road seemed to be absorbed
and drawn down into the ground, and the horsemen, horses, guns sloshing
through the mud, and the tall, jostling riflemen with rolled-up greatcoats
seemed to grow higher on the road than the houses.

Once, in one of these small towns, the doctor took over a supply of
British medications abandoned during the retreat by officers of Kappel's formation[1] and seized as war booty.

It was a dark, rainy, two-coloured day. All that was lit up seemed white,
all that was not lit up – black. And in his soul there was the same gloom of
simplification, without the softening of transitions and half-tones.

The road, utterly destroyed by frequent troop movements, was a stream
of black muck that could not be crossed everywhere on foot. The street
could be crossed in a few places, very far from each other, to reach which
one had to make big detours on both sides. It was in such conditions that
the doctor met, in Pazhinsk, his onetime fellow traveller on the train, Pelageya Tyagunova.

She recognised him first. He could not at once determine who this woman
with the familiar face was, who was casting ambiguous glances at him from
across the road, as from one bank of a canal to the other, now fully resolved
to greet him, if he recognised her, now showing a readiness to retreat.

After a moment he remembered everything. Together with images of the
overcrowded freight car, the multitudes being driven to forced labour, their
convoy, and the woman passenger with plaits thrown over her breast, he
saw his own people in the centre of the picture. The details of the family trip
of two years ago vividly crowded around him. The dear faces, for which he
felt a mortal longing, stood before him as if alive.

With a nod of the head he gave a sign that Tyagunova should go a little
further up the street, to a place where it could be crossed on stones sticking
up from the mud, went to the place himself, crossed over to Tyagunova, and
greeted her.

She told him many things. Reminding him of the handsome, unspoiled boy Vasya, illegally taken into the party of forced labourers, who had ridden in the same carriage with them, Tyagunova described for the doctor her life in the village of Veretenniki with Vasya's mother. Things were very good for her with them. But the village flung it in her face that she was a stranger, an outsider in the Veretenniki community. She was reproached for her supposed intimacy with Vasya, which they invented. She had to leave, so as not to be pecked to death. She settled in the town of Krestovozdvizhensk with her sister, Olga Galuzina. Rumours that Pritulyev had been seen in Pazhinsk lured her there. The information proved false, but she got stuck living there, having found a job.

Meanwhile misfortunes befell people who were dear to her heart. From Veretenniki came news that the village had been subjected to a punitive expedition for disobeying the law on food requisitioning.[2] Apparently the Brykins' house had burned down and someone from Vasya's family had perished. In Krestovozdvizhensk the Galuzins' house and property had been confiscated. Her brother-in-law had been imprisoned or shot. Her nephew had disappeared without a trace. At first, after the devastation, her sister Olga went poor and hungry, but now she works for her grub with peasant relations in the village of Zvonarsk.

As it happened, Tyagunova worked as a dishwasher in the Pazhinsk pharmacy, the property of which the doctor was about to requisition. The requisition meant ruin for everyone who fed off the pharmacy, including Tyagunova. But it was not in the doctor's power to cancel it. Tyagunova was present at the handing over of the goods.

Yuri Andreevich's cart was brought into the backyard of the pharmacy, to the doors of the storeroom. Bundles, bottles sleeved in woven wicker, and boxes were removed from the premises.

Along with the people, the pharmacist's skinny and mangy nag mournfully watched the loading from its stall. The rainy day was declining. The sky cleared a little. For a moment the sun appeared, squeezed between clouds. It was setting. The dark bronze of its rays sprayed into the yard, sinisterly gilding the pools of liquid dung. The wind did not stir them. The dungy wash was too heavy to move. But the rainwater flooding the roadway rippled under the wind and was tinged with cinnabar.

And the army walked and walked along the edges of the road, stepping or driving around the deepest lakes and potholes. In the seized batch of medicines a whole jar of cocaine turned up, the sniffing of which had lately been the weakness of the partisan chief.

3

The doctor was up to his neck in work among the partisans. In winter typhus, in summer dysentery, and, besides that, the growing influx of wounded on days of fighting in the renewed military activity.

In spite of failures and the predominance of retreats, the ranks of the partisans were constantly replenished by new insurgents from the places the peasant horde passed through and by deserters from the enemy camp. During the year and a half that the doctor had spent with the partisans, their army had grown tenfold. When Liberius Mikulitsyn mentioned the numbers of his forces at the meeting in the underground headquarters in Krestovozdvizhensk, he exaggerated them about ten times. Now they had reached that size.

Yuri Andreevich had assistants, several fresh-baked medical orderlies with appropriate experience. His right-hand men in the medical unit were the captured Hungarian Communist and military doctor Kerenyi Lajos, known in camp as Comrade Layoff, and the Croat medic Angelyar, also an Austrian prisoner of war. With the former Yuri Andreevich spoke German; the latter, born in the Slavic Balkans, just managed to understand Russian.

4

According to the international convention of the Red Cross, army doctors and those serving in medical units did not have the right to armed participation in the military actions of the belligerents. But once, against his will, the doctor had to violate this rule. The skirmish that had started caught him in the field and forced him to share the fate of the combatants and shoot back.

The partisan line, in which the doctor, surprised by enemy fire, lay next to the detachment telephonist, occupied the edge of a forest. At the partisans' back was the taiga, ahead was an open clearing, a bare, unprotected space, across which the Whites were moving to the attack.

They were approaching and were already close. The doctor saw them very well, the face of each one. They were boys and young men from the non-military strata of the capitals and older men mobilised from the reserves. But the tone was set by the former, the young ones, the first-year students and high school boys recently enlisted as volunteers.

The doctor did not know any of them, but the faces of half of them seemed to him habitual, seen, familiar. They reminded him of his former schoolmates. Could it be that these were their younger brothers? Others he seemed to have met in street or theatre crowds in years gone by. Their expressive, attractive physiognomies seemed close, kindred.

Doing their duty, as they understood it, inspired them with enthusiastic daring, unnecessary, defiant. They walked in a strung-out, sparse line, drawn up to full height, outdoing the regular guards in their bearing, and, braving the danger, did not resort to making rushes and then lying flat in the field, though there were unevennesses in the clearing, bumps and hummocks behind which they could have hidden. The bullets of the partisans mowed them down almost to a man.

In the middle of the wide, bare field over which the Whites were advancing stood a dead, burned tree. It had been charred by lightning or fire or split and scorched by previous battles. Each advancing volunteer rifleman cast glances at it, struggling with the temptation to get behind its trunk so as to take aim more safely and accurately, then ignored the temptation and went on.

The partisans had a limited number of cartridges. They had to use them sparingly. There was an order, upheld by mutual agreement, to shoot at close range, from the same number of rifles as there were visible targets.

The doctor lay unarmed in the grass, watching the course of the battle. All his sympathy was on the side of the heroically dying children. In his heart he wished them success. They were offspring of families probably close to him in spirit, to his upbringing, his moral cast, his notions.

The thought stirred in him to run out to them in the clearing and surrender and in that way find deliverance. But it was a risky step, fraught with danger.

While he was running to the middle of the clearing, holding his hands up, he could be brought down from both sides, shot in the chest and the back, by his own as a punishment for committing treason, by the others, not understanding his intentions. He had been in similar situations more than once, had thought over all the possibilities, and had long recognised these plans for salvation as unfeasible. And, reconciling himself to the ambiguity of his feelings, the doctor went on lying on his stomach, facing the clearing, and, unarmed, watched from the grass the course of the battle.

However, to look on and remain inactive amidst the fight to the death that was seething around him was inconceivable and beyond human strength. And it was not a matter of loyalty to the camp to which his captivity chained him, nor of his own self-defence, but of following the order of what was happening, of submitting to the laws of what was being played out before and around him. It was against the rules to remain indifferent to it. He had to do what the others were doing. A battle was going on. He and his comrades were being shot at. It was necessary to shoot back.

And when the telephonist next to him in the line jerked convulsively and then stretched out and lay still, Yuri Andreevich crawled over to him, removed his pouch, took his rifle, and, returning to his place, began firing it shot after shot.

But pity would not allow him to aim at the young men, whom he admired and with whom he sympathised. And to fire into the air like a fool was much too stupid and idle an occupation, contradictory to his intentions. And so, choosing moments when none of the attackers stood between him and his target, he began shooting at the charred tree. Here he had his own method.

Taking aim and gradually adjusting the precision of his sights, imperceptibly increasing the pressure on the trigger, but not all the way, as if not counting on ever firing, until the hammer fell and the shot followed of itself, as if beyond expectation, the doctor began with an accustomed accuracy to knock off the dry lower branches and scatter them around the dead tree.

But, oh horror! Careful as the doctor was not to hit anybody, now one, now another of the attackers got between him and the tree at the decisive moment and crossed his line of sight just as the gun went off. Two he hit and wounded, but the third unfortunate, who fell not far from the tree, paid for it with his life.

Finally the White commanders, convinced of the uselessness of the attempt, gave the order to retreat.

The partisans were few. Their main forces were partly on the march, partly shifted elsewhere, starting action against a much larger enemy force. The detachment did not pursue the retreating men, so as not to betray their small numbers.

The medic Angelyar brought two orderlies to the edge of the forest with a stretcher. The doctor ordered them to take care of the wounded, and went himself to the telephonist, who lay without moving. He vaguely hoped that the man might still be breathing and that he might be brought back to life. But the telephonist was dead. To make finally sure of it, Yuri Andreevich unbuttoned the shirt on his chest and began listening to his heart. It was not beating.

The dead man had an amulet on a string round his neck. Yuri Andreevich removed it. In it there turned out to be a piece of paper, decayed and worn at the edges, sewn into a scrap of cloth. The doctor unfolded its half-detached and disintegrating parts.

The paper contained excerpts from the ninety-first psalm, with those changes and errors that people introduce into prayers, gradually moving further from the original as they recopy it. The fragments of the Church Slavonic text on the paper were rewritten in Russian.[3]

In the psalm it is said: 'He that dwelleth in the secret place of the most High.' In the paper this became the title of a spell: 'Dwellers in Secret'. The verse of the psalm 'Thou shalt not be afraid . . . of the arrow that flieth by day' was misinterpreted as words of encouragement: 'Have no fear of the arrow flying by thee.' 'Because he hath known my name,' says the psalm. And the paper: 'Because he half knows my name.' 'I will be with him in trouble, I will deliver him' in the paper became: 'It will be winter and trouble, I will shiver for him.'

The text of the psalm was considered miracle-working, a protection against bullets. Troops already wore it as a talisman in the last imperialist war. Decades went by, and much later arrested people started sewing it into their clothing, and convicts in prison repeated it to themselves when they were summoned to the investigators for night interrogations.

From the telephonist, Yuri Andreevich went to the clearing, to the body of the young White Guard he had killed. The features of innocence and an all-forgiving suffering were written on the young man's handsome face. 'Why did I kill him?' thought the doctor.

He unbuttoned the dead man's greatcoat and opened its skirts wide. On the lining, in calligraphic lettering by a careful and loving hand, no doubt a mother's, there was embroidered 'Seryozha Rantsevich' – the first and last name of the dead man.

Through the opening of Seryozha's shirt a little cross fell and hung outside on a chain, with a medallion, and also some flat little gold case or snuff box with a damaged lid, as if pushed in by a nail. The little case was half open. A folded piece of paper fell out of it. The doctor unfolded it and could not believe his eyes. It was the same ninety-first psalm, only typed and in all its Slavonic genuineness.

Just then Seryozha moaned and stretched. He was alive. As it turned out later, he had been stunned by a slight internal contusion. A spent bullet had hit the face of his mother's amulet, and that had saved him. But what was he to do with the unconscious man?

The brutality of the fighting men had by that time reached the extreme. Prisoners were never brought alive to their destination, and enemy wounded were finished off on the spot.

Given the fluctuating make-up of the forest militia, which new volunteers kept joining, and old members kept deserting and going over to the enemy, it was possible, by preserving the strictest secrecy, to pass Rantsevich off as a new, recently joined-up ally.

Yuri Andreevich took the outer clothing off the dead telephonist and, with the help of Angelyar, whom the doctor initiated into his plan, put it on the young man, who had not regained consciousness.

Together with his assistant, he nursed the boy back to health. When Rantsevich was fully recovered, they let him go, though he did not conceal from his saviours that he would return to the ranks of Kolchak's army and continue fighting the Reds.

5

In the autumn the partisans camped at Fox Point, a small wood on a high knoll, under which a swift, foaming river raced, surrounding it on three sides and eroding the bank with its current.

Before the partisans, Kappel's troops had wintered there. They had fortified the wood with their own hands and the labour of the local inhabitants, but in spring they had abandoned it. Now the partisans settled into their unblown-up dugouts, trenches, and passages.

Liberius Averkievich shared his dugout with the doctor. For the second night he engaged him in conversation, not letting him sleep.

'I wish I knew what my esteemed parent, my respected *Vater*, my *Papachen*, is doing now.'

'Lord, I simply can't stand that clowning tone,' the doctor sighed to himself. 'And he's the very spit and image of his father!'

'As far as I have concluded from our previous talks, you came to know Averky Stepanovich sufficiently well. And, as it seems to me, are of a rather good opinion of him. Eh, my dear sir?'

'Liberius Averkievich, tomorrow we have a pre-election meeting at the stamping ground. Besides that, the trial of the moonshining orderlies is upon us. Lajos and I haven't prepared the materials for that yet. We're going to get together tomorrow in order to do so. And I haven't slept for two nights. Let's put off our discussion. Be a good heart.'

'No, still, let's get back to Averky Stepanovich. What do you say about the old man?'

'Your father is still quite young, Liberius Averkievich. Why do you speak of him like that? But for now I'll answer you. I've often told you that I have trouble making out the separate gradations of the socialistic infusion, and I don't see any particular difference between Bolsheviks and other socialists. Your father is of the category of people to whom Russia owes the troubles and disorders of recent times. Averky Stepanovich is of the revolutionary type and character. Like you, he represents the Russian fermenting principle.'

'What is that, praise or blame?'

'I beg you once again to put off the dispute to a more convenient time. Besides that, I draw your attention to the cocaine that you have again been sniffing without restraint. You wilfully appropriated it from the stock I'm in charge of. We need it for other purposes, not to mention that it's a poison and I'm responsible for your health.'

'You weren't at the study group again yesterday. Your social nerve has atrophied, as in illiterate peasant women or inveterately narrow-minded philistines or bigots. And yet you're a doctor, well-read, and it seems you even do some writing yourself. Explain to me, how does that tally?'

'I don't know. It probably doesn't tally, but there's no help for it. I deserve to be pitied.'

'A humility worse than pride. Instead of smiling so sarcastically, you'd do better to familiarise yourself with the programme of our courses and recognise your arrogance as inappropriate.'

'Good lord, Liberius Averkievich! What arrogance!? I bow down before your educative work. The survey of questions is repeated in the announcements. I've read it. Your thoughts about the spiritual development of the soldier are known to me. I admire them. Everything you say about the attitude of a soldier of the people's army towards his comrades, towards the weak, towards the defenceless, towards women, towards the idea of purity and honour – it's all nearly the same as what formed the Dukhobor community, it's a kind of Tolstoyism,[4] it's the dream of a dignified existence, which filled my adolescence. Who am I to laugh at such things?

'But, first, the ideas of general improvement, as they've been understood since October, don't set me on fire. Second, it's all still so far from realisation, while the mere talk about it has been paid for with such seas of blood that I don't think the end justifies the means. Third, and this is the main thing, when I hear about the remaking of life, I lose control of myself and fall into despair.

'The remaking of life! People who can reason like that may have been around, but they've never once known life, never felt its spirit, its soul. For them existence is a lump of coarse material, not yet ennobled by their touch, in need of being processed by them. But life has never been a material, a substance. It is, if you want to know, a continually self-renewing, eternally self-recreating principle, it eternally alters and transforms itself, it is far above your and my dim-witted theories.'

'And yet attending meetings and socialising with our splendid, wonderful people would, I dare say, raise your spirits. You wouldn't fall into melancholy. I know where it comes from. You're depressed that they're beating us and you don't see any light ahead. But, my friend, one must never give way to panic. I know things that are much more terrible, concerning me personally – they're not to be made public for now – and yet I don't lose heart. Our failures are of a temporary nature. Kolchak's downfall is inevitable. Remember my words. You'll see. We'll win. So take heart.'

'No, this is beyond anything!' the doctor thought. 'What infantilism! What shortsightedness! I endlessly repeat to him about the opposition of our views, he took me by force and keeps me with him by force, and he imagines that his failures should upset me, and his calculations and hopes should fill me with high spirits. What self-blindness! The interests of the revolution and the existence of the solar system are the same for him.'

Yuri Andreevich cringed. He made no reply and only shrugged his shoulders, not even trying to conceal that Liberius's naïveté had overflowed the measure of his patience and he could hardly control himself. That did not escape Liberius.

'You are angry, Jupiter, therefore you are wrong,' he said.

'Understand, understand, finally, that all this is not for me. "Jupiter", "Don't give way to panic", "Whoever says A must say B", "The Moor has done his work, the Moor can go"[5] – all these banalities, all these phrases are not for me. I'll say A, but I won't say B, even if you burst. I grant that you're all bright lights and liberators of Russia, that without you she would perish, drowned in poverty and ignorance, and nevertheless I can't be bothered with you, and I spit on you, I don't like you, and you can all go to the devil.

'The rulers of your minds indulge in proverbs, but they've forgotten the main one, that love cannot be forced, and they have a deeply rooted habit of liberating people and making them happy, especially those who haven't asked for it. You probably fancy that there's no better place in the world for me than your camp and your company. I probably should even bless you and thank you for my captivity, for your having liberated me from my family, my son, my home, my work, from everything that's dear to me and that I live by.

'Rumours have reached us of the invasion of Varykino by an unknown, non-Russian unit. They say it's been devastated and looted. Kamennodvorsky doesn't deny it. My family and yours supposedly managed to escape. Some mythical slant-eyed people in quilted jackets and papakhas crossed the ice of the Rynva in a terrible frost, and, without an ill word spoken, shot everything alive in the village, and then vanished as mysteriously as they appeared. What do you know about it? Is it true?'

'Nonsense. Made up. Unverified gibberish spread by gossip mongers.'

'If you're as kind and magnanimous as you are in your exhortations about the moral education of the soldiers, set me free. I'll go in search of my family – I don't even know if they're alive or where they are. And if not, then please stop talking and leave me alone, because all the rest is uninteresting to me, and I can't answer for myself. And, finally, devil take it, don't I have the right simply to want to sleep?'

Yuri Andreevich lay prone on the bunk, his face in the pillow. He tried as hard as he could not to listen to Liberius justifying himself, continuing to reassure him that by spring the Whites would certainly be crushed. The civil war would be over, there would be freedom, prosperity, and peace. Then no one would dare to keep the doctor. But until then he had to bear with it. After all they had endured, after so many sacrifices and so much waiting, they would not have long to wait now. And where would the doctor go? For his own sake it was impossible right now to let him go anywhere.

'He keeps grinding away, the devil! Giving his tongue a workout! How can he not be ashamed to chew the same cud for so many years?' Yuri Andreevich sighed to himself in indignation. 'He loves listening to himself, the golden-tongue, the wretched dope addict. Night isn't night for him, there's no sleep, no life where he is, curse him. Oh, how I hate him! As God is my witness, I'll kill him some day.

'Oh, Tonya, my poor girl! Are you alive? Where are you? Lord, she must have given birth long ago! How did the delivery go? Whom have we got, a boy or a girl? My dear ones, how are you all? Tonya, my eternal reproach and my guilt! Lara, I'm afraid to name you, so as not to breathe out my soul along with your name. Lord! Lord! And this one here keeps speechifying, he won't shut up, the hateful, unfeeling brute! Oh, some day I'll lose control and kill him, kill him.'

6

Indian summer was over. The clear days of golden autumn set in. The little wooden tower of the volunteers' undestroyed blockhouse jutted up from the ground in the western corner of Fox Point. It was there that Yuri Andreevich had arranged to meet his assistant, Dr Lajos, to discuss some general matters. Yuri Andreevich went there at the appointed time. While waiting for his colleague, he began pacing the dirt rim of the collapsed entrenchment, went up and into the watchtower, and looked through the empty loopholes of the machine-gun nest at the forest spreading beyond the river into the distance.

Autumn had already sharply marked the boundary between the coniferous and deciduous worlds in the forest. The first bristled in its depths like a gloomy, almost black wall; the second shone through the open spaces in fiery, wine-coloured patches, like an ancient town with a fortress and gold-topped towers, built in the thick of the forest from its own timber.

The earth in the ditch, under the doctor's feet, and in the ruts of the forest road, chilled and hardened by the morning frost, was thickly strewn and choked with fallen willow leaves, dry, small, as if clipped, rolled into little tubes. Autumn smelled of those bitter brown leaves and of a multitude of other seasonings. Yuri Andreevich greedily breathed in the complex spiciness of ice-cold preserved apples, bitter dryness, sweet dampness, and blue September fumes, reminiscent of the smoky steam of a campfire doused with water or a just-extinguished blaze.

Yuri Andreevich did not notice how Lajos came up to him from behind.

'Greetings, colleague,' he said in German. They got down to business.

'We have three points. The moonshiners, the reorganisation of the infirmary and the pharmacy, and third, at my insistence, the treatment of mental illnesses out of hospital, in field conditions. Maybe you don't see the need for it, but, from my observations, we're going out of our minds, my dear Lajos, and the modern sorts of madness take on an infectious, contagious form.'

'A very interesting question. I'll get to it later. Right now the thing is this. There's ferment in the camp. The fate of the moonshiners arouses sympathy. Many are also worried about the fate of families who flee the villages from the Whites. Some of the partisans refuse to leave the camp in view of the approaching train of carts with their wives, children, and old people.'

'Yes, we'll have to wait for them.'

'And all that before the election of a joint commander over our units and others not subordinate to us. I think the only real candidate is Comrade Liberius. A group of young men is putting up another, Vdovichenko. He's supported by a wing alien to us, which has sided with the circle of the moonshiners – children of kulaks and shopkeepers, deserters from Kolchak. They're especially noisy.'

'What do you think will happen with the orderlies who made and sold moonshine?'

'I think they'll be sentenced to be shot and then pardoned, the sentence being made conditional.'

'Anyhow, we're just chattering away. Let's get down to business. The reorganising of the infirmary. That's what I'd like to consider first of all.'

'Very good. But I must say that I find nothing surprising in your suggestion about psychiatric prophylaxis. I'm of the same opinion myself. Mental
illnesses of a most typical kind have appeared and spread, bearing definite
features of the time, and directly caused by the historical peculiarities of the
epoch. We have a soldier here from the tsarist army, very politically conscious, with an inborn class instinct – Pamphil Palykh. He's gone mad precisely from that, from fear for his family in case he's killed and they fall into
the hands of the Whites and have to answer for him. Very complex psychology. His family, it seems, is following in the refugee train and catching up
with us. Insufficient knowledge of the language prevents me from questioning him properly. Find out from Angelyar or Kamennodvorsky. He ought to
be examined.'

'I know Palykh very well. How could I not! At one time we kept running
into each other at the army council. Dark-haired, cruel, with a low brow. I
don't understand what you find good in him. He's always for extreme measures, strictness, executions. And I've always found him repulsive. All right.
I'll see to him.'

7

It was a clear, sunny day. The weather was still, dry, as it had been the whole
previous week.

From within the camp the vague noise of a big human settlement came
rolling, like the distant rumble of the sea. One could hear by turns the footsteps of men wandering in the forest, people's voices, the blows of axes, the
ding of anvils, the neighing of horses, the yelping of dogs, and the crowing
of cocks. Crowds of tanned, white-toothed, smiling folk moved about the
forest. Some knew the doctor and nodded to him; others, unacquainted
with him, passed by without greeting.

Though the partisans would not agree to leave Fox Point until their families running after them in carts caught up with them, the latter were already
within a few marches of the camp, and preparations were under way in the
forest for quickly pulling up stakes and moving further to the east. Things
were repaired, cleaned, boxes were nailed shut, wagons counted, their condition inspected.

In the middle of the forest there was a large, trodden-down glade, a sort
of barrow or former settlement, locally known as the stamping ground.
Military meetings were usually called there. Today, too, a general assembly
was set up there for the announcement of something important.

In the forest there were still many trees that had not turned yellow. In the
deepest part it was almost all still fresh and green. The sinking afternoon

sun pierced it from behind with its rays. The leaves let the sunlight through, and their undersides burned with the green fire of transparent bottle glass.

On the open grass next to his archive, the liaison officer Kamenno-dvorsky was burning the looked-over and unnecessary paper trash of the regimental office inherited from Kappel, along with his own partisan accounts. The bonfire was placed so that it stood against the sun. It shone through the transparent flames, as through the green of the forest. The fire itself could not be seen, and only by the undulating, mica-like streams of hot air could it be concluded that something was burning.

Here and there the forest was gaily coloured with ripe berries of all sorts: the prettily pendant berries of lady's-smock, brick-brown, flabby elderber-ries, the shimmering white-crimson clusters of the guelder rose. Dragonflies, their glassy wings tinkling, floated slowly through the air, speckled and transparent, like the fire and the forest.

Since childhood Yuri Andreevich had loved the evening forest shot through with the fire of sunset. In such moments it was as if he, too, let these shafts of light pass through him. As if the gift of the living spirit streamed into his breast, crossed through his whole being, and came out under his shoulder blades as a pair of wings. That youthful archetype, which is formed in every young man for the whole of life and serves him forever after and seems to him to be his inner face, his personality, awakened in him with its full primary force, and transformed nature, the forest, the evening glow, and all visible things into an equally primary and all-embracing likeness of a girl. 'Lara!' – closing his eyes, he half whispered or mentally addressed his whole life, the whole of God's earth, the whole sunlit expanse spread out before him.

But the immediate, the actual, went on, in Russia there was the October revolution, he was a prisoner of the partisans. And, without noticing it him-self, he went up to Kamennodvorsky's bonfire.

'Destroying the records? They're still not burnt?'

'Far from it! There's stuff enough for a long time yet.'

With the toe of his boot the doctor pushed and broke up one of the piles. It was the telegraph correspondence of White headquarters. The vague notion that he might run across the name of Rantsevich among the papers flashed in him, but he was disappointed. It was an uninteresting collection of last year's ciphered communiqués in incomprehensible abbreviations, like the following: 'Omsk genquasup first copy Omsk stareg map Omsky thirty miles Yenisei never received.' He scattered another pile with his foot. Out of it crawled the protocols of old partisan meetings. On top lay a paper: 'Highly urgent. On leaves. Re-election of members of the review committee.

Current business. In view of insufficient charges of the Ignatodvortsy schoolmistress, the army council thinks . . .'

Just then Kamennodvorsky took something from his pocket, handed it to the doctor, and said:

'Here's the schedule for your medical unit when we come to breaking camp. The carts with the partisan families are already close by. The dissension in the camp will be settled today. We can expect to leave any day now.'

The doctor cast a glance at the paper and gasped:

'That's less than they gave me last time. And there are so many more wounded! Those who are ambulant or bandaged can walk. But they're an insignificant number. How am I to transport the badly wounded? And the medications, and the cots, the equipment?'

'Squeeze yourself in somehow. We've got to adjust to circumstances. Now about something else. There's a general request to you from everybody. We have a seasoned, tried comrade here, devoted to the cause and an excellent fighter. Something's gone wrong with him.'

'Palykh? Lajos told me.'

'Yes. Go and see him. Look into it.'

'Something mental?'

'I suppose so. Some sort of fleetlings, as he puts it. Apparently hallucinations. Insomnia. Headaches.'

'Very well. I'll go at once. I have some free time now. When does the meeting begin?'

'I think they're already gathering. But why you? You see, I'm not going. They'll do without us.'

'Then I'll go to Pamphil. Though I'm so sleepy I'm ready to drop. Liberius Averkievich likes to philosophise at night; he's worn me out with talking. How do I get to Pamphil? Where is he quartered?'

'You know the young birch grove behind the filled-in pit? Birch saplings.'

'I'll find it.'

'There are some commanders' tents in a clearing. We assigned one to Pamphil. In expectation of his family. His wife and children are coming to him in the train. So he's in one of the commanders' tents. With the rights of a battalion commander. For his revolutionary merits.'

8

On the way to Pamphil the doctor felt that he could not go any further. He was overcome by fatigue. He could not fight off his sleepiness, the result of a lack of sleep accumulated over several nights. He could go back for a nap in the dugout. But Yuri Andreevich was afraid to go there. Liberius could come at any moment and disturb him.

He lay down in one of the not overgrown places in the forest, all strewn with golden leaves that had fallen onto the clearing from the surrounding trees. The leaves lay cross-hatched like a chequerboard in the clearing. The sun's rays fell in the same way onto their golden carpet. This double, criss-crossed motleyness rippled in one's eyes. It lulled one to sleep, like reading small print or murmuring something monotonous.

The doctor lay on the silkily rustling leaves, putting his hand under his head on the moss that covered the gnarled roots of a tree like a pillow. He dozed off instantly. The motley sun spots that put him to sleep covered his body stretched out on the ground with a chequered pattern and made him undiscoverable, indistinguishable in the kaleidoscope of rays and leaves, as if he had put on the cap of invisibility.

Very soon the over-intensity of his wish and need to sleep woke him up. Direct causes work only within commensurate limits. Deviations from the measure produce the opposite effect. Finding no rest, his wakeful conscious-ness worked feverishly in idle. Fragments of thoughts raced and whirled in circles, almost knocking like a broken machine. This inner turmoil tor-mented and angered the doctor. 'That scoundrel Liberius,' he thought indig-nantly. 'It's not enough for him that there are hundreds of reasons now for a man to go off his head. By his captivity, by his friendship and idiotic babble, he needlessly turns a healthy man into a neurasthenic. Some day I'll kill him.'

A colourful folding and opening little scrap, a brown speckled butterfly, flew by on the sunny side. The doctor followed its flight with sleepy eyes. It alighted on what most resembled its colouring, the brown speckled bark of a pine tree, with which it merged quite indistinguishably. The butterfly imperceptibly effaced itself on it, just as Yuri Andreevich was lost without trace to an outsider's eye under the net of sunlight and shadow playing over him.

The usual round of thoughts came over Yuri Andreevich. It was indirectly touched upon in many medical works. About will and expediency as the result of improving adaptation. About imitative and protective colouring. About the survival of the fittest, and that the path laid down by natural selection is perhaps also the path of the formation and birth of conscious-ness. What is a subject? What is an object? How give a definition of their identity? In the doctor's reflections, Darwin met with Schelling,[6] and the passing butterfly with modern painting, with impressionist art. He thought of creation, the creature, creativity, and mimicry.

And he fell back to sleep, and after a minute woke up again. He was awakened by soft, muffled talk not far away. The few words that reached him were enough for Yuri Andreevich to understand that something secret and illegal was being arranged. The conspirators obviously did not notice him, did not suspect his proximity. If he were to stir now and betray his presence, it would cost him his life. Yuri Andreevich kept quiet, froze, and began to listen.

Some of the voices he knew. These were the scum, the riff-raff of the partisans, the hangers-on, the boys Sanka Pafnutkin, Goshka Ryabykh, Koska Nekhvalenykh, and Terenty Galuzin, who sided with them – the ringleaders of all nastiness and outrage. With them was also Zakhar Gorazdykh, a still shadier type, involved with the moonshine case, but temporarily left out of it for having betrayed the chief culprits. Yuri Andreevich was surprised by the presence of a partisan from the 'silver company', Sivobluy, who was one of the commander's personal guards. By a tradition stemming from Razin and Pugachev,[7] this retainer, owing to the trust Liberius put in him, was known as 'the ataman's ear'. So he, too, was in the conspiracy.

The conspirators were making arrangements with men sent from the enemy's advance patrols. The parleyers could not be heard at all, they discussed things so softly with the traitors, and only by the pauses in the whispering of the accomplices could Yuri Andreevich guess that the enemy representatives were speaking.

The drunkard Zakhar Gorazdykh talked most of all, in a hoarse, rasping voice, using foul language all the time. He was probably the main instigator.

'Now listen, you guys. Above all it's got to be on the quiet, in secret. If anybody drops out and rats, see this knife? With this knife here I'll spill his guts. Understand? Now for us it's not here, not there, whichever way we turn it's the high oak tree. We've got to earn our pardon. We've got to pull a stunt like the whole world never saw, out of the old rut. They want him alive, tied up. We hear their chief, Gulevoy, is coming to this forest.' (They told him the right way to say it; he did not quite hear and corrected it to 'General Galeev'.) 'There won't be no more chances like this. Here are their delegates. They'll tell you everything. They say he's got to be delivered tied up and alive, without fail. Ask the comrades yourselves. Speak up, you guys. Tell 'em something, brothers.'

The strangers, the ones sent, began to speak. Yuri Andreevich could not catch a single word. By the length of the general silence, the thoroughness of what was being said could be imagined. Again Gorazdykh spoke:

'You hear, brothers? Now you can see for yourselves what a little treasure, what a sweet little potion we've run into. Do we have to pay for it with our lives? Is he a human being? He's a freak, a holy fool, a sort of runt, or a hermit. I'll teach you to guffaw, Tereshka! What are you baring your teeth for, you sin of Sodom? It's not for your jeers I'm talking. Yes. He's like a young hermit. Give in to him and he'll make a total monk, a eunuch, out of you. What's his talk all about? Driving from our midst, away with foul language, fight drunkenness, attitude towards women. Can we live like that? My final word. Tonight at the river crossing, where the stones are laid out. I'll lure him into the open. We'll fall on him in a heap. Is it so tricky to deal with him? Nothing to it. Where's the hitch? They want him alive. Tied up. If I see it's not coming off our way, I'll take care of him myself, bump him off with my own hands. They'll send their own men to help out.'

The speaker went on developing the plan for the conspiracy, but he began to move off with the others, and the doctor could not hear them any more.

'They mean Liberius, the scoundrels!' Yuri Andreevich thought with horror and indignation, forgetting how many times he himself had cursed his tormentor and wished for his death. 'The villains are going to hand him over to the Whites or kill him. How can I prevent it? Go up to the bonfire as if by chance and, without naming anybody, inform Kamennodvorsky. And somehow warn Liberius about the danger.'

Kamennodvorsky was no longer in his former place. The bonfire was going out. Kamennodvorsky's assistant was there to see that the fire did not spread.

But the attempt did not take place. It was stopped. As it turned out, they knew about the conspiracy. That day it was fully uncovered and the conspirators were arrested. Sivobluy had played a double role in it, as sleuth and seducer. The doctor felt still more disgusted.

9

It became known that the fleeing women and children were now just two marches away. At Fox Point they were preparing to meet their families soon and after that to raise camp and move on. Yuri Andreevich went to see Pamphil Palykh.

The doctor found him at the entrance to his tent with an axe in his hand. In front of the tent was a tall pile of young birches cut down for poles. Pamphil had not yet trimmed them. Some had been cut right there and, falling heavily, had stuck the sharp ends of their broken branches into the damp soil. Others he had brought from not far away and piled on top. Trembling and swaying on the resilient branches crushed underneath, the birches lay neither on the ground nor on each other. It was as if they were warding off

Pamphil, who had cut them down, with their hands and barring the entrance of the tent to him with a whole forest of live greenery.

'In expectation of our dear guests,' said Pamphil, explaining what he was doing. 'The tent will be too low for my wife and children. And it gets flooded when it rains. I want to prop up the top with stakes. I've cut some planks.'

'There's no use thinking they'll let your family live in the tent with you, Pamphil. Where have you ever seen non-military, women and children, staying in the middle of an army? They'll be placed somewhere at the edge, with the train. Go to see them in your free time, if you like. But to have them in a soldier's tent is unlikely. But that's not the point. They say you've grown thin, stopped eating and drinking, don't sleep? Yet you look pretty good. Only a bit shaggy.'

Pamphil Palykh was a stalwart man with black tousled hair and beard and a bumpy forehead that gave the impression of being double, owing to a thickening of the frontal bone that went around his temples like a ring or a brass hoop. This gave Pamphil the unkindly and sinister appearance of a man looking askance or glancing from under his brows.

At the beginning of the revolution, when, after the example of the year 1905, it was feared that this time, too, the revolution would be a brief event in the history of the educated upper classes, and would not touch the lowest classes or strike root in them, everything possible was done to propagandise the people, to revolutionise them, alarm them, arouse and infuriate them.

In those first days, people like the soldier Pamphil Palykh, who, without any agitation, had a fierce, brutal hatred of the intelligentsia, the gentry, and the officers, seemed a rare find to the rapturous left-wing intelligentsia, and were greatly valued. Their inhumanity seemed a miracle of class consciousness, their barbarity a model of proletarian firmness and revolutionary instinct. Such was the established reputation of Pamphil. He was on the best standing with partisan chiefs and party leaders.

To Yuri Andreevich this gloomy and unsociable strongman seemed a not quite normal degenerate, owing to his general heartlessness, and the monotony and squalor of whatever was close to him and could interest him.

'Let's go into the tent,' Pamphil invited.

'No, why? Anyway, I can't get in. It's better in the open air.'

'All right. Have it your way. In fact, it's a hole. We can chat sitting on these staves' (so he called the trees heaped lengthwise).

And they sat on the birch trunks, which moved springily under them.

'They say a tale's quickly told, but doing's not quickly done. But my tale's not quickly told either. In three years I couldn't lay it all out. I don't know where to begin.

'Well, so then. I was living with my wife. We were young. She saw to the house. I had no complaints, I did peasant work. Children. They took me as a soldier. Drove me flank-march to war. So, the war. What can I tell you about it? You saw it, comrade medic. So, the revolution. I began to see. The soldier's eyes were opened. The German's not the foreigner, the one from Germany, but one of our own. Soldiers of the world revolution, stick your bayonets in the ground, go home from the front, get the bourgeoisie! And stuff like that. You know it all yourself, comrade army medic. And so on. The civil war. I merge into the partisans. Now I'll skip a lot, otherwise I'll never finish. Now, to make a long story short, what do I see in the current moment? He, the parasite, has moved the first and second Stavropol regiments from the front, and the first Orenburg Cossack regiment as well. Am I a little kid not to understand? Didn't I serve in the army? We're in a bad way, army doctor, we're cooked. What does the scoundrel want? He wants to fall on us with the whole lot of them. He wants to encircle us.

'Now at the present time I've got a wife and kids. If he overpowers us now, how will they get away from him? Is he going to make out that they're not guilty of anything, that they're not part of it? He's not going to look into that. He'll twist my wife's arms, torment her, torture my wife and children on my account, tear their little joints and bones apart. Go on, eat and sleep after that. Say you're made of iron, but you'll still crack up.'

'You're an odd bird, Pamphil. I don't understand you. For years you've been doing without them, didn't know about them, didn't grieve. And now, when you may see them any day, instead of being glad, you sing a dirge for them.'

'That was then, but this is now – a big difference. The white-epauletted vermin are overpowering us. But I'm not the point. It's the grave for me. Serves me right, clearly. But I can't take my dear ones with me to the next world. They'll fall into the foul one's paws. He'll bleed them drop by drop.'

'And that's why you have these fleetlings? They say some sort of fleetlings appear to you.'

'Well, all right, doctor. I haven't told you everything. Not the main thing. Well, all right, listen to my prickly truth, don't begrudge me, I'll tell it all straight to your face.

'I've done in a lot of your kind, there's a lot of blood on my hands from the masters, the officers, and it's nothing to me. I don't remember numbers or names, it's all flowed by like water. But one little bugger won't get out of my head, I bumped off one little bugger and can't forget him. Why did I destroy the lad? He made me laugh, he was killingly funny. I shot him from laughter, stupidly. For no reason.

'It was during the February revolution. Under Kerensky. We were rioting. It happened at the railroad. They sent us a young agitator, to rouse us for the attack with his tongue. So we'd make war to a victorious conclusion. A little cadet comes to pacify us with his tongue. Such a puny fellow. He had this slogan: to a victorious conclusion. He jumped with his slogan onto a fire-fighting tub that was there at the station. So he jumped up on the tub to call us to battle from higher up, and suddenly the lid gave way under his feet and he fell into the water. A misstep. Oh, how funny! I just rolled with laughter. I thought I'd die. Oh, it was killing. And I had a gun in my hands. And I was laughing my head off, and that was it, no help for it. Same as if he was tickling me. Well, so I aimed and – bang – right on the spot. I don't understand myself how it came out that way. As if somebody nudged my arm.

'So there's my fleetlings. By night I seem to see that station. It was funny then, but now I'm sorry.'

'Was it in the town of Meliuzeevo, the Biriuchi station?'

'I forget.'

'Was it a riot with the people of Zybushino?'

'I forget.'

'What front was it? At what front? The western?'

'Something like that. It's all possible. I forget.'

Part Twelve

THE FROSTED ROWAN

I

The families of the partisans had long been following the body of the army in carts, with their children and chattels. At the tail of the refugee train, far behind, countless herds of cattle were driven, mostly cows, some several thousand of them.

Along with the partisans' wives a new person appeared in the camp, an army wife, Zlydarikha or Kubarikha, a cattle doctor, a veterinarian, and secretly also a sorceress.

She went about in a forage cap cocked to one side and the grey-green greatcoat of the Royal Scots Fusiliers, from the British uniforms supplied to the Supreme Ruler, and assured people that she had had these things made from a prisoner's hat and smock, and that the Reds had supposedly freed her from the jail in Kezhem, where Kolchak had held her for some unknown reason.

At that time the partisans were halted in a new place. It was assumed that this would be a brief halt, until the area was reconnoitred and a place was found for a long and settled wintering over. But later on circumstances took a different turn and forced the partisans to stay there and spend the winter.

This new halting place was in no way like the recently abandoned Fox Point. It was dense, impassable forest, the taiga. To one side, away from the road and the camp, there was no end to it. During the first days, while the army was setting up a new bivouac and preparing to live in it, Yuri Andre-evich had more leisure. He went deep into the forest in several directions with the aim of exploring it and convinced himself that it would be very easy to get lost in it. Two spots caught his attention, and he remembered them from that first round.

At the way out of the camp and the forest, which was now autumnally bare and could be seen through, as if gates had been thrown open into its emptiness, there grew a solitary, beautiful, rusty-red-leafed rowan tree, the only one of all the trees to keep its foliage. It grew on a mound above a low, hummocky bog, and reached right up to the sky, into the dark lead of the pre-winter inclemency, the flatly widening corymbs of its hard, brightly glowing berries. Small winter birds, bullfinches and tomtits, with plumage bright as frosty dawns, settled on the rowan tree, slowly and selectively pecked the larger berries, and, thrusting up their little heads and stretching their necks, swallowed them with effort.

Some living intimacy was established between the birds and the tree. As if the rowan saw it all, resisted for a long time, then surrendered, taking pity on the little birds, yielded, unbuttoned herself, and gave them the breast, like a nurse to a baby. 'Well, what can I do with you? Go on, eat, eat me. Feed yourselves.' And she smiled.

The other place in the forest was still more remarkable.

It was on a height. This height, like a drumlin, ended on one side in a sheer drop. It seemed that below, under the drop, there should have been something other than what was above – a river, or a ravine, or an abandoned, unmowed meadow overgrown with grass. However, below there was a repetition of the same thing as above, only at a dizzying depth, on another level, where the treetops were low down under one's feet. This was probably the result of a landslide.

It was as if this severe, cloud-propping, mighty forest had stumbled once, just as it was, and plunged down, and should have fallen through the earth into Tartarus, but at the decisive moment had miraculously kept itself on earth and now, safe and sound, could be seen rustling below.

But this forest height was remarkable not for that, but for another particularity. It was shut in all around its edge by vertical blocks of granite standing on end. They were like the flat-trimmed slabs of prehistoric dolmens. When Yuri Andreevich came to this platform for the first time, he was ready to swear that the place and its stones were not of natural origin at all, but bore the traces of human hands. Here in ancient times there might have been some sort of pagan shrine of unknown idol worshippers, the place of their rituals and sacrifices.

In this place on a cold, grey morning the death sentence was carried out on the eleven men found guilty of the conspiracy and the two moonshining orderlies.

Some twenty men from among the partisans most loyal to the revolution, with a core of special guards from headquarters, brought them here. The convoy closed in on the condemned men in a semicircle and, pointing their rifles, at a quick, close-packed pace, pushed them, drove them into the rocky corner of the platform, from which they had no way out except to leap into the abyss.

The interrogations, the long imprisonment, and the humiliations they had been subjected to had deprived them of their human image. They were shaggy, blackened, exhausted, and frightful as ghosts.

They had been disarmed at the very beginning of the investigation. It did not occur to anyone to search them a second time before the execution. That seemed like an unnecessary meanness, a mockery of people in the face of death.

Suddenly Rzhanitsky, a friend of Vdovichenko's, who was walking beside him and, like him, was an old ideological anarchist, fired three times at the line of the convoy, aiming at Sivobluy. Rzhanitsky was an excellent shot, but his hand shook from agitation and he missed. Again the same delicacy and pity for their former comrades kept the guards from falling upon Rzhanitsky or responding to his attempt by shooting ahead of time, before the general command. Rzhanitsky had three unspent shots left, but in his excitement, perhaps forgetting about them and vexed at having missed, he hurled his Browning against the stones. The blow fired off the Browning a fourth time, wounding the condemned Pachkolia in the foot.

The orderly Pachkolia cried out, clutched his foot, and fell, uttering quick shrieks of pain. Pafnutkin and Gorazdykh, who were nearest to him, picked him up, held him under the arms, and dragged him, so that he would not be trampled by his alarmed comrades, because they no longer knew what they were doing. Pachkolia went towards the stony edge, where the condemned men were being crowded, hopping, limping, unable to step on his wounded foot, and kept crying out. His inhuman howls were infectious. As if on signal, they all lost control of themselves. Something unimaginable began. Swearing poured out, prayers and entreaties were heard, curses resounded.

The adolescent Galuzin, throwing from his head the yellow-braided high school cap he was still wearing, sank to his knees and like that, without getting up from them, crept backwards in the crowd towards the frightful stones. He bowed quickly to the ground in front of the convoy, cried and sobbed, pleading with them half unconsciously, in singsong:

'I'm guilty, brothers, have mercy on me, I won't do it again. Don't destroy me. Don't kill me. I haven't lived yet, I'm too young to die. I want to go on living, I want to see mama, my mama, one more time. Forgive me, brothers, have mercy. I'll kiss your feet. I'll carry water for you on my back. Ah, terrible, terrible – mama, mama, I'm lost.'

From the midst someone wailed, no one could see who:

'Dear, good comrades! How can it be? Come to your senses. We've shed blood together in two wars. We stood, we fought for the same cause. Have pity, let us go. We'll never forget your kindness, we'll earn it, we'll prove it in action. Are you deaf that you don't answer? Aren't you Christians?'

To Sivobluy they shouted:

'Ah, you Judas, you Christ-seller! What sort of traitors are we compared to you? May you be throttled yourself, you dog, you three-time traitor! You swore an oath to your tsar and you killed your lawful tsar, you swore loyalty to us and you betrayed us. Go and kiss your Forester devil, till you betray him. And you will betray him.'

Vdovichenko remained true to himself even on the verge of the grave. Holding high his head with its grey, flying hair, he loudly addressed Rzhanitsky, like communard to communard, for everyone to hear:

'Don't humiliate yourself, Boniface! Your protests won't reach them. These new Oprichniki,[1] these executioners of the new torture chambers, won't understand you. Don't lose heart. History will sort it all out. Posterity will nail the Bourbons of the commissarocracy and their black cause to the pillory. We die martyrs to ideas at the dawn of the world revolution. Long live the revolution of the spirit! Long live universal anarchy!'

A volley of twenty guns, produced on some soundless command caught only by the firing squad, mowed down half of the condemned men, most of whom fell dead. The rest were finished off with a second volley. The boy, Terenty Galuzin, twitched longer than anyone else, but in the end he, too, lay still, stretched out on the ground.

2

The idea of shifting camp for the winter to another place further east was not renounced at once. Reconnoitring and scouting out the area to the other side of the high road, along the watershed of the Vytsk-Kezhem, went on for a long time. Liberius often absented himself from camp to the taiga, leaving the doctor alone.

But it was already too late to move, and there was nowhere to move to. This was the time of greatest unsuccess for the partisans. Before their final collapse, the Whites decided to have done with the irregular forest units at one blow, once and for all, and, in a general effort on all fronts, surrounded them. The partisans were hemmed in on all sides. This would have been a catastrophe for them if the radius of the circle had been smaller. They were saved by the intangible vastness of the encirclement. On the doorstep of winter, the enemy was unable to draw its flanks through the boundless, impassable taiga and surround the peasant troops more tightly.

In any case, movement anywhere at all became impossible. Of course, if there had existed a plan of relocation that promised definite military advantages, it would have been possible to break through, to fight their way out of the encirclement to a new position.

But no such plan had been worked out. People were exhausted. Junior commanders, disheartened themselves, lost influence over their subordinates. The senior ones gathered every evening in military council, offering contradictory solutions.

They had to abandon the search for another wintering site and fortify their camp for the winter deep inside the thicket they occupied. In wintertime, with the deep snow, it became impassable for the enemy, who were in short supply of skis. They had to entrench themselves and lay in a big stock of provisions.

The partisan quartermaster, Bisyurin, reported an acute shortage of flour and potatoes. There were plenty of cattle, and Bisyurin foresaw that in winter the main food would be meat and milk.

There was a lack of winter clothes. Some of the partisans went about half dressed. All the dogs in the camp were strangled. Those who knew how to work with leather made coats for the partisans out of dogskin with the fur on the outside.

The doctor was denied means of transportation. The carts were now in demand for more important needs. During the last march, the gravely ill had been carried on foot for thirty miles on stretchers.

Of medications, all Yuri Andreevich had left were quinine, iodine, and Glauber's salts. The iodine necessary for operations and dressings was in crystals. It had to be dissolved in alcohol. They regretted having destroyed the production of moonshine, and the less guilty moonshiners, who had been acquitted, were approached and charged with repairing the broken still or constructing a new one. The abolished making of moonshine was set going anew for medical purposes. People in the camp only winked and shook their heads. Drunkenness reappeared, contributing to the developing degradation in the camp.

The level of distillation they achieved reached almost two hundred proof. Liquid of such strength dissolved the crystal preparations very well. At the beginning of winter, Yuri Andreevich used this same alcohol, infused with quinine bark, to treat cases of typhus, which set in again with the coming of cold weather.

3

In those days the doctor saw Pamphil Palykh and his family. His wife and children had spent the whole previous summer fleeing along dusty roads under the open sky. They were frightened by the horrors they had lived through and expected new ones. Their wanderings had put an indelible stamp on them. Pamphil's wife and the three children, a son and two daughters, had light, sun-bleached, flaxen hair and white, stern eyebrows on dark, weather-beaten, tanned faces. The children were too small to bear any signs of what they had endured, but from their mother's face the shocks and dangers she had experienced had driven all the play of life and left only the dry regularity of the features, the lips pressed into a thread, the strained immobility of suffering, ready for self-defence.

Pamphil loved them all, especially the children, to distraction, and with a deftness that amazed the doctor sculpted wooden toys for them with the corner of a sharply honed axe – hares, bears, cocks.

When they arrived, Pamphil cheered up, took heart, began to recover. But then it became known that, owing to the harmful influence the presence of the families had on the mood of the camp, the partisans would be obliged to separate from their kinfolk, the camp would be freed of unnecessary nonmilitary appendages, and the refugee train would set up camp for the winter, under sufficient guard, somewhere further away. There was more talk about this separation than actual preparation for it. The doctor did not believe in the feasibility of the measure. But Pamphil turned gloomy and his former fleetlings returned.

4

On the threshold of winter, for several reasons, the camp was gripped by a long stretch of anxiety, uncertainty, menacing and confusing situations, strange incongruities.

The Whites carried out the plan of surrounding the insurgents. At the head of the accomplished operation stood the generals Vitsyn, Quadri, and Basalygo. These generals were famous for their firmness and inflexible resolution. Their names alone instilled terror in the wives of the insurgents in the camp and in the peaceful population, who still had not left their native places and remained behind in their villages, outside the enemy line.

As has already been said, it was impossible to see how the enemy circle could be tightened. On that account they could rest easy. However, to remain indifferent to this encirclement was also not possible. Submission to circumstances would morally strengthen the enemy. It was necessary to attempt to break out of the trap, unthreatening as it was, for the sake of military display.

To that end large forces of the partisans were detached and concentrated against the western bend of the circle. After many days of hot fighting, the partisans inflicted a defeat on the enemy and, breaching their line at that point, came at them from the rear.

Through the freed space formed by the breach, access to the insurgents was opened in the taiga. New crowds of refugees came pouring in to join them. This influx of peaceful country people was not limited to direct relations of the partisans. Frightened by the punitive measures of the Whites, all the neighbouring peasantry moved from their places, abandoning their hearths and naturally drawing towards the peasant forest army, in which they saw their defence.

But in the camp they were trying to get rid of their own hangers-on. The partisans could not be bothered with the newcomers and strangers. They went out to meet the fugitives, stopped them on the road, and turned them aside, towards the mill in the Chilim clearing, on the Chilimka River. This cleared space, formed from the farmsteads that had grown up around the mill, was called the Steadings. The plan was to set up a winter camp for the refugees in these Steadings and store the provisions allotted to them.

While these decisions were being made, things were taking their own course, and the camp command could not keep up with them.

The victory over the enemy had complications. Having let the partisan group that had beaten them pass into their territory, the Whites closed in and restored their breached line. For the unit that got to the rear of them and was separated from their own forces, the return to the taiga after their foray was cut off.

Something was also going wrong with the refugee women. It was easy to miss them in the dense, impassable thicket. Those sent to meet them lost track of the fleeing women and came back without them, while the women in a spontaneous flow moved deep into the taiga, performing miracles of resourcefulness on their way, felling trees on both sides, building bridges and log paths, making roads.

All this went contrary to the intentions of the forest headquarters and turned Liberius's plans and projects upside down.

5

That was what he was raging about as he stood with Svirid not far from the high road, a small stretch of which passed through the taiga in that place.

His officers were standing on the road, arguing about whether or not to cut the telegraph lines that ran along it. The last decisive word belonged to Liberius, and he was chattering away with a wandering trapper. Liberius waved his hand to let them know that he would come to them presently, that they should wait and not go away.

For a long time, Svirid had been unable to stomach the condemnation and shooting of Vdovichenko, guilty of nothing except that his influence rivalled Liberius's authority and introduced a split in the camp. Svirid wanted to leave the partisans, to live freely by himself as before. But not a chance. He had got himself hired, had sold himself – he would meet the same fate as the executed men if he left the Forest Brotherhood now.

The weather was the most terrible that could be imagined. A sharp, gusty wind carried torn shreds of clouds, dark as flakes of flying soot, low over the earth. Suddenly snow began to pour from them with the convulsive haste of some white madness.

In a moment the distance was covered by a white shroud, the earth was spread with a white sheet. The next moment the sheet burnt up, melted away. The soil appeared, black as coal, as did the black sky drenched from above with the slanting streaks of distant downpours. The earth could not take any more water into itself. In moments of brightening, the clouds parted, as if to air out the sky, windows were opened on high, shot through with a cold, glassy whiteness. The standing water, unabsorbed by the soil, responded from the ground with the same thrust-open casements of puddles and lakes, filled with the same brilliance.

The drizzle slid like smoke over the turpentine-resinous needles of the evergreen forest without penetrating them, as water does not go through oilcloth. The telegraph wires were strung with beadlike raindrops. They hung crowded, one against another, and did not fall.

Svirid was among those who had been sent into the depths of the forest to meet the refugee women. He wanted to tell his chief about what he had witnessed. About the muddle that resulted from the clash of different, equally impracticable orders. About the atrocities committed by the weakest, most despairing part of the horde of women. Young mothers, trudging on foot, carrying bundles, sacks, and nursing babies, losing their milk, run off their feet and crazed, abandoned their children on the road, shook the flour out of the sacks, and turned back. Better a quick death than a long death from starvation. Better the enemy's hands than the teeth of some beast in the forest.

Others, the stronger ones, gave examples of endurance and courage unknown to men. Svirid had many more things to report. He wanted to warn the chief about the danger of a new insurrection hanging over the camp, more threatening than the one that had been crushed, but found no words, because the impatience of Liberius, who hurried him irritably, completely deprived him of the gift of speech. And Liberius interrupted Svirid every moment, not only because people were waiting for him on the road and nodding and shouting to him, but because in the last two weeks he had been constantly addressed with such considerations and knew all about it.

'Don't hurry me, comrade chief. I'm no talker as it is. The words stick in my teeth, I choke on them. What am I saying to you? Go to the refugee train, talk some sense into these runaway women. It's all gone haywire with them there. I ask you, what is it with us, "All against Kolchak!" or female slaughter?'

'Make it short, Svirid. See, they're calling me. Don't lay it on thick.'

'Now there's this demon woman, Zlydarikha, deuce knows who the wench is. Sign me up to look after the cattle, she says, I'm a vitalinarian . . .'

'Veterinarian, Svirid.'

'Like I said – a vitalinarian, to treat animals in their vitals. But now you can forget your cattle, she's turned out to be a heretic witch from the Old Believers,[2] serves cow liturgies, leads the refugee women astray. It's your own fault, she says, see where you get when you go running after the red flag with your skirts pulled up. Next time don't do it.'

'I don't understand what refugees you're talking about. Our partisan wives, or some others?'

'Others, sure enough. The new ones, from different parts.'

'But there was an order for them to go to the Steadings, to the Chilim mill. How did they wind up here?'

'The Steadings, sure. There's nothing but ashes left of your Steadings, it's all burned down. The mill and the whole place is in cinders. They got to Chilimka and saw a barren waste. Half of them lost their minds, howled away, and went back to the Whites. The others swung round and are coming here, a whole train of them.'

'Through the thicket, through the bog?'

'Ever heard of axes and saws? Our men were sent to protect them – they helped out. Some twenty miles of road have been cut. With bridges, the hellcats. Talk about wenches after that! They do such things, the shrews, it takes you three days to figure it out.'

'A fine goose you are! Twenty miles of road, you jackass, what's there to be glad about? It plays right into Vitsyn's and Quadri's hands. The way into the taiga is open. They can roll in their artillery.'

'Cover them. Cover them. Send a covering detachment, and that's the end of it.'

'By God, I could have thought of that without you.'

6

The days grew shorter. By five o'clock it was getting dark. Towards dusk
Yuri Andreevich crossed the road in the place where Liberius had wrangled
with Svirid the other day. The doctor was heading for the camp. Near the
clearing and the mound on which the rowan tree grew, considered the
camp's boundary marker, he heard the mischievous, perky voice of
Kubarikha, his rival, as he jokingly called the quack wisewoman. His com-
petitor, with loud shrieks, was pouring out something merry, rollicking,
probably some folk verses. There were listeners. She was interrupted by
bursts of sympathetic laughter, men's and women's. Afterwards everything
became quiet. They all probably left.

Then Kubarikha began to sing differently, to herself and in a low voice,
thinking she was completely alone. Taking care not to step into the swamp,
Yuri Andreevich slowly made his way in the darkness down the footpath
that skirted the boggy clearing in front of the rowan tree, then stopped as if
rooted to the spot. Kubarikha was singing some old Russian song. Yuri
Andreevich did not know it. Might it be her own improvisation?

A Russian song is like water in a mill pond. It seems stopped up and
unmoving. But in its depths it constantly flows through the sluice gates, and
the calm of its surface is deceptive.

By all possible means, by repetitions, by parallelisms, it holds back the
course of the gradually developing content. At a certain limit, it suddenly
opens itself all at once and astounds us. Restraining itself, mastering itself,
an anguished force expresses itself in this way. It is a mad attempt to stop
time with words.

Kubarikha was half singing, half speaking:

> A little hare was running over the white world,
> Over the white world, aye, over the white snow.
> He ran, little flop-ears, past a rowan tree,
> He ran, little flop-ears, and complained to the rowan.
> Me, I'm a hare, and my heart's all timid,
> My heart's all timid, it's so easily frightened.
> I'm a hare and I'm scared of the wild beast's track,
> Of the wild beast's track, of the hungry wolf's belly.
> Have pity on me, rowan bush,
> Rowan bush, beautiful rowan tree.
> Don't give your beauty to the wicked enemy,
> To the wicked enemy, to the wicked raven.
> Strew your red berries in handfuls to the wind,

To the wind, over the white world, over the white snow,
Roll them, scatter them to the place I was born in,
To the last house there by the village gate,
To the last window there, aye, in the last room,
Where my little recluse has hidden away,
My dearest one, my longed-for one.
Speak into the ear of the one I long for
A hot word, an ardent word for me.
I languish in chains, a soldier-warrior,
I lose heart, a soldier, in this foreign land.
But I'll escape yet from this bitter bondage,
Escape to my berry, to my beautiful one.[3]

7

The army wife Kubarikha was putting a spell on a sick cow belonging to Pamphil's wife, Agafya Fotievna, known as Palykha or, in simple speech, Fatevna. The cow had been taken from the herd and put in the bushes, tied to a tree by the horns. The cow's owner sat by its front legs on a stump, and by the hind legs, on a milking stool, sat the sorceress.

The rest of the countless herd was crowded into a small clearing. The dark forest stood around it in a wall of triangular firs, tall as the hills, which seemed to sit on the ground on the fat behinds of their broadly spread lower branches.

In Siberia they raised a certain prize-winning Swiss breed. Almost all of the same colours, black with white spots, the cows were no less exhausted than the people by the privations, the long marches, the unbearable crowding. Squeezed together side by side, they were going crazy from the crush. In their stupefaction, they forgot their sex and, bellowing, climbed onto one another like bulls, straining to drag up the heavy weight of their udders. The heifers they covered up, raising their tails, tore away from underneath them and, breaking down bushes and branches, ran towards the thicket, where old shepherds and herdboys rushed shouting after them.

And, as if locked into the tight circle outlined by the treetops in the winter sky, the snowy black and white clouds over the forest clearing crowded just as stormily and chaotically, rearing and piling up on each other.

The curious, standing in a bunch further off, annoyed the wisewoman. She looked them up and down with an unkindly glance. But it was beneath her dignity to admit that they were hampering her. Her artistic vanity stopped her. And she made it look as if she did not notice them. The doctor observed her from the back rows, hidden from her.

It was the first time he had taken a good look at her. She was wearing her inevitable British forage cap and grey-green interventionist greatcoat with the lapels casually turned back. However, with the haughty features of suppressed passion, which gave a youthful blackness to the eyes and eyebrows of this no-longer-young woman, the extent of her indifference to what she was or was not wearing was clearly written on her face.

But the appearance of Pamphil's wife astonished Yuri Andreevich. He barely recognised her. She had aged terribly in a few days. Her bulging eyes were ready to pop from their sockets. On her neck, stretched like a shaft, a swollen vein throbbed. That was what her secret fears had done to her.

'She gives no milk, my dear,' said Agafya. 'I thought she was in between, but no, it's long since time for milk, but she's still milkless.'

'In between, hah! Look, there's an anthrax sore on her teat. I'll give you some herbal ointment to rub in. And, needless to say, I'll whisper in her ear.'

'I've got another trouble – my husband.'

'I can put a charm on him to stop him playing around. It can be done. He'll stick to you, there'll be no tearing him off. Tell me your third trouble.'

'He doesn't play around. It'd be good if he did. The trouble's just the opposite, that he clings to me and the children with all his might, his soul pines for us. I know what he thinks. He thinks they'll separate the camps, and we'll be sent the other way. Basalygo's men will lay hands on us, and he won't be there to protect us. They'll torture us and laugh at our torments. I know his thoughts. He may do something to himself.'

'I'll think on it. We'll quench your grief. Tell me your third trouble.'

'There is no third. It's just the cow and my husband.'

'You're poor in troubles, mother! See how merciful God is to you. Couldn't find your like with a candle in daylight. Two sorrows on your poor little head, and one of them's a pitying husband. What'll you give for the cow? And I'll start reciting.'

'What do you want?'

'A loaf of bread and your husband.'

People burst out laughing around them.

'Are you making fun of me?'

'Well, if that's too much, I'll knock off the bread. We'll settle on the husband alone.'

The laughter around them increased tenfold.

'What's the name? Not the husband's, the cow's.'

'Beauty.'

'Half the herd here is called Beauty. Well, all right. God bless us.'

And she began to recite a spell on the cow. At first her sorcery really had to do with cattle. Then she got carried away and gave Agafya a whole lesson in magic and its use. Yuri Andreevich listened spellbound to this delirious tissue, as he had once listened to the flowery babble of the driver Vakkh, when they came from European Russia to Siberia.

The army wife was saying:

'Auntie Morgesya, come be our guest. Not tomorrow but today, take the sickness away. Frumpkin, mumpkin, away with the lumpkin. Beauty, don't flinch, you'll tip over the bench. Forget your bad dream and give us a stream. Witchery, twitchery, stir your kettles, scrape off the scab and throw it in the nettles. Sharp as a sword is the wisewoman's word.

'You've got to know everything, Agafyushka, biddings, forbiddings, spells for avoiding, spells for defending. You look now and think it's the forest. But it's the unclean powers coming to meet the angelic host, just like ours with Basalygo's.

'Or, for instance, look where I'm pointing. Not there, my dear. Look with your eyes, not with the back of your head, look where I point my finger. There, there. What do you think it is? You think it's the wind twisty-twining one birch branch around another? You think it's a bird decided to build a nest? As if it was. That's a real devilish thing. It's a water nymph making a wreath for her daughter. She heard people going by and left off. Got scared. At night she'll finish plaiting it, you'll see.

'Or, again, take your red banner. What do you think? You think it's a flag? And yet, see, it's not a flag at all, it's the plaguie-girl's fetching raspberry kerchief – fetching, I say, and why is it fetching? To wave and wink at the young lads, to fetch young lads for the slaughter, for death, to inflict the plague on them. And you believed it was a flag – come to me, prolety and poorlety of all lands.

'Now you've got to know everything, Mother Agafya, everything, everything, and I mean everything. What bird, what stone, what herb. A bird, now, for instance – that bird there would be a fairy-starling. That animal there would be a badger.

'Now, for instance, if you've a mind to make love to somebody, just say so. I'll cast a pining spell on anybody you like. Your chief here, the Forester, if you like, or Kolchak, or Ivan Tsarevich.[4] You think I'm boasting, lying? But I'm not lying. Well, look, listen. Winter will come, the blizzard will send whirlwinds thronging over the fields, it will spin up pillars. And into that snowy pillar, into that snow-whirl I'll stick a knife for you, plunge it into the snow up to the hilt, and pull it out of the snow all red with blood. Have you ever seen such a thing? Eh? And you thought I was lying. And how is it, tell me, that blood can come from a stormy whirl? Isn't it just wind, air, snowy powder? But the fact is, my pet, that the storm is not wind, it's a changeling she-werewolf that's lost her young one, and searches for him in the field, and weeps because she can't find him. And my knife will go into her. That's why the blood. And with this knife I'll cut out the footprint of anybody you like, and take it and sew it to your hem with silk. And be it Kolchak, or Strelnikov, or some new tsar, he'll follow in your tracks wherever you go. And you thought I was lying, you thought – come to me, barefooty and prolety of all lands.

'Or else, for instance, stones fall from the sky now, fall like rain. A man steps out of his house and stones fall on him. Or some have seen horsemen riding in the sky, the horses touching the rooftops with their hooves. Or there were magicians in olden times would discover: this woman's got grain in her, or honey, or marten fur. And the knights in armour would bare the woman's shoulder, like opening a coffer, and with a sword take from her shoulder blade a measure of wheat, or a squirrel, or a honeycomb.'

A great and powerful feeling is sometimes met with in the world. There is always an admixture of pity in it. The object of our adoration seems the more the victim to us, the more we love. In some men compassion for a woman goes beyond all conceivable limits. Their responsiveness places her in unrealisable positions, not to be found in the world, existing only in imagination, and on account of her they are jealous of the surrounding air, of the laws of nature, of the millennia that went by before her.

Yuri Andreevich was educated enough to suspect in the sorceress's last words the beginning of some chronicle, the Novgorod or the Ipatyev,[5] which layers of distortion had rendered apocryphal. For centuries they had been mangled by witch doctors and storytellers, who transmitted them orally from generation to generation. Still earlier they had been confused and garbled by scribes.

Why, then, did the tyranny of the legend fascinate him so? Why did he react to the unintelligible nonsense, to the senseless fable, as if it were a statement of reality?

Lara's left shoulder had been opened. As a key is put into the secret door of an iron safe built into a cupboard, her shoulder blade had been unlocked by the turn of a sword. In the depths of the revealed inner cavity, the secrets kept by her soul appeared. Strange towns she had visited, strange streets, strange houses, strange expanses drew out in ribbons, in unwinding skeins of ribbons, ribbons spilling out in bundles.

Oh, how he loved her! How beautiful she was! Just as he had always thought and dreamed, as he had needed! But in what, in which side of her? In anything that could be named or singled out by examination? Oh, no, no! But in that incomparably simple and impetuous line with which the

Creator had outlined her entirely at one stroke, from top to bottom, and in that divine contour had handed her to his soul, like a just-bathed child tightly wrapped in linen.

But now where is he and how is it with him? Forest, Siberia, partisans. They are surrounded, and he will share the common lot. What devilry, what fantasy! And again things grew dim in Yuri Andreevich's eyes and head. Everything swam before him. At that moment, instead of the expected snow, rain began to drizzle. Like a poster on an enormous length of fabric stretched over a city street, there hung in the air from one side of the forest clearing to the other the diffuse, greatly magnified phantom of an astonishing, adored head. And the head wept, and the increasing rain kissed it and poured over it.

'Go,' the sorceress said to Agafya, 'I've put a spell on your cow, she'll get well. Pray to the Mother of God. For she is the chamber of light and the book of the living word.'[6]

8

Fighting was going on at the western border of the taiga. But the taiga was so immense that it all seemed to be playing out at the far confines of the state, and the camp lost in its thicket was so populous that, however many of its men went to fight, still more always remained, and it was never empty.

The noise of the distant battle barely reached the thick of the camp. Suddenly several shots rang out in the forest. They followed each other in quick succession and all at once turned into rapid, disorderly gunfire. Those surprised in the place where the shooting was heard dashed off in all directions. Men from the camp reserves ran to their carts. Turmoil ensued. Everyone began to put themselves into military readiness.

Soon the turmoil died down. It turned out to be a false alarm. But now again people began streaming towards the place where the shooting had been. The crowd grew. New people joined those already there.

The crowd surrounded a bloody human stump that was lying on the ground. The mutilated man was still breathing. He had had his right arm and left leg chopped off. It was inconceivable how, with his remaining arm and leg, the wretch had managed to crawl to the camp. The chopped-off arm and leg, terrible, bloody lumps, were tied to his back, as was a wooden plank with a long inscription which, among choice curses, said that this had been done in revenge for the atrocities of such-and-such Red detachment, to which the partisans of the Forest Brotherhood had no relation. Besides which, it was added that the same would be done to all of them, unless the partisans submitted by the term stated and laid down their arms before the representatives of the troops of Vitsyn's corps.

Bleeding profusely, faltering, with a weak voice and a thick tongue, losing consciousness every moment, the mangled, suffering man told of the tortures and ordeals in the court-martial and punitive units to the rear of General Vitsyn. The hanging to which he had been condemned had been replaced, in the guise of mercy, by cutting off his arm and leg and sending him to the partisan camp to terrify them. He had been carried as far as the advance posts of the camp's sentry line, then put on the ground and told to crawl by himself, while they urged him on from a distance by firing in the air.

The tortured man could barely move his lips. To make out his indistinct mumbling, they bent down and leaned over him to listen. He was saying:

'Watch out, brothers. He's broken through you.'

'We've sent a covering detachment. There's a big fight there. We'll hold him.'

'A breakthrough. A breakthrough. He wants to do it unexpectedly. I know. Aie, I can't go on, brothers. See, I'm losing blood, I'm spitting blood. It's all over for me.'

'Lie there, catch your breath. Keep quiet. Don't let him talk, you brutes! You see it's bad for him.'

'He didn't leave a living spot on me, the bloodsucker, the dog. You'll bathe in your own blood for me, he says, tell me who you are. And how can I tell him, brothers, when I'm a real diselter if there ever was one. Yes. I went over from him to you.'

'You keep saying "him". Which of them worked on you like this?'

'Aie, brothers, my insides are on fire. Let me catch my breath a little. I'll tell you right now. The ataman Bekeshin. Colonel Strese. Vitsyn's men. You here in the forest don't know anything. There's groaning in the city. They boil iron out of living people. They cut living people up for straps. They drag you who knows where by the scruff of the neck. It's pitch-dark. You feel around – it's a cage, a railroad carriage. More than forty people in just their underwear. The cage keeps opening and a paw comes in. The first one it falls on. Out he goes. Same as a chicken to be slaughtered. By God. One gets hanged, another gets a bayonet, another gets interrogated. They beat you to a pulp, sprinkle salt on your wounds, pour boiling water over you. If you puke or shit your pants, they make you eat it. And what they do with little kids, with women – oh, Lord!'

The wretched man was at his last gasp. He did not finish, cried out, and gave up the ghost. Somehow they all understood it at once and began taking their hats off and crossing themselves.

In the evening more news, much more horrible than this, spread through the camp.

Pamphil Palykh had been in the crowd that stood around the dying man. He had seen him, heard his story, read the inscription full of threats on the plank.

His constant fear for the fate of his family in case of his death came over him to an unprecedented degree. In imagination he already saw them handed over to slow torture, saw their faces disfigured by torment, heard their moans and calls for help. To deliver them from future sufferings and shorten his own, in a frenzy of anguish he finished them off himself. He cut down his wife and three children with that same razor-sharp axe with which he had carved wooden toys for the girls and his beloved son, Flenushka.[7]

It is astonishing that he did not lay hands on himself right after he did it. What was he thinking of? What could lie ahead for him? What prospects, what intentions? He was clearly deranged, an irrevocably finished being.

While Liberius, the doctor, and the members of the military council sat discussing what was to be done with him, he wandered freely about the camp, his head lolling on his chest, looking from under his brows with his dull yellow eyes and seeing nothing. A witless, vagrant smile of inhuman, invincible suffering never left his face.

No one pitied him. Everyone recoiled from him. Voices were raised calling for lynch law against him. They were not seconded.

There was nothing for him to do in the world. At dawn he disappeared from the camp, as an animal maddened by rabies flees from its own self.

9

Winter had long since come. It was freezing cold. Torn-up sounds and forms appeared with no evident connection from the frosty mist, stood, moved, vanished. Not the sun we are accustomed to on earth, but the crimson ball of some other substitute sun hung in the forest. From it, strainedly and slowly, as in a dream or a fairy tale, rays of amber yellow light, thick as honey, spread and on their way congealed in the air and froze to the trees.

Barely touching the ground with rounded soles, and at each step awakening a fierce creaking of the snow, invisible feet in felt boots moved in all directions, while the figures attached to them, in hoods and sheepskin jackets, floated through the air separately, like luminaries circling through the heavenly sphere.

Acquaintances stopped, got into conversation. They brought their faces close to each other, crimson as in a bathhouse, with frozen scrub brushes of beards and moustaches. Billows of dense, viscous steam escaped in clouds from their mouths and in their enormity were incommensurate with the frugal, as if frostbitten, words of their laconic speech.

On a footpath Liberius and the doctor ran into each other.

'Ah, it's you? Long time no see! I invite you to my dugout this evening. Spend the night. We'll talk, just like the old days. There's new information.'

'The messenger's back? Any news of Varykino?'

'The report doesn't make a peep about my family or yours. But I draw comforting conclusions precisely from that. It means they saved themselves in time. Otherwise there would have been mention of them. Anyhow, we'll talk about it when we meet. So I'll be waiting for you.'

In the dugout the doctor repeated his question:

'Just tell me, what do you know about our families?'

'Again you don't want to look beyond your nose. Ours are evidently alive, in safety. But they're not the point. There's splendid news. Want some meat? Cold veal.'

'No, thanks. Don't get sidetracked. Stick to business.'

'Big mistake. I'll have a go at it. There's scurvy in the camp. People have forgotten what bread and vegetables are. We should have done better at organising the gathering of nuts and berries in the autumn, while the refugee women were here. I was saying, our affairs are in splendid shape. What I've always predicted has come true. The ice has broken. Kolchak is retreating on all fronts. It's a total, spontaneously unfolding defeat. You see? What did I say? And you kept whining.'

'When did I whine?'

'All the time. Especially when we were pressed by Vitsyn.'

The doctor recalled that past autumn, the execution of the rebels, Palykh's murder of his wife and children, the bloody carnage and human slaughter of which no end was in sight. The atrocities of the Whites and the Reds rivalled each other in cruelty, increasing in turns as if multiplied by each other. The blood was nauseating, it rose to your throat and got into your head, your eyes were swollen with it. This was not whining at all, it was something else entirely. But how explain it to Liberius?

There was a smell of fragrant smoke in the dugout. It settled on the palate, tickled the nose and throat. The dugout was lighted by paper-thin splinters set in an iron trivet on a tripod. When one went out, the burnt end fell into a bowl of water underneath, and Liberius set up and lit a new one.

'See what I'm burning. We're out of oil. The wood's too dry. The splinter burns up quickly. Yes, there's scurvy in the camp. You categorically refuse the veal? Scurvy. Where are you looking, doctor? Why don't you gather the staff, shed light on the situation, give a lecture to the superiors about scurvy and the means of fighting it?'

'Don't torment me, for God's sake. Exactly what do you know about our families?'

'I've already told you that there's no exact information about them. But I didn't finish telling you what I know of the general military news. The civil war is over. Kolchak is utterly crushed. The Red Army is driving him down the railroad line, to the east, to throw him into the sea. Another part of the Red Army is hastening to join us, so that together we can start destroying his many scattered units in the rear. The south of Russia has been cleared. Why aren't you glad? Isn't that enough for you?'

'Not true. I am glad. But where are our families?'

'They're not in Varykino, and that's a great blessing. As I supposed, Kamennodvorsky's summer legends – remember those stupid rumours about the invasion of Varykino by some mysterious race of people? – have not been confirmed, but the place is completely deserted. Something seems to have happened there after all, and it's very good that both families got away in good time. Let's believe they're safe. According to my intelligence, that's the assumption of the few people left.'

'And Yuriatin? What's going on there? Whose hands is it in?'

'Also something incongruous. Undoubtedly a mistake.'

'What, precisely?'

'Supposedly the Whites are still there. It's absolutely absurd, a sheer impossibility. I'll make that obvious to you right now.'

Liberius set up a new splinter and, folding a crumpled, tattered, large-scale map so that the right section showed and unnecessary parts were turned back, began to explain, pencil in hand.

'Look. In all these sectors the Whites have been driven back. Here, and here, and here, all around. Are you following attentively?'

'Yes.'

'They can't be towards Yuriatin. Otherwise, with their communications cut, they'd inevitably fall into a trap. Their generals can't fail to understand that, however giftless they are. You're putting your coat on? Where are you going?'

'Excuse me for a moment. I'll be right back. It smells of shag and wood fumes here. I don't feel well. I'll catch my breath outside.'

Climbing up and out of the dugout, the doctor used his mitten to brush the snow off the thick log placed by the entrance as a seat. He sat down on it, leaned forward, and, propping his head in both hands, fell to thinking. As if there had been no winter taiga, no forest camp, no eighteen months spent with the partisans. He forgot about them. Only his family stood there in his imagination. He made conjectures about them, one more terrible than the other.

Here is Tonya going across a field in a blizzard with Shurochka in her arms. She wraps him in a blanket, her feet sink into the snow, she barely manages to pull them out, and the snowstorm covers her, the wind throws her to the ground, she falls and gets up, too weak to stand on her legs, weakened and giving way under her. Oh, but he keeps forgetting, forgetting. She has two children, and she is nursing the younger one. Both her arms are taken up, like the refugee women of Chilimka who lost their minds from grief and a strain that was beyond their endurance.

Both her arms are taken up, and there is no one around who can help. No one knows where Shurochka's papa is. He is far away, always far away, apart from them all his life, and is he a papa, are real papas like that? And where is her own father? Where is Alexander Alexandrovich? Where is Nyusha? Where are all the rest? Oh, better not to ask yourself these questions, better not to think, better not to go into it.

The doctor got up from the log, intending to go down into the dugout. Suddenly his thoughts took a different direction. He decided not to go back down to Liberius.

He had long ago stashed away some skis, a bag of rusks, and everything necessary for an escape. He had buried these things in the snow outside the guarded boundary of the camp, under a big silver fir, which he had also marked with a special notch to be sure. He headed there, down a footpath trampled in the snowdrifts. It was a clear night. A full moon was shining. The doctor knew where the guards were posted for the night and successfully avoided them. But by the clearing with the ice-covered rowan tree a sentry called to him from a distance and, standing straight on his skis as they gathered momentum, came gliding towards him.

'Stop or I'll shoot! Who are you? Give the password.'

'What, are you out of your mind, brother? It's me. Don't you recognise me? I'm your Doctor Zhivago.'

'Sorry! Don't be angry, Comrade Zhivak. I didn't recognise you. But even though you're Zhivak, I won't let you go any further. Everything's got to be done right.'

'Well, as you will. The password is "Red Siberia", and the response is "Down with the interventionists".'

'That's another story. Go wherever you like. Why the devil are you wandering about at night? Sick people?'

'I'm not sleepy, and I got thirsty. I thought I might stroll about and eat some snow. I saw this rowan tree with frozen berries on it. I wanted to go and chew some.'

'There's a squire's whim for you, to go berrying in winter. Three years we've been beating and beating, and haven't beaten it out of you. No consciousness. Go and get your rowan berries, oddball. What do I care?'

And, picking up more and more speed, the sentry went off, standing straight on his long, whistling skis, and moved away over the untouched snow further and further beyond the bare winter bushes, skimpy as balding heads. And the footpath the doctor was following brought him to the just-mentioned rowan tree.

It was half covered with snow, half with frozen leaves and berries, and it stretched out two snowy branches to meet him. He remembered Lara's big white arms, rounded, generous, and, taking hold of the branches, he pulled the tree towards him. As if in a conscious answering movement, the rowan showered him with snow from head to foot. He was murmuring, not realising what he was saying, and unaware of himself:

'I shall see you, my beauty, my princess, my dearest rowan tree, my own heart's blood.'

The night was clear. The moon was shining. He made his way deeper into the taiga, to his secret silver fir, dug up his things, and left the camp.

Part Thirteen

OPPOSITE THE HOUSE WITH FIGURES

I

Bolshaya Kupecheskaya Street descended the crooked hill to Malaya Spasskaya and Novosvalochny. The houses and churches of the higher parts of the town peered down on it.

At the corner stood the dark grey house with figures. The huge quadrangular stones of its foundation, cut on a slant, were blackened with freshly pasted-up issues of government newspapers, government decrees and resolutions. Stopping for a long time on the sidewalk, small groups of passers-by silently read this literature.

It was dry after the recent thaw. Turning cold. The frost was noticeably hardening. It was quite light at a time when, just recently, it would have been getting dark. Winter had recently departed. The emptiness of the vacated space was filled with light, which would not go away and lingered through the evenings. It stirred you, drew you into the distance, frightened and alerted you.

The Whites had recently left the town, surrendering it to the Reds. The shooting, the bloodshed, the military alarms were over. That, too, frightened and alerted you, like the departure of winter and the augmentation of the spring days.

The notice that the passers-by in the street read by the light of the lengthened day announced:

'For the information of the populace. Work booklets for those eligible can be obtained for 50 rubles each in the Provisions Section of the Yuriatin City Council, at 5 Oktiabrskaya, formerly General-gubernatorskaya, Street, room 137.

'Non-possession of a work booklet, or incorrect or, still more so, false entries, will be punished with full wartime severity. Precise instructions for the use of work booklets are published in the BYEC, No. 86 (1013), of the current year and posted in the Provisions Section of the Yuriatin City Council, room 137.'

Another announcement reported on the sufficiency of food supplies available in the city, though they had supposedly been concealed by the bourgeoisie in order to disorganise distribution and sow chaos in the matter of provisioning. The announcement ended with the words:

'Those caught hoarding and concealing food supplies will be shot on the spot.'

A third announcement offered:

'In the interests of the correct organising of food distribution, those not belonging to exploiter elements are to unite into consumers' communes. Details can be obtained in the Provisions Section of the Yuriatin City Council, 5 Oktiabrskaya, formerly General-gubernatorskaya, Street, room 137.'

The military were warned:

'Those who have not surrendered their weapons or who carry them without a proper, newly issued permit, will be prosecuted with the full severity of the law. Permits can be exchanged in the Yuriatin Revolutionary Committee, 6 Oktiabrskaya, room 63.'

2

A wild-looking man with a sack on his back and a stick in his hand, emaciated, long unwashed, which made him look swarthy, came up to the group of readers. His long hair had no grey in it yet, but his dark blond beard was turning grey. It was Doctor Yuri Andreevich Zhivago. His winter coat had probably long since been taken off him on the way, or else he had traded it for food. He was in someone else's old clothes, with sleeves too short to keep him warm.

In his sack there remained an unfinished crust of bread, given him in the last outlying village he had passed through, and a hunk of lard. About an hour earlier, he had entered the city from the side of the railway, and it had taken him a whole hour of trudging to get from the city gates to this intersection, so weak he was and exhausted from walking the past few days. He stopped often and barely kept himself from falling to the ground and kissing the stones of the city, which he had had no hope of ever seeing again, and the sight of which delighted him as if it were a living being.

For a very long time, half his journey on foot, he had gone along the railroad tracks. It was all left in neglect and inactive, and all covered with snow.

His way had led him past whole trains of the White Army, passenger and freight, overtaken by snowdrifts, the general defeat of Kolchak, and the exhaustion of fuel supplies. These trains, stopped in their course, forever standing, and buried under snow, stretched in an almost unbroken ribbon for many dozens of miles. They served as strongholds for armed bands of highway robbers, a refuge for criminal and political fugitives in hiding, the involuntary vagabonds of that time, but most of all as common graves and collective burial sites for those who died of cold and the typhus that raged all along the railway line and mowed down whole villages in the area.

This time justified the old saying: Man is a wolf to man. A wayfarer turned aside at the sight of another wayfarer; a man would kill the man he met, so as not to be killed himself. There were isolated cases of cannibalism. The human laws of civilisation ended. Those of beasts were in force. Man dreamed the prehistoric dreams of the caveman.

Solitary shadows, occasionally sneaking along the roadside, fearfully crossing the path far ahead, and whom Yuri Andreevich carefully avoided when he could, often seemed familiar to him, seen somewhere. He fancied they belonged to the partisan camp. In most cases he was mistaken, but once his eye did not deceive him. The adolescent who crawled out of the snowdrift that covered the body of an international sleeping car, and who, having satisfied his need, darted back into the drift, was in fact from the Forest Brotherhood. He was Terenty Galuzin, supposedly shot dead. He had not been killed, had lain in a deep faint, come to, crawled from the place of execution, hidden in the forest, recovered from his wounds, and now, secretly, under another name, was making his way to his family in Krestovozdvizhensk, hiding from people in snowbound trains as he went.

These pictures and spectacles made the impression of something outlandish, transcendent. They seemed like parts of some unknown, otherplanetary existences, brought to earth by mistake. And only nature remained true to history and showed itself to the eye as the artists of modern times portrayed it.

There were some quiet winter evenings, light grey, dark pink. Against the pale sunset, black birch tops were outlined, fine as handwriting. Black streams flowed under a grey mist of thin ice, between banks of white heaped snow, moistened from beneath by dark river water. And now such an evening, frosty, transparently grey, tender-hearted as pussy-willow fluff, promised to settle in after an hour or two opposite the house with figures in Yuriatin.

The doctor was going up to the board of the Central Printing Office on the stone wall of the house to look over the official information. But his gaze kept falling on the other side and up towards the several windows on the second floor of the house opposite. These windows giving onto the street had once been painted over with whitewash. In the two rooms inside, the owners' furniture had been stored. Though frost covered the lower parts of the windowpanes with a thin, crystalline crust, he could see that the glass was now transparent and the whitewash had been removed. What did this change mean? Had the owners returned? Or had Lara gone away, and there were new tenants in the apartment, and everything in it was different now?

The uncertainty agitated the doctor. He was unable to control his agitation. He crossed the street, went into the hall through the front door, and began to go up the main stairs, so familiar and so dear to his heart. How often he had remembered, in the forest camp, the openwork pattern of the cast-iron steps, down to the last curlicue. At some turn of his ascent, as he looked through the openwork under his feet, he could see old buckets, tubs, and broken chairs piled up under the staircase. This repeated itself now, too. Nothing had changed, everything was as before. The doctor was almost grateful to the stairs for this faithfulness to the past.

Once there had been a doorbell. But it had broken and ceased to work already in former times, before the doctor's forest captivity. He was about to knock on the door, but noticed that it was locked in a new way, with a heavy padlock hanging on rings, crudely screwed into the panelling of the old oaken door, with its fine trimming fallen off in places. Formerly such barbarity had not been allowed. Locks had been mortised into the doorway and had worked well, and if they broke, locksmiths had existed to repair them. This insignificant detail spoke in its own way of a general, greatly advanced deterioration.

The doctor was certain that Lara and Katenka were not at home, and perhaps were not in Yuriatin, and perhaps were not even in this world. He was prepared for the most terrible disappointments. Only for the sake of a clear conscience, he decided to feel in the hole that he and Katenka had been so afraid of, and he tapped his foot on the wall, so that his hand would not come upon a rat in the opening. He had no hope of finding anything in the prearranged place. The hole was stopped up with a brick. Yuri Andreevich removed the brick and stuck his hand inside. Oh, wonder! A key and a note. A rather long note on a big piece of paper. The doctor went over to the window on the landing. A still greater wonder, still more incredible! The note was written to him! He read quickly:

'Lord, what happiness! They say you're alive and have turned up. They saw you in the neighbourhood and came running to tell me. Supposing you'd hurry to Varykino first of all, I'm going there myself with Katenka. In any case the key is in the usual place. Wait for me to come back, don't go anywhere. Ah, yes, you don't know, I'm now in the front part of the apartment, in the rooms that give onto the street. But you'll figure that out yourself. The house is empty, there's lots of room, I had to sell part of the owners' furniture. I'm leaving some food, mostly boiled potatoes. Put an iron or something heavy on the lid of the pot, as I've done, to protect it from the rats. I'm out of my mind with joy.'

Here ended the front side of the note. The doctor did not notice that there was writing on the other side of the paper. He brought the page unfolded on his palm to his lips and then, without looking, folded it and put it in his pocket along with the key. A terrible, wounding pain was mixed with his mad joy. Since she had gone straight to Varykino, without any hesitation, it meant that his family was not there. Besides the anxiety this detail caused him, he also felt an unbearable pain and sadness for his family. Why did she not say a word about them and where they were, as if they did not exist at all?

But there was no time for thinking. It was beginning to get dark outside. He had to do many things while there was still light. Not the least concern was familiarising himself with the decrees posted in the street. This was a serious time. Out of ignorance, you could pay with your life for violating some mandatory decree. And not opening the apartment and not taking the sack from his weary shoulder, he went down and outside and approached the wall pasted all over with printed matter.

3

This printed matter consisted of newspaper articles, the records of speeches at meetings, and decrees. Yuri Andreevich glanced cursorily at the titles. 'On the Rules of the Requisition and Taxation of the Propertied Classes'. 'On Workers' Control'. 'On Factory Committees'. These were the instructions of the new power that had come to the town to abolish the preceding order found there. They were a reminder of the immutability of its foundations, perhaps forgotten by the inhabitants during the temporary rule of the Whites. But Yuri Andreevich's head began to spin from the endlessness of these monotonous repetitions. What year did these headlines belong to? The time of the first upheaval, or a later period, after some intervening rebellions of the Whites? What were these inscriptions? From last year? The year before last? At one time in his life he had admired the unconditional quality of this language and the directness of this thinking. Could it be that he had to pay for this imprudent admiration by never seeing anything else in his life but these frenzied cries and demands, unchanging in the course of long years, becoming ever more impractical, incomprehensible, and unfeasible? Could it be that for a moment of too-broad sympathy he had enslaved himself forever?

He came upon a fragment from some report. He read:

'Information about famine testifies to the incredible inactivity of the local organisations. The facts of abuse are obvious, the speculation is monstrous, but what has been done by the bureau of the local trade union leaders, what has been done by the heads of municipal and regional factory committees? Unless we conduct massive searches in the warehouses of the Yuriatin freight station and along the Yuriatin–Razvilye and Razvilye–Rybalka lines, unless we take severe measures of terror, down to shooting speculators on the spot, there will be no escape from famine.'

'What enviable blindness!' thought the doctor. 'What bread are they talking about, when there has long been none in nature? What propertied classes, what speculators, when they've long been abolished by the sense of previous decrees? What peasants, what villages, if they no longer exist? What obliviousness to their own designs and measures, which have long left no stone upon stone in life! What must one be, to rave year after year with delirious feverishness about non-existent, long-extinct themes, and to know nothing, to see nothing around one!'

The doctor's head was spinning. He fainted and fell unconscious on the pavement. When he came to his senses, people helped him to get up and offered to take him wherever he indicated. He thanked them and declined the help, explaining that he only had to go across the street.

4

He went up the stairs again and started opening the door to Lara's apartment. It was still quite light on the landing, not a bit darker than when he had first gone up. He noted with grateful joy that the sun was not hurrying him.

The click of the unlocking door caused turmoil inside. The space left empty in the absence of people met him with the clanging and rattling of overturned and falling tin cans. Rats fell smack on the floor and scattered in all directions. The doctor felt ill at ease from a sense of helplessness before these loathsome creatures, which probably bred here by the thousand.

And before making any attempt to settle down for the night, he decided first of all to protect himself from this pestilence, and, finding some easily isolated and tightly closing door, to stop all the rat holes with broken glass and scraps of sheet metal.

From the front hall he turned left, to a part of the apartment unknown to him. Passing through a dark room, he found himself in a bright one, with two windows giving onto the street. Just opposite the windows, on the other side, the house with figures stood darkly. The lower part of its wall was pasted over with newspapers. Their backs to the windows, passers-by stood reading the newspapers.

The light in the room and outside was one and the same, the young, unseasoned evening light of early spring. The commonality of the light inside and outside was so great that it was as if there were no separation between the room and the street. Only in one thing was there a slight difference. In Lara's bedroom, where Yuri Andreevich was standing, it was colder than outside on Kupecheskaya.

When Yuri Andreevich was nearing town during his last march, and was walking through it an hour or two earlier, the immense increase of his weakness had seemed to him the sign of an imminently threatening illness, and it had frightened him.

Now the uniformity of light in the house and in the open delighted him for no reason. The column of cold air, one and the same outside and inside, made him akin to the passers-by in the evening street, to the moods of the town, to life in the world. His fears went away. He no longer thought he would fall ill. The evening transparency of the all-pervading spring light seemed to him a pledge of distant and generous hopes. He believed that everything was for the better, that he would achieve everything in life, would find and reconcile everybody, would think everything through and express it. And he waited for the joy of seeing Lara as for the nearest proof.

Mad excitement and unbridled restlessness replaced his previously failing strength. This animation was a surer symptom of beginning illness than the recent weakness. Yuri Andreevich could not stay put. He was again drawn outside, and here is the reason why.

Before settling himself in here, he wanted to have his hair cut and his beard shaved. With that in mind, he looked into the windows of the former barbershops as he went through the city. Some of them were empty or occupied by other businesses. Others, which corresponded to their former purpose, were under lock and key. There was nowhere for him to have a shave and a haircut. Yuri Andreevich had no razor of his own. Scissors, if he could find Lara's, might help him out of his difficulty. But, rummaging through everything in her dressing table with nervous haste, he did not find any scissors.

He remembered that there had once been a sewing shop on Malaya Spasskaya. He thought that, if the establishment had not ceased to exist and still went on working, and if he managed to get there before they closed, he could ask one of the seamstresses for scissors. And he went out again.

5

His memory had not deceived him. The shop was still in its former place; the work went on. The shop occupied a commercial space on the ground floor, with a window running the whole width of it and an entrance from the street. Through the window one could see inside to the opposite wall. The seamstresses worked in full view of the passers-by.

The room was terribly crowded. In addition to the actual workers, some amateur seamstresses, ageing ladies from Yuriatin society, had probably got places in order to obtain the work booklets spoken of in the decree on the wall of the house with figures.

Their movements could be distinguished at once from the efficiency of the real seamstresses. The shop worked only for the army, making padded trousers, quilted coats and jackets, and such clownish-looking overcoats as Yuri Andreevich had already seen in the partisan camp, tacked together from dog pelts of different colours. The clumsy fingers of the amateur seamstresses had a hard time doing the unaccustomed near-furrier's work, as they put the edges turned back for hemming under the needles of the sewing machines.

Yuri Andreevich knocked on the window and made a sign with his hand to be let in. He was answered in signs that orders were not taken from private persons. Yuri Andreevich would not give up and, repeating the same gestures, insisted that he should be let in and listened to. By negative gestures he was given to understand that they had urgent business and he should leave off, not bother them, and go on his way. One of the seamstresses showed perplexity on her face and in a sign of vexation held her hand out palm up, asking with her eyes what, in fact, he wanted. With two fingers, index and middle, he showed the cutting movement of scissors. His gesture was not understood. They decided it was some sort of indecency, that he was teasing them and flirting with them. With his ragged look and strange behaviour, he made the impression of a sick or crazy man. In the shop they giggled, exchanged laughs, and waved their hands, driving him away from the window. It finally occurred to him to look for the way through the courtyard, and, having found it and the door to the shop, he knocked at the back entrance.

6

The door was opened by an elderly, dark-faced seamstress in a dark dress, stern, perhaps the head of the establishment.

'Look, what a bother! A real punishment. Well, be quick, what do you want? I have no time.'

'I need scissors. Don't be surprised. I want to ask to use them for a moment. I'll cut my beard here in front of you and give them back with gratitude.'

Mistrustful astonishment showed in the seamstress's eyes. It was undisguisedly clear that she doubted the mental faculties of her interlocutor.

'I come from far away. I've just arrived in town. I'm overgrown. I'd like to have my hair cut. But there isn't a single barbershop. I think I could do it myself, but I don't have any scissors. Lend them to me, please.'

'All right. I'll give you a haircut. Only watch yourself. If you've got something else on your mind, some clever trick, changing your looks as a disguise, something political, don't blame us. We won't sacrifice our lives for you, we'll complain in the proper place. It's no time for things like that.'

'Good heavens, what fears you have!'

The seamstress let the doctor in, took him to a side room no wider than a cupboard, and a minute later he was sitting on a chair, as in a barbershop, all wrapped in a sheet that was tight on his neck and tucked in behind his collar.

The seamstress went to fetch her instruments and a little later came back with scissors, a comb, several clippers of different sizes, a strop and a razor.

'I've tried everything in my life,' she explained, seeing how amazed the doctor was that all this turned out to be in readiness. 'I used to work as a barber. During the war, as a nurse, I learned how to shave and give haircuts. First we'll chop the beard off with scissors, and then we'll shave it clean.'

'And when it comes to the hair, cut it short, please.'

'I'll try. Such an intellectual, and pretending to be a know-nothing! We don't count in weeks now, but in tens of days. Today is the seventeenth, and on numbers with a seven barbers have the day off. As if you didn't know.'

'I honestly didn't. Why should I pretend? I told you. I come from far away. I'm not from here.'

'Sit still. Don't jump. It's easy to get cut. So you're a newcomer? How did you get here?'

'On my own two feet.'

'Along the high road?'

'Partly, and the rest by the railway line. There's no end of trains under the snow! All sorts, deluxe, special.'

'Well, there's just a little bit left. I'll snip it off, and that's it. On family business?'

'What family business! I was working for the former union of credit associations. A travelling agent. They sent me around on inspection. I got stuck devil knows where in eastern Siberia. No way to get back. There are no trains. I had to go on foot, no help for it. I walked for a month and a half. The things I've seen, it would take more than a lifetime to tell.'

'And you oughtn't to tell. I'm going to teach you a bit of wisdom. Now wait. Here's a mirror. Take your hand from under the sheet and hold it. Look at yourself. Well, how do you find it?'

'I think you've cut too little. It could be shorter.'

'It won't hold its shape. As I said, you oughtn't to tell anything. It's better to keep mum about all that now. Credit associations, deluxe trains under the snow, agents and inspections – it's better if you even forget the words. You'll get into a real mess with them! Don't put your foot in it, it's not the season. Better lie that you're a doctor or a teacher. Well, there, I've chopped your beard off roughly, now we'll give you a real shave. We'll soap you up, zip-zap, and you'll get ten years younger. I'll go and put some water on to boil.'

'Who is this woman!' the doctor thought while she was away. 'There's a feeling that we may have some points of contact and I should know her. Something I've seen or heard. She probably reminds me of someone. But, devil take it, who precisely?'

The seamstress returned.

'Well, now we'll have a shave. Yes, so it's better never to say anything unnecessary. That's the eternal truth. Silence is golden. About those special trains and credit associations. Better to invent something about being a doctor or a teacher. And as for seeing all sorts of sights, keep it to yourself. Who'll be surprised at it now? Does the razor bother you?'

'It hurts a little.'

'It scrapes, it must scrape, I know. Bear with it, dearie. No way to avoid it. Your hair has grown and turned coarse, the skin's not used to it. Yes. Sights won't surprise anybody now. People have been tried and tested. We've drunk our cup of grief. Such things went on here under the Whites! Robberies, murders, abductions. Hunting people down. For instance, there was this petty satrap, from Sapunov's men, and, you see, he took a dislike to a certain lieutenant. He sends soldiers to ambush him near the Zagorodny woods, across from Krapulsky's house. He's disarmed and taken under escort to Razvilye. And Razvilye at that time was the same for us as the provincial Cheka is now. Golgotha. Why are you shaking your head? Scrapes, does it? I know, dearie, I know. Nothing to be done. Here I've got to shave against the grain, and your hair's stiff as bristles. Stiff. A tricky place. His wife is in hysterics. The lieutenant's wife. "Kolya! My Kolya!" And goes straight to the chief. Only "straight" is just a manner of speaking. Who's going to let her? Connections. A woman on the next street had access to the chief and interceded for everybody. He was an exceptionally humane man, not like the others, compassionate. General Galiullin. And all around there was lynch law, atrocities, dramas of jealousy. Just like in Spanish novels.'

'She's talking about Lara,' the doctor guessed, but by way of precaution he said nothing and did not enter into more detailed questioning. Yet when she said 'Just like in Spanish novels', she again reminded him terribly of someone. Precisely by this inappropriate phrase, spoken out of place.

'Now, of course, it's quite a different story. Let's say there's still more than enough investigations, denunciations, executions even now. But the idea is totally different. First, they're new to power. They've been ruling less than no time, they still haven't acquired a taste for it. Second, whatever you may say, they're for the simple folk, that's where their strength lies. There were four of us sisters, including me. And all working women. Naturally we lean towards the Bolsheviks. One sister died, she was married to a political. Her husband worked as a manager at one of the local factories. Their son, my nephew, is the leader of our village rebels – a celebrity, you might say.'

'So that's what it is!' it dawned on Yuri Andreevich. 'She's Liberius's aunt, Mikulitsyn's notorious sister-in-law, hairdresser, seamstress, switchwoman, a jack-of-all-trades whom everybody knows. I'll keep quiet like before, however, so as not to give myself away.'

'My nephew was drawn to the people from childhood. He grew up near his father, among the workers at the Mighty Sviatogor. The Varykino factories, maybe you've heard of them? Ah, what are we doing, the two of us! I'm a forgetful fool! Half the chin's smooth, the other half unshaven. I'm talking away. And what are you doing, not stopping me? The soap on your face has dried up. I'll go and heat some water. It's grown cold.'

When Tuntseva came back, Yuri Andreevich asked:

'Varykino – it's some sort of blessed backwater, a wild place, where no shocks ever reach?'

'Well, "blessed", so to speak. That wild place got into maybe a worse pickle than we did. Some bands of men passed through Varykino, no one knows who. They didn't speak our language. They went from house to house, taking people out and shooting them. And then left without a word.

The bodies just stayed there unattended on the snow. It happened in the winter. Why do you keep jumping all the time? I almost cut your throat with the razor.'

'But you said your brother-in-law lived in Varykino. Did he, too, suffer from these horrors?'

'No, why? God is merciful. He and his wife got out of there in time. The new wife, the second one. Where they are, nobody knows, but it's certain they're safe. Recently there were new people there. A Moscow family, visitors. They left even earlier. The younger man, a doctor, the head of the family, disappeared without a trace. Well, what does it mean, "without a trace"? It's just a way of speaking, that it was without a trace, so as not to get upset. But in reality we've got to assume he's dead, killed. They searched and searched, but didn't find him. Meanwhile the other man, the older one, was called home. He's a professor. Of agronomy. I heard he got a summons from the government. They passed through Yuriatin before the Whites came for the second time. You're up to it again, dear comrade? If you fidget and jump like that under the razor, it won't be long before the client's throat is cut. You ask too much from a barber.'

'So they're in Moscow!'

7

'In Moscow! In Moscow!' echoed in his soul with every step, as he went up the cast-iron stairs for the third time. The empty apartment met him again with an uproar of leaping, tumbling, scattering rats. It was clear to Yuri Andreevich that he would not get a wink of sleep next to these vermin, however worn out he was. He began his preparations for the night by stopping up the rat holes. Fortunately, there were not so many of them in the bedroom, far less than in the rest of the apartment, where the floors and baseboards were in less good condition. But he had to hurry. Night was falling. True, there waited for him on the kitchen table, perhaps in expectation of his coming, a lamp taken down from the wall and half filled, and, next to it in an open matchbox, several matches, ten in number, as Yuri Andreevich counted. But the one and the other, the kerosene and the matches, he had better use sparingly. In the bedroom he also discovered a night lamp – a bowl with a wick and some traces of lamp oil, which the rats had probably drunk almost to the bottom.

In some places, the edges of the baseboards had come away from the floor. Yuri Andreevich filled the cracks with several layers of broken glass, the sharp ends pointing inwards. The bedroom door fitted well to the doorstep. It could be closed tightly and, when shut, totally separated the room with the stopped-up holes from the rest of the apartment. In a little more than an hour, Yuri Andreevich managed to do it all.

A tile stove cut off one corner of the bedroom, with a tile cornice that did not reach the ceiling. In the kitchen there was a supply of firewood, about ten bundles. Yuri Andreevich decided to rob Lara of a couple of armloads, and going on one knee, he began to pile the wood on his left arm. He brought it to the bedroom, set it down by the stove, familiarised himself with its mechanism, and quickly checked the condition it was in. He wanted to lock the door, but the lock turned out to be in disrepair, and therefore, tucking in some paper to make it tight and keep it from opening, Yuri Andreevich unhurriedly began making a fire in the stove.

While putting wood into the firebox, he saw a mark on the butt end of one of the logs. He recognised it with surprise. It was the trace of an old brand mark, the two initial letters K and D, which indicated what warehouse the logs came from before they were cut up. Long ago, when Krüger was still there, they had branded with these letters the ends of logs from the Kulabyshev plot in Varykino, when the factory sold off its extra unneeded fuel supplies.

The presence of this sort of firewood in Lara's household proved that she knew Samdevyatov and that he looked after her, just as he had once supplied all the needs of the doctor and his family. This discovery was a knife in the doctor's heart. He had been burdened by Anfim Efimovich's help even before. Now the embarrassment of these favours was complicated by other feelings.

It was unlikely that Anfim was Larissa Fyodorovna's benefactor just for the beauty of it. Yuri Andreevich pictured Anfim Efimovich's free and easy ways and Lara's recklessness as a woman. It could not be that there was nothing between them.

In the stove the dry Kulabyshev wood was beginning to burn furiously, with a concerted crackling, and as it caught fire, Yuri Andreevich's jealous blindness, having started from weak suppositions, arrived at complete certainty.

But his soul was tormented on all sides, and one pain came to replace another. He had no need to drive these suspicions away. His thoughts, without effort, of themselves, jumped from subject to subject. Reflections about his family, rushing upon him with renewed force, overshadowed his jealous fits for a time.

'So you're in Moscow, my dear ones?' It already seemed to him that Tuntseva had certified their safe arrival for him. 'Meaning that you repeated that

long, difficult trip without me? How was the journey? What sort of business
was Alexander Alexandrovich summoned for? Probably an invitation from
the Academy to start teaching there again? What did you find at home?
Come now, you don't mean that home still exists? Oh, Lord, how difficult
and painful! Oh, don't think, don't think! How confused my thoughts are!
What's wrong with me, Tonya? I seem to be falling ill. What will become of
me and of you all, Tonya, Tonechka, Tonya, Shurochka, Alexander Alexandrovich? O Light that never sets, why hast Thou rejected me from Thy presence?[1] Why are you borne away from me all my life? Why are we always
apart? But we'll soon be united, we'll come together, right? I'll reach you on
foot, if it can't be otherwise. We'll see each other. Everything will go well
again, right?

'But how can the earth not swallow me up, if I keep forgetting that Tonya
was supposed to give birth and probably did give birth? It's not
the first time that I've shown this forgetfulness. How did her delivery go?
How did she give birth? They stopped in Yuriatin on their way to Moscow.
True, Lara doesn't know them, but still this seamstress and hairdresser,
a total stranger, wasn't ignorant of their fate, yet Lara doesn't say a word
about them in her note. What strange inattention, smacking of indifference! As inexplicable as passing over in silence her relations with Samdevyatov.'

Here Yuri Andreevich looked around at the walls of the bedroom with a
different, discerning eye. He knew that, of the things standing or hanging
around him, not one belonged to Lara, and that the furnishings of the former owners, unknown and in hiding, in no way testified to Lara's taste.

But all the same, be that as it may, he suddenly felt ill at ease among the
men and women in enlarged photographs gazing from the walls. A spirit of
hostility breathed on him from the crude furnishings. He felt himself foreign
and superfluous in this bedroom.

And he, fool that he was, had remembered this house so many times, had
missed it, and had entered this room, not as a space, but as his yearning for
Lara! How ridiculous this way of feeling probably was from outside! Was
this how strong, practical people like Samdevyatov, handsome males, lived
and behaved and expressed themselves? And why should Lara prefer his
spinelessness and the obscure, unreal language of his adoration? Did she
have such need of this confusion? Did she herself want to be what she was
for him?

And what was she for him, as he had just put it? Oh, to this question he
always had the answer ready.

There outside is the spring evening. The air is all marked with sounds.

The voices of children playing are scattered at various distances, as if to signify that the space is alive throughout. And this expanse is Russia, his incomparable one, renowned far and wide, famous mother, martyr, stubborn, muddle-headed, whimsical, adored, with her eternally majestic and disastrous escapades, which can never be foreseen! Oh, how sweet it is to exist! How sweet to live in the world and to love life! Oh, how one always longs to say thank you to life itself, to existence itself, to say it right in their faces!

And that is what Lara is. It is impossible to talk to them, but she is their representative, their expression, the gift of hearing and speech, given to the voiceless principles of existence.

And untrue, a thousand times untrue, was all that he had said about her in a moment of doubt. How precisely perfect and irreproachable everything is in her!

Tears of admiration and repentance clouded his vision. He opened the door of the stove and stirred inside with a poker. He pushed the burning, pure heat to the very back of the firebox and moved the as yet unburnt logs towards the front, where the draught was stronger. For some time he did not close the door. He enjoyed feeling the play of warmth and light on his face and hands. The shifting glimmer of the flames finally sobered him. Oh, how he missed her now, how he needed at that moment something tangible that came from her!

He took her crumpled note from his pocket. He unfolded it the other side up, not the way he had read it earlier, and only now noticed that there was writing on the other side as well. Having smoothed out the crumpled paper, he read in the dancing light of the burning stove:

'About your family you know. They are in Moscow. Tonya gave birth to a daughter.' This was followed by several crossed-out lines. Then there was: 'I crossed it out, because it's silly in a note. We'll talk our fill face-to-face. I'm in a hurry, running to get a horse. I don't know what I'll do if I don't get one. With Katenka it will be hard . . .' The end of the phrase was smudged and he could not make it out.

'She ran to get a horse from Anfim, and probably got it, since she's gone,' Yuri Andreevich reflected calmly. 'If her conscience weren't completely clear on that account, she wouldn't have mentioned that detail.'

8

When the fire burned out, the doctor closed the flue and had a bite to eat. After eating he was overcome by a fit of invincible drowsiness. He lay down

on the sofa without undressing and fell fast asleep. He did not hear the deafening and shameless uproar the rats raised outside the door and walls of the
room. He had two oppressive dreams, one after the other.

He was in a room in Moscow, facing a glass door locked with a key,
which, to make sure, he also held shut by pulling the door handle towards
him. Outside the door, his boy Shurochka, in a child's coat, sailor's trousers
and hat, pretty and miserable, thrashed and wept, asking to be let in. Behind
the child, showering him and the door with spray, was a roaring and rumbling waterfall, either from burst pipes, an everyday phenomenon of that
epoch, or perhaps there really was some wild mountain gorge coming right
up to the door, with a furiously rushing stream and an age-old accumulation
of cold and darkness.

The crash and roar of falling water frightened the boy to death. What he
was crying could not be heard; the noise drowned out the boy's cries. But
Yuri Andreevich could see that his lips were forming the word 'Papa! Papa!'

Yuri Andreevich's heart was breaking. He wished with all his being to
seize the boy in his arms, press him to his breast, and run off with him without looking back. But, flooding himself with tears, he pulled the handle of
the locked door towards him, not letting the boy in, sacrificing him to falsely
understood feelings of honour and duty before another woman, who was
not the boy's mother and who at any moment might come into the room
from the other side.

Yuri Andreevich woke up in sweat and tears. 'I have a fever. I'm falling
ill,' he thought at once. 'It's not typhus. It's some sort of heavy, dangerous
fatigue that has taken the form of a sickness, some illness with a crisis, as in
all serious infections, and the whole question is what will win out, life or
death. But how I want to sleep!' And he fell asleep again.

He dreamed of a dark winter morning on a busy lit-up street in Moscow,
by all tokens before the revolution, judging by the early street animation,
the ringing of the first trams, the light of the street lamps that streaked with
yellow the grey, pre-dawn snow on the pavements.

He dreamed of a long, drawn-out apartment with many windows, all on
one side, low over the street, probably on the second floor, with curtains
lowered to the floor. In the apartment people in travelling clothes slept in
various postures without undressing, and there was disorder, as on a train,
leftover food on greasy, spread-out newspapers, gnawed bones of roast
chicken, wings and legs, lay about, and on the floor in pairs, taken off for
the night, stood the shoes of relatives and acquaintances, passers-by and
homeless people, come for a short stay. The hostess, Lara, in a hastily tied
dressing gown, rushed about the apartment from one end to the other,

bustling quickly and noiselessly, and he followed on her heels, being a nuisance, trying giftlessly and inappropriately to clarify something, and she no longer had a moment for him, and to all his explanations she merely responded in passing by turning her head to him, by quiet, perplexed glances and innocent bursts of her incomparable, silvery laughter, the only forms of intimacy still left to them. And how distant, cold, and attractive she was, to whom he had given everything, whom he preferred to everything, and in contrast to whom he diminished and depreciated everything!

9

Not he, but something more general than he, sobbed and wept in him with tender and bright words, which shone like phosphorus in the darkness. And together with his weeping soul, he himself wept. He felt sorry for himself.

'I'm falling ill, I am ill,' he reflected in moments of lucidity, between the spells of sleep, feverish raving, and oblivion. 'It's some kind of typhus after all, not described in textbooks, which we didn't study in medical school. I must prepare something, I must eat, otherwise I'll die of hunger.'

But at the first attempt to raise himself on one elbow, he became convinced that he had no strength to stir, and either lay in a faint or fell asleep.

'How long have I been lying here, still dressed?' he reflected in one of these flashes. 'How many hours? How many days? When I collapsed, spring was beginning. And now there's frost on the window. So loose and dirty it makes the room dark.'

In the kitchen, rats overturned plates with a clatter, ran up the wall on the other side, let their heavy hulks drop to the floor, their weepy contralto voices squealing disgustingly.

And again he slept, and woke up to discover that the windows in the snowy net of frost were suffused with a rosy, burning glow, which shone in them like red wine poured in crystal glasses. And he did not know and asked himself what glow this was, of dawn or sunset?

Once he imagined human voices somewhere quite near, and he lost heart, deciding that this was the beginning of madness. With tears of pity for himself, he murmured against heaven in a voiceless whisper for having turned away from him and abandoned him. 'O Light that never sets, why hast Thou rejected me from Thy presence, and why has the alien darkness surrounded me, cursed as I am?'

And suddenly he realised that he was not dreaming and this was the fullest truth, that he was undressed and washed, and was lying in a clean shirt, not on the sofa, but on a freshly made bed, and that, mingling her hair with his and his tears with hers, Lara was weeping with him, and sitting by his bed, and leaning towards him. And he fainted from happiness.

10

In his recent delirium he had reproached heaven for its indifference, but now heaven in all its vastness had descended to his bed, and two big woman's arms, white to the shoulders, reached out to him. His vision went dark with joy and, as one falls into oblivion, he dropped into bottomless bliss.

All his life he had been doing something, had been eternally busy, had worked about the house, had treated people, thought, studied, produced. How good it was to stop doing, striving, thinking, and to give himself for a time to this working of nature, to become a thing himself, a design, a work of her merciful, exquisite, beauty-lavishing hands!

Yuri Andreevich was recovering quickly. Lara nourished him, nursed him by her care, by her swan-white loveliness, by the moist-breathed, throaty whispering of her questions and answers.

Their hushed conversations, even the most trifling ones, were as filled with meaning as Plato's dialogues.

Still more than by the communion of souls, they were united by the abyss that separated them from the rest of the world. They both had an equal aversion to all that was fatally typical in modern man, his studied rapturousness, his shrill elation, and that deadly winglessness which is assiduously spread by countless workers in the sciences and the arts, so that genius will go on being an extreme rarity.

Their love was great. But everyone loves without noticing the unprecedentedness of the feeling.

For them, however – and in this they were exceptional – those instants when the breath of passion flew like a breath of eternity into their doomed human existence, were moments of revelation and of learning ever new things about themselves and life.

11

'You absolutely must return to your family. I won't keep you for a single extra day. But you see what's going on. As soon as we merged with Soviet Russia, we were swallowed up by its devastation. Siberia and the East are plugging its holes. You don't know anything. During your illness there have been such changes in town! The stores from our warehouses are being transported to the centre, to Moscow. For her it's a drop in the ocean, these supplies disappear into her as into a bottomless barrel, while we're left without provisions. The mails don't work, passenger transportation has ceased, express trains loaded with grain are all that run. There's murmuring in town again, as there was before the Gajda uprising,[2] and again the Cheka rages in response to the signs of discontent.

'So where are you going to go like that, skin and bones, your soul barely keeping in your body? And on foot again? You won't make it! Recover, get your strength back, then it's another matter.

'I won't venture to give advice, but in your place, before setting out for your family, I'd find a job for a while, in your speciality of course, they value that, I'd go to our board of health, for example. It's still in the old medical centre.

'Otherwise, judge for yourself. The son of a Siberian millionaire who blew his brains out, your wife the daughter of a local industrialist and landowner. Was with the partisans and ran away. Whatever you say, that's quitting the military-revolutionary ranks, it's desertion. In no case should you stay out of things, with no legal status. My situation isn't very firm either. And I'm also going to work, I'm joining the provincial education department. The ground's burning under my feet, too.'

'How do you mean? What about Strelnikov?'

'It's burning because of Strelnikov. I told you before how many enemies he had. The Red Army is victorious. Now the non-party military, who were close to the top and know too much, are going to get it in the neck. And lucky if it's in the neck and not in the back, so as to leave no traces. Among them, Pasha is in the first rank. He's in great danger. He was in the Far East. I heard he escaped and is in hiding. They say he's being sought. But enough about him. I don't like to cry, and if I add even one more word about him, I can feel I'll start howling.'

'You loved him, even now you still love him very much?'

'But I'm married to him, he's my husband, Yurochka. He has a lofty, shining character. I'm deeply guilty before him. I didn't do anything bad to him, it would be wrong to say so. But he's of enormous importance, a man of great, great uprightness, and I'm trash, I'm nothing beside him. That's my guilt. But enough of that, please. I'll come back to it myself some other time, I promise. How wonderful your Tonya is! A Botticelli. I was there at her delivery. She and I became terribly close. But of that, too, some other time, I beg you. Yes, so, let's the two of us find work. We'll both go to work. Each month we'll get billions in salary. Until the last coup, we were using Siberian money. It was abolished quite recently, and for a long time, all through your

illness, we lived without currency. Yes. Just imagine. It's hard to believe, but
we somehow managed. Now a whole trainload of paper money has been
delivered to the former treasury, about forty carriages, they say, not less. It's
printed on big sheets in two colours, blue and red, like postage stamps, and
divided into little squares. The blue ones are worth five million a square, the
red ones ten million. They fade quickly, the printing is bad, the colours run.'

'I've seen that money. It was introduced just before we left Moscow.'

12

'What were you doing so long in Varykino? There's nobody there, it's
empty. What kept you there?'

'Katenka and I were cleaning your house. I was afraid you'd stop there
first thing. I didn't want you to find your home in such a state.'

'What state? Messy, disorderly?'

'Disorder. Filth. I cleaned it.'

'How evasively monosyllabic. You're not telling everything, you're hiding
something. But as you will, I won't try to find out. Tell me about Tonya.
How did they christen the girl?'

'Masha. In memory of your mother.'

'Tell me about them.'

'Let me do it sometime later. I told you, I can barely keep back my tears.'

'This Samdevyatov, the one who gave you the horse, is an interesting figure. What do you think?'

'Most interesting.'

'I know Anfim Efimovich very well. He was a friend of our house here, he
helped us in these new places.'

'I know. He told me.'

'You're friends, probably? He tries to be useful to you, too?'

'He simply showers me with kindnesses. I don't know what I'd do without him.'

'I can easily imagine. You're probably in close, friendly relations, on simple terms? He's probably making up to you for all he's worth?'

'I'll say. Relentlessly.'

'And you? Sorry. I'm overstepping the limits of the permissible. What
right do I have to question you? Forgive me. It's indelicate.'

'Oh, please. You're probably interested in something else – what sort of
relations we have? You want to know whether anything more personal has
crept into our good acquaintance? Of course not. I'm obliged to Anfim Efimovich for a countless number of things, I'm roundly in debt to him, but

even if he showered me with gold, if he gave his life for me, it wouldn't bring me a step closer to him. I have an inborn hostility to people of that alien cast. In practical matters, these enterprising, self-assured, peremptory people are irreplaceable. In matters of the heart, such strutting, moustachioed male self-satisfaction is disgusting. I understand intimacy and life quite differently. But that's not all. In the moral respect, Anfim reminds me of another, far more repulsive man, who is to blame for my being this way, thanks to whom I am what I am.'

'I don't understand. Just how are you? What are you getting at? Explain. You're the best of all people in the world.'

'Ah, Yurochka, how can you? I'm being serious with you, and you pay me compliments like in a drawing room. You ask how I am? I'm broken, I have a crack in me for all my life. I was made a woman prematurely, criminally early, and initiated into life from its worst side, in the false, boulevard interpretation of a self-confident ageing parasite from former times, who profited from everything and allowed himself everything.'

'I can guess. I supposed there was something. But wait. It's easy to imagine your unchildish pain of that time, the fear of frightened inexperience, the first offence of an immature girl. But that's a thing of the past. I mean to say – to grieve over it now is not your concern, it's that of the people who love you, like myself. It's I who should tear my hair and feel desperate at being late, at not being with you then already, so as to prevent what happened, if it is truly a grief for you. Astonishing. It seems I can be deeply, mortally, passionately jealous only of what is beneath me or distant from me. Rivalry with a superior man calls up totally different feelings in me. If a man close to me in spirit and whom I love should fall in love with the same woman as I, I would have a feeling of sad brotherhood with him, not of dispute and competition. Of course, I wouldn't be able to share the object of my adoration with him for a second. But I would withdraw with a feeling of suffering quite different from jealousy, not as smouldering and bloody. The same would happen if I should run into an artist who won me over with his superior ability in works similar to mine. I would probably renounce my search and not duplicate his attempts, which had defeated me.

'But I've got sidetracked. I don't think I'd love you so deeply if you had nothing to complain of and nothing to regret. I don't like the righteous ones, who never fell, never stumbled. Their virtue is dead and of little value. The beauty of life has not been revealed to them.'

'And I'm thinking precisely of that beauty. It seems to me that what's needed in order to see it is intact imagination, primary perception. And that is just what was taken from me. Perhaps I would have formed my own view

of life, if I hadn't seen it, from the very first steps, with someone else's vulgar-
ising stamp on it. But that's not all. Because of the interference in my just-
beginning life of an immoral, self-gratifying mediocrity, my subsequent
marriage to a big and remarkable man did not work out, though he loved
me deeply and I responded in the same way.'

'Wait. Tell me about your husband later. I told you, jealousy is usually
aroused in me by an inferior, not an equal. I'm not jealous of your husband.
But that one?'

'What "that one"?'

'That profligate, the one who ruined you. Who is he?'

'A well-known Moscow lawyer. He was my father's associate, and after
papa's death he supported mama materially, when we were living in
poverty. A bachelor with a fortune. I'm probably making him far too interesting and unsuitably significant by besmirching him like this. A very ordinary phenomenon. If you like, I'll tell you his last name.'

'Never mind. I know it. I saw him once.'

'Really?'

'One time in a hotel room, when your mother poisoned herself. Late in
the evening. We were still children, schoolboys.'

'Ah, I remember that time. You came and stood in the dark, in the front
hall of the room. I might never have recalled that scene myself, but you
helped me once to bring it back from oblivion. You reminded me of it, I
think, in Meliuzeevo.'

'Komarovsky was there.'

'Was he? Quite possible. It was easy to find me with him. We were often
together.'

'Why are you blushing?'

'From the sound of "Komarovsky" on your lips. From the unwontedness
and the unexpectedness.'

'A comrade of mine was with me, a schoolmate. Here's what he told me
right then in the hotel room. He recognised Komarovsky as a man he had
seen one time by chance, in unforeseen circumstances. Once, while on a
journey, this schoolboy, Mikhail Gordon, was eyewitness to the suicide of
my father – a millionaire industrialist. Misha was travelling on the same
train with him. My father threw himself from the moving train with the
intention of ending his life, and he was killed. He was in the company of
Komarovsky, his lawyer. Komarovsky had encouraged my father's drinking,
got his affairs embroiled, driven him to bankruptcy, pushed him onto the
path of ruin. He's to blame for his suicide and for my being left an orphan.'

'It can't be! What a portentous detail! Is it really true? So he was your evil

genius, too? How that brings us together! Simply some sort of predestination!'

'It's of him that I'm insanely, irremediably jealous over you.'

'What? Why, I not only don't love him. I despise him.'

'Do you know your whole self so well? Human nature, especially
woman's, is so obscure and contradictory! In some corner of your aversion,
you may be in greater subjection to him than to any other man, whom you
love by your own goodwill, without constraint.'

'How horrible, what you're saying. And, as usual, you say it so pointedly
that this unnaturalness seems like the truth to me. But then how terrible
it is!'

'Calm yourself. Don't listen to me. I wanted to say that with you I'm jealous of what is obscure, unconscious, of something in which explanations
are unthinkable, of something that cannot be puzzled out. I'm jealous of
your toilet things, of the drops of sweat on your skin, of infectious diseases
borne on the air, which may affect you and poison your blood. And, as of
such an infection, I'm jealous of Komarovsky, who will one day take you
from me, just as one day we will be separated by my death or yours. I know
that this must seem like a heaping up of obscurities to you. I can't say it in a
more orderly and comprehensible way. I love you wildly, insanely, infinitely.'

13

'Tell me more about your husband. "One writ with me in sour misfortune's
book", as Shakespeare says.'

'Where is it from?'

'*Romeo and Juliet.*'[3]

'I told you a lot about him in Meliuzeevo, when I was searching for him.
And then here in Yuriatin, when you and I first met and I learned from your
own words that he had wanted to arrest you on his train. I think I told you,
but maybe I didn't and it only seems so to me, that I saw him once from a
distance when he was getting into a car. But you can imagine how protected
he was! I found him almost unchanged. The same handsome, honest, resolute face, the most honest of any I've ever seen in the world. Not a trace of
showing off, a manly character, a complete absence of posturing. He was
always that way, and has remained that way. And yet I noticed one change,
and it alarmed me.

'It was as if something abstract had entered into that look and dis-
coloured it. A living human face had turned into the embodiment, the principle, the portrayal of an idea. My heart was wrung when I noticed it. I

realised it was the consequence of the powers whose hands he had given himself into, sublime but deadening and merciless powers, which some day would also not spare him. It seemed to me that he was marked, and that this was the finger of doom. But maybe I'm confused. Maybe your expressions sank into me, when you described your meeting to me. Besides the feelings we have in common, I also borrow a lot from you!'

'No, tell me about your life before the revolution.'

'Early in childhood I began to dream of purity. He was its realisation. We were almost from the same courtyard. He and I and Galiullin. I was his child-hood passion. He swooned, he went cold when he saw me. It's probably not good for me to say it and know it. But it would be still worse if I pretended not to know. I was his childhood passion, that enslaving infatuation which one conceals, which a child's pride doesn't allow him to reveal, and which is written without words on his face and is obvious to everybody. We were friends. He and I are people as different as you and I are similar. Right then I chose him with my heart. I decided to join my life with this wonderful boy's as soon as we had both made our way, and mentally I became engaged to him right then.

'And think what abilities he has! Extraordinary! The son of a simple switchman or railroad watchman, through nothing but his own giftedness and persistent work he achieved – I was about to say the level, but I should say the summit of contemporary university knowledge in two fields, mathematics and the humanities. That's no joke!'

'In that case, what upset your domestic harmony, if you loved each other so much?'

'Ah, how hard it is to answer that. I'll tell you about it right now. But it's astonishing. Is it for me, a weak woman, to explain to you, who are so intelligent, what is now happening with life in general, with human life in Russia, and why families fall apart, yours and mine among them? Ah, as if it's a matter of people, of similarities and dissimilarities of character, of loving and not loving. All that's productive, settled, all that's connected with habitual life, with the human nest and its order, all of it went to rack and ruin along with the upheaval of the whole of society and its reorganisation. All everyday things were overturned and destroyed. What remained was the un-everyday, unapplied force of the naked soul, stripped of the last shred, for which nothing has changed, because in all times it was cold and trembling and drawing towards the one nearest to it, which is just as naked and lonely. You and I are like Adam and Eve, the first human beings, who had nothing to cover themselves with when the world began, and we are now just as unclothed and homeless at its end. And you and I are the last reminder of all those countless great things that have been done in the world in the many thousands of years between them and us, and in memory of those vanished wonders, we breathe and love, and weep, and hold each other, and cling to each other.'

14

After a pause, she went on much more calmly:

'I'll tell you. If Strelnikov became Pashenka Antipov again. If he stopped his madness and rebellion. If time turned backwards. If somewhere far away, at the edge of the world, the window of our house miraculously lit up, with a lamp and books on Pasha's desk, I think I would crawl there on my knees. Everything in me would be aroused. I would not resist the call of the past, the call of faithfulness. I would sacrifice everything. Even what's most dear. You. And my intimacy with you, so easy, so unforced, so self-implied. Oh, forgive me. I'm not saying the right thing. It's not true.'

She threw herself on his neck and burst into tears. But very soon she came to herself. Wiping her tears, she said:

'But it's the same voice of duty that drives you to Tonya. Lord, how miserable we are! What will become of us? What are we to do?'

When she had completely recovered, she went on:

'Anyhow, I haven't answered you yet about why our happiness fell apart. I understood it so clearly afterwards. I'll tell you. It won't be a story only about us. It became the fate of many people.'

'Speak, my bright one.'

'We were married just before the war, two years before it began. And we had just started living by our own wits, setting up house, when war was declared. I'm convinced now that it's to blame for everything, all the subsequent misfortunes that keep overtaking our generation to this day. I remember my childhood well. I caught the time when the notions of the previous, peaceful age were still in force. It was held that one should trust the voice of reason. What was prompted by conscience was considered natural and necessary. The death of a man at the hands of another was a rarity, an extraordinary phenomenon, out of the common run. Murders, it was supposed, happened only in tragedies, in detective novels, and in newspaper chronicles of events, not in ordinary life.

'And suddenly this leap from serene, innocent measuredness into blood and screaming, mass insanity, and the savagery of daily and hourly, lawful and extolled murder.

'Probably this never goes unpaid for. You probably remember better than

I do how everything all at once started going to ruin. Train travell, food supplies for the cities, the foundations of family life, the moral principles of consciousness.'

'Go on. I know what you'll say further. How well you analyse it all! What a joy to listen to you!'

'Then untruth came to the Russian land. The main trouble, the root of the future evil, was loss of faith in the value of one's own opinion. People imagined that the time when they followed the urgings of their moral sense was gone, that now they had to sing to the general tune and live by foreign notions imposed on everyone. The dominion of the ready-made phrase began to grow – first monarchistic, then revolutionary.

'This social delusion was all-enveloping, contagious. Everything fell under its influence. Our home couldn't stand against this bane either. Something in it was shaken. Instead of the unconscious liveliness that had always reigned with us, a dose of foolish declamation crept into our conversations, some ostentatious, mandatory philosophising on mandatory world themes. Could a man as subtle and self-demanding as Pasha, who could so unerringly distinguish essence from appearance, pass by this insidious falseness and not notice it?

'And here he committed a fatal error, which determined everything beforehand. He took the sign of the time, the social evil, for a domestic phenomenon. He attributed the unnatural tone, the official stiffness of our discussions to himself, he ascribed them to his being a dry stick, a mediocrity, a man in a case.[4] To you it probably seems incredible that such trifles could mean anything in our life together. You can't imagine how important it was, how many stupid things Pasha did because of that childishness.

'He went to the war, something nobody demanded of him. He did it to free us from himself, from his imaginary burden. That was the beginning of his follies. With some youthful, misdirected vanity, he took offense at something in life that one doesn't take offense at. He began to pout at the course of events, at history. He began to quarrel with it. And to this day he's settling accounts with it. Hence his defiant extravagances. He's headed for certain ruin because of that stupid ambition. Oh, if only I could save him!'

'How incredibly purely and deeply you love him! Go on, go on loving him. I'm not jealous of him, I won't hinder you.'

15

Summer came and went imperceptibly. The doctor recovered. Temporarily, in expectation of his supposed departure for Moscow, he took three posts.

The quickly progressing devaluation of money forced him to juggle several jobs.

The doctor rose at cockcrow, stepped out on Kupecheskaya, and went down it past the Giant picture house to the former printing shop of the Ural Cossack army, now renamed the Red Typesetter. At the corner of City Square, on the door of Administrative Affairs, he came upon a plaque reading 'Claims Office'. He crossed the square diagonally and came to Malaya Buyanovka Street. Past the Stanhope factory, through the hospital backyard, he arrived at the dispensary of the Military Hospital – the place of his main job.

Half his way lay under the shady trees hanging over the street, past whimsical, mostly wooden little houses with steeply cocked roofs, lattice fences, wrought-iron gates, and carved platbands on the shutters.

Next to the dispensary, in the former hereditary garden of the merchant's wife Goregliadova, stood a curious little house in old Russian taste. It was faced with faceted, glazed tiles, the triangular facets coming together to form a peak pointing outwards, as in ancient Moscow boyar mansions.

Three or four times in the ten-day week, Yuri Andreevich left the dispensary and went to the former Ligetti house on Staraya Myasskaya, to meetings of the Yuriatin regional health commission, which was housed there.

In a totally different, remote quarter stood the house donated to the town by Anfim's father, Efim Samdevyatov, in memory of his late wife, who had died in childbed giving birth to Anfim. In that house the Institute of Gynaecology and Obstetrics founded by Samdevyatov used to be located. Now it accommodated the Rosa Luxemburg[5] accelerated course in medicine and surgery. Yuri Andreevich taught general pathology and several noncompulsory subjects there.

He came back from all these duties at night, worn out and hungry, to find Larissa Fyodorovna in the heat of household chores, at the stove or over a tub. In this prosaic and homely appearance, dishevelled, with her sleeves rolled up and her skirts tucked up, she was almost frightening in her regal, breathtaking attractiveness, more so than if he were suddenly to find her about to go to a ball, standing taller, as if she had grown on her high heels, in an open, low-cut dress and wide, rustling skirts.

She cooked or did laundry and then with the remaining soapy water washed the floors in the house. Or, calm and less flushed, she ironed and mended her own, his, and Katenka's linen. Or, having finished with the cooking, laundry, and tidying up, she gave lessons to Katenka. Or, burying herself in textbooks, she occupied herself with her own political re-education, before going back to the newly reformed school as a teacher.

The closer this woman and girl were to him, the less he dared to see them as family, the stricter was the prohibition imposed upon his way of thinking by his duty to his family and his pain at being unfaithful to them. In this limitation there was nothing offensive for Lara and Katenka. On the contrary, this non-family way of feeling contained a whole world of respect, excluding casualness and excessive familiarity.

But this split was always tormenting and wounding, and Yuri Andreevich got used to it as one gets used to an unhealed, often reopening wound.

16

Two or three months passed like this. One day in October Yuri Andreevich said to Larissa Fyodorovna:

'You know, it seems I'll have to quit my job. It's the old, eternally repeated story. It starts out as if nothing could be better. "We're always glad of honest work. And still more of thoughts, especially new ones. How can we not encourage them? Welcome. Work, struggle, seek."

'But experience shows that what's meant by thoughts is only their appearance, a verbal garnish for the glorification of the revolution and the powers that be. It's tiresome and sickening. And I'm no master in that department.

'And in fact they're probably right. Of course I'm not with them. But it's hard for me to reconcile the thought that they're heroes, shining lights, and I'm a petty soul, who stands for darkness and the enslavement of men. Have you ever heard the name of Nikolai Vedenyapin?'

'Well, of course. Before I met you, and later, from what you've often told me. Simushka Tuntseva mentions him often. She's his follower. But I'm ashamed to say I haven't read his books. I don't like works devoted entirely to philosophy. I think philosophy should be used sparingly as a seasoning for art and life. To be occupied with it alone is the same as eating horseradish by itself. But forgive me, I've distracted you with my stupid talk.'

'No, on the contrary. I agree with you. That way of thinking is very close to me. Yes, so, about my uncle. Maybe I've really been spoiled by his influence. But they themselves shout with one voice: a brilliant diagnostician, a brilliant diagnostician! And it's true I'm rarely mistaken in determining an illness. But that is precisely their detested intuition, which is alleged to be my sin, an integral knowledge that includes the whole picture.

'I'm obsessed by the question of mimicry, the external adaptation of organisms to the colour of their environment. Here, hidden in this adjustment of colour, is the astonishing transition from the internal to the external.

'I ventured to touch on it in my lectures. And off it went! "Idealism, mysticism! Goethe's *Naturphilosophie,* neo-Schellingism!"[6]

'I've got to quit. I'll turn in my resignation from the health commission and the institute, and try to hang on at the hospital until they throw me out. I don't want to frighten you, but at times I have the feeling that I'll be arrested one of these days.'

'God forbid, Yurochka. Fortunately, we're still far from that. But you're right. It won't hurt to be more careful. As far as I've noticed, each time this young power installs itself, it goes through several stages. In the beginning it's the triumph of reason, the critical spirit, the struggle against prejudices.

'Then comes the second period. The dark forces of the "hangers-on", the sham sympathisers, gain the majority. Suspiciousness springs up, denunciations, intrigues, hatred. And you're right, we're at the beginning of the second phase.

'No need to look far for an example. Two former political prisoners from the workers have been transferred from Khodatskoe to the board of the revolutionary tribunal here, a certain Tiverzin and Antipov.

'They both know me perfectly well, and one simply happens to be my father-in-law, my husband's father. But in fact it's only quite recently, since their transfer here, that I've begun to tremble for my and Katenka's lives. Anything can be expected of them. Antipov has no great liking for me. They're quite capable of destroying me and even Pasha one fine day in the name of higher revolutionary justice.'

The sequel to this conversation took place quite soon. By that time a night search had been carried out at 48 Malaya Buyanovka, next to the dispensary at the widow Goregliadova's. In the house they found a cache of arms and uncovered a counter-revolutionary organisation. Many people in town were arrested; the searches and arrests were still going on. In connection with this, it was whispered that some of the suspects had escaped across the river. Considerations were expressed, such as: 'What good will it do them? There are rivers and rivers. There are, it must be said, certain rivers. In Blagoveshchensk-on-Amur, for instance, on one bank there's Soviet power, and on the other – China. You jump into the water, swim across, and adyoo, it's the last they see of you. That, you might say, is a river. A totally different story.'

'The atmosphere is thickening,' said Lara. 'For us the safe time is past. We'll undoubtedly be arrested, you and I. What will happen to Katenka then? I'm a mother. I must forestall misfortune and think up something. I must have a decision ready on that account. I lose my reason when I think of it.'

'Let's consider. What will help here? Are we able to prevent this blow? After all, it's a matter of fate.'

'There's nowhere and no chance for escape. But we can withdraw somewhere into the shadows, into the background. For instance, go to Varykino. I keep thinking about the house in Varykino. It's pretty far away, and everything's abandoned there. But there we wouldn't be in full view of everyone, as we are here. Winter's coming. I'll take on the work of wintering there. We'd gain a year of life before they get us, and that's something. Samdevyatov would help me keep a connection with town. Maybe he'd agree to hide us. Eh? What do you say? True, there isn't a soul there now, it's eerie, deserted. At least it was in March when I went there. And they say there are wolves. Frightening. But people, especially people like Antipov or Tiverzin, are more frightening now than wolves.'

'I don't know what to tell you. You yourself keep sending me to Moscow, persuading me not to put off going. It's become easier now. I made enquiries at the station. They've evidently waved their hand at the black-marketeers. Evidently not all the stowaways are taken off the trains. They've grown tired of shooting people; shootings have become rarer.

'It troubles me that all my letters to Moscow have gone unanswered. I must get there and find out what has happened with my family. You keep saying that yourself. But then how understand your words about Varykino? Would you really go to that frightening wilderness without me?'

'No, without you, of course, it's unthinkable.'

'And yet you're sending me to Moscow?'

'Yes, that's indispensable.'

'Listen. Do you know what? I have an excellent plan. Let's go to Moscow. You and Katenka together with me.'

'To Moscow? You're out of your mind. Why on earth? No, I have to stay. I must be in readiness somewhere nearby. Pashenka's fate is being decided here. I must wait for the outcome, so as to be at hand in case of need.'

'Then let's give some thought to Katenka.'

'From time to time Simushka stops by to see me, Sima Tuntseva. We were talking about her the other day.'

'Well, of course. I often see her at your place.'

'I'm surprised at you. Where are men's eyes? If I were you, I'd certainly have fallen in love with her. So enchanting! Such fine looks! Tall. Shapely. Intelligent. Well-read. Kind. Clear-headed.'

'On the day I returned here from captivity, her sister, the seamstress Glafira, shaved me.'

'I know. The sisters live together with the eldest, Avdotya, the librarian.

An honest, hard-working family. I want to persuade them, in the worst case, if you and I are picked up, to take Katenka into their charge. I haven't decided yet.'

'But really only in the most hopeless case. And God grant that such a misfortune is still a long way off.'

'They say Sima's a bit odd, not all there. In fact, one has to admit that she's not an entirely normal woman. But that's owing to her depth and originality. She's phenomenally well educated, only not like the intelligentsia, but like the people. Your views and hers are strikingly similar. I would trust Katya to her upbringing with an easy heart.'

17

Again he went to the station and came back with nothing for his pains. Everything remained undecided. He and Lara were faced with uncertainty. It was a cold, dark day, as before the first snow. The sky over the intersections, where it spread wider than over the streets drawn out lengthwise, had a wintry look.

When Yuri Andreevich came home, he found Simushka visiting Lara. A talk was going on between the two that bore the character of a lecture read by the guest to the hostess. Yuri Andreevich did not want to disturb them. Besides, he wanted to be alone for a while. The women were talking in the next room. The door was ajar. A floor-length curtain hung from the lintel, through which he could hear every word of their conversation.

'I'll sew, but don't pay any attention to that, Simushka. I'm all ears. In my time I took courses in history and philosophy at the university. The structure of your thought is after my own heart. Besides, listening to you is such a relief for me. These last few nights we haven't had enough sleep, because of various worries. My motherly duty towards Katenka is to assure her safety in case of possible troubles with us. I have to think soberly about her. I'm not particularly strong in that. It makes me sad to realise it. I'm sad from fatigue and lack of sleep. Your conversation calms me down. Besides, it's going to snow any moment. When it snows, it's such a pleasure to listen to long, intelligent reasoning. If you glance out of the window when it's snowing, it seems like somebody's coming towards the house through the courtyard, doesn't it? Begin, Simushka. I'm listening.'

'Where did we stop last time?'

Yuri Andreevich did not hear Lara's reply. He began to follow what Sima was saying.

'It's possible to make use of the words "culture" and "epochs". But they are so differently understood. In view of the uncertainty of their meaning, we won't resort to them. Let's replace them with other expressions.

'I'd say that a human being is made up of two parts. Of God and work. The development of the human spirit breaks down into separate works of enormous duration. They were realised in the course of generations and followed one after the other. Egypt was such a work, Greece was such a work, the biblical prophets' knowledge of God was such a work. Such a work – the latest in time, not yet supplanted by anything else, performed by the entire inspiration of our time – is Christianity.

'In order to present to you in all its freshness and unexpectedness, not as you yourself know and are used to it, but more simply, more directly, what it brought that was new and unprecedented, I'll analyse several fragments of liturgical texts with you, very few and brief ones.

'Most hymns are formed by juxtaposing images from the Old and New Testaments. Instances from the old world – the burning bush, the exodus of the Jews from Egypt, the youths in the fiery furnace, Jonah in the belly of the whale, and so on – are compared with instances from the new, for example, the Mother of God's conception and the Resurrection of Christ.

'In this frequent, almost constant matching, the oldness of the old, the newness of the new, and their difference appear with particular distinctness.

'In a whole multitude of verses, the virgin motherhood of Mary is compared with the crossing of the Red Sea by the Jews. For instance, in the verses of "In the Red Sea, a type of the virgin bride was figured" it is said: "After Israel's passage, the sea remained impassable; after Emmanuel's birth the undefiled one remained intact."⁷ In other words, the waters of the sea closed after the crossing of Israel, and the Virgin remained intact after giving birth to the Lord. What sort of incidents are made parallel here? Both events are supernatural, both are equally recognised as miracles. In what did these two different times, the ancient, primitive time and the new, post-Roman time, which was far more advanced, see a miracle?

'In the one case, by the command of the people's leader, the patriarch Moses, and by the swinging of his magic rod, the sea opens up, lets a whole nation pass across it, a countless multitude, hundreds of thousands, and when the last one has crossed, closes again, and covers and drowns the pursuing Egyptians. A spectacle in the ancient spirit, the elements obedient to the magician's voice, the great thronging multitudes, like Roman armies on the march, the people and their leader, things visible and invisible, stunning.

'In the other case, a maiden – an ordinary thing, the ancient world wouldn't have paid attention to it – secretly and quietly gives life to a child, brings life into the world, the miracle of life, the life of all, He who is "the

Life of all", as he was later called. Her childbirth is unlawful not only from the point of view of the scribes, being outside wedlock. It also contradicts the laws of nature. The maiden gives birth not by force of necessity, but by miracle, by inspiration. It is that very inspiration upon which the Gospel, by opposing the exception to the rule and the feast to the everyday, wants to build a life contrary to all constraint.

'What an enormously significant change! How is it that for heaven (because it is in the eyes of heaven that this must be evaluated, before the face of heaven, in the sacred framework of uniqueness in which it is all accomplished) – how is it that for heaven a private human circumstance, negligible from the point of view of antiquity, became equivalent to the migration of an entire people?

'Something shifted in the world. Rome ended, the power of numbers, the necessity, imposed by arms, of living en masse, as a whole population. Leaders and nations became things of the past.

'The person, the preaching of freedom came to supplant them. An individual human life became God's story, filling the space of the universe with its content. As it's said in one of the hymns of the Annunciation, Adam wanted to become God and made a mistake and did not become Him, but now "God becomes man, so as to make Adam God".'[8]

Sima went on:

'I'll tell you something else on that same theme in a moment. But meanwhile a small digression. In relation to the care for workers, the protection of mothers, the struggle with the power of capital, our revolutionary time is an unprecedented, unforgettable time, with achievements that will abide for a long time, forever. As for the understanding of life, the philosophy of happiness that's being propagated now, it's simply hard to believe that it's spoken seriously, it's such a ridiculous remnant. These declamations about leaders and people could send us back to Old Testament times of cattle-breeding tribes and patriarchs, if they had the power to reverse the course of time and throw history back thousands of years. Fortunately, that's impossible.

'A few words about Christ and Mary Magdalene. This isn't from the Gospel account of her, but from the prayers of Holy Week, I think from Holy Tuesday or Wednesday. But you know that without me, Larissa Fyodorovna. I simply want to remind you of a thing or two, and not at all to lecture you.

'"Passion" in Slavonic, as you know perfectly well, first of all means "suffering", the Passion of our Lord, "the Lord goeth to His voluntary passion" (that is, to His voluntary suffering). Besides that, the word is used in the later Russian meaning of vices and lusts. "Having enslaved the dignity of my soul to passions, I turned into a beast", "Having been expelled from paradise, let us strive to enter it by abstention from passions", and so on. I'm probably very depraved, but I don't like the pre-Easter readings in that line, devoted to harnessing sensuality and mortifying the flesh. It always seems to me that these crude, flat prayers, lacking in the poetry proper to other spiritual texts, were composed by greasy, fat-bellied monks. And the point is not that they themselves did not live by their own rules and deceived others. Suppose they even lived according to conscience. The point isn't them, but the content of these texts. These laments give unnecessary significance to various infirmities of the body and to whether it is well-fed or famished. It's disgusting. Here a dirty, inessential secondariness is raised to an undue, inappropriate height. Forgive me for putting off the main thing like this. I'll reward you presently for the delay.

'It has always interested me why the mention of Mary Magdalene is placed just before Easter, on the threshold of Christ's end and His resurrection. I don't know the reason, but the reminder of what life is comes so timely at the moment of taking leave of it and on the threshold of its return. Now listen with what genuine passion, with what directness regardless of anything, this mention is made.

'There's a debate about whether it's Mary Magdalene, or Mary of Egypt, or some other Mary. Whoever she may be, she asks the Lord: "Loose my debt as I have loosed my hair." That is: "Release me from guilt, just as I have released my hair." How materially the thirst for forgiveness, for repentance, is expressed! You can touch it with your hands.

'And there is a similar exclamation in another hymn for the same day, a more detailed one, which we can refer with greater certainty to Mary Magdalene.

'Here, with terrible tangibility, she laments for her past, for the fact that every night her former, inveterate habits flare up in her. "For I live in the night of licentiousness, shrouded in the dark and moonless love of sin." She asks Christ to accept her tears of repentance and incline His ear to the sighing of her heart, so that she may wipe His most pure feet with her hair, with which the stunned and ashamed Eve covered herself in paradise. "Once Eve heard Thy footstep in paradise in the cool of day and in fear ran and hid herself. But now I will tenderly embrace those pure feet and wipe them with the hair of my head." And suddenly, right after this about her hair, an exclamation is wrung from her: "Who can measure the multitude of my sins, or the depth of Thy judgements?" What intimacy, what equality of God and life, of God and a person, of God and a woman!'⁹

18

Yuri Andreevich had come back tired from the station. This was his one day off every ten days. Usually on those days he made up in sleep for the whole week. He sat leaning back on the sofa, at times half reclining or stretching out full length on it. Though he listened to Sima through surging waves of drowsiness, her reasoning delighted him. 'Of course, it's all from Uncle Kolya,' he thought, 'but how talented and intelligent she is!'

He jumped up from the sofa and went to the window. It gave onto the courtyard, as did the one in the next room, where Lara and Simushka were now whispering indistinctly.

The weather was worsening. It was getting dark in the courtyard. Two magpies flew into the yard and began flying around, looking for a place to alight. The wind slightly fluffed and ruffled their feathers. The magpies alighted on the lid of a rubbish bin, flew over to the fence, came down to the ground, and began walking about the yard.

'Magpies mean snow,' thought the doctor. At the same time he heard Sima tell Lara behind the curtain:

'Magpies mean news,' Sima was saying. 'You're going to have guests. Or receive a letter.'

A little later the doorbell on its wire, which Yuri Andreevich had recently repaired, rang outside. Larissa Fyodorovna came from behind the curtain and with quick steps went to the front hall to open the door. From her conversation, Yuri Andreevich understood that Sima's sister, Glafira Severinovna, had come.

'Do you want your sister?' asked Larissa Fyodorovna. 'Simushka's here.'

'No, not her. Though why not? We'll go together, if she's ready to go home. No, I've come for something else. There's a letter for your friend. He can be thankful I once worked at the post office. It passed through so many hands and landed in mine through an acquaintance. From Moscow. It took five months to come. They couldn't find the addressee. But I know who he is. I gave him a shave once.'

The letter, long, on several pages, crumpled, soiled, in an unsealed and disintegrating envelope, was from Tonya. The doctor was not fully conscious of how he came to be holding it; he had not noticed Lara handing it to him. When the doctor began to read the letter, he still remembered what town he was in, and in whose house, but as he read, he began to lose that awareness. Sima came out, greeted him, and began saying goodbye. Mechanically, he made the proper response, but paid no attention to her.

Her leaving fell out of his consciousness. He was gradually becoming more fully oblivious of where he was and what was around him.

'Yura,' Antonina Alexandrovna wrote to him, 'do you know that we have a daughter? She was christened Masha, in memory of your late mother, Marya Nikolaevna.

'Now about something else entirely. Several well-known social figures, professors from the CD Party and socialists of the right, Melgunov, Kiesewetter, Kuskova, some others, as well as Uncle Nikolai Alexandrovich Gromeko, papa, and we as members of his family, are being deported from Russia.[10]

'This is a misfortune, especially in your absence, but we must submit and thank God for such a soft form of exile in such a terrible time, for it could be much worse. If you had been found and were here, you would come with us. But where are you now? I am sending this letter to Antipova's address, she will hand it on to you, if she finds you. I suffer from uncertainty, whether afterwards, when – if it is so fated – you are found, they will extend to you, as a member of our family, the permission to leave that we have all been granted. It is my belief that you are alive and will be found. My loving heart tells me so and I trust its voice. It is possible that, by the time you are discovered, the conditions of life in Russia will have softened, and you will be able to obtain separate permission for a trip abroad, and we will all gather again in one place. But as I write it, I myself do not believe that such happiness can come true.

'The whole trouble is that I love you and you do not love me. I try to find the meaning of this condemnation, to interpret it, to justify it, I rummage, I delve into myself, going through our whole life and everything I know about myself, and I cannot see the beginning and cannot recall what I did and how I brought this misfortune upon myself. You look at me somehow wrongly, with unkind eyes, you see me twistedly, as in a distorting mirror.

'And yet I love you. Ah, how I love you, if only you could imagine! I love every peculiarity in you, all that is advantageous and disadvantageous, all your ordinary aspects, dear in their unusual combination, your face ennobled by inner content, which without that might seem unattractive, your talent and intelligence, which have as if taken the place of a total lack of will. All this is dear to me, and I do not know a man who is better than you.

'But listen, do you know what I shall tell you? Even if you were not so dear to me, even if I did not like you so much, still the deplorable truth of my coldness would not have been revealed to me, still I would think that I loved you. From fear alone of the humiliating, annihilating punishment that non-love is, I would unconsciously beware of realising that I did not love you. Neither I nor you would ever find it out. My own heart would conceal it from me, because non-love is almost like murder, and I would be unable to deal such a blow to anyone.

'Though nothing has been finally decided yet, we are probably going to Paris. I will get to those far-off lands where you were taken as a boy and where papa and my uncle were brought up. Papa sends his greetings. Shura has grown, he's not so handsome, but he has become a big, strong boy and always cries bitterly, inconsolably, at the mention of you. I can't go on. My heart is bursting with tears. So, farewell. Let me make the cross over you for this whole unending separation, the trials, the uncertainty, for the whole of your long, long, obscure path. I do not blame you for anything, I do not have a single reproach; shape your life as you want it to be, so long as it is good for you.

'Before leaving the dreadful and, for us, so fateful Urals, I came to know Larissa Fyodorovna quite closely. I owe her my thanks, she was constantly there when it was hard for me, and helped me during the delivery. I must tell you frankly that she is a good person, but I do not want to play the hypocrite – she is the complete opposite of me. I was born into this world to simplify life and seek the right way through, and she in order to complicate and confuse it.

'Farewell, I must end. They have come to take the letter and it is time to pack. Oh, Yura, Yura, my dear, my darling, my husband, father of my children, what is all this? We will never, ever see each other again. There, I have written these words, do you clearly make out their meaning? Do you understand, do you understand? They are hurrying me, and it is a sure sign that they have come to take me to my execution. Yura! Yura!'

Yuri Andreevich looked up from the letter with an absent, tearless gaze, not directed anywhere, dry from grief, devastated by suffering. He saw nothing around him, he was conscious of nothing.

Outside the window it began to snow. Wind carried the snow obliquely, ever faster and ever denser, as if trying all the while to make up for something, and the way Yuri Andreevich stared ahead of him through the window was as if it were not snow falling but the continued reading of Tonya's letter, and not dry starlike flakes that raced and flashed, but small spaces of white paper between small black letters, white, white, endless, endless.

Yuri Andreevich involuntarily moaned and clutched his chest. He felt faint, made several hobbling steps towards the couch, and collapsed on it unconscious.

Part Fourteen

IN VARYKINO AGAIN

Winter settled in. Snow fell in big flakes. Yuri Andreevich came home from the hospital.

'Komarovsky's come,' Lara said in a failing, husky voice, coming to meet him. They stood in the front hall. She had a lost look, as if she had been beaten.

'Where? To whom? Is he here?'

'No, of course not. He was here in the morning and wanted to come in the evening. He'll show up soon. He needs to talk with you.'

'Why has he come?'

'I didn't understand all he said. He says he was passing through on his way to the Far East and purposely made a detour and turned off at Yuriatin in order to see us. Mainly for your sake and Pasha's. He talked a lot about you both. He insists that all three of us, that is, you, Patulia, and I, are in mortal danger, and that only he can save us, if we listen to him.'

'I'll leave. I don't want to see him.'

Lara burst into tears, tried to fall on her knees before the doctor, embrace his legs, and press her face to them, but he prevented her, holding her back by force.

'Stay for my sake, I implore you. I'm not at all afraid of finding myself face-to-face with him. But it's hard. Spare me from meeting him alone. Besides, he's a practical man, he's been around. Maybe he really will give us some advice. Your loathing for him is natural. But I beg you, overcome yourself. Stay.'

'What's the matter, my angel? Calm yourself. What are you doing? Don't throw yourself on your knees. Stand up. Be cheerful. Drive away this obsession that pursues you. He's frightened you for life. I'm with you. If need be, if you tell me to, I'll kill him.'

Half an hour later evening fell. It became completely dark. For six months already, the holes in the floor had been stopped up everywhere. Yuri Andreevich watched for the forming of new ones and blocked them in time. They acquired a large, fluffy cat, who spent his time in immobile, mysterious contemplation. The rats did not leave the house, but they became more cautious.

In expectation of Komarovsky, Larissa Fyodorovna cut up the black rationed bread and put a plate with a few boiled potatoes on the table. They intended to receive the guest in the previous owners' dining room, which had kept its purpose. In it stood a big oak dining table and a big, heavy sideboard of the same dark oak. On the table, castor oil burned in a vial with a wick in it – the doctor's portable lamp.

Komarovsky came in from the December darkness all covered with the snow that was falling heavily outside. Snow fell in thick layers from his fur coat, hat, and galoshes, and melted, forming puddles on the floor. The snow that stuck to his moustaches and beard, which Komarovsky used to shave but now had let grow, made them look clownish, buffoonish. He was wearing a well-preserved jacket and waistcoat and well-creased striped trousers. Before greeting them or saying anything, he spent a long time combing his damp, flattened hair with a pocket comb and wiping and smoothing his wet moustaches and eyebrows with a handkerchief. Then silently, with an expression of great significance, he held out his two hands simultaneously, the left to Larissa Fyodorovna and the right to Yuri Andreevich.

'Let's consider ourselves acquaintances,' he addressed Yuri Andreevich. 'I was on such good terms with your father – you probably know. He gave up the ghost in my arms. I keep looking closely at you, searching for a resemblance. No, clearly you didn't take after your papa. He was a man of an expansive nature. Impulsive, impetuous. Judging by appearances, you are more like your mother. She was a gentle woman. A dreamer.'

'Larissa Fyodorovna asked me to hear you out. She says you have some business with me. I yielded to her request. Our conversation has been forced upon me against my will. I would not seek your acquaintance by my own inclination, and I do not consider us acquainted. Therefore let's get down to business. What do you want?'

'Greetings, my good ones. I feel everything, decidedly everything, and understand everything thoroughly, to the end. Forgive my boldness, but you're awfully well suited to each other. A harmonious couple in the highest degree.'

'I must interrupt you. I ask you not to interfere in things that do not concern you. No one has asked for your sympathy. You forget yourself.'

'Don't you flare up at once like that, young man. No, perhaps you're like your father after all. The same pistol and powder. Yes, so with your permission, I congratulate you, my children. Unfortunately, however, you are children not only in my expression, but in fact, who don't know anything, who don't reflect on anything. I've been here for only two days and have learned more about you than you yourselves suspect. You're walking on the edge of an abyss without thinking of it. If the danger isn't somehow averted, the days of your freedom, and maybe even of your lives, are numbered.

'There exists a certain Communist style. Few people measure up to it. But no one so clearly violates that way of living and thinking as you do, Yuri Andreevich. I don't understand – why stir up a hornets' nest? You're a mockery of that world, an insult to it. It would be fine if it were your secret. But there are influential people from Moscow here. They know you inside and out. You're both terribly distasteful to the local priests of Themis. Comrades Antipov and Tiverzin are sharpening their claws for Larissa Fyodorovna and you.

'You are a man – a free Cossack, or whatever it's called. Madcap behaviour, playing with your own life, is your sacred right. But Larissa Fyodorovna is not a free person. She's a mother. She has a young life, a child's destiny, in her hands. She's in no position to fantasise, to live in the clouds.

'I wasted a whole morning talking to her, persuading her to take the local situation more seriously. She refuses to listen to me. Use your authority, influence Larissa Fyodorovna. She has no right to toy with Katenka's safety, she should not disregard my arguments.'

'Never in my life have I tried to persuade or compel anyone. Especially people close to me. Larissa Fyodorovna is free to listen to you or not. That's her business. Besides, I have no idea what you're talking about. What you call your arguments are unknown to me.'

'No, you remind me more and more of your father. Just as intractable. So, then, let's go on to the main thing. But since it's a rather complex matter, arm yourselves with patience. I beg you to listen and not to interrupt.

'Big changes are being prepared at the top. No, no, I have it from the most reliable sources, you can trust me. They have in mind a switch to more democratic tracks, concessions to general legality, and that in the very near future.

'But precisely as a result of that, the punitive institutions liable to abolition will become all the more ferocious towards the end and will hasten to settle their local accounts. You are next in line to be annihilated, Yuri

Andreevich. Your name is on the list. I'm not joking when I say it, I saw it myself, believe me. Think about saving yourself, otherwise it will be too late.

'But this is all a preface so far. I go on to the essence of the matter.

'In Primorye, on the Pacific Ocean, a gathering of political forces that have remained loyal to the deposed Provisional Government and the disbanded Constituent Assembly is taking place. Members of the Duma, social figures, the most prominent of the former zemstvo activists, businessmen, industrialists are coming together. The generals of the volunteer armies are concentrating what remains of their forces there.

'The Soviet government turns a blind eye to the emergence of the Far Eastern republic. The existence of such a formation on its outskirts is advantageous to it as a buffer between Red Siberia and the outside world. The government of the republic will be mixed. Moscow has negotiated more than half the seats for Communists, so that with their aid, at the right time, they can carry out a coup and take the republic in hand. The scheme is perfectly transparent, and the only thing is to be able to take advantage of the remaining time.[1]

'Before the revolution I used to conduct the affairs of the Arkharov brothers, the Merkulovs, and other trading and banking houses in Vladivostok. I'm known there. An unofficial emissary of the forming government brought me, half secretly, half with official Soviet connivance, an invitation to enter the Far Eastern government as minister of justice. I accepted and am on my way there. All this, as I've just said, is happening with the knowledge and silent consent of Soviet power, though not so openly, and there should be no noise about it.

'I can take you and Larissa Fyodorovna with me. From there you can easily make your way to your family by sea. Of course, you already know about their deportation. A story that made a noise, the whole of Moscow is talking about it. I promised Larissa Fyodorovna to ward off the blow hanging over Pavel Pavlovich. As a member of an independent and recognised government, I'll seek out Strelnikov in eastern Siberia and assist in his transfer to our autonomous region. If he doesn't manage to flee, I'll suggest that he be exchanged for some person detained by the allies who is of value for the central power in Moscow.'

Larissa Fyodorovna had difficulty following the content of the conversation, the meaning of which often escaped her. But at Komarovsky's last words, concerning the safety of the doctor and Strelnikov, she came out of her state of pensive non-participation, pricked up her ears, and, blushing slightly, put in:

'You understand, Yurochka, how important these plans are for you and Pasha?'

'You're too trusting, my dear friend. One can hardly take things promised for things performed. I'm not saying that Viktor Ippolitovich is consciously pulling our leg. But it's all still in the air! And now, Viktor Ippolitovich, a few words from me. I thank you for your attention to my fate, but can you possibly think I'll let you arrange it? As for your taking care of Strelnikov, Lara has to think it over.'

'What are you driving at? Either we go with him, as he suggests, or we don't. You know perfectly well that I won't go without you.'

Komarovsky sipped frequently from the diluted alcohol Yuri Andreevich had brought from the dispensary and set on the table, munched the potatoes, and gradually became tipsy.

2

It was already late. Relieved now and then of its snuff, the wick of the lamp flared up with a crackle, brightly lighting the room. Then everything sank into darkness again. The hosts wanted to sleep and had to talk things over alone. But Komarovsky would not leave. His presence was wearying, like the oppressive sight of the heavy oak sideboard and the dispiriting, icy December darkness outside the window.

He looked not at them, but somewhere over their heads, fixing his drunken, rounded eyes on that distant point, and with a sleepy, thick tongue ground away at something endlessly boring, all about one and the same thing. His hobbyhorse was now the Far East. He chewed the cud about it, developing before Lara and the doctor his reflections on the political significance of Mongolia.

Yuri Andreevich and Larissa Fyodorovna had not caught the point at which the conversation had landed on this Mongolia. The fact that they had missed how he skipped over to it increased the tiresomeness of the alien, extraneous subject.

Komarovsky was saying:

'Siberia – truly a New America, as they call it – conceals in itself the richest possibilities. It is the cradle of the great Russian future, the pledge of our democratisation, prosperity, political health. Still more fraught with alluring possibilities is the future of Mongolia, Outer Mongolia, our great Far Eastern neighbour. What do you know about it? You're not ashamed to yawn and blink with inattention, and yet it has a surface of over a million square miles, unexplored minerals, a country in a state of prehistoric virginity, which the greedy hands of China, Japan, and America are reaching for, to the detriment of our Russian interests, recognised by all our rivals under any division of spheres of interest in this remote corner of the globe.

'China takes advantage of the feudal and theocratic backwardness of Mongolia, influencing its lamas and *khutukhtas*. Japan leans on local serf-owning princes – *khoshuns* in Mongolian. Red Communist Russia finds an ally in the person of the *khamdzhils,* in other words, the revolutionary association of rebellious Mongolian shepherds. As for me, I would like to see Mongolia really prosperous, under the rule of freely elected *khurultai*. Personally, we ought to be concerned with the following. One step across the Mongolian border, and the world is at your feet, and you're free as a bird.'

This verbose reasoning on an intrusive subject that had no relation to them exasperated Larissa Fyodorovna. Driven to the point of exhaustion by the boredom of the prolonged visit, she resolutely held out her hand to Komarovsky in farewell and, without beating around the bush, said with unconcealed hostility:

'It's late. Time for you to go. I want to sleep.'

'I hope you won't be so inhospitable as to put me out at such an hour. I'm not sure I'll find my way at night in a strange, unlit town.'

'You should have thought of that earlier and not gone on sitting. Nobody was keeping you.'

'Oh, why do you speak so sharply with me? You didn't even ask whether I have anywhere to stay here.'

'Decidedly uninteresting. No doubt you can stick up for yourself. If you're inviting yourself to spend the night, I won't put you in our bedroom, where we sleep together with Katenka. And in the others there'll be no dealing with the rats.'

'I'm not afraid of them.'

'Well, as you like.'

3

'What's wrong, my angel? You haven't slept for so many nights now, you don't touch your food at the table, you go around as if in a daze. And you keep thinking, thinking. What's haunting you? You shouldn't give such free rein to troubling thoughts.'

'The hospital caretaker Izot was here again. He's carrying on with a laundress in the house. So he stopped by to cheer me up. "A terrible secret," he says. "Your man can't avoid the clink. He'll be put away any day now, so be ready. And you, hapless girl, after him." "Where did you get that, Izot?" I asked. "Don't worry," he says, "you can count on it. People from the hex-com told me." "Hexcom", as you may have guessed, is his version of "excom", the executive committee.'

Larissa Fyodorovna and the doctor burst out laughing.

'He's quite right. The danger is ripe and at our doorstep. We must disappear at once. The only question is where exactly. There's no use thinking about going to Moscow. The preparations are too complicated, and they'll attract attention. It has to be done hush-hush, so that nobody notices anything. You know what, my joy? I think we'll avail ourselves of your idea. We have to drop from sight for a while. Let the place be Varykino. We'll go there for two weeks, a month.'

'Thank you, my dearest, thank you. Oh, how glad I am! I realise how everything in you must go against such a decision. But I wasn't talking about your house. Life in it would really be unthinkable for you. The sight of the empty rooms, the reproaches, the comparisons. As if I don't understand? To build happiness on another's suffering, to trample on what is dear and sacred to your heart. I could never accept such a sacrifice from you. But that's not the point. Your house is such a ruin that it would hardly be possible to make the rooms fit to live in. I was sooner thinking of the Mikulitsyns' abandoned place.'

'All that is true. Thank you for your sensitivity. But wait a minute. I keep wanting to ask and keep forgetting. Where is Komarovsky? Is he here, or has he already left? Since I quarrelled with him and kicked him out, I've heard nothing more of him.'

'I don't know anything either. But let him be. What do you want with him?'

'I keep coming back to the thought that we should have treated his suggestion differently. We're not in the same position. You have a daughter to look after. Even if you wanted to perish with me, you'd have no right to allow yourself to do it.

'But let's get back to Varykino. Naturally, to go to that wild backwater in harsh winter, with no supplies, with no strength, with no hopes, is the maddest madness. But let's be mad, my heart, if there's nothing left us but madness. Let's humble ourselves once more. Let's beg Anfim to give us a horse. Let's ask him, or not even him but the dealers who work for him, to lend us some flour and potatoes, as a debt not justifiable by any credit. Let's persuade him not to buy back the good service he has rendered us by coming to visit right away, at once, but to come only at the end, when he needs the horse back. Let's stay alone for a little while. Let's go, my heart. In a week we'll cut and burn a whole stand of trees, which would be enough for an entire year of conscientious housekeeping.

'And again, again. Forgive me for the confusion that keeps breaking through my words. How I'd like to talk to you without this foolish pathos! But we really have no choice. Call it what you like, death really is knocking at our door. The days at our disposal are numbered. Let's use them in our own way. Let's spend them on taking leave of life, on a last coming together before separation. Let's bid farewell to all that was dear to us, to our habitual notions, to how we dreamed of living and to what our conscience taught us, bid farewell to hopes, bid farewell to each other. Let's say once more to each other our secret night words, great and pacific as the name of the Asian ocean. It's not for nothing that you stand at the end of my life, my secret, my forbidden angel, under a sky of wars and rebellions, just as you once rose up under the peaceful sky of childhood at its beginning.

'On that night, a girl in the last year of high school, in a coffee-coloured uniform, in the semi-darkness behind the partition of a hotel room, you were exactly as you are now, and as stunningly beautiful.

'Often, later in life, I tried to define and name that light of enchantment that you poured into me then, that gradually dimming ray and fading sound that suffused my whole existence ever after and became, owing to you, the key for perceiving everything else in the world.

'When you, a shadow in a schoolgirl's uniform, stepped out of the darkness of the hotel room's depths, I, a boy who knew nothing about you, understood with all the torment of a force that answered yours: this slight, skinny girl is charged to the utmost, as with electricity, with all conceivable femininity in the world. If you go near her or touch her with your finger, a spark will light up the room and either kill you on the spot or electrify you for your whole life with a magnetically attractive, plaintive craving and sorrow. I was all filled with wandering tears, all my insides glittered and wept. I felt a mortal pity for the boy I was, and still more pity for the girl you were. My whole being was astonished and asked: If it's so painful to love and absorb electricity, how much more painful it is to be a woman, to be the electricity, to inspire love.

'Here at last I've said it out loud. It could make you lose your mind. And the whole of me is in it.'

Larissa Fyodorovna was lying on the edge of the bed, dressed and feeling unwell. She was curled up and had covered herself with a shawl. Yuri Andreevich was sitting on a chair next to her and speaking quietly, with long pauses. At times Larissa Fyodorovna raised herself on her elbow, propped her chin in her hand, and gazed open-mouthed at Yuri Andreevich. At times she pressed herself to his shoulder and, not noticing her tears, wept quietly and blissfully. She finally drew towards him, hanging over the edge of the bed, and whispered joyfully:

'Yurochka! Yurochka! How intelligent you are! You know everything, you guess about everything. Yurochka, you are my fortress, my refuge, and my foundation – God forgive my blasphemy. Oh, how happy I am! Let's go, let's go, my dear. Once we're there, I'll tell you what's troubling me.'

He decided that she was hinting at her supposed pregnancy, probably imaginary, and said:

'I know.'

4

They drove out of town in the morning of a grey winter day. It was a week-day. People walked down the streets about their business. They frequently met acquaintances. At bumpy intersections, next to the old pump houses, women who had no wells near their houses lined up with their buckets and yokes set aside, waiting their turn to draw water. The doctor reined in Savraska, a smoky yellow, curly-haired Viatka horse, who was straining forward, and steered him carefully to avoid the crowding housewives. The sleigh picked up speed, slid sideways off the humpbacked, water-splashed, and icy pavement, rode onto the pavements, the bumpers hitting lamp posts and hitching posts.

At full speed they overtook Samdevyatov walking down the street, flew past him, and did not look back to see if he recognised them and his horse and shouted anything after them. In another place, similarly, without any greeting, they left Komarovsky behind, having ascertained in passing that he was still in Yuriatin.

Glafira Tuntseva shouted all the way across the street from the opposite pavement:

'And they said you left yesterday. Go trusting people after that. Off to fetch potatoes?' – and, with a gesture showing that she had not heard their answer, she waved goodbye behind them.

For Sima's sake they tried to pull up on a hillside, in an awkward place, where it was hard to stop. The horse had to be held back all the time without that, by tugging tightly on the reins. Sima was wrapped from head to foot in two or three shawls, which lent her figure the rigidity of a round log. With straight, unbending steps she came to the sleigh in the middle of the pavement and said goodbye, wishing them a safe journey.

'We must finish our talk when you get back, Yuri Andreevich.'

They finally drove out of town. Though Yuri Andreevich had occasionally ridden on this road in winter, he mainly remembered it as it was in summer and now did not recognise it.

The sacks of provisions and other luggage were placed deep in the hay at the front of the sleigh, under the dashboard, and tied securely. Yuri Andreevich drove either kneeling on the bottom of the broad sleigh, in local parlance a *koshovka,* or sitting sideways, his feet in Samdevyatov's felt boots hanging over the edge.

In the afternoon, when winter's deceptiveness made it seem that the day was coming to an end long before sunset, Yuri Andreevich started whipping Savraska mercilessly. She shot off like an arrow. The *koshovka* flew up and down like a boat, bobbing over the unevenness of the much-used road. Katya and Lara were wearing fur coats, which hindered their movements. As the sleigh leaned or jolted, they shouted and laughed their heads off, rolling from one side of the sleigh to the other and burying themselves in the hay like unwieldly sacks. At times, for the fun of it, the doctor purposely rode one runner over the snowbank on the edge of the road, turning the sleigh on its side and throwing Lara and Katya out into the snow without doing them any harm. After being dragged by the reins a few steps along the road, he would stop Savraska, set the sleigh back on both runners, and get a scolding from Lara and Katya, who would shake themselves off and climb into the sleigh, laughing and pouting.

'I'll show you the place where the partisans stopped me,' the doctor promised, when they had driven far enough from town, but he was unable to keep his promise, because the winter bareness of the forest, the deathly calm and emptiness all around, changed the place beyond recognition. 'Here it is!' he soon cried, mistaking the first Moreau and Vetchinkin billboard, which stood in a field, for the second one in the forest, where he had been taken. When they raced past this second one, which was still in its former place, in the woods by the Sakma intersection, the billboard could not be made out through the scintillating lattice of thick hoarfrost, which turned the forest into a filigree of silver and niello. And they did not notice the billboard.

They flew into Varykino while it was still light and stopped at the Zhivagos' old house, since it was the first on the road, closer than the Mikulitsyns'. They burst into the room hurriedly, like robbers – it would soon be dark. Inside it was already dark. In his haste, Yuri Andreevich did not make out half the destruction and filth. Some of the familiar furniture was intact. In deserted Varykino there was no one left to carry through the destruction that had been begun. Of their household things Yuri Andreevich found nothing. But he had not been there at his family's departure, he did not know what they had taken with them and what they had left behind. Meanwhile Lara was saying:

'We must hurry. Night is coming. There's no time to reflect. If we settle here, then the horse must be put in the barn, the provisions in the front hall, and we here in this room. But I'm against such a decision. We've talked enough about it. It will be painful for you and therefore for me. What's this, your bedroom? No, the nursery. Your son's little bed. Too small for Katya. On the other hand, the windows are intact, no cracks in the walls or ceiling. And a magnificent stove besides, I already admired it on my last visit. And if you insist that we stay here after all, though I'm against it, then – off with my coat and straight to work. The heating first of all. Heat, heat, heat. Day and night non-stop to begin with. But what's the matter, my dear? You don't answer anything.'

'Just a moment. It's nothing. Forgive me, please. No, you know, we'd really better have a look at the Mikulitsyns'.'

And they drove further on.

5

The Mikulitsyns' house was locked with a padlock hanging from the eye of the door bar. Yuri Andreevich pried at it for a long time and ripped it off, with splintered wood clinging to the screws. As in the previous house, they barged in hurriedly and went through the rooms with their coats, hats, and felt boots on.

Their eyes were immediately struck by the stamp of order on the objects in certain parts of the house – for instance, in Averky Stepanovich's study. Someone had been living here, and quite recently. But who precisely? If it was the owners or some one of them, what had become of them, and why had they locked the outside door with a padlock instead of the lock in the door? Besides, if it was the owners, and they had been living there long and permanently, the house would have been in order throughout and not in separate parts. Something told the intruders that it was not the Mikulitsyns. But in that case who was it? The doctor and Lara were not troubled by the uncertainty. They did not start racking their brains over it. As if there were not enough abandoned dwellings now with half the furniture pilfered? Or enough fugitives in hiding? 'Some White officer being pursued,' they agreed unanimously. 'If he comes, we'll live together, we'll work things out.'

And again, as once before, Yuri Andreevich stood as if rooted to the threshold of the study, admiring its spaciousness and astonished at the width and convenience of the desk by the window. And again he thought how such austere comfort probably disposes one and gives one a taste for patient, fruitful work.

Among the outbuildings in the Mikulitsyns' yard there was a stable built right onto the barn. But it was locked, and Yuri Andreevich did not know what state it was in. So as not to lose time, he decided to put the horse in the easily opened, unlocked barn for the first night. He unharnessed Savraska, and when she cooled down, he gave her water that he brought from the well. Yuri Andreevich wanted to give her some hay from the bottom of the sleigh, but the hay had turned to dust under the passengers and was unfit for horse feed. Luckily, he found enough hay along the walls and in the corners of the wide hayloft over the barn and stable.

They slept that night under their fur coats, without undressing, blissfully, deeply, and sweetly, as children sleep after a whole day of running about and playing pranks.

6

When they got up in the morning, Yuri Andreevich began to gaze admiringly at the tempting desk by the window. His hands were itching to get to work over a sheet of paper. But he chose to enjoy that right in the evening, when Lara and Katenka had gone to bed. And meanwhile he had his hands full just putting two rooms in order.

In dreaming of his evening's work, he did not set himself any important goals. A simple passion for ink, an attraction to the pen and the occupation of writing, possessed him.

He wanted to scribble, to set down lines. At first he would be satisfied with recalling and writing down something old, unrecorded, only so as to warm up his faculties, which had been standing inactive and drowsing in the interim. And later, he hoped, he and Lara would manage to stay on there longer, and he would have plenty of time to take up something new and significant.

'Are you busy? What are you doing?'

'Heating and heating. Why?'

'I need a tub.'

'If we keep the place this warm, we won't have wood enough for more than three days. We've got to go and look in our former Zhivago shed. What if there's more there? If there's enough left, I'll make several trips and bring it here. Tomorrow I'll see to it. You asked for a tub. Imagine, my eye fell on one somewhere, but where – it's gone clean out of my head, I can't place it.'

'It's the same with me. I saw one somewhere and forgot. Probably not in the right place, that's why I've forgotten. But let it be. Mind you, I'm heating a lot of water for cleaning. What's left I'll use to do some laundry for me and Katya. Let me have all your dirty things at the same time. In the evening, when we've put the place in order and can see what else needs to be done, we'll wash ourselves before going to bed.'

'I'll collect my laundry right now. Thanks. I've moved the wardrobes and heavy things away from the walls, as you asked.'

'Good. Instead of a tub, I'll wash it in the dish basin. Only it's very greasy. I'll have to scrub the fat off the sides.'

'Once the stove is heated, I'll close it and go back to sorting the remaining drawers. At each step I find new things in the desk and chest. Soap, matches, pencils, paper, writing materials. And also unexpected things in plain sight. For instance, a lamp on the desk, filled with kerosene. It's not the Mikulitsyns', that I know. It's from some other source.'

'Amazing luck! It's all him, our mysterious lodger. Like out of Jules Verne. Ah, well, how do you like that, really! We're babbling and chattering away, and my cauldron's boiling over.'

They were bustling, rushing here and there about the rooms, their hands full, busy, bumping into each other or running into Katenka, who kept getting in the way and under their feet. The girl wandered from corner to corner, hindering their cleaning, and pouted when they told her so. She was chilled and complained of the cold.

'Poor modern-day children, victims of our Gypsy life, unmurmuring little participants in our wanderings,' thought the doctor, while saying to the girl:

'Well, forgive me, my sweet, but there's nothing to shiver about. Stuff and nonsense. The stove is red-hot.'

'The stove may be hot, but I'm cold.'

'Then bear with it, Katyusha. In the evening I'll heat it a second time hot as can be, and mama says she'll also give you a bath, do you hear? And meanwhile – here, catch!' And he poured out on the floor a heap of Liberius's old toys from the cold storeroom, broken or intact, building blocks, coaches, trains, and pieces of ruled cardboard, coloured and with numbers in the squares, for games with chips and dice.

'Well, how can you, Yuri Andreevich!' Katenka became offended like a grown-up. 'It's all somebody else's. And for little kids. And I'm big.'

But a minute later she was settled comfortably in the middle of the rug, and under her hands the toys of all sorts turned into building materials, from which Katenka constructed a home for her doll Ninka, brought with her from town, with greater sense and more permanence than those strange, changing shelters she was dragged through.

'What domestic instinct, what ineradicable striving for a nest and order!' said Larissa Fyodorovna, watching her daughter's play from the kitchen.

'Children are unconstrainedly sincere and not ashamed of the truth, while we, from fear of seeming backward, are ready to betray what's most dear, to praise the repulsive, and to say yes to the incomprehensible.'

'The tub's been found,' the doctor interrupted, coming in with it from the dark front hall. 'In fact, it wasn't in the right place. It's been sitting on the floor under a leak in the ceiling, evidently since autumn.'

7

For dinner, prepared for three days ahead from their freshly started provisions, Larissa Fyodorovna served unheard-of things – potato soup and roast lamb with potatoes. Katenka relished it, could not eat enough, laughed merrily and frolicked, and then, full and languid from the heat, covered herself with her mother's plaid and fell fast asleep on the sofa.

Larissa Fyodorovna, straight from the stove, tired, sweaty, half asleep like her daughter, and satisfied with the impression produced by her cooking, was in no rush to clear the table and sat down to rest. Having made sure that the girl was asleep, she said, leaning her breast on the table and propping her head with her hand:

'I'd spare no strength and I'd find happiness in it, if only I knew that it's not in vain and is leading to some goal. You must remind me every moment that we're here to be together. Encourage me and don't let me come to my senses. Because, strictly speaking, if you look at it soberly, what is it we're doing, what's going on with us? We raid someone else's home, break in, take charge, and urge ourselves on all the while so as not to see that this is not life, it's a theatrical production, not serious but "pretend", as children say, a puppet comedy, a farce.'

'But, my angel, you yourself insisted on this journey. Remember how long I resisted and did not agree.'

'Right. I don't argue. So now it's my fault. You can hesitate, ponder, but for me everything must be consistent and logical. We went into the house, you saw your son's little bed and felt ill, you almost swooned from the pain. You have the right to that, but for me it's not allowed, my fear for Katenka, my thoughts about the future must give way before my love for you.'

'Larusha, my angel, come to your senses. It's never too late to think better of it, to change your mind. I was the first to advise you to take Komarovsky's words more seriously. We have a horse. If you want, we can fly off to Yuriatin tomorrow. Komarovsky is still there, he hasn't left. We saw him in the street from the sleigh, and I don't think he noticed us. We'll probably find him.'

'I've said almost nothing, and you already have displeased tones in your voice. But tell me, am I not right? We could hide just as insecurely, at random, in Yuriatin. And if we were seeking salvation, then it should have been for certain, with a thought-out plan, as, in the end, was suggested by that well-informed and sober, though repulsive, man. While here I simply don't know how much closer we are to danger than anywhere else. A boundless, windswept plain. And we're alone as can be. We may get snowbound overnight and be unable to dig ourselves out in the morning. Or our mysterious benefactor who visits the house may drop in, turn out to be a robber, and put his knife in us. Do you have any sort of weapon? No, you see. I'm frightened of your light-heartedness, which you've infected me with. It muddles my thinking.'

'But in that case what do you want? What do you order me to do?'

'I don't know myself how to answer you. Keep me in submission all the time. Constantly remind me that I'm your blindly loving, unreasoning slave. Oh, I'll tell you. Our families, yours and mine, are a thousand times better than we are. But is that the point? The gift of love is like any other gift. It may be great, but without a blessing it will not manifest itself. And with us it's as if we were taught to kiss in heaven and then sent as children to live in the same time, so as to test this ability on each other. A crown of concord, no sides, no degrees, no high, no low, equivalence of the whole being, everything gives joy, everything becomes soul. But in this wild tenderness, lying in wait every moment, there is something childishly untamed, illicit. It's a self-willed, destructive element, hostile to peace in the home. My duty is to fear it and not to trust it.'

She threw her arms around his neck and, fighting back her tears, finished:

'You understand, we're in different positions. Wings were given you so as to fly beyond the clouds, and to me, a woman, so as to press myself to the ground and shield my fledgling from danger.'

He terribly liked everything she said, but did not show it, so as not to fall into excessive sweetness. Restraining himself, he remarked:

'Our bivouac life really is false and overwrought. You're profoundly right. But we didn't invent it. A frantic casting about is everybody's lot, it's the spirit of the time.

'I myself have been thinking today, since morning, about approximately the same thing. I'd like to make every effort to stay on here longer. I can't tell you how much I miss work. I don't mean agricultural work. Once our whole household here threw itself into it, and it succeeded. But I wouldn't be able to repeat that again. It's not what I have in mind.

'Life on all sides is gradually being put in order. Maybe some day books will be published again.

'Here's what I've been thinking over. Couldn't we arrange it with Samde-vyatov, on conditions profitable for him, to keep us supplied for six months, on the pledge of a work I would promise to write during that time, a text-book on medicine, let's suppose, or something artistic, a book of poems, for example. Or let's say I undertake to translate some world-famous foreign book. I have a good knowledge of languages, I recently read an advertise-ment from a big Petersburg publisher who specialises in bringing out works in translation. Work like that would probably acquire an exchange value that could be turned into money. I'd be happy to busy myself with some-thing of that sort.'

'Thank you for reminding me. I was also thinking of something like that today. But I don't believe we can hold out here. On the contrary, I have a presentiment that we'll soon be carried somewhere further on. But while this stopover is at our disposal, I have something to ask you. Sacrifice a few hours for me during the next few nights and, please, write down every-thing you've recited to me from memory at various times. Half of it has been lost, the other half has never been written down, and I'm afraid you'll forget it all afterwards and it will perish, as you say has often happened to you before.'

8

By the end of the day they had all washed with hot water, left over in abun-dance from the laundry. Lara bathed Katenka. Yuri Andreevich, with a blissful feeling of cleanness, sat at the desk by the window with his back to the room in which Lara, fragrant, wrapped in a bathrobe, her wet hair wound turbanlike in a Turkish towel, was putting Katenka to bed and set-tling for the night. All immersed in the foretaste of impending concentra-tion, Yuri Andreevich perceived everything that was going on through a veil of softened and all-generalising attention.

It was one o'clock in the morning when Lara, who until then had been pretending, actually fell asleep. The changed linen on her, on Katenka, and on the bed shone, clean, ironed, lacy. Even in those years Lara somehow contrived to starch it.

Yuri Andreevich was surrounded by blissful silence, filled with happiness and breathing sweetly with life. The light of the lamp cast its calm yellowness on the white sheets of paper, and its golden patches floated on the surface of the ink in the inkstand. The frosty winter night shone pale blue outside the window. Yuri Andreevich stepped into the next room, cold and unlit, from which he could better see outside, and looked through the window. The light of the full moon bound the snowy clearing with the tangible viscosity of egg white or white sizing. The luxuriance of the winter night was inexpressible. There was peace in the doctor's soul. He went back to the bright, warmly heated room and got down to writing.

In a sweeping script, taking care that the appearance of the writing conveyed the living movement of his hand and did not lose its personality, becoming soulless and dumb, he recalled and wrote out in gradually improving versions, deviating from the previous ones, the most fully formed and memorable poems, 'The Star of the Nativity', 'Winter Night', and quite a few others of a similar kind, afterwards forgotten, mislaid, and never found again by anyone.

Then, from settled and finished things, he went on to things once begun and abandoned, entered into their tone, and began to sketch out their continuation, without the least hope of finishing them now. Then he warmed up, got carried away, and went on to new things.

After two or three easily poured-out stanzas and several similes that he was struck by himself, the work took possession of him, and he felt the approach of what is known as inspiration. The correlation of forces that control creative work is, as it were, stood on its head. The primacy no longer belongs to man and the state of his soul, for which he seeks expression, but to the language in which he wants to express it. Language, the homeland and receptacle of beauty and meaning, itself begins to think and speak for man and turns wholly into music, not in terms of external, audible sounds, but in terms of the swiftness and power of its inner flow. Then, like the rolling mass of a river's current, which by its very movement polishes the stones of the bottom and turns the wheels of mills, flowing speech itself, by the force of its own laws, on its way, in passing, creates metre and rhyme and thousands of other forms and constructions, still more important, but as yet unrecognised, unconsidered, unnamed.

In such moments Yuri Andreevich felt that the main work was done not by him, but by what was higher than him, by what was above him and guided him, namely: the state of world thought and poetry, and what it was destined for in the future, the next step it was to take in its historical development. And he felt himself only the occasion and fulcrum for setting it in motion.

He was delivered from self-reproach; self-dissatisfaction, the feeling of his own nonentity, left him for a while. He looked up, he looked around him.

He saw the heads of the sleeping Lara and Katenka on the snow-white pillows. The cleanness of the linen, the cleanness of the rooms, the purity of their profiles, merging with the purity of the night, the snow, the stars, and the moon into one equisignificant wave, passed through the doctor's heart, making him exult and weep from the feeling of the triumphant purity of existence.

'Lord! Lord!' he was ready to whisper. 'And all this for me! How have I deserved so much? How have You allowed me to approach You, how have You let me wander onto Your priceless earth, under Your stars, to the feet of this reckless, luckless, unmurmuring, beloved woman?'

It was three o'clock in the morning when Yuri Andreevich raised his eyes from the desk and the paper. From the detached concentration he had gone into over his head, he was returning to himself, to reality, happy, strong, at peace. Suddenly, in the silence of the distant expanses that spread beyond the window, he heard a mournful, dismal sound.

He went into the unlit next room to look out of the window from there. During the hours he had spent writing, the windowpanes had become thickly frosted over, and he could see nothing through them. Yuri Andreevich pulled away the rolled-up rug placed at the bottom of the front door to stop the draught, threw his coat over his shoulders, and went out to the porch.

The white fire with which the snowy expanse was enveloped and blazing in the light of the moon blinded him. At first he could not focus his eyes and saw nothing. But after a moment he heard a drawn-out, hollow, whining howl, muffled by the distance, and then he noticed at the edge of the clearing, beyond the ravine, four elongated shadows no bigger than little dashes.

The wolves were standing side by side, their muzzles turned towards the house, and, raising their heads, were howling at the moon or at its silver reflection in Mikulitsyn's windows. For a few moments they stood motionless, but as soon as Yuri Andreevich realised they were wolves, they lowered their behinds like dogs and trotted away from the clearing as if the doctor's thought had reached them. The doctor had no time to figure out in which direction they had vanished.

'Unpleasant news!' he thought. 'That's all we needed. Can they have a lair somewhere nearby, quite close to us? Maybe even in the ravine? How frightening! And unfortunately there's also Samdevyatov's Savraska in the stable. It's probably the horse they scented.'

He decided for the time being to say nothing to Lara, so as not to frighten her, went in, locked the front door, closed the hall doors connecting the cold and warm parts of the house, stopped all the cracks and openings, and went to the desk.

The lamp was burning as brightly and welcomingly as before. But he no longer felt like writing. He could not calm down. Nothing but wolves and other threatening complications went through his mind. And he was also tired. At that moment Lara woke up.

'And you're still burning and glimmering, my dear, bright candle!' Lara said softly in a moist, sleep-congested whisper. 'Sit here next to me for a minute. I'll tell you the dream I had.'

And he put out the lamp.

9

Again a day went by in quiet madness. A child's sled turned up in the house. Flushed Katenka, in her little fur coat, laughing loudly, came sliding onto the uncleared paths of the front garden from the ice hill the doctor had made for her, packing the snow down tightly with a shovel and pouring water over it. A smile fixed on her face, she endlessly climbed back up the hill, pulling her sled on a string.

It was freezing cold and getting noticeably colder. Outside it was sunny. The snow turned yellow under the noontime rays, and into its honey yellowness poured a sweet sediment of orange thickness from the early-falling evening.

With yesterday's laundry and bathing, Lara had filled the house with dampness. The windows were covered with crumbly hoarfrost, the steam-dampened wallpaper was covered from floor to ceiling with black streaks. The rooms became dark and cheerless. Yuri Andreevich carried firewood and water, continued the unfinished examination of the house with unceasing discoveries all the time, and helped Lara, who had been busy since morning with constantly emerging household chores.

Time and again in the heat of some task their hands came together and remained that way, the load picked up to be carried was set down before it reached its destination, and a haze of invincible tenderness rushed to disarm them. Time and again everything dropped from their hands and left their heads. Minutes passed and turned into hours, and it was getting late, and they both came to their senses, horrified, remembering the neglected Katenka or the unfed and unwatered horse, and they rushed headlong to make up for and amend what had been left undone, and suffered from remorse.

The doctor's head throbbed from lack of sleep. It was filled with a sweet haze, like a hangover, and there was an aching, blissful weakness in his whole body. He waited impatiently for evening to go back to his interrupted night's work.

The preliminary half of the work was performed for him by that sleepy mist that filled him, and covered everything around him, and enwrapped his thoughts. The general diffuseness it imparted to everything went in the direction that preceded the exactness of the final embodiment. Like the vagueness of first drafts, the languid idleness of the whole day served as a necessary preparation for a labourious night.

The idleness of fatigue left nothing untouched, untransformed. Everything underwent changes and acquired a different look.

Yuri Andreevich felt that his dreams of a more settled life in Varykino were not to be realised, that the hour of his separation from Lara was at hand, that he would inevitably lose her, and after that the incentive to live, and maybe even life itself. Anguish gnawed at his heart. But still greater was his longing for the coming of evening and the desire to weep out this anguish in expressions that would make everyone weep.

The wolves he had been remembering all day were no longer wolves in the snow under the moon, but became the theme of wolves, the representation of a hostile power that had set itself the goal of destroying the doctor and Lara or driving them from Varykino. The idea of this hostility, developing, attained such force by evening as if the tracks of an antediluvian monster had been discovered in Shutma and a fairy-tale dragon of gigantic proportions, thirsting for the doctor's blood and hungering for Lara, were lying in the ravine.

Evening came. As he had yesterday, the doctor lit the lamp on the desk. Lara and Katenka went to bed earlier than the day before.

What he had written during the previous night fell into two categories. The familiar things, in newly revised versions, were written out in clean, calligraphic copies. The new things were sketched out with abbreviations and ellipses, in an illegible scrawl.

In deciphering these daubs, the doctor felt the usual disappointment. Last night these fragmentary drafts had moved him to tears and astounded him by the unexpectedness of certain strokes of luck. Now it was just these imaginary strokes of luck that stopped him and upset him, standing out sharply as too forced.

All his life he had dreamed of an originality that was smoothed over and muted, externally unrecognisable and hidden under the cover of conventional and habitual form; all his life he had striven to elaborate this restrained, unpretentious style, through which the reader and listener would grasp the content without noticing what enabled them to do so. All his life he had worked for this inconspicuous style, which would attract no one's attention, and kept being horrified at how far he still was from this ideal.

In yesterday's sketches he had wanted, using means of a simplicity verging on prattle and reaching the intimacy of the lullaby, to express his mixed mood of love and fear and anguish and courage, so as to have it pour out as if apart from words, by itself.

Now, the next day, looking through these trials, he found that they lacked a supporting plot that would join the disconnecting lines together. Gradually reworking what he had written, Yuri Andreevich began in the same lyrical manner to tell the legend of Egory the Brave.[2] He started with a sweeping pentameter that allowed for great scope. But the euphony characteristic of this metre, regardless of content, annoyed him by its conventional, false melodiousness. He abandoned the pompous metre with its caesura, cramming his lines into four feet, the way one struggles against verbosity in prose. Writing became more difficult and more alluring. The work went at a livelier pace, but still some superfluous garrulity got into it. He forced himself to shorten the lines still more. The words were crowded into trimeters, the last traces of sleepiness fell from the writer, he awakened, took fire, the narrowness of the available space itself told him how to fill it. Subjects barely named in words began to stand out in relief within the frame of reference. He heard the pace of a horse stepping over the surface of the poem, as one can hear the clop of a horse's amble in one of Chopin's ballades. St George galloped on horseback across the boundless expanse of the steppe; Yuri Andreevich saw him from behind growing smaller as he moved away. Yuri Andreevich wrote with feverish haste, barely managing to set down the words and lines arriving all in their place and apropos.

He did not notice how Lara got out of bed and came over to the desk. She seemed delicate and slender and taller than she really was in her floor-length nightgown. Yuri Andreevich gave a start when she unexpectedly rose up beside him, pale, afraid, and, stretching out her arm, asked in a whisper:

'Do you hear? A dog is howling. Two, even. Ah, how frightening, what a bad omen! Let's wait somehow till morning, and then leave, leave. I won't stay here a moment longer.'

An hour later, after much persuasion, Larissa Fyodorovna calmed down and went back to sleep. Yuri Andreevich went out to the porch. The wolves were closer than the night before and vanished still more quickly. And again Yuri Andreevich had no time to make out which way they went. They stood in a group, he had no time to count them. He fancied there were more of them.

10

The thirteenth day of their stay in Varykino arrived, in its circumstances no different from the previous ones. Wolves had howled in the same way in the

evening, after disappearing for a time in the middle of the week. Again taking them for dogs, Larissa Fyodorovna had resolved in the same way to
leave the next morning, frightened by the bad omen. In the same way states
of equilibrium alternated in her with fits of anguished uneasiness, natural in
a hard-working woman unaccustomed to daylong outpourings of the heart
and the idle, impermissible luxury of immoderate caresses.

Everything repeated itself exactly, so that when, on that morning of the
second week, Larissa Fyodorovna again, as so many times before, began
preparing for the return trip, one might have thought the week and a half
they had lived through in the interim had never been.

Again it was damp in the rooms, which were dark owing to the bleakness
of the grey, overcast day. The cold had lessened; at any moment snow might
start pouring from the dark sky covered with low clouds. Yuri Andreevich
was succumbing to the mental and physical fatigue caused by a continual
lack of sleep. His thoughts were confused, his strength was undermined,
weakness made him feel chilled, and, shivering and rubbing his hands, he
paced the unheated room, not knowing what Larissa Fyodorovna would
decide and what, according to her decision, he would have to undertake.

Her intentions were not clear. Right then she would have given half her
life for the two of them not to be so chaotically free, but forced to submit to
any strict order, established once and for all, for them to go to work, to have
duties, to be able to live sensibly and honestly.

She began her day as usual, made the beds, tidied up and swept the
rooms, made breakfast for the doctor and Katya. Then she began to pack
and asked the doctor to hitch up the horse. She had taken a firm and inflexible decision to leave.

Yuri Andreevich did not try to dissuade her. Their return to town in the
heat of the arrests there after their recent disappearance was completely
foolhardy. But it was scarcely more reasonable to sit there alone and
unarmed in the midst of this dreadful winter desert, full of its own menace.

Besides that, the last armloads of hay, which the doctor had raked up in
the nearby sheds, were coming to an end, and there were no more to be
expected. Of course, had it been possible to settle here more permanently, the
doctor would have made the rounds of the neighbourhood and seen to
replenishing the stock of fodder and provisions. But for a brief and problem-
atic stay, it was not worthwhile starting such reconnoitring. And, waving his
hand at it all, the doctor went to harness up.

He was not skilful at it. Samdevyatov had taught him how. Yuri Andreevich kept forgetting his instructions. With inexperienced hands he nevertheless did all that was needed. Having fastened the bow to the shafts with a
studded leather strap, he tied its metal-tipped end in a knot on one of the

shafts, winding it round several times, then, placing his leg against the horse's side, he pulled and tightened the ends of the collar, after which, having finished the rest, he brought the horse to the porch, tethered her, and went to tell Lara that they could make ready.

He found her in extreme disarray. She and Katenka were dressed to leave, everything was packed, but Larissa Fyodorovna was wringing her hands and, holding back tears and asking Yuri Andreevich to sit down for a moment, throwing herself into the armchair, then getting up, and – frequently interrupting herself with the exclamation 'Right?' – spoke very quickly, in an incoherent patter, on a high, singsong, and plaintive note:

'It's not my fault. I myself don't know how this came about. But we really can't go now. It will be dark soon. Night will find us on the road. There in your dreadful forest. Right? I'll do what you tell me, but myself, of my own will, I can't decide on it. Something's holding me back. My heart isn't in it. Do as you know best. Right? Why are you silent, why don't you say something? We lolled around all morning, spent half the day on God knows what. Tomorrow it won't be the same, we'll be more careful, right? Maybe we should stay one more day? We'll get up early tomorrow and set out at daybreak, at seven or even six in the morning. What do you think? You'll heat the stove, do some writing here for one extra evening, we'll spend one more night here. Ah, it would be so incomparable, so magical! Why don't you answer? Again I'm at fault for something, wretch that I am!'

'You're exaggerating. It's still long before dark. It's quite early. But let it be your way. Very well. Let's stay. Only calm yourself. Look how agitated you are. Really, let's unpack, take our coats off. Here Katenka says she's hungry. We'll have a bite to eat. You're right, leaving today would be too unprepared, too sudden. Only don't fret and don't cry, for God's sake. I'll start the stove right now. But first, since the horse is harnessed and the sleigh is at the porch, I'll go and fetch the last firewood from the Zhivagos' shed, there's not a stick left here. Don't cry. I'll be back soon.'

11

In the snow in front of the shed there were several circles of sleigh tracks from Yuri Andreevich's former comings and turnings. The snow by the porch was trampled and littered from his carrying wood two days earlier.

The clouds that had covered the sky in the morning had scattered. It became clear. Cold. The Varykino park, which surrounded these parts at various distances, was close to the shed, as if in order to peer into the doctor's face and remind him of something. The snow lay deep that winter, higher than the doorstep of the shed. It was as if the lintel lowered itself, the shed seemed to be hunched over. A slab of accumulated snow hung from the roof almost down to the doctor's head, like the cap of a giant mushroom. Directly above the slope of the roof, its sharp end as if stuck into the snow, burning with a grey heat all around its semicircular outline, stood the young, just-born crescent moon.

Though it was daytime and quite light, the doctor had a feeling as if he were standing on a late evening in the dark, dense forest of his life. There was such gloom in his soul, so sad he felt. And the young moon, a foreboding of separation, an image of solitude, burned before him almost on the level of his face.

Yuri Andreevich was falling off his feet with fatigue. Flinging wood through the door of the shed into the sleigh, he seized fewer pieces at a time than he usually did. In such cold, to touch the icy logs with snow clinging to them was painful, even through mittens. His brisk movements did not warm him up. Something had stopped inside him and snapped. He roundly cursed his talentless fate and prayed to God to keep and safeguard the life of this wondrous beauty, sad, submissive, and simple-hearted. And the crescent moon went on standing over the shed, burning without heat and shining without light.

Suddenly the horse, turning in the direction she had been brought from, raised her head and neighed, first softly and timidly, then loudly and confidently.

'What's she doing?' the doctor wondered. 'Why on earth? It can't be from fear. Horses don't neigh from fear, what stupidity. She's not such a fool as to give herself away to the wolves with her voice, if she can scent them. And so cheerfully. It must be in anticipation of home. She wants to go home. Wait, we'll set off at once.'

In addition to the load of firewood, Yuri Andreevich took some chips from the shed for kindling and a big piece of birch bark that fell whole from a log, rolled up like a boot top. He covered the wood pile with a bast mat, tied it down with rope, and, striding beside the sleigh, drove it all back to the Mikulitsyns' shed.

The horse neighed again, in response to the clear neigh of a horse somewhere in the distance, in the other direction. 'Where is that from?' the doctor wondered, rousing himself. 'We thought Varykino was deserted. It means we were mistaken.' It could not have entered his head that they had visitors, that the horse's neighing was coming from the direction of the Mikulitsyns' porch, from the garden. He led Savraska in a roundabout way through backyards, towards the outbuildings of the factory's farmsteads, and from behind the hillocks, which hid the house, could not see the front part.

Without haste (why should he be in a hurry?), he dumped the firewood in the shed, unhitched the horse, left the sleigh in the shed, and led the horse to the cold, empty stable beside it. He put her in the right corner stall, where it was less draughty, and bringing several armloads of the remaining hay from the shed, piled it onto the slanted grating of the manger.

He walked towards the house with a troubled soul. By the porch stood a well-fed black stallion hitched to a very wide peasant sleigh with a comfortable body. An unfamiliar fellow in a fine jacket, as smooth and well-fed as the horse, strolled around the horse, patting him on the sides and examining his fetlocks.

Noise could be heard in the house. Unwilling to eavesdrop and unable to hear anything, Yuri Andreevich involuntarily slowed his pace and stood as if rooted to the spot. He could not make out the words, but he recognised the voices of Komarovsky, Lara, and Katenka. They were probably in the front room, by the entrance. Komarovsky was arguing with Lara, and, judging by the sound of her replies, she was agitated, weeping, and now sharply objected to him, now agreed with him. By some indefinable sign, Yuri Andreevich imagined that Komarovsky had just then brought the talk around precisely to him, presumably in the sense that he was an untrustworthy man ('a servant of two masters', Yuri Andreevich fancied), that it was not clear who was dearer to him, his family or Lara, and that Lara could not rely on him, because by entrusting herself to him, she would be 'chasing two hares and falling between two stools'. Yuri Andreevich went into the house.

In the front room, indeed, still in a floor-length fur coat, stood Komarovsky. Lara was holding Katenka by the collar of her coat, trying to pull it together and failing to get the hook through the eye. She was cross with the girl, shouting that she should stop fidgeting and struggling, while Katenka complained: 'Gently, mama, you're choking me.' They all stood dressed and ready to leave. When Yuri Andreevich came in, Lara and Viktor Ippolitovich rushed simultaneously to meet him.

'Where did you disappear to? We need you so much!'

'Greetings, Yuri Andreevich! Despite the rudenesses we exchanged last time, I've come again, as you see, without invitation.'

'Greetings, Viktor Ippolitovich.'

'Where did you disappear to for so long? Listen to what he says and decide quickly for yourself and me. There's no time. We must hurry.'

'Why are we standing? Sit down, Viktor Ippolitovich. Where did I disappear to, Larochka? But you know I went to fetch wood, and then I saw to the horse. Viktor Ippolitovich, I beg you to sit down.'

'Aren't you struck? How is it you don't show any surprise? We were sorry that this man left and we hadn't seized upon his offers, and now he's here before you and you're not surprised. But still more striking is his fresh news. Tell him, Viktor Ippolitovich.'

'I don't know what Larissa Fyodorovna has in mind, but for my part I'll say the following. I purposely spread the rumour that I had left, and stayed for a few more days, to give you and Larissa Fyodorovna time to rethink the questions we had touched upon and on mature reflection perhaps come to a less reckless decision.'

'But we can't put it off any longer. Now is the most convenient time for leaving. Tomorrow morning – but better let Viktor Ippolitovich tell you himself.'

'One moment, Larochka. Excuse me, Viktor Ippolitovich. Why are we standing here in our coats? Let's take them off and sit down. This is a serious conversation. We can't do it harum-scarum. Forgive me, Viktor Ippolitovich. Our disagreement touches upon certain delicate matters. To analyse these subjects is ridiculous and awkward. I never even thought of going with you. Larissa Fyodorovna is another matter. On those rare occasions when our anxieties were separable and we remembered that we were not one being but two, with two different destinies, I thought that Lara should consider your plans more attentively, especially for Katya's sake. And she constantly did just that, coming back again and again to those possibilities.'

'But only on condition that you come, too.'

'We have the same difficulty imagining our separation, but perhaps we must overcome ourselves and make this sacrifice. Because there can be no talk of my going.'

'But you don't know anything yet. First listen. Tomorrow morning . . . Viktor Ippolitovich!'

'Clearly, Larissa Fyodorovna has in mind the information I brought and have already told her. An official train of the Far Eastern government is standing under steam on the tracks at Yuriatin. It arrived yesterday from Moscow and tomorrow it continues on its way. It's the train of our Ministry of Transportation. It is half made up of international sleeping cars.

'I must be on that train. Places have been put at my disposal for persons invited to join my working team. We'll roll along in full comfort. Such an occasion will not present itself again. I know you don't throw words to the wind and will not change your refusal to come with us. You're a man of firm decisions, I know. But all the same. Bend yourself for Larissa Fyodorovna's sake. You heard, she won't go without you. Come with us, if not to Vladivostok, at least to Yuriatin. And there we'll see. But in that case we have to hurry. We mustn't lose a minute. I have a man with me, I'm a poor driver. The five of us, counting him, won't fit into my sleigh. If I'm not mistaken, you have Samdevyatov's horse. You said you drove her to fetch firewood. Is she still harnessed up?'

'No, I unhitched her.'

'Then hitch her up again quickly. My driver will help you. Though, you know . . . Well, devil take the second sleigh. We'll make it in mine somehow. Only for God's sake be quick. Take the most necessary things for the road, whatever you've got at hand. Let the house stay as it is, unlocked. We must save the child's life, not go looking for locks and keys.'

'I don't understand you, Viktor Ippolitovich. You talk as if I had agreed to come. Go with God, if Lara wants it that way. And don't worry about the house. I'll stay, and after your departure I'll tidy things and lock up.'

'What are you saying, Yura? Why this deliberate nonsense, which you don't believe yourself? "If Larissa Fyodorovna has decided." He himself knows perfectly well that without his participation in the trip, there is no Larissa Fyodorovna in the works and none of her decisions. Then what are these phrases for: "I'll tidy the house and take care of everything."'

'So you're implacable. Then I have another request. With Larissa Fyodorovna's permission, may I have a couple of words with you in private, if possible?'

'Very well. If it's so necessary, let's go to the kitchen. You don't object, Larusha?'

12

'Strelnikov has been seized, given a capital sentence, and the sentence has been carried out.'

'How terrible. Can it be true?'

'So I've heard. I'm sure of it.'

'Don't tell Lara. She'll go out of her mind.'

'Of course I won't. That's why I invited you to another room. After this execution, she and her daughter are in direct, imminent danger. Help me to save them. Do you flatly refuse to accompany us?'

'I told you so. Of course.'

'But she won't go without you. I simply don't know what to do. In that case I'll ask you for help of another sort. Pretend in words, deceitfully, that you're ready to give in, that you may be persuaded. I can't picture your parting to myself. Neither here on the spot, nor at the station in Yuriatin, if you really were to go to see us off. We must make it so that she believes you're also coming. If not now, along with us, then some time later, when I offer you a new opportunity, which you will promise to make use of. You must be able to give her a false oath on it. But these are not empty words on my part. I assure you on my honour that, at the first expression of your desire, I will undertake to deliver you from here to us and send you further on, wherever you like. Larissa Fyodorovna must be certain that you're accompanying us. Convince her of it with all your power of persuasion. Let's say you pretend that you're running to hitch up the horse and insist that we set out at once, without waiting, while you harness up and overtake us on the road.'

'I'm shaken by the news of Pavel Pavlovich's execution and can't come to my senses. I'm having trouble following your words. But I agree with you. After Strelnikov has been dealt with, by our present-day logic, the lives of Larissa Fyodorovna and Katya are also in danger. One of us is certain to be deprived of freedom, and therefore, one way or the other, we'll be separated. It's true, then, that it's better if you separate us and take them somewhere far away, to the ends of the earth. Right now, as I say this to you, things are going your way anyhow. I probably won't be able to bear it and, surrendering my pride and self-love, will obediently come crawling to you to receive her from your hands, and life, and a way by sea to my family, and my own salvation. But let me sort it all out. The news you've reported has stunned me. I'm overwhelmed by suffering, which deprives me of the ability to think and reason. Maybe by obeying you I'm committing a fatal, irrevocable error that will horrify me all my life, but in the fog of pain that robs me of strength the only thing I can do now is mechanically agree with you and obey you blindly and will-lessly. And so, for the sake of her good, I'll pretend now and tell her that I'm going to hitch up the horse and overtake you, and I'll stay here alone by myself. Only one small thing. How are you going to go now, with night falling? It's a forest road, there are wolves around, you must be careful.'

'I know. I have a rifle and a revolver. Don't worry. And, incidentally, I brought a bit of alcohol along in case of cold. A good amount. Want some?'

13

'What have I done? What have I done? Given her away, renounced her, surrendered her. Run headlong after them, overtake them, bring her back. Lara! Lara!

'They can't hear. The wind's against me. And they're probably talking loudly. She has every reason to be cheerful, calm. She's let herself be deceived and doesn't suspect the delusion she's in.

'These are probably her thoughts. She's thinking. Everything has turned out in the best possible way, just as she wanted. Her Yurochka, a fantastic and obstinate man, has finally softened, praise God, and is now setting out with her for some safe place, to people wiser than they, under the protection of law and order. Even if, to stand on his mettle and show his character, he turns pigheaded and refuses to get on their train tomorrow, Viktor Ippolitovich will send another one for him in the nearest future.

'And now, of course, he's already in the stable hitching up Savraska, his confused, disobedient hands trembling with agitation and haste, and will immediately whip her up to full speed behind them, so as to overtake them while they're still in the fields, before they get into the forest.'

That was probably what she was thinking. And they had not even said goodbye properly. Yuri Andreevich had only waved his hand and turned away, trying to swallow the pain that stuck like a lump in his throat, as if he were choking on a piece of apple.

The doctor, his coat thrown over one shoulder, was standing on the porch. With his free hand, not covered by the coat, he squeezed the neck of a turned porch post just under the ceiling with such force as if he were trying to strangle it. With all his consciousness he was riveted to a distant point in space. There, a short stretch of the road could be seen, going uphill between a few scattered birches. On that open space the light of the low, already setting sun was falling at that moment. There, into that lit-up strip, the racing sleigh should come at any moment out of the shallow depression they had dipped into for a short time.

'Farewell, farewell,' the doctor repeated soundlessly, senselessly, in anticipation of that moment, forcing the nearly breathless sounds from his chest into the frosty evening air. 'Farewell, my only beloved, lost forever!'

'Here they come! Here they come!' his white lips whispered with impetuous dryness, when the sleigh shot up from below like an arrow, passing one birch after another, and began to slow down and – oh, joy! – stopped by the last one.

Oh, how his heart pounded, oh, how his heart pounded, his legs gave way under him, and he became all soft as felt from agitation, like the coat that was slipping from his shoulder! 'Oh, God, it seems You have decided to return her to me? What's happened there? What's going on there on that distant line of sunset? Where is the explanation? Why are they standing there? No. All is lost. They've set off. Racing. She probably asked to stop for a moment for a farewell look at the house. Or maybe she wanted to see whether Yuri Andreevich had already set out and was speeding after them? They're gone. Gone.

'If they have time, if the sun doesn't set beforehand' (he wouldn't be able to see them in the darkness), 'they'll flash by one more time, the last one now, on the other side of the ravine, in the clearing where the wolves stood two nights ago.'

And now this moment came and went. The dark crimson sun still rounded over the blue line of the snowdrifts. The snow greedily absorbed the pineapple sweetness the sun poured into it. And now they appeared, swept by, raced off. 'Farewell, Lara, till we meet in the other world, farewell, my beauty, farewell, my fathomless, inexhaustible, eternal joy.' And now they vanished. 'I'll never see you again, never, never in my life, I'll never see you again.'

Meanwhile, it was getting dark. The crimson-bronze patches of light the sunset scattered over the snow were swiftly fading, going out. The ashen softness of the expanses quickly sank into the lilac twilight, which was turning more and more purple. Their grey mist merged with the fine, lacy handwriting of the birches along the road, tenderly traced against the pale pink of the sky, suddenly grown shallow.

The grief in his soul sharpened Yuri Andreevich's perceptions. He grasped everything with tenfold distinctness. His surroundings acquired the features of a rare uniqueness, even the air itself. The winter evening breathed an unprecedented concern, like an all-sympathising witness. It was as if there had never been such a nightfall until now, and evening came for the first time only today, to comfort the orphaned man plunged into solitude. It was as if the woods around stood on the hillocks, back to the horizon, not simply as a girdling panorama, but had just placed themselves there, having emerged from under the ground to show sympathy.

The doctor almost waved away this tangible beauty of the hour, like a crowd of importunate commiserators; he was almost ready to whisper to the sunset's rays reaching out to him: 'Thanks. Don't bother.'

He went on standing on the porch, his face to the closed door, turning away from the world. 'My bright sun has set,' something within him repeated and re-echoed. He had no strength to utter this sequence of words aloud without convulsive spasms in the throat interrupting them.

He went into the house. A double monologue, two sorts of monologue, started and played out in him: a dry, seemingly businesslike one with respect to himself, and an expansive, boundless one addressed to Lara. This is how his thoughts went: 'Now I'll go to Moscow. The first thing is to survive. Not to surrender to insomnia. Not to fall asleep. To work at night to the point of stupefaction, until I drop from fatigue. And another thing. To heat the bedroom at once, so as not to be needlessly cold at night.'

But he also talked to himself like this: 'My unforgettable delight! As long as the crooks of my arms remember you, as long as you're still on my hands and lips, I'll be with you. I'll shed tears about you in something worthy, abiding. I'll write down my memory of you in a tender, tender, achingly sorrowful portrayal. I'll stay here until I've done it. And then I'll leave myself. This is how I'll portray you. I'll set your features on paper, as, after a terrible storm that churns the sea to its bottom, the traces of the strongest, farthest-reaching wave lie on the sand. In a broken, meandering line the sea heaps up pumice stones, bits of cork, shells, seaweed, the lightest, most weightless things it could lift from the bottom. This is the line of the highest tide stretching endlessly along the shore. So the storm of life cast you up to me, my pride. And so I will portray you.'

He went into the house, locked the door, took off his coat. When he went into the room that Lara had tidied up so well and with such care in the morning, and in which everything had now been turned upside down again by her hasty departure, when he saw the rumpled, unmade bed and things lying about in disorder, thrown on the floor and chairs, he sank to his knees before the bed like a little boy, leaned his whole breast against its hard edge, and, burying his face in the hanging end of the coverlet, wept with a childish ease and bitterness. This did not go on for long. Yuri Andreevich stood up, quickly wiped his tears, looked around with a distractedly astonished and wearily absent gaze, took out the bottle Komarovsky had left, uncorked it, poured half a glass, added water, mixed in some snow, and with a pleasure almost equal to his just-shed, inconsolable tears, began drinking this mixture in slow, greedy gulps.

14

Something incongruous was taking place in Yuri Andreevich. He was slowly losing his mind. He had never yet led such a strange existence. He neglected the house, stopped looking after himself, turned nights into days, and lost count of the time that had passed since Lara's departure.

He drank and wrote things devoted to her, but the Lara of his verses and notes, as he struck out and replaced one word with another, kept moving further away from her true prototype, Katenka's living mother, who was now travelling with Katya.

Yuri Andreevich did this crossing out from considerations of precision and power of expression, but it also answered to the promptings of inner restraint, which did not allow him to reveal personal experiences and unfictitious happenings too openly, so as not to wound or offend the direct participants in what had been written and lived through. Thus what was visceral, still pulsing and warm, was forced out of the poems, and instead of the bleeding and noxious, a serene breadth appeared in them, raising the particular case to a generality familiar to all. He did not strive for this goal, but this breadth came of itself like a comfort sent to him personally by the traveller, like a distant greeting from her, like her appearance in a dream, or like the touch of her hand on his brow. And he loved this ennobling stamp on his verses.

With this lament for Lara, he also finished scribbling down his stuff from various periods about all sorts of things, about nature, about everyday life. As had always happened to him before as well, a multitude of thoughts about personal life and the life of society descended upon him while he worked, simultaneously and in passing.

He again thought that his notion of history, of what is known as the course of history, was not at all the same as the accepted one, and that he pictured it as similar to the life of the vegetable kingdom. In winter, under snow, the bare branches of a deciduous forest are as scraggly and pathetic as the hairs on an old man's wart. In spring the forest is transformed in a few days, rises to the clouds; one can lose oneself, hide oneself in its leafy maze. This transformation is achieved by a movement that surpasses in speed the movements of animals, since animals do not grow as quickly as plants, and that can never be observed. A forest does not move; we cannot catch it, cannot surprise it changing place. We always find it immobile. And it is in the same immobility that we find the eternally growing, eternally changing life of society, history, in its unobservable transformations.

Tolstoy did not carry his thought through to the end when he denied the role of initiators to Napoleon, to rulers, to generals.[3] He thought precisely the same, but he did not voice it with full clarity. No one makes history, it is not visible, just as it is impossible to see grass grow. Wars, revolutions, tsars, Robespierres – these are its organic stimulants, its fermenting yeast. Revolutions are produced by men of action, one-sided fanatics, geniuses of self-limitation. In a few hours or days they overturn the old order. The upheavals last for weeks, for years at the most, and then for decades, for centuries, people bow down to the spirit of limitation that led to the upheavals as to something sacred.

With his lament for Lara, he also lamented that far-off summer in Meliuzeevo, when the revolution was a god come down from heaven to earth, the god of that time, that summer, and each one went mad in his own way, and the life of each existed by itself and not as an explanatory illustration confirming the rightness of superior politics.

With this sketching out of various odds and ends, he again verified and noted down that art always serves beauty, and beauty is the happiness of having form, while form is the organic key to existence, for every living thing must have form in order to exist, and thus art, including tragic art, is an account of the happiness of existing. These reflections and notes also brought him happiness, so tragic and filled with tears that his head grew weary and ached from it.

Anfim Efimovich came to call on him. He also brought vodka and told him about the departure of Antipova with her daughter and Komarovsky. Anfim Efimovich came by rail on a handcar. He scolded the doctor for not taking proper care of the horse and took her back, despite Yuri Andreevich's request to bear with him for three or four more days. Instead he promised to come in person and fetch the doctor after that time and remove him from Varykino for good.

Sometimes, writing away, working away, Yuri Andreevich suddenly remembered the departed woman in all distinctness and lost his head from tenderness and the keenness of deprivation. As once in childhood, amidst the splendour of summer nature, he had fancied that he heard the voice of his dead mother in the trilling of the birds, so his hearing, accustomed to Lara, grown used to her voice, now sometimes deceived him. 'Yurochka,' he sometimes heard in an auditory hallucination from the next room.

Other sensory deceptions also befell him during that week. At the end of it, in the night, he suddenly woke up after an oppressive, absurd dream about a dragon's lair under the house. He opened his eyes. Suddenly the bottom of the ravine was lit up with fire and resounded with the crack and boom of someone firing a gun. Surprisingly, a moment after this extraordinary occurrence, the doctor fell back to sleep, and in the morning he decided that he had dreamed it all.

15

Here is what happened a little later during one of those days. The doctor finally heeded the voice of reason. He said to himself that if one has set oneself the goal of doing oneself in at all costs, one could find a more effective and less tormenting way. He promised himself that as soon as Anfim Efimovich came for him, he would immediately leave the place.

Before evening, while it was still light, he heard the loud crunch of someone's footsteps on the snow. Someone was calmly walking towards the house with brisk, resolute strides.

Strange. Who could it be? Anfim Efimovich would have come with a horse. There were no passers-by in deserted Varykino. 'It's for me,' Yuri Andreevich decided. 'A summons or a request to come to town. Or to arrest me. But how will they take me? And then there should be two of them. It's Mikulitsyn, Averky Stepanovich,' he surmised, rejoicing, recognising his guest, as he thought, by his gait. The man, who was still a riddle, paused for a moment at the door with the broken-off bar, not finding the expected padlock on it, and then moved on with assured steps and knowing movements, opening the doors before him and closing them carefully, in a proprietary way.

These strangenesses found Yuri Andreevich at his desk, where he sat with his back to the entrance. While he was getting up from his chair and turning his face to the door so as to receive the visitor, the man was already standing on the threshold, stopped as if rooted to the spot.

'Whom do you want?' escaped from the doctor with an unconsciousness that did not oblige him to anything, and when no answer followed, Yuri Andreevich was not surprised.

The man who had come in was strong and well-built, with a handsome face. He was wearing a short fur jacket, fur-lined trousers, and warm goatskin boots, and had a rifle slung over his shoulder on a leather strap.

Only the moment of the stranger's appearance was unexpected for the doctor, not his coming. His findings in the house and other tokens had prepared Yuri Andreevich for this meeting. The man who had come in was obviously the one to whom the supplies in the house belonged. In appearance he seemed to be someone the doctor had already seen and knew. The visitor had probably also been forewarned that the house was not empty. He was not surprised enough to find it inhabited. Maybe he had been told whom he would meet inside. Maybe he himself knew the doctor.

'Who is he? Who is he?' The doctor painfully searched his memory. 'Lord help me, where have I seen him before? Can it be? A hot May morning in some immemorial year. The railway junction in Razvilye. The ill-omened carriage of the commissar. Clarity of notions, straightforwardness, strictness of principles, rightness, rightness, rightness. Strelnikov!'

16

They had been talking for a long time already, several hours straight, as only Russians in Russia talk, in particular those who are frightened and anguished, and those who are distraught and frenzied, as all people were then. Evening was coming. It was getting dark.

Besides the uneasy talkativeness that Strelnikov shared with everybody, he also talked incessantly for some other reason of his own.

He could not have enough of talking and clung with all his might to the conversation with the doctor, so as to avoid solitude. Did he fear pangs of conscience or sad memories that pursued him, or was he tormented by dissatisfaction with himself, which makes a man unbearable and hateful to himself and ready to die of shame? Or had he taken some dreadful, irrevocable decision, with which he did not want to be left alone, and the fulfilment of which he kept postponing as long as possible by chatting with the doctor and being in his company?

However it was, Strelnikov was hiding some important secret that weighed on him, while giving himself in all the rest to the most lavish outpourings of the heart.

This was the sickness of the age, the revolutionary madness of the epoch. In thought everyone was different from his words and outward show. No one had a clear conscience. Each with good reason could feel himself guilty, a secret criminal, an unexposed deceiver. On the slightest pretext, a rage of self-castigating imagination would play itself out to the uttermost limits. People fantasised, denounced themselves, not only under the effect of fear, but also drawn on by a destructively morbid inclination, of their own free will, in a state of metaphysical trance and passion for self-condemnation that, once set loose, could not be stopped.

How much of this evidence, written and oral, given on the point of death, had been read and heard in his time by the prominent military, and sometimes also court-martial, figure Strelnikov. Now he himself was possessed by a similar fit of self-exposure, re-evaluated himself entirely, put a bottom line to everything, saw everything in a feverish, distorted, delirious misinterpretation.

Strelnikov was telling it all without order, jumping from confession to confession.

'It was near Chitá. Were you struck by the curiosities I stuffed the cupboards and drawers in this house with? It's all from war requisitions, which we carried out when the Red Army occupied eastern Siberia. Naturally, I didn't drag it on my back myself. Life always pampered me with loyal, devoted people. These candles, matches, coffee, tea, writing materials, and all the rest are partly from Czech military property, partly Japanese and English. Wonders of the world, right? "Right?" was my wife's favourite expression, as you've probably noticed. I didn't know whether to tell you this at once, but now I'll confess. I came to see her and our daughter. I wasn't told in time that they were here. And now I'm too late. When I learned about your intimacy with her from gossip and reports, and the name Doctor Zhivago was first uttered, I remembered in some inconceivable way, out of the thousands of faces that have flashed past me in these years, a doctor of that name who was once brought to me for interrogation.'

'And you were sorry you didn't have him shot?'

Strelnikov let this remark go unnoticed. Perhaps he did not even hear his interlocutor interrupt his monologue with his own insertion. He went on distractedly and pensively.

'Of course, I was jealous of you, and I'm jealous now. How could it be otherwise? I've been hiding in these parts only in recent months, after my other covers failed far to the east. I was supposed to be court-martialled on a false accusation. The outcome was easy to predict. I didn't know myself to be guilty of anything. There was a hope that I might vindicate myself and defend my good name in the future under better circumstances. I decided to quit the field in good time, before I was arrested, and meanwhile to hide, wander about, live like a hermit. Maybe I would have saved myself in the end. A young rascal who wormed his way into my confidence did me a bad turn.

'I was going west through Siberia on foot, in winter, hiding, starving. I buried myself in the snow, spent nights in snow-covered trains, of which there were endless chains standing under the snow then along the Siberian main line.

'In my wanderings, I ran into a vagabond boy who supposedly had survived after being shot by the partisans in a line of other men executed at the same time. He supposedly crawled from under the pile of corpses, caught his breath, recovered, and then began moving about from one lair to another, like myself. At least that's what he told me. A scoundrelly adolescent, full of vices, backward, one of those dunces who get thrown out of school for inability.'

The more details Strelnikov gave, the better the doctor recognised the boy.

'First name Terenty, last name Galuzin?'

'Yes.'

'Then all that about the partisans and the execution is true. He didn't invent any of it.'

'The only good feature the boy had was that he madly adored his mother. His father had perished as a hostage. He learned that his mother was in prison and would share the father's lot, and decided to do anything to free her. In the provincial Cheka, where he came pleading guilty and offering his

services, they agreed to forgive him everything for the price of some important information. He pointed out the place where I was hiding. I managed to
forestall his betrayal and disappear in time.

'With fantastic efforts, with thousands of adventures, I crossed Siberia
and came here, to places where I'm known to everybody and am least of all
expected to appear, such boldness not being presumed on my part. And
indeed they spent a long time searching for me around Chitá, while I was
hiding in this house or some other refuge in the area. But now it's the end.
They've tracked me down here, too. Listen. It's getting dark. I don't like the
time that's coming, because I lost my sleep long ago. You know what a torment that is. If you haven't burned up all my candles – excellent stearin candles, right? – let's talk a bit longer. Let's talk as long as you can, with every
luxury, all night long, with candles burning.'

'There are candles. Only one pack has been opened. I burned the
kerosene I found here.'

'Do you have any bread?'

'No.'

'What did you live on? However, I'm asking a stupid question. On potatoes. I know.'

'Yes. There's all you could want here. The owners of the place were experienced and provident. They knew how to store them. They're all safe in the
cellar. Didn't rot or freeze.'

Suddenly Strelnikov began talking about the revolution.

17

'All this is not for you. You won't understand it. You grew up differently.
There was the world of the city's outskirts, a world of railroad tracks and
workmen's barracks. Filth, overcrowding, destitution, the degradation of
man in the labourer, the degradation of women. There was the gleeful,
unpunished impudence of depravity, of mama's boys, well-heeled students,
and little merchants. The tears and complaints of the robbed, the injured,
the seduced were dismissed with a joke or an outburst of scornful vexation.
This was the olympianism of parasites, remarkable only in that they did not
trouble themselves about anything, never sought anything, neither gave nor
left the world anything!

'But we took up life like a military campaign, we moved mountains for
the sake of those we loved. And though we brought them nothing but grief,
we did not offend them in the least, because we turned out to be even
greater martyrs than they were.

'Before I go on, though, it is my duty to tell you this. The point is the following. You must leave here without delay, if you hold your life dear. The round-up is closing in on me, and whatever its end may be, you'll be implicated with me, you're already part of my affair by the fact of our conversation. Besides, there are a lot of wolves here, I shot at them the other day.'

'Ah, so that was you shooting?'

'Yes. You, of course, heard it? I was on my way to another refuge, but before I came to it, I realised by various signs that it had been discovered and the people there had probably been killed. I won't stay long with you, I'll just spend the night and leave in the morning. So, then, with your permission, I'll go on.

'But could it be that Tverskaya-Yamskaya Streets⁴ and fops in cocked caps and trousers with foot straps racing about with their girls in dashing cabs existed only in Moscow, only in Russia? The street, the evening street, the evening street of that age, the trotters, the dapple greys, existed everywhere. What unified the epoch, what shaped the nineteenth century into a single historical segment? The birth of socialist thought. Revolutions took place, selfless young men mounted the barricades. Publicists racked their brains over how to curb the brutal shamelessness of money and raise up and defend the human dignity of the poor man. Marxism appeared. It discovered what the root of the evil was and where the cure lay. It became the mighty force of the age. All this was the Tverskaya-Yamskaya of the age, and the filth, and the shining of sanctity, and the depravity, and the workers' quarters, the leaflets and barricades.

'Ah, how beautiful she was as a young schoolgirl! You have no idea. She often visited her girlfriend in a house inhabited by workers of the Brest railway. That's how the railway was named originally, before several subsequent renamings. My father, presently a member of the Yuriatin tribunal, worked then as a trackman on the station section. I visited that house and met her there. She was a young girl, a child, but the apprehensive thought, the anxiety of the age, could already be read on her face, in her eyes. All the themes of the time, all its tears and injuries, all its impulses, all its stored-up revenge and pride, were written on her face and in her posture, in the mixture of her girlish modesty and bold shapeliness. An accusation of the age could be pronounced on her behalf, with her mouth. You'll agree, that's not a trifling thing. It's a sort of predestination, a marking out. One must have it from nature, one must have the right to it.'

'You speak wonderfully about her. I saw her at that time, just as you describe her. The schoolgirl was united in her with the heroine of an unchildish mystery. Her shadow flattened itself on the wall in a movement of apprehensive self-defence. That's how I saw her. That's how I remember her. You've put it strikingly well.'

'You saw and remember? But what did you do about it?'

'That's another question entirely.'

'So, you see, all this nineteenth century, with all its revolutions in Paris, several generations of Russian emigration, starting with Herzen,[5] all the plotted regicides, realised and unrealised, all the workers' movements of the world, all the Marxism in the parliaments and universities of Europe, all the new system of ideas, the novelty and hastiness of its conclusions, the mockery, all the additional pitilessness developed in the name of pity, all this was absorbed and in a generalised way expressed by Lenin, so as to fall upon the old in a personified retribution for what had been done.

'Beside him rose the unforgettably immense image of Russia, which suddenly blazed up in the eyes of all the world like a candle of atonement for all the woes and adversities of mankind. But why am I saying all this to you? For you it's a clanging cymbal,[6] empty sounds.

'For the sake of this girl I went to the university, for her sake I became a teacher and came to work in this Yuriatin, which was as yet unknown to me. I swallowed stacks of books and acquired a mass of knowledge, to be useful to her and to be at hand in case she needed my help. I went to war, so as to conquer her again after three years of marriage, and then, after the war and my return from captivity, I took advantage of my being considered dead and, under an assumed name, immersed myself totally in the revolution, to pay back in full for everything she had suffered, to wash clean these sad memories, so that there would be no return to the past, so that Tverskaya-Yamskaya would be no more. And they, she and my daughter, were next door, right here! What effort it cost me to suppress the desire to rush to them, to see them! But I wanted first to carry my life's work to its conclusion. Oh, what I'd give now for just one look at them! When she came into a room, it was as if a window was thrown open, the room was filled with light and air.'

'I know how dear she was to you. But, forgive me, do you have any idea of how she loved you?'

'Sorry. What did you say?'

'I said, do you have any idea to what extent you were dear to her, dearer than anyone in the world?'

'Where did you get that?'

'She said it to me herself.'

'She? To you?'

'Yes.'

'Forgive me. I suppose this request is unrealisable, but if it is permissible within the bounds of modesty, if it is within your power, please recall as far as possible precisely what she said to you.'

'Very willingly. She called you an exemplary man, whose equal she had never seen, of a uniquely high authenticity, and said that if the vision of the home she once shared with you glimmered again on the far horizon, she would crawl to its doorstep on her knees from anywhere at all, even the ends of the earth.'

'Sorry. If this does not encroach on something inviolable for you, can you remember when and in what circumstances she told you that?'

'She was tidying this room. Then she went outside to shake out the rug.'

'Forgive me, but which one? There are two here.'

'The larger one.'

'She couldn't do it alone. Did you help her?'

'Yes.'

'You held opposite ends of the rug, and she threw herself back, waving her arms high, as on a swing, and turned away from the flying dust, squinting and laughing. Right? How well I know her habits! And then you started walking towards each other, folding the heavy rug first in two, then in four, and she joked and pulled all sorts of antics while you did it. Right? Right?'

They got up, walked over to different windows, started looking in different directions. After some silence, Strelnikov went up to Yuri Andreevich. Catching hold of his hands and pressing them to his breast, he went on with the former hastiness:

'Forgive me, I understand that I'm touching something dear, cherished. But, if I may, I'll ask more questions. Only don't go away. Don't leave me alone. I'll soon go away myself. Think, six years of separation, six years of inconceivable self-restraint. But it seemed to me that not all of freedom had been conquered yet. I would achieve that first, and then I would belong wholly to them, my hands would be unbound. And now all my constructions have come to nothing. Tomorrow they'll seize me. You're close and dear to her. Maybe you'll see her some day. But no, what am I asking? It's madness. They'll seize me and won't allow me to vindicate myself. They'll fall upon me all at once, stopping my mouth with shouts and abuse. Don't I know how it's done?'

18

At last he would have a good night's sleep. For the first time in a long while Yuri Andreevich did not notice how he fell asleep as soon as he stretched out on his bed. Strelnikov spent the night with him. Yuri Andreevich gave him a place to sleep in the next room. In those brief moments when Yuri Andreevich woke up to turn on his other side or pull up the blanket that had slipped to the floor, he felt the strengthening power of his healthy sleep and delightedly fell asleep again. During the second half of the night, he began to have short, quickly changing dreams from the time of his childhood, sensible and rich in detail, which it was easy to take for reality.

Thus, for instance, his mother's watercolour of the Italian seacoast, which hung on the wall, suddenly tore off, fell on the floor, and the sound of breaking glass awakened Yuri Andreevich. He opened his eyes. No, it was something else. It must be Antipov, Lara's husband, Pavel Pavlovich, whose last name is Strelnikov, scarifying wolves in Shutma again, as Vakkh would say. Ah, no, what nonsense. Of course, it was the painting falling off the wall. There it is in splinters on the floor, he confirmed, as his dream returned and continued.

He woke up with a headache from having slept too long. He could not figure out at first who and where in the world he was.

Suddenly he remembered: 'Strelnikov spent the night with me. It's already late. I must get dressed. He's probably up already, and if not, I'll rouse him, make coffee, we'll have coffee together.'

'Pavel Pavlovich!'

No answer. 'It means he's still asleep. Fast asleep, though.' Yuri Andreevich unhurriedly got dressed and went into the next room. Strelnikov's military papakha was lying on the table, but he himself was not in the house. 'Must have gone for a walk,' thought the doctor. 'Without his hat. To keep himself in shape. And I've got to put a cross on Varykino today and go to town. But it's too late. I overslept again. Just like every morning.'

Yuri Andreevich started a fire in the stove, took the bucket, and went to the well for water. A few steps from the porch, obliquely across the path, having fallen and buried his head in a snowdrift, lay Pavel Pavlovich. He had shot himself. The snow under his left temple was bunched into a red lump, soaked in a pool of spilled blood. The small drops of blood spattered around had rolled up with the snow into little red balls that looked like frozen rowan berries.

Part Fifteen

THE ENDING

I

It remains to tell the uncomplicated story of the last eight or nine years of Yuri Andreevich's life, in the course of which he declined and went more and more to seed, losing his knowledge and skil as a doctor and as a writer, would emerge from this state of depression and despondency for a short time, become inspired, return to activity, and then, after a brief flash, again fall into prolonged indifference towards himself and everything in the world. During these years his long-time heart ailment, which he himself had diagnosed earlier, though he had no idea of the degree of its seriousness, advanced greatly.

He arrived in Moscow at the beginning of the NEP,[1] the most ambiguous and false of Soviet periods. He was more emaciated, overgrown, and wild than at the time of his return to Yuriatin from his partisan captivity. Along the way he had again gradually taken off everything of value and exchanged it for bread, plus some cast-off rags, so as not to be left naked. Thus, as he went, he ate up his second fur coat and his two-piece suit and appeared on the streets of Moscow in a grey papakha, foot cloths, and a threadbare soldier's greatcoat, which, lacking its buttons, which had all been cut off, had turned into a wraparound prisoner's robe. In this outfit, he was in no way distinguishable from the countless Red Army soldiers whose crowds flooded the squares, boulevards, and train stations of the capital.

He did not arrive in Moscow alone. A handsome peasant youth, dressed like himself in soldier's clothes, had followed on his heels everywhere. In this guise they appeared in those surviving Moscow drawing rooms where Yuri Andreevich had spent his childhood, where he was remembered and received with his companion, following delicate enquiries into whether they had gone to the bathhouse after the trip – typhus was still raging – and where Yuri Andreevich was told, in the first days of his appearance, the circumstances of his family's leaving Moscow for abroad.

They both shunned people, but from acute shyness they avoided the chance of appearing singly as guests, when it was impossible to be silent and one had to keep up the conversation. Usually their two lanky figures showed up at a gathering of their acquaintances, hid in some inconspicuous corner, and silently spent the evening without taking part in the general conversation.

In the company of his young comrade, the tall, thin doctor in homely clothes looked like a seeker of truth from the common people, and his constant attendant like an obedient, blindly devoted disciple and follower. Who was this young companion?

2

For the last part of the trip, closer to Moscow, Yuri Andreevich had gone by rail, but the first, much bigger part he had made on foot.

The sight of the villages he passed through was no better than what he had seen in Siberia and the Urals during his flight from forest captivity. Only then he had passed through that region in winter, and now it was the end of summer and the warm, dry autumn, which was much easier.

Half the villages he passed through were deserted, as after an enemy campaign, the fields abandoned and unharvested, and in fact these were the results of war, of civil war.

For two or three days at the end of September, his road followed the steep, high bank of a river. The river, flowing towards Yuri Andreevich, was on his right. To the left, from the road to the cloud-heaped skyline, unharvested fields spread far and wide. They were broken up here and there by deciduous forests, with a predominance of oaks, elms, and maples. The forests ran down to the river in deep ravines, and cut across the road with precipices and steep descents.

In the unharvested fields, the rye, not holding to the overripe ears, flowed and spilled from them. Yuri Andreevich filled his mouth with handfuls of the grain, which he had difficulty grinding with his teeth, and fed on it on those especially difficult occasions when the possibility did not present itself for boiling the grain into porridge. His stomach poorly digested the raw, barely chewed feed.

Yuri Andreevich had never in his life seen rye of such a sinister dark brown, the colour of old, dull gold. Ordinarily, when reaped in time, it is much lighter.

These flame-coloured fields, burning without fire, these fields calling for help with a silent cry, were bordered with cold tranquillity by the big sky, already turned towards winter, over which, like shadows over a face, long stratus snow clouds with black middles and white sides ceaselessly drifted.

And everything was in movement, slow, regular. The river flowed. The road went the opposite way. The doctor strode along it. The clouds drew on in the same direction as he. But the fields did not remain motionless either. Something was moving about on them; they were covered by a tiny, restless, disgusting swarming.

Mice had bred in the fields in unprecedented, as yet unheard-of numbers. They scurried over the doctor's face and hands and ran up his trouser legs and sleeves when night overtook him in the fields and he had to lie down and sleep somewhere by a boundary. Swarms of the enormously multiplied, glutted mice darted underfoot on the road by day and turned into a slippery, squealing, slithering mush when stepped on.

Frightening, shaggy village mongrels gone wild, who exchanged looks among themselves as if holding a council on when to fall upon the doctor and tear him to pieces, trudged after him in a pack at a respectful distance. They fed on carrion, but did not scorn the mouse flesh teeming in the fields, and, glancing at the doctor from afar, confidently moved after him, expecting something all the time. Strangely, they would not enter the forest, and on approaching it would drop behind little by little, turn tail, and vanish.

Forest and fields were complete opposites then. The fields were orphaned without man, as if they had fallen under a curse in his absence. Delivered from man, the forests stood beautiful in their freedom, like released prisoners.

Usually people, mainly village children, do not let hazelnuts ripen fully, but break them off while they are still green. Now the wooded hillsides and ravines were completely covered with untouched, rough, golden foliage, as if dusty and coarsened from autumnal sunburn. Out of it stuck handsomely bulging clusters of nuts, three or four at a time, as if tied in knots or bows, ripe, ready to fall from their common stem, but still holding to it. Yuri Andreevich cracked and ate them endlessly on his way. His pockets were stuffed with them, his sack was filled with them. For a week nuts were his chief nourishment.

It seemed to the doctor that the fields he saw were gravely ill, in a feverish delirium, but the forests were in a lucid state of recovery, that God dwelt in the forests, but the devil's mocking smile snaked over the fields.

3

In those same days, in that part of the journey, the doctor entered a burned-down village deserted by its inhabitants. Before the fire, it had been built in only one row, across the road from the river. The river side had remained unbuilt on.

In the village a few intact houses could be counted, blackened and scorched on the outside. But they, too, were empty, uninhabited. The other cottages had turned into heaps of coal from which black, sooty chimneys stuck up.

The steep banks of the riverside were pitted with holes where the villagers had extracted millstones, which had been their livelihood. Three such unfinished, round millstones lay on the ground across from the last cottage in the row, one of the intact ones. It was also empty, like all the rest.

Yuri Andreevich went into it. The evening was still, but it was as if a wind burst into the cottage as soon as the doctor stepped inside. On the floor wisps of hay and tow crawled in all directions, on the walls shreds of unstuck paper fluttered. Everything in the cottage moved, rustled. It was swarming with mice, like the whole area around, and they squeaked and scurried all over it.

The doctor left the cottage. The sun was going down behind the fields. The warm, golden glow of the sunset flooded the opposite bank, the separate bushes and backwaters stretching the glitter of their fading reflections into the middle of the river. Yuri Andreevich crossed the road and sat down to rest on one of the millstones that lay on the grass.

Above the edge of the bank a light brown, shaggy head appeared, then shoulders, then arms. Someone was coming up the path from the river with a bucket of water. The man saw the doctor and stopped, showing to the waist above the line of the bank.

'Want a drink, my good man? Don't hurt me and I won't touch you.'

'Thanks. Yes, I'll have a drink. Come all the way up, don't be afraid. Why should I touch you?'

The water carrier, having come up over the bank, turned out to be a young adolescent. He was barefoot, ragged, and dishevelled.

Despite his friendly words, he fastened his anxious, piercing gaze on the doctor. For some inexplicable reason, the boy was strangely excited. In his excitement, he set the bucket down, suddenly rushed towards the doctor, stopped halfway, and began to murmur:

'It can't be . . . It can't be . . . No, it's impossible, I'm dreaming. But I beg your pardon, comrade, allow me to ask you anyway. It seems to me that you're somebody I knew once. Ah, yes! Yes! Uncle doctor?!'

'And who would you be?'

'You don't recognise me?'

'No.'

'We were on the train from Moscow with you, in the same car. Herded off to labour camp. Under convoy.'

It was Vasya Brykin. He fell down before the doctor, started kissing his hands, and wept.

The burned-down place turned out to be Vasya's native village Veretenniki. His mother was no longer living. When the village was raided and burned down, Vasya hid in an underground cave where a stone had been cut out, but his mother thought Vasya had been taken to town, went mad with grief, and drowned herself in that same river Pelga on the bank of which the doctor and Vasya now sat conversing. Vasya's sisters, Alenka and Arishka, according to unconfirmed information, were in another district, in an orphanage. The doctor took Vasya with him to Moscow. On the way he told Yuri Andreevich all sorts of horrors.

4

'That's last autumn's winter crop spilling out. We'd just sowed it when the disasters began. When Auntie Polya left. Do you remember Auntie Palasha?'

'No. I never knew her. Who is she?'

'What do you mean, you don't know Pelageya Nilovna! She was on the train with us. Tyagunova. Open face, plump, white.'

'The one who kept plaiting and unplaiting her hair?'

'The plaits, the plaits! Yes! That's it. The plaits!'

'Ah, I remember. Wait. I met her afterwards in Siberia, in some town, in the street.'

'You don't say! Auntie Palasha?'

'What is it, Vasya? You're shaking my hands like a madman. Watch out, you'll tear them off. And you're blushing like a young maiden.'

'Well, how is she? Tell me quickly, quickly.'

'She was safe and sound when I saw her. Told me about you. That she stayed with you or visited you, as I recall. But maybe I've forgotten or confused something.'

'Well, sure, sure! With us, with us! Mama loved her like her own sister. Quiet. Hard-working. Good with her hands. While she lived with us, we were in clover. They hounded her out of Veretenniki, gave her no peace with their slander.

'There was a muzhik in the village, Rotten Kharlam. He played up to

Polya. A noseless telltale. She didn't even look at him. He bore me a grudge for that. Said bad things about us, me and Polya. So she left. He wore us out. And then it started.

'A terrible murder took place hereabouts. A lonely widow was murdered at a forest farmstead over by Buiskoe. She lived alone near the forest. She went around in men's boots with tabs and rubber straps. A fierce dog ran around the farmstead chained to a wire. Named Gorlan. The farming, the land, she managed by herself, without helpers. Then suddenly winter came when nobody was expecting it. Snow fell early. Before the widow had her potatoes dug out. She comes to Veretenniki. "Help me," she says, "I'll give you a share, or pay you."

'I volunteered to dig her potatoes. I come to her farmstead, and Kharlam's already there. He invited himself before me. She didn't tell me. Well, it was nothing to fight over. We set to work together. The worst weather for digging. Rain and snow, sleet, muck. We dug and dug, burned potato greens to dry the potatoes with warm smoke. Well, we dug them all out, she paid us off honestly. She let Kharlam go, but winked at me, meaning she had more business with me, I should come later or else stay.

'I came to her another time. "I don't want my potatoes confiscated as surplus by the state," she said. "You're a good lad," she said, "you won't give me away, I know. See, I'm not hiding from you. I could dig a pit myself and bury them, but look what's going on outside. It's winter – too late to think about it. I can't manage by myself. Dig a pit for me, you won't regret it. We'll dry it, fill it up."

'I dug her a pit the way a hiding place should be, wider at the bottom, like a jug, the narrow neck up. We dried and warmed the pit with smoke, too. Right in the middle of a blizzard. We hid the potatoes good and proper, covered the pit with dirt. Done to a tee. I keep mum about the pit, sure enough. Don't tell a living soul. Not even mama or my little sisters. God forbid!

'Well, so. Hardly a month went by – there was a robbery at the farmstead. People walking past from Buiskoe told about it, the house wide open, everything cleaned out, the widow nowhere to be seen, the chain broken and the dog Gorlan gone.

'More time went by. During the first winter thaw, on New Year's Day, the eve of St Basil's,[2] it was pouring rain, which washed the snow off the hillocks, melted through to the ground. Gorlan came and started scraping the dirt with his paws on the bare spot where the pit with the potatoes was. He dug away, scattered the top layer, and there were the mistress's feet in their shoes with straps. See, what a frightful thing!

'Everybody in Veretenniki pitied the widow, talked about her. Nobody thought of blaming Kharlam. And how could they? Who'd think of such a thing? If it was him, where would he get the pluck to stay in Veretenniki and strut around like a peacock? He'd have made tracks for somewhere far away.

'The village kulaks, the ringleaders, were glad of this villainy at the farmstead. They began stirring up the village. See, they said, what townies come up with! There's a lesson for you, a warning. Don't hide bread, don't bury potatoes. And these fools all keep at it – forest robbers, they dream up some kind of forest robbers at the farmstead. Simple folk! Go on listening to these townies. They'll show you better than that, they'll starve you to death. If you villagers know what's good for you, you'll follow us. We'll teach you a thing or two. They'll come to take what's yours, earned with your own sweat, and you'll say, what extra, we haven't got a single grain of rye for ourselves. And if they try anything, go for the pitchfork. And anybody who's against the community, look out! The old men made a buzz, started boasting, held meetings. And that was just what telltale Kharlam wanted. He snatched his hat and was off to town. And there psst-psst-psst. See what's doing in the village, and you just sit and gawk? What's needed there is a committee of the poor. Give the order, and I'll set brother against brother in no time. And he hightailed it from these parts and never showed his face again.

'All that happened after that, happened of itself. Nobody set it up, nobody's to blame. They sent Red Army soldiers from town. And an itinerant court. And got at me straight off. Kharlam blabbed. For escaping, and for avoiding labour, and for inciting the village to mutiny, and for murdering the widow. And they locked me up. Thanks be, I thought of taking up a floorboard and got away. I hid underground in a cave. The village was burning over my head – I didn't see it. My dearest mama threw herself into a hole in the ice – I didn't know it. It all happened of itself. The soldiers were put in a separate cottage and given drink, they were all dead drunk. During the night somebody got careless and set the house on fire, the ones next to it caught. The villagers jumped out of the burning houses, but the visitors, nobody set fire to them, they just got burned alive to a man, that's clear. Those from Veretenniki weren't driven from their burned-down places. They ran away themselves, frightened that something more might happen. Those cheating ringleaders told them again that every tenth man would be shot. I didn't find anybody here, they're all scattered, knocking about the world somewhere.'

5

The doctor and Vasya arrived in Moscow in the spring of 1922, at the beginning of the NEP. The days were warm and clear. Patches of sunlight reflected from the golden cupolas of the Church of the Saviour fell on the cobbled square, where grass was growing in the cracks between cobbles.

The ban on private enterprise was lifted, and free trade was permitted within strict limits. Deals were done on the scale of commodity circulation among junkmen in a flea market. The dwarf scope of it encouraged speculation and led to abuse. The petty scrambling of the dealers produced nothing new, it added nothing material to the city's desolation. Fortunes were made by pointlessly reselling the same things ten times over.

The owners of a few rather modest private libraries would bring the books from their bookcases to some one place. Would make application to the city council asking to open a bookselling cooperative. Would request space for same. Would obtain use of a shoe warehouse that had stood empty since the first months of the revolution or a florist's greenhouse also closed since then, and under these spacious vaults would try to sell their meagre and haphazard collections.

The wives of professors, who even earlier in difficult times had secretly baked white rolls for sale in defiance of the prohibition, now openly sold them in some place registered as a bicycle repair shop all those years. They changed landmarks,[3] accepted the revolution, and began saying 'You bet', instead of 'Yes' or 'Very well'.

In Moscow Yuri Andreevich said:

'You'll have to start doing something, Vasya.'

'I suppose I'll study.'

'That goes without saying.'

'I also have a dream. I want to paint mama's face from memory.'

'Very good. But for that you must know how to draw. Have you ever tried?'

'In Apraksin, when my uncle wasn't looking, I fooled around with charcoal.'

'Well, all right. With any luck. We'll give it a try.'

Vasya turned out to have no great ability at drawing, but an average one was enough to allow him to study applied art. Through connections, Yuri Andreevich got him enrolled in the general education programme of the former Stroganov school, from which he was transferred to the department of polygraphy. There he studied lithographic techniques, typography and bookbinding, and graphic design.

The doctor and Vasya combined their efforts. The doctor wrote little books the size of one printer's sheet on the most varied questions, and Vasya printed them at school as work counted for his examinations. The books, published in a small number of copies, were distributed through newly opened second-hand bookstores, founded by mutual acquaintances.

The books contained Yuri Andreevich's philosophy, explanations of his medical views, his definitions of health and unhealth, his thoughts about transformism and evolution, about personality as the biological basis of the organism, his reflections on history and religion, close to his uncle's and to Simushka's, sketches of the Pugachev places he had visited, and his stories and poems.

His works were set forth accessibly, in spoken form, though far from the goals set by popularisers, because they contained disputable, arbitrary opinions, insufficiently verified, but always alive and original. The little books sold. Fanciers valued them.

At that time everything became a speciality, verse writing, the art of literary translation, theoretical studies were written about everything, institutes were created for everything. Various sorts of Palaces of Thought and Academies of Artistic Ideas sprang up. Yuri Andreevich was the staff doctor in half of these bogus institutions.

The doctor and Vasya were friends for a long time and lived together. During this period they took many rooms and half-ruined corners one after another, in various ways uninhabitable and uncomfortable.

Just after his arrival in Moscow, Yuri Andreevich visited his old house in Sivtsev, which, as he learned, his family had never stopped at in passing through Moscow. Their exile had changed everything. The rooms reserved for the doctor and his family had other tenants, and there was nothing left of his or his family's belongings. People shied away from Yuri Andreevich as from a dangerous acquaintance.

Markel had risen in the world and no longer passed his time in Sivtsev. He had been transferred to Flour Town as a superintendent, one of the benefits of the job being a manager's apartment for himself and his family. However, he preferred to live in the old porter's lodge with a dirt floor, running water, and an enormous Russian stove that nearly filled the whole space. In all the buildings of the quarter, the water and heating pipes burst in winter, and only in the porter's lodge was it warm and did the water not freeze.

At that time a cooling off took place in the relations between the doctor and Vasya. Vasya had become extraordinarily developed. He began to speak and think not at all as the barefoot and shaggy boy had spoken and thought in Veretenniki on the river Pelga. The obviousness, the self-evidence of the truths proclaimed by the revolution attracted him more and more. The doctor's not entirely clear, figurative speech seemed to him the voice of error, condemned, aware of its weakness, and therefore evasive.

The doctor went around to various departments. He solicited for two causes: for the political rehabilitation of his family and their legal return to the motherland; and for a foreign passport for himself, with permission to go to Paris to fetch his wife and children.

Vasya was surprised at how lukewarm and limp this petitioning was. Yuri Andreevich was in too much of a hurry to establish ahead of time the failure of the efforts he made, announcing too confidently and almost with satisfaction the uselessness of any further attempts.

Vasya disapproved of the doctor more and more often. The latter did not take offence at his fair reproaches. But his relations with Vasya were deteriorating. Finally their friendship broke down and they parted ways. The doctor left Vasya the room they shared and moved to Flour Town, where the all-powerful Markel obtained for him the end of the Sventitskys' former apartment. This end part consisted of the Sventitskys' old out-of-use bathroom, a room with one window next to it, and a lopsided kitchen with a half-ruined and sagging back entrance. Yuri Andreevich moved there and after that abandoned medicine, grew unkempt, stopped seeing acquaintances, and started living in poverty.

6

It was a grey winter Sunday. The smoke from the chimneys did not rise in columns above the roofs, but seeped in black streams from the vent windows, through which, despite the prohibition, people continued to stick the iron pipes of their stoves. The city's everyday life was still not settled. The inhabitants of Flour Town went about as unwashed slovens, suffered from boils, shivered, caught cold.

On the occasion of Sunday, the family of Markel Shchapov was all assembled.

The Shchapovs were having dinner at that same table on which, in the time of the distribution of bread by ration cards, in the mornings at dawn, they used to cut up the small bread coupons of all the tenants with scissors, sort them, count them, tie them in bundles or wrap them in paper by categories, and take them to the bakery, and then, on coming back, they would chop, cut, crumble, and weigh out the portions for the quarter's inhabitants. Now all that had become a thing of the past. The rationing of provisions was replaced by other forms of accounting. Those sitting at the long table ate with appetite, smacking their lips, chewing and chomping.

Half of the porter's lodge was taken up by the Russian stove towering in the middle, with the edge of a quilted coverlet hanging off its shelf.

On the front wall by the entrance there was a sink with a tap for running water sticking out over it. There were benches along the sides of the lodge with chattels in sacks and trunks stuffed under them. The left side was occupied by the kitchen table. Over it, nailed to the wall, hung a cupboard for dishes.

The stove was burning. It was hot in the porter's lodge. In front of the stove, her sleeves rolled up to the elbows, stood Markel's wife, Agafya Tikhonovna, using long, far-reaching tongs to move the pots in the oven closer together or further apart at need. Her sweaty face was alternately lit up by the breathing fire of the stove, then veiled by steam from the cooking. Having pushed the pots aside, she took from the depths a meat pie on an iron sheet, with one deft movement flipped it bottom side up, and pushed it back to brown for a moment. Yuri Andreevich came into the lodge with two buckets.

'Enjoy your meal.'

'Welcome to you! Sit down, be our guest.'

'Thank you, I've had my dinner.'

'We know your dinners. Sit down and eat something hot. Don't scorn it. There are potatoes baked in a clay pot. A savoury pie. Wheat kasha.'

'No, really, thank you. Forgive me, Markel, for coming so often and making your place cold. I want to store up a lot of water at once. I scrubbed the zinc bathtub at the Sventitskys' till it shines; I'll fill it up, and the big pots as well. I'll come some five times now, maybe ten, and after that I won't bother you for a long time. Forgive me for coming so often, I have nobody else but you.'

'Help yourself, we won't miss it. There's no syrup, but as much water as you like. It's free. We don't deal in it.'

The people at the table guffawed.

When Yuri Andreevich came for the third time, for his fifth and sixth bucketful, the tone had changed slightly and the talk went differently.

'My sons-in-law are asking who you are. I tell them – they don't believe me. Go ahead, take the water, don't hesitate. Only don't spill it on the floor, you gawk. See, the doorstep's wet. It'll freeze, and it won't be you who breaks it up with a crowbar. And shut the door tighter, you lummox – there's a draught from outside. Yes, I tell my sons-in-law who you are, and they don't believe me. So much money gone to waste on you! You studied and studied, and what was the use?'

When Yuri Andreevich came for the fifth or sixth time, Markel frowned:

'Well, once more, if you please, and then basta. You've got to know the limits, brother. Marina here, our youngest one, defends you, otherwise I'd pay no attention to what a noble Freemason you are and lock the door. Do you remember Marina? There she is, at the end of the table, the dark-haired one. See, she's getting red in the face. Don't offend him, papa, she says. As if anybody's bothering you. Marina's a telegraph girl at the central telegraph, she understands when it's foreign words. He's miserable, she says. She'll go through fire for you, she pities you so much. But is it my fault if you didn't turn out? You shouldn't have gone off to Siberia and abandoned your home in a time of danger. It's your own fault. Here we sat out all this famine, all this White blowkade, we didn't waver, and we survived. The blame's on you. You didn't keep Tonka, so she's wandering abroad. What is it to me? It's your business. Only don't get offended if I ask what you need all this water for. Were you hired to make a skating rink in the courtyard? Eh, I can't even get angry at a sad sack like you.'

Again there was guffawing at the table. Marina glanced around at her family with a displeased look, blushed, and started reprimanding them. Yuri Andreevich heard her voice, was struck by it, but did not understand its secret yet.

'There's a lot of cleaning to be done in the house, Markel. I have to tidy up. Wash the floors. Do some laundry.'

There was surprise at the table.

'Aren't you ashamed even to say such things, let alone do them, as if you're a Chinese laundry or something!'

'Yuri Andreevich, if you'll allow me, I'll send my daughter to you. She'll come to your place, do the laundry, the scrubbing. If you need, she can mend things. Don't be afraid of the gentleman, dear daughter. You see how well-breeded he is, not like some others. He wouldn't hurt a fly.'

'No, what are you saying, Agafya Tikhonovna, there's no need. I'll never agree that Marina should dirty and soil herself for me. Why should she work for me? I'll see to it all myself.'

'You can dirty yourself, and I can't? You're so intractable, Yuri Andreevich. Why do you wave me away? And if I invite myself as a guest, will you really drive me out?'

Marina might have become a singer. She had a pure, melodious voice of great pitch and strength. Marina spoke softly, but in a voice that was stronger than conversation required and that did not merge with Marina, but could be conceived as separate from her. It seemed to come from another room, to be located behind her back. This voice was her defence, her guardian angel. One does not want to insult or sadden a woman with such a voice.

THE ENDING   427

With this Sunday water carrying the doctor's friendship with Marina
began. She often came to help him around the house. One day she stayed
with him and never went back to the porter's lodge. Thus she became the
third, not officially registered, wife of Yuri Andreevich, who was not
divorced from the first. Children came along. Father and mother Shchapov,
not without pride, began to call their daughter a doctor's wife. Markel
grumbled that Yuri Andreevich did not marry Marina in church or sign up
in the register office. 'What, are you daft?' his wife protested. 'With Antonina alive, what would that be? Bigamy?' 'You're a fool yourself,' replied
Markel. 'Why look at Tonka? Tonka's the same as if she doesn't exist. No
law will defend her.'

Yuri Andreevich sometimes said jokingly that their intimacy was a novel
of twenty buckets, as there are novels of twenty chapters or twenty letters.

Marina forgave the doctor his strange quirks, which had already formed
by then, the whims of a man gone to seed and aware of his fall, and forgave
the dirt and disorder that he spread around him. She put up with his grumbling, sharpness, irritability.

Her self-sacrifice went still further. When through his fault they fell into
voluntary, self-created poverty, Marina, so as not to leave him alone in those
intervals, would abandon her job, where she was so valued and where she
was eagerly taken back after these forced interruptions. Submitting to Yuri
Andreevich's fantasy, she would go with him through the courtyards looking for odd jobs. They did woodcutting for tenants living on various floors.
Some of them, particularly the speculators grown rich at the beginning of
the NEP and people of science and art who were close to the government,
began fixing up their apartments and furnishing them. One day Marina and
Yuri Andreevich, stepping carefully on the rugs in their felt boots, so as not
to track in sawdust from outside, brought a load of firewood to the study of
an apartment owner, who was insultingly immersed in some reading and
did not bestow so much as a glance on the sawyers. The lady of the house
negotiated, gave orders, and paid them.

'What is the swine so riveted to?' The doctor became curious. 'What is he
marking up so furiously with his pencil?' Going around the desk with the
firewood, he peeked over the reading man's shoulder. On the desk lay Yuri
Andreevich's little books in Vasya's early art school editions.

7

Marina and the doctor lived on Spiridonovka. Gordon was renting a room
nearby on Malaya Bronnaya. Marina and the doctor had two girls, Kapka

and Klashka. Kapitolina (Kapka) was going on seven; the recently born Klavdia was six months old.

The beginning of the summer of 1929 was hot. Acquaintances from two or three streets away ran to visit each other without hats or jackets.

Gordon's room was strangely organised. In its place there used to be a fashionable dressmaker's shop with two sections, a lower and an upper one. From the street, these two levels had a single plate-glass window. The gold inscription on the glass gave the dressmaker's last name and the nature of his occupation. Inside, behind the glass, there was a spiral staircase from the lower to the upper section.

Now this space had been divided in three.

By means of an additional floor, the shop had gained an intermediary entresol, with a window strange for an inhabited room. It was a metre high and was at floor level. It was covered with remnants of the gold lettering. Through the spaces between them, the legs of those in the room could be seen up to the knees. Gordon lived in this room. Sitting with him were Zhivago, Dudorov, Marina and the children. Unlike the adults, the children filled the entire window frame. Soon Marina and the children left. The three men remained alone.

They were having a conversation, one of those lazy, unhurried summer conversations conducted among schoolmates whose friendship dates back countless years. How are they usually conducted?

There are some who possess a sufficient stock of words and are satisfied with it. They speak and think naturally and coherently. Only Yuri Andreevich was in that position.

His friends were lacking in necessary expressions. They did not possess the gift of speech. To make up for their poor vocabulary, they paced the room as they talked, smoked cigarettes, waved their arms, repeated the same thing several times. ('That's dishonest, brother; dishonest is what it is; yes, yes, dishonest.')

They were not aware that the excessive dramatics of their intercourse in no way signified ardour and breadth of character, but, on the contrary, expressed an insufficiency, a blank.

Gordon and Dudorov belonged to a good professional circle. They spent their lives among good books, good thinkers, good composers, good, always, yesterday and today, good and only good music, and they did not know that the calamity of mediocre taste is worse than the calamity of tastelessness.

Gordon and Dudorov did not know that even the reproaches that they showered on Zhivago were suggested to them not by devotion to their friend and the wish to influence him, but only by their inability to think freely and guide the conversation as they willed. The speeding cart of the conversation carried them where they had no wish to go. They were unable to turn it and in the end were bound to run into something and hit against something. And so, rushing at full speed, they smashed with all their sermons and admonitions into Yuri Andreevich.

He could see clearly the springs of their pathos, the shakiness of their sympathy, the mechanism of their reasonings. However, he could not very well say to them: 'Dear friends, oh, how hopelessly ordinary you and the circle you represent, and the brilliance and art of your favourite names and authorities, all are. The only live and bright thing in you is that you lived at the same time as me and knew me.' But how would it be if one could make such declarations to one's friends! And so as not to distress them, Yuri Andreevich meekly listened to them.

Dudorov had recently finished his first term of exile and come back. He was restored to his rights, of which he had been temporarily deprived. He received permission to resume his lectures and university occupations.

Now he initiated his friends into his feelings and state of soul in exile. He spoke with them sincerely and unhypocritically. His observations were not motivated by cowardice or extraneous considerations.

He said that the arguments of the prosecution, his treatment in prison and after leaving it, and especially his one-on-one interviews with the interrogator had aired out his brain and re-educated him politically, that his eyes had been opened to many things, that he had grown as a human being.

Dudorov's reasonings were close to Gordon's heart precisely in their triteness. He nodded his head sympathetically to Innokenty and agreed with him. The stereotyped character of what Dudorov said and felt was just what Gordon found especially moving. He took the imitativeness of these copybook sentiments for their universality.

Innokenty's virtuous orations were in the spirit of the time. But it was precisely the conformity, the transparency of their hypocrisy that exasperated Yuri Andreevich. The unfree man always idealises his slavery. So it was in the Middle Ages; it was on this that the Jesuits always played. Yuri Andreevich could not bear the political mysticism of the Soviet intelligentsia, which was its highest achievement, or, as they would have said then, the spiritual ceiling of the epoch. Yuri Andreevich concealed this feeling from his friends as well, so as not to quarrel.

But he was interested in something quite other, in Dudorov's account of Vonifaty Orletsov, his cell mate, a priest and a follower of Tikhon.[4] The arrested man had a six-year-old daughter, Christina. The arrest and subsequent trial of her beloved father were a shock to her. The words 'servant of a cult' and 'disenfranchised' and the like seemed to her a stain of dishonour. It may be that in her ardent child's heart, she vowed to wash this stain from her father's name some day. This goal, so far removed and set so early, burning in her as an inextinguishable resolution, made of her even then a childishly enthusiastic follower of everything that seemed to her most irrefutable in Communism.

'I'm leaving,' said Yuri Andreevich. 'Don't be angry with me, Misha. It's stuffy in here, and hot outside. I don't have enough air.'

'You can see the vent window on the floor is open. Forgive us for smoking. We always forget that we shouldn't smoke in your presence. Is it my fault that it's arranged so stupidly here? Find me another room.'

'Well, so I'm leaving, Gordosha. We've talked enough. I thank you for caring about me, dear comrades. It's not a whimsy on my part. It's an illness, sclerosis of the heart's blood vessels. The walls of the heart muscle wear out, get thin, and one fine day can tear, burst. And I'm not forty yet. I'm not a drunkard, not a profligate.'

'It's too early to be singing at your funeral. Nonsense. You'll live a long while yet.'

'In our time the frequency of microscopic forms of cardiac haemorrhages has increased greatly. Not all of them are fatal. In some cases people survive. It's the disease of our time. I think its causes are of a moral order. A constant, systematic dissembling is required of the vast majority of us. It's impossible, without its affecting your health, to show yourself day after day contrary to what you feel, to lay yourself out for what you don't love, to rejoice over what brings you misfortune. Our nervous system is not an empty sound, not a fiction. It's a physical body made up of fibres. Our soul takes up room in space and sits inside us like the teeth in our mouth. It cannot be endlessly violated with impunity. It was painful for me to hear you tell about your exile, Innokenty, how you grew during it, and how it re-educated you. It's as if a horse were to tell how it broke itself in riding school.'

'I'll stand up for Dudorov. You've simply lost the habit of human words. They've ceased to reach you.'

'That may well be, Misha. In any case, excuse me, let me go. It's hard for me to breathe. By God, I'm not exaggerating.'

'Wait. That's nothing but dodging. We won't let you go until you give us a straight, sincere answer. Do you agree that you've got to change, to mend your ways? What do you intend to do in that respect? You ought to clarify your relations with Tonya and with Marina. They're living beings, women capable of suffering and feeling, and not some bodiless ideas hovering in your head in arbitrary combinations. Besides, it's a shame that a man like you should go to waste uselessly. You must wake up from your sleep and indolence, rouse yourself, make out what's around you without this unjustified haughtiness, yes, yes, without this inadmissible arrogance, find a job, take up practice.'

'Very well, I'll answer you. I myself have often thought in that same spirit lately, and therefore I can promise you a thing or two without blushing for shame. It seems to me that everything will get settled. And quite soon. You'll see. No, by God. Everything's getting better. I have an incredible, passionate desire to live, and to live means always to push forward, towards higher things, towards perfection, and to achieve it.

'I'm glad, Gordon, that you defend Marina, as before you were always Tonya's defender. But I have no dispute with them, I don't make war on them or anybody else. You reproached me at first that she addresses me formally in response to my informality and calls me by my name and patronymic, as if it doesn't weigh on me as well. But the deeper incoherence that underlies that unnaturalness has long been removed, everything's smoothed over, and equality has been re-established.

'I can tell you some more good news. They've started writing to me from Paris again. The children have grown; they feel quite at ease among their French peers. Shura is finishing their primary school, *école primaire*. Manya is just beginning. I don't know my daughter at all. For some reason I have the feeling that, despite their receiving French citizenship, they will soon return, and everything will be set right in some unknown way.

'By many tokens, my father-in-law and Tonya know about Marina and the girls. I didn't write to them about it. These circumstances must have reached them from elsewhere. Alexander Alexandrovich is naturally offended in his paternal feelings; it's painful for him on account of Tonya. That explains the nearly five-year break in our correspondence. I did correspond with them for a while after I came to Moscow. And suddenly they stopped answering. Everything stopped.

'Now, quite recently, I've begun to receive letters again from there. From all of them, even the children. Warm, tender letters. Something's softened. Maybe there are changes with Tonya, some new friend. God grant it's so. I don't know. I also sometimes write to them. But I really can't go on. I must leave or I'll start suffocating. Goodbye.'

The next day Marina came running to Gordon more dead than alive. She had no one to leave the children with and carried the little one, Klasha, wrapped tightly in a blanket, pressing her to her breast with one hand, and with the other dragged the lagging and protesting Kapka by the hand.

'Is Yura here, Misha?' she asked in a voice not her own.
'Didn't he spend the night at home?'
'No.'
'Well, then he's at Innokenty's.'
'I was there. Innokenty has classes at the university. But his neighbours know Yura. He didn't show up there.'
'Then where is he?'
Marina placed the swaddled Klasha on the sofa. She became hysterical.

8

For two days Gordon and Dudorov never left Marina's side. They took turns keeping watch on her, afraid of leaving her alone. In the intervals they went in search of the doctor. They ran around to all the places they supposed he might be wandering in, went to Flour Town and to the Sivtsev house, visited all the Palaces of Thought and Houses of Ideas that he had ever worked in, went to see all the old acquaintances they had any idea of and whose addresses they were able to find. The search yielded no results.

They did not inform the police, so as not to remind the authorities of a man who, though he was registered and had no criminal record, was, in the notions of that time, far from exemplary. They decided to put the police on his trail only in the last extremity.

On the third day, Marina, Gordon, and Dudorov received letters at different times from Yuri Andreevich. They were full of regrets regarding the anxieties and fears he had caused them. He begged them to forgive him and to calm themselves, and adjured them by all that was holy to stop their search for him, which in any case would lead to nothing.

He told them that with the aim of the speediest and fullest remaking of his life, he wanted to be left alone for a time, in order to go about his affairs in a concentrated way, and once he was somewhat set in his new pursuits and was convinced that, after the break that had taken place, there would be no return to the old ways, he would leave his hiding place and return to Marina and the children.

He told Gordon in his letter that he had transferred money for Marina to his name. He asked him to hire a nanny for the children, so as to free Marina to go back to work. He explained that he was wary of sending money directly to her address, for fear that the sum showing on the notice would expose her to the danger of being robbed.

The money soon came, far exceeding the doctor's scale and the standards of his friends. A nanny was hired for the children. Marina was taken back at the telegraph. For a long time she could not calm down, but, being

accustomed to Yuri Andreevich's past oddities, she finally reconciled herself to this new escapade as well. Despite Yuri Andreevich's pleas and
warnings, his friends and Marina continued to search for him, and his pre-
diction kept being confirmed. They did not find him.

9

And meanwhile he was living a few steps away from them, right under their
noses and in full view, within the narrow circle of their search.

When he left Gordon's on the day of his disappearance, it was still light.
He went down Bronnaya, heading for his home in Spiridonovka, and at
once, before going a hundred steps, ran into his half-brother, Evgraf
Zhivago, coming in the opposite direction. Yuri Andreevich had not seen
him for more than three years and knew nothing about him. As it turned
out, Evgraf was in Moscow by chance, having arrived quite recently. As
usual, he dropped from the sky and was impervious to questions, getting off
with silent little smiles and jokes. Instead, passing over petty everyday
details, after two or three questions to Yuri Andreevich, he straight away
entered into all his sorrows and quandaries, and right there, at the narrow
turns of the crooked lane, amidst the jostling of passers-by going in both
directions, he came up with a practical plan of how to help his brother and
save him. Yuri Andreevich's disappearance and remaining in hiding were
Evgraf's idea, his invention.

He rented a room for Yuri Andreevich in a lane that was then still called
Kamergersky, next to the Art Theatre. He provided him with money and
took steps to have the doctor accepted at some hospital, in a good position
that would open prospects for scientific work. He protected his brother in
every way in all the aspects of his life. Finally, he gave his brother his word
that his family's unsettled position in Paris would be resolved in one way or
another. Either Yuri Andreevich would go to them, or they would come to
him. Evgraf promised to take all these matters upon himself and arrange
everything. His brother's support inspired Yuri Andreevich. As always
before, the riddle of his power remained unexplained. Yuri Andreevich did
not even try to penetrate this mystery.

10

The room faced south. Its two windows looked onto the roofs opposite the
theatre, beyond which, high above the Okhotny Ryad, stood the summer
sun, leaving the pavement of the lane in shadow.

The room was more than a place of work for Yuri Andreevich, more than his study. In this period of devouring activity, when his plans and projects could not find enough room in the notes piled on his desk, and the images of his thoughts and visions hung in the air on all sides, as an artist's studio is encumbered with a multitude of started works turned face to the wall, the doctor's living room was a banquet hall of the spirit, a storeroom of ravings, a larder of revelations.

Fortunately, negotiations with the hospital authorities were taking a long time; the moment of starting work kept being put off to an indefinite future. He could take advantage of this opportune delay and write.

Yuri Andreevich began putting in order what had already been written, fragments he remembered, or what Evgraf found somewhere and brought to him, part of them in Yuri Andreevich's own manuscripts, part in someone else's typewritten copies. The chaotic state of the material made Yuri Andreevich squander his energy even more than his own nature predisposed him to do. He soon abandoned this work and, instead of reconstructing the unfinished, went on to writing new things, carried away by fresh sketches.

He composed rough drafts of articles, like those fleeting notes from the time of his first stay in Varykino, and wrote down separate pieces of poems that came to him, beginnings, ends, and middles all mixed up, unsorted. Sometimes he could barely manage his rushing thoughts; the first letters of words and the abbreviations of his swift handwriting could not keep up with them.

He hurried. When his imagination grew weary and the work began to lag, he speeded it and whipped it up with drawings in the margins. They represented forest clearings and city intersections with the billboard 'Moreau and Vetchinkin. Seeders. Threshers' standing in the middle of them.

The articles and poems were on one theme. Their subject was the city.

II

Afterwards this note was found among his papers:

'In the year '22, when I returned to Moscow, I found her emptied and half ruined. As she came out of the ordeals of the first years of the revolution, so she has remained to this day. Her population has thinned out, new houses are not built, the old ones are not renovated.

'But even in that state, she remains a big modern city, the only inspiration of a new, truly contemporary art.

'The disorderly listing of things and notions, which look incompatible and are placed side by side as if arbitrarily, in the symbolists, Blok,

Verhaeren, Whitman, is not at all a stylistic caprice. It is a new order of impressions observed in life and copied from nature.

'Just as they drive sequences of images through their lines, so a busy city street of the end of the nineteenth century sails along and draws past us its crowds, coaches, and carriages, and then, at the beginning of the next century, the cars of its electric trams and subways.

'Pastoral simplicity has no source in these conditions. Its false artlessness is a literary counterfeit, an unnatural mannerism, a phenomenon of a bookish order, picked up not in the countryside, but from the bookshelves of academic libraries. The living language, live-formed and answering naturally to the spirit of today, is the language of urbanism.

'I live on a crowded city intersection. Summer Moscow, blinded by the sun, her asphalt courtyards scorching, the windows of the upper floors scattering reflections and breathing in the flowering of clouds and boulevards, whirls around me and makes my head spin and wants me, for her glory, to make the heads of others spin. To that end she has brought me up and given art into my hands.

'Constantly noisy, day and night, the street outside my wall is as closely connected with the contemporary soul as the opening overture is with the theatre curtain, filled with darkness and mystery, still lowered, but already set aglow by the flames of the footlights. Ceaselessly stirring and murmuring outside the doors and windows, the city is a vastly enormous introduction to the life of each of us. It is just along these lines that I would like to write about the city.'

In the notebook of Zhivago's poems that has been preserved, no such poems are to be found. Perhaps the poem 'Hamlet' belonged to that category?

12

One morning at the end of August, Yuri Andreevich got on the tram at the stop on the corner of Gazetny Lane, to go up Nikitskaya from the university to Kudrinskaya Square. He was going for the first time to his job at the Botkin Hospital, which was then called Soldatenkovskaya. It was all but his first visit to it in an official capacity.

Yuri Andreevich was not in luck. He got on a defective tramcar which was meeting with all kinds of disasters. First a cart with its wheels stuck in the grooves of the rails held it up by blocking the way. Then faulty insulation under the floor or on the roof of the tramcar caused a short circuit and something crackled and burned.

The driver would stop the tram and with wrenches in his hands would come down from the front platform and, going around the tramcar, would crouch down and immerse himself in repairing its mechanism between the wheels and the rear platform.

The ill-fated tramcar blocked traffic along the whole line. The street was filled with trams it had already made stop and newly arriving and gradually accumulating ones. Their line reached the Manège and stretched back further. Passengers from the tramcars behind came to the front one that was the cause of it all, hoping to gain something by it. On that hot morning, the jam-packed tramcar was cramped and stifling. A black and purple cloud crept from behind the Nikitsky Gates, rising ever higher in the sky over the crowd of passengers running across the pavement. A thunderstorm was approaching.

Yuri Andreevich was sitting on a single seat on the left side of the tramcar, squeezed up against the window. The left-hand pavement of Nikitskaya, where the Conservatory was, remained in his view all the time. Willy-nilly, with the dulled attention of a man thinking about something else, he stared at the people walking or riding on that side and did not miss a single one.

A grey-haired old lady in a light straw hat with cloth daisies and cornflowers, and in a tight-fitting old-fashioned lilac dress, puffing and fanning herself with a flat parcel she carried in her hand, trudged along that side. She was tightly corseted, weary from the heat, and, sweating profusely, kept wiping her wet lips and eyebrows with a small lace handkerchief.

Her path lay parallel to that of the tram. Yuri Andreevich had already lost sight of her several times when the repaired tram started up again and got ahead of her. And she returned to his field of vision several times, when a new breakdown stopped the tram and the lady caught up with it.

Yuri Andreevich recalled school problems on the calculation of the time and order of arrival of trains starting at different moments and moving at different speeds, and he wanted to recall the general method of solving them, but failed to do so and, without finishing, skipped from these memories to other, much more complicated reflections.

He thought about several existences developing side by side, moving next to each other at different speeds, and about one person's fate getting ahead of another's fate in life, and who outlives whom. He imagined something like a principle of relativity in the arena of life, but, getting thoroughly confused, he dropped these comparisons as well.

Lightning flashed, thunder rolled. The luckless tram got stuck yet again on the descent from Kudrinskaya to the Zoological Garden. The lady in purple appeared a little later in the frame of the window, went past the tram, began to move off. The first big drops of rain fell on the pavement, and on the lady. A gust of dusty wind dragged over the trees, brushing leaves against leaves, began tearing the lady's hat off and tucking her skirts under, and suddenly died down.

The doctor felt a rush of debilitating nausea. Overcoming his weakness, he got up from the seat and began jerking the window straps up and down, trying to open the window. It did not yield to his efforts.

They shouted to the doctor that the frame was screwed permanently to the jamb, but, fighting against the attack and seized by some sort of anxiety, he did not take these shouts as addressed to him and did not grasp their meaning. He continued his attempts and again tugged at the frame in three different movements, up, down, and towards himself, and suddenly felt an unprecedented, irreparable pain inside, and realised that he had torn something internally, that he had committed something fatal, and that all was lost. At that moment the tram began to move, but having gone a little way down Presnya, it stopped again.

By an inhuman effort of will, staggering and barely making his way through the congested throng standing in the aisle between the seats, Yuri Andreevich reached the rear platform. They snarled at him and would not let him pass. He fancied that the breath of air had refreshed him, that perhaps all was not lost yet, that he felt better.

He began to squeeze through the crowd on the rear platform, provoking more abuse, kicks, and anger. Paying no attention to the shouts, he broke through the crowd, climbed down from the standing tram onto the pavement, took one step, another, a third, collapsed on the cobbles, and did not get up again.

Noise, talk, arguments, advice arose. Several persons got down from the platform and surrounded the fallen man. They soon established that he was not breathing and that his heart had stopped. People from the pavements came over to the little group around the body, some reassured, others disappointed that the man had not been run over and that his death had no connection with the tram. The crowd grew. The lady in purple also came up to the group, stood for a while, looked at the dead man, listened to the talk, and went on. She was a foreigner, but she understood that some suggested carrying the body into the tramcar and taking it to the hospital, while others said that the police must be called. She went on without waiting to see what decision they would come to.

The lady in purple was the Swiss subject Mademoiselle Fleury from Meliuzeevo, now very, very old. For twelve years she had been pleading in writing for the right to leave for her native country. Quite recently her efforts had been crowned with success. She had arrived in Moscow to obtain an exit visa. She was going that day to pick it up at the consulate, fanning herself with her documents tied with a ribbon. And she went on, getting ahead of the tram for the tenth time and, without knowing it in the least, went ahead of Zhivago and outlived him.

13

Through the doorway from the corridor one could see the corner of the room, with a table standing at an angle to it. From the table to the doorway peered the narrowing lower end of a crudely hollowed-out, boatlike coffin, with the dead man's feet resting against it. This was the same table at which Yuri Andreevich used to write. There was no other in the room. The manuscripts had been put in the drawer, and the table had been put under the coffin. The pillows under the head had been plumped up high, the body in the coffin lay as if on the rising slope of a hill.

It was surrounded by a multitude of flowers, whole bushes of white lilacs, rare at that season, cyclamens, cineraria in pots and baskets. The flowers blocked the light from the windows. The light barely seeped through the flowers onto the dead man's waxen face and hands, onto the wood and lining of the coffin. On the table lay a beautiful pattern of shadows that seemed as if it had just stopped swaying.

The custom of burning the dead in a crematorium was widespread by then.[5] In hopes of obtaining a pension for the children, out of concern for their future at school, and from an unwillingness to damage Marina's situation at work, they renounced a church funeral and decided to have nothing but a civil cremation. Application had been made to the relevant organisations. Representatives were expected.

In expectation of them, the room stood empty, as premises are vacated between the departure of old tenants and the moving in of new ones. The silence was broken only by the decorous tiptoeing and accidental shuffling of those who came for the leavetaking. They were few, but still far more than one might have expected. The news of the death of a man almost without name had spread all around their circle with miraculous speed. A good number of people turned up who had known the dead man at various periods of his life and at various times had lost track of or forgotten him. His scientific thought and his muse were found to have a still greater number of unknown friends, who had never seen the man they were drawn to, and who came to look at him for the first time and to give him a last parting glance.

In those hours when the general silence, not filled by any ceremony, became oppressive in that almost tangible lack, the flowers alone were a substitute for the missing singing and the absent rite.

They did not simply blossom and give off fragrance, but, as if in a chorus, perhaps hastening the corruption by it, poured out their perfume and, endowing everyone with their sweet-scented power, seemed to perform something.

The kingdom of plants so easily offers itself as the nearest neighbour to the kingdom of death. Here, in the earth's greenery, among the trees of the cemetery, amidst the sprouting flowers rising up from the beds, are perhaps concentrated the mysteries of transformation and the riddles of life that we puzzle over. Mary did not at first recognise Jesus coming from the tomb and took him for the gardener walking in the cemetery. ('She, supposing him to be the gardener . . .')[6]

14

When the dead man was brought to his last address in Kamergersky, his friends, informed of his death and shaken by the news, came running from the front entrance to the wide open door of the apartment with Marina, half-crazed by the terrible news. She was beside herself for a long time, thrashed on the floor, and beat her head against the edge of a long chest with a seat and back that stood in the front hall and on which the body was laid until the coffin came and the untidied room was put in order. She was bathed in tears and whispered and cried out, choking on the words, half of which escaped her against her will like the wailing of mourners. She babbled at random, the way simple people lament, not embarrassed by or noticing anyone. Marina clutched at the body and could not be torn away from it, so that the dead man could be transferred to the room, now tidied and freed of extra furniture, to be washed and placed in the delivered coffin. All that was yesterday. Today the violence of her suffering had eased, giving way to dull dejection, but she was still as beside herself as before, said nothing, and was oblivious of herself.

She had sat there through all the rest of the previous day and that night without going anywhere. Here Klava had been brought to her to be nursed and taken away, and Kapka had come with her young nanny and then gone.

She was surrounded by her own people, by Dudorov and Gordon, as grief-stricken as herself. Her father, Markel, quietly sobbing and deafeningly blowing his nose, came and sat with her on the bench. Here also came her weeping mother and sisters.

And there were two persons in this human flow, a man and a woman, who stood out from them all. They claimed no greater closeness to the dead man than those listed above. They did not vie in their grief with Marina, her daughters, and the dead man's friends, and acknowledged their precedence. These two had no claims, but had some entirely special rights of their own to the deceased. These incomprehensible and undeclared powers with which the two were somehow invested were of concern to no one, and no one disputed them. Precisely these people had apparently taken upon themselves the cares of the funeral and its arrangement from the very beginning, and had seen it through with such unruffled calm as though it gave them satisfaction. This loftiness of spirit struck everyone's eye and produced a strange impression. It seemed that these people were involved not only in the funeral, but in the death itself, not as perpetrators or indirect causes, but as persons who, after the fact, accepted this event, reconciled with it, and did not see it as having the greatest importance. Some knew these people, others guessed about them, still others, who were in the majority, had no idea who they were.

But when this man, whose keen, narrow Kirghiz eyes aroused curiosity, and this effortlessly beautiful woman came into the room where the coffin was, all who sat, stood, or moved about in it, not excepting Marina, without objection, as if by arrangement, cleared the premises, stepped aside, got up from the chairs and stools placed along the walls, and, crowding together, went out to the corridor and the front hall, leaving the man and woman alone behind the closed doors, like two initiates called to perform in silence, without hindrance and undisturbed, something immediately concerned with the burial and vitally important. That is what happened now. The two, left alone, sat on two stools by the wall and began to talk business.

'What have you learned, Evgraf Andreevich?'

'The cremation is this evening. In half an hour people from the medical trade union will come for the body and take it to the union's club. The civil ceremony is scheduled for four. Not a single document was in order. His work record had expired, his old trade union card had not been exchanged, his dues hadn't been paid for several years. All of that had to be settled. Hence the red tape and delay. Before the body is taken from the house – incidentally, the moment isn't far off, we must be prepared – I'll leave you alone, as you asked. Forgive me. Do you hear? The telephone. One minute.'

Evgraf Zhivago went out to the corridor, overflowing with unknown colleagues of the doctor's, his schoolmates, minor hospital personnel, and publishing workers, and where Marina and the children, her arms around them, keeping them covered with the skirts of her coat (it was a cold day and there was a draught from the front door), sat on the edge of the bench waiting for the door to be opened again, the way a woman who has come to see an arrested man waits for the guard to let her into the prison reception room. It was crowded in the corridor. Some of those gathered could not get into it. The door to the staircase was open. Many stood, paced, and smoked in the front hall and on the landing. Those lower down the stairs talked the more loudly and freely the closer they were to the street. Straining his hearing on account of the subdued murmur, Evgraf, in a muffled voice, as decency required, covering the receiver with his palm, was giving answers over the telephone, probably about the order of the funeral and the circumstances of the doctor's death. He returned to the room. The conversation continued.

'Please don't disappear after the cremation, Larissa Fyodorovna. I have a great favour to ask of you. I don't know where you're staying. Don't leave me in ignorance about where to find you. I want in the nearest future, tomorrow or the day after, to start going through my brother's papers. I'll need your help. You know so much, probably more than anyone else. You let drop in passing that it's two days since you arrived from Irkutsk for a short stay in Moscow, and that you came up to this apartment by chance, knowing neither that my brother had been living here in recent months, nor what had happened here. Some of what you said I didn't understand, and I'm not asking for explanations, but don't disappear, I don't know your address. It would be best to spend the few days devoted to sorting the man-uscripts under the same roof, or not far from each other, maybe in two other rooms of the house. That could be arranged. I know the manager.'

'You say you didn't understand me. What is there to understand? I arrived in Moscow, left my things at the checkroom, walked through the old Moscow without recognising half of it – I'd forgotten. I walk and walk, go down Kuznetsky Most, up Kuznetsky Lane, and suddenly there's something terribly familiar – Kamergersky Lane. My husband, Antipov, who was shot, rented a room here as a student, precisely this room where you and I are sit-ting. Well, I think, let's have a look, maybe if I'm lucky the old owners are still alive. That there was no trace of them and everything was different, I learned later, the next day and today, gradually, from asking. But you were there, why am I telling you? I was thunderstruck, the street door was wide open, there were people in the room, a coffin, a dead man in the coffin. What dead man? I go in, go up to it, I thought – I've lost my mind, I'm dreaming. But you witnessed it all, right? Why am I telling you about it?'

'Wait, Larissa Fyodorovna, I must interrupt you. I've already told you that my brother and I did not suspect that so many amazing things were connected with this room. For example, that Antipov used to live in it. But still more amazing is an expression that just escaped you. I'll tell you at once what it was – forgive me. At one time, at the beginning of the civil war, I heard much and often about Antipov, or Strelnikov in his military-revolutionary activity, almost every day in fact, and I saw him in person once or twice, without foreseeing how closely he would touch me one day for family reasons. But, excuse me, maybe I didn't hear right, but I think you said, "Antipov, who was shot," in which case it's a slip of the tongue. Surely you know that he shot himself?'

'There's such a version going around, but I don't believe it. Pavel Pavlovich was never a suicide.'

'But it's completely trustworthy. Antipov shot himself in the little house from which, as my brother told me, you left for Yuriatin in order to continue on to Vladivostok. It happened soon after your departure with your daughter. My brother found him and buried him. Can it be that this information never reached you?'

'No. My information was different. So it's true that he shot himself? Many people said so, but I didn't believe it. In that same little house? It can't be! What an important detail you've told me! Forgive me, but do you know whether he and Zhivago met? Did they talk?'

'According to the late Yuri, they had a long conversation.'

'Can it be true? Thank God. It's better that way.' (Antipova slowly crossed herself.) 'What an astounding, heaven-sent coincidence! Will you allow me to come back to it and ask you about all the details? Every little thing is precious to me here. But now I'm not able to. Right? I'm too agitated. I'll be silent for a while, rest, collect my thoughts. Right?'

'Oh, of course, of course. Please do.'

'Right?'

'Surely.'

'Ah, I nearly forgot. You've asked me not to leave after the cremation. Very well. I promise. I won't disappear. I'll come back with you to this apartment and stay where you tell me to and for as long as necessary. We'll start going through Yurochka's manuscripts. I'll help you. It's true that I may be of use to you. That will be such a comfort to me! I feel all the nuances of his handwriting with my heart's blood, with every fibre. Then I also have business with you, I may have need of you, right? It seems you're a lawyer, or in any case have good knowledge of the existing practices, former and present. Besides, it's so important to know which organisation to address for which document. Not everybody knows these things, right? I'll have need of your advice about one dreadful, oppressive thing. It has to do with a child. But I'll tell you later, once we're back from the crematorium. All my life I've been searching for somebody, right? Tell me, if in some imaginary case it was necessary to find the traces of a child, the traces of a child placed in the hands of strangers to be brought up, is there some sort of general, nation-wide archive of existing children's homes and have they made, have they undertaken a national census or registration of homeless children? But don't answer me now, I beg you. Later, later. Oh, how frightening, how frighten-ing! What a frightening thing life is, right? I don't know how it will be later on, when my daughter comes, but for now I can stay in this apartment. Katyusha has shown extraordinary abilities, partly dramatic, but also musi-cal, imitates everybody wonderfully and acts out whole scenes of her own invention, but, besides, she also sings whole parts of operas by ear – an astonishing child, right? I want to send her to the preparatory, beginning classes of a theatre school or the Conservatory, wherever they take her, and place her in a boarding house, that's why I've come without her now, to set everything up and then leave. One can't tell everything, right? But about that later. And now I'm going to wait till my agitation calms down, I'll be silent, collect my thoughts, try to drive my fears away. Besides, we're keep-ing Yura's family in the corridor a horribly long time. Twice I fancied there was knocking at the door. And there's some movement, noise. Probably the people from the funeral organisation have come. While I sit here and think, you open the door and let the public in. It's time, right? Wait, wait. We need a little footstool beside the coffin, otherwise one can't reach Yurochka. I tried on tiptoe, it was very difficult. Marina Markelovna and the children will need it. And besides, it's required by the ritual. "And kiss me with the last kiss."[7] Oh, I can't, I can't. It's so painful. Right?'

'I'll let them all in presently. But first there's this. You've said so many mysterious things and raised so many questions that evidently torment you, that it's hard for me to answer you. One thing I want you to know. From the bottom of my heart, I willingly offer you my help in everything that worries you. And remember. Never, in any circumstances, must you despair. To hope and to act is our duty in misfortune. Inactive despair is a forgetting and failure of duty. I'll now let the people in to take their leave. You're right about the footstool. I'll find one and bring it.'

But Antipova no longer heard him. She did not hear how Evgraf Zhivago opened the door to the room and the crowd from the corridor poured in through it, did not hear him talk with the funeral attendants and the chief mourners, did not hear the rustle of people's movements, Marina's sobbing, the men's coughing, the women's tears and cries.

The swirl of monotonous sounds lulled her and made her feel sick. She kept a firm grip on herself so as not to faint. Her heart was bursting, her head ached. Hanging her head, she immersed herself in surmises, considerations, recollections. She went into them, sank, was as if transported temporarily, for a few hours, to some future age, which she did not know she would live to see, which aged her by decades and made her an old woman. She plunged into reflections, as if falling into the very depths, to the very bottom of her unhappiness. She thought:

'Nobody's left. One has died. The other killed himself. And only the one who should have been killed is left alive, the one she had tried to shoot but missed, that alien, useless nonentity who had turned her life into a chain of crimes unknown to her. And that monster of mediocrity hangs or hustles about the mythical byways of Asia, known only to stamp collectors, but none of my near and needed ones is left.

'Ah, but it was at Christmas, before her intended shooting of that horror of banality, that she had had a conversation with the boy Pasha in this room, and Yura, of whom they were now taking leave here, had not come into her life yet.'

And she began straining her memory to restore that Christmas conversation with Pashenka, but could recall nothing except the candle burning on the windowsill and the melted circle beside it in the icy crust of the windowpane.

Could she have thought that the dead man lying there on the table had seen that peephole from the street as he drove past and had paid attention to the candle? That from this flame seen from outside – 'A candle burned on the table, a candle burned' – his destiny had come into his life?

Her thoughts strayed. She mused: 'What a pity all the same that he won't have a church funeral! The burial service is so majestic and solemn! Most of the dead aren't worthy of it. But Yurochka was such a gratifying cause! He was so worthy of it all, he would so justify and repay that "making our funeral dirge the song: Alleluia"!'[8]

And she felt a wave of pride and relief, which always happened to her at the thought of Yuri and in the brief periods of her life close to him. The breath of freedom and light-heartedness that always issued from him came over her now. She impatiently got up from the stool she was sitting on. Something not quite comprehensible was going on in her. She wanted, with his help, to break free, if only for a short time, into the fresh air, out of the abyss of sufferings that entangled her, to experience, as she once had, the happiness of liberation. This happiness she dreamed, she imagined, as the happiness of taking leave of him, the occasion and the right to weep her fill over him, alone and unhindered. And with the haste of passion, she cast at the crowd a glance broken by pain, unseeing and filled with tears, as from burning eyedrops administered by an oculist, and they all stirred, blew their noses, began moving aside, and went out of the room, leaving her finally alone behind the closed door, and she, quickly crossing herself, went to the table and the coffin, stepped onto the footstool Evgraf had placed there, slowly made three big crosses over the body, and put her lips to the cold forehead and hands. She passed by the sensation that the cold forehead had become smaller, like a hand clenched into a fist; she managed not to notice it. She became still and for a few moments did not speak, did not think, did not weep, covering the middle of the coffin, the flowers, and the body with herself, her head, her breast, her soul, and her arms, as big as her soul.

15

She shook all over with repressed sobs. While she could, she fought them back, but suddenly it became beyond her strength, the tears burst from her and poured over her cheeks, her dress, her arms, and the coffin to which she pressed herself.

She said nothing and thought nothing. Successions of thoughts, generalities, facts, certainties, freely raced, sped through her, like clouds across the sky, as in the times of their former night-time conversations. It was this that used to bring happiness and liberation. An uncerebral, ardent, mutually inspired knowledge. Instinctive, immediate.

She was filled with such knowledge now as well, an obscure, indistinct knowledge of death, a preparedness for it, an absence of perplexity before it. As if she had already lived twenty times in the world, had lost Yuri Zhivago countless times, and had accumulated a whole heart's experience on that account, so that everything she felt and did by his coffin was apropos and to the point.

Oh, what love this was, free, unprecedented, unlike anything else! They thought the way other people sing.

They loved each other not out of necessity, not 'scorched by passion', as it is falsely described. They loved each other because everything around them wanted it so: the earth beneath them, the sky over their heads, the clouds and trees. Everything around them was perhaps more pleased by their love than they were themselves. Strangers in the street, the distances opening out during their walks, the rooms they lived or met in.

Ah, it was this, this was the chief thing that united them and made them akin! Never, never, even in moments of the most gratuitous, self-forgetful happiness, did that most lofty and thrilling thing abandon them: delight in the general mould of the world, the feeling of their relation to the whole picture, the sense of belonging to the beauty of the whole spectacle, to the whole universe.

They breathed only by that oneness. And therefore the exaltation of man over the rest of nature, the fashionable fussing over and worshipping of man, never appealed to them. Such false principles of social life, turned into politics, seemed to them pathetically home-made and remained incomprehensible.

16

And so she began to take leave of him in the simple, ordinary words of a brisk, informal conversation, which breaks up the framework of reality and has no meaning, as there is no meaning in the choruses and monologues of tragedies, in verse, in music, and in other conventions, justified only by the conventionality of emotion. The conventionality in the present case, which justified the tension of her light, unpreconceived talk, was her tears, in which her everyday, unfestive words plunged, bathed, floated.

It seemed that these words wet with tears stuck together of themselves in her tender and quick prattle, as the wind rustles silky and moist foliage tousled by a warm rain.

'So we're together once more, Yurochka. This is how God granted that we meet again. How terrible, just think! Oh, I can't! Oh Lord! I weep and weep! Just think! So again it's something of our sort, from our arsenal. Your going, my end. Again something big, irrevocable. The riddle of life, the riddle of death, the enchantment of genius, the enchantment of nakedness – that, yes, if you please, that we understood. But petty worldly squabbles like recarving the globe – sorry, we pass, it's not in our line.

'Farewell, my great and dear one, farewell, my pride, farewell, my swift, deep river, how I loved your daylong splashing, how I loved to throw myself into your cold waves.

'Remember how I said goodbye to you that time, there, in the snow? How you deceived me! Would I ever have gone without you? Oh, I know, I know, you forced yourself to do it, for the sake of my imaginary good. And then everything went to rack and ruin. Lord, what a cup I drank there, what I endured! But you don't know anything. Oh, what have I done, Yura, what have I done! I'm such a criminal, you have no idea! But it wasn't my fault. I was in the hospital for three months then, for one of them unconscious. Since then there's been no life for me, Yura. There's no peace for my soul from pity and torment. But I'm not telling, I'm not revealing the main thing. I can't name it, I haven't got strength enough. When I come to this point in my life, my hair stands on end from horror. And, you know, I can't even swear I'm quite normal. But, you see, I don't drink, as many do, I didn't set out on that path, because a drunken woman is the end, it's an unthinkable thing, right?'

And she said something more and wept and suffered. Suddenly she raised her head in surprise and looked around. There had long been people in the room, anxiousness, movement. She got down from the footstool and, staggering, stepped away from the coffin, passing her palm over her eyes, as if to squeeze out the remaining unwept tears and shake them onto the floor.

Some men went up to the coffin and lifted it on three cloths. The carrying out began.

17

Larissa Fyodorovna spent several days in Kamergersky Lane. The sorting of papers she had talked about with Evgraf Andreevich was begun with her participation, but not brought to an end. The conversation with Evgraf that she had asked for also took place. He learned something important from her.

One day Larissa Fyodorovna left the house and did not come back again. Evidently she was arrested on the street in those days and died or vanished no one knew where, forgotten under some nameless number on subsequently lost lists, in one of the countless general or women's concentration camps in the north.

Part Sixteen

EPILOGUE

I

In the summer of 1943, after the breakthrough on the Kursk bulge and the liberation of Orel,[1] Gordon, recently promoted to second lieutenant, and Major Dudorov were returning separately to their common army unit, the first from a service trip to Moscow, the second from a three-day leave there.

They met on the way back and spent the night in Chern, a little town, devastated but not completely destroyed, like most of the settlements in that 'desert zone' wiped off the face of the earth by the retreating enemy.

Amidst the town's ruins, heaps of broken brick and finely pulverised gravel, the two men found an undamaged hayloft, where they made their lair for the night.

They could not sleep. They spent the whole night talking. At dawn, around three in the morning, the dozing Dudorov was awakened by Gordon's pottering about. With awkward movements, bobbing and waddling in the soft hay as if in water, he was gathering some underthings into a bundle, and then, just as clumsily, began sliding down the hay pile to the doorway of the loft on his way out.

'What are you getting ready for? It's still early.'

'I'm going to the river. I want to do me some laundry.'

'That's crazy. We'll be in our own unit by evening; the linen girl Tanka will give you a change of underwear. What's the rush?'

'I don't want to put it off. I've been sweating, haven't changed for too long. The morning's hot. I'll rinse it quickly, wring it out well, it'll dry instantly in the sun. I'll bathe and change.'

'All the same, you know, it doesn't look good. You must agree, you're an officer, after all.'

'It's early. Everybody around is asleep. I'll do it somewhere behind a bush. Nobody will see. And you sleep, don't talk. You'll drive sleep away.'

'I won't sleep any more as it is. I'll go with you.'

And they went to the river, past the white stone ruins, already scorching hot in the just-risen sun. In the middle of the former streets, on the ground, directly in the hot sun, sweaty, snoring, flushed people slept. They were mostly locals, old men, women, and children, left without a roof over their heads – rarely, solitary Red Army soldiers who had lagged behind their units and were catching up with them. Gordon and Dudorov, watching their feet so as not to step on them, walked carefully among the sleepers.

'Talk softly, or we'll wake up the town, and then it's goodbye to my laundry.'

And they continued their last night's conversation in low voices.

2

'What river is this?'

'I don't know. I didn't ask. Probably the Zusha.'

'No, it's not the Zusha. It's some other.'

'Well, then I don't know.'

'It was on the Zusha that it all happened. With Christina.'

'Yes, but in a different place. Somewhere downstream. They say the Church has canonised her a saint.'

'There was a stone building there that acquired the name of "The Stable". In fact it was the stable of a collective farm stud, a common noun that became historical. An old one, with thick walls. The Germans fortified it and turned it into an impregnable fortress. The whole neighbourhood was exposed to fire from it, and that slowed our advance. The stable had to be taken. Christina, in a miracle of courage and resourcefulness, penetrated the German camp, blew up the stable, was taken alive and hanged.'

'Why Christina Orletsova, and not Dudorova?'

'We weren't married yet. In the summer of forty-one we gave each other our word that we would get married once the war was over. After that I moved about with the rest of the army. My unit was being endlessly trans-ferred. What with these transfers, I lost sight of her. I never saw her again. I learned of her valiant deed and heroic death like everybody else. From newspapers and regimental orders. They say they're going to set up a monu-ment to her somewhere here. I've heard that General Zhivago, the brother of the late Yuri, is making the rounds of these parts, gathering information about her.'

'Forgive me for bringing her up in our conversation. It must be painful for you.'

'That's not the point. But we keep babbling away. I don't want to hinder you. Get undressed, go into the water, and do your work. And I'll stretch out on the bank with a blade of grass in my teeth, I'll chew and think, and maybe take a nap.'

A few minutes later, the conversation picked up again.

'Where did you learn to wash clothes like that?'

'From necessity. We had no luck. Of all the penal camps, we landed in the most terrible one. Few survived. Beginning from our arrival. The party was taken off the train. A snowy waste. A forest in the distance. Guards, rifles with lowered muzzles, German shepherds. Around that same time, new groups were driven in at various moments. They formed us into a wide polygon the size of the whole field, facing out, so as not to see each other. The order came: on your knees, and don't look to the sides or you'll be shot, and then began the endless, humiliating procedure of the roll-call, which was drawn out for long hours. Kneeling down the whole time. Then we stood up, other parties were taken elsewhere, and we were told: "Here's your camp. Settle in as you can." A snowy field under the open sky, a post in the middle, an inscription on the post: "Gulag 92 Y N 90" and nothing more.'

'No, for us it was easier. We were lucky. I was serving my second term, which usually followed on the first. Besides, the article was different and so were the conditions. After my release, my rights were restored, as they were the first time, and I was again allowed to lecture at the university. And I was mobilised in the war with the full rights of a major, not in a penal unit like you.'

'Yes. A post with the number "Gulag 92 Y N 90" and nothing else. At first we broke off laths for huts with our bare hands in the freezing cold. And, you won't believe it, but we gradually built the place up for ourselves. We cut wood for shacks, surrounded ourselves with palings, set up punishment cells, watchtowers – all by ourselves. And we started logging. Tree felling. We felled trees. Eight of us would hitch ourselves to the sledge, load it with logs, sinking up to our chests in the snow. For a long time we didn't know that war had broken out. They concealed it. And suddenly – an offer. Volunteer for penal battalions at the front and, if you chance to come out of the endless battles alive, you'll all go free. And then attacks, attacks, miles of electrified barbed wire, mines, mortars, month after month under a hail of fire. It was not for nothing that in these companies we were known as "the condemned". We'd be mowed down to a man. How did I survive?

How did I ever survive? But, imagine, that whole bloody hell was happiness compared to the horrors of the concentration camp, and not at all owing to the harsh conditions, but to something else entirely.'

'Yes, brother, you've drunk a bitter cup.'

'It wasn't just washing clothes you could learn there, but anything you like.'

'An amazing thing. Not only compared to your convict's portion, but in regard to the whole previous life of the thirties, even in freedom, even in the well-being of university activity, books, money, comfort, the war came as a cleansing storm, a gust of fresh air, a breath of deliverance.

'I think collectivisation was a false, unsuccessful measure, and it was impossible to acknowledge the mistake. To conceal the failure, it was necessary to cure people, by every means of intimidation, of the habit of judging and thinking, and force them to see the non-existent and prove what was contrary to evidence. Hence the unprecedented cruelty of the Ezhovshchina, the promulgation of a constitution not meant to be applied, the introduction of elections not based on the principle of choice.[2]

'And when the war broke out, its real horrors, real danger, and the threat of real death were beneficial in comparison with the inhuman reign of fiction, and brought relief, because they limited the magic power of the dead letter.

'Not only people in your situation, at forced labour, but decidedly everybody, in the rear and at the front, breathed more freely, with a full breast, and threw themselves rapturously, with a feeling of true happiness, into the crucible of the fierce fight, deadly and salutary.

'The war is a special link in the chain of revolutionary decades. The action of causes that lay directly in the nature of the upheaval came to an end.

'The indirect results began to tell, the fruits of the fruits, the consequences of the consequences. A tempering of character derived from calamity, non-indulgence, heroism, readiness for the great, the desperate, the unprecedented. These are fantastic, stunning qualities, and they constitute the moral flower of the generation.

'These observations fill me with a feeling of happiness, in spite of the martyr's death of Christina, of my wounds, of our losses, of all this high, bloody price of the war. The light of self-sacrifice that shines on her end and on the life of each of us helps me to endure the pain of Orletsova's death.

'Just when you, poor fellow, were enduring your countless tortures, I was released. At that time, Orletsova was studying history at the university. The nature of her scholarly interests placed her under my guidance. Much earlier, after my first term in the camps, when she was still a child, I had paid attention to this remarkable girl. While Yuri was still alive, remember, I told you about her. Well, so now she turned up among my auditors.

'The custom of students publicly criticising teachers had just come into fashion then. Orletsova fervently threw herself into it. God only knows why she picked on me so ferociously. Her attacks were so persistent, bellicose, and unjust that other students in the department occasionally rose up and defended me. Orletsova was a remarkable satirist. Under an imaginary name, in which everybody recognised me, she mocked me to her heart's content in a wall newspaper. Suddenly, by complete chance, it turned out that this deep-rooted hostility was a form of camouflage for a young love, strong, hidden, and long-standing. I had always felt the same.

'We spent a wonderful summer in forty-one, the first year of the war, just on the eve of it and soon after it was declared. Several young students, boys and girls, and she among them, had settled in a summer place outside Moscow, where my unit was later stationed. Our friendship began and took its course in the circumstances of their military training, the forming of sub-urban militia units, Christina's training as a parachutist, the repulsing of the first German air raids by night from the rooftops of Moscow. I've already told you that we celebrated our engagement there and were soon parted by the beginning of my displacements. I never saw her again.[3]

'When there were signs of a favourable change in our affairs, and the Germans began to surrender by the thousand, I was transferred, after two wounds and two stays in the hospital, from the anti-aircraft artillery to seventh division headquarters, where there was a demand for people with a knowledge of foreign languages, and where I insisted that you, too, should be sent, after I fished you up as if from the bottom of the sea.'

'The linen girl Tanya knew Orletsova well. They met at the front and were friends. She told many stories about Christina. This Tanya has the same manner of smiling with her whole face as Yuri had, have you noticed? For a moment, the turned-up nose and angular cheekbones disappear, and the face becomes attractive, pretty. It's one and the same type, very widespread among us.'

'I know what you're talking about. Maybe so. I hadn't paid attention.'

'What a barbaric, ugly name, Tanka Bezocheredeva, "Tanka Out-of-Turn". In any case it's not a surname, it's something invented, distorted. What do you think?'

'She did explain it. She was a homeless child, of unknown parents. Probably somewhere in the depths of Russia, where the language is still pure and unsullied, she was called Bezotchaya, meaning "without father". Street kids, for whom this derivation was incomprehensible, and who get everything from hearing and distort it, remade the designation in their own way, closer to their actual vulgar parlance.'

3

It was not long after the night Gordon and Dudorov spent in Chern and their night-time conversation there. Overtaking the army in the town of Karachevo, which had been razed to its foundations, the friends found some rear units that were following the main forces.

The clear and calm weather of the hot autumn had settled in for more than a month without interruption. Bathed in the heat of the cloudless blue sky, the fertile black soil of Brynshchina, the blessed region between Orel and Bryansk, was burnished to a chocolate-coffee colour by the play of sunlight.

The town was cut by a straight main street that merged with the high road. On one side of it lay collapsed houses, turned by mines into heaps of building rubble, and the uprooted, splintered, and charred trees of orchards flattened to the ground. On the other side, across the road, stretched empty plots, probably little built upon to begin with, before the town's destruction, and spared more by the fire and powder blasts because there was nothing there to destroy.

On the formerly built-up side, the shelterless citizens poked in the piles of still-smouldering ashes, digging things up and carrying them to one place from the far corners of the burned-down site. Others hastily burrowed into dugouts and sliced layers of earth so as to cover the upper parts of their dwellings with sod.

On the opposite, unbuilt side there were white tents, a crowd of trucks and horse-drawn wagons of various second-line services, field hospitals strayed from their division headquarters, confused units of every sort of depot, commissariat, supply dump, lost and looking for each other. There, too, relieving themselves, snatching something to eat, sleeping, and then trudging further west, were companies of skinny, ill-nourished adolescent draftees in grey forage caps and heavy grey coats, with wasted, sallow faces, bloodless from dysentery.

The town, blown up and half reduced to ashes, went on burning and exploding in the distance, where timed charges had been planted. Now and then men digging in their gardens interrupted their work, stopped by a trembling of the ground under their feet, straightened their bent backs, leaned on the handles of their spades and, turning their heads in the direction of the blast, rested, looking off that way for a long time.

There, first in pillars and fountains, then in lazy, ponderous swellings, the grey, black, brick-red and smokily flaming clouds of airborne trash ascended into the sky, thinned out, spread into plumes, scattered, and settled back down to earth. And the workers took up their work again.

One of the clearings on the unbuilt side was bordered with bushes and covered completely by the shade of the old trees growing there. The clearing was fenced off from the rest of the world by this vegetation, like a covered courtyard standing by itself and immersed in cool twilight.

In the clearing, the linen girl Tanya, with two or three persons from her regiment and several self-invited fellow travellers, as well as Gordon and Dudorov, had been waiting since morning for a truck sent for Tanya and the regimental property she was in charge of. It was stowed in several boxes piled up in the clearing. Tatiana kept an eye on them and did not move a step away, but the others also stayed close to the boxes, so as not to miss the possibility of leaving when it presented itself.

The wait had lasted a long time, more than five hours. The waiting people had nothing to do. They were listening to the incessant chatter of the garrulous girl, who had seen a lot. She had just told them about her meeting with Major General Zhivago.

'That's right. Yesterday. Brought in person to the general. Major General Zhivago. He was passing through here and made enquiries about Christina, asked questions. Of eyewitnesses who knew her personally. They pointed me out. Said I was her friend. He summoned me. So I'm summoned, brought to him. Not scary at all. Nothing special, just like everybody else. Slant-eyed, dark. So what I knew, I laid out. He listened, said thank you. And you yourself, he says, where from and what sort? I, naturally, hemmed and hawed and nay-sayed him. What's there to boast of? A homeless child. And so on. You know it yourselves. Correctional institutions, vagrancy. But he won't hear of it, go ahead, he says, don't be embarrassed, there's no shame in it. So I said the first timid word or two, then more, he nods away, I got bolder. And I do have things to tell. If you heard, you wouldn't believe it, you'd say – she's making it up. Well, it was the same with him. Once I finished, he got up and paced up and down the cottage. You don't say, he says, what wonders. Well, here's the thing, he says. I've got no time now. But I'll find you, don't worry, I'll find you and summon you again. I simply never thought I'd hear such things. I won't leave you like this, he says. I'll have to clarify a thing or two, various details. And then, he says, for all I know I may yet put myself down as your uncle, promote you to a general's niece. And send you to study in any school you like. By God, it's true. Such a jolly leg-puller.'

Just then a long, empty cart with high sides, such as is used in Poland and western Russia for transporting sheaves, drove into the clearing. The pair of horses hitched to the shafts was driven by a serviceman, a *furleit* in the old terminology, a soldier of the cavalry train. He drove into the clearing, jumped down from the box, and started unhitching the horses. Everyone except Tatiana and a few soldiers surrounded the driver, begging him not to unhitch and to drive them where they told him – not for free, of course. The soldier protested, because he had no right to dispose of the horses and cart and had to obey the orders he had been given. He led the unhitched horses somewhere and never came back again. Everyone who had been sitting on the ground got up and went to sit in the empty cart, which was left in the clearing. Tatiana's story, interrupted by the appearance of the cart and the negotiations with the driver, was taken up again.

'What did you tell the general?' asked Gordon. 'Repeat it for us, if you can.'

'Sure, why not?'

And she told them her horrible story.

4

'And it's true I've got things to tell. I'm not from simple folk, I was told. Either other people told me, or I tucked it away in my heart, only I heard that my mama, Raissa Komarova, was the wife of a Russian minister, Comrade Komarov, who was hiding in White Mongolia. He wasn't my father, wasn't my kin, you can only suppose, this same Komarov. Well, of course, I'm an uneducated girl, grew up an orphan, with no father or mother. It may seem funny to you that I say it, well, I'm only saying what I know, you've got to put yourselves in my position.

'Yes. So, it all happened, what I'm going to tell you now, beyond Krushitsy, at the other end of Siberia, beyond Cossack country, closer to the Chinese border. When we – our Red Army, that is – started approaching the main town of the Whites, this same Komarov the minister put mama and all their family on a special reserved train and had it take them away, because mama was forever frightened and didn't dare take a step without him.

'And he didn't even know about me, Komarov didn't. Didn't know there was anybody like me in the world. Mama produced me during a long absence and was scared to death that somebody might let it slip to him. He terribly disliked having children around, and shouted and stamped his feet that it was all just filth in the house and a big bother. I can't stand it, he shouted.

'Well, so, as I was saying, when the Red Army was approaching, mama sent for the signalman's wife, Marfa, at the Nagornaya junction, three stops away from that town. I'll explain right away. First the Nizovaya station, then the Nagornaya junction, then the Samsonovsky crossing. I see now how mama got to know the signalman's wife. I think Marfa came to town to sell vegetables and deliver milk. Yes.

'And I'll say this. It's obvious there's something I don't know here. I think they tricked mama, told her something else. Described God knows what, it was just temporary, a couple of days, till the turmoil calmed down. And not for me to be in strangers' hands forever. To be brought up forever. My mama couldn't have given away her own child like that.

'Well, you know how they do with children. "Go to auntie, auntie will give you gingerbread, auntie's nice, don't be afraid of auntie." And how I cried and thrashed afterwards, how my child's little heart was wrung, it's better not to speak of it. I wanted to hang myself, I nearly went out of my mind in childhood. Because I was still little. They must have given Auntie Marfusha money for my keep, a lot of money.

'The farmstead at the post was a rich one, a cow and a horse, well, and of course all sorts of fowl, and a plot for a kitchen garden as big as you like, and free lodgings, needless to say, a signalman's house, right by the tracks. From our parts below, the train could barely go up, had trouble making the climb, but from your Russian parts it went at high speed, had to put on the brakes. In autumn, when the forest thinned out, you could see the Nagornaya station like on a plate.

'The man himself, Uncle Vassily, I called daddy, peasantlike. He was a jolly and kind man, only much too gullible, and when he was under the influence, he ran off at the mouth – like they say, the hog told the sow, and the sow the whole town. He'd blurt out his whole soul to the first comer.

'But I could never get my tongue to call his wife mother. Whether because I couldn't forget my own mama, or for some other reason, only this Auntie Marfusha was so scary. Yes. So I called the signalman's wife Auntie Marfusha.

'Well, time went by. Years passed. How many, I don't remember. I'd already started to run out to the trains with a flag. To unharness a horse or bring home a cow was no mystery to me. Auntie Marfusha taught me to spin. To say nothing of the cottage. To sweep the floor, to tidy up, or to cook something, to mix the dough, was nothing to me, I could do it all. Ah, yes, I forgot to tell you, I was also nanny to Petenka. Our Petenka had withered legs, he was just three, he lay there and couldn't walk, so I was nanny to Petenka. And now so many years have gone by and it still gives me shivers, how Auntie Marfusha used to look sideways at my healthy legs, as if to say, why weren't mine withered, it would be better if mine were withered and not Petenka's, as if it was my evil eye that had spoiled Petenka, just think, what malice and darkness there are in the world.

'Listen, now, that was all just flowers, as they say, what comes next will make you gasp.

'It was the NEP then, and a thousand rubles were worth a kopeck. Vassily Afanasievich went down with the cow, got two bags of money – kerenki, they were called, ah, no, sorry – lemons, they were called lemons – got drunk, and went sounding off about his riches all over Nagornaya.

'I remember, it was a windy autumn day, the wind tore at the roof and knocked you off your feet, the locomotives couldn't make it uphill, the wind was so against them. I see an old woman, a wanderer, come down the hill, the wind tearing at her skirt and kerchief.

'The wanderer walks up, groaning, clutching her stomach, asking to come inside. We put her on the bench – ohh, I can't, she yells, I can't, it's stomach cramps, it's the death of me. And she begs us, take me to the hospital, for Christ's sake, you'll be paid, I won't stint on money. Daddy hitched up Udaloy, put the old woman on the cart, and drove to the zemstvo hospital, ten miles from the railway line.

'After a time, maybe long, maybe short, Auntie Marfusha and I went to bed, we hear Udaloy neighing under the window and our own cart driving into the yard. It was a bit early for that. So. Auntie Marfusha lit a lamp, threw on a bed jacket, and, not waiting for daddy to knock, lifted the latch.

'She lifts the latch, and there's no daddy on the doorstep, but a stranger, a dark and scary muzhik, and he says: "Show me," he says, "where the money for the cow is. I took care of your husband in the forest," he says, "but I'll spare you, woman, if you tell me where the money is. And if you don't tell, you know what'll happen, don't blame me. You'd better not dawdle. I've got no time to hang around."

'Oh, saints alive, dear comrades, what a state we were in, put yourselves in our position! We tremble, more dead than alive, can't speak from fright, such a horror! First of all, he's murdered Vassily Afanasievich, he says so, cut him down with an axe. Secondly, we're alone in the house with a robber, we've got a robber here, it's clear he's a robber.

'Here, obviously, Auntie Marfusha went right off her head, her heart broke for her husband. But we had to hold out, not show anything.

'Auntie Marfusha started by throwing herself at his feet. Have mercy, she says, don't destroy us, I have no idea about this money, what are you talking about, it's the first I hear of it. But the cursed fellow wasn't so simple as to be handled just by talk. And suddenly the thought popped into her head how to outwit him. "Well, all right," she says, "have it your way. The cash," she says, "is down below. I'll open the trapdoor, and you," she says, "can go down." But the devil sees through her cleverness. "No," he says, "it's your house, you hunt it up. Go yourself," he says. "Whether it's down below or on the roof, as long as I get the money. Only," he says, "remember, don't try to cheat me, tricks go down bad with me."

'And she to him: "Good heavens, don't be so suspicious. I'd gladly go, but I'm too clumsy. Better," she says, "if I stand on the top step and hold the light for you. Don't be afraid, for your assurance I'll send my daughter down with you" – me, that is.

'Oh, saints alive, dear comrades, think for yourselves what I felt when I heard that! Well, I thought, that's it. My eyes went dim, I felt I was falling, my legs gave way under me.

'But again the villain wouldn't be played for a fool, he looked at the two of us out of the corner of his eye, squinted, twisted his whole mouth and bared his teeth, meaning, there's no way you're going to trick me. He saw she didn't care about me, so I wasn't her own blood, and he grabbed Petenka with one hand, and with the other opened the trapdoor – "give me light," he says, and with Petenka he goes down the ladder into the cellar.

'And I think Auntie Marfusha was already barmy then, didn't understand anything, was already touched in the head. As soon as the villain went down below with Petenka, she slammed the lid, that is, the trapdoor, back in place and locked it, and started moving a heavy trunk onto it, nodding to me, help, I can't do it, it's too heavy. She moved it, and sat herself down on the trunk, overjoyed, fool that she was. Just as she sat down on the trunk, the robber started shouting from inside, and there was a bang-bang under the floor, meaning you'd better let me out, or I'll finish off your Petenka right now. We couldn't make out the words through the thick boards, but the sense wasn't in the words. He roared worse than a beast of the forest, to put fear into us with his big voice. Yes, he shouts, now it'll be the end of your Petenka. But she doesn't understand a thing. She sits and laughs and winks at me. Shout away, every dog has his day, but I'm sitting on the trunk and the key's clutched in my fist. I try to get at Auntie Marfusha this way and that. I shout in her ear, push her, want to dump her off the trunk. We must open the trapdoor and save Petenka. Too much for me! Could I do anything against her?

'So he beats on the floor, he beats, time goes by, and she sits on the trunk rolling her eyes and doesn't listen.

'After a while – oh, saints alive, oh, dear saints alive, the things I've seen and suffered in my life, but I don't remember any such horror, all my life long I'll hear Petenka's pitiful little voice – Petenka, that angelic little soul, crying and moaning from underground – he just bit him to death, the fiend.

'Well, what am I to do, what am I to do now, I think, what am I to do with the half-crazed old woman and this murderous robber? And time's going by. I only just thought it when I heard Udaloy neighing outside the window, he was standing there hitched up all the while. Yes. Udaloy neighed as if he wanted to say, come on, Tanyusha, let's gallop off quickly to some good people and ask for help. I look out, it's already getting light. Have it your way, Udaloy, I think, thanks for the suggestion – you're right, let's run for it. And I only just thought it when, hah, I hear, it's like somebody's talking to me again from the forest: "Wait, Tanyusha, don't rush, we'll handle this matter differently." And again I'm not alone in the forest. Like a cock singing out something I knew, a familiar engine whistle called to me from below, I knew this engine by its whistle, it was always standing in Nagornaya under steam, it was called a pusher, to push freight trains up the hill, but this was a mixed train, it went by every night at that time – so I hear the familiar engine calling me from below. I hear it and my heart leaps. Can it be, I think, that I'm out of my mind like Auntie Marfusha, since a living creature and a speechless machine talk to me in clear Russian language?

'Well, why stand thinking, the train was already close, there was no time to think. I grabbed the lantern, because it still wasn't very light, and rushed like mad to the tracks, swinging the lantern back and forth.

'Well, what more can I say? I stopped the train, thanks to its being slowed down by the wind, well, simply speaking, it was creeping along. I stopped the train, the engineer I knew, he stuck himself out of the window of his cabin, asked something; I didn't hear what he asked on account of the wind. I shout to the engineer, the railway post's been attacked, there's been murder and robbery, the robber's in the house, do something, comrade uncle, we need urgent help. And as I was saying it, Red Army soldiers got out of the cars onto the tracks one after another, it was a military train, the soldiers came down the tracks, said: "What's the matter?" – wondering what the story was, why the train had been stopped in the forest on a steep hill at night.

'They learned about it all, dragged the robber from the cellar, he squealed in a high voice, higher than Petenka's, have mercy, good people, he said, don't kill me, I won't do it again. They dragged him to the tracks, tied his legs and arms to the rails, and ran the train over him alive – lynch law.

'I didn't go to the house for my clothes, it was so scary. I begged – dear uncles, take me on the train. They took me with them on the train and drove off. Afterwards, it's no lie, I went around half the world, foreign and our own, with homeless children, I've been everywhere. Such freedom, such happiness I got to know, after the woes of my childhood! But, true, there was all sorts of trouble and sin. That was all later, I'll tell about it some other time. But then a railway worker from the train went to the signalman's house to take charge of the government property and give orders about Auntie Marfusha, to arrange her life. They say she later died insane in the madhouse. But others say she got better and came out.'

Long after hearing all that, Gordon and Dudorov were silently pacing up and down on the grass. Then a truck arrived, turning awkwardly and cumbersomely from the road into the clearing. The boxes were loaded onto the truck. Gordon said:

'You realise who this linen girl Tanya is?'

'Yes, of course.'

'Evgraf will look after her.' Then, pausing briefly, he added: 'It has already been so several times in history. What was conceived as ideal and lofty became coarse and material. So Greece turned into Rome, so the Russian enlightenment turned into the Russian revolution. Take Blok's "We, the children of Russia's terrible years",[4] and you'll see the difference in epochs. When Blok said that, it was to be understood in a metaphorical sense, figuratively. The children were not children, but sons, offspring, the intelligentsia, and the terrors were not terrible, but providential, apocalyptic, and those are two different things. But now all that was metaphorical has become literal, and the children are children, and the terrors are terrifying – there lies the difference.'

<h1 style="text-align:center">5</h1>

Five or ten years went by, and one quiet summer evening they were sitting again, Gordon and Dudorov, somewhere high up by an open window over the boundless evening Moscow. They were leafing through the notebook of Yuri's writings put together by Evgraf, which they had read many times and half of which they knew by heart. As they read, they exchanged observations and abandoned themselves to reflections. Midway through their reading it grew dark, they had difficulty making out the print and had to light the lamp.

And Moscow below and in the distance, the native city of the author and of half of what had befallen him, Moscow now seemed to them, not the place of these events, but the main heroine of a long story, which they had reached the end of that evening, with the notebook in their hands.

Though the brightening and liberation they had expected after the war did not come with victory, as had been thought, even so, the portents of freedom were in the air all through the post-war years, constituting their only historical content.

To the ageing friends at the window it seemed that this freedom of the soul had come, that precisely on that evening the future had settled down tangibly in the streets below, that they themselves had entered into that future and henceforth found themselves in it. A happy, tender sense of peace about this holy city and about the whole earth, about the participants in this story who had lived till that evening and about their children, filled them and enveloped them in an inaudible music of happiness, which spread far around. And it was as if the book in their hands knew it all and lent their feelings support and confirmation.

Part Seventeen

I

Hamlet

The hum dies down. I step out on the stage.
Leaning against a doorpost,
I try to catch the echoes from far off
Of what my age is bringing.

The night's darkness focuses on me
Thousands of opera glasses.
Abba Father, if only it can be,
Let this cup pass me by.

I love the stubbornness of your intent
And agree to play this role.
But now a different drama's going on –
Spare me, then, this once.

But the order of the acts has been thought out,
And leads to just one end.
I'm alone, all drowns in pharisaism.
Life is no stroll through a field.

2

March

The sun heats up to the seventh sweat,
And the ravine, gone foolish, rages.
Like the work of a robust barnyard girl,
Spring's affairs are in full swing.

The snow wastes away with anaemia
In the branchwork of impotent blue veins,
But life is steaming in the cowshed,
And the pitchfork's teeth are the picture of health.

Oh, these nights, these days and nights!
The drumming of drops towards the middle of day,
The dwindling of icicles on the eaves,
The sleepless babbling of the brooks!

Everything wide open, stables and cowshed,
Pigeons peck up oats from the snow,
And the lifegiver and culprit of it all –
Dung – smells of fresh air.

3

Holy Week

Still the gloom of night around.
Still so early in the world,
The stars are countless in the sky,
And each of them as bright as day,
And if the earth were able to,
It would sleep its way through Easter
To the reading of the psalms.

Still the gloom of night around.
So early an hour in the world,
The square lies like eternity
From the crossroads to the corner,
And the light and warmth of dawn
Are still a millennium away.

The earth's still bare as bare can be,
With nothing to put on at night
To go and swing the bells outside
And there back up the choristers.

And from Great and Holy Thursday
Right to Holy Saturday,
Water bores the riverbanks
And twines in whirlpools round itself.

And the woods are undressed, uncovered,
And at the service of Christ's Passion,
Like the ranks of people praying,
Stand trunks of pine trees in a crowd.

And in town, with very little
Space, as at a local meeting,
Trees, stark naked, stand and look
Through the church's grillwork gates.

And their gaze is filled with terror.
The cause of their alarm is clear.
Gardens are coming through the fence,
The order of the earth is shaken:
It is God they're burying.

And they see light by the royal doors,
A black pall and a row of candles,
Tear-stained faces – suddenly
The procession of the cross
Comes to meet them with the shroud,
And two birches by the gate
Are forced to step aside for it.

And the procession makes its way
Around the yard and down the walk,
And brings to the chapel from outside
Spring, and springtime conversation,
And air that smacks of blessed bread,
And of spring's intoxication.

And March squanders its hoard of snow
On cripples crowding by the porch,
As if a man came out to them
Carrying the ark, and opened it,
And gave away all to the very last.

And the singing goes on till dawn,
And, when it has sobbed its fill,
The reading of psalms and the epistle
Reaches more softly from inside
To vacant plots under the lamps.

But at midnight creature and flesh
Fall silent, hearing the springtime rumour
That the moment the weather clears
Death itself may be overcome
By the effort of the Resurrection.

4

White Night

I am dreaming of a far-off time,
A house over on the Petersburg Side.
The daughter of a modest steppe landowner,
You're taking courses, you were born in Kursk.

You're sweet, you have admirers.
On this white night the two of us,
Having settled on your windowsill,
Are looking down from your skyscraper.

Street lights like gas butterflies,
Morning touched by a first tremor.
What I am softly telling you
Is so much like the sleeping distance!

We are gripped by the very same
Timid loyalty to the secret
As Petersburg spreading its panorama
Beyond the boundless river Neva.

Far off at the dense confines,
On this white night in the spring,
Nightingales fill the forest's limits
With their thunderous hymns of glory.

The crazy trilling surges, rolls,
The voice of the little homely bird
Awakens ecstasy and turmoil
In the depths of the enchanted wood.

In those parts, night, the barefoot pilgrim,
Making her way along the fence,
Draws after her from the windowsill
A trail of overheard conversation.

To the echoes of talk heard aloud,
In orchards fenced with wooden palings,
Bending apple and cherry boughs
Clothe themselves in whitish flowers.

And the trees, like white apparitions,
Pour in a crowd out to the road,
Waving as if to bid farewell
To the white night that has seen so much.

5

Bad Roads in Spring

Sunset's fires were burning down.
A man on horseback dragged himself
Over a bad road through the pines
To a far-off farmstead in the Urals.

The horse's spleen was tossed about,
The splashing of its iron shoes
Was echoed in its wake by water
In the sinkholes of the springs.

When the rider dropped the reins
And went on at a walking pace,
The flooding waters spread nearby
With all their roar and rumbling.

Someone laughed, someone wept,
Stone against stone crashed and crumbled,
Tree stumps torn out by the root
Toppled into the whirling pools.

And at sunset's conflagration,
In the far-off, blackened branches,
Like the tolling of the tocsin,
A nightingale sang furiously.

Where the widowed willow bowed
Her headdress over the ravine,
Like old Nightingale the Robber,
He whistled in the seven oaks.

What calamity, what ladylove
Was this ardour destined for?
At whom did he fire off his load
Of grapeshot in the thickset wood?

A demon, he seemed, about to step
From the camp of fugitives from hard labour
And go to meet the local posts
Of partisans, mounted or on foot.

Earth and sky, forest and field
Tried to snare this rarest sound,
These measured shares of madness, pain,
Happiness, and suffering.

6

A Final Talk

Life has come back as causelessly
As once it was strangely broken off.
I am here on the same old street
As then, that summer day and hour.

The same people and the cares the same,
And the fire of sunset not yet cooled,
As when death's evening hastily
Nailed it to the wall of the Manège.

Women in cheap workday clothes
In the same way wear out their shoes at night.
And later the garrets crucify them
In the same way on the iron roofs.

Here one with a weary gait
Slowly emerges on the threshold
And, climbing up from the half basement,
Goes diagonally across the yard.

I again ready my excuses,
And again it's all the same to me.
And the neighbour woman skirts the backyard,
Leaving the two of us alone.

Don't cry, don't pucker your swollen lips,
Don't gather them in wrinkles.
You'll reopen the dried-up scab
Of your spring fever sore.

Take your palm off of my breast,
We are high-tension wires,
Watch out, or by accident we may be
Thrown together again.

Years will pass, you will get married,
And forget all this disorder.
To be a woman is a giant step,
To drive men mad – heroic.

While at the miracle of a woman's arms,
Shoulders, and back, and neck,
I've stood in reverence all my life
Like a devoted servant.

But howsoever night may bind me
With its anguished coil,
Strongest of all is the pull away,
The passion for a clean break.

7

Summer in Town

Talk in half whispers,
And with fervent haste
She gathers her hair up
In a shock from the nape.

A woman in a helmet
Looks from under the big comb,
Tossing back her head
With its plaits and all.

But the night outside is hot
And promises bad weather,
And, shuffling as they pass,
Pedestrians head for home.

Abrupt thunder comes
With sharp reverberations,
And the wind flutters
The curtains of the windows.

A hushed stillness follows,
But it's sultry as before,
And lightning as before
Rummages in the sky.

And when the intense, radiant
Morning heat dries up
The puddles on the boulevards
After the night's downpour,

The still-flowering lindens,
Fragrant, centuries old,
Look gloweringly around them,
Having had too little sleep.

8

Wind

I'm no more, but you're still alive,
And the wind, complaining, weeping,
Sways the forest and the dacha,
Not each pine tree separately,
But all in their entirety,
With all the boundless distances,
Like the hulls of sailing ships
On the smooth surface of a harbour.
And it's not out of mere bravado,
Nor out of pointless fury, but

So as in anguish to find words
To make for you a lullaby.

9

Hops

Under a willow twined with ivy
We seek shelter from the rain.
Our shoulders are covered by a raincoat,
And my arms are twined about you.

I was wrong. These thick bushes
Are wound not with ivy, but with hops.
Better, then, let's take this raincoat
And spread it out wide under us.

10

Indian Summer

The currant leaf is coarse as canvas,
There's laughter in the house and the clink of glass,
There's chopping there, and pickling, and peppering,
And cloves are put into the marinade.

The forest, like a scoffer, flings this noise
As far away as the precipitous slope
Where the hazel grove burnt by the sun
Looks as if a bonfire's heat had scorched it.

Here the road descends into a gully,
Here you feel pity for the dry old snags
And for the poor ragpicker, Mistress Autumn,
Who sweeps it all down into the ravine.

And because the universe is simpler
Than some clever thinker might suppose,
Because the grove is feeling so crestfallen,
Because it is all coming to its end.

Because it is senseless to stand blinking
When everything before you is burnt down,
And the white autumnal soot
Draws its cobwebs across the window.

There's a way from the garden through the broken fence,
And it loses itself among the birches.
Inside there's laughter and the noise of housework,
And the same noise and laughter far away.

II

A Wedding

Cutting through the yard outside,
Guests came to make merry
In the bride's house until dawn
With a concertina.

Back behind the masters' doors,
Doubled with felt lining,
The snatches of small talk died down
Between one and seven.

Just at dawn, the deep of sleep,
Slumber, slumber, slumber,
The accordion struck up afresh
Going from the wedding.

The accordionist poured out anew
Music from his squeeze box,
The clap of hands, the flash of beads,
The din of merrymaking.

And again, again, again
The chattering chastushka
Burst right into the sleepers' bed
From the joyous feasting.

And one woman white as snow
Amidst the noise and whistling
Floated again like a peahen
Swaying her hips in rhythm.

Tossing back her haughty head,
And with her right hand waving,
She went dancing down the road –
Peahen, peahen, peahen!

Suddenly the heat and noise of play,
The stomping of the round dance,
Went plunging into Tartarus
And vanished in a twinkling.

The noisy yard was waking up,
And the busy echo
Mixed itself into the talk
And the peals of laughter.

Into the sky's immensity,
A whirl of blue-grey patches,
A flock of pigeons went soaring up,
Rising from the dovecote.

Just as if someone half-asleep
Suddenly remembered
To send them, wishing many years,
After the wedding party.

For life is only an instant, too,
Only the dissolving
Of ourselves, like the giving of a gift,
Into all the others.

Only a wedding that bursts its way
Through an open window,
Only a song, only a dream,
Only a blue-grey pigeon.

12

Autumn

I've let the family go its ways,
All those close to me have long dispersed,
And the usual solitude
Fills all of nature and my heart.

And so I'm here with you in the cabin,
In the unpeopled and deserted forest.
The paths and trails, as in a song,
Are half submerged in undergrowth.

Now the log walls gaze in sorrow
At us alone. We never promised
To take the obstacles, if we perish,
We shall do it openly.

We sit down at one, get up at three,
I with a book, you with your sewing,
And at dawn we won't have noticed
How at some point we stopped kissing.

Rustle, leaves, rustle and fall
Still more splendidly and recklessly,
Let yesterday's cup of bitterness
Brim over with the anguish of today.

Attachment, attraction, loveliness!
Let's be scattered in September's noise!
Bury yourself in autumnal rustling!
Freeze in place, or lose your mind!

You shed your dress in the same way
A grove of maples sheds its leaves,
When you fall into my embrace
In your robe with silken tassels.

You are the blessing of a fatal step,
When life's more sickening than illness,
Yet courage is the root of beauty,
And that's what draws us to each other.

13

A Tale

Once in olden times,
In a faery land,
A horseman made his way
Over the thorny steppe.

He was hastening to battle,
And far across the steppe,
Out of the dust a forest
Darkly rose to meet him.

An aching in his bosom,
A gnawing in his heart:
Fear the watering place,
Tighten the saddle girth.

The rider did not listen
And rode on at full speed,
Going ever faster
Towards the wooded knoll.

Turning at the barrow,
He entered a dry gap,
Passed beside a meadow,
Rode over a hill.

And finally reached a hollow,
And by a forest path
Came upon animal footprints
And a watering place.

And deaf to any warning,
And heedless of his sense,
He led his steed down the bankside
To water him at the stream.

———

By the stream – a cave,
Before the cave – a ford.
What seemed like flaming brimstone
Lighted the cave mouth.

And from that crimson screen,
Which hid all from view,
A distant call resounded,
Coming through the pines.

Then straight across the gully
The startled rider sent
His horse stepping surely
Towards the summoning cry.

And what the rider saw there
Made him clutch his lance:
The head of a dragon,
A long tail all in scales.

Its maw was spewing fire,
Spattering light about,
In three rings round a maiden
Its twisting length was wound.

The body of the serpent,
Like a whip's lash,
Swayed about, just grazing
The shoulder of the girl.

The custom of that country
Was to bestow the prize
Of a captive beauty
On the monster in the woods.

The local population
Had agreed to pay this tax
Each year to the serpent
In ransom for their huts.

The serpent wound and bound her
And tightened on her neck,
Having received this tribute
To torture as it liked.

With a plea the horseman
Looked to the lofty sky
And prepared for battle,
His lance set at the tilt.

———

Tightly shut eyelids.
Lofty heights. Clouds.
Waters. Fords. Rivers.
Years and centuries.

The rider, without helmet,
Knocked down in the fight,
The faithful steed tramples
The serpent with his hoof.

Steed and dragon body
There upon the sand.
The rider is unconscious,
And the maiden stunned.

The heavenly vault at noonday
Shines with a tender blue.
Who is she? A royal princess?
A daughter of the earth? A queen?

First in a flood of happiness
Her tears pour out in streams,
Then her soul is mastered
By sleep and oblivion.

He first feels health returning,
But then his veins go still,
For his strength is failing
From loss of so much blood.

Yet their hearts keep beating.
And now she, and now he
Tries to awaken fully,
And then falls back to sleep.

Tightly shut eyelids.
Lofty heights. Clouds.
Waters. Fords. Rivers.
Years and centuries.

14

August

This morning, faithful to its promise,
The early sun seeped through the room
In an oblique strip of saffron
From the curtains to the couch.

It covered with its burning ochre
The nearby woods, the village homes,
My bedstead and my still moist pillow,
The edge of wall behind the books.

Then I remembered the reason why
My pillowcase was slightly damp.
I had dreamed you were walking through the woods
One after another to see me off.

You walked in a crowd, singly, in pairs,
Then someone remembered that today
Was the sixth of August, old style,
The Transfiguration of Our Lord.

Ordinarily a flameless light
Issues on this day from Tabor,
And autumn, clear as a sign held up,
Rivets all gazes to itself.

And you walked through little, beggarly,
Naked, trembling alder scrub
To the spicy red woods of the graveyard
Burning like stamped gingerbread.

The sky superbly played the neighbour
To the hushed crowns of its trees,
And distances called to each other
In the drawn-out voices of the cocks.

Death, like a government surveyor,
Stood in the woods among the graves,
Scrutinising my dead face,
So as to dig the right-sized hole.

You had the physical sensation
Of someone's quiet voice beside you.
It was my old prophetic voice
Sounding, untouched by decay:

'Farewell, azure of Transfiguration,
Farewell, the Second Saviour's gold.
Ease with a woman's last caress
The bitterness of my fatal hour.

'Farewell, years fallen out of time!
Farewell, woman: to an abyss
Of humiliations you threw down
The challenge! I am your battlefield.

'Farewell, the sweep of outspread wings,
The wilful stubbornness of flight,
And the image of the world revealed in words,
And the work of creation, and working miracles.'

15

A Winter Night

It snowed, it snowed over all the world
From end to end.
A candle burned on the table,
A candle burned.

As swarms of midges in summertime
Fly towards a flame,
Snowflakes flew from the dark outside
Into the window frame.

The blizzard fashioned rings and arrows
On the frosty glass.
A candle burned on the table,
A candle burned.

Shadows lay on the ceiling
In the candlelight,
Crossings of arms, crossings of legs,
Crossings of destiny.

And two little shoes dropped down
With a thump on the floor,
And wax tears from the night-light
Dripped on a dress.

And all was lost in the snowy murk,
Hoary and white.
A candle burned on the table,
A candle burned.

It blew at the candle from the corner,
And the heat of seduction
Raised up two wings like an angel,
Cruciform.

It snowed through all of February,
And time and again
A candle burned on the table,
A candle burned.

16

Separation

The man looks from the threshold,
Not recognising his home.
Her departure was more like flight.
Havoc's traces are everywhere.

All the rooms are in chaos.
The extent of the destruction
Escapes him because of his tears
And an attack of migraine.

Some humming in his ears since morning.
Is he conscious or dreaming?
And why does the thought of the sea
Keep coming to his mind?

When God's world cannot be seen
Through the hoarfrost on the windows,
The hopelessness of anguish resembles
The waste of the sea twice over.

She was as dear to him
In her every feature
As the coast is near the sea
Along the line of breakers.

As waves drown the reeds
In the aftermath of a storm,
So her forms and features
Sank to the bottom of his soul.

In years of affliction, in times
Of unthinkable daily life,
She was thrown to him from the bottom
By the wave of destiny.

Amidst obstacles without number,
Past dangers in its way,
The wave bore her, bore her
And brought her right to him.

And now here is her departure,
A forced one, it may be.
Separation will devour them both,
Anguish will gnaw their bones.

And the man looks around him:
At the moment of leaving
She turned everything upside down,
Emptying the dresser drawers.

He wanders about and till nightfall
Keeps putting scattered scraps
Of fabric and pattern samples
Back into the drawer.

And pricking himself on a needle
Stuck into some sewing,
All at once he sees the whole of her
And quietly starts to weep.

17

Meeting

Snow will cover the roads,
It will heap up on the rooftops.
I'll go out to stretch my legs:
You're standing near the door.

Alone in an autumn coat,
Without hat, without warm boots,
You're fighting back agitation
And chewing the wet snow.

Trees and lattice fences
Go off into the murk.
Alone amidst the snowfall,
You stand at the corner.

Water runs from your kerchief
Down your sleeve to the cuff,
And drops of it like dewdrops
Sparkle in your hair.

And a flaxen strand
Illuminates: your face,
Your kerchief and your figure,
And that skimpy coat.

Snow moist on your lashes,
Anguish in your eyes,
And your entire aspect
Is formed of a single piece.

As if with iron dipped
In liquid antimony,
You have been engraved
Into my very heart.

And the meekness of those features
Is lodged in it forever,
And therefore it's no matter
That the world's hard-hearted.

And therefore everything
On this snowy night is doubled,
And I can draw no boundary
Between myself and you.

But who are we, where from,
If of all these years
There remains only gossip,
And we're no longer here?

18

The Star of the Nativity

It was winter.
Wind was blowing from the steppe.
And the infant was cold there in the grotto
On the slope of the hill.

He was warmed by the breathing of the ox.
Domestic animals
Stood about in the cave,
And a warm mist floated above the manger.

Shaking bed straw from their sheepskin capes
And grains of millet,
Shepherds on the cliff
Stood looking sleepily into the midnight distance.

Far off there was a snowy field and graveyard,
Fences, tombstones,
A shaft stuck in a snowdrift,
And the sky over the cemetery, full of stars.

And alongside them, unknown till then,
More bashful than an oil lamp
In a watchman's window,
A star glittered on the way to Bethlehem.

It blazed like a haystack, quite apart
From heaven and God,
Like the gleam of arson,
Like a burning farm, a fire on a threshing floor.

It raised itself up like a flaming rick
Of straw and hay amidst
The entire universe,
Which took alarm at the sight of this new star.

A reddish glow spread out above it
And had a meaning,
And three stargazers
Hastened to the call of the unprecedented light.

After them came camels bearing gifts.
And harnessed asses, one smaller than the other,
Moved down the hillside with little steps.

And in a strange vision of the time to be,
All that came later rose up in the distance,
All the thoughts of the ages, the dreams, the worlds,
All the future galleries and museums,
All pranks of fairies, all tricks of sorcerers,
All the Christmas trees on earth, all children's dreams.

All the flicker of gleaming candles, all the paper chains,
All the magnificence of gaudy tinsel . . .
. . . All the more fiercely the wind blew from the steppe . . .
. . . All the apples, all the golden balls.

Part of the pond was hidden by the tops of the alders,
But part of it was perfectly visible from there,
Through the nests of jackdaws and the treetops.
The shepherds could make out very well
How the asses and camels went past the dam.
'Let's go with them to worship the miracle,'
They said, wrapping their leather coats around them.

Scuffling through the snow made them hot.
Across the bright clearing, like sheets of mica,
The tracks of bare feet led behind the hovel.
At these tracks, as at the flame of a candle end,
The sheepdogs growled in the light of the star.

The frosty night was like a fairy tale.
And from the heaped-up snowdrifts, all the while,
Someone invisibly slipped into their ranks.
The dogs trudged on, looking warily around,
And pressed to the herdboy, and expected trouble.

Down the same road, over the same country,
Several angels walked in the thick of the crowd.
Bodilessness made them invisible,
But their tread left the imprints of their feet.

By the stone a throng of people crowded.
Daybreak. Cedar trunks outlined themselves.
'And who are you?' asked Mary.
'We're of the tribe of shepherds and heaven's envoys.
We've come to offer up praises to you both.'
'You can't all go in together. Wait by the door.'

In the pre-dawn murk, as grey as ash,
Drivers and shepherd boys stamped about,
The men on foot cursed the men on horseback,
At the hollowed log of the water trough
Camels bellowed, asses kicked.

Daybreak. Dawn was sweeping the last stars
Like specks of dust from the heavenly vault.
And only the Magi of that countless rabble
Would Mary allow through the opening in the rock.

He slept, all radiant, in the oaken manger,
Like a moonbeam in the wooden hollow,
Instead of a sheepskin coat, he had for warmth
The ox's nostrils and the ass's lips.

They stood in shadow, like the twilight of a barn,
Whispering, barely able to find words.
Suddenly, in the darkness, someone's hand
Moved one of the Magi slightly to the left
Of the manger. He turned: from the threshold, like a guest,
The star of the Nativity looked in at the maiden.

19

Dawn

You meant everything in my destiny.
Then came war, devastation,
And for a long, long time there was
No word of you, no trace.

And after many, many years
Your voice has stirred me up again.
All night I read your Testament,
As if I were reviving from a faint.

I want to go to people, into the crowd,
Into their morning animation.
I'm ready to smash everything to bits
And put everybody on their knees.

And I go running down the stairs,
As if I'm coming out for the first time
Onto these streets covered with snow
And these deserted pavements.

Everywhere waking up, lights, warmth,
They drink tea, hurry for the tram.
In the course of only a few minutes
The city's altered beyond recognition.

In the gateway the blizzard weaves
A net of thickly falling flakes,
And in order to get somewhere on time,
They drop their breakfast and rush off.

I feel for them, for all of them,
As if I were inside their skin,
I myself melt as the snow melts,
I myself knit my brows like morning.

With me are people without names,
Trees, children, stay-at-homes.
Over me they are all the victors,
And in that alone lies my victory.

20

Miracle

He was walking from Bethany to Jerusalem,
Already weighed down by sad presentiments.

The prickly brush on the steep hillside was scorched,
Over a nearby hut the smoke stood still,
The air was hot and the rushes motionless,
And the Dead Sea was an unmoving calm.

And in a bitterness that rivalled the bitterness of the sea,
He was going with a small throng of clouds
Down a dusty road to someone's house,
Going to town, to a gathering of his disciples.

And he was so deep in his own thoughts
That the fields in their wanness smelled of wormwood.
All fell silent. He stood alone in the midst,
And the countryside lay flat, oblivious.
Everything mixed together: the heat and the desert,
And the lizards, and the springs and rivulets.

A fig tree rose up not far away
With no fruit on it, only leaves and branches.
And he said to it: 'What good are you?
Is your stupor of any earthly use to me?

'I hunger and thirst, and you are a sterile blossom.
Meeting with you is more cheerless than with stone.
Oh, how galling you are and how ungifted!
Stay that way until the end of time.'

A shudder of condemnation ran down the tree,
Like a flash of lightning down a lightning rod,
And the fig tree was reduced to ashes.

If the leaves, the branches, roots, and trunk
Had found themselves a free moment at that time,
Nature's laws might have managed to intervene.
But a miracle is a miracle, and a miracle is God.
When we're perturbed, in the midst of our disorder,
It overtakes us on the instant, unawares.

21

The Earth

Spring comes barging loutishly
Into Moscow's private houses.
Moths flutter behind the wardrobe
And crawl over the summer hats,
And fur coats are put away in trunks.

Pots of wallflowers and stock
Stand on the wooden mezzanines,
There's a breath of freedom in the rooms,
And the garrets smell of dust.

And the street enjoys hobnobbing
With the nearsighted window frame,
And the white night and the sunset
Can't help meeting by the river.

And in the corridor you can hear
What's happening in the wide outdoors,
What April says to the dripping eaves
In a random conversation.

He can tell a thousand stories
About the woes of humankind,
And dawn feels chilly along the fences,
And draws it all out endlessly.

And that same mix of fire and fright
Outside and in our cosy dwellings,
And the air everywhere is not itself,
And the same transparent pussy willows,
And the same swelling of white buds
At the window and at the crossroads,
In the workshop and in the street.

Then why does the distance weep in mist,
And why does the humus smell so bitter?
In that precisely lies my calling,
So that the expanses won't be bored,
So that beyond the city limits
The earth will not languish all alone.

It is for that my friends and I
Get together in early spring,
And our evenings are farewells,
Our little feasts are testaments,
So that the secret stream of suffering
Can lend warmth to the chill of being.

22

Evil Days

When in the last week
He was entering Jerusalem,
Thundering hosannas met him,
People ran after him with branches.

But the days grow more grim and menacing,
Love will not touch hearts.
Brows are knitted scornfully,
And now it's the afterword, the end.

The sky lay over the courtyards
With all its leaden weight.
The Pharisees sought evidence,
Twisting before him like foxes.

And the dark powers of the temple
Hand him to the scum for judgement.
And with the same ardour as they praised him
Earlier, they curse him now.

The crowd from the plot next door
Peered in through the gates,
Jostling and shoving each other
As they waited for the outcome.

And a whisper crept through the neighbours,
And rumours came from all sides,
And childhood and the flight into Egypt
Were recalled now like a dream.

He remembered the majestic hillside
In the desert, and that height
From which Satan tempted him
With power over all the world.

And the marriage feast at Cana,
And the miracle that astonished the guests,
And the misty sea he walked on
To the boat, as over dry land.

And a gathering of the poor in a hovel,
And the descent into the dark cellar,
Where the candle died of fright
When the raised man stood up . . .

23

Magdalene

I

At nightfall my demon's right here
In payment for my past.
Memories of depravity
Come and suck at my heart,
Of when, a slave of men's fancies,
I was a bedevilled fool,
And the street was my only shelter.

A few minutes remain,
And then comes sepulchral silence.
But, before they pass,
Having reached the brink, I take
My life and smash it before you
Like an alabaster vessel.

Oh, where would I be now,
My teacher and my Saviour,
If eternity had not been waiting
By night at the table for me,
Like a new client, lured
Into the nets of my profession?

But explain to me what sin means,
Death, hell, and flaming brimstone,
When, before the eyes of all,
I've grown into you like a graft on a tree
In my immeasurable anguish.

When I rest your feet, Jesus,
Upon my knees, it may be
That I am learning to embrace
The four-square beam of the cross
And, feeling faint, strain towards your body,
Preparing you for burial.

24

Magdalene

II

People are tidying up before the feast.
Away from all that fuss,
I wash your most pure feet
With myrrh from a little flask.

I feel for and do not find your sandals.
I can see nothing for my tears.
Loosened strands of hair
Fall over my eyes like a veil.

I rested your feet on my skirt
And poured tears over them, Jesus,
I wound them in a necklace of beads,
Buried them in the burnous of my hair.

I see the future in such detail
As if you had made it stop.
I am now able to predict
With a sybil's prophetic clairvoyance.

Tomorrow the veil in the temple
Will fall, we will huddle in a circle
To one side, and the earth will sway underfoot,
Perhaps out of pity for me.

The ranks of the convoy will re-form,
The cavalry will begin their departure.
Like a whirlwind in a storm, this cross
Will tear into the sky overhead.

I'll throw myself at the foot of the crucifix,
Go numb and bite my lip.
For the embrace of all too many
You have spread your arms wide on the cross.

For whom on earth is there so much breadth,
So much torment and such power?
Are there so many souls and lives in the world?
So many villages, rivers, and groves?

But three such days will go by
And push me down into such emptiness,
That in this terrible interval
I'll grow up to the Resurrection.

25

The Garden of Gethsemane

The bend of the road was lighted up
By the indifferent glitter of distant stars.
The road went around the Mount of Olives,
Down below it flowed the Kedron.

The little meadow broke off halfway,
Beyond it the Milky Way began.
The grey, silvery olive trees tried
To step on air into the distance.

At the end was someone's garden plot.
Leaving his disciples outside the wall,
He said, 'My soul is sorrowful unto death,
Tarry here and watch with me.'

He renounced without a struggle,
As things merely borrowed for a time,
His miracle-working and omnipotence,
And was now like mortals, like us all.

Now night's distance seemed the verge
Of annihilation and non-being.
The expanse of the universe was uninhabited,
And the garden only was the place for life.

And, peering into those dark gulfs,
Empty, without beginning or end,
And sweating blood, he prayed to his Father
That this cup of death might pass.

Having eased his mortal anguish with prayer,
He went back out. There, on the ground,
His disciples, overcome with sleep,
Lay about among the roadside weeds.

He woke them: 'The Lord has granted you
To live in my days, but you lie sprawling.
The hour of the Son of Man has struck.
He will give himself into the hands of sinners.'

He had barely said it when, who knows from where,
A crowd of slaves and vagabonds appeared,
Torches, swords, and at their head – Judas,
With a treacherous kiss upon his lips.

Peter rushed the cut-throats with his sword
And lopped off the ear of one. He hears:
'Disputes can never be resolved with iron.
Put your sword back in its place, man.

'Could my Father not provide me
With hosts of winged legions? Then,
Having touched not a hair upon my head,
My enemies would scatter without a trace.

'But the book of life has reached a page
Dearer than all that's sacred.
What has been written must now be fulfilled.
Then let it be fulfilled. Amen.

'For the course of the ages is like a parable,
And can catch fire in its course.
In the name of its awful grandeur, I shall go
In voluntary suffering to the grave.

'I shall go to the grave, and on the third day rise,
And, just as rafts float down a river,
To me for judgement, like a caravan of barges,
The centuries will come floating from the darkness.'

NOTES

The notes that follow are indebted to the commentaries by E. B. Pasternak and E. V. Pasternak in volume 4 of the Complete Collected Works *in eleven volumes published by Slovo (Moscow, 2004). Biblical quotations, unless otherwise specified, are from the Revised Standard Version.*

Book One

PART ONE

1. *Memory Eternal:* The chanted prayer of 'Memory Eternal' *(Vechnaya Pamyat),* asking God to remember the deceased, concludes the Orthodox funeral or memorial service *(panikhida)* and the burial service. Pasternak places it here to introduce the central theme of the novel. Psalm 24:1 ('The earth is the Lord's . . .') and the prayer 'With the souls of the righteous dead, give rest, O Saviour, to the soul of thy servant' come at the end of the burial service.

2. *The Protection:* Dating events by church feasts was customary in Russia (as elsewhere) until the early twentieth century, and even later. Pasternak alternates throughout the novel between civil and religious calendars. The feast of the Protective Veil (or Protection) of the Mother of God falls on 1 October. The Russian Orthodox Church, and the Russian state until 1917, followed the Julian rather than the Gregorian calendar, which have a difference of thirteen days between them. Thus 1 October by the Julian calendar is 14 October by the Gregorian calendar, and the October revolution of 1917 actually broke out on 7 November.

3. *The Kazan Mother of God:* This feast, which commemorates the miracle-working icon of the Virgin found in Kazan in 1579, is celebrated on 8–21 July.

4. *zemstvo:* A local council for self-government introduced by the reforms of the emperor Alexander II in 1864.

5. *Tolstoyism and revolution:* 'Tolstoyism', an anti-state, anti-church, egalitarian social doctrine of the kingdom of God on earth, to be achieved by means of civil disobedience and non-violent resistance, was developed in the polemical writings of Leo Tolstoy and his disciples in the last decades of the nineteenth century. A number of revolutionary movements appeared during the same period in Russia, some more or less Marxist, others populist.

6. *Soloviev:* Vladimir Soloviev (1853–1900) was a poet, philosopher, and literary critic. His work, of major importance in itself, also exerted a strong influence on the poetry of the Russian symbolists and the thinkers of the religious-philosophical revival in the early twentieth century.

7. *the capitals:* The old capital of Russia was Moscow; St Petersburg, founded by the emperor Peter the Great in 1703, became the new capital and remained so until the 1917 revolution. Exclusion from both capitals was a disciplinary measure taken against untrustworthy intellectuals under the old regime and again under Stalin.

PART TWO

1. *The war with Japan* . . . : The Russo-Japanese War (10 February 1904–5 September 1905), fought for control of Manchuria and the seas around Korea and Japan, ended in the unexpected defeat of Russia at the hands of the Japanese. The Russian situation was made more difficult by increasing social unrest within the country. On 22 January 1905, which came to be known as 'Bloody Sunday', the Orthodox priest Gapon led a large but peaceful procession to the imperial palace in Petersburg to present a petition asking for reforms in the government. The procession was fired upon and many people were killed. Further disturbances then sprang up all across the country and spread to the armed forces. In August 1905 the emperor Nicholas II allowed the formation of a State Duma (national assembly). But the Duma's powers were so limited that it satisfied none of the protesting parties, and in October came a general strike, as a result of which the emperor was forced to sign the so-called October Manifesto, which laid the foundations for a constitutional monarchy. This satisfied the Constitutional Democratic (CD) Party and other liberals, but not the more radical parties.

2. *Yusupka* . . . *Kasimov bride:* It was common until recently for Tartars like Gimazetdin Galiullin to work as yard porters in Russian apartment blocks. Gimazetdin's son Osip (Yusupka) will play an important role later on. *The Kasimov Bride* (1879) is a historical novel by Vsevolod Soloviev (1849–1903), brother of the philosopher (see part 1, note 6). In the fifteenth century, the town of Kasimov, now in Riazan province, was the capital of the Kasimov Tartar kingdom.

3. *Wafangkou:* At the battle of Wafangkou (14–15 June 1904), the Russian forces of General Stackelberg, who was attempting to relieve Port Arthur, were roundly defeated by the Japanese under General Oku.

4. *Your dear* . . . *boy:* An altered quotation from Tchaikovsky's opera *The Queen of Spades* (1890), with a libretto by Modest Tchaikovsky, based on the story by Alexander Pushkin.

5. *a manifesto:* The October Manifesto of 1905 (see note 1 above).

6. *a papakha:* A tall hat, usually of lambskin and often with a flat top, originating in the Caucasus.

7. *Gorky* . . . *Witte:* Maxim Gorky (1868–1936), a major figure in Russian literature and in the radical politics of the time, was one of a group of writers who wrote to inform the chairman of the council of ministers, Count Sergei Witte (1849–1915), of the peaceful character of Father Gapon's demonstration on 22 January 1905 (see note 1 above). Witte, who brilliantly negotiated the peace with Japan in September 1905, was also the author of the October Manifesto.

8. *The Meaning* . . . *Sonata:* Leo Tolstoy's story *The Kreutzer Sonata* (1889), a study of sensuality and jealousy, is a violent attack on the relations between the sexes in modern society. *The Meaning of Love* (1892–94), by the philosopher

Vladimir Soloviev (see part 1, note 6), is an affirmation of the physical-spiritual union of sexual love.

9. *fauns . . . "let's be like the sun"*: Vyvolochnov refers to some of the favourite motifs in *fin de siècle* poetry and book design. One such book was *Let's Be Like the Sun* (1903), the best-known work of the symbolist poet Konstantin Balmont (1867–1942).

10. *Lev Nikolaevich . . . Dostoevsky:* In his polemical treatise *What Is Art?*, Tolstoy (Lev Nikolaevich, i.e., Leo) attacks the 'all-confusing concept of beauty' in art, and replaces it with the notion of 'the good'. The phrase 'Beauty will save the world' is commonly but wrongly ascribed to Dostoevsky. In fact, it comes from Dostoevsky's novel *The Idiot* (1868), where it is attributed to the hero, Prince Myshkin, by Aglaya Epanchina. Vassily Rozanov (1856–1919), philosopher, diarist, and critic, was one of the major figures of the period leading up to the revolution. He was deeply influenced by Dostoevsky.

11. Faust . . . *Hesiod's hexameters: Faust,* a monumental cosmic drama in two parts, is considered the masterwork of the German poet Johann Wolfgang von Goethe (1749–1832). Part 1 was published in 1808 and part 2 in 1832. Pasternak translated the two parts of *Faust* between 1948 and 1953, in alternation with his work on *Zhivago.* The ancient Greek poet Hesiod, author of *Works and Days* and *The Theogony,* is thought to have lived in the later eighth century BC.

12. *Katerina's in* The Storm: The Russian playwright Alexander Ostrovsky (1823–1886) wrote and staged his play *The Storm* in 1859. The heroine Katerina says, in a famous monologue in act 5, scene 4, 'Where to go now? Home? No, whether home or the grave, it's all the same to me.'

13. *The psalm:* Psalm 103, which opens with the words quoted here, is sung as the first of three antiphons at the start of the Orthodox liturgy.

14. *the nine beatitudes:* The beatitudes from the Sermon on the Mount (Matthew 5:3–12) are sung as the third antiphon of the Orthodox liturgy.

15. *Presnya days:* The armed riots of workers in the Presnya district of Moscow during December were the last incidents of the 1905 revolution.

16. *bashlyks:* A bashlyk is a hood of Tartar origin with long tails that can be tied round the neck like a scarf.

17. The Woman or the Vase: The title of a painting by G. I. Semiradsky (1843–1902), which depicts a market in ancient Rome, where a customer is trying to decide whether to buy a slave woman or a costly vase.

18. *dacha:* The word *dacha,* in its broadest sense, refers to a country dwelling, which can be anything from a rented room in a cottage, to a privately owned country house, to a complex of buildings as significant as the Krüger estate referred to here.

19. *Theosophist:* The spiritual teaching known as Theosophy ('God-wisdom'), first propounded by Helena Petrovna Blavatsky (1831–1891), is an esoteric doctrine of human perfectibility through communion with a 'Spiritual Hierarchy' drawn from all of the world's religions. It was especially popular in intellectual circles during the later nineteenth century, in Russia, Europe, and the United States.

20. *Cui's nephew:* César Cui (1835–1918), Russian composer, was one of a group of composers known as 'the Five' or 'the Mighty Little Bunch' *(Moguchaya Kuchka),* the other four being Balakirev, Mussorgsky, Rimsky-Korsakov, and Borodin.

PART THREE

1. *'Askold's grave'* . . . *Oleg's steed:* The actual grave is said to be the burial place of the Kievan prince Askold, still to be seen on the steep bank of the river Dnieper. Askold was killed in 882 by Oleg, the successor to Rurik, founder of the first dynasty of Russian rulers. These events were the subject of an opera composed by Alexei Verstovsky (1799–1862). It was predicted that Oleg's death would be caused by his favourite horse. As it turned out, he died from the bite of a snake that hid in the skull of his horse long after its death.

2. *John the Theologian:* St John, the author of the fourth Gospel, known as John the Theologian in Orthodox tradition, was also the author of the book of Revelation, from which Zhivago quotes ('and death shall be no more, neither shall there be mourning nor crying nor pain any more', Revelation 21:4).

3. *vodka and pancakes* . . . : In the week before the beginning of the Great Lent, the forty-day fast period preceding Holy Week and Easter, it is the Russian custom to eat pancakes *(bliny)* with all sorts of fish and cream toppings, accompanied by vodka.

4. *Egyptian expedition* . . . *Fréjus:* The ultimately unsuccessful expedition of the French army in Egypt lasted from 1798 to 1801, but Napoleon led it only until August of 1799, when news of unrest in Paris drew him back to the capital. He landed at the port of Fréjus in the south of France on 9 October 1799, and a month later led a bloodless coup against the then-ruling Directoire and set up the Consulat, with himself as first consul.

5. *Blok:* Alexander Blok (1880–1921), one of the greatest Russian poets, was a leader of the symbolist movement. In an autobiographical sketch written near the end of his life, Pasternak noted: 'A number of writers of my age as well as myself went through the years of our youth with Blok as our guide' (*I Remember,* translated by David Magarshack, New York, 1959). Blok is an important presence in *Doctor Zhivago,* where he is referred to a number of times.

6. *panikhidas:* See part 1, note 1. During the prayers over a dead person before burial, the panikhida may be repeated several times.

7. *'Holy God* . . . *have mercy on us':* This prayer, known as the trisagion, is sung repeatedly after the funeral service as the coffin is carried out.

PART FOUR

1. *Erfurt Programme* . . . *Plekhanov:* The Erfurt Programme was a plan of action adopted by the German Social Democratic Party at its conference in Erfurt in 1891, based on a simplified or 'vulgar' Marxist analysis. Presented a year later in *The Class Struggle,* by Karl Kautsky (1854–1938), one of the authors of the programme, it became widely influential in the years before the 1917 revolution. Georgi Plekhanov (1857–1918), revolutionary activist and Marxist theorist, was one of the founders of the Russian Social Democratic Labour Party. At the second party conference in 1903, Plekhanov broke with Lenin, who headed the Bolsheviks ('Majority'), and joined the Mensheviks ('Minority'), who tended to be more moderate.

2. *mad Gretchen:* In the first part of Goethe's *Faust* (see part 2, note 11), Faust sees the young Gretchen (Margarete) in the street and asks Mephistopheles to procure her for him. Gretchen's purity makes the task difficult, but Faust succeeds in the

end. Gretchen becomes pregnant, drowns her baby, is condemned to death, and awaits execution in prison, where Faust sees her for a last time.

3. *Eruslan Lazarevich:* A hero of so-called lubok literature. A lubok is a folk woodcut or steel engraving, a form of broadside combining illustrations and text, produced in the seventeenth and eighteenth centuries and later.

4. *the Gypsy Panina:* Varya Panina (1872–1911) was a famous Gypsy singer, whose voice had great depth and musicality. She began singing in Moscow restaurants and gave her first public concert, which was a huge success, in 1902, at the Hall of the Nobility in Petersburg. Alexander Blok called her 'the celestial Varya Panina'. The words 'led under the golden crown' refer to the Orthodox wedding service, during which the bride and groom stand under crowns held by their attendants.

5. *second autumn . . . action:* The Eighth Army under General Alexei Brusilov (1853–1926) had occupied Galicia in 1914, but had been forced to withdraw during a general retreat. In 1915, the Eighth Army entered the Carpathians and moved towards Hungary, but again was forced to withdraw due to circumstances elsewhere.

6. *the Lutsk operation:* Also known as the 'Brusilov Offensive', this was the liberation of the city of Lutsk, in north-west Ukraine, by four Russian armies under the command of General Brusilov on 4–7 June 1916.

7. *Krestovozdvizhensky Hospital:* The hospital is named for the feast of the Elevation of the Holy Cross *(Krestovozdvizhenie),* which falls on 14–27 September and commemorates the finding of the true cross in Jerusalem by the empress Helen, mother of Constantine the Great, in AD 326. Hospitals in Russia before the revolution were often named for church feasts.

8. *friend Horatio:* Cf. Shakespeare's *Hamlet,* act 1, scene 5, lines 165–66: 'There are more things in heaven and earth, Horatio, / Than are dreamt of in your philosophy.' After an abandoned earlier attempt in 1923–24, Pasternak translated *Hamlet* in 1939 at the request of the famous director Vsevolod Meyerhold. Meyerhold was arrested and shot before he could produce the play. A production in 1943 at the Moscow Art Theatre was cancelled owing to the death of the director, the venerable Nemirovich-Danchenko, and the first performance finally took place in 1954, at the Pushkin Theatre in Leningrad. Pasternak's work on the play over the years (there were twelve versions among his papers) left a deep mark on *Doctor Zhivago.* In his essay 'Translating Shakespeare', Pasternak wrote: 'From the moment of the ghost's appearance, Hamlet gives up his will in order to "do the will of him that sent him". *Hamlet* is not a drama of weakness, but of duty and self-denial . . . What is important is that chance has allotted Hamlet the role of judge of his own time and servant of the future' (translated by Manya Harari, in *I Remember,* New York, 1959).

9. *Brusilov . . . on the offensive:* See note 6 above.

10. *St Tatiana's committee:* A benevolent association formed at the beginning of the war, under the honorary chairmanship of the grand duchess Tatiana Konstantinovna Romanova, to aid those at the front and the families of the wounded or dead.

11. *Wilhelm:* Kaiser Wilhelm II (1859–1941) ruled as the last German emperor and king of Prussia from 1888 to 1918, when he was forced to abdicate.

12. *Dahl:* Vladimir Ivanovich Dahl (1801–1872) was an eminent Russian lexicographer, compiler of the four-volume *Explanatory Dictionary of the Great Russian Language* (1863–1866). He was a proponent of native as opposed to imported vocabulary.

13. *equal before God:* A reference to Paul's epistle to the Galatians 3:28: 'There is neither Jew nor Greek, there is neither slave nor free, there is neither male nor female; for you are all one in Christ Jesus.'

PART FIVE

1. *black earth region:* The region of rich black soil *(chernozem)* extending from the north-east Ukraine across southern Russia.

2. *Provisional Government:* When the February revolution of 1917 (23–27 February–8–12 March) brought about the abdication of Nicholas II and the end of imperial Russia, a provisional government was created, composed of an alliance of non-Communist liberal and socialist parties headed by Prince Georgi Lvov (1861–1925), who was a Constitutional Democrat. In July 1917, Prince Lvov was replaced by the Socialist Revolutionary (SR) Alexander Kerensky (1881–1970). The intent of the Provisional Government was to create a democratically elected executive and assembly, but its programme was opposed by Lenin and the Bolsheviks, and in October 1917 the Provisional Government was brought down by the Bolshevik revolution.

3. *the Time of Troubles:* The period in Russian history from the death of the last representative of Rurik's dynasty, the tsar Fyodor Ivanovich, in 1598, to the election in 1613 of the tsar Mikhail Romanov (1596–1645), founder of the new dynasty. The government was taken over by Boris Godunov (1551–1605), brother-in-law and chief adviser to the late tsar. His rule, from 1598 to 1603, was a time of great unrest, famine, factional struggles, international conspiracies, and false claims to the throne.

4. *Raspou . . . Trease:* As the author has just said, Mlle Fleury swallows the endings of Russian words, including in this case the name of Grigory Rasputin (1869–1916), a bizarre holy man who attached himself to the imperial family, and the word 'treason.'

5. *death penalty was reinstated:* Among the first acts of the Provisional Government (see note 2 above) was the abolition of the death penalty. But in July 1917, owing to difficulties in the continuing war with Germany and the problem of mass desertions, special military courts were established and the death penalty was reinstated. It was abolished again by the Bolsheviks, and again quickly reinstated.

6. *Pechorin-like:* Grigory Alexandrovich Pechorin, the protagonist of the novel *A Hero of Our Time* (1839–1841), by Mikhail Lermontov (1814–1841), is a world-weary, cynical, cold-hearted, but also courageous, sensitive, and melancholic army officer.

7. *State Duma:* See part 2, note 1. The Fourth Duma sat from 1912 to 1917. During the February revolution, it sent a commission of representatives to replace the imperial ministers, leading to the creation of the Provisional Government (see note 2 above).

8. *People's Will Schlüsselburgers:* People's Will *(Narodnaya Volya)* was a revolutionary terrorist organisation of the later nineteenth century, responsible among other things for the assassination of the emperor Alexander II in 1881. Their programme was non-Marxist, aimed at a peasant revolution bypassing capitalism. Some of its members, released from prison in the early twentieth century, helped to form the Socialist Revolutionary (SR) Party. The Schlüsselburg Fortress, on the Neva near Lake Ladoga, was used as a political prison.

9. *Bolsheviks and Mensheviks:* See part 4, note 1.

10. *Balaam:* The story of Balaam and his ass is told in Numbers 22:21–35. The Moabite prophet Balaam fails to see the angel of God barring his way, but his she-ass does see the angel and finally cries out to warn him.

11. *Lot's wife:* Ustinya has confused the story of Balaam with the story of Lot, who was saved by the Lord when Sodom and Gomorrah were destroyed, but whose wife was turned into a pillar of salt when she looked back at the cities (Genesis 19:1–26).

12. *the land question:* One of the major questions facing the Provisional Government was the redistribution and continued cultivation of land seized from the former landowners, made especially urgent by the decline in farm production during the war years. In May 1917, *Izvestia,* the newspaper of the Petrograd Soviet, expressing Menshevik and SR views, published a lead article headlined 'All land to the people'.

13. *the accursed questions:* Dostoevsky coined this phrase *(prokliatye voprosy)* for the ultimate questions of human existence – the nature of man, the existence of God, the problem of evil, the meaning of life, the riddle of death – 'the great Russian questions', as Nicolà Chiaromonte called them, which Pasternak raises again in *Doctor Zhivago,* 'when it seemed that history . . . had suppressed them forever' ('Pasternak's Message', in *Pasternak: Modern Judgements,* edited by Donald Davie and Angela Livingstone, Nashville and London, 1970).

14. *in Paul . . . 'interpretation':* The reference is to Paul's first epistle to the Corinthians 14:5 and 13: 'Now I want you all to speak in tongues, but even more to prophesy . . . Therefore, he who speaks in a tongue should pray for the power to interpret.'

15. *Petenka Verkhovensky . . . the Futurists:* Pyotr ('Petenka') Verkhovensky is the young radical organiser, theorist, and mystificator in Dostoevsky's novel *Demons* (1872), who came to signify the empty babbler and demagogue. The Russian Futurists were a group of poets and artists who embraced the ideas of the Italian writer F. T. Marinetti (1876–1944) in his *Futurist Manifesto* of 1908 and shared his enthusiasm for dynamism, speed, and machines. In 1912, David Burlyuk, Velimir Khlebnikov, Alexei Kruchenykh, Vladimir Mayakovsky, and others issued their own manifesto, *A Slap in the Face of Public Taste.*

16. *mushroom rain:* A warm rain with sunshine that is thought to encourage the growth of mushrooms.

PART SIX

1. *annexates and contributses:* 'Annexations' and 'contributions' were controversial terms in discussions of the Brest-Litovsk treaty of March 1918 between the new Russian Soviet Federal Socialist Republic (RSFSR) and Germany, Austria, and Turkey, ending Russia's participation in World War I. The Russian negotiators, headed by Leon Trotsky (Lev Bronstein, 1879–1940), wanted no annexations of Russian territory and no payments of war reparations, but eventually agreed to both. The treaty was broken eight and a half months later.

2. *Saint-Just:* Louis de Saint-Just (1767–1794) was a French revolutionary and a close associate of Robespierre, with whom he was executed on 9 Thermidor (17 July 1794), bringing an end to the Reign of Terror.

3. War and Peace . . . The Backbone Flute: These and *Man*, mentioned a little later, are titles of books of poetry by Vladimir Mayakovsky (1893–1930) published during the years of the war and the revolution. Pasternak had great admiration for these early poems and for their author.

4. *Ippolit* . . . The Adolescent: Ippolit is the consumptive rebel in Dostoevsky's *The Idiot*, Raskolnikov is the hero of *Crime and Punishment*; the first-person narrator-hero of *The Adolescent* is Arkady Dolgoruky. They are all rootless young intellectuals in great inner turmoil.

5. *Mme Roland's before the Convention*: Manon Roland (1754–1793), an ardent republican and admirer of Plutarch, kept a salon in Paris that had considerable political influence and was frequented mainly by the party of the Girondins, who opposed the violent measures of the Montagnards. She was executed along with other Girondins on 31 October 1793. Her *Memoirs* are an important record of the time. The revolutionary National Convention governed France from September 1792 to October 1795.

6. *two left SR names*: That is, the names of two left-leaning members of the Socialist Revolutionary Party (see part 5, note 8). The pseudonyms themselves are absurd, as was often the case at that time.

7. *to a victorious conclusion*: A watchword of Kerensky and the Provisional Government, who pledged to continue the war with Germany after the February revolution. The more radicalised workers and armed forces were aligned with the Bolsheviks in opposing the war.

8. *Antaeus . . . an old Bestuzhevist*: The mythological giant Antaeus kept his immense strength as long as he touched the earth. Hercules, who was unable to defeat him by throwing him to the ground, discovered his secret, held him up in the air, and crushed him to death. The historian Konstantin Bestuzhev-Riumin founded the St Petersburg Higher Women's Courses, which opened in 1878 and were named for their director. This was the first institution of higher education for women in Russia.

9. *the days following the Dormition*: The feast of the Dormition (in the West the Assumption) of the Mother of God falls on 15–28 August, which in Russia is already the beginning of autumn.

10. *Hegel and Benedetto Croce*: Georg Wilhelm Friedrich Hegel (1770–1831) was a philosophical idealist and the creator of an integral philosophical system that was of great influence on nineteenth- and twentieth-century thought. Benedetto Croce (1866–1952) was an Italian philosopher and critic, an idealist deeply influenced by Hegel, and politically a liberal.

11. *the October fighting*: That is, the outbreak of the October revolution of 1917 (see part 1, note 2, and part 5, note 2).

12. *the time of the civil war*: The Russian Civil War (1918–1923) broke out after the Bolsheviks assumed power and withdrew from the alliance opposed to the Central Powers in World War I. The Red Army was confronted by various forces from the former empire, known collectively as the White Army, made up of army officers, cadets, landowners, and foreign forces opposed to the revolution. The main White leaders were Generals Yudenich, Denikin, and Wrangel and Admiral Kolchak. Their units fought not only with the Red Army, but also with the Ukrainian nationalist Green Army and the Ukrainian anarchist Black Army led by General Nestor Makhno. The Whites eventually lost on all fronts, and the major fighting ended in 1922 with the Red Army's capture of Vladivostok, though the last pocket

of White resistance in the Far East capitulated only in June 1923. The events of the civil war form the backdrop of most of book 2 of *Doctor Zhivago*.

13. *Mary Magdalene:* One of the followers of Jesus, and, according to all four Gospels, the first or one of the first to see him after his resurrection (Matthew 28:1–10; Mark 16:1–10; Luke 24:1–11; John 20:1–18).

PART SEVEN

1. *coupons . . . distribution centre:* As a result of the acute shortages that followed the war and the revolution, the authorities of the first socialist republic created closed stores where the privileged could obtain supplies in exchange for special coupons. The practice continued throughout the Soviet period.

2. *kerenki:* A nickname for banknotes issued by the Provisional Government in 1917 and by the Russian state bank until 1919, from the name of Alexander Kerensky (see part 5, note 2).

3. *labour conscripts from Petrograd:* By a decree issued in December 1918, all able-bodied citizens of the RSFSR were obliged to work on state construction projects. The name of St Petersburg was changed to Petrograd in 1914, after the outbreak of World War I. In 1924 it became Leningrad, and in 1991 it became St Petersburg again.

4. *stormy petrels:* In 1901, Maxim Gorky (see part 2, note 7) published a poem entitled 'The Song of the Stormy Petrel', in which the petrel symbolises the working class as a revolutionary force. He was arrested for publishing it but soon set free. The poem, which was one of Lenin's favourites, became a battle song of the revolution.

5. *Pugachevism . . . Pushkin's perception . . . Aksakovian:* Emelian Pugachev (1742–1775) was a Don Cossack who led a rebellion in 1773–1774, claiming the throne under the pretence that he was the tsar Peter III. Alexander Pushkin wrote *The History of Pugachev* (1834) and a fictional treatment of the same events in his short novel *The Captain's Daughter* (1836). The Aksakov family, the father Sergei (1791–1859) and his two sons, Konstantin (1817–1860) and Ivan (1823–1886), were writers belonging to the group known as Slavophiles, who favoured the native and local traditions of Russian life as opposed to Western influences. Sergei Aksakov, who was born in Ufa, the capital of Bashkiria, over a thousand miles east of Moscow on the border of Asia, gives a detailed description of Russian patriarchal life, hunting, fishing, flora, and fauna in his *Family Chronicle* (1856).

6. *kulaks:* The word *kulak*, Russian for 'fist', was a derogatory name applied to well-off peasants who owned their own land, a group that emerged after the agricultural reforms of 1906. The Bolsheviks declared them the 'class enemy' of poor peasants and subjected them to various forms of persecution and extermination.

7. *ataman:* A general title given to Ukrainian military leaders, related to the word *hetman*, and possibly derived from the German *Hauptmann*. During the Russian Civil War it was used as a title for various Cossack leaders and acquired a negative tone.

8. *the Greens:* See part 6, note 12.

9. *the Cheka:* An abbreviation of the Russian words for Extraordinary Commission (the full title was All-Russian Extraordinary Commission for Combating Counter-revolution and Sabotage), the first Soviet state security organisation (secret police), founded in December 1917 and headed by Felix Dzerzhinsky, known as

'Iron Felix' (1877–1926). By 1921 the Cheka numbered 200,000 men. In 1922 it became the GPU (State Political Administration).

Book Two

PART EIGHT

1. *St Akulina's day:* St Aquilina of Byblos (281–293), martyred during the reign of Diocletian, is commemorated on 7–20 April.

2. *a Social Democrat:* See part 4, note 1.

3. *the Demidovs:* The family of the Demidovs was one of the most distinguished in Russia, second only to the imperial family in wealth and known for its philanthropy. Anatoli Nikolaevich Demidov (1813–1870) acquired the Italian title of Prince of San Donato and built a villa in Florence.

4. *Blessed is the man . . . :* The first half of the sentence is from the opening of Psalm 1 ('Blessed is the man who walks not in the counsel of the wicked . . .'); the rest is a jocular rhyme.

5. *Suvorov:* Field Marshal Alexander Suvorov (1729–1800) was reputed never to have lost a battle. He was only the fourth man in Russian history to be awarded the highest rank, that of generalissimo. The fifth and last was Joseph Stalin.

6. *SR . . . Constituent Assembly:* On 12 November 1917, an All-Russian Constituent Assembly was democratically elected to draw up a constitution for Russia. The SR Party won a large majority of the seats, almost twice as many as the Bolsheviks. After meeting for one day on 5 January 1918, the assembly was dissolved on orders from Lenin.

7. *our White-Stoned Mother:* Moscow was known endearingly as 'the White-Stoned Mother' of the Russian people, because of the white stone used in building the churches of the Kremlin.

8. *Hebrew youths . . . Mazeppa:* The book of Daniel 3:8–30 tells the story of the three Hebrew men thrown into the fiery furnace by the Babylonian king Nebuchadnezzar for refusing to worship his golden idol. Mazeppa (1644–1709) was a hetman of the Cossacks in the Ukraine, who first served Peter the Great and then joined the Swedes against him. The name came to be a general derogatory epithet.

9. *the dark waters . . . secrecy:* The phrases and rhythms are loosely based on Psalm 18:11: 'He made darkness his covering around him, his canopy thick clouds dark with water.'

10. *the year of Griboedov's death:* Alexander Griboedov (b. 1795), Russian poet, playwright, and diplomat, author of the verse comedy *Woe from Wit*, was killed on 11 February 1829, while on an official mission to Persia.

PART NINE

1. *Tyutchev:* Pasternak felt a strong affinity with the work of the poet Fyodor Tyutchev (1803–1873), whose poem 'The Summer of 1854' Zhivago slightly misquotes from memory.

2. *Dostoevsky's* Demons . . . *the Communist Manifesto:* Dostoevsky's 1872 novel was, among other things, a forceful attack on the radicals and nihilists of the later nineteenth century. The Communist Manifesto, written by Karl Marx and Friedrich Engels and published in 1848, set forth the revolutionary programme of the German Communist League.

3. *Pray fervently . . . he is her glory:* The first words come from an Orthodox prayer to the Mother of God; the rest are from the Song of the Mother of God (the Magnificat), Luke 1:46–55.

4. *Arzamas . . . adolescent:* Arzamas was a literary society formed by a group of friends in Petersburg in 1815, which the young Pushkin, who was then fifteen himself, soon joined. From 1821 to 1823, he lived mainly in Kishinev, the capital of the recently annexed Bessarabia, where he was in military service.

5. *Nekrasov:* Nikolai Nekrasov (1821–1877), the major poet of the 'prose age' of Dostoevsky and Tolstoy, was a man of radical leanings and deep social conscience. His best work often captures the style of the folk song.

6. *I am a bourgeois . . . my fine self:* Zhivago refers to Pushkin's poem 'My Genealogy' (1830), where the words 'I am a bourgeois' are repeated as a refrain. The second passage is from stanza 18 of 'Onegin's Journey', a section that Pushkin later cut from his novel in verse *Evgeny Onegin* (1823–1830).

7. *Nightingale the Robber:* A monstrous figure, part bird, part man, who appears in the medieval Russian epic *Ilya Muromets and Nightingale the Robber,* from which Zhivago proceeds to quote.

8. *In Turgenev somewhere:* Turgenev's late collection, *Literary Reminiscences* (1874), includes a piece entitled 'About Nightingales'.

9. *Chekhovian schoolboys . . . :* In an early story, 'Boys', Chekhov describes the scheme of two schoolboys to run off to America and become Indians.

10. *My soul . . . sleeping:* The words, which Pasternak gives in Church Slavonic, come from the Great Canon of St Andrew of Crete (650–712), an Orthodox penitential canon sung during the Great Lent (see part 3, note 3).

PART TEN

1. *Kolchak:* Admiral Alexander Kolchak (1874–1920) supported the Provisional Government after the February revolution and opposed the Bolsheviks. In 1918 he became a member of the Siberian Regional Government (White), and when it was overthrown by a military coup, he was appointed head of state with dictatorial powers and given the title of Supreme Ruler. Kolchak's brutal repressions and mass executions aroused dislike even among potential allies, including the Czech Legion, the British, and the Americans. When the Regional Government was taken over by a pro-Bolshevik faction, Kolchak was condemned and executed, despite orders to the contrary from Moscow.

2. *Vozdvizhensky Monastery . . . Great Lent:* The monastery, like the town and the hospital earlier, is named for the feast of the Elevation of the Holy Cross (see part 4, note 7). The words quoted are the start of one of the hymns of the feast. Holy Week follows the forty days of the Great Lent and leads to Easter.

3. *church time:* The time of day in the church is reckoned as in Jewish practice, the day starting at nightfall (6 p.m.).

4. *Holy Thursday . . . the Twelve Gospels:* Holy Thursday commemorates the Last Supper and the betrayal and arrest of Jesus. On the night of Holy Thursday, the matins of Holy Friday are served, including a reading of twelve composite passages from the four Gospels describing the trial and crucifixion of Jesus.

5. *Leibochka's little tricks:* In March 1918, Trotsky (see part 6, note 1) was made People's Commissar for Army and Navy Affairs and Chairman of the Supreme Military Council – that is, the commander-in-chief of the Red Army at the start of the civil war. Galuzina uses the diminutive of Leib, Trotsky's first name in Yiddish.

6. *Kubarikha . . . Medvedikha . . . Zlydarikha:* Fanciful nicknames suggestive, respectively, of a spinning top, a she-bear, and a wicked person.

7. *Kirghiz and Buryat:* Peoples from Central Asia. The Kirghiz, a Turkic people living in the area of the Tian Shan mountains, were brought under Soviet power in 1919. The Buryat are a northern Mongolic people who live in Siberia.

8. *the former cooperative labourist:* That is, a member of the Labour Group *(Trudoviki)* in the Duma, affiliated with the SR party and headed by Kerensky, part of whose programme was the idea of cooperative farm labour.

9. *Convention . . . Thermidorians:* The French revolutionary National Convention, which sat from 1792 to 1795, held executive power during the First Republic, with Robespierre, Marat, and Danton among its prominent members and the Reign of Terror as its political means. It was brought down by the so-called Thermidorian reaction (see part 6, notes 2 and 5) and replaced by the Directoire.

10. *kulichi . . . paschas:* Foods traditionally eaten in celebration of Easter. A *kulich* is a tall, cylindrical cake, usually decorated with fruit and icing, and *pascha* is a moulded sweet dish made from fresh white cheese, butter, sugar, eggs, and cream, with various dried fruits, nuts, and flavourings.

11. *Many years:* The prayer wishing a person 'Many Years' is sung on name days or for congratulations on various occasions.

12. *Miliukov:* Pavel Miliukov (1859–1943), statesman and liberal historian, and a prominent member of the Constitutional Democratic Party, was elected to the Duma, became a member of the Provisional Government after the February revolution, and served as foreign minister from March to May 1917. He was known to be a powerful orator.

13. *the Black Hundred:* The name of a counter-revolutionary movement in Russia, formed in 1900 from conservative intellectuals, officials, landowners, and clergy, with a reputation for being anti-Semitic and anti-Ukrainian. It grew weaker after 1907 and was finally abolished following the February revolution.

PART ELEVEN

1. *Kappel's formation:* General Vladimir Kappel (1883–1920), who sided with the Constitutional Democratic Party after the February revolution, was put in command of the so-called Komuch White Army Group in 1918 ('Komuch' is an abbreviation of Committee of Members of the Constituent Assembly). After the execution of Admiral Kolchak (see part 10, note 1), he commanded the remnants of the White Army in Siberia and led them in a retreat across the frozen Lake Baikal, an episode known as the Great Siberian Ice March. He died of frostbite.

2. *the law on food requisitioning:* In January 1919, a decree was issued calling for the requisitioning without compensation of what was described as 'surplus agricultural produce'. The procedure was open to abuse and resulted in great unrest among the peasants, which was brutally suppressed.

3. *Church Slavonic . . . Russian:* The language of the Russian and some other Orthodox Churches is Church Slavonic. Ultimately derived from Middle Bulgarian, it differs from Russian, which leads to misunderstandings such as those that follow here. The lines quoted are from Psalm 91 in the King James Version.

4. *Dukhobor community . . . Tolstoyism:* The Dukhobors (meaning 'Spirit-Fighters', a name coined by their opponents) emerged as a Christian sect in Russia in the eighteenth century, but may go back further. They rejected the authority of state and church, the Bible as divine revelation, and the divinity of Christ, lived in egalitarian farming communities, and refused military service, for which they were repeatedly persecuted. Their beliefs are close to the teachings of Tolstoyism (see part 1, note 5), and in fact Tolstoy contributed money to their cause when they petitioned to move to western Canada in the late nineteenth century.

5. *You are angry, Jupiter . . . the Moor can go:* The saying about Jupiter, which is proverbial in Russia, comes from the Latin: *Iuppiter iratus ergo nefas* ('Jupiter is angry, therefore he is [it is] wrong'), which is attributed to Lucian of Samosata (ca. AD 125–180 AD). The phrase about the Moor, also proverbial, comes from *The Conspiracy of Fiesco in Genoa* (1783), a play by the German poet and playwright Friedrich Schiller (1759–1805).

6. *Darwin met with Schelling:* Charles Darwin (1809–1882) formulated the principle of natural selection in the process of biological evolution in his *Origin of Species* (1859). The German idealist philosopher Friedrich Schelling (1775–1854), a friend and later a critic of Hegel, proposed the idea, in his *Philosophy of Nature* (*Naturphilosophie*, 1797), that the ideal springs from the real in a dynamic series of evolutionary processes. Zhivago's thoughts thus unite naturalist and idealist notions of evolution.

7. *Razin and Pugachev:* Stepan ('Stenka') Razin (1630–1671) was a Cossack who led a band of robbers in the late 1660s. He was joined by discontented peasants and non-Russian peoples like the Kalmyks and in 1670 went into open rebellion against the Russian state. After some successes, he was defeated and captured, and in 1671 he was executed in Moscow. For Pugachev, see part 7, note 5.

PART TWELVE

1. *Oprichniki:* An order of special troops organised by Ivan the Terrible (1530–1584), loyal to him alone, living on their own separate territory (the name comes from an old Russian word meaning 'apart' or 'separate'), and opposed to the traditional nobility (boyars). They were given unlimited power and used it ruthlessly. Their number increased from 1,000 in 1565 to 6,000 in 1572, when the tsar abolished the order.

2. *a heretic witch from the Old Believers:* The Old Believers, also known as Raskolniki (from the Russian word *raskol*, 'schism'), separated themselves from the Russian Orthodox Church in protest against the reforms introduced by the patriarch

Nikon in 1653. Women among the Old Believers sometimes took the role of 'Mothers of God' or 'Brides of Christ'.

3. *A little hare . . . my beautiful one:* According to the commentary of E. B. and E. V. Pasternak, this 'folk song' is entirely the work of Pasternak himself.

4. *Kolchak . . . Ivan Tsarevich:* For Kolchak, see part 10, note 1. Ivan Tsarevich ('Ivan the Prince') is a hero of Russian folk tales, often the third of three sons, who struggles with Koshchei the Deathless, goes to catch the Firebird, and eventually marries the princess.

5. *Or else, for instance . . . the Novgorod or the Ipatyev . . . :* Kubarikha's speech, as well as what she speaks about, is drawn from texts collected by Alexander Afanasiev (1826–1871) in his *Poetic Notions of Nature Among the Slavs* (1865–69). The Novgorod Chronicle, covering the years from 1016 to 1471, is the oldest record of the Novgorod Republic; the Ipatyev Chronicle contains material going back to the twelfth and thirteenth centuries. It is a major source for the early history of southern Russia.

6. *the book of the living word:* The verse comes from a hymn from the service for the Nativity of the Mother of God, but Kubarikha connects the Slavonic word *zhivotnogo* ('living') with the Russian word *zhivotnoe* ('animal') and applies it to the cow.

7. *He cut down . . . Flenushka:* Pasternak based the stories of the butchered man and of Pamphil Palykh on published accounts of partisan life during the war with Kolchak.

PART THIRTEEN

1. *O Light . . . presence?:* The first line of the fifth hymn of the canon in the eighth tone, sung at matins. Zhivago repeats it along with the second line a little further on.

2. *the Gajda uprising:* Radola Gajda (born Rudolf Geidl, 1892–1948) joined the Czech Legion in Russia in 1917. During their evacuation across Siberia in 1918, violence broke out between the Czechs and the Bolsheviks, and Gajda and his troops combined with Kolchak's forces, but in July 1919, after a falling out with Kolchak, he was dismissed. He then involved himself in a mutiny of SRs, which came to be known by his name, and when it failed, he escaped from Siberia and made his way back to Czechoslovakia, where he later took up the cause of fascism.

3. Romeo and Juliet: The words are spoken by Romeo in his last speech (act 5, scene 3, line 82). Pasternak quotes from his own translation, made during the early years of World War II.

4. *a man in a case:* Lara is referring to the hero of Chekhov's story 'The Man in a Case' (1898), who for Russians typifies a man physically and mentally trapped in his own narrow views and inhibitions.

5. *Rosa Luxemburg:* The political writer and activist Rosa Luxemburg (1871–1919) became a member of the Social Democratic Party of Germany (see part 4, note 1), and in 1914, with Karl Liebknecht (1871–1919), founded the antiwar Spartakusbund ('Spartacus League', from Liebknecht's pen name, Spartacus), which on 1 January 1919, became the German Communist Party. She was shot along with Liebknecht and others after the crushing of the Spartacist uprising later

that same month, and thus became one of the first martyrs of the Communist cause.

6. *Goethe's . . . neo-Schellingism:* In his *Naturphilosophie,* Goethe, like Schelling (see part 11, note 6), sought to establish a universal order of metaphysical as well as pragmatic validity.

7. *In the Red Sea . . . remained intact:* The quotations come from the Dogmatik (Hymn to the Mother of God) in the fifth tone, sung at vespers. The earlier references are to the Old Testament books of Exodus, Daniel (see part 8, note 8), and Jonah.

8. *to make Adam God:* The quotation comes from verses sung in the second tone at the vespers of the Annunciation. The essential notion that 'God became man so that man could become God' is attributed to several early church fathers, among them St Irenaeus of Lyons (second century) and St Athanasius of Alexandria (293–373).

9. *Christ and Mary Magdalene . . . God and a woman:* This entire passage is based on the traditional identification of Mary Magdalene with the woman taken in adultery in John 8:3–11, and with the unnamed woman who anoints Christ's feet from an alabaster flask and wipes them with her hair in Matthew 26:6–13, Mark 14:3–9, and Luke 7:36–50. In John's version of this incident (12:1–8), the woman is Mary, the sister of Martha and Lazarus, who is neither a prostitute nor the Magdalene. Sima mentions this confusion herself. St Mary of Egypt was indeed a repentant prostitute, but she lived in the fourth century. Sima goes on to quote hymns from the matins of Holy Wednesday, the middle of Holy Week, in which the woman with the alabaster vessel confesses to having been a harlot. The longest of these hymns, from which Sima quotes most fully, known as 'The Hymn of Cassia', is attributed to the Byzantine abbess and hymnographer Cassia (ca. 805–867). Zhivago's two poems about Mary Magdalene follow the same tradition.

10. *Several well-known social figures . . . deported from Russia:* Tonya's letter mixes real people with the fictional Gromeko family: S. P. Melgunov (1879–1956) was a historian, a Constitutional Democrat, and an outspoken opponent of the Bolsheviks; A. A. Kiesewetter was also a historian and a leader of the CD Party; and E. D. Kuskova was a journalist and member of the Committee to Aid the Hungry. Deportation became Lenin's preferred way of dealing with prominent ideological opponents. In the autumn of 1922 he loaded some 160 intellectuals, including the philosophers Nikolai Berdyaev, Semyon Frank, Sergei Bulgakov, Ivan Ilyin, and Fyodor Stepun, on the so-called 'Philosophy Steamer' and shipped them to Europe.

PART FOURTEEN

1. *In Primorye . . . the remaining time:* Primorye, more fully the Primorsky Krai, or 'Maritime Territory', is the extreme south-east region of Russia, bordering on China, North Korea, and the Sea of Japan, with its capital at Vladivostok. The remnants of Kappel's forces (see part 11, note 1), with other White groups, set up a government there, known as the Provisional Primorye Government, which lasted from late May 1921 to October 1922, when the Red Army took Vladivostok and effectively ended the civil war.

2. *Egory the Brave:* The name for St George in Russian oral epic tradition. The

image of St George slaying the dragon figures on both the Moscow and the Russian coats of arms, and in Zhivago's poem, 'A Tale'.

3. *Tolstoy . . . generals:* Zhivago is thinking of Tolstoy's commentaries on the moving forces of history in *War and Peace,* particularly in the second epilogue to the novel.

4. *Tverskaya-Yamskaya Streets:* Four parallel streets north of the centre of Moscow.

5. *Herzen:* Alexander Herzen (1812–1870), the illegitimate son of a wealthy landowner, was a pro-Western writer and publicist, often called 'the father of Russian socialism'. In 1847, having inherited his father's fortune, he left Russia and never returned. Abroad he edited the radical Russian-language newspaper *Kolokol* ('The Bell') and wrote a number of books, the most important of which is the autobiographical *My Past and Thoughts* (1868).

6. *a clanging cymbal:* A phrase from Paul's first epistle to the Corinthians (13:1): 'If I speak in the tongues of men and of angels, but have not love, I am a noisy gong or a clanging cymbal.'

PART FIFTEEN

1. *the NEP:* That is, the New Economic Policy, established by a decree of 21 March 1921, which allowed for some private enterprise on a small scale, following the ravages of War Communism, which had tried to remove the market economy entirely. Peasants were also allowed to sell their surplus, which previously had been requisitioned without compensation (see part 11, note 2). The policy was abandoned by Stalin in 1928, in favour of the first Five-Year Plan and the forced collectivisation of agriculture.

2. *the eve of St Basil's:* The feast of St Basil of Caesarea (330–379), a major Orthodox theologian and author of a liturgy that is still in use, is celebrated on 1–14 January, the day of his death.

3. *They changed landmarks:* The reference is to a movement of liberals in the White Russian emigration named for a collection of essays entitled *Smena Vekh* ('Change of Landmarks'), published in Prague in 1921, which proposed a resigned acceptance of the October revolution and the Soviet regime and called on émigrés to return to Russia.

4. *Tikhon:* Tikhon (Vassily Bellavin, 1865–1925), elected patriarch of the Russian Orthodox Church in 1917, was the first patriarch since the reforms of Peter the Great eliminated the position in 1721 and brought the Church under state control. The Bolsheviks did not welcome Tikhon, who protested against many of their acts, and he was imprisoned from 1922 to 1923. He was canonised by the Russian Orthodox Church in 1989.

5. *The custom . . . was widespread by then:* Cremation, which was not an Orthodox practice, was introduced after the revolution. But Zhivago's acquaintances follow the old practice of laying out the body at home, in an open coffin on a table, surrounded by flowers.

6. *She . . . the gardener:* See John 20:1–18, the account of Mary Magdalene meeting the risen Christ.

7. *the last kiss:* From a hymn sung near the end of the Orthodox burial service,

which speaks in the voice of the dead person: 'Come, all you who loved me, and kiss me with the last kiss. For nevermore shall I walk or talk with you.'

8. *making . . . the song: Alleluia:* Words of a hymn from the funeral or memorial service: 'For dust thou art, and unto dust shalt thou return. Whither we mortals all shall go, making our funeral dirge the song: Alleluia.'

PART SIXTEEN

1. *the Kursk bulge . . . Orel:* This major battle, fought in July 1943, ended in a decisive Soviet victory and set the Russian army on the offensive for the duration of the war. The city of Orel was liberated on 5 August of that year.

2. *Ezhovshchina:* The period of the most intense purges of the Communist Party and the Soviet government, in 1937–1938, named for Nikolai Ezhov (1895–1940), head of the NKVD, including the internal security forces, which ran the prisons and labour camps.

3. *I never saw her again:* The story of Christina Orletsova is based on the life of an actual girl named Zoya Kosmodemyanskaya, an account of which was preserved in Pasternak's archive.

4. *Blok's "We, the children . . ."* : See part 3, note 5. The poem, written on 8 September 1914, at the outbreak of World War I, begins: 'Those born in obscure times / Do not remember their path. / We, the children of Russia's terrible years / Are unable to forget anything.'

NOTES TO THE POEMS OF YURI ZHIVAGO

6. *A Final Talk*
The Manège is a large, rectangular, neoclassical building in the centre of Moscow, near Red Square, built in the early nineteenth century, which originally served as a riding academy and later became a concert and exhibition space.

9. *Hops*
The Russian word for hops, *khmel,* also means intoxication.

11. *A Wedding*
A *chastushka* is a form of Russian folk poetry, usually quatrains in trochaic metre with alternating four and three stress lines, rhyming ABCB, often racy, political, or nonsensical, sung to the accompaniment of the accordion or balalaika.

14. *August*
The Feast of the Transfiguration (see Matthew 17:1–8, Mark 9:2–8, Luke 9:28–36) is celebrated on 6–19 August, when there are already signs of autumn in Russia. It is popularly referred to as the 'Second Saviour'.

20. *Miracle*
See Matthew 21:18–22, Mark 11:12–23.

23 and 24. *Magdalene*
See part 13, note 9.

25. *The Garden of Gethsemane*
See Matthew 26:36–46, Mark 14:32–42, Luke 22:39–48.

THE HISTORY OF VINTAGE

The famous American publisher Alfred A. Knopf (1892–1984) founded Vintage Books in the United States in 1954 as a paperback home for the authors published by his company. Vintage was launched in the United Kingdom in 1990 and works independently from the American imprint although both are part of the international publishing group, Random House.

Vintage in the United Kingdom was initially created to publish paperback editions of books bought by the prestigious literary hardback imprints in the Random House Group such as Jonathan Cape, Chatto & Windus, Hutchinson and later William Heinemann, Secker & Warburg and The Harvill Press. There are many Booker and Nobel Prize-winning authors on the Vintage list and the imprint publishes a huge variety of fiction and non-fiction. Over the years Vintage has expanded and the list now includes great authors of the past – who are published under the Vintage Classics imprint – as well as many of the most influential authors of the present. In 2012 Vintage Children's Classics was launched to include the much-loved authors of our youth.

penguin.co.uk/vintage-classics

Collect all the titles in the Vintage Classic Russians Series

War and Peace by Leo Tolstoy
Anna Karenina by Leo Tolstoy
Crime and Punishment by Fyodor Dostoevsky
Doctor Zhivago by Boris Pasternak
Life and Fate by Vasily Grossman
The Master and Margarita by Mikhail Bulgakov